THE REMNANT

THE REMNANT

BY MARY LA CROIX

AVON
PUBLISHERS OF BARD, CAMELOT AND DISCUS BOOKS

THE REMNANT is an original publication of Avon Books. This work has never before appeared in book form.

Excerpts from THE DEAD SEA SCRIPTURES edited by Theodor H. Gaster. Copyright © 1956, 1964 by Theodor H. Gaster. Reprinted by permission of Doubleday and Company, Inc.

Scripture texts used in this work are taken from THE NEW AMERICAN BIBLE. Copyright © 1970 by the Confraternity of Christian Doctrine, Washington, D.C. and are used by license of said copyright owner. No part of THE NEW AMERICAN BIBLE may be reproduced in any form without permission in writing from the Confraternity of Christian Doctrine, Washington, D.C. All rights reserved. See Scripture Index for reference.

Verbatim and paraphrased extracts from the Edgar Cayce readings are reprinted by permission. Copyright © 1971 by Edgar Cayce Foundation, Virginia Beach, Virginia.

The author would also like to acknowledge EDGAR CAYCE'S STORY OF JESUS by Jeffrey Furst, EDGAR CAYCE'S STORY OF THE ORIGIN AND DESTINY OF MAN by Lytle Robinson and THERE WILL YOUR HEART BE ALSO by Dr. William McGarey.

Geneological charts appear at the end of the narrative.

AVON BOOKS
A division of
The Hearst Corporation
959 Eighth Avenue
New York, New York 10019

First Avon Printing, March, 1981

AVON TRADEMARK REG. U.S. PAT. OFF. AND IN
OTHER COUNTRIES, MARCA REGISTRADA, HECHO EN U.S.A.

Printed in the U.S.A.

For Dick

PART I
JUDITH

Chapter 1

Phinehas shaded his eyes with his arm and stole a quick squinting glance at the sun. It was only mid-morning and already the sun was a blazing white fire, beating down upon the tortured earth and bouncing back into the air in shimmering waves of heat. Only an occasional breeze stirred the barley fields and touched his hot sweaty face with a cool but fleeting caress. Insects hummed and buzzed in the still air. Clusters of tiny gnats hovered around his head; he swatted at them and blew through his mouth in a futile attempt to chase them away. The path was powder-dry, and every step he took sent little clouds of dust swirling up beneath his tunic to cling to his legs and irritate his skin until his sweat turned into rivulets of mud. Birds wheeled and called overhead, sounding a cacophony of complaint against the heat and grating on Phinehas' ears. Little burrowing rodents scurried across the path, annoying Phinehas with their smallness and ability to hide among the sheaves from the relentless glare of the sun.

Phinehas was hot and cross and sweaty and dirty, and he longed for the hills and trees of Cana. His eyes ached from the white glaring sun flashing like streaks of silver upon the barley and burned from the dust and his own salty sweat. His beard itched, and his hair lay matted beneath the hood of his mantle. His leg muscles ached and his feet were two fiery coals. He sighed into his beard and thought Elkatma had been right; they should have made the journey earlier in the season before the sun dipped so low toward earth that it broiled a man alive. But he had had to keep the child a few weeks longer.

He groaned at the thought of the child, and his heart

contracted in a spasm of grief. The child! His darling, his beloved, his very heart! By the time that hellish sun had set he would have given her up, given her away—bone of his bone, flesh of his flesh, heart of his heart. His throat constricted and closed around a hard knot of grief, and his eyes welled and reddened as he struggled to keep the tears from spilling over his cheeks. His tears would only upset Elkatma and remind her of her own grief, and wouldn't ease the ache in his breast. He pulled his rough sleeve across his eyes and straightened his shoulders with a determined shrug. He'd not think of the child now, he'd think of happier times, times when he and Elkatma had been children and had travelled along this very path, young and oblivious to the sun and dust and flies and aching joints and burning feet, with nothing in their young heads but the joy of life and the excitement of the journey.

Phinehas and Elkatma had lived in the little village of Cana all their lives. Their families were close friends, closer than most because they adhered to the teachings and beliefs of the Pious Ones on Mt. Carmel and so were looked upon as outcasts by their orthodox Jewish neighbors. There were one or two other families in Cana who believed as they did, and they all lived like a tiny community within a larger community, sharing everything they owned as though they were one family. Elkatma had been like his cherished little sister, her brothers had been his brothers, her mother his mother, and Phinehas' family likewise had been hers.

The boys had chased across the hills of Galilee, tending the sheep and helping their fathers plant and harvest their crops. They had sat side by side in the synagogue school, learning the Torah by rote and bearing the sting of the rod more often than the other boys of Cana because their fathers held to the tenets of the Pious Ones. They'd endured the taunts of the other boys and the scorn and contempt of the scribes with silent pride, their mutual suffering and humiliation welding their friendship into a lifelong, ironclad bond.

Except for school, their lives had been carefree and happy. The Carmelites regarded children as precious souls to be taught and nurtured with tender care: cruelty,

anger, and injustice were nonexistent within their group.
Children were disciplined with loving firmness and taught
to obey out of love instead of fear. They'd worked hard,
for life was meager, and each willing hand added to the
good of all; even the smallest toddler was made to feel
needed and useful. In sharing all things, they never knew
want or hunger. If famine and drought should strike, they
knew that Carmelites from other villages would come to
their aid, and so they lived in security and freedom from
fear, except of those who hated them for their religious
beliefs.

Even that was not so bad. Sneers and scorn could be
tolerated, and physical violence against the sect was extremely rare in Galilee. The majority of the Galileans were
Gentile, or of a mixture of Jewish and Gentile blood
through centuries of intermarriage, and only a few of the
hundreds of small villages, such as Cana, Nazareth, and
Capernaum, could be said to be mostly Jewish. The Gentiles scorned the Carmelites and laughed at their crazy
claim to other-worldly powers, but didn't hold the murderous hate for them as did the wholly Jewish Judeans.

For the most part, Phinehas and Elkatma had had a
happy childhood, but the best times of all had been the
annual trek down this dusty path across the Plain of Es-
draelon to the winding road along the Kishon River, then
westward to the majestic Great Sea and up the steep path
to the summit of Mt. Carmel. Sometimes they'd be joined
by other families from Asochis, Bethsaida, Capernaum, or
Sepphoris, and then they became a holiday caravan of
laden, braying asses, laughing, shouting youngsters, and
wailing babes. Over all the melee, the men's deep voices
could be heard, expounding the finer points of the Torah,
condemning the fatuous customs of the pagans, and chastising their shouting, scuffling sons who ran in and out
among their legs disturbing their heady talk and causing
them to stumble and trip over small, brown bodies.

The atmosphere of the quiet house of study on Mt.
Carmel had changed during the summer to an almost
carnival air, for then the priests and monks relaxed their
rigid rule for a few weeks and welcomed their Brothers
from the camps in the villages and cities of Palestine. A
city of tents sprang up beneath the towering pines and

oaks, and the Mount came alive with family life. The air was permeated with the odors from a hundred cooking pots mingling with the acrid smell of campfire smoke. The onslaught of hammer and saw against wood, and chisel and maul against stone rang out across the sea, carrying with it the singsong chant of young voices memorizing the Psalms and the Torah with help from kindly priests and monks who carried no rod to chastise tender backs. Here the Law was learned out of love and not out of force and fear.

All who gathered on this Holy Mount of Elijah had been dedicated from birth to render their services to the purposes and aims of the Brotherhood. Whatever God-given talents they had were laid at the feet of the Saints, to be used in whatever capacity would best further the Cause, to help prepare the Way, to promote the conditions necessary to make possible the entrance into the earth of the Holy One, the Son, the Messiah. Back into the centuries, into the mists of time before the recollections of man, the promise had been made that the Son would be given to redeem all Israel from her sins, that a time would come when the Evil One, Belial, would be bound, and the sons of men would be freed from his grasp, and death would rule no more.

In the cool breezes on Mt. Carmel the men would bend their backs to cutting down the lofty pine and cedar trees and hauling them up to the temple compound where carpenters would strip them of their bark, then plane and hew them into boards from which they fashioned doors and benches, tables, beams, and cupboards, and the myriad other things needed by the Holy Ones. Stonemasons, tanners, butchers, winemakers, millers, pottery workers, dyers, parchment makers, plasterers, painters, craftsmen of every kind, as well as men to till the soil, thatch the roofs, clean the stone, and whitewash the walls came to Mt. Carmel to advance the Cause.

The women also gave their talents. Wool was spun and dyed and woven into curtains, blankets, robes, and winter mantles. The white linen tunics worn by the priests and monks were made in every size, and carefully stored in the communal warehouse. Vegetables and fruits were dried and stored for winter use. The younger boys fished the streams that cut through the dense forest floor and brought their catch to the women, who dried and salted them down in great wooden barrels.

Everyone worked with a festive air, with flying hands and gladsome hearts and untiring backs, for this was the purpose of their being alive. This was why they were in the earth. They were the Elect, the Chosen Ones, destined before their conception in the womb to help make way for the coming of the Lord.

In the midst of all this activity stood the temple. One could not think of Mt. Carmel without envisioning the temple. It was small compared to the Jerusalem temple, and could not boast of gold or jewels or other riches as could the other, but ah! the reverence and holiness one felt there! Set on the very summit of the Mount, with all of Palestine spread before its face and the Great Sea standing guard at its back, it seemed to wait in solemn majesty for the day when the Messiah would enter through its doors.

It was an edifice of peace and harmony, a bulwark of ancient truth, a sentinel against a cruel and pagan world, a beacon reaching out into all the corners of the earth to summon the pure of heart, the longing souls, the searching minds, whispering to them on the winds, "*here here here* you will find rest and peace." Not, *here* will you find the stench of the burning fat of hypocrisy rising to assault the sensibilities of the Lord. The Lord had said to Isaiah, "I have had enough of whole burnt rams and fat of fatlings; in the blood of calves, lambs, and goats I find no pleasure." On the Mount, only the sweet, pungent scent of incense rose with the morning mists, carrying with it hymns of praise and thanksgiving, the supplications and prayers of the pure in heart, the adoration and faith of a chosen few who kept the Law of their fathers and who remembered the spiritual meaning of that Law.

Familiar waves of excitement began to rise in Phinehas' breast. His chest seemed to tighten and his breath came in short, laboring pants. His heart quickened; the blood drained from his legs, leaving them weak and trembling, then rushed to his head and pounded in his ears where it distorted his vision and thickened his tongue. His step faltered and he leaned for a moment against the donkey, deeply inhaling the hot arid air, willing his heart to be calm, and swallowing hard at the sudden onrush of saliva in his mouth. In a moment the spell was over, and he was left with a deep and profound peace. His long lean body stood upright and the strength returned to his legs. His vision cleared and his heart beat normally. The chatter and call of the birds and the buzz of the flies fell sharply upon his ears. Elkatma and the child marched steadily before him and had noted nothing, thanks be to God.

He had never told anyone, not even Elkatma, of this strange malady that overtook him whenever he thought of the prophecies and of the Messiah. On the day he had seen the holy vision he had been alone in his fields and no one knew that hours had passed from the time the Messenger had left him until he had regained his senses. He'd found himself lying prostrate on the ground, drained of all his strength and trembling in all his parts. He'd lain there and wept until the strength returned to his limbs and gave wings to his feet as he'd flown over the hills to Elkatma.

It had been natural that he and Elkatma marry, for they'd loved one another all of their lives, but the years had passed and their union bore no fruit. How they had prayed for and dreamed of a child! A child full of grace and zeal for the Lord, a child tall and strong, with hair as golden as the setting sun and eyes as blue as the Sea of Galilee. A child who would run over the hills and delight in all he saw and smelled and touched and heard, because it was given by the Lord. A child who would grow strong of limb and courageous of heart and would be a servant of the Lord to His people.

Phinehas had grown old with his dreams, and Elkatma's womb had ceased its life-giving flow. They'd bowed to the will of the Lord in sorrow, but not in despair.

Then he had had the vision! It had been a day such as today, hot and still with the sky bleached white by the blazing sun. Phinehas had been pulling weeds in the barley field, and had straightened to rest his back and wipe the sweat from his eyes when he looked into the face of an angel! He'd known at once that it was an angel. No ordinary man in Galilee dressed in robes of such shimmering whiteness, or was so tall and beautiful, or emitted such an aura of loving peace. Phinehas had never known such fear! Even after the angel had raised his hand in blessing and said, "Fear not, Phinehas. You are favored by the Lord," Phinehas had been sure he'd die of fright. The angel told him that God had heard their prayers and that the child he and Elkatma had longed for would be born to them and would grow to be a leader and teacher to all their people and would be greatly blessed by the Lord.

Phinehas chuckled aloud without realizing it, remembering Elkatma's face when he'd told her. Now Elkatma turned at the sudden sound and said crossly, "You find the heat comical, then, old fool?"

Embarrassed, Phinehas made a gesture with his hand as though to brush away the intrusion of her voice.

"I only clear the dust from my throat," he growled.

Elkatma grunted and turned back to the business of walking, leaving him alone again with his thoughts.

Such joy he'd seen on the woman's face, and then for a moment doubt, as she remembered her age and lifeless womb. But just as quickly she had remembered Sara and Hannah.

They'd left at once for Mt. Carmel to raise up prayers of thanksgiving in the temple and to tell the Holy Ones of the visitation from the Lord. All the Elect had rejoiced and joined in hymns of praise for this wondrous thing that was being done for them. But when the child had been brought forth from Elkatma's womb there was consternation and doubt among the Brotherhood, for the child was female. How could a girl fulfill the promises that had been given? Questions were raised as to the validity of the vision, and some of the Brotherhood had looked upon Phinehas with scorn and derision, contending that the vision had been the wanderings of an old man's mind. Enos, the priest and Prefect of the Community at Mt. Carmel, had admonished them, saying no one knew the ways of the Lord, and he counseled all to wait and watch the child, for if she were indeed a favored one of the Lord, it would soon be made manifest for all to see.

Phinehas had named her Judith instead of Judah, as he had planned to name his son, and she was all that they had dreamed of, and more. Her hair was as golden as sun-ripened wheat, and her eyes a fathomless blue set wide under long, flaxen lashes. She was fair-skinned—not the stark marble-white of the Greeks, nor the soft, translucent ivory of the Galileans, but more the rosy tone of the rain-washed hills of Galilee.

She was a striking child. Her unusual coloring and tall stature set her apart from other girls her age. Their neighbors in Cana who were not of the Brotherhood and knew nothing of the prophecy of the angel thought her strange and moody, and sometimes looked at her askance. She didn't join in the childish games with the other village children, but preferred to dog Phinehas' steps, begging him for stories of her people's sojourn in the earth. She never tired of hearing of how God called Abraham out of the corrupt idol-worshipping city of Ur to wander with his flocks through lonely hills and plains and deserts where he could better hear the word of God and raise a tribe free from the destructive metropolitan influences. She thrilled to the story of the barren Sara who, like her own mother, had brought forth a child in her old age through the promise of an angel of the Lord.

As soon as Judith was old enough to understand, Phinehas and Elkatma had told her of the circumstances surrounding her birth and had begun to prepare her for the unknown role she was to play. Every evening Phinehas sat with the child, teaching her the Law, the Prophets, and the oral traditions of her people. Judith's young mind was quick and keen. She understood and absorbed everything Phinehas taught. Now, though she was only eight years old, Phinehas had taught her all he knew. They had dedicated her to the Lord as Elkanah and Hannah had dedicated Samuel, and now the time had come for them to keep their promise to the Lord and take her to the school on Mt. Carmel. The kindly monks would teach her things far beyond the reach of Phinehas' knowledge, and Judith would learn, he knew. Already she became impatient when Phinehas had to admit he didn't know the answers to her surprising questions, and her eagerness to leave them and go to Mt. Carmel made them wince. Phinehas knew the child loved them, but her zeal for knowledge of the Lord was greater.

Phinehas sighed deeply and gave the faltering donkey a sharp rap on the rump, making the poor animal bear the punishment for the irritation he felt. Was he jealous because the child loved the Lord more than himself? Was that not what he and Elkatma had prayed for all those years? He hadn't known then the strength and depth of love a parent could feel for a child, and what if he had? Would he still have given his promise to return her to Him? He felt disgusted and ashamed of himself. He silently asked forgiveness for the weakness of his flesh, but on the other hand, he reasoned, he had good cause for his reluctance.

These were troubled times. He had been sixteen years old when Pompey rode into Jerusalem with his legions, flooding the land with fear and hate. Rome was an exacting mistress and kept a careful eye on all her varied subjects. The Jews' religion was their government and their daily life. There were so many sects and interpretations of the Law that the Romans were hard-pressed to sort them out and understand them. The sects were continually quarreling among themselves, and their volatile, stubborn nature often led to disturbances and riots. Rome refused to tolerate such behavior and so ruled with an iron fist and choking rein.

The Pharisees and Sadducees struggled for control of the temple and the Sanhedrin. The Zealots exhorted their neighbors to open warfare. The Samaritans loathed all the Jews, and threatened every one who crossed their borders. All of them despised the Carmelites, whom they considered heretical and blasphemous, and took every opportunity to charge them with those sins and bring them to trial before the Sanhedrin.

It helped a little that King Herod was somewhat kindly disposed toward the sect. The story went that once, when he was but a child and on his way to school, a Carmelite by the name of Manahem had saluted him as King of the Jews. Manahem was well-known for his foreknowledge of future events, and he proceeded to tell young Herod how his reign would come about and develop over the years. Herod had dismissed Manahem's prophecy then, but as the years went by and the prophecy had come to pass, Herod remembered and now gave at least a verbal honor to the sect. But Herod had his problems, too. He trod the troubled waters of trying to be friends with Rome and also with the Sadducees and Pharisees, and any sympathy he might have for the Elect was hidden from the ears and eyes of influential rulers.

The Brotherhood met in secret now, and no longer openly spoke of their aims and purposes. A careless word dropped in the ears of a hostile neighbor could mean charges brought before the Sanhedrin. Phinehas had told his neighbors in Cana that they were journeying to visit friends in the wilderness of Judea, and had left before dawn to avoid any undue questioning. He had told the same story last night at the inn in Asochis.

Phinehas now smiled ruefully and shook his head. Human souls were such a paradox. The whole nation writhed and groaned under foreign rule and the ignominy of an Idumean king. In the great temple in Jerusalem daily sacrifice was made, imploring the Most High to relieve them of their oppressors, and the cry arose from every corner of Palestine for the Messiah.

The land was rife with prophets proclaiming the Kingdom of the Lord, and cults and sects were constantly being formed and disbanded as the people followed this prophet and that, hoping each was the Messiah, until they became disillusioned with one and sought another. The Romans were right in calling them stiff-necked Jews, thought Phinehas. They heaped ashes on their heads and wailed outside the city walls, belaboring their plight and exhorting deliverance from their enemies, but refused to turn their hearts to the truth and give aid to the Brotherhood whose very purpose through the ages had been to bring about the conditions that would enable their prayers and supplications to be answered. Even the proud and haughty Sadducees, who maintained that a man was born and lived and died and that was that, held a secret hope for the Messiah in their arrogant and unbelieving souls.

The Romans called the Brotherhood "the Essenes," the Expectant Ones, and the Pharisees had taken up the term in ridicule, contending that a man would have to be mad even to consider the thought that God would send the King of Glory through such a ragged bunch of blasphemers who refused to offer the blood sacrifices, followed a calendar of feasts all their own, and performed feats of healing and divination through what they called sorcery. The Brotherhood didn't mind being called Essenes, for surely they were Expectant Ones, but they called themselves the "Covenanters," for the Messiah would be a priestly Messiah, a teacher of righteousness like their founder, and would bring a new testament, a new revelation from God before he destroyed the Evil One and the Sons of Darkness and gathered to himself the Sons of Light and established his Kingdom on the earth.

Yes, these were troubled times, and whoever led the Essenes would bear the brunt of all the punishments and harassments. If the Messiah were to come during Judith's generation, what would that mean for his child? Who could ever forget the sight of a Roman execution by crucifixion! What if Judith— He couldn't even think of such a horror.

Phinehas gave the poor donkey a savage thrust with his walking stick and cast such thoughts from his mind. Better to be like Elkatma—to walk and not think, and let God take care of tomorrow!

Chapter 2

The sun was hanging far out across the sea when the dense forest which covered Mt. Carmel abruptly ended and they found themselves in the temple clearing. Judith gasped and stared in speechless wonder. Phinehas had described the temple and the school, the life of the priests and monks who lived there, the scribes who copied the sacred Scriptures, and the library which held the precious scrolls, but no words could describe the beauty and peace and holiness that assailed Judith's senses and made her tremble as did her first sight of the place where she would spend her life.

From the time she had first learned to talk she had begged Phinehas and Elkatma to tell her about this hidden, sacred place and the ancient prophets who had lived in caves far from the world of men, spending their days in prayer and fasting and leaving Carmel only to bring a message to the people from the Lord. How she'd loved to hear how Samuel had begun the school to teach the children of Israel the mysteries and wisdom of the ages! Now the stories were real to her, and she was one who had come to learn.

The temple stood at the crest of the Mount. Its blocks of white limestone were cut and fit so precisely that it looked as though the entire temple had been carved from one massive rock. Two limestone-walled courts encircled the temple, each with twelve arched gates representing the Twelve Tribes of Israel and the twelve phases of man's sojourn on earth. The courts and temple were rectangular in shape, with four gates on each side and three in back overlooking the Great Sea. The main gate at the eastern end of the temple was double the size of the other gates, for this was the gate of Judah, and it was from the tribe of Judah that the Messiah would come.

The temple itself was two stories high, with many arched windows that let in the light of the sun and the cooling breezes from the sea. Each arch was lined with sun-faded, red clay bricks, and their dusty rose softened the glare of the shimmering white stone. A pathway of the same red brick, as wide as the gate of Judah, led from the complex of buildings on the cleared slope below through both courts to the base of the twelve wide steps rising to the second-story porch. Great carved cedar doors opened from the porch onto the holy recesses of the upper floor.

The whole temple glowed with rosy warmth in the setting sun, and long shadows from branches bowing in the gentle breeze played upon its walls. It seemed alive, pulsating, beckoning, and Judith could barely restrain from running through the inviting gates.

The temple's hypnotic spell was broken as an old man with a tall, thin frame and a flowing white beard approached them with long quick strides and clasped Phinehas in a crushing embrace.

"Peace be with you!" he cried as he kissed Phinehas on each cheek. Phinehas returned the greeting, and as the old man turned to Elkatma his merry eyes softened and moistened. "Ah, Elkatma. It is a long time since we have seen our beloved sister in God."

Elkatma held his bony hand and said, "Too long, Enos, old friend, but to bring the child to visit Carmel would only have brought ridicule upon her from the other children in the village and thus draw her thoughts away from God and His purpose for her in this generation. We thought it best to keep her mind free from worry and worldly cares while she is yet so young. She will have enough of those when she is older and, pray God, can bear them better."

Enos nodded understandingly and turned to Judith. Judith returned his scrutiny with a gaze as steady as his own. She guessed this was Enos, priest and leader of all the Essenes, and that his approval was imperative to her acceptance at the school on Mt. Carmel.

"Welcome to Mt. Carmel, Judith. We have looked forward to admitting you into our school for a long time. I saw you admiring our temple. Do you like it?"

"Oh yes!" Judith breathed. "It is beautiful. It seems to smile and beckon to me as though it has waited for me as I have longed and waited for it."

Enos smiled and laid his hand upon her head and felt the heavy, silken hair beneath it. She was tall for her age, standing level to his shoulder, and her piercingly blue eyes held a depth and maturity unusual in a child so young. She has a woman's face and voice, thought Enos. Though she is only eight years old, she makes me feel as though she knows everything, has felt everything, has experienced everything, and so, perhaps, she has.

Enos cupped her chin in his hand and studied her face. Her skin was brown and moist, her mouth wide and full and set with purpose, her jaw square and firm—she was not a child which one could mold and bend at will, but a child of iron who would use her will and healthy body for a singleness of purpose. Nothing would deter her once she found that purpose. It was now in his hands to guide this child to make that purpose one with God's.

"Tomorrow I will take you to the temple and teach you myself of what it means. But for now, come. The sun is setting and it will soon be time for the evening meal. Do you wish to go to the lodging for the students, or would you rather stay with your mother and father?" Enos turned to Phinehas. "A tent has been prepared for you and Elkatma, and we wish for you to stay as long as possible. Not many of the Brotherhood can come to Carmel in these troubled times, and we are overjoyed that you are here."

Judith fought a battle between wanting to start her new life at once and wanting to stay with her parents, whom she knew were suffering over leaving their only child. Her love for Elkatma won out and she said, "I'll go with my mother to the tent."

Elkatma shook her head. She spoke quickly, though her voice caught. "You'll go to the Lodgement. You are no longer just a young girl. Today you become a handmaid of the Lord. We shall see you every day that we are here, but you must begin to fulfill the promise given by the angel."

Enos was pleased to see the child put her parents'
wishes before her own. She has been taught well, he
thought. She is kind and perceives the pain of others, and
shows strength to endure disappointments.

They walked along the red brick walk toward the compound below. The walk was lined with rows of flowers
and the lawns were green and finely manicured. Flowering
shrubs had been planted between the walk and the court
walls, and the air was profuse with their perfume.

Judith looked through each gate they passed, awed by
the simple beauty inside the courts. Fountains bubbled
and splashed with cool, clear water, and beds of flowers
had been planted and carefully tended throughout the
court. Here and there trees had been left standing, and
wooden benches encircled their trunks. There were also
benches hewn from stone, and a few were occupied by
white-robed monks or scribes studying small scrolls and
writing on wax tablets. She caught a glimpse of a group of
girls little older than herself putting their needlework into
linen sewing bags, their lessons finished for the day.

Judith grimaced and fervently hoped she wouldn't have
to learn to sew. How wonderful it would be to read and
study in that peaceful place! If only she had been a boy
she could have become a monk, but she was a girl and
they would want her to cook and sew and learn all the
other arts of homemaking. The prospect was abhorrent to
her. She lifted her chin defiantly and thought she would
not, could not, for she had no inclination toward keeping
house or cooking meals. She wanted to study! Judith
sighed. There were so many things to learn, and she wanted
to know them all. She couldn't be bothered with mundane
things like sewing; it took too much time, and even if she
studied all her life she still wouldn't know all the things
she longed to know.

They met a young monk with curly, black hair and a
short beard who stepped aside to let them pass, bowing
gravely at Enos as he did so. His smooth cheeks above his
beard flushed when his eyes met Judith's, but when he
realized she was only a child, he smiled delightfully. Judith returned his smile, instantly liking him, and after he
had passed, she asked Enos who he was.

"That is Joseph ben Jacob of Nazareth," Enos answered. "He was a student at the City of Salt before the earthquake. He returned home when the Brothers were forced to leave the destruction, and when he reached the age of manhood, came here to Mt. Carmel and joined the Brotherhood as a monk. He is a most gifted carpenter, even surpassing his father, who was regarded as the best in Galilee. You admired the great temple doors, Judith. They were carved by Joseph."

Judith was impressed. She turned and watched the young man walk hurriedly away. His white robes swirled at his ankles and his long, waving, black hair bounced against his shoulders. She hoped she would see him again.

Enos was saying, "We believe each soul has its own particular gift to give in service to God and men. Unfortunately, too many use their gifts to satisfy self and for aggrandizement of the body, much to the loss to their souls. Joseph is doubly gifted, for not only is he an artist in wood, but he is also blessed with the most humble and gentle of natures, and is dearly beloved by everyone, and most of all, I think, by God."

Judith was dismayed at the jealousy she felt. She had no particular talents, and she was far from being humble and gentle. She was stubborn and strong-willed and was known to argue vehemently to get her own way. As though he could read her thoughts, Enos went on. "Ah. If all the souls upon the earth were as Joseph! But they are not, and so we have great need of people of a stronger mien to teach and admonish and stem the growing tide of the Sons of Darkness. A strong will and eloquent tongue can be an excellent force for good, if tempered with piety and charity and love for one's fellow man."

Judith felt better, and smiled at Enos gratefully. As they neared the farthest gate, the girls Judith had seen inside the court came out, led by a young woman about twenty years of age. She was tall and big-boned, with a large, open, friendly face. Enos introduced her to Phinehas and Elkatma, then turned to Judith.

". . . and this is their daughter Judith, who will be a student in our school. I was just bringing her to the House of Lodgement, but since the hour is late, perhaps she could go with you and get acquainted on the way."

The woman's name was Eloise. Judith stared at her and

thought she looked like one enormous block. Her large, square face was framed with thick chestnut hair flowing over strong, square shoulders. She grasped Judith's shoulders with big square hands and studied her with merry eyes, a smile playing upon her generous mouth. "Judith!" she cried. "What a lovely name. And so tall!" She turned to the other girls. "Here is competition for your games. I'll bet Judith will outrace you all, with those long legs."

The girls laughed and crowded around her. "Maybe she could beat even Nathan," one girl sighed dreamily. They all broke into gales of easy laughter, with Eloise laughing loudest of all.

"Come, Judith," Eloise chortled, "we'll explain this mysterious Nathan along the way."

Judith was bewildered and confused. She had never been a part of a group her own age, and didn't know exactly how to act. In Cana she was considered strange, and the other girls had kept their distance. These girls were welcoming her without reservation and with no suspicion in their eyes. Their teasing was merry and kind, and their faces an open invitation to be one of them. She felt suddenly shy and tongue-tied. She looked to her father for support and Phinehas smiled and nodded to her, *go*. One of the girls grabbed her hand and she found herself being pulled along as one of the group.

Elkatma watched her leave. "She's never had a friend," she said sadly.

Enos touched Elkatma's shoulder sympathetically. "Here she will have many, for our children know that God is no respecter of persons, that a soul is unique and fills a place which only that particular soul can fill. They also know the circumstances of Judith's birth, and being older than she, will help her in every way they can."

He then left Phinehas and Elkatma at their tent and invited them to eat their evening meal as his guests in the dining hall for the priests and monks in the temple. They entered the courts through the northwestern gate of Naphtali and stood uncertainly at the door until a smiling white-robed monk gestured for them to follow and led them to the far end of the room to a table directly in front of the raised dais of the priests' table. Phinehas and Elkatma flushed, embarrassed at being so honored.

The room was long, stretching the entire width of the temple. The walls were plastered white with niches cut into the stone which held small, polished brass oil lamps. The table where Phinehas and Elkatma sat was parallel to the priests' table, but the others were laid out in the opposite way. They were low and finely made of pine and cedar, and the evening sun reflected on the burnished wood with a warm, inviting glow. Colorfully dyed rush mats on which they sat added a cheerful note to the otherwise white room. A lectern stood on a raised stone dais before the door to the passage which led through the rest of the main floor. It was made of lemonwood and delicately carved with cherubim whose uplifted faces looked adoringly at a wooden cross, crowned by a golden sunburst. Phinehas wondered if it, too, was the work of the gifted Joseph.

The monks were filing in, silently taking their assigned places according to rank. The higher ranking sat nearest to the priests' table, and so on down to the lowest. They were all dressed uniformly in flowing white robes. Phinehas was astonished to see the long, aquiline face of an Egyptian, the smooth, yellow skin and hooded eyes of an Indu, and across the room, a black, compassionate face from the depths of darkest Africa. Why, these men are from all over the world, thought Phinehas. Why would such men as these come to Mt. Carmel?

Enos and two other priests who Phinehas recognized as Judas and Mathias took their places, and as though on cue, the youngest members of the Brotherhood, who had not yet earned the privilege to eat with the others, filed in carrying earthenware wine vessels and huge trays laden with loaves of white bread. They served the wine and bread, beginning with the priests and then going to Phinehas and Elkatma and on through the ranks of monks. No one spoke, for it was the rule that silence be kept throughout the meal, and after, that it be broken only according to rank and with permission of the others.

When all had been served, Enos stood and spread his hands above the cup and intoned the blessing. He raised the cup with outstretched arms as an offering to the Lord. He drank, and then broke the bread, following the ritual of the wine, his deep, rich voice blending with the evening song of birds and the soughing of the pines. The young monks returned with kettles of steaming stew which they ladled into plain pottery bowls placed before each, again beginning with the priests. After the stew came trays of grapes, apples, and melons, and plates of cheeses and bowls of ripe, salty olives. The fare was simple, but the stew was thick and delicately seasoned, the fruit was fresh and chilled, and the cheese sharp and aged exactly right. Phinehas and Elkatma ate with relish as a senior monk stood at tht lectern and read the Word of the Lord from a huge scroll.

When the meal was finished, Enos asked Phinehas to walk with him. They strolled through the courts and out the Gate of Ephraim where Elkatma pled weariness and retired to the tent. The night was warm and clear and the first stars began to wink in the velvet sky. The scent of laurel and jasmine and earth drifted in the still night air, carrying with it the poignant song of a nightingale. It was a tranquil night, soft and surprisingly cool after the heat of the day. They walked across the verdant lawn and through the trees that hid the temple from the sea until they reached the rocky bluff that jutted out over the dark water far below.

They stood for a while in companionable silence, drinking in the cool night air and basking in the contentment of one another's company. When Enos spoke, his voice was musing and gentle. He didn't look at Phinehas, but stared out across the black expanse of sea as though he saw a vision of the words he spoke somewhere on its farthest shore.

"I come here often, Phinehas, to look across the sea and wonder at God's plan for man. Sometimes I wonder why He created such a miserable lot, for surely in His wisdom He knew we would become the greedy, sinful selfish beasts we are. I look across the sea and think of all the souls out there, writhing in the misery of poverty and disease and hopelessness, endlessly searching for that fleeting thing called happiness. I sometimes weep for the hardness of their hearts and think, if only they would listen and know that they are strangers on this earth, and that all their search for gold and riches and the pleasures of the flesh only drives them farther from their true abode, which is with God. I hear their mournful cry riding on the waves and in the very air around me, and their groans assail my ears as the groans of the slaves in Egypt must have assailed the ears of the Lord. My heart is heavy with their woes. The rich lanquish in their luxurious homes, caring only for the silks upon their skin and jewels upon their fingers. Their women spend hours in front of mirrors, dabbling in their paint pots and arranging their hair to find the most provocative style. Their tables are laden with rich foods and delicacies and they gorge themselves, trying to diminish a gnawing hunger which cannot be satisfied with food."

Enos had begun to pace back and forth. His voice seemed to Phinehas to have suddenly become old and tired. Enos had always been so vibrant and full of enthusiasm. It wasn't like him to take such a pessimistic view of the world. He was obviously deeply troubled, and Phinehas guessed that these thoughts had been brewing in his mind for a long time. Phinehas didn't comment, but listened quietly without interruption, wise in knowing that speech could often be a cleansing purge for a troubled soul.

"There is such a longing in the souls of men," Enos continued urgently. "A yearning, searching, restlessness that their minds cannot comprehend. They think, 'perhaps if I had a different wife or husband I would be more content,' and so they take a mistress or a lover or frequent the brothels and try to forget their loneliness by wallowing in lust. Some take opium or drink strong wine, numbing their brains in a vain attempt to escape the torment of their thoughts. Our people tell me that even in Jerusalem the number of writs of divorce presented to the Sanhedrin increases at an appalling rate, and the abortionists are getting rich. Young women flaunt their breasts and hair like brazen hussies in the brothels and think they are being smart and fashionable. Our young men wear the Greek hat of the athletes and take part in all the pagan games, unashamed of their nakedness, but ashamed of the mark of Abraham."

Enos sat on a stone next to Phinehas and buried his face in his hands. His voice broke with emotion and his shoulders drooped in desolation. The moon had risen over the trees and its silvery light played on the face of the dark sea and outlined Enos' pitiful form.

"I despair for the world of men, Phinehas. My spirit weeps for their very souls. Our youth have become idolators, turning away from the God of their fathers from Pharisaic rigidness which chokes a man's free will. And who can blame them, truthfully? Religion has become a meaningless ritual, a gigantic list of dos and don'ts that our youth look upon with scorn. They see the outward act of sacrifice and ritual, but the Pharisees have thrown away the key to the meaning of the act, or else they feel that the common folk have no right to use that key because of their unwashed poverty or lack of means to bribe a priest. They teach a God of wrath and little mercy, and weave graphic pictures of the torments they will suffer for eternity unless they follow the smallest letter of the Law. But then they interpret the Law so finely that people find it impossible to follow it in the world of men, and so they turn away in helplessness and despair. The Sadducees tell them the soul is not immortal, and reincarnation a foolish myth, so why not 'eat, drink, and be merry,' for tomorrow they'll be food for worms. They hear the law of an eye for an eye, and 'He who lives by the sword shall die by the sword,' and then they look around and see that thieves and murderers and adulterers are getting richer by the day and living in fine houses with slaves to tend their every need, while they who try to live by the Law go to bed hungry each night and watch their children die of the disease of poverty."

Enos' voice rang with bitterness and anger, and his hands trembled in his agitation. "What am I to do, Phinehas? How can I give them faith when they have no faith, and hope where there is no hope? We teach a God of love and mercy, a God who is just and forgiving. We tell them man makes his own destiny and what he sows in this life he will reap in the next. We know the truth and have the key! We know each soul is part of the Divinity, a part of God, whose natural state is spiritual and not a house of flesh. How do I give them meaning to their lives on earth, tell them that this world is but a school where each soul learns the lessons of the spirit by using this house of flesh to experience those ancient truths of patience, charity, and love?

"I want them to know, as surely as the sun rises and sets, that every time a man commits a crime against his fellows he does violence to his own soul! Each time he cheats and steals and lies and indulges in the sins of pride and hate and selfishness, he commits an outrage to his soul! And this violence and outrage must become manifest in the flesh, and so they suffer heart diseases, stomach ulcers, and cancers in their bowels, and then cry vengeance to the very gates of heaven to an unrelenting, uncompassionate God. But if we teach this openly, we are charged with blasphemy and stoned until there will be no one left to bear the light of truth."

Enos groaned. He leaned against a tree and his body sagged beneath its burden of distress. "I see the world being drawn into a morass of sin, a quicksand of oblivion from which there is no escape. I see the world as it was in Noah's day, when only by wiping man from the face of the earth could there be a new beginning."

He looked at Phinehas and whispered, "What am I to do, Phinehas? I am a priest, a servant of the Most High. I would die for all those souls if that would save them from destruction. What am I to do?"

Phinehas' heart ached for Enos' suffering. He frantically searched for the right words to ease him, patting his shoulder like one would a distressed child. "You ask too much, old friend. You ask to be the savior of the world, and only God can save the world. You've spent your life preparing for the One to do just that, and now in your old age you begin to despair, because you fear that you might not live to see the fruits of your life's work. But you are forgetting something, Enos. You're forgetting the immortality of your soul. You'll see and celebrate those fruits whether in this world of flesh or in the world of spirit."

Enos' voice was harsh. "Ah! But therein lies my sin, for I have not forgotten, but have lost hope, and bear the sin of unbelief and loss of faith that our Messiah will come." He buried his face in his hands and wept, horrible, strangled sobs which tore from deep in his throat.

Phinehas was aghast and bewildered. God help me, he silently begged. Use my mind and tongue to heal this, your faithful servant. After a few moments he felt the tension drain from Enos and he dried his eyes on his sleeve and mumbled an apology for having lost his control.

The moon was full beyond the trees and shone directly on them from its perch above the sea. They could see one another clearly. Phinehas waited until he was sure Enos had fully regained his composure, and then said gently, "Do you remember Ann, wife of Joachim of Cana?" Enos nodded. "Ann gave birth to a child this spring," Phinehas continued. "A baby girl whom she named Mary."

Enos straightened and looked disinterestedly at Phinehas. "I remember Joachim died some time ago. So Ann has found a husband then," he said politely.

Phinehas shook his head. "Two years and more have passed since Joachim was gathered to our fathers." He looked steadily into Enos' eyes and said slowly and deliberately, "Ann has found no husband."

A look of shock crossed Enos' face. "What are you saying, Phinehas!" he cried incredulously. "Ann and Joachim were often here on Mt. Carmel and worshipped in our temple. Ann was a pious and most holy woman. Her devotion to the Lord was an example to us all, and her patience and her charity were unsurpassed, and now you tell me she has committed such a sin?" Enos groaned and pulled his robes as though to rent them. "This is more than I can bear. If one whom I regarded as the saintliest of saints could fall into the clutches of Belial, what will happen to those souls who are weak and helpless in his hands and have no armor of the Lord? Why have you chosen now to tell me such a thing? You are my oldest and my closest friend and this night I have bared my soul to you, for there is none other who could share my sorrow, and now you heap ashes on my head and add increase to my grief. Have you no pity in your heart?"

Phinehas flinched under Enos' anger, but then ignored his outburst and continued in a steady voice. "Ann claims that she is free from sin. She says she has lain with no man. She claims an angel of the Lord visited her in her time of mourning and promised her a child, a child who would be consecrated to the Lord from her infancy and would be filled with the Holy Spirit from her mother's womb. He instructed her to call her name Mary."

Enos was astonished. "What tale is this you tell me?"

"Ann lives in her sister Ismeria's house and only those of the Brotherhood knew of her condition. Elkatma assisted at the birth and brought the babe forth from Ann's womb. She said it was a wondrous child of perfect form and beauty. She came forth without a cry, and as she lay in Elkatma's arms, Elkatma said it seemed as though the babe recognized her and regarded her with the eyes of a wise, old woman instead of the vacant eyes of a newborn babe.

"When Cana heard about the child, there were many whispered tales. Some thought Ann must be insane, and in her insanity forgot the moment of her indiscretion. Others thought she must have been abused, and shame and fear of ridicule forced her to invent the story of the angel. None were willing to publicly charge her with adultery because of the many acts of charity she performed, and because of their love and gratitude towards her. Ann is aware of what is whispered in the town, but takes it all serenely and has unmoveable faith in the Lord. She sings praises to His Holy Name and spends her days in prayer and thanksgiving.

"When her time of purification passed, she took the child to Capernaum to Anna the prophetess, so she might bless the child and advise Ann as to the child's upbringing. It is said that as Ann was nearing the city gates, Anna was reading the stars for three prominent men of the city. Knowing nothing of the child, or even that they were coming, Anna suddenly gave a cry of joy, and leaping up, left the three men, to their astonishment, and hurried to the gates where she greeted Ann with open arms. She took the child and called her 'blessed of all women,' and prophesied the child would bring great sorrow and great joy into the world and all the generations would call her holy."

Enos was speechless. A thousand thoughts raced through his mind and he gestured feebly to Phinehas to say no more. "Be still, Phinehas," he croaked. "Let me think. Let me absorb what you have just told me." He began to pace among the rocks and trees, combing his fingers through his hair, tugging at his beard and mumbling under his breath.

Finally he stopped in front of Phinehas, but Phinehas
held up his hand. "Before you speak, I would tell you one
more tale." He told Enos of the strange weakness that
overcame him whenever he thought of the Messiah. He
told him of his reaction in the field on the day the messenger from God had appeared to him, and how again,
only this day, he'd had to steady himself against the poor
donkey to keep from falling to the ground. "When Elkatma returned that night from delivering Ann's child and
told me all that had transpired, I again felt the weakness
and stumbled out into the cool night air. When I had
regained my strength, I went up to the roof of my house.
My heart was full and my eyes could not contain their
tears of joy, though my mind knew not why. I began to
pray unto the Lord, but my words could not express the
emotions in my soul. I fell to my knees in ecstasy and my
spirit prayed in unknown tongues."

Enos gave an exultant cry and threw his arms around
Phinehas. "You have restored my faith, old friend. Surely
God has heard my cry and sent you to me on this night!
We are old men, Phinehas, and may not live to see our
great Messiah, but God in all His mercy has granted that
we see the beginning of His wondrous Day, and for that I
give Him praise and thanksgiving. You saw the faces of
our brothers from distant lands?" Phinehas nodded. "They
bring us missives from wise men across the earth which
I've had no heart to even read. Now I must hurry back
and search their contents and read again the prophecies
and study all the signs and visions given through our
people, for surely this child Mary is a most momentous
sign!

"Oh! I am shamed that I have wallowed in my self-pity
and my lack of faith that the Lord God would rescue His
children from this vale of tears. Who am I, mere man of
clay, that I thought I could bring to pass the glorious Day
of the Lord? Only the Creator of the Universe knows the
hour of His coming. He put all the signs of His coming
Day before my eyes, and through the anguish that lingered in my heart, I refused to see them. I have sinned
against the Lord and against my very soul. Blessed is the
Lord, and Blessed be His holy Name, that He has sent His
servant Phinehas to open my blinded eyes and melt my

hardened heart, and allowed me once more to walk in His path of light and see the glorious works He has performed!"

Enos pulled Phinehas to his feet. The long journey of the day and the heightened emotion of the last hours had sapped Phinehas' strength, and he staggered as he tried to stand. Enos steadied him and cried out in alarm, "Are you unwell, my friend?"

"No," said Phinehas. "I am only weary to the marrow of my bones. This day and night has drained me, and I long for sleep."

"I've added thoughtlessness to my already many sins!" wailed Enos.

Phinehas laughed. "I'm sickened by your 'many sins,' old fool. Forget them as the Lord has already forgotten, and tend to the task at hand. Help me to my good wife and my bed and then be off to search your learned books and counsel with your wise men from afar. I'm a simple man who needs his rest, so off with you and leave me to dream my dreams in peace."

Enos threw his head back and laughed heartily, then put his arm about Phinehas' shoulders and led him back along the path toward the temple. Enos spoke excitedly all the way, but Phinehas hardly heard him. He could only think of his bed and Elkatma's warm body at his back.

When the eastern sky began to leaden with the promise of a new dawn, Enos was still in the temple library pouring over scrolls and missives, his wonder and excitement growing every hour. He rolled a scroll and took it into the storage room beneath the temple porch and mounted the spiral steps which led to the upper story and his rooms. He took a clean white tunic from a peg on the wall and made his way silently back down the stairs and to the baths. After he had washed himself clean physically, and symbolically of his sins, he returned to his rooms and dressed himself in his priestly robes to perform the morning worship. He dropped the violet robe over his head, the golden bells tinkling as it fell to his sandaled feet, and slipped into the heavy Breastpiece of Decision, settling the ephod on his chest and tying the embroidered belt. He settled the tall miter on his head and tied the gold plate with a velvet ribbon. He met Judas and Mathias, dressed in white robes with purple sashes and turbans wound tightly around their heads, on the stairs.

They left the temple through the far gate and followed the path outside the courts to the front of the temple. The white-robed and hooded monks lined the red brick walk at the entrance to the gate of Judah, waiting for the priests to lead them in procession to the altar of the Lord. The people had gathered in the inner court before the temple porch, and as the sun's first rays burst through the stately pines, they joined their voices in singing the glorious Psalms of David.

The sleepless night had not tired Enos; on the contrary, he had never felt more wide awake. His jubilant voice rang above the others and he feared his exultation would overflow in a shocking display of joyful laughter. He saw Phinehas standing down below with Elkatma and Judith by his side, and fought an impulse to wink his eye and shout to Phinehas the things he'd read that night. He marvelled at his blindness and failure to see the signs that God had wrought. He wanted to laugh at the frailty of the human mind to comprehend the ways of the Lord, and knew now that only through God's gifts of wisdom and knowledge could man begin to understand. He flushed in his embarrassment at the audacity of the sons of men who in their arrogance thought they could rule the world and even all the universe through their own house of flesh, and gave no thought to God's great plan and knew not that all their childish effort came to naught unless guided by the hand of God. Who were kings and princes, rulers in rich houses, and merchants with their treasures wrought in gold? Nothing, save but souls lost upon a lonely planet, far away from home, ever searching for the map to chart their way back to that misty, long-forgotten point of their beginning. But now, thought Enos, that map is on the way! For certainly the signs pointed to the imminent arrival of the Messiah! He would bring with Him a new covenant, a new teaching from the Lord, and the sons of men would at long last know who they were and whence they came, and how they could return.

Enos mused upon how the Messiah would come. As a priest? A king, such as the glorious David? Would He lead the Sons of Light to war with the Sons of Darkness and overthrow the Herodians and the pagan rule of Rome and establish the supremacy of God once more in Israel? Would He be a teacher who would enlighten the Sons of Light as to the mysteries of the ages? In any event, they must be prepared for all possibilities. The Scriptures seemed to point to two Messiahs, one a priest, such as Aaron, and one a king, such as David.

Enos thrilled to the thought of the massive amount of work to be done and the preparations to be made. His hands and body mechanically enacted the worship ritual, but his mind raced to the days and weeks ahead. His body and mind, which only hours ago he had considered worn and dulled, now flowed with renewed vigor and life. He looked down again at Phinehas and thought, *And what part will his child have to play in all of this?*

Chapter 3

Enos caught Phinehas' eye as he led the procession out of the temple, and with an imperceptible movement of his head, indicated to him to follow. Phinehas whispered a few words to Elkatma and then entered the lower level of the temple through the dining hall and met Enos in the long, center passage.

"You are looking well this morning," he said jokingly to Enos. "A sleepless night seems to fare well with you."

"A sleepless night which restores a man's spirit fares well with every soul," answered Enos. He turned to Judas and Mathias. "I wish to hold a meeting in the library as soon as possible. Judas, would you inform the scribes that I would like to use the library this morning and help them to set up their work in one of the other rooms? Also, if Zermada is in the library, please ask her to stay. Mathias, I would like Shalmar and Philo to join us, and also our three brothers who are visiting from distant lands."

The two priests nodded and hurried away, wondering at the change in Enos. For weeks he had been sluggish and despondent, almost reluctant to make decisions and issue orders, as though he'd lost all confidence in his ability to do so. Today he was charged with energy and wore an air of contagious excitement.

Enos and Phinehas continued down the corridor. "Zermada is a Syrophoenician woman," said Enos. "She is a gifted astrologer and has studied extensively with the wise men of the far eastern nations. She is also a dreamer and a prophetess, and her knowledge and insight have been invaluable to us in determining the conditions necessary for the entry of the Messiah. She journeys to Carmel often to confer with us and compare the knowledge of the eastern lands with the conclusions we have drawn. Being a Syrophoenician, she can move freely through the land without obstruction from the Romans."

They had reached the spiral stairway and Enos beckoned to Phinehas. "Come and help me out of these robes, Phinehas."

Phinehas was surprised. Very few laymen were invited into the private upper rooms in the temple. He hesitated and then followed Enos up the stairs. Enos' room was large but sparsely furnished. A narrow, uncomfortable-looking cot jutted out from an end wall, with a small, rough table beside it littered with candle stubs and odd pieces of parchment. A long uncarved table stretched between two windows on the south wall and was piled high with scrolls and inkpots and rolls of unused parchment. The single wooden chair looked hard and uninviting. Enos' few articles of clothing hung on pegs, and the floor was bare, with not even a rush mat by the cot to keep bare feet from freezing during the cold winter months.

Phinehas suppressed a shiver at such austerity. Even Elkatma and I, poor as we were, have more comfort than this, he thought. He helped Enos out of the elaborate robes and was even more surprised when he said, "I may want you to handle the sacred books at the meeting, Phinehas, so come and we will wash our hands in the waters of purification."

They went out onto the porch to the brazen laver. It was a large, circular bowl filled with water blessed by the priests. On the lower sides of the bowl were two spigots which let the water run into the huge, saucerlike pedestal beneath, for the rule required that the hands must be washed in clean, flowing water. Phinehas was embarrassed at being so singularly honored as to take part in the ritual which, in the Jerusalem temple, was reserved only for priests. The Essenes believed that all the Sons of Light were priests in the eyes of God, even though they did not perform the priestly duties in the temple. Each Saint was called to a specific purpose, whether it be marriage and parenthood, tilling the fields, healing, or any other vocation, but the main purpose was to be a priest and spread the Word of the Lord. Phinehas knew all of this, but he still felt out of place taking part in the ritual, especially when Judas, Mathias, and Philo joined them on the porch.

Philo was the recorder for the Brotherhood. It was his duty to keep each member's genealogy and to record all the visions, dreams, healings, and visitations of the Elect. He was small, fine-boned, and not much younger than Enos and Phinehas. Somber and stern, he instructed the people in how to conduct their material as well as their spiritual lives according to the Law, and lamented when he saw them laughing and enjoying this sojourn on earth, for he considered such behavior frivolous and unbecoming to the Sons of Light. He acted as overseer to the scribes and kept them at their labors even in the relaxed atmosphere of summer. He'd glanced at Phinehas with surprise, as though wondering what a peasant was doing performing the sacred ritual, and then ignored him as he slowly and meticulously washed his hands.

Judas and Mathias were younger by at least ten or fifteen years. Judas was of medium height and well-fed. He was calm and kindly, with a mischievous twinkle in his eye. He wore a perpetual half-smile that invited teasing about the large, perfectly round, bald spot at the crown of his head. He was well-liked by the monks, particularly the younger ones who found him eager to help them adjust to the rigid, monastic way of life. He smiled at Phinehas and bid him good morning, not in the least disconcerted by his presence. Phinehas returned the smile and wondered if Judas was ever disconcerted.

Not so with Mathias. He was in a perpetual state of disquietude. He was tall and thin and constantly moving. His voice was high-pitched and static and grated on one's ears. His full beard was stiff and wiry and looked as though it was going to take flight from his face in a fit of nervousness. His eyes darted from one man to the other, and he looked fleetingly at Phinehas with a combination of fear and annoyance. Any break in the routine upset Mathias. His amazingly intelligent mind retained every bit of information it had ever received, and Phinehas could see him frantically searching that storehouse of information for a clue as to why Phinehas was here. For all his eccentric ways, everyone was fond of Mathias. Enos called him his walking library, and admitted he didn't know what he'd do without him.

They finished the ritual washing and went downstairs. Everyone who had been summoned to the library had assembled and were seated according to rank. Enos lifted his arms and spread his hands in a prayer of thanksgiving. He entreated the Lord to send His spirit into their midst, to inspire them to truth, to open their minds and hearts to understanding, to open their eyes to see and their ears to hear the wondrous workings of the Lord. Enos lowered his arms and they meditated in silence until he opened the meeting with the traditional greeting.

"Peace be with you. I have brought you here this morning that we might counsel together and pool our knowledge and wisdom to learn the will of the Lord. From ancient days our forefathers have preserved a record of God's dealings with men on earth, of all His visitations and revelations to the Children of Light. At the break of dawn in every Jewish Household the cry is heard, 'Hear, O Israel. The Lord thy God is One.' The Sons of Darkness understand Israel to refer to only those of Hebrew blood and of the faith of Judaism, but we of the Brotherhood know, through the mercy of God's revelation, that 'Israel' refers to all the Sons of God, a race of souls called to manifest the will of God in the world of flesh on earth. These souls are in all the wordly nations and all the wordly religions, and so I believe it the hand of Divine Providence that many of the different creeds and nations are represented here on Mt. Carmel today. We know God imparts His knowledge and wisdom in part to all such different sects and peoples, and it has, for many ages, been the aim and purpose of the Brotherhood to combine the revelations given by the Lord to all the Sons of God dwelling in the earth and thus learn of His divine will.

"Each of you has a special gift and special knowledge which I will now ask you to share with all the others, that we might discern the meaning and truth of God's word. For many generations, the primary function of the Brotherhood has been, through interpreting the signs and portents of the Lord, to make manifest those conditions necessary that the promised Messiah might enter the earth. This is why we are gathered here today, to review the signs of the past, and try to discern the signs to come, for my spirit tells me the Day of the Lord is truly drawing nigh and there is much to do and many preparations to make, lest the Most High find His watchmen asleep at the gate.

"Our brother Phinehas of Cana has brought me a tale which my heart perceives as a sign from the Most High. After I had heard Phinehas' tale of recent events in Cana, my spirit rejoiced and I spent the remaining hours of the night here in the library, studying again the words of the prophets, and reading and rereading the signs and portents of the heavens. As I read, my excitement and my conviction that this was indeed a most momentous sign grew hourly."

A low murmur travelled through the room at these last exciting words. They looked questioningly at Phinehas, who flushed at being singled out.

"Would any wish to speak at this point?" Enos asked.

No one moved for a moment, and then the black-skinned Ethiopian stood. He bowed to Enos and to the others. He spoke in a soft, rich voice, slowly and carefully forming the unfamiliar Hebrew words. "My people also feel a momentous time is near at hand. We calculate the numbers of the times and read our ancient words of old and conclude the earth is moving rapidly to a new age. On my journey to your lands I found refuge from the elements with many of our brothers, both in monasteries and in village camps, and even those souls who till the soil and tend their flocks and know little of the movements of the stars or of the mysteries handed down of old also feel a stirring in the air. They too confess a sense of change, an undefinable spirit moving across the face of the earth."

The others nodded in agreement as he sat down, and the Egyptian rose to his feet. "My people concur with this appraisement. We too feel the stirrings in the souls of men. My land possesses the wisdom of the ages, preserved in the Great Pyramid, the key of which is known only to the Brotherhood. We study the phases and movements of the earth in conjunction with the history of man, and in comparing the temper of the present times with the signs and symbols contained in the Great Pyramid, we have drawn the conclusion that the time is approaching when a Great Initiate will be forthcoming into the world of men. My people are beginning to prepare for the instruction and initiation of One who will become the Master of Masters."

Enos intertwined his fingers over his breast and rocked back and forth on his heels. "My soul is edified by your words, my brothers, and lends strength to my conviction regarding the events which have taken place in Cana. Before we continue, let me ask Phinehas to enlighten you concerning this matter, and perhaps his story will add to your conclusions."

Phinehas stumbled to his feet. His hands trembled and tiny beads of sweat appeared on his brow. He had never spoken at a formal meeting before such distinguished men as these and he was extremely nervous. He said a silent prayer for help and stammered thanks to Enos for allowing him the honor, and then haltingly he began to tell the story of Ann of Cana. The others leaned forward on their benches, eagerly trying to catch every word, and an audible intake of breath was heard when Phinehas related that the expectant Ann had been without betrothed or husband. As he spoke, a feeling of truth and rightness seemed to flow through Phinehas, and his voice gained strength and conviction. He told the tale with simple clarity and Enos was filled with pride in his old friend. Phinehas ended the story with his own experience of speaking in strange tongues and then sat down. His audience sat in stunned silence and stared at him and at Enos, and then all began to speak at once, a thing unheard of in the strictly ordered Rule of the Essenes.

Enos raised his hand and admonished them to silence. "I understand your amazement and agitation, and realize there is much here to absorb, as I myself felt the same when I first heard this tale last night. The fifth hour is soon upon us. I suggest we go to our baths and morning meal and ponder this quietly in our minds and form our thoughts before we hold discussion upon this matter. Let us ask God to guide our thoughts and lead us on the path of truth so when we reconvene we may counsel together in a thoughtful and orderly manner."

Philo didn't hear Enos' prayer. His mind raced, and he was furious that Enos should allow himself to be duped by a country bumpkin and a woman who obviously was making a futile attempt to cover up her sin. He was shamed that such a piece of sordid nonsense should be presented before their distinguished brothers from the East as a matter of such importance. They would think them all as stupid and unlearned as this peasant from Cana, and that their beloved leader was no more than a doddering old fool, grasping in desperate senility at any straw that hinted at the coming of the Messiah.

Zermada caught Shalmar's eye and raised her brows in puzzled question. Shalmar answered by a slight shrug of his shoulders and wished he could discuss this turn of events with her before the morning meal, but knew he'd have to honor Enos' request for silent contemplation and wait until after the evening prayers to speak to her alone.

Mathias nervously pulled at his thumbs and twitched at the prospect of the uproar this would cause among the Brothers. The very thought of arguments and heated discussions made his ulcer bite, and the taste of gall rose in his throat. He wished they'd never heard of this Ann and her mewling child, or of Phinehas of Cana. Hadn't this man caused enough trouble with his visions and special children already? He longed only for peace and orderliness, and now Enos would surely ask him for his opinion, and what was he going to say then? All he could do was pray he wouldn't be asked to speak until he could see which way the wind blew, for to be the lone dissenting voice was unthinkable to him, even if that's what he felt. To be the only one in agreement with Enos would be equally distasteful. Well, he'd have to wait and see.

Judas was the only one who took the impact of the tale calmly. He bowed his head to Enos' prayer and a bemused smile played upon his mouth. Why not? he thought. Simply because he knew of no woman conceiving without the aid of man, that didn't mean it couldn't happen! Didn't Melchizedek appear on earth with neither mother nor father, and weren't all things possible with the Lord? He looked around the room and noted the emotions rampant in each face, until his eyes came to rest on Enos. He looked at him with affection and thought again, why not! Judas had seen the listlessness and despair into which Enos had fallen these past months, and thought that anything which would relieve him of his agony could not all be the works of Belial. He suppressed a chuckle at the thought of what would happen when this news made its mysterious way from camp to camp, for nothing was hidden for long from their Brothers in the towns. The buzzing of whispered gossip would be louder than the Lord's own beehive! I have a feeling, he thought, that our ordered, contemplative way of life is about to come to a close, especially if this is true. And if it proved a hoax, what of it! At least for a time the Brothers would be moved to action and time would prove if this were of God or no.

At the finish of the prayer, they hurried to the baths and donned clean, white robes in which to eat the morning meal. The temple area was deserted, for the summer people had already assembled in their communal dining hall in the complex of buildings below the temple. In the old days, when many of the Elect had come to Carmel for the summer, they had eaten at their tents, but now with the political atmosphere being so oppressive, few families ventured to the Holy Mount, and so those that did ate together with the students. The monks were already seated in the temple hall and the others hurried in. Enos intoned the blessing over the wine and broke the bread. The morning meal consisted of only one dish which the younger initiates served. One monk read from the sacred Scriptures while another stood beside him and expounded upon the hidden meaning of the words.

The monks felt the tension in the air and noticed that the usually relaxed meal was being gulped down hurriedly, and so followed suit. They didn't know what had taken place in the library, but whatever it was, it must have been explosive. They looked at Phinehas curiously, because it was highly irregular for a guest to join them for the morning repast. They surmised that whatever was taking place, it had much to do with this simple farmer from Cana.

Joseph of Nazareth also wondered. He remembered the tall, blond child who had smiled at him the day before, and of the furor her birth had caused eight years before. Her birth had split the Brotherhood into two dissenting camps, one who believed Phinehas' tale of his vision, and the other who scoffed at the ravings of an old man. Perhaps the child had shown unusual abilities and gifts, and the leaders were now having to reassess their stand regarding the girl. According to her father, the angel had prophesied the girl would become a leader of her people and a great teacher. Joseph smiled and wondered how the Brotherhood would accept the leadership of a female, particularly in this day when women were considered almost unclean and little more than chattels of their husbands and fathers. He had heard the women jokingly call the Jerusalem priests the "bleeding Pharisees" because they turned their faces to the wall so quickly upon meeting a female on the streets that they bumped their noses and caused them to bleed. The women in the Brotherhood were treated far better than those outside, for the Essenes knew the soul had no sex, but there were those who still felt that only an inferior soul would choose to incarnate in a female body. As for himself, Joseph thought he'd have no objection to a female leader. He thought with fondness of his gentle mother, God bless her departed soul, and could feel no objection whatsoever in his heart.

After the meal and the ritual washing of hands, Enos again stood at the head of the small assembly in the library. "I hope you have had time to absorb the events of the morning, somewhat," he said. "Shalmar, would you be the first to share your thoughts with us?"

Shalmar hesitated a moment, not at all sure what his thoughts were. "I am a student of the beliefs and religions of all men on earth, and while I can find no parallel to such a conception in the faith of the Jews, there are legends of such from other faiths."

He nodded to the Hindu. "The great prophet Buddha Gautama's mother is said not to have lain with her husband for eighteen months before his birth. In the scriptures of Zend and Zoroaster there is mention of a virgin giving birth, and of course in the complex pantheon of the Greeks and Romans one can find evidence of such. While we consider their gods as myths, we realize there is a grain of God's truth in all things. In our own Law, I find no such evidence, though we are aware of the twinness of the soul, its positive and negative, aggressive and passive attributes, as well as its being both male and female. I am also reminded of the ancient tradition regarding the beginning of creation when the soul could occupy all manner of material bodies and had the ability to use its influence to change the form of that body. In conclusion, I draw no conclusion at this point."

Everyone laughed at Shalmar's feeble joke, and he added, "I find it in the realm of possibility, but I feel we must proceed with extreme caution, lest we fall into a trap laid by Belial."

The Hindu asked permission to speak. "What Shalmar says is true—there is the traditional story of the unusual birth of the Buddha, and the idea of a virgin birth is not unknown in the world of men, though it is certainly not a generally accepted truth. I too feel we must proceed with caution, but proceed."

Enos thanked him and asked, "Is it agreed that there is enough evidence to proceed? I should like to hear any dissenting voice."

Philo rose without waiting for permission from Enos. His voice trembled and his face was flushed with anger. "I must dissent! I feel this is foolishness, a stumbling block laid before us by Belial! A woman conceiving without the seed of man is unthinkable and an affront to the Lord, our God. We are tottering on the brink of grave sin, and if we lend any credence whatsoever to such a sordid affair, and if this news leaks out among the camps as all happenings on the Mount are wont to do, I foresee an epidemic of wantonness among the women who can then claim the fruits of their sins were visited upon them by an angel of the Most High. I think it borders on blasphemy!"

The others received his outburst in embarrassed silence, and doubt began to grow until Judas slowly stood and regarded them all with his bemused smile. Enos took a deep breath and silently thanked God for this gentle man who stood beside him. Judas never failed in his ability to soothe ruffled feathers and smooth troubled waters. He squeezed Philo's shoulder in a brotherly caress. "Thank you, Brother Philo. God in His mercy is indeed good to send us such a soul as you. We weak vessels of clay sometimes allow ourselves to be carried away to the heights of folly by our ardent desires, and so we have great need of such a one to bring us back to earth so we might examine the evidence with minds unclouded by our emotions."

Philo flushed under this high praise and the anger faded from his eyes. Judas rubbed his hands together as though relishing the job ahead and said enthusiastically, "Now then! Let us proceed with order and see just what we have here in our laps." The others laughed and leaned back in

their seats and the tension in the room disappeared. "First,
I think, we should discuss this Ann of Cana and see if
we find any evidence of cunning or guile in our sister.
Enos, would you or Phinehas tell us what you know of
Ann?"

Enos looked at Phinehas, who gestured to him to speak.
They were all seated at a large table in the center of the
room and the sun was pouring through the high arched
windows. Enos didn't stand. He decided to preserve the
now-relaxed atmosphere and keep the meeting as informal
as possible. He spoke lightly and with ease, as though he
were speaking of nothing more startling than the heat of
the day.

"I know Ann very well," he began. "Prior to Joachim's
death they spent nearly every summer with us on Mt.
Carmel. Joachim was an extraordinary gardener, though
his livelihood in Cana was through his flocks. It is due
largely to his efforts that we now have our lovely gardens
and the beauty that surrounds our beloved temple. Ann
was the most pious and saintly of souls. She was a leader
among the women of the Brotherhood and was constantly
sought out for her wise counsel. The family lived mod-
estly in Cana, though Joachim owned an extremely large
flock, for most of his profits found its way into the pockets of the poor or into our temple treasury. Their gener-
osity of worldly goods and time and labors were un-
matched by any other.

"Ann and Joachim had three children. The oldest, Zebedee, is married and lives outside the city walls of Jerusalem. He is a wholesale fisherman. He owns a small fleet of
boats on the Sea of Galilee, plus a number of stalls in the
market places in Jerusalem. The palace of the High Priest
and the Fortress Antonia are among his clientele, and so
you can see that his business is very large and lucrative.
Zebedee provides work for many people and is a generous
and fair employer. He is wealthy and highly respected
among the ruling class in Jerusalem. He is not an active
member of the Brotherhood, for his wife Salome is of the
priestly family of Levites and so there is some dissension
there. Ann's oldest daughter, Mary Josie, who is called
simply Josie, is married to Marcus ben Cleopas of Jerusalem, another influential and well-known family. The

youngest daughter Salone is but a young girl, and is still with her mother.

"Ann and Salone make their home in Cana with Ann's sister Ismeria. This is not due to any selfishness or lack of charity on the part of Zebedee or Josie, but Ann was loath to leave her beloved Galilee to live in the heat and noise of the city. Also, she and her sister have always been particularly dear to one another, and since Ismeria is also a widow, it seemed natural that Ann and Salone should join her household. Ismeria has two daughters— Mary, born shortly before her father's death four years ago as the final manifestation of the love in that union, and Elizabeth. I believe some of you know Elizabeth, who attended our school here on Mt. Carmel." The other priests and Philo nodded. "Elizabeth has married Zachariah ben Berachiah who is a priest in the division of Abijah in the Jerusalem temple. He does not embrace our tenets, but is a good and godly soul who does not object to his wife's preference, and allows her to journey to Carmel to celebrate our feasts. He maintains his home in Ain Karim, a village in the hills of Judea, to protect Elizabeth from any slights she might have to endure from the wives of other Jerusalem priests in regard to her beliefs."

Enos sat back and ran his fingers through his hair. "There is little else I can tell you as far as facts regarding Ann. I believe her to be completely truthful, and for her to commit a sin against God to be unthinkable. If Ann had committed a sin of impurity, I believe without question she would confess that sin and make a public atonement, but never would she blaspheme by deliberately inventing the tale of the visitation of an angel and that the child was conceived without the seed of man!"

Everyone in the room was quiet for some minutes, each absorbed in his own thoughts. Then Phinehas spoke. "Everything you heard from Enos is true. I have lived as a neighbor to Ann all of my life, and I wholeheartedly agree with him in regard to the purity of her charactor. Even the Sons of Darkness who reside in Cana do nothing to cause her embarrassment, though of course they believe she has committed a grave sin."

Judas added, "I also concur with Phinehas and Enos, for I too know Ann well. And while I do not say that all

came to pass as Ann believes, I do know in my heart that
this is no deliberate deception on her part. She may be the
victim of Belial, but she would never knowingly perpetrate
an untruth."

The Egyptian rose and walked to the window. He
stared for some time at the beauty beyond, then turned
and said. "There are mysteries which are far beyond the
comprehension of man. We men of dust can do no more
than search and delve and pray to the Creator for enlightenment as far as our feeble minds can accept it. Anything
is possible to the King of all the Universe. My counsel is
to search and probe and try to discern the heart of God."
He bowed to Philo. "Our brother Philo is right to counsel
caution, though I feel we must trust the love and compassion of the Lord, for if we proceed in purity of heart and
purpose, I am convinced the One God will overlook the
deed and remember only the purpose for which it was
committed."

Mathias had been silent throughout the entire meeting.
He had wriggled in his seat and thought he would expire
during Philo's violent outburst. He saw they were now all
in agreement, at least on the issue of whether to pursue
this thing or not, so he felt it was safe to speak since even
Philo seemed mollified and willing to proceed. "I agree. I
agree," he said in his high, reedy voice. "I think absolutely
we should proceed, but keep in mind it is a search and
that we are not at all prepared to aver it as truth. Absolutely."

Enos suppressed a smile and tried to sound gravely
impressed by what Mathias had to say. He had noted the
younger priest's acute discomfort throughout the day, and
felt pity for the poor soul who simply couldn't bear to
express his own opinions for fear they would be in conflict
with someone else's. "Thank you, Mathias. You are absolutely right as usual. We have sat for many hours, and I
for one am growing stiff in my ancient joints. I suggest we
adjourn for a few minutes to walk about a bit and refresh
ourselves and then resume."

His suggestion met with wholehearted approval and
they left the temple and stepped out into the fresh, mid-
afternoon air.

Phinehas was the last to return to the library and wearily found his place at the table. It had been a long and tiring day for him. He was a man of movement, used to spending his days in the labor of his hands, tilling his tiny fields and tending his meager flock. He was not accustomed to sitting for hours indoors, and he longed for the heat of the sun upon his back and the feel of a hoe or flail in his hands. He wondered about Judith and how she was adjusting to her first day on Mt. Carmel, and wished he could talk to Elkatma. He'd thought of asking Enos if he might be excused from further participation in the meeting, but on second thought decided that Enos knew him well enough so that if he had no more need of him he would have told him so.

Philo and Mathias were busy gathering inkpots and quills and rolls of clean parchment, for Enos had asked that a record of the proceedings be made. When all were ready, Enos asked Zermada to share with them all the astrological signs that might point to the imminent entry of the Messiah.

Phinehas knew nothing about astrology and couldn't follow the strange terms Zermada used. She explained how certain periods were found to come in cycles, and then launched into a long discourse on the position of the stars that stand in the dividing ways between the Universal, and those outside the spheres, which made no sense to Phinehas whatever. Zermada was expounding on the position of the polar star as it moved in relation to the southern clouds and how this made for the signs of a new age approaching which she called the "Piscean Age," whose symbol would be the fish. At this Phinehas inwardly smiled. Would the lowly fish then be the sign of the Great Messiah? This age, according to Zermada, would be upon them in approximately ten to fifteen years. Ah, thought Phinehas, I am an old man and will not see this new age in this world. He then thought about Judith. In ten years she would be a woman of eighteen. He wondered what role she would play in the drama to unfold, and wistfully wished he could be with her. He looked around the room at the intent interest in the faces of the others, and for a moment regretted that he was not a more learned man and therefore able to better understand what it all meant. He could tell it was of vast importance, for even the eternal calm of Judas seemed shaken.

The Ethiopian gave a long report on numerology which Phinehas understood even less than astrology. The room was very warm, and only a light breeze stirred the late afternoon air. Phinehas felt his eyes grow heavy and struggled not to fall asleep. He knew that to do so during a session was a grave infraction of the Rule. Any monk who did so was deprived of a fourth of his food ration and excluded from the sacred meal for thirty days. Phinehas didn't know if this particular rule would apply to himself, as he was not an initiated monk, but the ignominy and embarrassment of such an act would be punishment enough.

When Shalmar and Judas discussed the Holy Scriptures, Phinehas became alert. Here at last was a subject he knew as well as any, and could follow the words with ease. They were searching out the words of the prophets whose hidden meaning would pertain to this day and age, and Phinehas grew more and more excited as the Scriptures seemed to speak of his own generation. They had the scroll of the prophet Isaiah before them, and as Judas read the words, Shalmar revealed their possible connection to this generation.

" 'Your country is waste, your cities burn with fire; your land before your eyes strangers devour.' "

Shalmar explained: "This could refer to the famine of four years ago, and the fire to the burning of the sun which laid waste to the crops and flocks of the land. The strangers are the Romans who extort exorbitant taxes that the people cannot pay, and so confiscate our lands and divide it among their friends and cohorts."

" 'Your princes are rebels and comrades of thieves, each one of them loves a bribe and looks for gifts.' "

"The princes are the Jerusalem priests, pandering to the Romans who rob the pockets of the poor, and selling forgiveness and salvation to those who can afford to pay for them."

" 'In days to come, the mountain of the Lord's house shall be established as the highest mountain and raised above the hills. All nations shall stream toward it.' "

"This could refer to the Brotherhood and Mt. Carmel, where all nations come to learn the heart of God."

" 'My people, a babe in arms will be their tyrant, and women will rule them.' "

"Perhaps this refers to the child of Ann called Mary, and to Judith, the daughter of Phinehas who was prophesied by an angel to become the leader of her people."

At this Phinehas gasped and felt weak. A sense of foreboding flooded over him. He thought of the persecutions the Brotherhood endured from the Herodians and the leaders of the Jerusalem temple, and his heart constricted with dread. If Judith became the leader of the Brotherhood, then it would be she who would have to undergo the harassments and abuses such as Enos had been subjected to over the years. Though Mt. Carmel was now considered a part of Phoenicia and thus was under Roman rule, this did not insure her safety from the Pharisees. The Romans seldom meddled in the religious affairs of the Jews, but the Pharisees exerted great control over the masses and the Romans were prone to placate them by listening to their whinings and making a weak attempt to carry out their mewling demands. Also, if the Messiah came in the order of David to restore Israel to a rule only under God, there was sure to be revolt and war, and Judith, as leader of the Brotherhood, would be the first to suffer retribution. The Romans would never stand for revolt, and their swords were swift and mighty in revenge. They were noted for their justice, yes, but also for their cruelty in dealing with rebellion. Phinehas quaked at the very thought of his child in the hands of Roman infidels.

The rest of the words whirled past Phinehas' ears like the drone of bees, but he heard nothing but the pounding of his own heart until he heard his name called, and he pulled himself out of his tumultuous reverie to stare at Enos, who was looking at him queerly. For a moment he wondered why, and then realized that Enos must have asked him something. "I'm sorry. My mind has strayed," he stammered, embarrassed.

"We wonder, Phinehas, if you remember the weather conditions on the day the angel visited you in the fields," said Judas.

"The weather? Why, I don't recall. The wheat was beginning to turn and so the day must have been hot and sunny as they always are that time of year," Phinehas said slowly, remembering. "I had gone to the fields to check the heads to estimate the yield and pull out the weeds. I was standing midway in the field and was looking down among the shafts, for I had suddenly smelled the strongest scent of violets and thought I might pick a bunch for Elkatha to surprise her." Phinehas' eyes widened and he said excitedly, "Now I remember! I heard a crash of thunder followed by a flash of lightning and for a moment was afraid, for it was not the season for rain and feared some unnatural storm would ruin my stand of barley. Then I saw the angel, standing in a misty light in the midst of my barley field and I fell to my face in the dirt. The sight of his glorious countenance threw all remembrance of the storm from my mind until this moment."

The others stared at him in silence until he feared he had uttered something shocking, and then Phinehas was amazed as Philo suddenly gave a strangled cry and bolted from his seat and threw himself at Phinehas' feet.

"Phinehas, my brother!" Philo croaked. "Forgive me! All these years I have never believed you and thought you naught but an old fool, and now God has revealed to me my folly and my sin. I have borne a grudge against you in my heart and have regarded you with a stiff neck and impatience in my thoughts. I humbly confess my sin to you and to all the Brothers, and ask for your forgiveness. I shall make atonement by voluntarily excluding myself from the sacred food of the masters and deprive myself of one-fourth of my food ration for one year!"

Phinehas was aghast! Philo was a teacher, a rabbi of the highest rank, while he, Phinehas was only a poor peasant, and now the rabbi was lying prostrate at his feet! Phinehas reached down and lifted Philo to his feet with one quick swoop and said harshly, to cover his embarrassment, "On your feet, man! Forgiveness for what sin? I see no sin in you nor feel the need to hand out any forgiveness! Are you a man so weak in purpose that you instantly embrace every tale that assaults your ears? No! You are a man who waits and mulls and ponders such in the deepness of his soul and waits until a sign from God reveals the truth to him. You are a man of strength and balance who keeps the Brotherhood on an even keel and protects us all from being buffeted hither and yon as the wind is wont to blow."

Philo was bewildered and looked at Enos. "Phinehas

speaks true, Philo," Enos replied. "There will be no voluntary punishment! We see today the beginning of a new age, the culmination of the works begun by our fathers in generations past. The Sons of Light are few compared in number to the Sons of Belial. We need men of steady minds and stout hearts, not one whose mind and body is weak from deprivation of his food."

"I too felt the same as you," Mathias said in a conciliatory tone. "I never truly believed Phinehas' story either, but I do not feel this is a sin against the Lord. Phinehas could have unwittingly fallen into a trap laid by Belial, but if the vision were of God, I reasoned, it would be known in His own season. Come, sit down and calm yourself."

Phinehas was relieved to see Philo do as Mathias said, but was puzzled. "Philo, what was it I said that dispelled your unbelief?" he asked.

"The thunder and the lightning and the scent of flowers in the field. I am the recorder of all such visitations to our people, and invariably such important visits from the realms above are preceded by such signs. Thus I knew you spoke truly and it was indeed of God," Philo answered.

The hour was growing late and the sun hung far out across the sea. Enos gave a brief summation of the proceedings of the day and it was agreed that they be presented before the Council of Twelve. Philo was charged with the duty of dispatching his monks to summon the Twelve to Mt. Carmel, and after Enos offered up a prayer of thanksgiving, they adjourned, each exhausted by the long, intense day, but exulting in the promise of the days and years to come.

The Council of Twelve agreed that, disregarding Ann's claim, the signs did point to a new age and to the coming of the Messiah. Word was circulated among the Brotherhood throughout Palestine that all who wished could dedicate their daughters as possible channels through which the Messiah might be made manifest in the flesh. Many were dedicated, and out of the many, twelve were chosen. The girls had to be in perfect health, both physically and mentally. Philo diligently searched every genealogy chart for any hint of genetic deformity or disease. Anna, the old prophetess from Capernaum, read their astrological charts to determine what each girl's purpose was in this generation and what personality and character traits each child was likely to develop. A student of phrenology kneaded each head in search for clues of character and ability, and a detailed account was drawn of each child.

Ann of Cana presented the infant Mary as a possible channel, which caused an uproar from some members. They felt a child born under such circumstances was impure and unworthy of such honor, but little Mary was perfect in every way and passed every test, so had to be accepted. Nine years after Mary's birth, the twelve chosen girls came to Mt. Carmel to enter into a period of intensive study and training to prepare one of them to become the mother of the Messiah.

Chapter 4

For the first few days Judith thought she was living out all her dreams of Mt. Carmel. Eloise outfitted her in the uniform short, white tunic worn by all permanent residents on Mt. Carmel, and assigned her a cell in the House of Lodgement for the girls. The cell was tiny—long and narrow with only one small window at the end, covered by a faded blue curtain which could be pushed back to let in the light and drawn to shield the cell from the House of Lodgement for boys next door. A straw pallet lay on the stone floor along one wall, covered by a rough linen sheet and one worn, thin blanket. The pillow was thin and limp, and for some reason made Judith feel a little forlorn. A small sturdy table was next to the pallet, holding a tiny brass lamp, a wax tablet, and a stylex. Judith bit her lower lip in anticipation of the hours she'd spend there studying.

Eloise took her on a tour of the whole compound, pointing out the baths and the communal dining hall where she'd take her meals. Judith learned that the students were all assigned various tasks in the compound, everyone taking turns in the kitchens and dining hall, helping in the storehouse and with keeping the grounds. Judith hid her dismay at that news. She detested any kind of household chores, and Elkatma had never insisted upon them but had freed her to run with Phinehas to the fields and flocks where he could teach her as he worked.

Enos kept his promise and showed her through the temple. It was patterned after the tabernacle Moses had set up in the wilderness, and everything had a mystical, spiritual meaning which added an air of sacred majesty to its simple beauty. The library and its adjoining storeroom fascinated Judith. Here the monks worked every day, copying the sacred Scriptures and keeping the records of all the Elect. She was intrigued to learn that the Brotherhood maintained communities throughout the world, and that all followed the same basic Rule, though with variations to suit each particular circumstance. Each community employed different emphasis on interpretation and purpose, but basically they were the same, and Mt. Carmel served as the headquarters and a kind of clearing house for the different schools of thought.

The library was Philo's realm of authority, and Enos, sensitive to Philo's jealous zeal for his position, allowed him to explain its function to Judith. Philo had no particular liking for children, but Judith's enthusiasm and delight in his work pleased him. She asked sensible, intelligent questions and seemed to grasp the fact that while the temple was the soul of all the Brotherhood, the library was its heart and mind. She praised him on small details that most adult visitors overlooked, and even made a suggestion or two that were quite worthy of consideration. He watched her leave the temple and was surprised to find himself hoping she would come again.

The only dampening to darken Judith's euphoria was the thought that Phinehas and Elkatma had to return to Cana, but her eagerness to begin her new life, and their promise to visit Carmel as often as possible, dissolved the lump in her throat and she was even able to smile as Elkatma's sturdy back disappeared down the steep incline of the path above the sea. That night she slept soundly and arose in the morning trembling with expectation of her first real day in school. By the end of the day she was both disillusioned and frightened. School was not at all the way she had imagined it would be, and sometime during the night it seemed as though Judith of Phinehas got lost and only an anonymous student was left in her place.

The day had begun innocently enough. The rule of silence until after the morning worship was difficult, but Judith knew she'd get used to that in time, and she'd also get over her acute embarrassment at the ritual baths taken every morning and evening. She wasn't however, prepared for the shock of being regarded as simply another student among many. She found she was expected to follow the same schedule and classes that the other students followed, and to her chagrin, she found them all useless and time-wasting.

She was also confronted with a variety of relationships to deal with. She'd led a singular, isolated life in Cana. For eight years the only company she'd known was that of her parents and their few friends, and now she was bewildered by so many people all openly accepting her as one of them. They overwhelmed her with their sudden smiles and gentle teasing, and she felt tongue-tied and inadequate under their barrage of words. It was worse with the students than with the adults. She felt shy and awkward with children her own age. She didn't know how to talk to them or how to play their games. She found their conversation dull and their games silly and childish.

She hid her impatience at the slow, tedious method of learning by rote, doggedly joining in the singsong chant with the others as they memorized the Scriptures word by word. Over and over they chanted, until she thought the monotony would make her lose her mind. She knew the Scriptures before she came to Mt. Carmel, but her fear of being different kept her silent. How she longed to be turned loose in the library to devour the scrolls and trap their contents forevermore in her eager mind. She burned with questions left unasked, and she sometimes had to stop herself from contradicting her teachers.

She endured the hateful sewing and cooking classes, blinking away tears of frustration when the needle insisted on jabbing her fingers instead of the fabric and spoiled the fine linen with drops of blood. She forced herself to make a humble apology when her cooking pot revealed an inedible mess instead of their morning meal, and chafed under the stupidity of learning to cook when she had no intention of doing so in the future.

The days wore on in unbearable boredom, each day the same as the day before. She was always with the other students, and never had a moment to herself. She struggled to sort out the different personalities and to react to them in an appropriate manner. By the end of the day she was too tired to think, and she fell on her pallet in the dreamless sleep of escape.

She wanted so much to be like the others. She learned their games and pretended to enjoy them. She forced herself to talk of silly, ordinary things, to whisper gossip in another girl's ear and to laugh at their pranks and jokes, but she secretly thought it was all nonsense and not at all funny. She came to dread the few hours when the students were free from classes and chores, and lived in fear that they would discover how she felt and rebuff her, and she'd again be an outcast as she'd been in Cana. Her pretense made her feel dishonest, and she knew her father would be ashamed of her if he knew. She felt guilty in front of her teachers as she led them to believe she was no different from any other student, when in her heart she knew how unlike them she was.

She became homesick for Galilee, for the hills that stretched as far as the eye could see and challenged her long legs to run from crest to valley to crest again until they trembled with exhaustion and her heart beat against her ribs in exhilaration. She missed Phinehas and Elkatma and their easy, indulgent ways. She'd always been free. She could do as she wished and go where she wanted, and each day had held forth the promise of surprise.

Here she felt as though she were suffocating. There was so much to learn and so little time to learn it all, and she was only going over the same old ground, or doing useless things like sewing. Even the worship services were beginning to grate on her nerves. She never was allowed time to go off by herself to talk with God alone. There was an emptiness inside of her, a great hole that ached and hurt, not unlike the way she'd felt when Phinehas and Elkatma had returned to their home. She tried to explain it to Joseph. "It's like being hungry but nothing looks good, and so you just keep rummaging about in the cupboard with a pain in your stomach."

Joseph had thrown his head back and laughed, but even he didn't know how to help her. He had become her special friend. She could talk to him without measuring her words, and she didn't have to pretend with him. He accepted her for exactly what she was, and moreover, approved. If it hadn't been for Joseph's sympathetic ear, Judith would probably have rebelled even sooner than she did.

The first time she found herself fleeing the compound, she'd simply bolted without conscious thought, and could hardly believe she had done so. Once she was in the forest, she decided that since she'd already committed an unheard-of act, she might as well stay and enjoy herself. She stayed the whole day, splashing in the streams and marvelling at the myriad wild flowers and strange plants. She delighted at the forest animals who looked at her with wary eyes and then strangely seemed to accept her as one of them, as though something in her wild, free spirit touched their own. It was a glorious day, the happiest since she'd come to Carmel. She sat on the bank of a gurgling stream for hours, watching the sunlight filter through the great pines, thinking nothing, hearing nothing, letting herself stretch and expand until she became one with her surroundings and had no need to hear or see or touch. She prayed the way she used to in Cana, a two-way discussion with a kind, understanding, interested God, not too unlike her father.

The aching emptiness disappeared.

At the end of the day she trudged sadly back to the compound where she faced a worried, angry Eloise. She accepted Eloise's admonishments and punishment gladly, sick with shame because she had been so weak as to run away, and vowed to herself that henceforth she would be good and never, never disobey again.

Judith tried hard to keep that promise, but it wasn't long before a bird's song and the smell of pine and earth beckoned and she found herself once again running through the trees with the wind in her hair. Now she was sent to Enos, who scolded her severely, shaming her with talk of responsibility and mature obligations. A part of her rebelled even at his scolding, and she knew that she would run away again. She thought of being sent home to Cana in disgrace, and was anguished at the vision of Phinehas' and Elkatma's grief. She couldn't, she wouldn't, shatter all their dreams—yet that tiny, mocking voice whispered that she would.

The conflict between her will and spirit began to take its toll. She grew thin and listless. She couldn't eat. She tossed and turned upon her pallet and cried out as phantoms invaded her dreams. She hugged the poor, limp pil-

low and cried with her fist in her mouth so no one would
hear.

At first, Judith's teachers thought her acute unhappiness was a simple case of homesickness. It was the custom
among the Essenes not to accept students until they were
ten years of age, but an exception had been made in
Judith's case, and they wondered if it had not been a
mistake. They redoubled their efforts to keep her occupied, and made sure that she was never left alone to brood
about her home. Instead of helping, it only seemed to
make matters worse. They finally offered to send her
home, and were bewildered by her violent no, not knowing that to be sent home would be for Judith the ultimate
failure.

There was no way she could explain how she felt. She
couldn't tell them that their school bored her, or that she
found their constant presence suffocating and their conversation and games nonsense. She couldn't insult them
when they had all been so kind and accepting of her. Her
mind was so confused she couldn't have put her feelings
into words even if she had wanted to, and to explain the
subtleties of human emotions was beyond the ability of an
eight-year-old. Matters went from bad to worse until Joseph broke his confidence with Judith and carried the
whole sorry tale to Enos.

Enos was dismayed at their failure to recognize the
cause of Judith's misery, and blamed himself particularly
for not taking the time to question Phinehas and Elkatma
about the child they'd left in his care. They'd all been so
excited by the events disclosed in that day-long meeting,
and afterward so preoccupied by its results, that no one
had given Judith a second thought. He quickly called
Judith's teachers and the other leaders on Mt. Carmel
together, and they decided to let the child follow her
inclinations, to let her choose what she wanted to do and
what she wanted to study. They all agreed that to try to
tame her spirit would only result in breaking her will, and
in doing so they faced the possibility of thwarting her
soul's purpose in this generation.

And choose she did! She sat at the feet of Shalmar and
learned the teachings of the East and the traditions from
India and Egypt and the Persian lands and all those lands

around their borders. She dogged Philo's steps and read all of the records that he kept, and learned to copy the sacred Scriptures on long, rolled, leather scrolls. She climbed the spiral stairway to the temple roof and listened as astrologers described the heavens and told of their message. She trailed after Enos and Judas and bombarded them with questions, and they were amazed at her discernment and insight into their hidden meanings.

Then she'd suddenly have had enough and would flee to the cool, dark forest or tramp the sands on the shore of the sea, to think and muse and ponder and put together all she'd learned. Sometimes she'd stay out all night, not returning until late the next day. The first time night fell without her return, panic ensued. A search party was formed and they combed the forest until they found her curled up asleep in an ancient cave. Judith couldn't understand why everyone had worried so about her, or why they came searching for her. Didn't God take care of all His children? No harm could come to her without the will of God, and since He had sent her onto the earth for an express purpose, surely nothing could happen to her until that purpose was fulfilled.

Judith bloomed under her new-found freedom. Her energy was boundless, and her thirst for knowledge phenomenal. Her mind was like a gigantic sponge, absorbing every lesson instantly, as long as it was something she wanted to know. She had an uncanny ability to separate the wheat from the chaff, discarding useless bits of information as easily as one would discard an old coat, forgetting it as soon as she heard it and going on to the next.

She became a favorite of everyone on the Mount. Her obsession to know everything led her to every facet of life on Carmel, and she was as much at home in the carpentry shop or working the wine press as she was in her beloved library. Even the other students recognized Judith's uniqueness, and her freedom provoked neither jealousy nor resentment. Once she was no longer forced to be in the constant company of others, she enjoyed their chatter and their games. She was a loyal friend, never breaking a confidence and never choosing special friends to the exclusion of others. She made no distinction between male or female and was as at ease with the boys as she was with the girls.

Her popularity and strong personality soon set the tone for the whole community, and the pulse of the Mount rose and fell with her moods. When Judith was happy, the whole Mount was happy. It was a joy to see her somber, child-woman's face suddenly break into a smile, like an unexpected flood of sunshine on a gloomy day. Her merry laughter was infectious, inviting them all to join in her absolute joy at being alive.

Judith couldn't bear injustice or petty meanness, and when these occurred her eyes faded to a glacial blue and her cold, controlled anger was like a frost descending upon the Mount. She never railed or flew into a fit of temper—they wished she would, for anything would have been better than her stony stare and tight, closed face. They avoided her when she was angry, fearful of her silence and ashamed of the incident that caused it. Her anger was as infectious as her joy, and the instigator had better be prepared for his glowering companions.

As much as they dreaded her anger, her rare fits of despair were worse. She set almost impossible standards for herself, and when she couldn't live up to them, she grew melancholy and full of remorse. She mentally berated herself for what she thought was weakness and failure. Her eyes grew dark with grief and her mouth became a thin, white line. She'd disappear into the forest or to the sea to brood and weep with abject frustration, and the Mount suffered with her and waited in subdued silence until the storm had passed.

As Judith grew older and realized how everyone reacted to her moods, she tried to control her emotions, or at least to hide them, and to maintain an air of peace and serenity. She began to go to the sea every morning after the sunrise worship service. She felt a kinship with the sea, in its changeability and vastness, its unfathomable depth and mystery. It helped to spend a quiet time alone before the busy day began, to still her thoughts and feelings in meditation and to have a quiet talk with God. But though it helped, she still could not maintain the outward calm so desired by those of the Brotherhood.

It wasn't surprising that Judith's love for the forest should spark an interest in the plant life that grew there. She found an aging monk who could tell her the names and virtues and properties of each one, and her tiny cell was soon crammed with bottles and jars and little bags of seeds and clumps of leaves and roots hanging from the rafters to dry. She mixed herbs and boiled the essence out of roots. She commandeered the boys to build cages and pens for all the sick and injured animals and birds she found, and was so successful with her cures that it wasn't long before her patients included the residents of Mt. Carmel, as well as those of the forest.

Eloise deplored the state of chaos in the House of Lodgement. It was impossible to keep order when the hallway was lined with cages and the floor littered with straw—and the stench! She insisted that the menagerie go, and Judith insisted it stay, until Enos finally threw up his hands and gave Judith a small storage building to use as her infirmary.

It was quite by accident that Judith discovered she could heal without the use of brews and unguents. She'd found a squirrel lying in her path, its eyes glazed and the only sign of life an imperceptible twitch in its hind legs. She'd fallen to her knees and laid her hands on it to comfort it, and out of her pity had asked God to spare one of His tiny creatures. She'd felt the warmth flow into her hands and the trembling shudder which passed through her body, but didn't connect the sensations with what she was doing. When the little squirrel stirred and began to struggle beneath her hands, she'd released him and watched in amazement as he scampered up a tree. She tried to convince herself that he'd only been stunned, and wasn't dying, as she had thought, but Judith was not one to leave a mystery unsolved, and at the first opportunity had tried it again.

She told no one of the power she'd found in her hands —in fact, it frightened her, and she used it only when absolutely necessary, until one day a monk let an axe slip in his hand and slashed his ankle to the bone. Judith had been with Enos when they heard the cries, and had run with him to where the monk lay. The gash was long and deep, and another monk was desperately trying to staunch the flow of blood. Without thought, Judith pushed the monk aside and gently took the mangled ankle in her hands. She felt the familiar warmth in her hands and the surge of energy course through her veins. She seemed to

be in a trance as she closed her eyes to erase from her
mind all but a vision of the ankle as whole as it had been
before the accident. Her silent prayer was short and intense, and then she simply gave up her being to God's
healing work.

It was over in an instant, and she looked up to a ring of
shocked faces hovering over her. For a moment she
wondered why they looked at her so, and then she saw her
bloodied hands. With a short cry of dismay, she jumped
to her feet and fled to the sea, her heart pounding against
her ribs and her eyes blinded by tears. Now they knew,
and nothing would ever be the same again! Once more
she'd proved herself different from the others, and again
she'd have to endure their stares and whispers. She stayed
away from the compound for three days, until she finally
reconciled her will to God's and accepted the fate He had
in store for her.

News of such a miracle travels fast, and the Mount
became a place of pilgrimage for the sick and suffering.
The gift of healing was well-known in the sect of the
Essenes, but it was a gift developed over years of saintly
living and intense training. Surely it was a sign of God's
high favor when a mere girl spontaneously manifested
that gift. Judith's name was whispered wherever the Elect
met. Who was this extraordinary soul who had come into
their midst, and what did it mean? They recounted her
peculiar ways, embellishing them a little here and there
until it wasn't surprising that such rumors should reach
the ears of the Sons of Darkness.

The Jerusalem priests condemned her for being a sor-
ceress. They called her a child of Belial, and declared that
anyone who consorted with her was destined for Sheol.
But the common folk wondered. They feared the priests
and scribes, who held absolute authority on all religious
matters, but had an uneasy feeling that in this case they
might be wrong. The Jews' history was rife with individuals who possessed powers not of this world, but little or
nothing had happened for four hundred years which
could be regarded as a revelation from God. Couldn't it
be possible that the Most Holy had at long last turned His
face again to Israel? Particularly now when man had
reached such depths of depravity that the earth could no

longer sustain his wickedness, and the whole world sought a closer understanding of who they were and why they were here, having to endure such hardship and suffering. They might be poor and unlearned, but even they could read the signs and feel the air of doom that enveloped the earth. Only the Messiah could save the world from reverting to chaos.

They tentatively began to question, whispering by the village well or in the market place while fingering a piece of wool. A few grew bold enough to furtively attend the secret meetings of the Essenes, their hearts pounding with fear of being discovered, but their fear of disregarding a sign from the Lord outweighed their fear of the priests and scribes.

Judith deplored her notoriety. She knew she was an object of curiosity and a subject for gossip. She pretended she didn't care, and managed an air of indifference, ignoring the stares and whispers that followed her through the compound. But she did care! She hated being scorned and despised by the outside world, and she resented being treated with awe by her friends. She was embarrassed by the homage paid to her, and winced under the devoted eyes of those she healed. She brushed aside their gratitude, curtly reminding them that God healed, not she—she was only the instrument used.

She quickly learned that each gift brought its burden of responsibility. There was no longer time to run off to the forest for quiet days alone. Her menagerie had to go, as did the time she'd spent in the fields and winery, and all the other pursuits she'd loved so much. There simply weren't enough hours in the day, and she would not steal time away from her studies. Her morning meditation on the bluff above the sea was the only solitary time she had, and she found that those few moments of tranquility had become a necessity instead of an indulgence.

Healing was not her only gift. She realized she could easily read other people's minds, which made her feel like a trespasser in a private realm. She had to make a conscious effort to block out all the thoughts that came winging uninvited into her mind, and she didn't always succeed. It was a burden to have this ability, and except for the rare times that it was an aid to her in helping someone, she found it more of an annoying nuisance than a gift.

Judith also discovered she often knew things before they happened. She hated to look into someone's eyes and know that death was near, or that some tragedy was about to befall. She could see all their griefs and sorrows, and by seeing them, they were somehow transferred to herself, and she felt their pain as though it were her own. Not all the things she saw were unhappy, of course. She would also see a child being born or a marriage taking place, or even a financial success in the offing, and so she shared in the joys as well as in the sorrows. But it was distressing to see what others could not see.

Judith became noted for her wise counsel and found herself in the position of mediator and problem-solver. It was comparatively easy to guide someone on a safe course when she could see the past cause which induced the present effect, and could see into the future to determine the outcome of her advice. Very few on Mt. Carmel knew of Judith's ability to see into the past and the future, and those who came seeking her advice simply thought she had an old soul, wise beyond her years.

Enos knew, of course, and found Judith's prophetic gifts a boon. She knew it was possible to avoid many mistakes and problems in administering the affairs of the Elect, and they no longer feared a surprise visit by the Romans or Herod's barbarians. Judith's spiritual gifts and exceptional knowledge made her an invaluable asset to the Brotherhood, and by the time she was fifteen, she had quietly assumed a place among the leaders of the Essenes.

Her gifts played a major role in selecting the twelve girls who would serve as possible channels for the entry of the Messiah. Hundreds of children had been offered as candidates, and it was a mammoth task to meticulously screen each one. Judith's dreams and prophetic abilities often came to the rescue when a controversy arose. The leaders had learned to trust her intuitive judgments, and they turned to her when there was indecision about a candidate. Through the process of elimination they brought the number down to fifty, and then to twenty-five, until at last the twelve were chosen and the girls came to Mt. Carmel.

The residents at the Mount were at a fevered pitch of excitement the day the girls arrived, and Judith was no exception. Eight years of painstaking selection had resulted in twelve beautiful, physically and mentally perfect young girls. Judith studied them with a sense of satisfaction and inordinate pride. They were the cream of Israel and as varied as the lilies of the field. It was awesome to think that one of those lovely, smiling girls would one day carry the Messiah in her womb. She couldn't help but speculate which girl it would possibly be. The veil which hid the future had not been lifted this time, and Judith had to suffer the excitement of not knowing like everyone else.

She felt a special fondness for little Mary, daughter of Ann of Cana, but she knew that part of that was her empathy due to their similar backgrounds. Mary was not a favored choice of many of the Brotherhood. Controversy still raged over her legitimacy, and many looked at her with the same skeptical eyes that Judith remembered so well from her own childhood. She was also the smallest, and, at eight, the youngest of all the girls, and Judith vividly recalled her own homesickness. She also thought Mary was the most beautiful. Her coloring was extraordinary! The pale, ivory skin of the Galileans seemed even more translucent and fair when framed by Mary's unusual, red-gold hair that glowed in the sun like finely burnished copper. Her eyes were large—fringed with thick, curling lashes of spun gold—sometimes blue, and then again gray, with a steady gaze of complete serenity. Her movements were as fluid and graceful as a high-born princess, and her voice as sweet as a nightingale's song.

Judith looked away from Mary and shook her head to clear it of her bemusement. It wouldn't do to pick a favorite. When the time came, the Holy Spirit would make the final choice, and in the meantime she must discipline herself to be absolutely impartial. She studied the other girls, cataloguing each one as her eyes moved from one to the other.

There was Editha, daughter of Apsafar, an innkeeper in Bethlehem. She was tall and olive-skinned, with long straight hair as black as a raven's wing. At twelve, she was the oldest of the girls. Her dark, intelligent eyes, and full,

mature mouth made her beautiful as she moved with confidence and an air of assurance. Dependable and full of
good sense, Judith thought. She'll be helpful with the
younger ones.

Looking a little fearful was Rebkah, also from Bethlehem. The girls were friends, and it was obvious that
Editha was the dominant one. Rebkah clung to her and
followed her direction in everything.

Judith moved on to Andra and Abigale, both from
wealthy, prominent families in Jerusalem. She wondered
how they would adjust to the austerity of Mt. Carmel.
Andra was cool, blond, and aristocratic. She had a look of
fragility about her, but her jaw was strong and her brow
intelligent. Abigale had luxuriant, chestnut-colored hair,
and clear, friendly eyes. She had a classic face with high
cheek bones, a clear, smooth brow, and a finely molded
nose. Both girls displayed a graciousness that reflected
good breeding and a confidence cultivated over years of
moving in high social circles.

Judith smiled as her eyes rested on Josie, daughter of a
shepherd from Nazareth and only a few months older
than Mary. Josie was short and still retained vestiges of
baby fat. Her chubby cheeks were flushed with excitement
and her bright little eyes that darted to and fro missed
nothing. Her hair was dark brown and straight, and damp
wisps escaping from her headband clung to her face. She
had a stubborn little tilt to her chin, and Judith thought
she'd probably prove a handful. Josie had Mary by the
hand and was pointing to someone. Judith followed the
direction of her short stubby finger and saw Shem and
Mephibosheth, Josie's father and mother. Judith's smile
spread. They could have been Phinehas and Elkatma
standing there, so filled with pride. Shem, with his full,
flowing beard and colorful, striped shepherd's robe, and
Mephibosheth, short and squat beneath voluminous layers
of dun-colored wool—they were the salt of the earth, the
backbone of the race, the mature, first-planted root whose
fruit would undoubtedly prove rich and sweet.

Sophie was from Bethsaida, daughter of a fisherman,
and possessed an extraordinary talent for languages. Her
name meant "female scribe," and Judith thought she was
no doubt aptly named. She was dark blond, willowy, and

had a merry laugh and the open, easy manners of the Galileans.

Judith thought Zipporah also aptly named—"little bird" —for so she seemed as she chirped gaily and fluttered in and out among the girls. As was Rachel—"ewe." Rachel's father was also a shepherd, but from the Judean hills instead of Galilee, and Rachel's was a dusky beauty, earthy, strong-bodied, and even at eleven she looked the part of the eternal mother.

Kereth and Hannah were both from Capernaum, both good-humored and eager for adventure. Their skin was tanned by the sun reflecting from the sea, and they had a healthy, outdoor look of vitality.

Judith's eyes came to rest on the "Other Mary," Ismeria's daughter and cousin to Mary of Ann. She was a small, quiet, wistful girl, the second oldest of the twelve, but the least noticed. Judith remembered her as a toddler in Cana, never able to compete with the flamboyant, headstrong daughter of Phinehas. Later, when Judith had left, Mary of Ann was born and all the attention focussed on her. The Other Mary. Judith winced at the name. The poor girl had even lost her name when Ann's miraculous child had been born. It seemed amazing that the Other Mary showed no resentment whatever to her young cousin; in fact, she was devoted to Mary and didn't seem to have a jealous bone in her body. She was a dutiful, complacent girl, eager to please and always searching out ways in which to be helpful. Judith liked her immensely. She had an ethereal, other-worldly beauty, and for sheer goodness of heart, no one could compete. Judith resolved that the Other Mary would receive her due and never be overlooked again.

Despite her youth, Judith had been instrumental in setting up the program for the girls' training. Through her studies of all the teachings of man's relationship to the universal forces, and her ability to combine those teachings into one, she had set up a cohesive, practical program that would prepare the girls for any vocation they might choose. When the time came for the Spirit to indicate which one of the girls would become the mother of the Messiah, that girl would receive a more intensive training in regard to the care and training of the child, and the other eleven would be free to choose the manner and capacity in which to serve.

The girls were taught the rudiments of astrology, the movements and influences of the heavenly bodies in relation to man's activities. They studied eugenics and learned to read genealogical charts and to search them for any clues pertaining to inherited defects or diseases. They attended classes on numerology. They learned to read and write in Greek, Hebrew, Aramaic, and Latin, and to copy and interpret the Holy Scriptures.

They were schooled in the arts of homemaking and became adept with the needle and loom. They learned the nutritional values of foods and their preparation, and memorized the dietary laws of Judaism and those set down by the priest Ra-Ta in ancient Egypt. Judith taught them the healing properties of herbs and roots, how to prepare them, and what ills each would cure.

Most important of all, the girls were taught the things of the soul, the spirit, and the mind. They learned how to live in the spirit as they walked in the body of flesh. They learned of the purpose of the souls' sojourn on earth, and the spiritual lessons to be learned through the experiences in materiality. They were told of their own past generations or incarnations, and how these influenced the events they were now living, as self met self in the universal law of cause and effect. They learned to raise their consciousness to a spiritual level for a closer walk with God. Each child dutifully kept a record of her dreams and learned to interpret their symbols and meanings and to understand the message they conveyed.

The years flew by. The number of summer tents increased each year as the girls matured and the sense of expectation and tension grew. A new dormitory was erected, and the kitchens and dining hall expanded to accommodate the steadily increasing numbers of initiates into the Brotherhood. Leaders and representatives of the various branches of the Essenes from all over the world were frequent visitors to Mt. Carmel, as were great sages from all the ancient religions. They saw the signs and read the omens and knew an event of vast importance would soon take place on the Holy Mount.

The increased activity made ripples which flowed from

Carmel throughout the land, and the Herodians and the Jerusalem priests became alarmed and accelerated their attempts to discredit the sect. Mt. Carmel lay outside their judicial authority, and so they cunningly whispered their slanderous tales into Roman ears, arousing their suspicions with hints of rebellion and hidden caches of arms until Enos was hard pressed to convince them that the sect's purpose was entirely peaceful and that the Essenes had no quarrel with Rome.

A small contingent of Roman soldiers made regular forays to Mt. Carmel. They combed the forest and searched the ancient caves for evidence of treachery. They plundered the storehouses and treasury, and rifled the dormitories and outbuildings, all the while thoroughly enjoying the havoc they raised and the terror they struck in the Essenes' hearts. Their questioning of Enos and the other priests and elders was far from gentle, and the peace-loving Saints were forced to endure physical as well as mental and emotional abuse.

Those trying years tested the Essenes' patience and fortitude. Phinehas died, and Enos, persecuted and heavily burdened with responsibility, was left weak and trembling, seldom able to leave his cot. Judas assumed the temple duties and acted as the aged Enos' arms and legs, but it was Judith upon whom Enos relied to be his eyes and tongue. The people accepted her leadership as natural, knowing the faith and trust that Enos had in her, and even those who wondered at such authority given to a female refrained from voicing their questions as long as Enos maintained control.

Judith had long ago buried her ardent wish for anonymity, and accepted each new responsibility with resigned equanimity. She consecrated her life to the aims and purposes of the Essenes, and resolved to follow wherever the Spirit should lead. She never even considered the possibility of marriage. Her life was completely absorbed by her duties on Mt. Carmel, and she felt no longings for a home of her own or for children. No man had ever aroused her desire, nor she theirs. Indeed, men tended to shy away from any thoughts of intimacy with her. She was physically as tall and strong as they, and mentally and spiritually towered over them. They came eagerly for her counsel and friendship, regarded her as comrade, guide, and teacher with great affection and admiration, but could not conceive of her as a meek and dutiful wife who would share their bed and board.

She was wholly content with life as it was, days bursting with activity and nights alone in her cell for quiet contemplation. Each dawn promised surprise and challenge. Every season brought a new cycle of activity. Each year carried them a step closer to realizing the fulfillment of centuries of preparation.

Chapter 5

The Great Sea lay calm, placid, and brilliantly blue beneath a sky as blue as itself, thickly studded with puffs of fluffy, white clouds. The sun danced and played on the glassy surface, and gulls wheeled and called their raucous greetings to the new day. The gentle breeze was soft and balmy with the promise of spring, and the earth smelled fresh and clean, newly baptized and purified by the rains. Judith threw off the heavy mantle she'd automatically thrown over her shoulders and took an almost sensual pleasure in the sun's warmth on her back and bare arms. The winter had seemed exceptionally long and raw, and Judith had begun to feel as black as the weather, but this morning she felt buoyant, happy and alive. The unexpected sun and balmy air were welcome after weeks of dismal rain and gloomy overcast skies.

Judith settled herself comfortably on a sun-warmed rock and performed the breathing exercises to relax her mind and body for meditation. She closed her eyes and murmured her prayers. She banished all thoughts from her mind and waited for the blessed peace of nothingness to descend, but the sun teased her eyelids open, and thoughts of the busy day ahead crept unbidden into her mind.

She gave up trying to meditate, laughing aloud at the birds who were wiser than she. She stood and stretched. The warm breeze molded the sleeveless white tunic against her slim hips and full, high breasts, and lifted the long, heavy hair from her neck. She watched a few gaily colored sailing vessels slide across the glassy sea, probably manned by some private merchants taking advantage of the surprisingly clear day to sail from Caesaria up the coast to Ptolemais to trade their wares. Idly she wondered what it was like in that reputedly magnificent new city which Herod had built to honor Caesar Augustus. She had never been there, though it was only twenty five miles from Mt. Carmel. The only time she'd left the Mount in twelve years was to go to Cana when Phinehas had died. She wondered what it was like in all the great cities that bordered the sea—Athens, Rome, and particularly Alexandria, where the great library stood. How she'd love to go there one day! What secrets those massive archives held!

She picked up her mantle and started back toward the temple. This was no time to be daydreaming. In a few days Passover would be upon them, and there was much to do to prepare for the pilgrims who would celebrate the feast on Mt. Carmel. Each year since the arrival of the girls four years ago, the number of celebrants had grown, all eager to get a glimpse of the future mother of the Messiah. They'd waited for the Messiah for so long that it was almost impossible to believe that the time was actually near, and to see the chosen girls helped them to realize that the ancient dream was now becoming a reality.

A few had already arrived. Elkatma, Ann, Ismeria, and some of the other girls' families had come early to spend a few extra days with their daughters. Elizabeth and her own small daughter Adahr had arrived the night before with a group of families from Judea. She and Elizabeth had had little time to talk last night and Judith was eager to find her.

Elizabeth had become a regular visitor to Mt. Carmel since the Other Mary had been chosen as one of the twelve, and she and Judith had become close friends. Elizabeth was a number of years older than Judith, but she was open and honest and completely unaffected, nor did she feel the slightest bit inferior. She was one of the few who didn't stand in awe at Judith's unusual gifts and abilities, and treated her the same way she did everyone else. She understood Judith better than anyone, and didn't tiptoe around Judith's moods, but said exactly what she thought.

Judith was still thinking about Elizabeth as she entered the inner court. She heard Enos' quavering voice and turned, surprised, for Enos rarely left his room. Judas had evidently carried Enos' cot to the courts to take advantage of the warm sun. He was half sitting, propped by many pillows with a coverlet spread over him from his feet to his chest. His snowy beard and hair were freshly washed and combed, and a rich purple, woolen shawl was tucked closely around his shoulders. The girls were sitting in a half circle on the stone court floor before him, dressed alike in sleeveless white tunics like her own, pulled tight at the waist with multicolored woven sashes and matching headbands that held their free-flowing hair back from their eyes. The sun poured down upon them like a golden blessing and lit a misty halo above each bright, silky head. They made a pretty picture. Enos could have been an ancient patriarch surrounded by his beautiful, adoring granddaughters. Judith felt a rush of affection for them all, and a sentimental lump formed in her throat. Since Phinehas died, Enos had become a father to her, and the girls she loved as her own.

Judith stood still and watched them, spellbound by the simple beauty of the scene and lulled by the warmth of the sun. She suddenly lurched forward as though struck from behind and slapped her hand across her mouth to stop the anguished cry which fought to escape her throat. Enos was going to die! Soon! She'd seen Enos' death clearly in one of those sudden, unexpected flashes of foreknowledge which passed like a fleeting vision through her mind. The blood seemed to drain from her veins and she staggered, blinded by tears and assailed by grief as acute as physical pain. She felt a tight, restraining grip on her arm and through the mist of her tears saw Elizabeth beside her. She didn't know how long Elizabeth had been there, but the look on Elizabeth's face told Judith that she knew what had passed through her mind. Judith opened her mouth to speak and took an involuntary step towards Enos, but Elizabeth shook her head and strengthened her grasp on Judith's arm. Her eyes warned Judith to hold her tongue. "Look!" she whispered fiercely in Judith's ear.

Judith followed Elizabeth's glance and saw that the court had quietly filled with Carmelites, as though drawn by some invisible hand to bear witness to the scene before them. Through the blur of tears she saw Elkatma, Ann, and Ismeria, Apsafar and Shem with Sodaphe and Mephibosheth, Judas, Philo, Joseph, and monks with hoes and shepherd staffs still in their hands. She looked wonderingly back to Elizabeth who whispered tersely, "Listen!"

Enos and the girls were completely oblivious of the audience around them. Enos was speaking, his quavering voice carried clearly through the courts, and the girls were enraptured, their upturned faces aglow with innocence and childish awe. Judith swallowed, and blinked the tears away from her eyes. She forced herself to listen to Enos and realized he spoke of the Creation, of the beginning of Man and his search for God.

"God moved and the spirit came into activity. In the moving was light and then chaos. In this light came the creation of that which in the earth came to be matter; in the spheres about the earth, space, and time. In patience it has evolved through those activities until there are the heavens and all the constellations, the stars, and the universe as it is known. Then came materiality as such into the earth, through the spirit pushing itself into matter. Spirit became individualized and then became what we recognize in one another as individual entities. Spirit which uses matter, which uses every influence in the earth's environment for the glory of the Creative Forces, partakes of—and is a part of—the Universal Consciousness. As the entity, the individual, then applies itself, it becomes aware through patience, through time, through space, of its relationship to the Godhead. For God moved and said, 'Let there be light,' and there was light. Not the light of the sun, but rather that light which, through which, in which, every soul had, and has, and ever has had, its being.

"Let it be remembered that the earth was peopled by animals before it was peopled by man! First there was a mass, about which there arose a mist, and then the rising of the mist, with light breaking over it as it settled itself to be as a companion to those planets in the universe; as it began its natural rotations, with their varied effects upon various portions of the earth, as it slowly receded—and is still slowly receding—or gathers closer to the sun, it receives its impetus for awakening the elements that give life itself.

"In the matter of form, as we find, there were first those projections from the animal kingdom; for the thought-bodies gradually took form, and the various combinations classified themselves as gods or rulers over herds or fowls or fishes—in part, much in the form of the present-day man. These took on many sizes as to stature, from midgets to giants, for there were giants in the earth in those days, men as tall as ten to twelve feet, and well-proportioned throughout.

"In the beginning, as matter was impregnated with spirit of the Creative Influence, there came into being Man, in his environment that made for indwelling of the spirit with a soul that might be made one with that Creative Energy. That matter became impregnated with spirit arose from the very fact that spirit, separated, had erred, and only through the environment of matter or flesh might the attributes of the source of good be manifested. For the spirit of evil has not—did not—become manifest in matter; it has only been moved by, or upon, or through matter. Just as the process of time has moved in and through matter, so there has come to man, in the finite mind, the consciousness of the indwelling of soul, spirit, body.

"Man was made as man. There were, there are, as we find, only three of the creations—matter, force, and mind. All flesh is not one flesh, but the developing of one has always remained in the same pattern and only has been developed to meet the needs of man, for whom was made all that was made. Man's evolving has only been the gradual growth upward to the mind of the Maker. Man was made in the beginning, as the ruler over those elements which were prepared in the earth plane for his needs. When the plane became such that man was capable of being sustained by the forces and conditions, upon the face of the earth man appeared. And in man there is found all that may be found without, in the whole earth plane, and other than that, the soul of man is that which makes him above the animal, the vegetable, and the mineral kingdoms of the earth. For entities come not merely by chance. For the earth is a world of causation, and in the earth cause and effect are the natural law. And as each soul enters this material plane, it is to meet or give such lessons or truths that others may gain more knowledge of the purpose for which each soul enters. Then you as a soul entity in the beginning sought companionship with God, losing that companionship by choice of what would satisfy or gratify merely the material desire. Thus you enter again and again, coming to fulfill the law that brought that soul into being to be one with Him. All souls were created in the beginning, and are finding their way back to whence they came."

The cadence of Enos' voice spun a magical web of peace. The breeze died, the pines ceased their mournful soughing. Even the birds perched in the bare branches of the court oaks were quiet, as though they, too, strained to hear the old priest's words. Only the sound of a fountain bubbling nearby could be heard as it played an accompaniment to Enos' voice.

Lovely, silver-haired Andra interrupted Enos' narrative and asked, "Are all souls perfect, as created by God in the beginning? If so, where is there any need for development?"

"The answer to this may only be found in the evolution of life, in such a way as to be understood by the finite mind," said Enos. "In the First Cause or Principle, all is perfect. That portion of the whole, manifest in the creation of souls, may become a living soul and equal with the Creator. To reach that position, when separated from Him, it must pass through all stages of development in order that it may be one with the Creator."

"Is it the destiny of every spiritual entity to become eventually one with God?" asked Editha.

"Unless that entity wills its banishment. As with man: in giving him the soul there was given the will wherewith there might be manifested in the entity either the spiritual or the material. With the will, the entity, either spiritual or physical, may banish itself. God has not willed that any soul should perish. He gave the will to His creation, MAN, that man might be one with Him. As the meaning of destiny is Law, the compliance with the Law enables one to become the Law." Enos paused and looked solemnly at the young faces before him. "For will is the factor which affords the opportunity to choose what is for development or what is for retardation. As so oft has been indicated, there is today, now, set before you, before each and every soul-entity, that which is life or death, good or evil. Each soul chooses its manifestations."

"What was the reason for the Creation?" asked Josie.

"God's desire for companionship and expression."

Rebkah asked, "Was it originally intended that souls remain out of earthly forms?"

"The earth and its manifestations were only the expressions of God and not necessarily as a place of tenancy for the souls of men, until man was created to meet the needs of existing conditions."

Mary touched Enos' hand shyly, her voice as melodious as a silver bell in the clear morning air. "Is the body at birth aware of the destiny of the physical body?"

Enos took her small hand in his own and smiled. "God Himself knows not what man will destine to do with himself, else would He not have repented that He had made man! He has given man free will. Man destines the body! Man may hold an ideal at the time of birth that would determine his destiny." Enos sighed sadly. "So soon as man contemplates his free will, he thinks of it as a means of doing the opposite of God's will, though he finds that only by doing God's will does he find happiness. Yet, the notion of serving God sits ill with him, for he sees it as a sacrifice of his will. Only in disillusionment and suffering, in time, space, and patience, does he come to the wisdom that his real will is the will of God, and in its practice is happiness and heaven."

Enos pushed himself upright from the bed of pillows and his voice was urgent. "What has been given as the truest of all that has ever been written? God does not will that any soul should perish! But man, in his willfulness, harkens oft to that which would separate him from his Maker! He has not willed that any soul should perish, but from the beginning has prepared a way of escape! What, then, is the meaning of the separation? Bringing into being the various phases so that the soul may find in manifest forms the consciousness and awareness of its separation, and a return to itself, by that through which it passes in all the various spheres or stages of awareness. Thus the separation between light and darkness. Darkness, that it had separated—that a soul had separated itself from the light. Hence He called into being Light, and awareness began." He raised his face and pointed with a trembling, gnarled hand to the sea-blue sky and the billowy white clouds floating through it. "We look out and see the heavens, the stars, and, as the Psalmist has said:

'The heavens declare that glory of God and the firmament showeth His handiwork, as day unto day uttereth speech and night unto night showeth knowledge.' "

Exhausted, Enos fell back upon the pillows, and closed his eyes. The girls quietly waited for him to regain his strength and continue, but his breathing became even and rhythmical, and they realized he had fallen asleep. Mary gently pulled her hand away and silently signalled to the others and they tiptoed out of the court. The Carmelites watched as Judas rearranged the old priest's robes and then quietly returned to their daily tasks. Judith fled to the towering pines to grieve for the death she knew was soon to come.

There she wept until she had no more tears to shed. Then she pulled herself wearily to her feet, and started to walk slowly back to the compound when she met Elizabeth coming along the path toward her. Elizabeth started to speak, but changed her mind when she saw Judith's tear-reddened eyes and swollen mouth. She fell into step at Judith's side, and they didn't speak until they came to a small, rushing stream, where they sat on the grassy bank with their backs against a tree.

"They're looking for you," Elizabeth said gently.

Judith shrugged. It didn't seem to matter. She looked at Elizabeth curiously. "You know what I saw?"

"It doesn't take the gift of prophecy to know that Enos is dying. He's old and tired. He's done his work well and has earned his rest," said Elizabeth.

"I know," Judith said miserably. "It's just that I love him so. I want him to see the fulfillment of all he's worked so hard to bring about."

"He will! Does it matter if in the flesh or in the spirit? Or is it Judith, wanting the joy of sharing it with him?" Elizabeth retorted.

Judith managed a smile. "You know me very well, don't you?" she said ruefully.

Elizabeth laughed. "We know one another."

Judith sighed. There was nothing to be gained by talking about it. She steered away from the subject of Enos and said, "I hardly saw you last night. How are things with you? Adahr seems well and growing. How is Zachariah?"

"Adahr is my right hand, a good, dutiful child, but so

sober! I wish she found more joy in life. She dotes on her father, is fiercely possessive of him, but keenly feels his disappointment that he has no son. I sometimes think Adahr perversely blames herself that she was born a girl and not the son Zachariah so desires."

Judith frowned. "Does Zachariah say or do something to make her feel so?" she asked.

"No, no," Elizabeth said hurriedly. "He loves her. He's very understanding and kind with Adahr, but one cannot help knowing his obsession for a son."

"Perhaps you're wrong, then. It's more likely that it's simply Adahr's nature to be somber, and not that she's unhappy. Did Zachariah mind your coming to Carmel?"

Elizabeth's gray eyes clouded for a moment, and then she lowered her head to avoid Judith's steady gaze. Judith saw that a few gray strands mingled through the older woman's pale hair, and her profile had lost its fine, sharp lines and had grown a little heavy. She clearly saw how the Other Mary would look in her middle years, and, with a pang of remorse wondered if Elizabeth was right in fearing she would never bear Zachariah a son.

Elizabeth shrugged. "Of course, but he said little. We resolved that problem long ago. Zachariah loves me, though he is not a demonstrative man and cannot put his feelings into words. He could forbid me to come to Mt. Carmel, but shows his love for me by allowing me to come."

"How do you explain to Adahr that you and she come to Carmel, and her father goes to Jerusalem?" Judith asked.

"I have pointed out the differences in our beliefs. She knows the Law well, and I explain that we find different meanings in the words of the Scriptures. I tell her that when she is older, she can then choose her own way, but while she is still so young it is better that she be with me, since her father is a priest and has his temple duties to see to and cannot watch over her. She is only ten, but seems to accept my explanation. I don't really know how she feels or what she thinks; she says little. She does know there is love and giving and compromise between her father and me, so I don't think it is too terrible for her."

"You do well, Elizabeth, both you and Zachariah. You use your differences as a steppingstone and not a stumbling block in your marriage. This very difference between you has taught you to compromise, to understand and accept each other, even though you do not believe the same way. You both give of yourselves and make sacrifices to insure the other's peace of mind. That is the highest order of love, love that can allow the companion to be himself, to go his own way without feeling threatened."

Elizabeth sighed. "It is difficult, though, for a child to understand, and even for me. I sometimes long for Zachariah to change and follow my way, so we could truly be one. I am even angry with him sometimes and think of him as simply stubborn and deliberately refusing to acknowledge the truth, or I think of him as being weak and afraid for fear of losing his temple friends and of what they might say."

Judith looked alarmed and Elizabeth said quickly, "Have no fear. They are only passing thoughts. My life is in the hands of the Lord, His will be done. It is only when my heart longs for another child that such thoughts creep into my mind. If I could give Zachariah a son, I believe his heart would soften. I am getting old for childbearing. I fear I will never hold another babe to my breast."

Judith searched for words that would comfort Elizabeth, though she wondered if Elizabeth were not right. "You just said, 'His will be done.' If it is God's will, you will have another child. If it is God's will, Zachariah will join the Elect and be one of us. I pray for you each day, and God hears all the supplications of His children. If it is in His holy plan that you bear a son for His glory, such will be in His own time. Remember my mother and father, and your own mother who bore the Other Mary in her advanced years."

"I know and I do," said Elizabeth. "I haven't given up all hope, but sometimes I think Zachariah has. He doesn't talk to me or confide in me as he used to do, but then he has more on his mind than a barren wife who follows the Carmelites. Judea strains under Herod's erratic rule. One never knows where his anger will next lead him. The Sanhedrin is under terrible pressure from the whims of Rome and Herod, and Zachariah is in Jerusalem more often than at home."

"We feel those same pressures here," Judith admitted.

"We hope that Herod's young wife Theresa will be able to influence his attitude toward us. She's definitely sympathetic to our purpose and is in communication with the Mount through one of our women who poses as her handmaid."

"If only Herod would come to love her as he did Mariamme perhaps she could convince him to see our way. To be free from the constant threat of that tyrant would be like heaven itself," Elizabeth said dryly.

Judith laughed. "You forget that he loved Mariamme so much he murdered her. Even now her sons are imprisoned in Rome. That Son of Belial would kill his own children in his madness and lust for power."

"I look forward to the coming of the Messiah and His overthrowing of that evil soul," Elizabeth said heatedly.

"Herod is an old man, and our Messiah is not yet born. I doubt if Herod will yet be sitting on the throne by the time He reaches manhood," laughed Judith.

"That's true," sighed Elizabeth. "How do you think it will be when the Messiah comes?"

Judith thought deeply for a moment and then said, "Some, most of the Elect, look for Him to be a great king, such as David, who will lead us in war against the Sons of Darkness. They look to the heavenly hosts to join them in that war, to completely destroy the Evil One and usher in the peaceable kingdom over which the Messiah will rule. Indeed, the lines of battle are drawn up and the scrolls even now lie waiting in our libraries. Others look for Him to come as a priest, in the line of Aaron, to bring new revelations and understanding to the Elect in their struggle against Belial. Enos sees the possibility of two Messiahs, one a king and one a priest.

"As for myself, I'm not sure. The Scriptures say the Messiah will be from the root of Jesse, through the gate of Judah, and Judah is not a priestly tribe. In the morning, when I meditate by the sea, I feel myself become one with all the universe and know that even the Sons of Darkness are beloved by the Creator. My spirit speaks to me then and says that the Promised One will come to all who have life, and will be the salvation of all souls. How this will be accomplished has not been revealed to me, but I feel this will be the truth. The Messiah will come as an instrument of truth and a channel of God's love, and the world will

be changed. The hearts of men will be reformed and
peace will reign with all who believe. Peace may not come
to all the material world in the history of man, but all
who believe in the coming Messiah will receive the peace
of His love in their hearts."

"I hope you are right," said Elizabeth. "I have no wish
for war. I see the strength of Rome as the legions march
along the roads in Judea, and know the cruelty of Herod's
army. Herod would certainly throw in his lot with Rome.
I have no doubt that the Messiah, with God's help, would
triumph in the end, but at what cost?"

Elizabeth shuddered and Judith touched her shoulder.
What role would Zachariah play in that war? She got to
her feet and pulled Elizabeth up with her. "Come. I must
get back, or Judas will send out a search party soon."

"I remember he did that once," laughed Elizabeth.

Judith smiled broadly and linked her arm in Elizabeth's
as they made their way back to the temple.

Judith couldn't imagine what she would have done
without Elizabeth. The week of Passover served a dual
purpose for Mt. Carmel. It was a time of great activity
throughout all of Palestine. The roads were crowded with
pilgrims from all over the world making their way to
Jerusalem to commemorate the Exodus out of Egypt, and
no one questioned a family leaving their home during that
time. It was just naturally assumed that they were also
going to Jerusalem. The Essenes took advantage of the
general confusion and used the week to conduct the annual affairs of the sect.

It was almost impossible to accomplish so much in so
little time, but it was simply too dangerous for the elders
to come to Carmel more than was absolutely necessary.
Enos took part when he had to, but more often than not it
was Judith and Judas who represented him and served as his
tongue. Judith delegated her regular tasks of seeing that
everyone was housed and fed and entertained to Elizabeth
and Elkatma, and left the girls strictly in Eloise's capable
hands. Even so, on the last night of the feast she had
fallen on her pallet in a state of near exhaustion and
thanked God that the morning would herald the pilgrims'
own exodus.

That night she tossed and turned. Strange dreams and
visions flew through her sleeping mind, jerking her awake

to struggle to remember their content, but she couldn't hold on to them. All she could remember was light and sound, wonderful, brilliant, all-embracing light, and sounds of music and harmony unlike anything she'd ever known. She remembered color and texture, but couldn't find sense or meaning. She woke once to find her pillow wet and was amazed to discover it was with her own tears. Sometimes she'd awaken in a state of exquisite ecstasy—unbearable, uncontained joy that made her want to run and laugh and clasp the whole world to her breast. And then she'd awaken to such desolation she could only hug herself and moan, paralyzed by some unknown fear and dread, and horrible despair.

The last time she awoke the darkness had begun to lift and the pines were gray shadows against the sky. She stood at her window and wondered at the eerie night she'd passed through, and a shivery thrill of excitement made gooseflesh on her arms. Something wonderful was going to happen! She was sure of it. She could feel it in the very air!

She grabbed a clean white tunic and silently ran through the dormitory to the baths. She splashed the icy water over her body, quickly intoning the purification prayers. She dried herself with a piece of rough linen and slipped the tunic over her head. She ran back to her cell and slid her feet into wooden sandals, quickly tying the latchets about her ankles, and then ran a comb through her hair. She pulled a braided rope belt from a peg and knotted it about her waist as she hurried to the temple.

Judith was surprised when she reached the temple. It seemed she wasn't the only early one today. Almost everyone on the Mount had already gathered together, and the courts were full to bursting. The usual solemn, pious air of the sunrise worship had vanished this morning, and everyone was wide awake. They were smiling and nodding good morning and jostling one another in the push toward the temple gates. The monks were milling about outside the gate of Judah, waiting for Judas and Mathias to lead them in. Eloise was herding the girls along the walk, positioning them into a single line to make up the last of the procession. The girls took turns leading the others and choosing the hymn they would sing as they entered, and Judith noted that this morning the lot had fallen to Mary.

Judith was just about to enter the temple when she heard an audible intake of breath from the monks behind her. She turned and was astounded to see Enos. He was flanked by Judas and Mathias, and though his steps were slow and cautious, he was walking! A look of sheer delight at the furor he was causing shone on his face, and Judas was grinning like a little boy who had just perpetrated a huge joke. Mathias looked as nervous as a cat, chewing his lip and dancing along at Enos' side. Judith knew his ulcer was probably biting and that he thoroughly disapproved of Enos' appearance in the temple. He would be fearing Enos would stumble and fall, or faint and make himself ill, and all kinds of disasters would take place. Judith was delighted and wanted to cheer Enos on. Only the rule of silence until after the sunrise service stopped her from doing just that.

She slipped through the crowd and saw Elizabeth and Ann, who motioned to her to join them. A place by the foot of the porch steps was reserved for the girls' families so they could see their daughters and feel a part of the role they played in the ceremonies. All of them were here today. Judith squeezed in between Elizabeth and Ismeria and smiled down at Adahr who had moved to stand in front of her.

At the blast of the shofar, the multitude hushed. The outer gate of Judah swung open and Enos' quavering voice cut the silence as he began to chant the Hymn of Thanksgiving.

> "I give thanks unto Thee, O Lord,
> for Thou art my strength and my stronghold,
> and Thou hast delivered my soul
> from all works of unrighteousness.
> For Thou hast put truth in my heart
> and righteousness in my spirit,
> along with all gifts of Thy wisdom;
> and hast crushed the loins of them
> that have risen up against me.
> Thou bringest me cheer, O Lord,
> amid the sorrow of mourning,

words of peace amid havoc,
stoutness of heart when I faint,
fortitude in the face of affliction.
Thou has given free flow of speech
to my stammering lips;
stayed my drooping spirit
with vigor and strength;
made my feet to stand firm
when they stood where wickedness reigns."

Judith watched Enos advance with a surge of pride and love. The sky had lightened to a silvery white, and the violet robe and tall golden miter which Enos wore shimmered in a vaporous mist. The purple turbans and sashes worn by Judas and Mathias pulsed with life against the stark white of their robes, and the monks in white tunics formed a cloudlike trail behind them. The monks had joined their voices in the second verse of the hymn and the people in the third.

The priests and highest-ranking monks advanced up the steps to the porch and the others formed two columns on either side of the walk. The hymn ended, and the sudden silence caught and held the last resounding notes until Enos stepped to the edge of the porch and the tinkling golden bells at the hem of his robe released them to wing their way across the sea. Enos turned his face to the east, raised his arms and spread out his hands, and prayed aloud to the Lord.

The girls' high soprano voices rose from the outer gate of Judah, their clear, silver notes floating through the clean morning air with a piercing sweetness. All heads turned to watch as they moved in single file through the column of monks, each bearing a small golden vessel of incense as a gift to the Lord. Their white tunics seemed to drift along the walk and only their gold and purple and blue sashes and headbands were clearly defined in the gray, predawn light. Mary led them. Each fair, upturned face was a study of piety and childish innocence. Mary had chosen a Psalm of David, depicting the Lord's solemn entry into Zion, a hymn most appropriate for twelve chaste, untouched maidens.

"The Lord's are the earth and its fullness; the world and those who dwell in it. For He founded it upon the seas and established it upon the rivers. Who can ascend the mountain of the Lord? or who may stand in His holy place? He whose hands are sinless, whose heart is clean. Who desires not what is vain, nor swears deceitfully to His neighbor. He shall receive a blessing from the Lord, a reward from God His savior. Such is the race that seeks for Him, that seeks the face of the God of Jacob.

"Lift up, O gates, your lintels: reach up, you ancient portals, that the king of glory may come in! Who is this king of glory? The Lord, strong and mighty, the Lord, mighty in battle. Lift up, O gates, your lintels: reach up, you ancient portals, that the king of glory may come in! Who is this king of glory? The Lord of hosts; He is the king of Glory."

Mary had just lifted her slender, blue-slippered foot to the first step leading to the porch when the sun burst forth over the horizon, bathing the scene in purple and gold. The sudden brilliance forced the watchers to blink and shade their eyes. The golden vessels and brazen laver seemed to explode into blazing, flashing tongues of fire, and the bells at Enos' hem winked like burning sparks against his glowing, purple robe.

Judith felt the court floor tremble beneath her feet, and then a deafening roar of thunder crashed above the Mount, tearing through the air until it seemed as though the earth were being split and rent apart. A dazzling light flashed and struck the multitude. Its white brilliance obscured the radiance of the sun, making the hair on their heads and arms stand up, and shocking their flesh until the blood in their veins seemed to coagulate and cease to flow. They screamed and fell to their knees as panic and fear overwhelmed them.

In an instant it was over. The courts were a babble of incoherent hysteria. Judith pulled herself to her feet and looked to the girls. She drew in her breath with a gasp, for they seemed to have seen and felt nothing. They were still singing the Psalm of David, and Mary continued to lead them slowly up the stairs. Judith was dazed, overcome by a sense of unreality. She looked away from their serene, unshaken faces to search out Enos, but stopped as a long shadow blocked the sun and fell over the sedately marching girls.

A hush fell over the courts. Every eye looked to the

gate of Judah to see what cast such a shadow. The air was thick with fear, and a single moan of dread arose when their eyes saw absolutely nothing in the open gate. The shadow began to shorten, as though some invisible being were walking forward toward the temple. The sun followed in its wake, framing each girl in a bath of gold until only Mary was left in the shadow. The girls had come to the end of the Psalm and the silence was like a tangible entity that could be touched and held.

The shadow moved to Mary's side and became like a mist or a cloud or a vapor, and then took the shape of a man.

The girls fell to their knees. The people stood rooted where they were. A shuddering, a moan rippled through the courts.

A hand reached out to Mary and she took it with perfect calm. It led her up the remaining steps to the altar and turned her to face the people.

Mary lifted her face to the sun, though it glowed with a radiance all its own. Her red-gold hair shone like a fiery halo about her head, and her tunic shimmered like the sun on the waves of the sea. She raised her smooth, round arms and turned her palms upward to the Lord. She was filled with the Holy Spirit and her sweet, treble voice rained peace down upon them all and their fear and dread vanished under her spell as she sang praises unto the Lord.

"My being proclaims the greatness of the Lord, my spirit finds joy in God my savior, for He has looked upon His servant in her lowliness; all ages to come shall call me blessed. God who is mighty has done great things for me, holy is His name; His mercy is from age to age on those who fear him. He has shown might with his arm; He has confused the proud in their inmost thought. He has deposed the mighty from their thrones and raised the lowly to high places. The hungry He has given every good thing, while the rich He has sent empty away. He has upheld Israel His servant, ever mindful of his mercy; even as He promised our father, promised Abraham and His descendants forever."

The people took up her song. They sang in tongues unknown to men, in a language known only to God.

Their voices blended into one voice of perfect harmony which rang through the courts, and reverberated from the walls, in a surging wave of untold joy.

The Mother was chosen! The Messiah would come! Prepare the Way of the Lord!

Chapter 6

Judith sat by Enos' cot and listened to the sounds of revelry coming from the courts below. Torchlight flickered on the bare stone walls, adding their eerie, dancing light to the steady glow of a lone oil lamp on the table next to Enos' head. The lamplight cast dark shadows in the hollows of his cheeks. His thin, bony chest barely moved, and his pulse beneath Judith's searching fingers was ragged and irregular. He'd lain thus since early morning.

When the angel had indicated the Lord's choice for the blessed Mother, Enos had flung the great, carved temple doors wide. Judas and Mathias had followed him into the sacred recesses of the upper temple to the embroidered veil which hid the Holy of Holies. His jubilant hymn of praise and thanksgiving had echoed through the temple halls, ringing out over the courts and resounding above all the others with the last reserves of his strength and breath. He'd ended the hymn with a mighty "Amen" and then had fallen to the floor. The priests had carried him unconscious to his room and laid him on his cot where Judith had stayed by his side all day, but none of her potions or healing arts had sufficed to revive him.

Men had danced in the courts while the women laughed at their antics and clapped their hands and encouraged even the youngest child to stamp his feet and twirl his tunic in time to the music. The Mount rang with the Psalms of David and voices singing praise to the Lord. The pious Essenes had danced and embraced and thumped each other's backs. They wept and rejoiced and kissed one another's cheeks. All aches and pains and troubles and worries had disappeared. They'd gathered into groups

to talk about what they had seen and heard and felt.
Only by telling and retelling could their carnal senses
absorb the glorious event that had taken place in the
temple. Only by hearing the tale from others could their
minds accept what they had experienced. They needed the
confirmation of others to assure themselves that what they
had seen and heard was real. The rigid rule of the Brotherhood had been forgotten, and the rule of silence during
the meals became nonexistent as even the monks and
priests joined in the melee. But Enos had lain oblivious to
it all.

Judith felt surprisingly calm. She'd thought she'd never
be able to bear the loss of Enos, but today's events had
changed the temper of her heart, and now it seemed only
right and just. The signs foretold that a new cycle was
soon to begin. The choice of the Mother was the first sign
of a new era, and Enos' passing would signify the end of
the old. She laid her hand on Enos' brow and found it
cool and dry, like fine parchment.

A shout rose up from below, calling praises and blessings to Mary's name, followed by a thunderous cheer
which made Judith smile at the fickleness of the human
condition. The patience the Lord must have with His children! If it rained, they wished it would stop, when it
stopped, they prayed for rain. When the sun blazed, they
asked for clouds, and under the gloom of overcast skies,
watched for the sun to peep through. If they had been
given the right to vote for their choice yesterday, they
would never have chosen Mary, but today they sang
praise to her name. Today they declared with one voice
that they'd felt all along that Mary would be the Lord's
choice. They extolled her virtues and beauty. They vied
with one another to tell of her piety and humbleness of
heart.

Did she not volunteer for the most unpleasant tasks
such as cleaning the latrines and scrubbing the crusty,
greasy kettles until they shone, and all without the slightest sign of distaste or squeamishness? Did she not ask to
care for the aged and infirm, washing their wasted bodies
and changing their putrid dressings without a qualm?
They regaled the gentleness of her touch and declared that
her mere presence brought soothing relief to their pain-

racked flesh. All of this was true, though yesterday who would have remembered it, except those who lived with her on Mt. Carmel!

Judith's reverie was broken as the door opened and Judas came quietly into the room. His face was flushed and beads of perspiration glistened on his brow.

"Peace be with you, Judith," he said. "Is there no change?"

Judith shook her head. "You are breathless and smell of wine, Rabbi."

Judas flushed. He detected the faint note of accusation in Judith's tone and said defensively, "Enos would wish it so. We have waited centuries for this day. He would wish for us to express our joy with song and dancing, for in the years ahead I see increased persecution and hardship and little cause for rejoicing. The Sons of Darkness will not take lightly to our claims that the Messiah has come, and some of us are old and will not live to see the Messiah reach manhood and ascend the throne of Israel. Would Enos deprive us of our day for joy and wish instead for us to wear sackcloth and ashes and wail in grief that he is at last released from his body of flesh?"

Judith winced beneath his rebuke, knowing his words to be true. "Forgive me, Judas. Of course not. I am only weary to the bone from noise and clamor, and fear the days ahead without our rabbi's wise counsel."

Judas looked at her with pity and laid his hand on her shoulder in a gesture of forgiveness. "Go and eat. Refresh yourself. I will stay with Enos until you return. Sleep a little if you can."

Another shout assailed their ears and Judith laughed dryly. "Sleep! Only the dead could sleep!" Nevertheless, she did as Judas bid and pushed her way through the throngs of merrymakers, ignoring their calls to join their dances, and sighed with relief as the dormitory door closed behind her and muffled the clamor from the courts.

Elkatma was waiting for her in her cell and clucked and fussed as she pushed a glass of wine into Judith's hand before scurrying about to fix a dish of roasted lamb and tiny white onions. The rich aroma was tantalizing but the food tasted like dust in Judith's mouth. She forced herself to choke it down rather than enter into an argument with her mother.

The food and wine restored her somewhat, and the quiet, dimly lit cell revived her spirit. Elkatma had refrained from asking after Enos, seeing the answer in Judith's eyes when she'd first entered, but now that Judith had regained her strength, she asked, "What will come to pass now, my daughter?"

"That will depend upon Enos. If he dies, a new leader must be chosen. Messengers will have to be sent to all our Brothers in other lands, and a new order will come into being," Judith replied.

"Can you guess who the new leader will be? Judas, or perhaps Mathias?" Elkatma asked.

"Judas perhaps, but I think not Mathias. He is too erratic and excitable. I don't know. The Lord will point the way. He has long since sent the soul into the world who will guide the destiny of the Elect through the turbulent times of the Messiah. The Scriptures say His messenger will come before Him. Perhaps it will be he who leads us now."

Elkatma shook her head. "Many years lie ahead before the new order will come to pass. What of Mary? She is yet a child, hardly past the age of puberty. It will be some time yet before a child is conceived in her blessed womb."

"Mary will be separated from the other girls to receive special instruction and preparation to carry out her role. The others will be free to choose the way in which to serve. I have thought on this as I watched over Enos. I'm sure the girls will continue their studies here, at least for a time, for they are still young and haven't thought yet about what they will wish to do. Eloise is most qualified to assume the concentrated instruction of Mary. I'm sure Judas will agree with me on that point and appoint her to that task. Until a new leader is chosen, I will be inordinately occupied with aiding Judas, which means someone will have to assume Eloise's and my usual tasks here in the House of Lodgement."

Judith looked around the cell which was usually cluttered with scrolls and scattered clothing, and wondered at its neat orderliness since Elkatma had arrived. A sudden thought flashed through her mind and her eyes opened wide at the obvious solution to one problem. "What about you, Mother?" she asked excitedly.

Elkatma looked perplexed. "Me what?" she asked.

"Would you stay at Mt. Carmel? At least until a new leader is chosen, or until Enos is well. I need someone to act as a sort of overseer, or Mother Superior, someone to run the House of Lodgement. Someone to see that the rooms are cleaned and the supply cupboards are in order, that the girls' clothing is cared for and to get them up in the morning and make sure they are tucked in at night. They are so young. They need the reassurance of a mother-figure to listen to their problems, to confide in and to love them. Who could fill that role better than you?"

Elkatma was abashed. A twinge of fear prickled her skin's surface. Leave Cana? Such a thought had never occurred to her in all her life! It was a frightening thing even to think of abandoning the safe and familiar for an unknown and uncertain future. She was too old, too set in her ways. No! It was impossible. But she looked at Judith's excited, pleading face and wondered.

She walked to the window and stared out at the dark night, deep in thought for a long time. Without turning, she spoke softly. "Cana has been my home all of my life. To leave Galilee is to leave a part of my soul. But I am lonely there. With you here at Carmel and your father with God, I am lonely. I'm an old woman, and thought I had outlived my usefulness. I've often wondered why I live on, particularly with such good health and energy. I am not the least bit infirm and am often restless when time hangs heavy on my hands. Perhaps the Lord has work for me to do still. To be useful and needed again is an appealing thought. What does Cana hold for me except old memories of happy days long gone? I shall miss Ismeria and Ann, but here I would be with you."

Years seemed to have dropped from Elkatma's face as it glowed with excitement and resolve. "I once gave you up to the Lord, and now, blessed be His name, He rewards His faithful servant by giving you back to me again! Who am I to turn aside His gift? I will! Yes, I will stay."

Judith hugged her, and Elkatma's soft, square body felt warm and good in Judith's arms, and she was convinced that it had been an inspiration from God. "Thank you, Mother. I must get back to Enos."

She turned to leave and then paused at the door and said musingly, "God is indeed merciful and wise. Each time a loved one is taken from me, He eases my pain by giving another. When Phinehas died I found a father in Enos. Now as I am about to lose Enos, he restores to me my mother."

The night wore on and the clamor in the courts gradually diminished as the revelers grew weary and made their way to their tents. Mathias and Philo came to Enos' room, Mathias ashen-faced from punishing his tender stomach with too much wine and excitement, and Philo cross and disgruntled by the Essenes' blatant display of unbridled emotion and lack of decorum. Judith mixed Mathias a potion to ease his biting ulcer while Judas tried to soothe Philo's sense of outrage, assuring him that on the morrow the pilgrims would return to their homes and the Mount would resume its normal air of peace and piety.

A small group of monks led by Joseph of Nazareth stopped at Enos' door to inquire about their beloved Rabbi. Joseph was calm and serene in contrast to the others whose voices rasped from singing psalms and shouting praises to the Lord, and whose limbs trembled from the unaccustomed dancing. Judith had seen Joseph from Enos' window at random times throughout the day, always standing to one side, watching the celebration with a faint smile of amusement on his face, but never taking part unless he was unwillingly pulled into the melee.

Judith watched him now as he bent his tall frame down to hear Judas' softly spoken words, his black, bushy brows knit in concentrated concern. Joseph always stood in the background, silent, watching, never pushing himself forward to be noticed, yet one was always aware of his steady presence and quiet strength. Everyone seemed to know Joseph. Many of the Elect who visited Carmel could not name most of the monks, but Judith could think of none who did not know Joseph. Small groups always gathered in the carpentry shop, ostensibly to watch the magic that Joseph wrought in wood, but who were actually there to draw on Joseph's homely wisdom and to seek his advice.

Children especially were drawn to the tall, silent man. Students vied for the chance to help in the carpentry shop, and it was a usual sight during the summer months to see Joseph leading a gaggle of youngsters off to the forest to fish in the streams. Judith remembered herself as a child when Joseph had been the only one who had understood her acute unhappiness. She remembered the gentleness in his big, rough carpenter's hands as he'd brushed the hair back from her face and wiped the tears from her cheeks, and the compassion and understanding in his voice, and the love—that wonderful, depthless love—in his eyes.

Only once had Judith seen the terrible anger which Joseph kept hidden from the eyes of the world. A Roman contingent had thundered up the Mount, instilling fear and dread as they plundered the storehouses and defiled the holy temple with their prying eyes. They were an unusually vulgar and coarse group that day, and when their razing search discovered nothing of value, they'd turned their pleasure to abusing the aged leader of the Essenes. They had teased Enos with their spears, jabbing only hard enough to prick the surface of his skin and drawing a small trickle of blood. They'd jeered and mocked and laughed uproariously as they spit in his face and reddened his cheeks with their open palms, hugely enjoying the moans and looks of horror they elicited from the Carmelites whom they'd forced to watch the humiliating debacle.

Joseph had seemed to appear from nowhere, his face black with an awesome anger, with a huge axe gripped tightly in his hands. His eyes blazed. His voice had been hard and cold and threatening, not Joseph's voice at all. The veins in his neck protruded like thick cords as he told the officer in low, measured words that he had done his duty and could now remove his men from the Mount. Joseph had chosen his words with care. They were polite words, respectful, almost conversational, but delivered with a deadly, menacing calm that caused the Romans to back away a step or two, disconcerted and confused by the calculated authority that emanated from the huge Jew.

The officer had stared open-mouthed. His eyes had locked with Joseph's in a terrible, silent battle of wills for what had seemed an eternity to Judith. She'd been sure they'd kill him. She'd held her breath until her lungs felt as though they'd explode, until finally the Roman dropped his eyes. With a great show of bravado he spewed out a stream of vindictive insults which Joseph calmly ignored, and then ordered his men to horse and thundered back down the mountainside.

Judith had been dizzy with relief, but Joseph had returned to his shop as though nothing unusual had taken place.

She listened now as Joseph told Judas that the monks had formed a vigil of prayer for Enos before the Holy of Holies. She guessed at once that it had been done under Joseph's direction, and a rush of affection brought tears to her eyes.

When Joseph and the monks had gone, the silent night descended upon the room like a lonely shroud. No torchlight disturbed the steady glow of lamplight, and no shouts or song rose up from the courts. Judith and Judas watched over Enos in silence, each lost in thought and each silently intoning a prayer for Enos' soul.

In the last eerie hours before dawn, when the Mount slept the deep, unconscious sleep of the dead and even the wind ceased to stir the pines, Enos suddenly opened his eyes. They were clear and alert, unclouded by confusion or questioning of where he was or why. He tried to smile, a faint, tremulous quiver about his mouth. Judith splashed a little wine into a clay goblet and held it to his mouth, sliding her arm behind his head to give him support.

"Peace be with you, Rabbi," she smiled. "You've come back to us, then."

Enos drank thirstily, gulping the strength-giving warmth and unmindful of the slow trickle that stained his beard. The effort drained him and his full weight rested on Judith's arm as she eased him back onto the pillow.

Judas took his hand and said gently, "Do not try to speak, Enos. Rest yourself."

The wine strengthened him and brought a faint blush to his white, sunken cheeks. His laboring breath eased and his smile broadened a little as he shook his head weakly. "Soon I will rest the good sleep in the Lord. Now I will speak," he whispered.

Judith's eyes were awash with unshed tears. Enos' gnarled hand feebly sought hers and she grasped it hard. "Do not weep nor mourn for me, my daughter. I go to God with joy. Mary—?"

"She sleeps and is well. The people rejoiced in celebra-

tion all day and Mary accepted their homage with her
usual sweet serenity. Eloise watches over her," Judas answered reassuringly.

"Good. Good." He turned to Judith. "I knew Mary to
be the one. In a dream I saw Mary leading the other girls
and saw the angel take her by the hand. Each day I asked
Judas who would lead the girls to the altar, and when the
lot fell to Mary, I knew that to be the day."

Judith glanced at Judas, who affirmed Enos' statement.

Enos went on, his words hurried and choppy, as though
he must speak quickly for there was little time. "There
will be much for you to do. A new leader must be chosen.
God will direct you. Help Judas as you've helped me.
Troubled times are ahead. The Messiah. Protect Him. He
will have many enemies. Teach Him. Hear Him. He will
know. You must follow!"

Enos' voice had become shrill with urgency. He struggled to sit up, to impress what he must say upon them
both, but Judas pressed him back against the pillow. "We
know, Rabbi. We will. Do not excite yourself!" he
soothed.

Enos gasped, "Mary must be betrothed."

Judith frowned. "She is yet a child, Rabbi."

"Why so soon, Enos? Judith is right. Mary is only a
child. Surely there is time for that ahead," Judas said.

"My soul has flown through many spheres as my body
has lain here dying. My flesh is weak with dying, but I
remember! It must be soon." Enos pleaded.

It was not an uncommon experience among the Essenes
for the soul to leave the body and communicate with
other souls either on earth or in the world of spirit. Sometimes the experience was remembered as a dream, and
sometimes as a vision seen during a trancelike state of
meditation. But always, when remembered, it was as vivid
and real as though it had occurred while the person was
awake, and was distinguishable from ordinary dreams.
Neither Judith nor Judas questioned the veracity of Enos'
revelation in the least.

"Was it told to you who Mary's betrothed should be?"
Judith asked quietly.

"Joseph. Joseph ben John of Nazareth!"

Judith gasped. She put her hand to her throat and

looked at Judas, who was as stunned as she. They'd known, of course, that one day a companion would be selected for the Chosen One, but it had seemed pointless to give it any serious thought until the spirit had indicated the choice of the Mother. They had all mildly speculated on the possibilities for the companion, and had watched each year's candidates for initiation into the Brotherhood for some sign of unusual character or ability. But Joseph? They had never given Joseph a thought!

Judith collected herself and leaned over Enos who seemed to be sleeping. "Enos! Are you sure?" she demanded. But Enos had lapsed into unconsciousness and could no longer answer. She tried to revive him and when she could get no response, sank weakly onto the stool and looked at Judas with a bewildered, helpless look.

"The Scriptures say we must test the spirits," said Judas. "We must use all the methods possible and search every means at our disposal to be sure that Enos is right."

Judith nodded dumbly, her mind spinning with scenes she'd noted over the years but hadn't given any conscious thought to. Scenes of Joseph and children—throwing a ball, laughing, tossing small boys into the air, kissing a tiny cut finger, bouncing a chubby babe upon his knee, wiping a small, runny nose. Judith wanted to cry. Now that his name had been spoken, Joseph seemed the perfect choice to protect and care for gentle little Mary and the Son she was to bear.

Judith and Judas watched over Enos in silence, each trying to absorb the enormity of Joseph as the husband of Mary. The sky became lighter and the surrounding pines emerged from the darkness like ghostly giants assembling to protect the temple through the day. Enos' breath became more and more shallow, until finally, with an audible sigh, his soul took leave of his body, leaving it behind with an expression of eternal peace. Judas crossed his once strong, willing hands which had spent years in the service of his God, gently over his breast as Judith bent and kissed his brow, feeling only a deep, longing sorrow as she whispered, "Peace be with you, Rabbi. Until we meet again in God."

Chapter 7

Enos' body lay entombed in one of the ancient caves hidden in the Mount, buried according to Law before the sun set that same day. The mourners had wailed and rent their clothes in an expression of grief and then the next morning had quietly melted away to return to their homes.

The Mount lay under a shroud of silence. The monks went about their daily tasks with a quiet, silent resolve, speaking in whispers if they spoke at all. The students resumed their classes, but they too were subdued, repeating the Scriptures in hushed, mechanical tones, and filing in and out of the courts in a quiet, orderly manner instead of their usual exuberant pell-mell.

Judas sent letters to all the camps and communities informing them of Enos' passing and asking that the Deliberative and General Councils convene at once on Mt. Carmel to elect a new "Prince of the Entire Congregation," also called the Prefect.

Mary was separated from the other girls to begin the long and arduous training which would bring her body, mind, and spirit into perfect accord with the universal forces in order to permit entry of the Chosen One into the world. The other eleven chose to remain at Mt. Carmel, each dedicating her life to the aid and support of Mary and the child she would bear.

Time seemed suspended as they waited for the Councils to gather and sit in silent meditation until their collective spirits became as one, allowing the Spirit of the Lord to indicate His choice of the new leader. The Mount was immersed in a period of reflection, remembering the past and looking ahead into an unknown future.

Beneath that calm surface of quiet reflection flowed a current of uneasiness, an apprehensive wondering about who the new leader would be and what course he would chart for the Covenanters. How would he guide them through the turbulent years ahead as they waited for the Messiah to come and grow into manhood? They had waited centuries for this day, and now that it was upon them, they were filled with a mixture of joy and dread. Nothing would ever be the same again. Each life would be changed, but no one knew how.

Judith was no exception. For months she'd enjoyed the position of acting as Enos' right hand. She'd thrived on the responsibility Enos had thrust upon her, and knew herself to be fully qualified to handle any office in the Congregation. But she was a woman, and women did not hold administrative offices, and even if she had been a man, the Rule clearly stated that one must be twenty-five years old to be eligible to hold any office, and Judith was five years short. She knew with a sinking heart that as soon as a new prince was elected she would be relegated back into the obscure realm of the holy women, destined to carry out the orders of men and to take little part in the decision making. She plodded through the days, hiding her dejection as best she could.

She and Judas told no one except Mathias of Enos' certainty that Joseph of Nazareth was the Lord's choice for the husband of Mary. They diligently searched through all the records, keeping their purpose hidden from everyone until the new leader was chosen. They would present their findings to him, and he alone would decide how to proceed. They spent hours in the library, searching the Scriptures, sifting, filing, compiling any bits and pieces of information they could find, and on the day before the first arrivals appeared on Mt. Carmel, all three were satisfied with their mutual conclusion.

There was no way the Carmelites could have guessed the identity of their new Prefect. Who of them had ever heard of the Roman Jew named Aristotle? Aristotle! Tall, ascetic, arrogant, a man who looked down upon them with a bemused, half-smile as though he found them all a poor joke and their efforts nothing more than child's play. Even when the Council had been told that the Spirit had indicated the choice of the Mother, his self-contained expression had never changed, except for a slight rise of his eyebrows. When Judith and Judas had presented their findings regarding Joseph, so excited themselves by the importance of the revelation that their words emerged strained, his face had shown no reaction. He'd listened with polite interest, asking no questions, offering no comment, accepting the sheaves of parchment as though they contained nothing more than the daily work schedule, and then politely dismissed them with a few desultory words of gratitude for their long hours of work.

Who was this Aristotle of Rome? It was easy enough to find his records in the census from the Jewish enclave in Rome, for while there were many Jews in that pagan city, only a mere handful adhered to the teachings and purposes of the Essenes.

Aristotle was the third son in a family of five sons and three daughters. His father was a Roman citizen, respected and honored by the Romans for his business acumen, and loved and revered by the Jews for his charity and wisdom. The old man was a priest and a leader in the Roman synagogue which his vast wealth had helped to build. The daughters had married well, their considerable dowries enabling them to obtain husbands from the richest and most prominent Jewish families. The brothers were also married, and were involved in their father's complex holdings; each maintained a luxurious home in the rich section of the Jewish community. The mother had died many years before and the eldest daughter and her family lived with Aristotle's father and kept his home.

The father had afforded his children the best possible education. Their schooling in the synagogue had been augmented by private tutors who opened their eyes to the world of science, literature, and philosophy. Each of his sons had attended the rabbinical school, but it was only Aristotle who had gone on to the University in Alexandria where he had first learned of the school for prophets on Mt. Carmel, and of the Remnant who still squatted upon that Holy Mount to keep the torch of truth burning in a world blinded by the darkness of ignorance.

Aristotle had stayed on in Alexandria for a number of years, studying under the great masters and then travelling all over the world to seek out the wisdom and knowledge of all the great sages. He'd been initiated into the Great Brotherhood in Egypt, and had then returned to his father's house in Rome where he assumed the duties of priest and teacher, and secretly, the leader of the few Essenes.

The records showed that Aristotle was a holy man, endowed with many gifts of the spirit, and certainly was most qualified for the exalted position of Prince of the Entire Congregation. But who *was* Aristotle of Rome?

Aristotle had been at Mt. Carmel for some weeks and Judith felt she knew the answer to that question no better than she had when he'd first stepped foot on the Mount. He was an enigma—aloof, urbane, and never without that maddening, secretive, half-smile which reduced Judith to feeling like an ignorant peasant. He looked like a Roman with his short-cropped, curly black hair and finely trimmed beard that came to a point just below his chin. He irritated Judith with his sardonic, mocking eyes and fleshy, Jewish lips that quivered when she spoke to him, as though they wanted to laugh at the nonsense of a whimsical child. She knew he watched her, as he watched Eloise, Elkatma, and Anna and all the other holy women who dedicated their lives to the Elect, with a look of bemusement and indulgence, as though they were nothing but children playing the game of grownups, and not to be taken seriously. She found his manner with women despicable and outrageous and thought it was by the mercy of God that the man had never married, thus sparing some poor woman a life of misery.

Judith couldn't understand why nothing as yet had been done about Joseph. She and Judas had surely impressed on Aristotle the urgency in Enos' final command, but weeks had passed and nothing had been done. Nothing, anyway, that Judith was aware of, but then, since she was no longer in the inner circle of authority, what did she know? And what of the school and scriptorium?

In the months prior to Enos' passing, she and Enos had often discussed the need for a larger school and a scriptorium. Every year the number of initiates into the Brotherhood increased, and more and more families in the villages and camps were seeking the teachings of the Essenes in their longing for the Messiah and disillusionment with the corrupt Jerusalem priesthood. Now that the Mother had been chosen, and the imminent advent of the Messiah was a reality, it was vital that copies be made of the Holy Scriptures and other documents of the Essenes. When the final victory over the Sons of Darkness had been won and the Messiah ruled over all of Israel, there would be an urgent need for these writings for the instruction and edification of the surviving Sons of Light. It was true that it would be years before the Messiah reached manhood and the fulfillment of the Scriptures came to pass, but it would take years to accomplish such an undertaking. The facilities on Mt. Carmel were already becoming inadequate. New buildings should be erected to house the growing numbers of students. More monks should be trained in the exacting art of copying the Scriptures. Judith wasn't sure the Mount could support the steadily increasing population.

She had asked for permission to speak at the last session of the General Council and had pointed all of this out, recommending that a school, scriptorium, and monastery be founded upon a new site. The Council had unanimously adopted her recommendations and had charged Judas, Mathias, and Aristotle with the task of working out the details and bringing the plans to fulfillment.

But nothing had yet been done and Judith's impatience grew daily. All Aristotle seemed interested in was establishing his own comforts. A few strange monks had accompanied him to Mt. Carmel, which in itself annoyed her by the implication that he'd known he'd stay, and Aristotle had kept them busily employed in furnishing a room in the temple with Roman-style luxury and elegance. Judith heartily disapproved of such action and refused to inspect the crates and boxes which had been brought up to the Mount from Caesaria. She stomped about with pursed lips and glacial eyes, seething with anger that he should disregard the traditional austerity and piety of the Poor. Enos had lived as meagerly as the poorest brother in the camps, while Aristotle—!

A part of Judith deplored her attitude toward their new leader, and she knew that part of the reason for it was her own frustration at being shorn of all responsibility and authority and relegated back to the anonymity of one of the holy women.

She was bored. After months of days so full she could hardly find a minute to herself, she was suddenly in the ignoble position of having no position. She'd done her work too well after Enos' death. Eloise was in charge of Mary, Elkatma in charge of the House of Lodgement, teachers had been assigned to instruct the girls in all the various phases of their education, every man and woman had been assigned their specific duty, but she'd overlooked herself.

She hated herself for her avid dislike of Aristotle and was ridden with guilt because she knew she was jealous. She longed for Enos and was filled with self-loathing because her longing was really for her old position of authority. She prayed for God to heal her of the anger and resentment she felt, and implored His forgiveness for her weakness and lack of humility. But another part of her rebelled and burned with a sense of outrage that the aims and purposes of the Essenes were being taken so lightly.

Judith was sitting in the library supposedly copying the Scriptures, but making only a poor attempt. The scribes' scratching pens distracted her and the oppressive heat dulled her senses and made her head ache. She laid her pen down and walked stiffly to the window to look out on the baking court, wishing she was a child again and could run away to the cool, dark forest and leave her troubled thoughts behind. She heard a discreet cough and turned from the window to see Aristotle beckoning to her from the doorway. She was startled. He'd never summoned her before, and for a fleeting moment she thought it must be someone else he wanted. She glanced quickly around the room, but no one else seemed to notice him, and so she followed him out into the dim hallway. A knot of apprehension settled into the pit of her stomach and she wiped her sweating palms down the tunic over her thighs. Aristotle opened the door to the room next to the library and stood aside to allow Judith to enter first. She stepped inside and gasped, stunned to speechlessness.

The small, barren, functional room had been transformed. Color, shape, and texture flowed in a continuous weave of harmony, grace, elegance, and comfort. She stared, wide-eyed and open-mouthed. Her eyes flew over the room, struggling to bring the splashes of color and confusion of shapes into some kind of order.

An intricately carved and highly polished teakwood desk dominated the room. It was placed directly in front of the window, facing the door, so whoever sat on the plush green velvet-upholstered chair behind it need only raise his eyes to command a view of the entire room. A large silver tray rested on one corner of the huge desk, holding a finely etched, silver wine urn and matching goblets of such simple, graceful lines that Judith could hardly tear her eyes away from them. The sun, filtering through a silk curtain of the same soft green as the chair, reflected in the silver with prisms of color, all mirrored in the polished surface of the desk.

Judith took an involuntary step forward and looked down as her sandaled feet sunk into a thick, beautifully patterned Persian rug. Her eyes followed the rug until they came to the clawed feet of a Roman couch, sweeping the gracefully curved legs to rest on the plush, dusty rose, cushioned seat. She turned and found its mate on the opposite wall. Two chairs, both upholstered in rose and green stripes, sat invitingly on either side of the door. One brushed the skirt of her tunic and she had to fight the temptation to sink down upon it. Tiny marble tables were placed discreetly about the room like silent, unobtrusive servants waiting for their master's call. Corinthian copper lamps nestled in tiny niches recessed in the stark white walls, giving a splash of brightness to the otherwise softly subdued color scheme. In each corner stood a tall, marble pedestal adorned by an alabaster vase filled with blossoms. The flowers filled the room with a heady perfume and gave the illusion of cool, airy expanse.

Judith was floundering in confusion. The room drew her in, tantalizing, bewitching, and at the same time repulsing her. A part of her wanted to touch and examine and exclaim with delight at its subtle balance of line and color, and another part of her wanted to lash out and destroy. The room seemed to reflect its creator's sensitivity, a man who could make the peace and harmony in his soul become manifest in a room that soothed the eye by its serenity and beckoned the weary with its comfort. But to place such a room in the austere setting of Mt. Carmel was to mock and scorn and belittle. It exposed a streak of cruelty and a twisted, depraved sense of humor in that same soul. An icy fear swept into Judith's heart as she looked at Aristotle with bewilderment and disbelief. Who was this Aristotle of Rome?

He was looking down at her with his maddening, amused smile. His arms were crossed and he rocked back and forth on his heels, obviously delighted by Judith's astonishment.

"Do you like the room, Judith?" he asked.

Judith gaped at him. She thought he must be mad! "It's blasphemous!" she croaked. "We are 'The Poor'! We care not for the riches and luxuries of this world! You betray our ideals and bring shame to us by bringing the evil taint of the world into the purity of our community!"

Aristotle's head had snapped back as though she had slapped him. He visibly paled, and his eyes contracted into narrow slits with a dangerous gleam that made them look like the yellow eyes of a cat. Judith was too livid with rage to notice. She plunged on.

"How dare you! How dare you ask me if I like it! It is an abomination to the Lord!"

Aristotle grasped Judith's forearms in a grip of iron. He towered over her, his face contorted in anger. Judith winced with pain and shrank from him. She thought he was going to strike her. He yanked her toward him and pushed his face into her own. He spoke with cold, calculated fury, flinging his words into her face like hard pellets of stone.

"You are quick to judge, Judith of Phinehas. I have been led to believe that you are a woman of intelligence and foresight. Have you not asked yourself why the Council chose me to fill Enos' place at Mt. Carmel? You have many able priests in your land; did it never occur to you to question, why a Roman? Did it never occur to you that God has molded me for this role from my mother's womb?"

Aristotle suddenly released her, nearly flinging her away. Judith caught the striped chair to keep from falling, her heart pounding with fear of the terrible anger she'd evoked.

"You don't approve of me, do you?" Aristotle sneered. "The wonderful, gifted Judith of Mt. Carmel, whose name is spoken with awe in every camp and community throughout the Elect, thinks the Council has made a mistake! Who do you think you are, and who are you to sit in judgment over me! How dare *you* challenge the decision of the Council and of God, and how dare *you* question my motives and authority in what I do!"

Judith stared at him. Her face had gone white and she had a feeling in the pit of her stomach that everything he said was true. She was sickened by her own stupidity and lack of judgment. She rubbed her arms where Aristotle's fingers had left red, ugly marks, and wondered how she could ever breach the terrible gulf she'd created by her suspicion and jealousy.

Aristotle's eyes dropped to Judith's hands and the welts on her arms. His anger suddenly evaporated and his rigid body sagged. "Forgive me," he said thickly, "and may God forgive us both."

He sighed deeply and rubbed his hand across his eyes in a gesture so like Phinehas that Judith swallowed a little cry, and hot tears stung her lids. She lowered herself weakly into the chair, too drained to speak. Aristotle touched her shoulder briefly and then sat down on the divan with his elbows on his knees and his face buried in his hands. When he finally looked up, his face was calm and his voice, though urgent, was gentle and conveyed no resentment.

"Judith! Think, my dear, think! Rome rules the world! Herod and the Pharisees and the Sadducees are only puppets to Rome. Caesar plays his puppets with care, conceding to their whims and pretending to bow to their imagined power and feigned religious piety, but in all truth, Judith, Rome laughs at them behind their backs and even Roman women snicker behind their fancy fans at the Sadducees' wives who simper and mimic and try to worm their way into Roman society. Never forget it is Rome who rules! One word and Herod is in chains and Jerusalem razed to the ground. So why me, you ask? Why this room? Because I am a Roman! I know their customs, their manners, their traditions. I know what pleases them and what mollifies them. I know how to banter, to trade, to get what I want without seeming to, and I need this room to do it.

"The fact that I am an Essene will mean nothing to them, and why should it? Aren't the Jews always quarrelling over their precious Law and falling out to form different cults and sects because of it? They care nothing for my religious beliefs. They care only that I am a citizen of Rome and that I am my father's son, my father who is a friend of Caesar. They may find it curious that I chose to leave the luxury and richness of my father's house to attach myself to this lovely Mount, but they will only shrug their shoulders and think me some eccentric aesthetic who desires a scholar's life of contemplation. This room will prove to them that though I might be an eccentric, I am not a fanatic. This room will say to them that here is a man of taste and discernment who appreciates beauty and comfort, thus he must also be a man of reason and intelligence."

Aristotle stood and began to pace, his voice again angry. "From now on when soldiers from Rome or Herod's barbarians appear on the Mount, they will not find a pious, saintly, old man who would never raise a hand to defend himself. No! Now they will find a Roman citizen, a friend of Caesar, a man they will not dare to molest and abuse. I shall invite them into this room to wine and dine them and confound them with their own cunning usage of words. I shall personally guide them on an inspection of all our goods and rumored wealth, and send them on their way bemused with wine and convinced that the Poor are of no threat to Rome; we are only men who have wearied of the turmoils and stress in the world and have come to a holy mountain in search of peace and contemplation of the soul."

Judith couldn't help but smile at the picture Aristotle wove of his sly deception of the Sons of Darkness. He was standing in front of the window and the bright sun behind his back made it impossible for her to see his face. She suddenly felt fine—light and buoyant, as though a heavy load had just been lifted. At last she'd caught a glimpse of the true Aristotle who hid behind that maddening, sardonic smile, and that glimpse made her feel confident and excited. Life would not be dull with Aristotle as their leader. But first she must try to mend the wounds caused by their angry words.

She rose from the chair and walked idly around the room, aware that Aristotle watched her intently. She smoothed her hand over the plush velvet and examined the alabaster vases, inhaling the heady aroma wafting from their contents. She moved to the desk and smiled at her reflection in its polished top, and caressed the silky sheen of a silver goblet. She made her tour deliberately slow and critical, then lowered herself into a divan and regarded Aristotle with an unwavering stare.

"I could report you, you know," she said steadily, "for undermining my composure, and have you mulcted for one year."

Aristotle gave a slight start. That wasn't at all what he expected her to say, but then he bowed slightly and said, "And I, you, dear lady."

"Hmmm," Judith mused as she looked again around the room. "This is a room of great beauty and comfort. Perhaps we could ask to have our food ration cut to one-half and for exile to this room. I shouldn't mind starving here."

Aristotle watched as the girl's incredible eyes changed to the blue of the Galilee, and a smile, which began in the depths of that blue, grew and spread over her face until it burst into gales of laughter. His eyes widened and his mouth dropped. Then he joined her in her glee and they laughed until they were exhausted.

When Judith had caught her breath, she leaned forward and said in all seriousness. "Everything you said is true, Rabbi. We must beware of Rome. And no, the thought did not occur to me that that was why a Roman Jew was elected. I'm sorry. I apologize for my outburst and for my unforgivable rudeness, but most of all for my stupidity. Surely your appointment was guided by the Spirit, for none other could be better qualified."

Aristotle made a gesture with his hand that dismissed any further need for apology. He sat down behind the desk and studied Judith intently, as though trying to make up his mind whether or not to speak. When he finally did, his voice was brusque and authoritative.

"I am sending you on a journey. You will make the necessary arrangements as soon as possible. The rule for

travel will be set aside in this instance, for I wish for you
to appear as a wealthy Jewish woman journeying to visit
relatives in Alexandria. You will commission the seam-
stresses to prepare the proper clothing for such a guise, and
choose whatever jewelry, cloth, and other female adornments you need from the storehouse. Choose a woman to
travel with you as a handmaid. Shalmar will accompany
you as a protector, along with a few monks who will pose
as his retainers. Zermada is in Alexandria and you will
stay with her. I have already sent a message to inform her
of your arrival. Prepare for a stay of a number of months
and instruct the woman you choose accordingly. If the
treasury is lacking of any item you need, find it elsewhere."

Judith stared at him in astonishment. Her mind whirled.
A journey! To Alexandria? A thousand questions flooded
her mind, but she fought to control her tongue and answered a simple "Yes, Rabbi." The last hour had taught
her to have patience with this strange, alien priest, for she
had learned he did nothing without good reason.

Aristotle accepted her answer with amusement, knowing full well the turmoil he'd caused her, and was pleased
by her control. He walked to the center of the room
where Judith could see his face, and he smiled. His smile
no longer seemed mocking and condescending, but friendly
and even affectionate.

"You're an extraordinary woman, Judith. Your recom-
mendation to the Council regarding a school and scriptorium was truly an inspiration. The purpose of this
journey is to study other such facilities and to learn the
methods they employ and present a detailed report of
your own observations and opinions as to what we can do
here on Mt. Carmel. You are fully qualified for this work,
and as a woman, the easiest to disguise, thus causing little
or no suspicion from our enemies. You will be in complete authority. I suggest Alexandria as a start, but I will
leave it to your own judgment if you feel it necessary to
travel farther and investigate the methods of other lands
and peoples. Shalmar, Zermada, and all others will be
under your authority. As to what to look for, where to go,
how to handle the whole matter—that I leave in your
capable hands. I only ask that it be done quickly and that

you return to Carmel as soon as possible. However, do not shorten the time simply to return! If it takes a year or more, so be it."

Judith flushed under Aristotle's praise, and then as she listened to his description of the purpose of the journey, she could hardly contain her excitement. The scriptorium would become a reality! And the great university and library of Alexandria! Oh, yes! She knew what was needed for the scriptorium. A thousand things would have to be done. She stood up and began to pace back and forth and the words tumbled out of her mouth in an excited rush.

"We need more and better parchment, quills, and ink. A better method of preserving the scrolls. All the oral traditions of our people should be written and preserved. We must find a place to buy the supplies we need and a way to transport them to Mt. Carmel. Persian ink is said to be very good, though costly. If we could make it here, I'd have to find out how. The university at Alexandria must use a mammoth amount of writing materials. Zermada has told me there are records and books of such antiquity . . . if we could get permission to copy . . . there are many Jews there, perhaps,"

"Stop!" Aristotle laughed. "I can see I need not concern myself about your ability to accomplish this task. Now I have other duties to attend to, and so do you. Be off and do your thinking elsewhere."

Judith laughed and started out, but paused a moment at the door and turned back. "Might I suggest our old monastery in the wilderness of Judea as a possible site for the scriptorium and school? It lies above the Salt Sea and was called 'The City of Salt.' And one more thing—the inspiration was not mine, but Enos'." She softly closed the door and was gone.

Chapter 8

Judith sailed for Alexandria a few weeks later, and from there to Persia, India, and finally back again to Egypt. She studied the methods of making and preserving scrolls in each land she visited, and decided that the leather scrolls used in Egypt were superior to the others. She saw how the Egyptians wrapped the scrolls in linen and stored them in great earthenware jars to preserve them from the elements. She learned that a hot, dry climate was ideal for keeping the leather from disintegration, and became convinced that the City of Salt in the arid hills above the Salt Sea was the perfect location for such work.

They purchased a few jars to take back to Mt. Carmel for their own potters to use as models, and Judith drew up a minutely detailed record of how the hides were tanned and fashioned into scrolls. She visualized the City of Salt as one day being completely self-sustaining. They could make their own scrolls and jars, perhaps even keep a small flock and maintain their own farm. The possibilities for the new community were endless.

Judith found the world outside of Mt. Carmel beyond her wildest imaginings. Alexandria was typical of the cities she visited—turbulent, clamorous, wretchedly overcrowded, punishing her senses with color, noise, stench, and the everlasting dust and heat. It was a city of swarming flies and yapping dogs and braying camels and donkeys, of rumbling chariots and whinnying horses and brawling, drunken fights which broke out day and night. Merchants screamed their wares by day, and prostitutes haunted the alleys by night. Robberies and murders were commonplace. Sore-infested beggars beat their metal cups and plucked at her skirts when she passed on the streets.

She saw the horrors of the slave market where human flesh was auctioned to the highest bidder. She recoiled at the sight of slaves condemned to a life beneath the lash. She retched when she saw children, girls and boys, fingered and fondled by lascivious old men who lusted after their tender flesh.

The children broke her heart—filthy, ragged, starving, existing at the shadowy edge of humanity. They seemed to stay alive only by an animal cunning which helped them to steal and kill and escape the police. She wondered if they had homes and families, where they slept, and if anyone cared for or loved them. She blushed with shame as she remembered her own happy childhood in the sun-washed hills of Galilee, and prayed to God for those little souls cast into the bowels of Gehenna.

Zermada's house was up and away from the teeming squalor of the harbor area and market place, in an area of gracious homes and green gardens that overlooked Lake Mareotis, not far from the library and museum. Each day Judith and Shalmar walked beneath the wide, porticoed arcades surrounding the massive library and listened as masters and scholars expounded on every subject imaginable, each with his own following of disciples who pressed close to hear every pearl of wisdom dropped from the teacher's mouth.

Judith thought it the most exciting place in the world. The beauty of the buildings, built of gleaming white marble with intricately designed tiled floors, bubbling fountains, and lush gardens of exotic blooms in a riot of color, took her breath away. The interior of the library was the most impressive to Judith, for here were hundreds of thousands of scrolls, a massive collection of man's knowledge stretching back to a time long-forgotten by the modern mind. Judith found herself trembling with excitement when an aging curate led them to a vast room which held all the scrolls regarding religion.

The room was a veritable treasury of scrolls, far too numerous to count. It would take a lifetime, perhaps many lifetimes, to read and study them all. Judith felt a flash of jealousy that Aristotle had been able to spend even a few years here, while she was allowed only a few months. During her stay in Alexandria, Judith rarely missed spending the greater part of each day scanning

scroll after scroll, for there simply wasn't time to study
them thoroughly. She made note of any scroll that contained the slightest hint of a coming Anointed One, and
was astonished when she found such a doctrine in almost
every religion then known to man. Surely the One God
was the Father to all, and had revealed Himself to all His
children according to their understanding.

Judith regretted leaving Alexandria, but when spring
arrived they sailed on the Red Sea, around the coast of
Arabia, to Chaldea, Persia, and India.

Everywhere she went she was met by masters and sages
who through the mystical ways of the spirit knew of her
coming and of her purpose, and who sought her out. One
of the monks chosen by Aristotle to pose as a servant was
a man of many tongues, but Judith found they had no
need of an interpreter to converse with these men of wisdom. Even though she didn't know their language, she
understood them perfectly, and they, she.

All of the wise men knew that the earth was entering a
period when the Supreme Being would be made manifest
in the world. Like the Carmelites, they had read the signs
and studied the stars and searched through records of
great antiquity. The enlightened the world over felt the
stir of the Spirit and prepared for the Day of the Lord.
Judith was asked to repeat over and over again the story
of the choosing of Mary on the stair, and watched with a
full heart as old men wept tears of joy and sang praises
unto the Lord.

To sit at the feet of those great souls was even more
exciting and fulfilling than reading the scrolls in the library. In India they met a holy one who had not eaten for
years, but who radiated health and vigor. They watched
young monks with shaven heads sit for hours in strange,
unnatural positions, completely unaware of any discomfort and oblivious to the world around them. These young
monks could control the pace of their heartbeats and reg-
ulate the temperature of their bodies by using the power
of their minds. Judith and her entourage stared in disbelief as an Adept changed the atoms of the universe and
materialized a bowl of luscious, edible fruit from the air.

Shalmar looked upon these miracles with a skeptical
eye, but Judith wondered. Had not Elisha increased the
widow's oil? Had not Elijah put his head between his

knees until a rain-filled cloud appeared over the sea? Had God sent the cloud in answer to Elijah's prayer, or had Elijah summoned the cloud in the same way the Adept had called forth the fruit? How did twenty barley loaves feed a hundred people with some left over? Judith believed that whatever the Source of the wonders of India and those of her own people, it was undoubtedly the same.

The most thrilling experience of all occurred in a lonely little hut high in the Indian mountains when a wizened, loin-cloth-clad monk read from the Tripitaka:

"Monks, in the days when men live eighty thousand years, there will arise in the world a Buddha named Metteyyo, the Benevolent One, a Holy One, a supremely Enlightened One, endowed with wisdom in conduct; auspicious, knowing the universe, an incomparable Charioteer of men who are tamed, a Master of angels and mortals, a Blessed Buddha, even as I have now arisen in the world, a Buddha with these same qualities endowed. What he has realized by his own supernal knowledge he will publish to this universe with its angels, its fiends, and its archangels and to the race of philosophers and brahmins, princes and peoples; even as I now, having all this knowledge, do publish the same unto the same. He will preach his religion, glorious in its origin, glorious at the climax, glorious at the goal, in the spirit and the letter. He will proclaim a religious life, a wholly perfect and thoroughly pure; even as I now preach my religion and a like life do proclaim. He will keep up a society of monks numbering many thousand, even as I now keep up a society of monks numbering many hundred."

Was it the Messiah the great Siddhartha Gautama prophesied?

Judith kept journals of everything she saw and heard and read, and by the time she returned to Alexandria her journals were full. She now knew that there were many things which even the Covenanters did not know, and before she left those strange lands, she spoke with the sages about the possibility of one day teaching these things to the Messiah.

It was nearly a year before they returned to Zermada's house to rest and confirm the things they'd learned by a careful perusal of the records in the library. They took a barge to Memphis and then went by camel train to the

Great Pyramid where the Masters were initiated into the Great Brotherhood.

The trip down the wide river was slow and leisurely. They wound their way through lush green deltas and fertile valleys, occasionally pulling to shore to visit some of the many tiny villages which lay along the banks. Whole villages would come tumbling down the bank to greet them, bringing their crafts to sell and delicacies of food and drink to make them welcome.

Judith saw her first glimpse of the pyramids from far up the river. They rose skyward through the yellow haze like pointed, glowing white mountains. Shalmar had commissioned a guide and a donkey caravan to carry them from the river bank to the base of the pyramids, and Judith was so enthralled by the sight of them that she didn't mind the torturous ride, or the glaring heat and thick, yellow dust which choked her and burned her eyes.

She felt like an insignificant ant when she stood at the base of the towering Sphinx. She remembered her awe when as a child she had marvelled at the exact fit of the stones in the temple at Mt. Carmel, but they were nothing but pebbles as compared to the mammoth squares of stone in the pyramids. How could men have cut and moved those gigantic blocks of limestone?

Judith was lost in her thoughts when a deep, unfamiliar voice said from behind her, "They are quite wonderful, are they not?"

Judith turned to see who spoke and looked into the dark, aquiline face of a strange Egyptian. She had never seen him before, and yet she felt she knew him. He was dressed like a desert sheepherder in multicolored striped robes. A silk rope held the fringed *kufiyeh* on his head, pulled low over his broad, smooth brow, and simple, leather-thonged sandals adorned his feet. He studied her out of oval, hooded eyes—black, brooding eyes which seemed to bore through her flesh to see her very soul.

Judith was astonished and more than a little disconcerted. Who was he, and where did he come from? She'd seen no one when they arrived. She was more astonished when he said, "Peace be with you, Judith. Welcome to the Hall of the Initiates."

"You know me?" Judith gasped.

The Egyptian smiled and bowed. "We all know you,"

he said enigmatically. "May I offer you respite from the sun and a cooling drink to relieve your throat?"

Judith found she was trembling, but not out of fear. She swallowed and looked for Shalmar and the others who were walking toward the base of the pyramid.

"Never mind your friends. They will not miss you."

Judith stared at the Egyptian. She shivered and felt as though she was standing on the brink of a vast, unknown, realm of mystery. She was not afraid, in fact she was overwhelmingly curious, but even if she had been afraid, some inner compulsion forced her to follow him into the shadow of the pyramids.

He led her into a large tent, lavishly hung with silks and brocades, the floors covered with beautiful carpets and soft plump cushions. He gestured for her to recline and clapped his hands. Servants instantly answered his summons, bearing trays of fruits and wine, and after serving them, vanished behind the tapestries.

Judith had been speechless at the sight of such luxury in the middle of the desert. She finally found her tongue and stammered, "Who are you?"

The Egyptian smiled. "My name is unimportant. You would find it quite unpronounceable, in any event."

"Why are you here? You seemed to expect me."

"I am sent by the Brothers to tell of the pyramids, of their origin and purpose, and what they will mean to generations yet unborn."

A ripple of excitement flowed through Judith's veins. She guessed it would be futile to question him further. He'd tell her all she needed to know and no more. She sipped the wine and settled back on the cushions to listen. The Egyptian's voice was low and softly modulated. It had a hypnotic effect on her, and she felt transported to another time and place; his words became like visions which she saw instead of heard.

"You know, of course, the story of Creation when God created the heavens and earth, and then evolved the plant and animal kingdoms, long before the advent of man into the earth. Souls were created as spirit entities, particles of God Himself, in His image, and endowed with the gift of freedom of will. The souls watched the gradual development of life on the earth, delighting in the beauty and movement they saw taking place.

"Some souls were not satisfied with simply watching but desired to experience creation for themselves. They began to project themselves into the material earth as 'thought forms,' into the very rocks and trees, coexisting within various mineral and life forms, both animal and vegetable.

"For a long time souls had the ability to come and go through the various kingdoms of earth at will, but gradually they became so enmeshed in experiencing the physical sensations that they forgot how to use this ability and became trapped. They became hardened or set, much in the form of the existent human body of that day, with color that partook of their surroundings much in the manner of the chameleon in the present. Thus developed the five races, the yellow in the Gobi, white in the Carpathians, black in the plains or African lands, brown in the Andean, and red in the Atlantian land.

"These souls were able to use in their gradual development all the forces as were manifest in their individual surroundings, and those of the red race in the Atlantian land developed at a far faster rate than those in other lands. Remember that many of these souls inhabited animal bodies as well as that primitive, near-human one. Remember also that these conditions developed over eons of what we know of as time.

"These souls became known as the Sons of Belial, because through their obsession with the physical world, they forgot that they were created as spiritual beings, and in forgetting their creation, forgot their Creator.

"There were other souls who did not come into the physical world, but chose to remain in the spirit realm. These souls were called the Sons of the Law of One. The Sons of the Law of One saw what was happening to their brothers in the earth and desired to help them. Led by Adam, or Amelius as he was called in Atlantis, they drew on the image given by God for a body most perfect for souls to use while in the earth. Thus the human body of man was created.

"The Sons of the Law of One kept the race of man pure and did not cohabit with the Sons of Belial. They used their influence and teaching to bring the Sons of Belial to an awareness of who and what they really were. But as time went on, the Sons of Belial seduced the daughters of the Sons of the Law of One, bringing to these daughters the abilities for enjoying physical excess of every kind. The offspring of the Sons of Belial and the daughters of the Sons of the Law of One were grotesque monstrosities, part human, part beast, that we know today as the satyrs, mermaids, and nymphs of legend. These offspring were called the Sons and Daughters of Men.

"There were also in that land, Things, or automations, which were completely dominated and controlled by the Sons of Belial. These 'Things' performed all the manual labor that was necessary, for their minds had only evolved to about the level of our domesticated animal of today. They were in far worse straits than the slaves of today, for, having no will or thought of their own, they were outrageously exploited and subjugated by the Sons of Belial. This caused serious dissension between the Sons of Belial and the Sons of the Law of One, for the latter wished to free them from their servitude and mindlessness."

The Egyptian paused in his tale and looked at Judith through hooded eyes. A faint, cynical smile played at his mouth as he said ruefully, "It is much the same today. Evil versus good, spirituality versus materiality, the Children of Light war with the Sons of Darkness. All the corruption and oppression, debauchery and lust; the grasping, greedy lunge for power and riches were as evident in the world then as in the world today. Then, as now, there were a few good souls who, in remembering their Creator, fought to free man from the slavery of his passions and return him to his true abode which is with God. The battle continues. But let us return to Atlantis.

"The Atlantians were a people of industry and intelligence who learned to harness the forces of nature to generate power through the means of a great crystal, which they used for transportation, communications, and other marvelous technical innovations. They could transmit sound and images on the waves of ether, and had ships which flew through the air as well as on and under the sea. They possessed wonderful machines which freed men from arduous toil and provided for his ease and recreation. It all sounds quite wonderful, doesn't it? And yet man then, as now, had his problems.

"In that land, and indeed over most of the world, man

was beset by huge, gigantic animals and birds which made man's life on earth miserable and most precarious. Because of this, a meeting was called of the rulers and wise men of all the nations to find a way to rid the earth of this menace. The Sons of Belial attended this meeting and proposed the use of the great crystal to change the environment needed by these animals to survive. The Sons of the Law of One opposed this suggestion on the grounds that such methods could also destroy the world of men, but as usual, the world leaders followed the Sons of Belial. The result of this great experiment was world-wide earthquakes and volcanoes and tidal waves the like of which the earth had never seen before. The lands were broken up, the topography of the earth was changed, thousands of lives were lost, but the menace of the huge animals continued. The world leaders seemingly had learned their lesson, however, and for the next thousands of years fought the animals and birds with more conventional methods.

"A second like catastrophe occurred when the power of the great crystal was accidentally turned too high.

"Through all this period the dissension between the Sons of the Law of One and the Sons of Belial grew until open warfare broke out and again the crystal was used as a destructive force. The whole world had become one of such evil and destruction, such chaos and misery, that God solved the problem of man and beast by shifting the poles of the earth, freezing the animals in a blanket of ice and destroying the decadent land of Atlantis altogether. The lands broke up and fell into the sea, and the seas spilled over their appointed boundaries to cover lands not submerged, while dry lands appeared where before had only been water. It was the great flood, and the end of a civilization."

Judith couldn't help but shudder with horror at the vision of such suffering and fear the tale evoked in her mind. "Was no one spared?" she asked, aghast.

"Of course. Many. The Sons of the Law of One saw the advent of each catastrophe before it occurred, and many emigrated to other lands in order to escape, which brings us here, to the land of Egypt.

"About three hundred years before the final destruction and deluge, Egypt was ruled by King Raai. He was a spiritually minded ruler who brought peace and a broad understanding of universal laws to the people. He called a meeting of forty-four priests, seers, and astrologers to discuss methods of hastening man's development, both spiritually and physically. His teachings covered many phases of man's existence on the earth, and those teachings are inscribed in our Book of the Dead. It was this king, Raai, and his queen, Isai, who came to be worshipped as Ra and Isis.

"While King Raai was on the throne, Egypt was invaded by white men from a land called Arart in the Caucasian mountains, led by their king who was also called Arart, and guided by a priest named Ra-Ta. King Raai had no desire to plunge his people into war, and so immediately abdicated the throne in favor of Arart. However, some of the Egyptians, led by one Aarat, rebelled, and to restore peace to the land, Arart set up a governing Troika consisting of his son, then King Araaraat, the Egyptian Aarat, and the priest Ra-Ta. Under this troika Egypt became a powerful nation. Many people from India, Mongolia, and Atlantis migrated to Egypt to escape the earthquakes and disruptions then occurring in their own lands, making Egypt an amalgamation of many races. The Atlantians brought with them many 'Things,' and many of the Atlantians looked upon the native Egyptians as in the same class as those 'Things.'

"During the first part of the Rule of the Troika, the priest Ra-Ta was occupied with setting up spiritual codes and the worship of the One God. He built many temples for the spiritual and physical development of the masses. He often travelled to Atlantis to learn the tenets and methods of the Sons of the Law of One, and thus he became familiar with the problems regarding the 'Things,' and learned of the corruption of the Sons of Belial. He also learned of the coming submergence of those remaining portions of Atlantis and the need that a permanent record of that land be made.

"It was during this time that Ra-Ta supervised the building of the Temple of Sacrifice and the Temple Beautiful. These temples were built here, where we are now standing, and eventually were connected to the Sphinx."

"What happened to them?" Judith asked.

"Disintegrated, and in that sphere you may enter and

some have entered. These temples were designed for the development of those subhuman mixtures of part man, part beast, which were called the Sons of Men. The Temple Beautiful was for the purpose of training the Sons of Men in the various vocations, especially those of art and music.

"The Temple of Sacrifice was used more as a hospital, or infirmary, as we would call it today. It was here that the Sons of Men began to bring their hideous offspring and themselves to be purified of those appendages such as paws and claws, feathers and tails, and other such which set them apart from the society of men. Many methods were used to bring about this purification: surgery, medicines, diet, massage, and various manipulations. Vibrations from music and color were used—singing, dancing, chanting, and of course, deep meditation whereby the powers of the mind came into play. There was also a purification process involving the use of flames from the altar fires. This was a long process, taking six to seven years, and sometimes had to be continued through several incarnations of individual souls before a complete transformation could be effected. There was a gland, still existent in the animal kingdom today, which had to be eradicated from the bodies of the Sons of Men.

"The methods used would probably be called barbarous today, but taken in the light of spirituality were then morally ideal. You must think in terms of souls, each entering again and again into the earth. Without the use of such means to purify the race, you and I today could possibly be housed by a body with the lower limbs of a beast. Quite horrifying, is it not?

"These ministrations brought terrible mental and emotional anguish to those souls who were used for such experimentation. When the purifications were complete, they found themselves separated from their own kind, their loved ones, and yet were not accepted into the society of those of the pure human race, for they carried the stigma of having been one of those odd mixtures. Also, as part of this experimentation, the newly purified body was required to mate with a human so as to determine the manner of offspring this mating would produce. This was abhorrent to those souls, as they carried a natural mental repulsion to one another, such as you or I would experience if forced to mate with a beast of the field. However, when those entities did in fact produce a perfect human body and realized that by their sacrifice they were enabling other souls to enter through a pure vessel, a sense of peace and accomplishment pervaded and they dedicated themselves to the propagation of a pure race.

"Meanwhile, the strife which had occurred between Ra-Ta and his followers and those who wished to keep their control over the mixtures and 'Things' and the masses of poor, came to a head and resulted in the banishment of Ra-Ta. For ten years Ra-Ta was exiled to the Nubian lands, but Egypt writhed in a perpetual state of rebellion and civil war until the king was forced to recall him in order to restore peace to the land. It was after the recall of Ra-Ta that he began the building of these pyramids and the Sphinx.

"The Great Pyramid was built as a Hall of the Initiates for those souls who through the trials of many incarnations had been cleansed, or purified, of all avarice, hate, lust, and the like to the degree that they need never again incarnate on the earth, unless, of course, on a voluntary basis to help their less fortunate brothers also to reach that degree of purity.

"Ra-Ta, with the aid of Hermes, determined through mathematical, astronomical, and numerological means, as well as by inner inspiration, that this spot in the earth was the center of the universal activities of nature as well as of the spiritual forces. Here would be the least disturbance by the convulsive movements which came about in the earth. When the lines about the earth are considered from the standpoint of mathematical precisions, it will be found that the center is here at the Great Pyramid. The great stones were cut by means of forces and tools used by the Atlantians in those days, and were moved to the site by use of those forces in nature as make for iron to swim. Stone floats in the same manner. The Pyramid holds all the records from the beginnings of that given by the priest, Arart, Araaraat, and Ra. All changes that occurred in the religious thought in the world are shown there; in the variations in which the passage through the same is reached, from the base to the top, or to the open tomb and the top. These changes are signified both by the layer and the color, and the direction of the turn. The significance of the empty sarcophagus is that there will be no more death. Don't misunderstand or misinterpret! The interpretation of death will be made plain!

"The Pyramid of the Hall of Records and the Sphinx were built in the same way. The base of the Sphinx was laid out in channels, and in the corner facing the Great Pyramid may be found the wording of how this was founded, giving the history of the first invading ruler and the ascension of Araaraat to that position. The Hall of Records lies buried under the sands of time between or along that entrance from the Sphinx to the temple, or Great Pyramid, in a pyramid of its own. One day, in many generations to come, the Hall of Records will be uncovered and man will once again know the origins of his race.

"This Hall of Records contains a record of Atlantis from the beginning of those periods when the Spirit took form, or began the encasements in that land; and the development of the peoples throughout their sojourn, together with the record of the first destruction, and the changes that took place in the land. There is also the record of the sojournings of the peoples and their varied activities in other lands, and a record of the meetings of all the nations or lands, for the activities in the destructions that became necessary with the final destruction of Atlantis: and the building of the Pyramid of Initiation; together with whom, what, and where the opening of the records would come, that are as copies from the sunken Atlantis."

It took Judith a few moments to emerge from the almost trancelike state induced by the Egyptian's hypnotic voice and to realize that his recitation was finished. She felt strange and unsteady as she pushed herself up from the cushioned floor and drew back the flap of the tent to gaze upon the magnificent sight of the Great Pyramid. The Egyptian watched her but did not intrude upon her thoughts.

Without turning, Judith finally asked, "What happened to the Sons and Daughters of Men?"

"Destroyed by the deluge. Those in Egypt who escaped the greater destructions were eventually purified. In some remote unknown reaches of the earth, there can be found some remnants of their race. Some were very tiny, dwarflike humanoids, and some extremely large, apelike giants, and some of these remain hidden today, but very few," he answered.

"What of the Sons of Belial?"

He laughed and flung his arms in a wide arch. "Everywhere! The world is overrun with the Sons of Belial. Thanks to the Sons of the Law of One, they are now incarnated in pure, human bodies, but one can still recognize them by their works."

His laugh and the comical truth of his answer brought Judith back to reality. She left the doorway and returned to her seat. She took a sip of the surprisingly still-cool wine. She listened to the eerie, complete silence about her and again had the strange feeling that she had somehow slipped through a tear in time.

"And Amelius?" she asked.

The Egyptian's face changed. His features softened and his eyes seemed to melt with an infinite love, not unlike those of a man who has heard the name of his favorite child, or beloved wife. His voice held a note of piercing tenderness as he repeated the name after her.

"Amelius. It was for his sake that God introduced death into the world as a means of escape from the world into the realm of spirit to rest and reflect and assess before entering again. Amelius has come many times into the world, as Adam, as Melchizedek, as Zend, as Ur, as Asaph, as Jeshua, Joseph, Joshua, and more. He comes for our sake. He must become that which would be able to take the world, the earth, back to the source from which it came. He comes again now, in this day, to finish that begun in the beginning."

Judith's throat went dry. Her heart thudded against her ribs, and her palms were wet.

"The Messiah!" she whispered.

"Yes," the Egyptian said quietly. "The soul which will incarnate through the maiden Mary is Amelius, or Adam, the Greatest of the Great, the Leader of all souls. He comes freely into the world, to overcome the world, that by His example all souls might do the same and thus become one again with the Creator. He comes as a Light unto the world. He incarnates as the Way, the Truth, and the Light. He will become the First Begotten of the Father-Creator."

Judith felt paralyzed by the impact of the Egyptian's words. She fought to control her trembling and the tide of rising panic.

"Why do you tell me these things?" she cried.

"You have incarnated for the purpose of bringing to the conscious mind of the Son of Mary all that He must know to fulfill that which He began in the beginning. You will be His teacher and guide. There are many of us of the Brotherhood, both in this realm and in the realm of spirit who will help you. We are with you always, and when the time has come, you will send Him to us."

The enormity of such knowledge was too much to bear. The panic that had been building in Judith's soul broke through in a terrible cry of anguish. She plunged through the tent like a madwoman. She flung the flap aside and rushed headlong across the desert, stumbling and falling in the soft, shifting sand, mindless of the wind and grit that blinded and choked her. She ran until she could run no more, then fell with her face down in the burning sands.

Her hands took on a life of their own and dug into the sand as though to bury herself in the desert floor. She wept. Tearless, rasping sobs tore through her body with such painful, punishing intensity that when she finally lay still out of sheer exhaustion, she felt bruised and bleeding inside and out.

For a long time Judith lay without moving. The sun beat relentlessly down upon her, but she welcomed it as a sign that she was back in the realm of reality. The sun was real. The sand in her hands was real, and her sore, aching body was real.

She lifted her face and spat the grit from her mouth. She rolled over onto her back and stared into the brilliant blue sky above. A sense of total peace and tranquility surrounded her. Adam would come again, as the Son of Mary! And of Joseph, if Enos was right. He would come again to bring a new awareness to the souls of men of who and what they are. He would come as an example of all souls, of all their trials and tribulations, of all their failures and successes, culminating in Himself the final success of a pure, sinless soul, able to return to unity with the Father-Creator.

Judith trembled at the magnificence of what that meant. If Amelius could overcome the temptations of the flesh and bring His will into one with the Father, then so could they all! Even she, Judith, with all her weaknesses and petty jealousies, and flights of selfish fantasies and pride, could attain unity with the Father by following in Adam's footsteps. What hope he brings into the world! What love he must have to freely assume such a task!

How would Adam accomplish this? What means would he use to spread his teaching over the world? How long before the unification of all souls became a reality?

The Essenes believed the time had come for the world and all the universe to revert to chaos as in the beginning, but now Judith wondered. According to the Egyptian, it had been hundreds of thousands of years since Amelius first came to the earth to rescue his brothers. If it had taken all that time and so many incarnations for Adam to attain oneness with God, could the rest of us fulfill that promise in one generation? It seemed unlikely, but nothing was impossible to the Lord.

Judith thought of Amelius being born to beautiful little Mary, and then suddenly remembered her own role. She was to be His teacher! It would be her responsibility to lay the foundations of knowledge that would enable Adam to accomplish His final goal! The panic began to rise again and her knees involuntarily pulled up to her stomach and she groaned in fear and anguish. What if she should fail? What if she was lacking in the ability to teach the Anointed One!

Judith struggled to control her fear. She was capable! She must not doubt! She must put her trust in the Lord. She must remember how gentle little Mary had fully accepted the will of God. She had never feared, nor had such lack of faith! True, she didn't know the identity of the soul she would carry within her body, but she did know that He was the One whom they'd all waited and prepared for for centuries. Mary's responsibility was far greater than her own, but she did not quiver with fear like a silly, bashful bride beneath the wedding canopy!

Judith looked back to where the tent had stood. It was gone. The wind had erased every trace from the sand, as though it had never been. She saw Shalmar and the others walking along the base of the pyramid as they had been doing when she'd first gone with the Egyptian to his tent.

She knew intuitively that these last hours had not been passed in this world, and that Shalmar had never missed her. She got to her feet and brushed the dirt and sand from her face and clothes. The sky was beautiful; the sand was like gold. The pyramids rose like majestic monuments of truth against the azure sky.

"What a fool I am!" Judith said aloud to the wind and the sky. "I shall do what I have come to do!"

She suddenly wanted to laugh and run out of pure joy. She gathered her skirts up nearly to her knees and plunged through the soft, deep sand with galloping leaps.

"Taste and see the goodness of the Lord!" she cried.

Chapter 9

T wo years was a long time to be away from home, and Judith found many changes upon her return. Most of the twelve girls had left Mt. Carmel. Six were either married or betrothed, and Abigale and Andra had returned to their fathers' homes in Jerusalem.

The Other Mary was working in the orphanage on Mt. Carmel. She was a fey, pixielike girl who at seventeen looked little older than her young charges. She had a natural love and understanding for those little souls abandoned in the earth, and the sting of being left alone in an alien world was greatly eased by the Other Mary's gentle ministrations.

Sophia was true to her name and showed an aptitude for copying the Scriptures. She spent a few hours each day in the library under the exacting eye of the aging Philo, and though she was only fourteen, Judith could see that her work would soon surpass her own.

Josie, of course, could never be persuaded to leave Mary's side, and so was also at Mt. Carmel. She was a chubby, pretty girl who loved to cook and sew, and staunchly declared she would never marry but would spend her life in Mary's service. Judith had misgivings about Josie's fierce devotion to Mary, but said nothing, keeping in mind each soul's individual purpose in coming into the earth. Who knew but what Josie's purpose was to aid and comfort the mother of the Chosen One?

Mary was fourteen, and Judith's heart lurched in her breast when she saw her. She was breathtakingly lovely. Her red-gold locks fell in a mass of gentle waves over her narrow shoulders and framed her tiny, oval face like an angelic, golden halo. Her eyes were large and almond-shaped, first gray, then blue, and always with a depth of

serene compassion that was without end. She was small
and petite, but with a womanly softness that hid an iron-
hard strength and singular will.

Her outward beauty was as nothing compared to the
inner beauty which radiated from Mary's soul. She emitted an aura of holiness and purity that Judith had not
experienced in even the most saintly of the sages she'd
met in her travels. She felt young and awkward in Mary's
presence, as though Mary were the older and wiser, and
not herself.

Judith was not the only one so affected. The entire
Mount reflected Mary's influence. Carmel had always
been known as a holy place, and now the atmosphere was
one which made a visitor speak in hushed tones and shiver
as though he walked on hallowed ground. All the petty
jealousies and quarrels which were common in any community were simply nonexistent at Carmel as Mary's love
reached out and touched them all. It was as though the
hand of God lay over them as it shielded the chosen
Mother from every discordant influence.

Judith remembered everything that the Egyptian had
told her, and knew that only Mary could be a worthy
channel for the holy Amelius. The enormity of what was
soon to take place made her weak, and again she trembled
with fear lest she fail in the role she had chosen to play.

She wondered what Joseph would do if he knew all that
she knew. Judith had been shocked to learn that Joseph
had at first refused the role of Mary's betrothed. He considered the twenty-year difference in their ages too great,
arguing that a younger man would be more suitable. He
cited his vow to a life of chastity as a monk and a
servant of the Lord, and only a visitation from a messenger of God convinced him that he was indeed the chosen
father of the Messiah.

Joseph was now in Nazareth, the home of his childhood, preparing a home for Mary. He had opened a carpentry shop in the little village, and his work was in such
demand that he'd been forced to take on quite a few
apprentices.

The changes were not all domestic ones relating only to
the affairs on Mt. Carmel. Judith read the reports smuggled to the Essenes by Herod's young queen, Theresa,
with an increasing sense of apprehension.

The palace seethed with intrigues and plots and counterplots. Herod was an old man and suffered from pains in his lower regions. His sons each coveted the throne of Judea, and committed the most vicious calumnies against one another in attempts to ingratiate themselves into Herod's favor. Herod's family had long been notorious for their illicit romances, intrigues, and jealousies, and now that the king's days on earth were coming to a close, the rumors and slanders had intensified to the point where no one was above suspicion. The torture chambers rang with the screams of his victims. Heads rolled and blood flowed. No one was safe from his wrath. His state of mind, deteriorated by suspicion, fear, and pain, was such that no one dared to reason with him. Mariamme's sons had been brought to trial for regicide and strangled under their father's orders, causing Jew and Gentile alike to recoil in horror from the crazed king. Little wonder Caesar was reputed to have said, "I'd rather be Herod's pig than one of his sons!"

The ripples of fear and death flowed out from Herod's palace over all of Palestine. The people grumbled and openly complained about Herod's outrageous acts. Their hatred for him and all his house became a tangible, palpable thing, and the more Herod felt and saw their hatred, the greater his insanity grew.

The Deliberative and General Councils met and avidly listened to the account which Judith and Shalmar gave of their travels throughout the world. Judith's outline for the City of Salt was enthusiastically approved. The supervisor in each camp and village was given the charge of drawing up lists of members who would be willing to give of their time and talents to bring the City of Salt to fruition.

Herod's instability caused the priests and scribes to be doubly wary and intolerant of the "heretical" sects whose views differed from orthodox Jewry, and the bleak, desolate wilderness of Judea on the shores of the Salt Sea was an ideal site for the school and scriptorium. The site was nearly inaccessible, the heat intolerable, and water almost nonexistent, making it remote and isolated from the general populace. The actual building could be carried on in relative secrecy, and the barren hills themselves provided a natural fortress for the proposed community. There would be no chance of a surprise attack, and the bluffs contained many caves in which to hide if such an event became necessary.

The main obstacle to the site was the lack of water. Aqueducts would have to be built to transport fresh, clear water from the hills during the rainy season, and cisterns large enough to hold the enormous amount the community would need. It would be a difficult project, but not impossible, and when the reports began to come in from the camps and villages, the leaders at Mt. Carmel were amazed at the confidence and enthusiasm shown by the Brothers.

The City of Salt had become a Cause, a bond that united and welded their people together in the fulfillment of a common goal. The project aroused their imagination and gave them a tangible, valuable work to do while they waited for the Messiah. It gave them something other to think about than Herod and all their other enemies who seemed to press closer and closer. Men, women, and children were eager to help. Work units of two weeks duration were set up, comprised of those whose talents were needed at each stage of development, and by the time winter was upon them, the first walls were already up and Enos' dream had begun to materialize.

No one labored under the illusion that such an undertaking was not dangerous. It was highly dangerous! Every time a man left his home and ventured to travel the roads he risked the chance of being questioned by Herod's patrols or by the Romans who marched beneath the hated eagle. They avoided the inns lest a slip of the tongue evoke the suspicion of a priest or scribe, and depended on their fellow Essenes to provide them with food and shelter. The ancient greeting of "Peace be with you" became their password, and the hastily drawn outline of a fish, their secret sign.

The risks they took served to strengthen their resolve, and their faith that they were doing the will of God gave them courage. God was with them. His mighty arm protected them, and not one fell into the hands of the Sons of Belial.

Judith made many trips to the City of Salt and to the towns and villages to confer with supervisors and craftsmen. Aristotle had more or less put her in charge of the project, though any major decisions were left to the priests. Judith thought dryly that if she had been a man she no doubt could have authorized such decisions herself, but she had to be content with the thought that at least she had some authority, and more than any woman before her.

She was surprised at the honor she was paid by the Essenes she visited. The women were in awe of her and flew about in a nervous flurry to see to her comfort. The men hung back, shy of her beauty and disconcerted by the fact of having to deal in serious business with a female. Judith smiled at the latter and secretly took a perverse delight in their discomfort. About time they learned that female intelligence and ability were equal to their own! She put the women at ease by helping with the household chores and gossiping like any other woman, and dealt with the men with a forthright, businesslike manner that soon made them forget her sex.

Her fame as a healer and teacher had preceded her into the camps. They brought their sick to be healed, and crowded the house where she stayed to hear her recount the prophecies and promises made of old and point out how they spoke of this day and generation. Her quiet voice and absolute faith inflamed them with zeal. The coming Messiah was no longer a hope for some vague time in a faraway future, but was here and now, to be seen in their day!

The excitement and enthusiasm of those simple brothers was a wonder to behold. Judith's lists of volunteers for work on the City of Salt grew. The coffers in the communal treasury swelled. Everyone eagerly gave of what they could, from the poorest farmer's meager sack of wheat to the astonishingly large pouch of silver given by Mary's brother Zebedee.

Zebedee was a shock. Judith had naturally been curious about Mary's family. The Jews were an inordinately family-minded race and Judith was anxious to meet anyone who would have a lasting influence on the young Messiah. She had visualized Ann's son as being much the same as her daughters—quiet, gentle, and probably as fair as the girls. She could hardly believe that the swarthy, black-haired giant of a man who boomed a hearty welcome which Judith was sure reverberated from the very walls of Jerusalem was the son of saintly, pious Ann.

There was nothing of reticent awe for Judith in Zebedee, or in any of his household. He hauled her into his
house as though she were a long lost comrade, bawling
orders to his servants and bellowing for the presence of
his wife and sons. He hardly gave her to chance to exchange pleasantries with Salome or even to acknowledge
the presence of his sons before he began bombarding her
with questions about Mary and the City of Salt, as well as
Judith's travels abroad. Judith stammered like a school
girl beneath his barrage of questions, and finally gave up
trying to answer but just let the staccato flow of words
wash over her like a turbulent sea. Salome finally rescued
her by rebuking Zebedee for his lack of manners.

"Do you think our guest is one of your fishing cronies
from Galilee? Shame to you, Zebedee! Give the girl a
chance to catch her breath and put a little food in her
stomach!"

Zebedee was at once contrite and apologetic. A sharp
clap of Salome's hands brought the servants running, and
a "little food" turned out to be a virtual feast. It was easy
to see who ruled in the house of Zebedee.

Judith had never experienced a household like Zebedee's. She basked in the luxury of his house, and laughed
at his sons, Roael and James, who were as voluble and
boisterous as their father. She admired stately, aristocratic
Salome, who ruled his chaotic household with dignified
aplomb and still found time to partake in many charities
and temple affairs. They led an impulsive, disruptive life
with everyone coming and going until Judith wondered
how they could keep track of one another.

Beneath all the confusion and bantering arguments lay
a deep reverence for God and love for one another. The
Law was observed to the smallest letter. Zebedee used his
considerable power and influence to further social re-
forms that would make life easier for the poor and op-
pressed. They taught their sons tolerance of all men, to
live in accord with the growing pagan world around them
while keeping steadfast to the faith of their fathers.

On the day Judith left Zebedee's house, he walked
along with her and the young monk who always accompanied her. Zebedee was unusually quiet and subdued. His
heavy brows were knit with concern and his voice was
troubled.

"Tell me about this Joseph to whom my sister is betrothed. I know his brother Alphaeus of Capernaum, whom I deem a man of God, but I know little about the son of John who is to be my brother-in-law."

Judith told him everything she could about Joseph, ending with his refusal of Mary and then his vision. Zebedee listened closely, and, for once, without interruption. When Judith had finished, he spoke solemnly.

"It is a difficult thing for me to believe, that my sister shall bear the Messiah. And more so for Salome. You cannot imagine the grief and outrage I felt when I learned my widowed mother was with child. I accepted her explanation out of my love for her, but in my heart I was sickened. Now you tell me tales of more visions and visits of angels and I find it all incomprehensible. I am a simple man—a fisherman at heart, for all my wealth and prestige. I live in the world, a world of business and practicality and hard facts. I cannot understand these mysteries you put forth, yet my spirit tells me they are true."

They had come to the place of parting at the foot of the Mount of Olives. Zebedee's eyes swept upward over the Mount. The morning sun flashed silver upon the olive groves. Birds sang, and a gentle breeze whispered through the trees. Judith saw great sadness in Zebedee's eyes, and a sort of fatalistic acceptance of the fate which lay before them all. Her heart went out to him as he continued in a somber tone.

"My sister's life will be one of sorrow. Her Son will be hounded and persecuted by His enemies. Our ancestor David hid in the caves of Judea, but where will the Son of Mary find refuge in this evil world? His suffering will touch us all. I fear for my sons, and for Alphaeus' sons, and for all that generation yet unborn."

There was nothing Judith could say. Zebedee spoke as a visionary, and all he said was probably true. He turned and looked steadily into Judith's eyes.

"You have told me of visions. Now I'll tell you of one. This week Zachariah was in Jerusalem performing his week's tour of duty in the temple. The lot fell to him to enter the sanctuary of the Lord and offer incense. A full assembly of people was praying outside the sanctuary. Zachariah stayed inside the sanctuary far longer than usual, until the people began to wonder at the delay.

When he finally did come out, he could not speak, and by making signs to them, they realized that he had had a vision. He finished the time of his priestly service and then went home. He still could not speak."

"That's incredible!" Judith gasped. "What vision did he see?"

"No one seems to know. I myself questioned his closest friend, Simeon of Ain Karin, but even he did not know."

"Even if he could not speak, surely he could write!" Judith exclaimed.

"Evidently he did not wish to." Zebedee's manner suddenly reverted to his old exuberance. "I must leave you. The sun is high and my fish await. God go with you, and peace be unto you."

He pressed the pouch into her hand and was gone, loping easily down the pathway.

Judith met more of Mary's relatives. In Bethany she stayed with cousins of Ann and Ismeria, Syrus and his wife Eucharia. Syrus was the antithesis of Zebedee—quiet, scholarly, and somewhat other-worldly. Their small daughter Martha was a solemn, petulant child who reminded Judith of Elizabeth's Adahr, but the baby Lazarus was a gurgling, golden bundle of joy.

Syrus' younger brother Archaus lived with them, but he avoided Judith. He didn't approve of Syrus' connection with the Essenes. They were of an old, patrician family, and Archaus deplored having their name connected with a heretical sect. Judith sighed over the fact that so many families seemed to be at odds over their beliefs, and hoped the Promised One would put an end to such dissension.

Mary's sister Josie, her husband Marcus, and their two tiny daughters, Rhoda and Mary, visited Syrus' house while Judith was there, giving her a chance to see what kind of atmosphere Mary's child would experience in a family gathering. They were gentle people. Their talk was reverent and philosophical, and their attitudes toward one another were ones of loving concern.

Zebedee had sparked Judith's curiosity about Joseph's brother. Joseph seldom spoke of his family or of his life before he became a monk, so Judith decided to return home through Capernaum and Galilee. She and her companion crossed the Jordan at Jericho into the district of Perea in order to avoid Samaria, and then on into the

Decapolis until they reached the southern shore of the Sea of Galilee. They followed the eastern shoreline and skirted the Greek city of Hippos. The sun was hanging low to the earth when they reached the gates of Bethsaida, and so they stayed that night with one of Zebedee's crewmasters by the name of John.

John welcomed them into his tiny house and was full of admiration for his employer, which said much for Zebedee in these days. A fair employer who paid his men a decent wage was a rare treasure, and John knew it. He was honored to have a friend of his illustrious employer grace his house.

Since the next day was the Sabbath and no one could travel on that day, Judith had no choice but to stay in Bethsaida, a happenstance which turned out to be a wonderful occasion for her.

Bethsaida was a tiny fishing village at the northernmost point of the sea where the Jordan cascaded down from Mt. Hermon and spilled into the Galilee. The harbor was dotted with small fishing boats, their colorful sails furled as they lazily bobbed to and fro on the gentle waves. Graceful palm trees curtsied and bowed, and the lush grass rippled in a rhythmic dance to the wash of the waves breaking upon the sandy shore. The beach was alive with men and women and children who laughed and sang and called back and forth as they sorted and cleaned and cured the catch from the night before, and mended the nets and boats to make ready to sail again.

These people were the typical simple folk whom the Pharisees and Sadducees despised, poor and lax in their observance of the Law. Their days were filled with eking out a living from the temperamental Galilee, and there was little time left from their labors to observe the ritual washings and prayers so vital to the salvation of their souls, according to the priests. They kept the Sabbath as best they could and attended the synagogue as often as possible, but mostly their prayers were their thoughts and the cries from their hearts sent winging aloft to the ears of a merciful, loving God.

God was a real and ever-evident Presence in their lives. They saw Him in the sunset over the sea as He stretched a gossamer veil of pink, lavender, purple, and gold across the azure sky. They heard Him in the wind as it funnelled through the gap in the hills across the flat plain of Gennesaret, and whipped the sea into frothy foam which broke like thunder upon the shore. They heard His voice in the bleat of a lamb and in the laugh of a child, and in the groan of their nets, filled to breaking with the fruit from the sea. They tasted the Lord in the sweet, fragrant grape kissed by the sun while still on the vine, and in the honey which oozed from the comb.

The people worked hard, setting sail as soon as the moon was high, toiling through the night until the first pink glow of dawn sent them home, where the women and children waited to help sort and cure and pack the catch for market. It was often late afternoon before they could return to their homes to eat a meager meal and catch a few hours of sleep before it was time to sail again.

Sometimes the boats returned empty with their limp nets trailing dejectedly behind, outwitted by the wily fish who hid in the shoals and rocks in the depths of the sea. It was a hurtful thing for a man to return empty-handed. Their wives and children depended on each night's catch, and when the nets were empty, so were their hearts and spirits.

Judith was enchanted by the people of Bethsaida. She extended her stay, and each evening before the moon arose, John's little cottage filled to overflowing with those who hungered to hear of the God of Love whom they instinctively knew in their hearts.

Judith taught them of the sojourns of the soul, of how the souls sinned in the beginning and how God, through His love for them, prepared a way for their return. She told them of how each soul came to earth again and again to learn the lessons of truth, righteousness, and love until each attained that state of purity in which it was created. She taught that God willed for no soul to perish, for He knew and loved each one intimately from time forgotten. She gave them hope and confidence and faith. She instilled in them a new purpose for their lives. They understood that suffering and toil and poverty mattered little as long as they had love and justice and hope in their hearts.

But it was of the Messiah that they longed to hear. They absorbed her stories of His coming like a sponge a long time away from water. They begged to hear of the prophecies and of the work done at Mt. Carmel. An electrified excitement charged the room as she told of how a young girl had been chosen by an angel, and would bring forth the Messiah to the earth.

Judith could have stayed in Bethsaida forever, but she took her leave of John and his family. His four strapping, young sons, Simon, Andrew, Judas, and young John, walked part way to Capernaum with her, and she felt a sharp pang of regret when they left her.

Alphaeus, like Joseph, was also a carpenter, and was well-known and respected in Capernaum for his honesty and forthrightness. He was of the class of artisans, neither rich nor poor, and lived in a modest but comfortable, white-plastered, two-storied house set back from the noise and raucousness of the market square and wharf. He was entirely Jewish without the taint of Gentile blood, which gave him an added degree of stature and influence.

Alphaeus made no secret of his adherence to the Essenes, but neither did he try to sway others to his beliefs. He simply lived as he believed, and by his example many of his neighbors and friends came to lose their distrust and suspicions of the sect.

The Galileans were ripe for war to shake off the yoke of oppression inflicted by Rome and Herod, and looked to the Messiah to lead them. Only a king sent by God could lead them to victory. Judith felt a stab of fear for Mary's child, who these people hoped would be a great warrior. Could a son of the gentle Mary and Joseph wage bloody, destructive war as these people expected? Doubt settled within her, and she left Capernaum the next day in a state of depression and confusion.

They left the Sea of Galilee at Magdala, turning westward through Galilee to Cana. Galilee! Surely Galilee had been the Garden of Eden. It was a land of gently rolling hills, and wide, fertile valleys; a land of olive groves and terraced vineyards and patchwork quilts of barley fields. It was a land with soft skies overhead, and soft earth underfoot, and soft breezes which calmed and soothed the soul.

Judith was suddenly assailed by the uneasy thought that she should return to Carmel at once. Every mile which took her closer to home increased her sense of urgency until she bypassed Cana and her plan to visit a day or two with Ann and Ismeria and the newly wed Salone. She paused for only a few short hours with Joseph in Nazareth, and then pushed on to the Kishon river toward the Great Sea and up the northern face of the Mount toward home.

Chapter 10

Judith felt the tension in the air before she was even close to the compound clearing. Something was wrong! She left the monk to deal with the donkey and hurried on ahead. She was nearly running along the path when she rounded a bend and almost ran headlong into Judas.

"What is wrong?" she demanded, trying to catch her breath.

"A Roman patrol. They arrived yesterday. They're making an inventory of all our goods and poking their long noses into anything they please."

Icy fingers of fear clutched Judith's heart. "Where is Mary?"

"She's in the inner court with the other girls, attending a class on needlework. Aristotle gave orders that everyone is to continue as normal. Maybe you better go in. They didn't see you yesterday and might question where you were." Judas noticed Judith's deeply tanned skin which contrasted so strikingly with her sun-bleached hair. "They will certainly know they haven't seen you before," he said teasingly.

Judith shot him a look of disdain and hurried to the House of Lodgement where Elkatma helped her to quickly bathe and change. She pulled a long-sleeved white tunic over her head, and for the first time since she'd come to Carmel, felt it was too revealing. She grabbed a blue, sleeveless over-dress from a peg and pulled that on over the tunic. She tied a rope belt at her waist and ran a comb through her hair, carelessly slipping a blue band over her head to hold the curls back from her face. She gave Elkatma a quick hug and ran lightly up the steps to the temple.

She paused at the outer gate, then took a deep breath, said a prayer, and strode purposefully past two staring Romans and entered the lower level of the temple. She knocked boldly on Aristotle's door, and, at his bidding, strode in.

Aristotle was sitting behind his desk and a Roman tribune lounged on a divan.

"I beg your pardon for intruding, Rabbi," Judith said meekly, "but I thought I should let you know that I have returned."

Both men stood. Aristotle came around the desk.

"Peace be with you, Judith, and welcome home," said Aristotle. "As you see, we have guests. May I introduce Judith of Phinehas, Tribune. Judith is one of us here on Mt. Carmel, and has been visiting some of our Brothers in Galilee. It is most fortunate that her return is so timely, for she can answer your questions more accurately than I."

The tribune came toward her and bent over her hand. Judith was struck by his height. She had to tilt her head back to look into his face, which for her was an unusual experience.

He had a strong face, clean-shaven and deeply bronzed by the sun. His chin was square and purposeful, and a wide, sensuous mouth smiled disarmingly at her—a smile which crept into his coal-black eyes and stared at her in frank admiration.

His hair was black, tightly curled in a close-cropped cap about his head with a few longer ringlets that fell across his brow and in front of his ears. The hand that clasped hers was long and tapered and surprisingly graceful. His arms were bare, thickly furred, and bulged with long, ropelike muscles.

He was dressed in the usual Roman soldier's garb, a short linen tunic under a vest made of long leather strips which encircled his chest and came up over his shoulders, where they hooked onto the front piece by large brass buttons. A wide leather fringe fell from his waist to mid-thigh. His feet were shod in iron-soled sandals, and laced with leather latchets almost to his knees.

He held Judith's hand too long for propriety, and gazed at her in studied calculation. His grasp was firm and somehow possessive, and transmitted a strange, shivery thrill to Judith's own hand. He said to Aristotle, without taking his eyes from Judith's face, "I am sure the lady will prove to be most helpful."

The tribune's voice was deep and intimate. Judith felt a hot flush begin to creep up the back of her neck and she gently pulled her hand out of his grasp and quickly turned to Aristotle in order to hide her burning face.

"Will you take a glass of wine with us, Judith?" Aristotle asked.

Judith understood his offer as a command that she was to stay. She accepted the goblet and sat on the divan across the room from the Roman.

"What is it you wish to know, Tribune?" she asked, forcing her voice to be light and steady.

The Roman lounged back upon the divan in easy comfort and smiled. "I am called Justin. I have been assigned the task of making a study of the numbers and wealth of the various sects of the Hebrews for the purpose of taxation. This study is also to include an account of the beliefs and creeds of each sect, that Rome might better understand the temperament and personalities of her subjects."

He held his goblet out to be refilled. "Augustus is a man of justice. He desires peace throughout the empire, peace obtained by a fair and just rule. One can rule with fairness and justice only when one has an intimate knowledge of the underlying emotional attitudes of the populace."

Judith glanced at Aristotle, who slightly raised his eyebrows. "I see," she said dryly. "I commend Caesar for his desire for peace and justice, and assume he realizes that no nation takes easily to foreign rule. We Jews recognize only one Sovereign, and that is the Lord God. Any kings or judges that our people have had have been considered only a fleshly instrument used by the Lord through which He communicates with His people of Israel. Any Roman law which contradicts the Law of God will be met with resistance."

The smile disappeared from Justin's face. The woman is fearless, he thought. He seldom met with such open candor from the Jews.

"I can see where my report will be longer and more detailed than I had anticipated," he said dryly. He sipped the wine, then said, "I am told there are many different

sects among the Jews, and that each sect lives by laws of
their own which differ in content from the others. If this
be true, Rome will find it difficult to satisfy them all."

"Perhaps not," Judith answered. "Basically all Jews believe alike. We all use the same Scriptures and abide by
the same laws. Our differences lie in the interpretation and
outward, physical manifestation of those laws. Roman law
deals with the natural, physical man. Jewish law deals
with the inner, spiritual man. I think the two could possibly exist side by side, if given enough thought and effort."

"If Rome will conform to the Jews," said Justin.

Judith flashed a sudden, sunny smile at the tribune and
said, "I'm afraid so. It will not be easy. The Jews bitterly
resent Rome. We are an independent, unbending race. I
once heard my father call us 'stiff-necked,' and I think
perhaps he was right."

Aristotle laughed outright. "The Jewish mind, heart,
and soul is incomprehensible to the Gentile mind. There is
no division of religious and secular life to the Jew. They
are one and the same. The Jew's religion is his life. The
Roman lives a life of a soldier or businessman, house-
holder, husband, father, social being, and his religion is
distinct from these. To a Jew they are one, they cannot be
divided one from another, no more than blood from flesh."

"You pose a difficult task for me," said Justin.

"I should think the easiest way would be to make an
individual report on each sect, and once these are made,
to compile them into one, as much as you can."

The tribune lifted his goblet in mock salute. "An excellent suggestion." He set the goblet on one of the small
tables and stood. "I shall have to impose upon your hospitality for a time. I'll try to cause as little disturbance as
possible. My men should finish the inventory of goods
today, and I shall order them back to Caesarea and keep
only an aide or two with me here. Now if you will excuse
me, I shall see to their progress." He looked quizzically at
Judith. "We shall meet later."

As soon as the Roman had gone, Aristotle leaned back
in his chair and blew heavily through his mouth. "Thank
God. You did well, Judith."

Judith stood and replaced the goblet on the table beside
Aristotle's desk and stared out the window behind him. "I

don't think he'll cause much trouble," she said slowly. "He seems sincere and honest. There are some things we cannot tell him, of course. We must warn everyone that Mary is to be kept entirely inconspicuous, and under no circumstances can he learn that we expect the Messiah in this generation."

"You like him?" Aristotle asked in surprise.

"He is only carrying out his orders, and I think he sincerely wants to understand us. He strikes me as a just man, though perhaps a little pompous. No—confident is more the word. He certainly isn't sneering and rude like many of his fellow officers who have come here in the past. I found no trace of sadistic cruelty in his face or voice as I have seen in many other Romans."

"No. On that point I agree. I am also a Roman, and in different circumstances I think the tribune and I could be quite friendly. Before you came in, he and I had a lively discussion on One God versus many gods. Actually I found him quite receptive and open to our views. However, we must exert caution. His loyalty is to Rome!"

Judith nodded and sighed. A great weariness came over her, and she realized the sun was far below the western end of the temple and that she'd had no rest since before it had risen that day. She'd also had nothing to eat since mid-morning, and the effect of the wine on her empty stomach was going to her head.

"May I leave you, then? The strain of the past weeks seems to have caught up with me. May I give you my report on my journey tomorrow?" she asked.

"Of course. Of course," Aristotle exclaimed. "Rest and eat. I shall see you after tomorrow's morning worship."

Elkatma brought Judith's evening meal from the communal dining hall to her cell, and as soon as Judith had finished eating, she threw herself upon her cot and fell into a deep, dream-filled sleep in which she stood on the shores of the Galilee beside a tall, dark man whose face she could not see, but whose hand held her own as they watched the sun set into the sea.

The Roman tribune was not asleep. He sat on the ground before a small fire in front of his tent. The night was silent, the air still. The snap and crackle of the fire was the only sound to be heard on the Mount. His aide, Puloaus, was asleep, sprawled on the ground beside the fire with his mouth slack and a line of spittle crawling down his chin. Justin had sent the rest of the patrol back to Caesarea that afternoon, and only he and Puloaus remained.

Puloaus' inventory of the Essenes' goods lay across Justin's knees. There was nothing in the inventory of any value, only clothing, food, tools, bedding, some money, and a few jewels of little worth—just the normal necessities one would expect to find in any household of the poorer class.

The people here live meagerly, Justin thought. No one owns a house of his own, or indeed seems to own anything of his own. Everything is held in common. Their furnishings are simple and utilitarian, their daily fare meaner than that of the lowest foot soldier in Augustus' legions. The only place of any luxury at all is in the room where I interviewed their leader. That room had surprised Justin, but he believed Aristotle's candid explanation that it was solely for the purpose of receiving emissaries from Rome.

A strange man, this Rabbi Aristotle, Justin mused. He was well-educated, urbane, and the room testified that he had at one time been accustomed to the niceties of life. Why would a man like that give up position and wealth to live in such austere near-poverty? These people were a queer lot. From the two days Justin had spent on Mt. Carmel, he judged them to be intelligent, reasonable men. What inspired them to forego the pleasures of women and wine and a well-laden board? Admittedly, the peace and tranquility of life on the Mount held a certain attraction, but surely peace and tranquility could be had without giving up life's pleasures! There was something more, some mystery that he had not yet found, that drew men to this Mount to live in isolation from the world. Justin thought about his own restlessness and discontent. Perhaps they were like himself, disillusioned and bored unto death with the verities of the world.

Justin's family was of the equestrian class, and he had followed his father's career as a soldier in Caesar's army. He was only sixteen when his father had procured his commission for him, and those first years were ones of total absorption with army life. There was no aspect of that life which Justin did not enjoy. His young, healthy body plunged happily into the rigors and hardships endured in the field, and his amiable, good-natured manner won him many friends among the soldiery. He fought hard and fearlessly in battle. His innate sense of leadership, and his keen, decisive mind soon won him the attention and respect of his officers, and he found himself quickly promoted through the ranks. At age twenty-six, Caesar had ceremoniously bestowed the rank of tribune upon him and introduced him to the Senate as a son worthy to carry the name of his father. But Justin had become satiated with blood and death and suffering, and when his father died a short time later, army life had begun to pall, and Justin privately questioned what it all meant.

He had thought then to marry. Perhaps a wife and children would give meaning to his life, but the girl he chose had wished for a husband who would be at home occasionally, and so had married another.

Justin had expected his heart to be broken at the news, but surprisingly, it was not, and therefore he concluded that marriage was not for him. He'd tried to recapture his love and enthusiasm for army life, but the thrill and excitement was gone. It was like meat without salt, washed down with warm, flat beer.

Augustus' reign had brought an uneasy peace to the world. Three times the doors to the Temple of Janus were closed, signifying peace throughout the empire. With the cessation of war, Justin had time to observe and take part in the civilian life. He deplored the poverty and filth in Rome. His stomach churned at the rotting, fly-infested carcasses and fruit sold in the common market. He rebelled at the sight of slave gangs chained together and wincing under the lash as they tried to scrape human and animal excrement and vomit off the streets. The amphitheaters and circuses filled him with disgust. He found the bloody spectacles an outward sign of an inward depravity and decay in the people. He turned away from the games and other popular public diversions, and sought relief in the matters of the mind.

It was fashionable among the upper classes to pose an interest in the arts, literature, and philosophy. Justin attended a few plays, but thought them shallow and silly.

He dabbled in religion, but found little comfort in the legends of Jupiter, Juno, Mars, and Vesta. The gods, with their loves and hates and petty jealousies and caprices, were all too human for Justin's taste. His soul yearned for a more transcendent god than any offered by Rome and Greece.

He immersed himself in the philosophies of the Stoics and Epicureans in an effort to still the restless yearning in his heart, but they only seemed to intensify his longing. Justin didn't understand his own feelings. He didn't know what his heart cried out for, he only knew there was a growing void in his life and he did not know how to fill it. He often found himself standing before the altar of the "Unknown God" and wondering. Was there such a God? Where was He, and who was He? If he could find this God, could He still the burning need in Justin's soul?

Rome finally became so depressing for Justin that he filed a request for foreign duty. His request had been granted and he was ordered to Palestine, the land of the Jews, to compile a report on the temperament and attitudes of this strange, unfathomable people.

Before going out among them, Justin had versed himself in the Jews' religious lore that he might better understand them. He had procured copies of their sacred Scriptures, and as he poured over the scrolls, he began to feel a small excitement. Was this God of the Jews the "Unknown God"? For the first time in years he'd looked forward to an assignment with anticipation. When he'd learned that one sect, the Essenes, were quartered only a few miles north of Caesarea on Mt. Carmel, he'd decided to start with them, and here he was.

It was very late. The fire had died down and was nearly out. The moon was hidden behind a cloud and the darkness seemed filled with unseen presences. Justin, shivering, came out of his reverie. He drew his cloak tightly around his shoulders and poked, dishearteningly, at the coals. He yawned and stretched, then lay back with his hands under his head for a pillow and slept without dreaming.

The next afternoon Judith met with Justin in the library. He wanted to know, first of all, about the physical organization of the sect, and Judith provided him with lists of the numbers of priests, monks, teachers, students, and workers on Mt. Carmel. Then she gave him an outline of the councils and officers which made up the ruling body of the Essenes. She answered his questions truthfully, but with caution. She minimized the number of adherents in the villages and camps, and refrained from giving names. She didn't mention the City of Salt or the twelve girls who had been schooled on Mt. Carmel for a special purpose.

It was a fine day, and Judith found Justin an easy and amiable companion. Her nervousness of the day before had disappeared, she found herself enjoying the task of teaching the tribune the creeds and ways of her people. She had given him a copy of the Rule of the Order, and watched with amusement as he labored over the unfamiliar Hebrew.

Finally Justin laid it aside and said, "This is a most arduous document. Why don't you just tell me about yourselves?"

Judith smiled. "What do you know of our people?" she asked.

"Of the Essenes? Only that which I've learned in Caesarea. You are Jews, but an outcast sect. You refuse to worship and offer sacrifice in the Jews' beloved temple. You are extremely rigid in your beliefs and impose harsh judgments against the Jerusalem priests, which does not endear you to them. You do not marry and raise children of your own, but take other men's children and raise them up in your beliefs. You despise women, believing that they are troublesome and an enticement to sin, though I can see that this is a misconception."

Judith laughed. "Most of what you've heard is misconception. You are right to some extent in regard to our attitude toward women. I believe the Jews have more respect for women than the Gentile world, but still we are considered the inferior sex. The idea that women are inferior to men is difficult to dissipate when such has been the ingrained attitude for centuries, and it is also a comfortable way of life for men. Men find it most disagreeable to give up their role of superiority and authority over women. However, our teachings of the soul tell us that the soul knows no sex, that the soul is both male and female and can reach that stage of evolvement where it has the choice of the sex of a body in which to incarnate. The mental facilities and talents acquired by a soul through many incarnations belong to that soul, whether in a male or female body of flesh.

"As for marriage," Judith continued, "it is true that our monks do not marry, though they may if God so calls them, but most prefer, through choice, to dedicate their lives to the service of God without the distraction of their time and talents to marriage. I myself am not married, for I feel that I could not devote the time and energy necessary to a marriage and motherhood and to carrying out my work here at the same time. I think both would suffer. Many of our people are married and live normal lives throughout the villages and towns."

"I can understand that. I also am not wed and for the same reasons. The army has been my life," said Justin.

"I find that surprising," said Judith. "I thought the Romans were avid family men. Have you never considered marriage?"

Justin cleared his throat. "Once. The lady threw her bait to a more attractive fish," he said dryly.

Judith laughed. "Do I detect a note of wounded vanity?"

Justin shifted his position uncomfortably. "Perhaps," he said gruffly. "But what about you? You lecture me on the equality of men and women. Yet a man must combine career and family, but you admit that you are incapable of doing so."

Judith's eyes flashed with anger which did not go unnoticed by Justin. "I did not say I was incapable! I said I chose not to marry."

Justin shrugged his shoulders with a disbelieving look.

"As for 'taking' other men's children," Judith said testily, "we do not 'take' them. We provide a school for the children of our members who may choose to send them. It is not compulsory! Here they are taught many skills and arts which will enable them to earn a living or maintain a home, though the emphasis is on the Scriptures and the spiritual life God wills for them to live. The only children we 'take' are orphans who have no family to provide for them. We also have an infirmary and facilities for caring for the aged who are unable to care for themselves have no one else to care for them."

Justin was unimpressed. "Very commendable."

Judith regretted that she'd allowed the tribune to anger her, and now spoke lightly in order to hide it.

"What else did they tell you about us in Caesarea?"

"They say you practice mystical rituals and have strange powers. You are reputed to be healers and seers and to have the frightening capacity to see into a man's heart and soul. Most of all, you are a sect of fanatics who look for a Messiah who will restore Israel to its former glory. It is this which Rome looks upon with suspicion and anxiety, that your sect will cause uprisings and rebellions which will lead to war."

Justin looked at her gravely. "If this is true, let me warn you that war with Rome would be disastrous. Caesar would crush you like a beetle underfoot!"

Judith's anger flashed again. "When the Messiah comes we will follow His lead," she said hotly. "If He leads us into war, then it is with God at His side, and even Rome cannot stand against God."

She was enraged, both with herself for her outburst, which nearly admitted that the Messiah would lead them into war, and with Justin. How dare he speak of the Brotherhood in such contemptuous tones, and what gall to warn her that the Messiah would be no match for Rome! She was especially angered by the latter, for she discerned the grain of truth in what he said, and part of her anger stemmed from fear.

Angry silence lay thick in the room. Damnable woman! Justin thought. One moment she is as reasonable and intelligent as a man and the next as stubborn and illogical as a donkey. He searched for a question that would put them on a more neutral ground, and finally asked, "When and how did this sect originate?"

Judith sighed with relief at the question. Here at least there should be no controversy. "It was originally a school for prophets, first established on Mt. Carmel by Samuel, who was a prophet of the Lord during the reign of Saul. Samuel and his disciples would come to the peace and silence of the caves on Carmel to enter into a state of trance or deep meditation in which their souls could communicate with God and learn His will. This ability to enter into such profound silence was innate with Samuel, and he taught the technique to his disciples.

"They also learned the teachings regarding the soul and the purposes for the souls' incarnations into the realm of earth. These teachings were first given by Melchizedek, the High Priest of the Lord from Salem who blessed Abraham after his successful campaign against Chedor-laomer. When the soul of Samuel passed from his body of flesh, the school continued to exist under the leadership of Elijah and then Elisha, and so on down through the centuries."

"So you do practice mystical rituals and do pretend to strange powers!" Justin said accusingly.

"Our rituals are not so mystical, nor our powers so strange," Judith said gently. "These are innate in every soul—it is only that the carnal mind cannot or will not recognize them as such. Have you never felt strange urgings or yearnings for something that you cannot name in your own heart?"

Justin stared at her. How could she know that? he wondered, and decided it would be more prudent not to answer. It was unseemly for a Roman soldier in Caesar's legions to admit to any such weakness, and particularly to a woman!

Judith went on. "Every body of flesh walking upon the earth contains a soul. These souls are in various forms of development spiritually, but were created at the same moment from the same substance by the thought of God. Being of the same substance, they are as one entity, though individual in will and personality. It is the inherent craving of every soul to return to that blissful state of oneness with its Creator. In simple terms, we are all afflicted with a tragic case of homesickness!"

Justin snorted. "Why don't we all just go, then!"

"God is perfection. Souls were created in perfection, but through God's gift of free will, the souls desired to experience the rest of creation, the earth and all the universe. In doing so, selfishness was born, and from selfishness came all the other forms of sin, greed, hate, and lust in all its ramifications, not just sexual lust. Does not one spoiled fruit tend to contaminate the whole basket? Could the now-imperfect souls return to the perfect Oneness of the beginning and have that Oneness still maintain perfection?"

Justin didn't answer. Homesickness! The w

chord which responded in almost physical pain. He got up and walked to the window, where he stood staring out at the court.

Judith watched him. A shaft of sunlight touched his glossy curls and turned their blackness to an iridescent blue. A muscle beneath his ear knotted, disappeared, and then knotted again. She sensed he was going through some inner struggle and so she did not speak. She deliberately did not try to read his thoughts as she could sometimes do with others. Even though he was a Roman and thus an enemy of her people, she felt that somehow the discussion was no longer in the realm of a report to be given to Augustus, but had somehow turned to a personal level. To intrude upon his thoughts now would seem an invasion of privacy.

She studied him. His wide shoulders strained the leather straps which protected them from the archers' barbs. The edge of his short sleeves cut into his well-defined upper arms. His wide shoulders tapered to a narrow waist and hips, and his legs were long but thick, his muscular calves swelling through the tightly laced latchets.

What a wonderful body God has given this man, Judith thought, then blushed at the wanderings of her mind and silently chastised herself for allowing her thoughts such license.

Justin spoke without turning, trying to inject disbelief and scorn into his voice. "If what you say is true, and a man must be perfect in order to 'return home,' as you call it, then I think your God will be disappointed. Have you ever known a perfect man?"

Judith heard the sincerity that lay beneath the scorn in his voice, and felt pity for this huge man who suddenly seemed so vulnerable. She thought of Enos, and of Mary and Ann, and of her own parents, and chose her words carefully.

"Yes, a few. Not many. But this is on my own judgment. We vessels of flesh tend to play games with ourselves. We often say and act that which is in direct opposition to what is in our hearts. This we do out of fear —fear of ridicule, fear of punishment, fear of being singled out or seeming different from our comrades. When a man is drinking wine and laughing boisterously at lewd jokes with his comrades, we say, 'There is a lewd and debauched soul.' But perhaps inside he loathes the jokes, and the wine and atmosphere fill him with hidden disgust. Is he then a lewd and debauched soul, or is he only weak and pitiable?

"A priest posts notice of his fast in the temple and then rends his clothes and pours ashes on his head and moans aloud his misery, but in secret he eats fine morsels and drinks the best wine. Men say, 'There is a pious, holy man,' but in truth he is a hypocrite. I'm sure you've played these games yourself, as we all have."

Justin nodded, but did not turn away from the window.

Judith continued, "We judge by these outward acts and words, but God judges by what lies in the heart and soul. He knows the ways of our innermost selves better than we do ourselves. I think He is not so concerned with the outward acts, but more with the thoughts and feelings that have gone before."

Justin turned from the window and looked at her quizzically. "I don't understand."

Judith thought a moment and then said, "Why does a man steal? Does he steal in desperation to feed a starving family, or does he steal out of covetousness and greed? Does a man kill to save his own life or that of his loved ones, or does he kill out of jealousy and hatred? We judge the act. A man who steals is a thief. A man who kills is a murderer. God judges the thought which is manifested in the act."

"I see," said Justin. "Are we then to forego judgment? Are we not to have laws and rules of behavior? It seems to me if this were so, the world would become chaos!"

"Try to raise your thinking to a higher level of consciousness, Justin," Judith said impatiently, then flushed at her use of his given name.

Justin heard the slip and felt a strange sense of pleasure hearing it from Judith's lips. She remembers it, then, he thought with satisfaction.

Judith hurried on, hoping he hadn't noticed. "Of course we need laws and rules governing our behavior." She picked up the Rule of the Order. "You have just read our own Rule. Remember I said that all souls were in various stages of development? A soul in the lower s evolvement must first learn from the simpler, more mundane laws of man before he can understand the more subtle spiritual laws.

"You wondered how men could live under such stringent rules as this. It is because any souls who come here searching for a higher meaning to life have already learned the mundane laws and are ready to progress to the next step. A soul grows in spirituality as a body grows in strength. When a child is born, he requires only milk, but as he matures, he craves meat. When a child begins his lessons, he learns his letters and numbers, and then to read, and finally his mind demands the headier stuff of logic, philosophy, and the sciences."

"And when even those no longer satisfy him?" Justin asked slowly.

Judith smiled. "Then he comes to us, for then his soul begins to speak."

Chapter 11

Justin prolonged his stay at Mt. Carmel. The days turned into weeks and the Essenes, grown used to the presence of a Roman tribune in their midst, accepted him as one of them.

He moved among them freely, enjoying their gentle banter and stimulated by their serious talk. He came to share in their labors. He helped raise new buildings and sometimes took up a hoe or flail and worked alongside the Brothers in the fields and gardens they maintained. Always he was greeted with smiles and nods of welcome, and came to return their greeting of "Peace be with you" as naturally as if he'd always done so.

His body tingled with new vitality, and the clean pure air cleansed his lungs of the stench and putrid humors caused by city life. He bloomed with health. He felt young and vigorous and eager as he had not felt for years.

A sense of timelessness engulfed him. The Essenes lived an unhurried life, free from pressures and personal entanglements, and Justin's mind was free to roam and think and contemplate Judith's teachings.

The Essenes' philosophy fascinated him, tantalized his well-ordered Roman mind with its logic and reason. He studied their Scriptures and writings. He questioned the monks and priests, and observed all their rites and rituals. Their simple, unadorned form of worship appealed to him. He'd ever been repulsed by the act of animal sacrifice. His soul yearned for a God above the need for gifts of blood, a God transcendent over flesh and gold and other human riches, and Mt. Carmel stilled that yearning and filled the aching void around his heart.

Justin's stay at Mt. Carmel was not continuous. He made frequent trips to Caesaria to report to his superiors, and travelled throughout Judea and Galilee interviewing men of different sects and observing their rites and philosophies. But always he returned to the Mount.

Justin was not a fanciful man, nor was he accustomed to fooling himself. He was practical and saw the world and himself through realistic eyes, and so he knew that it wasn't only the heady philosophy and peaceful serenity of Mt. Carmel which drew him back again and again, but that a great portion of Carmel's attraction lay in Judith.

From the first moment he saw her, Justin knew that Judith was no ordinary woman. It came as no surprise when her beauty aroused his manhood, for many women had done the same, and Caesar's legionnaires were not known for their chastity. But with Judith, more than his desire had come to life. There was something about the disconcerting way she met him as an equal, a directness in her eye and unabashed honesty in her speech which challenged him. He took a perverse delight in provoking her. Her quick anger aroused him as much as her beauty, and her willingness to debate was as stimulating as a stolen caress. Yet he sensed in her a vulnerability, a virginal innocence which made him want to protect and comfort as one would a favored child.

Her complexities baffled him and kept his emotions in a state of turmoil. She was like alternating sips of fine, and then cheap, wine. One moment he felt warm and exhilarated, and the next his stomach soured and his head throbbed with exasperation. She could antagonize him to the point where he could hardly refrain from doing her violence, and then suddenly become as soft and gentle as one of the sloe-eyed does who sometimes appeared at the forest's edge. Her self-assurance and absolute faith in the truth of her religion was maddening, but her lack of confidence and fears of failure in her own character and abilities moved him to compassion.

Each time he left Carmel, Justin vowed to himself that he would not return. His emotions were becoming far too involved with that tall, golden-haired Jewess, and any dreams of a future with her were futile. Any advances he'd made toward deepening their friendship had been firmly rebuffed. The woman was a religious fanatic! Her life was dedicated to the Lord, and as far as she was concerned, the Lord was a jealous Master and would countenance no competition.

Justin thought it was a damnable shame for such a woman to deny her femaleness. What a sensation she would make in Caesar's court! Justin visualized her dressed in silks, cut in the most revealing, modish fashion, with those wheaten locks curled and piled high atop that long, queenly neck. The Empress Julia would turn livid with jealousy while the pious Augustus drooled with lust.

And the sons the two of them could make! Not to mention the pleasure to be had in their making, for under that austere, self-righteousness Justin sensed an earthy sensuality, wanting only to be awakened by a man as knowing and experienced as himself.

It was futile! Judith would never leave Carmel, and Justin was far from prepared to renounce his known way of life to spend his remaining days in isolation from the world. He could have simply taken her and satisfied his need, for after all, he was a Roman and she only a Jewess, and who would blame him?

But Justin wanted more than Judith's body. He wanted her mind and heart, her undivided thoughts and attention, and could settle for no less. It wrenched his heart and filled him with fury to know she'd never give her whole self over to his care. Though they never spoke of it outright, Judith left no doubt in his mind that the greater portion of her thoughts and devotion would ever go to the Essenes.

Why, he couldn't fathom. On the surface it seemed reasonable enough that Judith could easily combine her work and marriage, unless there was more to the Essenes' aims and purposes than she told. The more Justin probed, the more convinced he was that Mt. Carmel was more than just a religious retreat. He watched them carefully, especially a young maid called Mary whom everyone seemed to treat with special diffidence. He was determined that one day he would learn the secret that stood between him and his heart's desire, and when he did, what then? Could he betray these gentle people whom he'd come to love to Rome? Could he betray Judith? Could he betr~ the God of the Jews!

So went Justin's thoughts, in and out and a~

around until he thought he'd go mad. His soul embraced Judith's religion. His spirit bore witness when he heard the ancient truths, but his flesh rebelled. To join the sect and swear the oath of commitment and then to live with Judith in the camps and villages was one thing, but Judith and Mt. Carmel were one and the same in her eyes and she would never budge away from it. His pride would not permit him to be so subjugated to a woman. He was a man, and a Roman, and neither would have any part in accepting second place in any woman's life.

It may have eased Justin to know that Judith's thoughts and emotions were as much at war as his own. At first she had explained the tingling anticipation she felt each time she went to meet him in the library as the excitement of challenge in converting an important Roman away from paganism to a belief in the One, True God.

Justin was an eager, interested student. His questions were profound and searching. His sharp, methodical mind taxed Judith's knowledge to the utmost as he demanded a logical explanation of the merest point of the Law. He dug and searched and argued until Judith was exhausted, yet exhilarated, as his fresh point of view led to new insights on her own behalf.

Justin's extensive travels with Caesar's army had introduced him to the customs and religions of peoples in many lands. Unlike most of his comrades, he'd taken the time and trouble to learn the languages and creeds of those lands. His translations were surprisingly accurate for one with no formal training, and Judith couldn't help but speculate on what an asset he would be to the Brotherhood.

They spent hours in one another's company, usually in the presence of the other monks and scribes, but sometimes they walked alone to the sea or along the forest paths to escape the distraction of the others. Judith wouldn't admit to herself that she found those solitary walks so satisfying, nor that she looked forward to them with so much anticipation. It was at those times that Judith had so adroitly sidestepped Justin's tentative advances, telling herself that they were simply the reactions one would expect from any soldier, let alone a Roman. She refused to recognize her own accelerated heartbeat and warm rush of blood as anything more than a natural response of the flesh which she could easily subdue.

As time went on, Judith found her flesh was not so easy to overcome. She found herself disappointed when Justin did not try to take her hand or pull her into his arms. She felt her breath catch in her throat when he remarked upon her beauty, or made innuendoes regarding her desirability. She caught herself becoming flirtatious, taking care with her appearance in order to attract him, and the knowledge filled her with dismay.

Judith couldn't pinpoint when her feelings for Justin subtly changed. She watched him working side by side with the Brothers, laughing with them and speaking in his quick, excited way, and a well of tenderness enveloped her heart. It made her unduly happy when she saw how her friends smiled and welcomed him so openly, obviously liking him and trusting him.

An easy, bantering companionship had sprung up between Justin and Elkatma. He teased and flattered her outrageously, and Judith was shocked to see her mother coyly blush and return his joshing twofold. Also, Justin and Judas had struck up a special friendship, which, except for their differences in nationality and creed, was no surprise. Both were amiable and easygoing and in many ways much alike.

With Mathias, Justin was solicitous and understanding, ever finding time to listen to the priest's myriad of physical complaints. Even Philo liked the tribune in his sour, grudging way, and it was an absolute delight to listen to Justin and Aristotle as their tongues flashed fire in heady debate.

Everything Justin did seemed to give Judith pleasure. She was proud of his quick mind and his willingness to accept a new concept and to discard an old. It gave her inordinate joy to watch him write in his sure, firm hand. The unfamiliar letters forming with such decisive, easy flourish was to her a thing of beauty.

She liked the way he walked, and the graceful way he seemed to lounge instead of sit upon a divan. She liked the way his hair curled over his brow, the tautness of his muscles, and the knotting in his jaw when he was angry. She even took a perverse pleasure in his stubbornes his sometimes deliberate obtuseness in understanding a simple theory. He was exasperating and incomprehensible, yet displayed a bashful boyishness that Judith found infinitely appealing.

Judith finally forced herself to admit that she loved him, and it plunged her into a deep depression. It was impossible! It was not her destiny to love, and certainly not a Roman tribune! Her life had been planned before she entered Elkatma's womb, and this aberration of her heart could only be a flaw in her own personality or a trial sent by God to test her faith and loyalty.

Judith fought her heart and flesh with every weapon at her command. When Justin left Carmel, she chastised her flesh with fasting and distasteful manual labor. She cleansed her mind by isolation and constant meditation. Her knees became calloused by hours spent in fervent supplication to be released from this temptation, but always Justin returned, and always Judith met him with a glad heart in spite of her resolve.

When Justin left the last time, telling Judith it would probably be some months before he could return, if then, Judith had been weak with relief, but disconsolate before he disappeared among the trees. Her loneliness was staggering, and her yearning nearly beyond her ability to bear. However, it turned out that it was most fortunate that Justin had gone, for events began to accelerate and the Essenes found themselves drawn into a vortex which would eventually change the history of the world.

Judith's preoccupation with Justin had left her little time to think about anything else. When she'd first returned to Carmel from Galilee, she'd told Aristotle of Zachariah's vision, and Aristotle had sent an emissary to Ain Karim to investigate the matter. It was as Zebedee had said. Zachariah had indeed seen a vision and was now mute, but what he had seen or heard, he could not tell.

Judith had written to Elizabeth occasionally over the past months, but her replies had been vague and unsatisfactory, saying only that Judith was not to be concerned, that despite Zachariah's affliction, all was well and they were quite content. Judith had pushed the matter from her mind, reasoning that if Elizabeth needed her confidence, she would say so.

A few days after Justin left, Mary and Eloise were in the House of Lodgement spinning flax into linen threads which would then be loomed into the white cloth used for the summer tunics. It was a tiring chore, for one had to stand with the arms upraised for long periods of time.

"Our yarn bowls are nearly empty," said Eloise. "Take a rest while I run to the storehouse for more."

Mary smiled. Her shoulders ached and her hands and wrists were weary. She went to the open window and lifted her heavy red-gold hair, allowing the warm, spring sun to soothe her tired neck.

It was good to be alone for a change. Mary understood the Essenes' zeal in affording her constant protection; she was rarely left to herself. Even though they respected her need for privacy and solitary prayer, she knew they were always close by and ever watchful.

She watched two monks repairing the flat roof of the communal dining hall. They had spread a mixture of mud, straw, and lime over the roof and were now pulling a heavy stone cylinder over it to pack the mixture down so it could dry. Josie came out of the dining hall with a large jug balanced on her head and disappeared into the trees to bury the scraps and refuse left from the morning meal. Soon two of the holy women followed, each carrying a large basket of soiled linens to be washed in one of the sparkling streams.

Mary heard someone call her name and turned from the window to see a strange man standing in the center of the room. He was clad in a plain, brown robe with the hood pushed back from his face. He carried a rough, wooden walking staff, and wore the peasant's rope sandals on his feet. She was surprised that a stranger had been allowed to visit her unchaperoned. He had the gentlest of smiles, and his eyes were so kind and compassionate that Mary felt instantly drawn to him. A strong perfume of violets drifted through the open window, and Mary felt unaccountably happy.

"Peace be with you," she greeted him.

The man raised his right hand to her, as though in blessing. "Rejoice, O highly favored daughter! The Lord is with you. Blessed are you among women."

Mary was deeply troubled by his words and wondered what his greeting meant.

The man went on to say to her, "Do not fear, Mary. You have found favor with God. You shall conceive and bear a son and give him the name Jeshua. Great will be his dignity and he will be called Son of the Most High. The Lord will give him the throne of David his father. He will rule over the house of Jacob forever and his reign will be without end."

Mary said, "How can this be, since I do not know man?"

"The Holy Spirit will come upon you and the power of the Most High will overshadow you; hence the holy offspring to be born will be called Son of God. Know that Elizabeth, your kinswoman, has conceived a son in her old age; she who was thought to be sterile is now in her sixth month, for nothing is impossible with God."

Mary bowed and said, "I am the servant of the Lord. Let it be done to me as you say." When she raised her eyes, the man was gone and Mary realized she'd been visited by an angel of God.

When Eloise returned a few moments later, Mary was still standing where she had been when the angel left her, her hands clasped and her face aglow with ecstasy. Her eyes were huge and luminous, and staring as though she were in a trance. She didn't acknowledge Eloise's presence until the older woman touched her arm and said, "Mary? What is it, child? Why do you stand so?"

Mary's eyes cleared at the sound of Eloise's voice, and she cried joyously, "Eloise! I must go at once to my cousin Elizabeth. An angel of the Lord has appeared to me and told me that Elizabeth has conceived of a son! Blessed be the name of the Lord!"

Eloise was astounded! She stared at Mary in disbelief, unable to comprehend what she had said. She looked around the room as though to discover an angel lurking in the corner, and then back to Mary's rapturous face. Finally she grasped what Mary had told her. A weakness overcame her. For a moment she felt as though she would faint. Then the weakness passed and was replaced by excited joy. She took Mary's hand and said firmly, "Come! We must tell the others."

Forgetting all monastery decorum, they raced through the House of Lodgement and up the red brick walk to the temple. Judith and Judas were working in the library.

Eloise paused at the library door long enough to cry, "Come!" and they wonderingly obeyed and followed her down the hallway to Aristotle's reception room. Eloise knocked once, and then without waiting for an answer, pushed the door open and pulled Mary in behind her.

Aristotle was seated at the desk and looked up, momentarily annoyed by the intrusion, but when he saw Mary and noted the joy on the young girl's face, his annoyance changed to welcome and he greeted them jovially.

"Well, girls! What is all this excitement?"

He looked at Judith and Judas for some clue, but Judith only shook her head and Judas simply shrugged his shoulders.

"Mary has such news!" Eloise blurted. "I left her alone in the House of Lodgement for a moment while I went to the storage house for more yarn and while I was gone she was visited by an angel!"

There was shocked silence. They stared at Eloise and then at Mary, and like Eloise, knew by Mary's face that it was true.

Mary whirled to face Judith. "Elizabeth is with child! She is in her sixth month and she will bear a son! Oh, Judith! Is that not wonderful?"

"Elizabeth?" Judith repeated, wonderingly, then cried, "Elizabeth! That is wonderful! It's most marvelously wonderful! Her sixth month? But I only just a few days ago received a letter from her and she said nothing! Zachariah's vision! Of course! He must have been told that they would have a child!"

The three women laughed and embraced with glee. Judas scratched his head and Aristotle looked nonplussed.

"Ladies," Aristotle admonished, "I agree it is quite wonderful that your friend is with child, but isn't the visitation by an angel of the Lord just a tiny bit important?" They looked at him in surprise and then chagrin. "Come and sit down."

Aristotle led Mary to a divan and sat beside her. "Tell us exactly what happened, child."

Mary matter-of-factly related all that had occurred and all that had been said. Only when she told of the child Elizabeth was carrying did her voice betray her excitement. The prophecy regarding her own son she told with quiet serenity; this she would keep to ponder in her heart during quiet moments alone.

When she finished, no one spoke nor moved. A little, yellow-breasted bird landed on the window sill and trilled a sweet, lilting melody. The sun poured through the open window.

The memory of the strange Egyptian at the great pyramid rushed to Judith's mind. Amelius, Adam, Melchizedek, Zend, Ur, Asaph, Joseph, Joshua. Jeshua!

"Jeshua," Judas murmured. "Lord is Salvation."

Judith couldn't stop her tears. She rose and knelt before Mary, taking her slim white hand and pressing it against her own cheek.

"The Lord bless you and keep you! The Lord let His face shine upon you, and be gracious to you! The Lord look upon you kindly and give you peace!" Judith whispered, then rose and fled the room.

When Judith fled, they all separated, each to think, to ponder alone that which had come to pass. Each sought communication with God, to understand, to learn His will, and to seek direction as to what they should do.

They came together again after the evening meal, calmer now and able to think more clearly. They discussed the meaning of the message brought by the angel. His greeting to Mary seemed self-explanatory, though Mary flushed at being so exalted. That the child would be called "Son of the Most High" was puzzling, and that He would occupy the "throne of David" and "rule over the house of Jacob forever" seemed to denote the Davidic Messiah who would overthrow the Herodians and Romans and establish a theocracy in Israel once again and forever.

The words, "The Holy Spirit will come upon you and the power of the Most High will overshadow you," proved to be a mystery. Mary reminded them that these words were given in answer to her question, "How can this be, since I know not man?" Was this the manner of her own conception? They remembered Ann's declaration that the child she had borne had no human father! They recalled the teachings of old when souls in the beginning projected mind into matter. Could the forces of the Divine so stir a virginal womb? These were questions unanswerable by the limited carnal mind.

Then there was the news of Elizabeth to consider. Why should the fact that Elizabeth was with child be so important that an angel of God be sent to convey the news? They did not think that angels were given to mundane gossip, no matter how happy the content might be. What was the vision which Zachariah saw in the sanctuary, and why was he struck mute?

They searched the prophecies and pored over the Scriptures to trace again the foretold events. Judith read Malachi's last prophecy aloud.

"Lo, I will send you Elijah, the prophet, before the day of the Lord comes, the great and terrible day."

Could the son of Elizabeth and Zachariah be the soul of Elijah?

Throughout the discussions, Mary had been quiet, only inserting a pertinent comment and answering the questions put to her. When the discussion turned from the meaning of the message to what should be done, Mary quietly interrupted.

"I shall go to Elizabeth on the morrow."

"Mary, my dear. It may not be safe for you in Ain Karim. There are few of our people there—even Zachariah is not one of us," Aristotle replied, trying to dissuade her.

Mary smiled gently. "Do you think, Rabbi, that the Lord will not protect the vessel for His Chosen One? Please order the proper preparations for the journey, for I must go to Elizabeth at once."

This was a new Mary, no longer a humble, obedient child, but a young woman whose authority none of them could deny. Aristotle hesitated only a moment and then bowed his head in acquiescence, his action confirming the position of authority which Mary would hold for the rest of her life.

"It will be done as you request," he said gently.

Judith broke the uncomfortable silence which followed Aristotle's subtle acknowledgment of Mary's new authority.

"If Elizabeth's son is to be the forerunner to the Messiah, then it is vital that she be instructed as to the proper atmosphere to be maintained in the home both during her confinement and after the babe is brought forth, and to the upbringing of the child during his tender years."

"I agree," said Judas. "Two of our holy women, Margil and Anna, are exceptionally well-versed in our teachings on this matter. May I suggest that they accompany Mary to Ain Karim?"

Aristotle turned to Mary, deferring the question to her to answer.

Mary smiled. "I too shall need such instruction. It will be a pleasure to learn these things side by side with my cousin, and I know and love Margil and Anna well."

Aristotle's pleasure and approval of Mary shone in his face. He said to Judith, "And I think you should also go to Ain Karim for a time to help the women set up their program of study, though I wish for you to return to Mt. Carmel as soon as the task is accomplished."

"Thank you, Rabbi. I should very much like to go," said Judith.

Their leave-taking the next morning was a tearful one. The entire Mount was saddened by the prospect of Mary's absence, and Josie sobbed unabashedly at being separated from her beloved friend. Only Mary's continual assurances that she would return in a few months could calm the distraught girl.

They followed the same route through the Plain of Sharon that Judith had taken only a few months before, travelling as inconspicuously as possible. When they reached Zachariah's gate, Judith's conviction that Elizabeth's child was no ordinary soul was confirmed. They saw Elizabeth as she was just about to enter her house, and Mary called out to her. When Elizabeth heard Mary's greeting, the baby leaped in her womb. Elizabeth was filled with the Holy Spirit and cried out in a loud voice:

"Blest are you among women and blest is the fruit of your womb. But who am I that the mother of my Lord should come to me? The moment your greeting sounded in my ears, the baby leapt in my womb for joy. Blest is she who trusted that the Lord's words to her would be fulfilled."

Mary was also filled with the Holy Spirit, and sang again the canticle she had sung the morning she was chosen on the stair, and Anna too, spoke by the spirit and prophesied as to what would be the material experience for each in the earth.

Who could doubt that the Messiah was soon to come!

Chapter 12

After their arrival in Ain Karim, Judith immediately set up a schedule of study and prayer for Elizabeth and Mary. Since Ain Karim was only a few miles from Bethlehem, Rebkah and Editha were able to sit in on many of the lessons. Both girls were experiencing their first pregnancies. They were praying for sons who would eventually grow to aid the Messiah in His mission on the earth, and so were anxious to learn the correct thoughts and attitudes which would attract souls eager to fulfill that purpose.

Elizabeth's daughter Adahr was now of marriageable age. Though she declared she would not marry and leave her mother until Elizabeth's child was old enough to go to school, Adahr nevertheless recognized the opportunity for learning the invaluable lessons for maintaining a serene household and building a happy marriage for herself one day. She asked if her friend Eunice, a girl somewhat younger than herself, but her closest friend, could join her.

Eunice's family was originally from Galilee. Her ancestors were of those peoples who had united with the remnant left in the land of Zebulon during the period of captivity, thus being a mixture of Jew and Samaritan. However, with those adherents of the land becoming more and more imbued with the ideals and tenets of the Essenes, her family had then embraced that phase. Since there was little likelihood that Eunice would endanger her family by gossiping to others in Ain Karim of what was taking place in Zachariah's household, permission was granted.

Judith stayed in Ain Karim long enough to listen in on

the first few sessions and was satisfied that Judas had been right in recommending Margil and Anna.

"Hence the law is ever present," Anna read. "Like attracts like, like begets like. Hence there is the attraction as from the desires of those in the physical calling to the sources of generation in the flesh, to the sources of creation or of spirit in the spiritual realm. Then, know the attitude of mind, of self, of the companion, in creating the opportunity; for it depends upon the state of attitude as to the nature, the character that may be brought into material experience. Leave then the spiritual aspects to God. Prepare the mental and the physical body, according to the nature, the character of that soul being sought."

Margil used the story of Abraham and Sarah, and then of Isaac and Rebekah as examples of how the parents' thoughts and desires influence the nature of the soul who would incarnate.

"When Abraham and Sarah were given the promise of an heir through which the nations of the earth would be blessed, there were many years of preparation of these individuals, of the physical, mental, and spiritual natures. Again and again it is indicated as to how they each in their material concept attempted to offer a plan or way through which this material blessing from a spiritual source might be made manifest.

"Hence we find as to how the material or mental self, misunderstanding, misconstruing the spiritual promises, offered or effected channels through which quite a different individual entity was made manifest and through same, brought confusion, distress, disturbance one to another in the material manifestations.

"Abraham and Sarah were not content to wait until God saw fit to fulfill His promise. Sarah tried to bring the promise to fulfillment herself by offering Abraham her handmaiden, that the child might be born through her. But in doing so, we see all the dissension and problems such action brought about.

"Then we have that illustration in the sons of Isaac, when there were those periods in which there was to be the fulfilling of the promise to Isaac and Rebekah. We find that their minds differed as to the nature or character or channel through which there would come this promise;

when, as we understand, there must be the cooperation
spiritually, mentally, in order for the physical result to be
the same. Here we find a different situation taking place at
the time of conception, for both attitudes found expression. Hence twins were found to be the result of this long
preparation, and yet two minds, two opinions, two ideas,
two ideals. Hence we find that here it became necessary
that even the Divine indicate to the mother that channel
which was to be the ruler, or that one upon whom would
be bestowed the rightful heritage through which the
greater blessings were to be indicated to the world, to
humanity, to mankind as a whole.

"By this we can see the importance of the parents being
of one mind, of one ideal, of one thought as to the child
they desire. This should be a point of discussion between
them, and the preparation should be for both mother and
father."

Anna taught them the correct attitude to be maintained
in raising the child. "In these periods of unfoldment, instill that of right and justice, the child will grasp much
from observation."

"Train ye the child when he is young," she read. "And
when he is old he will not depart from the Lord. Train
him, train her, train them, rather in the sacredness of that
which has come to them as a privilege, which has come to
them as a heritage; from a falling away to be sure, but
through the purifying of the body in thought, in act, in
certainty, it may make for a peoples, a state, a nation that
may indeed herald the coming of the Lord. All of the God
ye may know lies within thyself. Do teach the child that,
and to communicate often with such. For thy body is
indeed the temple of the living God and there He may
meet thee. Do train the entity in these directions.

"If there is the proper manner used for the activities
with the entity, coercion or the breaking of the will or
demands will not be made. For we find that cooperation
may be had with the entity if there is love, and the practical answering as to why do this, why do that. Do not
answer the entity, especially in the early teen years, by
saying 'because I said so, or because it is right,' but explaining why you said so, and why it is right.

"Ponder well the expressions that arise from the emotions of a developing child; for as has been forever given, train them in the way they should go and when they are old they will not depart from the way!"

Judith listened to lessons on the atmosphere to be maintained in the home and between the parents themselves which would prove to be the most conducive in bringing about a physical, mental, and spiritual balance in a child.

"Know that though the world may appear large, there is not sufficient room in same for strife among those who would serve properly those forces that are to build in the life of each, for in humbleness of heart, humbleness of purpose must each present himself as wholly to blame for every element that may bring the seed of strife, and there can be no perfect union of strength with strife existent.

"Love is giving; it is growth. It may be cultivated or it may be seared. That of selflessness on the part of each is necessary. Remember, the union of body, mind, and spirit in such as marriage should ever be not for the desire of self, but as one. Love grows; love endures; love forgiveth; love understands; love keeps those things rather as opportunities that to others would become hardships. Then do not sit still and expect the other to do all the forgiving; but make it rather as the unison and the purpose of each to be that which is a complement one to the other, ever.

"Think not that there is any shortcut to peace or harmony, save in correct living. Ye cannot go against thine own conscience and be at peace with thyself, thy home, thy neighbor, thy God!

"This ye know, ye will never find harmony by finding fault with what the other does. Neither will the other find harmony without considering what the other will think, or be, or care for.

"And in love show the preference for that companionship, in the little things that make the larger life the bigger and better! And ever keep this in the inmost recesses of the heart, that in love the world was saved and made; in hate and indifference the world may be destroyed.

"The home is the nearest pattern in earth to man's relationship to his Maker!

"The home represents then, that which is as the haven, as the material representation of an abiding place, a home, for the developing of the mental, moral, and spiritual relationships of those therein, as a counterpart of that for which one longs in the heavenly home or in the spiritual kingdom."

Judith left Ain Karim in a contemplative, nostalgic mood, wishing every man and woman in the earth who desired marriage and children could hear and accept the simple, homely truths which were being taught in Zachariah's house.

The letters that Judith received from Ain Karim during the next weeks kept her informed of all that was taking place there, but most surprising, each told of the transformation taking place in Zachariah.

Zachariah's muteness had cut him off from the society of his old temple friends. He had taken to joining the women in their daily studies, more as a relief from boredom than from any interest or desire to learn. But as time passed and he watched Elizabeth and Mary grow in grace and spiritual beauty, and he saw his plain, somber daughter bloom into a lovely, smiling woman of charity and purpose, Zachariah came to believe, and with his belief came his own growth.

Zachariah had always been a pious, just man, but taciturn and aloof. Now he had softened, and his heart became filled with love of home and family and fellowman. His reserved love for his wife and daughter became an outward display of open affection. Now he reached for Elizabeth's hand in the company of others, or hugged his daughter tightly to his breast without the least embarrassment at publicly revealing his emotions.

His manner toward his neighbors changed, and he now walked among them as an equal and not as a lofty priest of high position. As he outwardly showed his love and concern, he received such in kind, and for the first time in his life, Zachariah basked in the knowledge that he was held in great affection by his friends and neighbors.

Judith thought the change in Zachariah was every bit as much a miracle as the fact that Elizabeth was with child.

Elizabeth grew heavy and cumbersome, and the Essenes went through their membership lists in search of a qualified nurse for her child. One of those selected as a possible candidate was a woman named Sofa. Sofa had been educated in her youth in the school at Mt. Carmel. She had married and raised a family, and now in her middle years was widowed and worked in the Jerusalem temple as one who kept certain portions of the temple in order for the activities of the priests. She knew Zachariah, and when she heard that a nurse was being sought, she longed to be the one chosen. When it was again the turn of Abijah to assume priestly duties, Sofa appealed to Zachariah and begged him to use his period of preparation as the one to offer sacrifice at the time when there would be the choosing of the nurse for the babe. Zachariah agreed.

On the morning that he was to offer sacrifice, Zachariah wore the Breastplate of Judgment. This was a pocketlike receptacle for holding the Urim and Thummin, made of brocaded linen and adorned with four rows of three precious stones, each stone representing a tribe of Israel. As Zachariah prayed, the symbol of the breastplate moved, indicating that the nurse for the child was to be Sofa. This method of leaving the choice to the forces of the Divine prevented any confusion or dissension among the Brotherhood, for many women desired the honor and privilege of that position. However, it was Sofa who went home with Zachariah when his tour of duty was over, and who became a member of his household.

Not everything that was taking place in Ain Karim was reported to Mt. Carmel. It was during those weeks that Mary noted the first stirrings of change taking place within her own body, but she kept that knowledge to herself.

As the concern and attention of the household centered on Elizabeth, Mary had more and more opportunity to quietly withdraw from the activities and to spend hours alone in meditation and prayer. Her thoughts were ever with God and the tiny life forming in her womb, and she moved unnoticed in a private realm of her own peace, serenity, and quiet joy. She told no one of what was taking place within her, but pondered those things in her heart.

Only Zachariah noticed the subtle change in Mary. He saw the darkening in her eyes, and how her slim, girlish figure had begun to gently curve and mold to blossoming womanhood. He had come to love Mary as a daughter, and Mary returned that love in full, for Zachariah had become the father she had never had. Often in those long, warm nights when they found sleep impossible because of the fullness in their hearts, they climbed to the roof of the

house and there under the canopy of stars and silvery
moonlight, they shared a silent communion with each
other and God.

Zachariah's esteem for Mary as the mother of the Messiah bordered on adoration. He realized that the most
precious of all beings was housed beneath his roof, and he
kept an ever-watchful eye on her, feeling deeply his responsibility as her protector. Sometimes the enormity of
what was actually taking place in his house overwhelmed
him, and he would weep copious tears and beat his breast
in uncontrollable joy. He wanted to sing and cry out to
the world the wonders he was observing, and thanked
God for his muteness that prevented him from giving in to
his joy and blurting out to the world those things that, for
now, must be kept secret.

Elizabeth delivered her child as summer first came to
bloom, and the whole village rejoiced that a son was born
to those who had nearly despaired of one. He was a big,
healthy, lusty boy who loudly proclaimed his entry into
the world. A thick shock of black hair curled over his
forehead, and a dark fuzz covered his chest. He clenched
his little fists and waved them defiantly at the world, and
seemed to howl in frustration at the helplessness of being
a babe. He was the delight and the joy of all the household, and Zachariah's pride knew no bounds.

Judith went to Ain Karim, and on the eighth day, the
whole village assembled for the child's circumcision.
Everyone naturally assumed the child would be named
Zachariah after his father, but when Elizabeth heard
this, she said, "No. He is to be called John."

They all argued with Elizabeth. None of her relatives
had that name, but Elizabeth was adamant. They finally
went to Zachariah and asked him what he wished the child
to be called. He reached for a tablet and stylex and wrote,
"His name is John." With that, Zachariah's mouth was
opened and he began to speak in praise of God, and, filled
by the Holy Spirit, began to prophesy.

"Blessed be the Lord the God of Israel because He
has visited and ransomed His people. He has raised a horn
of saving strength for us in the house of David His servant, as He promised through the mouths of His holy
ones, the prophets of ancient times: Salvation from our
enemies and from the hands of all our foes. He has dealt

mercifully with our fathers and remembered the holy covenant He made, the oath He swore to Abraham our father He would grant us: that, rid of fear and delivered from the enemy, we should serve Him devoutly and through all our days be holy in His sight. And you, O child, shall be called prophet of the Most High; for you shall go before the Lord to prepare straight paths for Him, giving His people a knowledge of salvation in freedom from their sins, all this is the work of the kindness of our God; He, the Dayspring, shall visit us in His mercy to shine on those who sit in darkness and in the shadow of death, to guide our feet into the way of peace."

Fear descended on all in the neighborhood; throughout the hill country of Judea these happenings began to be recounted to the last detail. All who heard stored these things up in their hearts, saying, "What will this child be?" and "Was not the hand of the Lord upon him?"

Judith also wondered. All the way back to Carmel she wondered what, in truth, it all meant, and what would happen to them all!

Judith didn't go back to Ain Karim when Elizabeth's forty days of seclusion ended, though Elizabeth's whole household traveled to Jerusalem to witness her purification and the ransoming of her first-born son from the Lord. Philo was ill and Aristotle had temporarily charged Judith with carrying out his duties in the library.

It was a happy caravan that wound its way over the Judean hills. Some of their neighbors and friends went with the household to share with Zachariah and Elizabeth the joy of presenting their long-awaited son in the temple. Zachariah was jubilant. At last the Lord had blessed him with a son, and to appear before his fellow priests with such a big, robust, perfect child was an incomparable triumph. His new-found belief in the purpose of the Essenes filled him with uncontained excitement. He strode at the head of the caravan with his close friend and neighbor, Simean, at his side. Simean was a Levite, but also an Essene, and he listened with amusement as Zachariah recounted the prophecies regarding the Messiah as though he himself had first discovered them, and excitedly expounded their meaning and pointed to those which were being fulfilled today.

Simean rejoiced that the Lord had opened Zachariah's eyes and heart to the light of truth, but felt a vague unease as Zachariah seemed determined to bring the good news to the attention of those of his own school of thought. He gently counseled caution, but being loathe to dampen Zachariah's joy, didn't press the issue.

They entered the city walls through the gate of the Essenes. This was the first time Zachariah had done so, and to him it was an outward act of faith in his belief in the tenets and purposes of the Brotherhood. Elizabeth wept tears of joy. All her prayers had been answered. Zachariah had come to believe as she believed, and her wondrous, longed-for son lay nestled in her arms.

Inside the walls, the members of the caravan parted, each to go to his place of lodging, to meet again in the morning at the temple for the presentation. Zachariah's household went to the Upper City to the home of Marcus and Josie. The Upper City was the part of Jerusalem where the wealthy and influential Jews and the higher-ranking Roman officials lived. Beautiful, spacious, white marble mansions lined broad, paved avenues, surrounded by walled, lush gardens for privacy. It was an area of luxury and ease, built after the Roman fashion with col-umned arcades and formally planted gardens.

Marcus was a wealthy young man. His father, Cleopas, was a rich and powerful Sadducee, held in high esteem, and an honored member of the Sanhedrin. Cleopas and Marcus secretly held to the tenets of the Essenes and provided any help they could without exposing their be-liefs to the others of their class. Marcus' home was not as lavish as many others. It stood on the eastern edge of the Upper City and was a comparatively modest, two-storied, limestone house with a large walled garden in front to set it back from the busy avenue.

Josie had sent a servant to watch for their arrival, and so was at the gate waiting when they came. She was overjoyed to see Mary, and clucked and exclaimed over John. She took the babe from Elizabeth's arms and bent low so her little girls, Rhoda and Mary, could marvel over their tiny cousin.

Josie was a larger, paler image of Mary, with the same red-gold hair and ivory skin, but more subdued in coloring and not as striking in feature. She was taller than Mary, and childbirth had given her a plump, matronly look. She had prepared a lavish feast to celebrate the birth of John, inviting Zebedee, Syrus, Archaus, and all their families, and the evening passed in joyous merrymaking.

In the morning they all met at the temple where a lamb was slaughtered in sacrifice and a pigeon given as a sin-offering for Elizabeth's purification. Then Zachariah presented John to the priests and proudly paid the five shekels which ransomed his son from the Lord.

Mary's joy for Elizabeth was overshadowed by a sense of foreboding. She thought of the reverent, quiet little temple on Mt. Carmel where one could pray in peace and silence, and then looked around at the immense lavishness of Herod's temple, and felt a sinking sensation. Thousands of workmen shouted and pounded and sawed and chiseled, making a clamorous, ear-shattering din. The massive Court of Gentiles was crammed with booths and stalls and pens of animals waiting to be sold for sacrifice, while money-changers called their values and knots of men gathered to exchange gossip and bet on races. Every type of business was being transacted in the House of the Lord.

The Court of Women proved no less clamorous, and Mary was amazed at the richness of the women's dress and the overpowering odor of perfumes and powders. She saw the grim, unsmiling faces of the poor, offering their meager sacrifices under the scornful gaze of the haughty priests, and she felt uncommonly depressed. Her temples throbbed, and her feeling of disquiet grew. She heaved a sigh of relief when John began to wail for his mother's breast and the women started back to Josie's.

Zachariah and Simean did not return with them. This was Zachariah's moment of triumph. He who had been mute and without a son and heir, had now returned to his fellow priests singing verbal praises of his first-born son.

They were in the Court of Priests, and Simean was thoroughly enjoying watching Zachariah boast of his child. Then his amusement changed to apprehension as Zachariah began to tell of the vision he had seen in the sanctuary.

The court was crowded with Pharisees and Sadducees

and minor priests. They lounged on tiered stone and wooden benches about the court walls, and were indulging Zachariah's extravagant praise of his son. Zachariah was standing in the center of the court, widely gesturing to emphasize his words. He spoke loudly and clearly, and as he began to speak of his vision, the languid priests became alert and leaned forward to hear every word.

"My brothers! I beg you to heed well my words. I am Zachariah ben Barachias. I am a priest of the tribe of Levi, of the class of Abijah. For many years my wife and I have been without the blessing of a son. For many years, we have made sacrifices and implored the Lord to bless us with a son, to be a comfort to our old age, and to bring glory to all of Israel. But after blessing us with a beautiful daughter, the Lord saw fit to close the womb of my wife, and, in His wisdom, waited until that day when the prophecies of old should be fulfilled, and her womb should again be opened."

A low murmur ran through the court as the priests wondered what ravings the old man was now spouting. Zachariah ignored the murmurs and went on.

"Once, when it was the turn of Abijah and I was fulfilling my functions as priest before God, it fell to me by lot to enter the sanctuary of the Lord and to offer incense. An angel of the Lord appeared to me, standing at the right of the altar of incense. I was deeply disturbed and overcome by fear, but the angel said to me, 'Do not be frightened, Zachariah, your prayer has been heard. Your wife Elizabeth shall bear a son whom you shall name John. Joy and gladness will be yours, and many will rejoice at his birth, for he will be great in the eyes of the Lord. He will never drink wine or strong drink, and he will be filled with the Holy Spirit from his mother's womb. Many of the sons of Israel will he bring back to the Lord their God. God himself will go before him, in the spirit and power of Elijah, to turn the hearts of fathers to their children and the rebellious to the wisdom of the just, and to prepare for the Lord a people well disposed.'

"I said to the angel, 'How am I to know this? I am an old man, my wife too is advanced in age.' The angel answered me. 'I am Gabriel, who stands in attendance before God. I was sent to speak to you and bring you this good news. But now you will be mute, unable to speak, until the day these things take place, because you have not trusted my words. They will all come true in due season.' I, Zachariah ben Barachias, tell these things as truth."

The priests' murmurings changed to an excited hum. Simean's fear grew as he saw the scorn and angry disbelief in the eyes of his fellow priests. He tried to catch Zachariah's eye, to warn him to stop, but Zachariah seemed oblivious to the danger in the air. He only felt the tumultuous joy in his heart, his joy in the knowledge that the prophecies were being fulfilled this day. He wanted to share this knowledge with those he had considered his friends, to offer them hope, to bring them to an awareness of the wondrous blessings the Lord was bestowing on this generation. He raised his arms for silence in the court and continued.

"Many of you saw me on that day and saw that my tongue was cleaved to the roof of my mouth. You saw with your own eyes that I was speechless and so you know I speak truth. I returned home to my wife, and it came to pass that my wife conceived in her old age and the son promised by the angel was born to us. On the day of my son's circumcision, the Lord loosened my tongue, and, filled with the spirit of the Lord, I began to prophesy."

The gates which led from the Court of Israel to the Court of Priests were crammed with Jews trying to hear what was taking place inside. Simean saw wonder and hope and excitement in some of their faces, but contempt and anger in others. The air was charged with tension. The murmurs had grown to a rumble. Some men called out for quiet, so the priest could be heard. Others cried for Zachariah to still his foolish tongue. The High Priest and his cohorts heard the disturbance and emerged from the sanctuary and stood on the porch, their cold eyes surveying the scene below.

Simean began to sweat beneath his robes. His hands trembled and his palms became sticky.

Zachariah paid no attention, but raising his voice above the rumbling, went on with his story, repeating the prophecies he had uttered upon naming the child John. "And you, O child, shall be called prophet of the Most High;

for you shall go before the Lord to prepare straight paths
for Him, giving His people a knowledge of salvation in
freedom from their sins, all this is the work of the kindness of our God; He, the Dayspring, shall visit us in His
mercy to shine on those who sit in darkness and in the
shadow of death, to guide our feet into the way of peace."

The courts erupted into an irate roar, but again Zachariah raised his arms to silence them. "My brothers! Hear
me out! Do not judge the words of the Lord! God in His
almighty mercy has found favor with this generation.
Hear the words of His servant, Zachariah ben Barachias."

Again the roar became a subdued rumble. Simean's
heart pounded in his ears. His stomach contracted in terror and he fought the bile rising in his throat. He prayed
to God to strike Zachariah mute again.

Zachariah cried, "In our land is a sect which the Romans call the Essenes, the Expectant Ones. These men,
our brother Jews, have borne the brunt of our scorn and
derision for centuries. We have hounded them and persecuted them, and tried to drive them from our land. These
men are good and holy men. Their purpose for centuries
has been to bring about the conditions necessary for the
Messiah to enter the earth. And for centuries we, their
brothers, through our unbelief, have tried to stop them.
We have sinned before God in our unbelief—"

Bedlam broke loose in the courts. Screams of "Blasphemer!" "The man is mad!" "Folly!" "Throw him out!"
rose above the roar. Some Sadducees started to chant,
"There is no reincarnation!" Others shouted, "Leave the
man speak!" "Quiet, that we may hear!" "At last we hear
truth!"

Simean was frantic. The priests and Jews had turned
into an angry mob. He saw the High Priest, his face
contorted with hatred, whisper to one of his cohorts who
slipped back into the sanctuary.

The priests spilled onto the floor of the court and were
arguing and shouting, shaking fists and shoving one another. Zachariah still stood where he had been speaking.
He looked bewildered and his mouth moved, but Simean
couldn't hear his words. Angry shouts and sounds of scuffling came from the Court of Israel. Simean was pushing
his way through the milling, angry men, trying to reach

Zachariah and pull him out of the court to safety, when the first blow was delivered and both courts dissolved into riot.

It was madness! Clubs and fists flew, and screams of pain and anger assailed the air.

Zachariah watched in horror. He had intended to bring them joy and hope and knowledge that God intended to deliver them from their enemies, and they had turned into a riotous, uncontrollable mob! He was sickened and bewildered. He cried out to them, begging, pleading with them, but no one listened.

Simean fought his way through the fighting. He was pushed and flailed. He fell again and again, each time fighting to regain his footing. He heard the clang of iron-clad sandals. Roman soldiers burst from the sanctuary door, emerging from the tunnel which connected the sanctuary to Herod's palace. Simean watched, frozen in fear, as the captain stopped and listened a moment to the High Priest. Then he barked orders to his men who tramped down the steps and joined in the melee.

Simean looked to where Zachariah had been and saw he was gone. He followed the High Priest's pointing arm and saw Zachariah scrambling up the long, stone steps to the altar in a desperate attempt to be seen and heard. The captain of the guard gestured to one of his men who drew an arrow from his quiver, inserted it in his bow, and aimed for Zachariah's back.

It was a dream, a nightmare! Everything moved in a slow, hazy motion. Every detail of the scene became sharp and clear and was burned into Simean's brain. The muscles of the soldier's arm bulged as he drew the bow. His eyes squinted to focus on his target. The arrow left the bow and floated lazily up and up through the air, then paused at the zenith of its flight and turned its barb downward. It seemed to hang in the air and then began its descent toward Zachariah's back.

A scream began in Simean's bowels and worked its way upward, filling every crevice of his being, filling his lungs and throat to bursting, clawing, tearing, ripping its way to become a long, shattering scream of "Noooooooo!"

As Zachariah reached the top of the altar, the arrow found its resting place and buried itself deep between Zachariah's shoulders. A look of bewilderment and disbelief spread over Zachariah's face. His outspread hands reached slowly upward and lazily closed on the horns of the altar. His head floated back, and his spine arched against the pain. A dark, ugly stain began to grow across his snow-white tunic. His hands languorously slipped from the altar horns and Zachariah tumbled over and over down the altar steps and settled in a heap at its feet.

Simean went wild. He fought and hit and kicked and bit and clawed his way through the rioting mob. A Roman truncheon landed across his shoulders, but he shrugged it off and beat his way toward the gates. Sweat ran in his eyes and mingled with furious tears, blinding him and forcing him to grope his way. The taste of blood rose from his aching throat and he realized he was screaming, "Madness! Madness!" over and over again. He fell again and again, insensible to what was happening and to the blows that rained over his body.

He finally found himself in the Court of Women and pushed his way blindly through the screaming females until he stumbled down the steps to the Court of Gentiles. He ran across the marble floors, stumbling and falling, until he burst through the Golden Gate and fell exhausted outside the city walls. He lay with his face pressed in the dirt and dug his nails into the earth. He wept. Great, rasping sobs tore his entrails and raked his already tortured throat.

"The fool! The fool! He should have known they wouldn't listen. They've killed him! They've killed a prophet of the Lord! May God curse them and all their generations forever!" Simean cried.

He wept until he vomited gall and blood and then, exhausted, lay still. A sadness carrying the weight of the world settled upon him. He lay a long time, too drained to feel or think. His robes were ragged and filthy. Vomit matted his beard, and blood dried in his hair and on his face. He became aware of pain shooting across his shoulders and down his legs. He looked at his arms and legs and saw ugly, black bruises and great, red welts beginning to appear. He was flooded with despair. The works and plans of centuries had come to naught. Better had the child never been born, than to bring about the murder of his father.

At the thought of John, Simean sat bolt upright. The child! He had to get the child out of Jerusalem!

He hauled himself to his feet and fought the blackness that threatened to envelop him. He reeled with nausea and his vision blackened with pain. He used the city wall as a support and started southward. His fear for John and Elizabeth gave him strength, and he began to run drunkenly for the Sheep Gate. He skirted the walls of the Fortress Antonia, and ran to the Fish Gate, where he reentered the city. He forced himself to think, to remember the way to Marcus' house, and then ran, oblivious to the stares and shouts of those along the way. He flung himself at Marcus' gate and crashed it open, falling full-length into the quiet, peaceful garden. A maid saw him and screamed, bringing the whole household running.

"Get the child! Get the child! Get out of Jerusalem!" he gasped. "They've murdered Zachariah! They've killed a prophet of the Lord!"

Then a black wave of pain engulfed him and Simean knew no more.

Chapter 13

Mary sat in Judith's accustomed place by the sea. Her slender face was pinched with grief, her skin the pallor of white marble. Her usually full, red mouth was only a tightly drawn white line. Her clenched fists lay unmoving in her lap, and her narrow, childish shoulders ached from the tension of her efforts to maintain her self-control.

She stared out over the calm Great Sea, oblivious to the sun playing games of hide-and-seek upon its glassy surface, or to the many-colored sails that bowed and curtsied like blossoms in a summer breeze. Instead she saw again the terrifying events of the past few days—scenes of horror and naked fear danced before her eyes in nightmarish confusion.

All of Mary's life had been spent with gentleness and loving care. She had never heard a quarrel, nor witnessed acts of hatred, fear, or lust in any form. She had never seen uncontrolled anger that resulted in physical blows or verbal abuse. Her life had been sheltered by kindly words and loving caresses, a haven of tranquility and peace. Nothing in all her life had prepared her for the horror she had just passed through.

Thank God that Marcus had been home when Simean had collapsed inside his gate. His cool, unruffled mind had grasped the situation immediately, and he'd quickly taken charge. Simean was carried into the house and put to bed and a servant sent running for a physician to tend to his wounds. Marcus had quietly marshalled all his servants, calmly giving orders and instructions to each. One he sent to summon Cleopas, others to prepare the women for their return to Ain Karim, and others to accompany the women.

His calm, quiet manner had been a soothing cushion during those first moments of shock, and had kept them all from teetering over the brink of hysteria and panic. Mary remembered how he'd kept the bewildered, terror-stricken Adahr constantly within the confines of his strong, protective arm, and how he'd spoken to Elizabeth with such compassion and loving understanding as he'd pressed upon her shock-numbed mind the urgency to remain calm and strong, and to get baby John out of Jerusalem.

What would they have done without Marcus, Mary wondered. As soon as Cleopas had arrived, Marcus personally took them home to Ain Karim, leaving Josie and his tiny daughters in his father's care. Mary now realized how difficult it must have been for Marcus to leave his family, not knowing how far-reaching the senseless anger in the temple would become, or what dangers Josie might have to face.

Mary could hardly remember the trip back to Ain Karim. It was like a nightmare with only the shreds of a few scenes remaining in her memory. She remembered Elizabeth riding on a donkey, clutching John to her breast, and Marcus striding by her side, still clinging to Adahr's hand. She remembered heat and dust and unbearable exhaustion, and sometimes Marcus' arms about her, encouraging and comforting, holding her together when she felt her whole being would fragment into a thousand, tiny pieces.

Cleopas had claimed Zachariah's body from the Sanhedrin, and after a hasty burial in Ain Karim, Marcus had brought them all to the safety and protection of Mt. Carmel.

Mt. Carmel lay under a shroud of grief. Zachariah's murder had thrown the Brotherhood into a state of confusion and terror. That he had been killed while clinging to the very horns of the altar was a sacrilege so horrible they could not even speak of it. They were numbed. Their eyes glazed with disbelief and they were unable to find words of comfort, too afraid of the answers to voice the questions that raged in every heart and soul. What did this mean to the purposes of the Covenanters? Was this the beginning of a wave of increased persecution toward the Elect? Would the Messiah enter into an atmosphere of

murder and persecution? What were they to do? All of
these questions had to be answered and preparations and
plans had to be made, but for the first days following the
murder, they reeled under shock and stared at one another with minds dulled with horror.

Elizabeth lay prostrate with grief. Her keening cries
hung in the air and pierced the hearts of the others with
sharp, physical pain. She suffered John to nurse when
Sofa laid him in her arms, but would not eat or sleep or
speak.

Adahr did not weep. She looked at the Brothers with
accusing eyes filled with hate, thinking that if her father
had not embraced the beliefs of those on Mt. Carmel he
would be alive still. She haunted the forest paths like a
wraith, trying to reconcile her love and anger toward her
mother. She clung to John with a fierce possession, regarding him as all she had left of Zachariah. Ann and
Ismeria, the Other Mary, and even Mary herself had tried
in every way they knew to console her, but Adahr only
listened in polite, stony silence, then returned to the forest
to nurse her bitter hatred alone.

Aristotle moved through the Mount with quiet authority, ordering the dazed monks to their work, keeping the
daily life on the Mount in order, knowing that work
would assuage their grief and be a balm to their fear.
Judas retreated into a silent world of untold sadness.
Mathias took to his bed, vomiting blood from his outraged ulcer, and the ailing Philo turned his face to the
wall and prepared to die.

Judith was of no help to anyone. For the first time in
her life her innate sense of purpose was shaken. She had
always had complete confidence in the steps she took to
prepare the way for the Messiah. Every contingency and
possibility had always been explored and planned for, and
any unforetold events had been dealt with in a calm,
orderly fashion. She firmly believed that any problem
could be solved with logic and reason and effort of
thought, combined with an unwavering faith in the Lord.
"The Lord will triumph." "Goodness will overcome evil."
"Light will prevail over darkness." These were the standards she lived by, but now she lived with doubt.

Anger, frustration, impatience—these were familiar
emotions to Judith, but doubt over the purpose for which

she had entered the realm of earth was alien to her, and rocked her convictions to their very roots. Now she found herself questioning her purpose, her reason for living. Were they all "chasing the wind"? Was it all "vanity of vanities"? Had their interpretation of the Scriptures been so wrong and such an affront to the Most High that He had allowed Zachariah to die so cruelly as to reveal to them His displeasure?

Such questions raged through Judith's mind, filling her with guilt for her lack of faith and plunging her into despair. She stumbled about in a daze like the others, her mind screaming a silent *why?* to the ears of an unanswering God.

Zachariah's death brought Justin to Mt. Carmel. He'd heard of the riot and of the murder of a priest in the temple at Jerusalem while he was in Caesarea. He knew nothing of Judith's intimate friendship with that priest's wife, but when he heard how the priest had been killed for proclaiming his belief in the sect of the Essenes, a cold knot of fear had grown in Justin's breast for the safety of the tall, golden-haired girl on Mt. Carmel. His heart had nearly broken when he'd looked into Judith's gray, tear-swollen face, and not caring what anyone might think, he crushed her in his arms and held her while she sobbed uncontrollably on his breast.

Justin's presence was comforting to Judith. She told him of her love and friendship for Elizabeth, and poured out her heart to Justin's sympathetic ears. She told him what had happened, leaving out the story of Zachariah's muteness and his prophecy concerning his son, telling only of Elizabeth's long years of barrenness and of Zachariah's pride and joy in his son, and that John's birth had brought about his belief in the teachings of the Essenes.

Justin privately thought the priest a fool for making his new-found beliefs public, but refrained from voicing his opinion aloud. He did admire the man for the courage of his convictions, but warned Judith that she and the others must not follow Zachariah's example. The Romans were disturbed by the events in Jerusalem, and Herod was furious that the Jews had once again put him in a bad light in Rome's eyes. Justin firmly cautioned Judith to take the utmost care, to keep their teachings to themselves, and to stay out of Judea, for the feelings against the Essenes ran high and the province was frought with danger for them.

Judith obediently agreed, thanking God that the Brotherhood had at least one friend among the Romans.

Justin's presence had bolstered everyone's spirits a little. He spoke at length with Judas and Aristotle, warning them as he had warned Judith. He spoke quietly and reassuringly to the monks, and teased the children into smiling a little. If only he could stay, Judith thought. But Justin had to return to Caesaria that same day.

Judith walked with Justin to the bottom of the incline where he had left his horse, and melted into dizzy, trembling joy when Justin suddenly pulled her roughly into his arms and kissed her hard upon her mouth. He flung himself upon the horse and thundered down the path without turning back, leaving her weak with a rush of desire and unbelievable happiness, yet more afraid than ever.

As Mary thought about the grief and terror of the others, her own disappeared. Her shoulders lost their rigidity and her hands lay placid in her lap. She mulled the past few days over and over in her mind, and as the events began to fall into sequence, she could comprehend all that had happened as a reality rather than as a fragmented nightmare. For the first time in days she could pray, not just a cry of terror, but a true communion with God. She thought of Elizabeth and Adahr, and of all the other broken, heartsick, fearful people on Mt. Carmel, and she implored the Lord to show her some way to bring surcease to their grief, to use her as a channel through which He could restore their faith and banish their fears.

A fluttering sensation in her womb brought Mary out of her reverie. She wondered and waited, and then again felt the movement deep inside her, this time firm and strong and unmistakably sure. Happiness washed over her. She laughed and cried out her gratitude to God. How good He was! He had shown her the way. He had answered her prayers and in such a wonderful, simple way.

Mary stood and hugged herself. She whirled about in her joy and then ran back along the path to the temple.

She went directly to Elizabeth's room. Ann and Ismeria, Judith, Adahr, the Other Mary, and Sofa with John in her arms were all there. Mary smiled when she entered, and went and sat on the edge of Elizabeth's bed. She was radiant with happiness, and they all looked at her with wonder.

With Elizabeth's hand in her own, and in her soft, melodious voice, she told Elizabeth of the love which had grown between Zachariah and herself. She recounted the words which the angel had spoken to her. Then she rose and unclasped the flowing mantle about her shoulders and let it drop to the floor. Her hands trembled as she pulled the white tunic tightly across her body so they could see her gently swelling womb.

"See, Elizabeth! God, the Master of all the Universe has not forgotten His children in their days of sorrow and tribulation. The promise of the Lord has been fulfilled. I have known no man, and yet the child grows in my womb. Zachariah guessed at this wondrous work of the Lord, and it was this knowledge, this absolute knowing that the Messiah had entered, which gave him such joy that he was compelled to prepare his friends for the Way of the Lord. That they did not perceive and accept the truth is cause for sorrow. That they slew him with his hands on the very horns of the altar is a sacrilege beyond belief. But grieve not for Zachariah or for yourselves, but thank God that Zachariah died in glory and in faith and that we can walk in light and not in darkness. Pray for those souls that will not hear, that cannot see, for they too are children of the Most High."

The others stood transfixed, unable to comprehend that she was with child. Mary seemed oblivious to their astonishment as she took John from Sofa's arms and idly twined his thick, black hair around her finger.

"Remember the words you spoke by the Spirit the day I first entered your house?" Mary mused. " 'Blest is the fruit of thy womb,' you said. Your son shall prepare the way for my son and together they shall bring salvation to all of Israel. Zachariah has given our sons an example of courage and faith unparalleled in the history of our people. You and I, all of us, must finish his work as Joshua finished the work of Moses. We must now raise our sons to be able to accomplish all that the Lord has set before them. Blessed be God in His wisdom and mercy!"

Word of Mary's pregnancy flew through the compound like the wind through the Plain of Gennesaret. Once again the people were asked to believe the impossible. Once again they were split into two camps, those who accepted and those who could not. But even those who doubted found new hope. Mary's news had banished their despair and dulled their grief, and the Mount catapulted to life. Mary had restored their faith that their purpose was indeed the will of God.

Judith believed in Mary without question. She had seen and experienced too many things which could not be explained by human thought to doubt for a moment that a virgin could conceive. She met with Judas, Aristotle, and Mathias, and the work on the City of Salt was accelerated. The child would soon be born and the need for a school and scriptorium had become a necessity. Elizabeth rose from her bed and assumed the care of John. Adahr took a slightly more skeptical attitude and clung even more zealously to her tiny brother.

Zebedee, like Justin, had also rushed to Mt. Carmel. Zebedee's anger was like a raging, destructive storm. His face was black with rage. He strode through the compound like a warrior going to battle, cursing the Jerusalem priests in thunderous, scathing terms, slamming his fist into his palm and kicking at any stone or branch that happened to be in his path. He roared in hatred and condemnation at men who would dare to kill a prophet upon the very altar of the Lord.

Zebedee's anger vanished when he learned that Mary was with child. Again he was forced to face the ugly fact that an unmarried woman in his household had been found with child. His heart sank and his spirit tumbled into the pit of despair. Ann tried to talk to him, to convince him that this was the will of God, but Zebedee only shook his head and stared at her without answering. When Ann saw that there was nothing she could say to relieve her son's suffering, she went to Mary. Mary listened to Ann's dismay with pity and concern, and immediately went in search of Zebedee.

She found him in the outer temple court. He was sitting on one of the stone benches, his shoulders slumped and his head bowed. His elbows rested on his thighs and his hands dangled limply between his knees. Mary paused a moment and watched him. He was the picture of dejection. Her heart ached for him and she wondered what she could say to this brother she hardly knew. She slowly walked across the court and gingerly sat down beside him. Zebedee seemed unaware of her until she spoke.

"Zebedee?" she said tentatively.

Zebedee slowly raised his head. When he saw it was Mary, he groaned and stared again at the court floor.

Mary touched his arm and said in a pleading voice, "Please, Zebedee, don't suffer so. It's all right. I assure you I have not played the harlot, nor have I been defiled."

Zebedee jerked his head toward her and demanded, "Will you take an oath that that is true?"

"No," Mary said firmly. "It is forbidden to take an oath. You can either believe me or not, but my word must stand."

Zebedee again hung his head and Mary sighed. "I know how difficult this is. I do not understand it myself, but the child stirs in my womb. He most assuredly lives. The angel said to me, 'The Holy Spirit will come upon you and the power of the Most High will overshadow you.' Can anyone understand this mystery? I, least of all, cannot; and yet it has happened."

Zebedee straightened and looked tiredly at Mary. "I have been thinking that perhaps I should have stayed in Cana. I should never have left our mother alone. Maybe then none of this would have happened."

Mary smiled at him with a twinkle in her eye. "Zebedee!" she said teasingly. "Are you so ominous a personage that even an angel of God would forbear to appear in your presence? Does the Lord God Himself quake before the dark, thunderous countenance of Zebedee ben Joachim?"

Zebedee snorted and Mary laughed. "Come, my brother. Smile for me. Judith tells me that you can be the most merry and optimistic of men, but all I have seen is thunderous rage and then dejection. Show your sister the gentle, carefree heart which she has heard so much about."

Zebedee slapped his thighs and stood. He faced Mary with indignation and said sternly, "Your feminine wiles will not work with me! Zebedee ben Joachim is not influenced by a young, pretty face, or by teasing words. Besides, you don't have to go home and face Salome with such news!"

Mary burst into laughter. "The mighty Zebedee fears his wife!"

Mary stood and took Zebedee's hands in her own. The laughing, teasing girl had gone. It was a woman's eyes which looked into his scowling face, and a woman's voice which spoke with tender understanding. "My brother is not so tough and heartless as he would have me believe. Do not worry about Salome. Judith tells me that she is kind and loyal and loves you to distraction. Salome may not believe, but she will keep an open mind and reserve her judgment. You know that if you can accept my child, Salome will also. As for your remaining in Cana, it wouldn't have mattered. Our mother would still have conceived and I would still be carrying the Messiah within my womb. God's will would not be deterred. He called you to Jerusalem for a purpose, even though that purpose is not yet revealed."

Zebedee wearily resumed his seat. For a while he didn't speak, but only studied this strange, unknown girl who was his sister. The sun glinted on Mary's hair, forming a halo of gold around her head. Her luminous, blue-gray eyes seemed to look straight through to his heart. He marvelled to himself at her youth and beauty and aura of innocence. She was so small and seemed so fragile, yet he sensed a strength and determination that belied her fragility. Nor could he deny the confidence and authority with which she spoke. He sighed and gingerly reached out his hand and brushed it lightly over Mary's womb.

"You believe you carry the Messiah," he said. Mary nodded. "And our mother believes, and Aristotle and Judith and Judas and Elizabeth and all the others?"

"Yes," Mary whispered.

Zebedee pulled on his beard and then said roughly, "Well, sit down then. The Mother of my Lord should get off her feet!"

Mary sat beside him and laid her head against his shoulder. "Thank you, Zebedee! I need you to believe in me. Sometimes I am afraid and it will be such comfort to know you are my friend."

Zebedee cleared his throat. He put one great arm around her and pulled her close, nearly crushing her with his embrace.

"Well, now," he said hoarsely. "Tell me about your life here. Are they good to you? Have you been happy?"

They talked a long time, getting to know one another

and to understand one another's feelings and hopes and desires for this life. By the time Zebedee left Mt. Carmel, he and Mary had formed a lasting friendship which would in years to come, sustain them through untold heartbreak and suffering.

As soon as Mary made her pregnancy known to the Brotherhood, a messenger was sent to Nazareth to summon Joseph to Mt. Carmel. Joseph could not accept the manner by which Mary's child had been conceived. He was determined not to marry her, but once again the forces of the Divine intervened.

An angel of the Lord appeared to Joseph in a dream and said to him, "Joseph, son of David, have no fear about taking Mary as your wife. It is by the Holy Spirit that she has conceived this child. She is to have a son and you are to name Him Jeshua, because He will save His people from their sins."

When Joseph awoke he did as the angel of the Lord had directed him. He came to Mt. Carmel and in the company of all of his friends, made Mary his wife. He took his bride home to the sleepy little village of Nazareth to live in simple obscurity until the day their son would become a man and lead all Israel to freedom.

The hot summer days melted into autumn. The tragic riot that had ended in the death of a priest at the altar was forgotten as throughout the land the people gathered the harvest. They celebrated the Feast of the New Moon which signified the beginning of the new year, and ten days later beat their breasts in penitence for their sins as a hush fell over the land on the Day of Atonement.

For eight days the populace of Palestine moved out of their homes and lived in tents and huts made out of palm fronds and grasses to commemorate their fathers' entry into the Promised Land. The nights turned chill and frosty and shepherds huddled in woolen robes against the cool night air.

The child in Mary's womb grew and stirred, and the universe held its breath and awaited the dawn of a New Age.

Three astrologers appeared on Mt. Carmel, causing a flurry of excitement and wonder. They looked like kings in beautiful, vibrantly colored robes of purple, gold, and sapphire blue, and their tall, plush velvet turbans glistened with discreetly embedded gems. They were wise men from Persia, India, and Egypt who had spent their lives watching and studying the movements of the heavenly bodies and relating their meaning to the lives of men.

Early in the summer they had observed an unusual phenomenon taking place in the heavens and had journeyed to the famous school of astrology in the city of Sippar in Babylonia. There they had watched in wonder and excitement as the planets Saturn and Jupiter moved into close conjunction in the constellation of Pisces. As the planets moved together they seemed to form one vast, brilliant star in the eyes of those who observed from the earth.

From ancient times Pisces had been known as the sign of the West, the sign of Israel, and the sign of the Messiah. These students of ancient wisdom and knowledge interpreted this phenomenon to signify the appearance of a mighty King in Israel, and through their calculations, knew this glorious star would soon make a final appearance in the heavens over Palestine. They had come to Carmel to the Brotherhood of the Elect, knowing that they too knew of such things and would help them find this wondrous King, that they might pay Him homage.

The Carmelites felt no fear in revealing their secrets to the astrologers, for they were also Israelites in the ancient meaning of that term, remnants of souls on earth who knew and preserved the truth of God. Indeed, the Carmelites, as well as being known by various other names, sometimes referred to those who shared their belief as the Remnant. They told the astrologers everything that had occurred on the Mount, from the selection of the twelve girls and the choosing of Mary on the stair to the birth of Elizabeth's son and the murder of Zachariah upon the altar.

The astrologers were still at Carmel when Justin's aide, Puloaus, and a small company of soldiers came to post notice of a decree published by Caesar Augustus ordering a census of all the Empire. Everyone over the age of fourteen was required to register in the town of the birth of his ancestors. This brought consternation to Judith and the others, for it meant that Joseph and Mary would have to journey to Judea to the little town of Bethlehem which was the home of David, since both were of the house and lineage of David. It would be a difficult journey for Mary, as her time of delivery was near. They would also be required to register their religious beliefs, and this caused alarm among the Brotherhood. Zachariah's death was still fresh in their minds and they feared the ridicule and persecution that would follow if Joseph proclaimed his adherence to the Essene thought.

Aristotle sent a messenger to Apsafar, Editha's father in Bethlehem, to elicit his aid. Apsafar owned a large inn in Bethlehem. Since Bethlehem lay on the main road which led from Jerusalem to Idumea, his inn was a popular resting place for merchants of many lands who traded with the Idumeans, and for the Roman soldiery who patrolled all the main roads of Palestine. High-ranking Jews also frequented the inn as they made pilgrimage to David's birthplace. All of this put Apsafar in a position of hearing all the news and different thought which prevailed throughout the land, which he in turn duly reported to the Essenes.

Apsafar was of both Jewish and Greek ancestry. He posed the attitude of a garrulous, simple, uneducated tavern-keeper, concerned only with the quality of his wine and the pleasure of his patrons. No one guessed that he was the supervisor of the Bethlehem Essenes, or that behind that facade of innocent indifference lay a keen, learned mind and a heart devoted to the advent of the Messiah. Apsafar was the Essenes' most valuable source of information regarding the temperament and thought of the Judean Jews.

Apsafar outlined a plan whereby Mary and Joseph would be relatively safe from the attention of the Romans and hostile Jews. He thought it would be most dangerous for them to stay at the inn, for it would be filled with Romans and Jews from every land and school of thought whose ancestors were of the line of David. Except for a few select members, even the Essenes of Bethlehem would not be told that Mary was in the city, for they could not risk a recurrence of the tragedy which had taken place in Jerusalem when Zachariah openly proclaimed the identity of his son. A series of codes and secret signals were planned so that Joseph would know what to do and whom to trust once he arrived in Bethlehem.

Aristotle approved the plan and the messenger was quickly dispatched to Joseph in Nazareth.

The days seemed to drag on with an unbearable slowness. Every night the Carmelites and astrologers climbed to the temple roof to watch as the planets drew closer and closer together. Judith suggested that the astrologers should go to Jerusalem to Herod and inquire of him where this king was prophesied to be born. Since she knew the Messiah would wrest his kingdom from the reins of the Herodians, and also knowing the insane jealousy with which Herod guarded his throne, she hoped his reaction would be such as to bring about an estrangement between his house and Rome. This way, when the Messiah claimed the throne of Israel they could count on sympathy to their cause from the Romans and possibly on their aid.

Aristotle and the others agreed. Word was sent to Theresa of the astrologers' coming and of their mission, and she gained permission from Herod to act as hostess to their august guests so she could keep the Essenes informed as to all that was said.

Herod welcomed the astrologers with lavish pomp and ceremony. It pleased his overblown sense of importance to be honored by a visit of personages of such renown. He felt complimented that the sages should come to him for the information they desired, and sent for priests and scribes from the temple to search the Scriptures for the birthplace of the Messiah.

Theresa reported that Herod was a congenial and solicitous host and put all of his authority at the disposal of the astrologers. He listened with avid interest to all the Magi said and feigned a fervent desire to see this wondrous Messiah, promising to give aid and sustenance to the Child. He implored the astrologers to return to him from their quest so that he too might go and pay homage to the Child, but inwardly he seethed with rage and jealousy and vowed to Theresa that no Jewish brat would sit on the throne of Israel.

The Carmelites were delighted that the plan was working so well. The seed of threat to his throne was planted in Herod's mind, and all they could do now was wait until the egotistical fool made some bungling move which would raise the ire and contempt of Rome.

The days grew shorter, the nights long and cold. The sun hung low in the sky and hid its warmth behind thick gray clouds. A gloomy mist hung in the air, whipped by the raw wind which blew from over the sea.

A runner from Nazareth brought the news that Mary and Joseph had left for Bethlehem. The Carmelites drew together in tension-filled anticipation. It had begun. There was nothing to do now but wait.

Chapter 14

For what seemed the one-hundredth time that day, Apsafar left the inn and strode through the milling corral to where Editha's husband Mark was stationed at the wide, wooden gate. He approached Mark anxiously and growled, "Nothing still?"

Mark shook his head and Apsafar sighed. He wiped his face on his once clean apron and scanned the sky. The air was sharp and the sky clear and cloudless. The soon-to-set sun cut huge clefts of shadow through the Judean hills.

"There will be a frost. A poor night for sleeping on the ground. They should have come yesterday. Why such a delay?" Apsafar whispered angrily.

Mark tried to relieve Apsafar's fears. "They'll travel slowly. It's a large caravan, and Mary's condition will slow them. A woman is hard to please when her time is near."

Apsafar laughed, thinking of Mark's own tiny son in the family's quarters above the inn. He clapped the younger man's shoulder and said, "You should know!"

Mark flushed at Apsafar's jibe and grinned. He said, "Joseph's helpers are with them and others of the house of David. No evil will befall so many. Besides, the roads are crowded. A patron told me only an hour ago that Jerusalem is ready to burst her walls with Jews from the tribe of Judah registering."

Apsafar couldn't argue with that point. All week long the road past the inn had been a continual sea of humanity as the Jews obeyed the edict from Rome and registered their goods and religion. Sleepy little Bethlehem had become a milling swarm of men, women, children, and beasts who created an ear-shattering cacophony and a nauseating, overpowering stench of human sweat and animal excrement. Roman soldiers were thick as flies, keeping the disgruntled crowds in order by cracking heads and barking orders.

The air was thick with the Jews' hatred. They bitterly resented having to list their worldly possessions just so Rome could levy even higher taxes to swell her coffers, and the very act of registering their religion seemed almost sacrilegious when they were forced to do so under contemptuous, sneering Roman eyes. The entire process was to the Jews an affront and an insult to the Lord God and His chosen people. Their fingers itched to curl around Roman throats, and their blood was hot to fight, but the Romans were many and well-armed and so they fought each other or drank themselves insensible.

Apsafar's inn was filled with such men. Family groups and men of learning and sensibility found lodging in private homes or pitched their tents outside the town, but the inn was a public house and drew the rebellious who sought to drown their frustration and helplessness in wine, and the rabble who used the census as an excuse to brawl and quarrel and indulge their taste for spirits.

Apsafar had guessed such would be the case, and for Mary to mingle with this despicable lot was unthinkable. He forbade even Editha and Sara to enter the inn this week. Sodaphe he needed to cook and help serve the louts, but her sharp tongue could cool any man's lust and her strong arm had sent lechers sprawling before. Lovely, gentle Mary would have caused a riot among such scum.

There was a cave behind the inn that Apsafar used as a stable for his beasts. Sodaphe and the girls had spent days cleaning it out and furnishing it with food and bedding. Mary and Joseph would stay there. It galled Apsafar to think of the future King of Israel being born in such mean surroundings, but it was warm and safe, and completely hidden from prying eyes and wagging tongues. Everything was ready. The plan to protect Mary and his own family from suspicion was good—nothing could go amiss. If only they would come! The waiting was getting on his nerves.

Apsafar sighed and said to Mark, "You are right. They'll come when they come, if it be the will of God."

He went back to the inn and shook his head at Sodaphe's questioning look. She was carrying a large tray laden with bowls of stew and loaves of bread to four Romans seated in a far corner. Apsafar was relieved to see them, even though he despised them, for their presence subdued the surly crowd and kept the arguing on a verbal level.

He went behind the serving table and poured a pitcher of his finest wine from a special barrel hidden in the back and took it to the Romans' table. Though he detested them, at least they had a taste for good wine, and he might need them before this accursed census was over. He set the pitcher on the table.

"Your inn is full, Innkeeper. The census will make you rich," said one.

"Bah!" spat Apsafar. "They are only rabble. They order the cheapest wine and beer I have and care only that it renders them senseless, and then quarrel with me over the price. It's a pleasure to serve someone who can tell the fruit of the vine from vinegar."

The soldiers laughed. Apsafar returned to his work, but his mind knew nothing of what his hands did. Each passing moment increased his worry. Twenty-four hours late! Something must have happened.

Sodaphe dropped a glass and Apsafar clamped his mouth over the rebuke that rushed to his tongue. He patted Sodaphe's clenched fist understandingly and picked it up for her. Poor Sodaphe. The waiting was harder for her, and the strain of keeping silent the worst of all.

The day was nearly gone when at last Mark entered with a barrel of wine upon his shoulder. Apsafar's heart lurched and his mouth went dry. Sodaphe shot him a quick uneasy glance and fled through the back door. Apsafar took the barrel from Mark with trembling hands.

"They've come," Mark whispered.

Apsafar set the barrel down on the floor and Mark left. He mopped his brow and dried his hands, and tried to quell the knotting in his belly. He busied himself with his work and forced himself not to watch the door. It seemed an eternity before a sudden hush fell over the room, telling him that Joseph had arrived.

Apsafar glanced up at the Galileans and let his eyes slide over Mary who clung to Joseph's arm. He feigned a look of contempt and then went back to his work.

The Galileans threaded their way through the crowded room amid whistles and catcalls and lewd remarks. Mary looked pale and frightened, and her eyes were dull with weariness. She blushed at the crude remarks made about her pregnancy, and her slender hands dug into Joseph's arm. The Romans smiled at the raw jokes flying back and forth across the room, and admired the beauty of the pale little Jewess. Joseph ignored the rabble and stood before the serving table, humbly waiting for Apsafar to notice them.

No sign of recognition showed in Apsafar's face when he finally turned to Joseph. "What do you want?" he asked roughly.

"I need a room. We've travelled far and my wife is weary," Joseph answered quietly.

Apsafar glanced at Mary and then let his eyes linger on Joseph, deliberately noting his poor peasant's robes and the center parting of his hair which signified he was a Galilean. The room had quieted; all were watching and listening to see how the innkeeper would handle the situation.

"I have no room," Apsafar said curtly. He turned back to his work and Joseph caught his arm.

"My wife's time has come. You must have one room left," Joseph said tersely.

"I have no room! The inn is full. See for yourself," Apsafar said as he waved his hand toward the rabble.

Joseph looked around. He saw the Romans in the corner, and the leers and hostility on the faces of the others. He felt the tension and danger in the room. His companions began to murmur, angered by the rude manner of the innkeeper and the filth spewed forth by his patrons. He looked back at Apsafar and met his steady gaze for a moment, and then let his face fall in defeat and disappointment. Mary plucked at his sleeve and whispered to him. Joseph looked into her pinched face and then back at Apsafar. "Can you direct me, then, to another place?"

"No," Apsafar said shortly. "Ask in the streets."

The rabble laughed, delighted that the innkeeper had put the wretched Galileans in their place, but some were disappointed that he hadn't given them a room, for the girl looked ripe to deliver and might have provided a story to tell when they returned home.

Joseph's young apprentices were furious. He quickly led them out of the inn where they implored him to let them go back and force that heartless swine to give him a room. Joseph refused. He sent them in search of lodging to distract them and cool their anger, then carefully lifted Mary to the little donkey's back. A spasm of pain fleetingly crossed her face, but then she smiled as Joseph squeezed her hand to reassure her.

He led the donkey through the swarming streets, searching the crowds until he saw the man he sought. Mark was making his way toward them with another barrel for Apsafar on his back, and as he approached, Joseph quickly stepped into his path. "Peace be with you," he murmured.

"And also with you," came the expected reply.

A relieved sigh escaped Joseph's throat. The answer was the right one. This was Apsafar's son-in-law. "I beg you, friend," Joseph said in his normal tone of voice, "can you guide me to a place of shelter? My wife's time is near and we must find shelter quickly."

Mark shifted the heavy barrel and pretended to think, then, waving his arm beyond the inn, he said, "There are caves behind the inn which are used as stables. They are dry and out of the night air. Perhaps you could find shelter there."

"Thank you! A cave is better than nothing at all. God go with you," said Joseph heartily.

Mark gave Joseph a curt nod and continued on his way. Joseph laid his hand on Mary's knee and grinned up at her. "So! We have shelter. If the carpentry business should ever fail, perhaps I could gain employment as an actor in the Roman theaters."

Mary laughed. Joseph found one of his helpers and sent him to find the others to tell them that shelter had been found for himself and Mary and for them to seek shelter for themselves.

Sodaphe and her daughters were waiting in the stable. They wasted little time with greetings as Joseph lifted Mary down from the donkey and carried her to a fresh straw pallet piled high with woolen blankets.

"Her pains have begun, Sodaphe," he said anxiously.

Sodaphe pushed him aside and knelt beside Mary. Her practiced hands quickly examined the panting girl and she nodded. "Good! We thought it might be so, and are prepared." She looked up at Joseph who stood white-faced and anxious. "Tend to the beasts and do not worry. Sara will go for the midwife."

She signaled Sara, who fled through the blanket that covered the opening to the cave. Editha knelt at Mary's other side and held a cup of cool water to her lips. "I too have a son, born only a few weeks ago."

Mary smiled weakly. "I know. I long to see him."

"I'll bring him to you soon. Our sons will be friends, brothers, as you and I are sisters. My son shall serve your son as I love and serve you."

Editha kissed Mary's cheek and then rose. "I must leave you for a while. My breasts are full, which means the nurse is trying to comfort a squalling, hungry babe. I'll be back as soon as I can."

The hours dragged. The midwife proved to be experienced and kind. Assisted by Sodaphe, she did everything she could to ease Mary and bring her labor to fruition as easily and quickly as possible.

Joseph paced the stable floor, shocked by the intensity of women's pain in giving birth. He sat by Mary and gave her his hands to use as leverage against the pain. His heart was wrung each time her frail body arched and convulsed against the outrage it was forced to endure. He marvelled at her courage. She never cried out, but somehow managed to smile and encourage him more than he seemed to comfort her. He was amazed at the intense love he felt for this small, very young girl whom he had doubted such a short time ago and had been reluctant to wed. He thought, if only he could take some of her pain unto himself, but all he could do was pray that the child would come soon and release her from her agony.

Apsafar was nearly at the end of his tether. The long wait for Joseph's arrival had been bad enough, but now the long-awaited one was being born in his own stable and his nerves were frazzled. The rabble seemed overly loud and obnoxious this night and Apsafar had no patience with their drunkenness and raucous laughter.

It was just at the midnight hour when one of the rabble staggered to the door and flung it open, flooding the room with eerie light. The light was so brilliant it hurt his drink-reddened eyes, and he cried out and fell to his knees. His cry and the sudden light startled everyone in the room, and they rushed to the door to see.

The planets had come together and formed what seemed to be a vast, brilliant star. It hung directly over the inn, and its radiance put the moon to shame and bathed the entire countryside with a shimmering silver glow. The patrons were momentarily paralyzed with fear. Some began to pray aloud and wailed that the day of doom had come upon them. Then someone shouted that it was only a comet passing close to earth. This was a natural enough explanation, one they could understand, and they grasped at it with relief. Their panic faded and they laughed at their own foolishness. Some went back to their wine, and others, sobered by the experience, went to their beds, but a few stayed and watched, not content with such a simple explanation.

Apsafar had followed the mad scramble to the door and pushed his way through the terrified rabble until he stood in the open corral. Mark was beside him, and the two men watched as the increasing brilliance gave the illusion that the star was slowly descending into the very heart of Bethlehem.

Mark clutched at Apsafar's arm and stammered with fear. "What is it, Apsafar? What does it mean?"

"It is the Star of Israel, the sign of the Messiah. Mary's travail is over. The Promised One is come."

Apsafar was so overcome that he could hardly speak. He lifted his head and let the light bathe his face. He closed his eyes and raised his arms in a gesture of prayer and supplication, as though to absorb its holiness and peace into his body. Tears coursed down his cheeks and his soul soared in exultation. He would have dropped to his knees and prayed aloud, but a Roman voice drew him back to himself and he quickly dashed his tears away lest they see.

"What say you, Innkeeper? Does the God of the Jews send a sign?"

Apsafar pulled himself together and snorted. "A comet, as they say, or perhaps a falling star. Why ask me? I am no astrologer! I deal in wine and lodging. My mind is filled with trying to please that cantankerous rabble which leaves no time to contemplate on heavenly phenomena."

The Romans laughed and went back to the inn. As soon as they were out of earshot, Mark whispered, "Listen, Apsafar! Do you hear? Listen!"

Apsafar cocked his head and strained his ears. At first he heard only the usual sounds of night, the rustle of restless beasts in the corral and the muted laughter from inside the inn. He heard a far-off murmur of voices coming from the town where others had been awakened by the light. But then as he strained, a new sound reached his ears. Music! Voices singing! He tried to concentrate.

The music grew louder. Not only voices, but instruments—strings and drums and trumpets, all blending in a harmony so beautiful that gooseflesh crawled on his arms and shivers raced down his back.

No mortals could make such sounds! Apsafar's entire being vibrated with the sound. It seemed to flow into his veins, filling him with a sweetness so profound his mortal flesh could not endure. He gave a strangled cry and fell full-face to the ground.

Then the music faded, and the night was completely still. Nothing moved. Only the light remained to assure Apsafar that it had not all been a dream—the light and Mark's senseless form stretched out beside him. He aroused Mark from his stupor and they stumbled back to the inn.

In the cave behind the inn, Sodaphe and Editha stood with Joseph at the doorway, awestricken by the panoply of light that bathed all of Judea. They listened to the music that seemed to come from everywhere, the trees and rocks and very earth, from the shimmering light that moved in sheets across the sky. They heard voices singing, "Peace on Earth! Good will to men!" and "Behold, a Son is given, and His name is Wonderful Counsellor!"

Joseph's tears fell unashamedly. "How is it that God can so love this world!" he whispered.

For the only time in her life, Sodaphe was speechless. She tore her eyes away from the star and looked to where Mary lay.

The cave was awash with the light from the star, but Mary's face shone so with joy she seemed to reflect the light back to heaven from whence it came. The babe lay asleep in the crook of her arm, his tiny face kissed by the light. Mary's red-gold hair spilled across the pillow, and the child's tiny fist clasped a small, curling lock.

Sara was standing entranced at the foot of the pallet. The wonder of the star was as naught compared to the wonder of the baby in Mary's arms. She was consumed with love. Her arms ached to hold him. She longed to touch his tiny hand and caress his downy cheek. She watched the pulse beat on the top of his head. His hair was the same red-gold as his mother's, and Sara wondered if his eyes were like Mary's also.

Mary's eyes fluttered open. She saw Sara, and understood the naked hunger on the girl's face. She beckoned to Sara and lifted the babe into the girl's arms.

Sara held her precious bundle to her breast and kissed his silky brow. At that moment she knew her life would be dedicated to Mary's child, and nothing else would ever have any importance to her. In some inexplicable way Mary's son commanded every ounce of love Sara ever had and ever would have. Any love she would try to give to a husband or child of her own would only be a sham and a shadow of the love she gave whole-heartedly to this child.

Sara began to weep. She wept with joy of a glory far surpassing what had been told of all the glories of her people in the days of old. She wished that all the world might know the beauty, joy, and glory of the Messiah's life in their own hearts, minds, and beings. She felt a new light, new vision, and a new experience being born in every cell of her being.

Mary watched and understood what was happening to Sara. She let her hold the child until Joseph approached the pallet and said, "There are some shepherds here. They wish to see the child. They saw the star and heard the music from the heavens and claim a choir of angels directed them here."

Mary smiled and took the babe from Sara's arms. "Let them come in. It is just for such men that our son is born. Let them see the One who will lead their souls to God."

As the lowly shepherds knelt in homage to a king they only understood within their hearts, a lone figure stood upon a parapet around a tower of the governor's palace in Caesarea. Justin had watched the advancing planets move slowly from east to west until they converged into one great star over the little town of Bethlehem.

Fear and excitement seemed to squeeze the very breath

from Justin's lungs and he struggled for air. He was seized by a trembling so violent that he had to hold on to the parapet wall to keep from falling. This was not a known phenomenon!

Everything that Judith had taught him came rushing into his mind, and he somehow knew in every fiber of his being that the miracle of the star had to do with Judith and the gentle people on Mt. Carmel. What was the secret that he'd always felt she withheld from him? What plot did they conspire to bring about that would manifest such a sign from God? A war with Rome?

Justin was gripped by cold terror. Judith could never win a war with Rome: Augustus would crucify her! If only he knew the meaning of the star, perhaps he could save her! His knuckles turned white as his grip on the wall tightened. Beads of sweat stood out on his brow and the cords of his huge neck bulged.

"What omen is this?" he cried aloud into the night. "What will happen in the world?"

He heard a voice, not with his ears, but in his mind. A voice he felt rather than heard, a voice that reverberated through his brain like thunder.

"It has begun!"

"What has begun? In the name of all the gods, tell me what?" But there was only silence and the night and the wondrous light over Judea.

The anguish of not knowing brought Justin to his knees. In frustration and helplessness he pounded his fists upon the parapet floor. A cry of grief and longing and need tore from his aching throat.

"Judith! Judith!"

Chapter 15

The planets parted and the light began to fade. By the first gray light before dawn there was nothing to testify to that wondrous night except the memories of those who had witnessed the glory of the star. Pious Jews spoke of the night's events in hushed tones, recalling other phenomena mentioned in their Scriptures, and quoting to one another the words of Balaam, son of Beor. "A star shall advance from Jacob, and a staff shall rise from Israel."

The Romans remembered the comet which appeared in the heavens when Julius Caesar was assassinated on the Ides of March, and shuddered with dread when they speculated on what dire event this omen foretold. The rabble laughed and scoffed and explained it away as the natural consequence of drinking too much wine.

Only the Essenes knew the truth. Judith and the Carmelites had watched from the temple roof. They didn't need a messenger to tell them that Mary's son had been born. The star told all, and the morning worship rang with songs of praise.

Rebkah had been waiting on the road that led from Jerusalem since long before anyone in Bethlehem stirred from their beds. She waited for the three astrologers Judith had sent to Herod, and who, as planned, would follow the star to Bethlehem. She was dressed as the poorest peasant, with a battered basket on her arm and a bright red, ragged shawl drawn over her head by which the astrologers would recognize her. She hid in a grove of ancient fig trees a short way from the inn. When she heard the sound of horses coming toward her, she stepped out onto the road and began to walk quickly back toward Bethlehem, her shoulders hunched and head bowed—she looked like nothing more than a peasant girl scurrying home to prepare the morning meal.

When the astrologers and their Roman escort drew abreast of her, one of the wise men reigned in his ungainly camel and called out to her.

"Girl! What do you here before the light of day?"

Rebkah stopped and clutched her basket in feigned fear. "Sir, I only go to glean before the owner of the field arises. I cause no harm."

"You need not fear us, child," the astrologer said kindly. "We only wish to know if there is an inn nearby where we can rest. Do you know of such?"

Rebkah nodded dumbly and ran before them until she brought them to Apsafar's corral. The astrologer offered her a silver coin. Rebkah stared at it with hungry eyes and then snatched it from his hand and fled.

The astrologers caused a flurry of excitement in Bethlehem as the people came out to stare at their rich robes and flowing beards, and the comical, awkward beasts they rode. When questioned by Roman and Jewish authorities alike, they explained that they had tracked the star from the lands of their birth and would stay in Bethlehem as long as the star remained visible to make charts and maps and calculations which they would study when they returned to their homelands. The officials saw the strange instruments and parchments filled with signs and symbols which made no sense to them, and accepted their explanation, letting them follow their curious profession in peace. Within a few days they were no longer objects of curiosity, and when two more men of wisdom, one from Persia and the other from India, arrived, they elicited little more than a passing glance.

When the census ended and the Romans and Herodians left Bethlehem, the astrologers remained. Each night they could be found on the roofs or in the hills, measuring and watching, and by day they stayed in their rooms in Apsafar's inn, ostensibly compiling their findings and setting them in order.

But the Essenes of Bethlehem knew who they were, and with one excuse or another, found their way to Apsafar's inn to listen in awe as the wise men explained the heavenly signs in accordance with prophecies of old.

The Persian, Achlar, by using the mathematical methods which had been handed down through the ages, as well as the teachings of the Persians from the days of Zend, Og, and Uhjltd, interpreted both the astrological and the natural laws for them. Ashtueil, the Indian, taught them how when the various forces of man are added to the creative forces necessary to keep the balance in the universal forces, the earth must bring forth that which would make man's balance of force with the Creative Energy as One. They praised the Elect for their efforts through prayer, faith, and purity of thought in bringing the vibrations of man into balance with those of the universe, thus making it possible for a pure and spotless vessel to be born into the world through which the Divine could become manifest.

These things were all reported to Mary and Joseph in the cave behind the inn.

When the census was over, their friends had pleaded with Mary and Joseph to leave, but Joseph had refused. The cave was warm and comfortable; it was better to stay hidden from unbelieving eyes. The fewer who knew of a child born on the night of the star, the better.

Mary was more than content to spend her forty days of seclusion in the quiet privacy of the cozy stable. The women visited her every day, bringing food and news, but there were long, happy hours with only Joseph and her babe. Those were peaceful, precious days for Mary, the only ones she would ever know as a simple wife and mother alone with her own little family.

When the babe was eight days old, he was circumcised according to the Law, and Joseph named him Jeshua, as had been dictated by the angel. There was no public celebration as there had been for Elizabeth's John, but every Essene household held their own private celebration, and "Jeshua ben Joseph" was whispered in every Essene ear.

Mt. Carmel marked the eighth day of Jeshua's life with a mingling of quiet joy and deep sorrow. Philo had never recovered from his shock at the manner of Zachariah's death, and on the same day that the long-awaited Messiah received the mark of Abraham, Philo's soul abandoned the realm of earth. Judith watched his body being entombed beside that of his old friend Enos, and was overcome by the curious sense of witnessing the passing of one age and the beginning of a new.

It surprised no one when Judith was elected to Philo's position of recorder for the sect, though it was the first time in the history of the Elect that a woman had been so honored. There were a few dissenting voices, of course, but only a few. She was the most revered and respected of all the holy women, and her gifts and abilities were beyond compare.

The Essenes were content. The Messiah had come, and those who would guide him to his ultimate goal were well-prepared for the task.

When the forty days of Mary's seclusion had passed, the astrologers could at last pay homage to the child whom they had come so far to see. They waited for the cover of darkness, then groped their way along the narrow path through the tangled underbrush to the cave.

The wise men had been told nearly everything there was to know about Mary and Joseph, but even so, they were not prepared for the humble simplicity they found. It seemed incongruous that the most exalted soul ever to enter the earth should be born in such meager surroundings, and of the unassuming, modest peasant couple who greeted them at the doorway. Only Mary's extraordinary beauty suggested they'd come to the right place.

Joseph bade them welcome and ushered them into the dimly lit cave and led them to a low, rough table to one side of the room. The richly dressed men lowered themselves to the plump cushions as Mary served wine and sweets like any other dutiful wife. They were startled when Mary poured herself a small portion and sat at the table with them, but quickly remembered that this was a household of the Essenes, and Essene women had far more privileges than those in the rest of the world.

At first the conversation was stilted and restrained. Mary's presence was disconcerting, and the astrologers were unsure as to what subjects to pursue with a lowly carpenter until Joseph led them to speak of the star and of the events which had led them to Bethlehem. From then on, the talk grew more and more lively. They jumped from subject to subject—numerology, astrology, religions from all lands, politics, and, of course, the education and upbringing of the child who slept in the manger. Mary entered the conversation often. She spoke with easy confidence, and, like Joseph, with a surprising knowledge of any subject.

The astrologers' initial awe of Mary slowly dissipated, and they looked at her now with affection and fatherly pleasure. They were also impressed by Joseph. His keen intelligence and quick understanding of the heart of a matter belied that he was only a simple carpenter. The wine warmed them. The peace and love which seemed to permeate the stable flowed about and through them until they were content and at ease. The conversation was so stimulating and satisfying that they almost forgot the purpose for which they had come, until a stirring and the mewling of an awakening babe came from the manger in the shadows across the room.

Mary smiled and rose. "Jeshua wishes to meet his honored guests. I'll bring him to you."

She took a lamp from the table and went to the far side of the stable, chasing the shadows before her as she went. The astrologers were amazed to see that the precious child slept in the midst of a few sheep, a pair of oxen, an aging cow and her calf, and a little gray donkey who seemed to stand guard over the shallow wooden manger.

Mary bent over the manger, tending to Jeshua's needs. She crooned and whispered in the baby's ear and he quieted at the sound of her voice. The astrologers stood to walk toward her as she straightened with the child in her arms, but as she turned and faced them, they stood transfixed.

An aura of light began to glow and shimmer around Mary and Jeshua, growing in brightness and intensity until the beasts and the manger and the walls of the cave receded from sight into a glowing white mist. Mary was smiling down at Jeshua. The babe was a tiny replica of his mother, with the same red-gold hair, the same piercing, knowing, blue-gray eyes. They seemed a vision out of time and space, a tear in the fabric of the universe where none else existed but the mother and child, and the ghostly echo of the haunting, celestial music which had filled the air on the night of the star.

The wise men fell to their knees in rapture, their souls transported to realms no body of flesh had known. They prostrated themselves to the floor of the cave and dared not look again at the vision before them. They were alarmed and terrified. They had seen a vision of Divine Holiness. What mortal would ever survive it?

Mary's sweet, melodious voice reached their ears and calmed their fear. They apprehensively raised their eyes and saw only a little Jewish girl and her first-born son. She drew near to them and held the babe out to them.

"See?" she murmured. "He is only a babe, our wonderful Jeshua. A babe like any other."

Joseph helped the men to their feet and they approached Mary timidly. Ashtueil stared into the babe's tiny face and then met Mary's serene, knowing gaze. His face turned ashen. His hands began to tremble uncontrollably and when he spoke his voice was barely audible. "I have seen the face of God!"

The others stared at him in shocked silence. No one moved or hardly dared to breathe, for the words were the words of blasphemy. Even the beasts seemed to sense the tension in the air and stood silently watching and unmoving.

Then the atmosphere changed. A sense of profound peace settled over them. The spirit of truth touched every soul, and those in that humble cave set deep into the hills of Judea knew in their hearts that Ashtueil's words were true.

The moment passed. Achlar cleared his throat and wiped his eyes on a piece of silk. He drew from his robes a delicately carved ivory box and presented it to Joseph as a gift for the child. The box contained a precious resin from a small, spiny tree in his land which was used as incense in solemn religious rites. The resin was called myrrh, and in the ancient mystery cults, represented the healing force in man's existence.

Ashtueil, following his colleague's lead, gave Joseph an exquisite, tiny, white alabaster urn, also filled with an incense called frankincense. It, too, was a resin from a tree in Persia, and represented the ethereal phase in the course of man. The three who had come from Herod's court offered gold to the child as a symbol of the materiality of man.

Thus the gifts brought to the child symbolized mind, body, and soul, the most precious and honored gifts which could be bestowed upon a person in the mystical, spiritual world of those men.

Joseph, knowing the meaning of such gifts, was overwhelmed. He tried to think of appropriate words to say, but could only stammer with confusion. The wise men waved aside his thanks, and bowing low before Mary and Jeshua, disappeared into the night.

The next morning the astrologers were gone from Bethlehem. They told Joseph that they had been warned in a dream not to return to Herod's court, and so left during the night and followed a secret route back to their homelands.

Mary and Joseph had little time to ponder the visit from the wise men, for it was time for them to go home. The others in the caravan who had accompanied them to Bethlehem had returned long before, but Mary's confinement had forced them to stay for forty days. They were both anxious to go. Joseph worried over his carpentry shop, and Mary was eager to present her son to her mother and friends in Galilee. But first they would go to Jerusalem to offer sacrifice for Mary's purification and to ransom their first-born from the Lord.

The Essenes had waited for that day throughout the entire time of their existence, and every one who could made the journey to Jerusalem to see the Messiah enter the House of God. All of the eleven girls chosen with Mary were there. Judas brought Eloise, Margil, Anna, and Judith from Mt. Carmel, for nothing could have stopped Mary's teachers from witnessing the event. Joseph's brother Alpheus joined with a group of Joseph's helpers and their friends and neighbors from Nazareth, bringing his own young sons so that one day they would remember, and follow their cousin Jeshua ben Joseph wherever he led.

Sara was so insistent that she see her beloved Jeshua ransomed from the Lord that Apsafar had been compelled to hire a man to oversee the inn so he could take her. He ranted and grumbled over the needless expense. Hadn't Sara spent the last forty days in the company of the child? Why more? But Sodaphe's sharp tongue had silenced his objections, and once Joseph and Mary were safely on their way, his own family followed.

Syrus and his family from Bethany came, with Lazarus jumping up and down in youthful exuberance while sober Martha frowned her disapproval. Zebedee and Salome waited at Josie's, where Mary and Joseph would stay, while Salone brought their mother and Ismeria to Mary's home in Nazareth to wait for them there. Everyone was in a festive mood.

Mary was the only one who didn't share the others' excitement. As soon as the walls of Jersualem loomed into sight, she was again overtaken by a sense of foreboding, just as she had been when she'd entered the city a few months before with Elizabeth and Zachariah. The city seemed threatening, as though warning her that once she passed through its walls it would swallow her up and she'd never come out again. She clutched Jeshua tightly to her breast and tried to dispel her gloom by telling herself it was only the memory of Zachariah's death that made her feel that way, but she knew it was more than that.

Mary hid her fears from everyone, telling no one, not even Joseph. She joined in the festivities with a forced gaiety, and if anyone noted her pale, strained face, they simply thought it weariness due to her recent confinement.

Nothing untoward happened to confirm Mary's fears. The pigeons were sacrificed and the shekels paid: everyone rejoiced when the Law was fulfilled. Only one incident marred the day.

They were all in the Court of Gentiles on their way out of the temple precincts when suddenly above the din of gaiety they heard a voice crying, "Make way! Make way!"

Those clustered around Mary and Jeshua parted, and an old man stumbled and shuffled his way toward them. Zebedee recognized him as Simeon, an old pious man who spent his days in the temple telling anyone who would listen how the Holy Spirit had revealed to him that he would not experience death until he had seen the Anointed of the Lord. When he stood before Mary, his rheumy old eyes filled with tears. He reached out to take Jeshua, and Mary, having pity for the harmless old man, allowed him to take the babe from her arms. He stared into Jeshua's face and then raised his own to heaven, tears flowing freely down his face.

"Now, Master," he cried, "you can dismiss your servant in peace; you have fulfilled your word. For my eyes have witnessed your saving deed displayed for all the peoples to see; a revealing light to the Gentiles, the glory of your people Israel."

Joseph and Mary and the others watched in astonishment, marvelling at the old man's words. Then Simeon gave Jeshua back to his mother's arms and raised his hand in blessing over them and said, "This child is destined to be the downfall and rise of many in Israel, a sign that will be opposed, and you yourself shall be pierced with a sword, so that the thoughts of many hearts may be laid bare."

It was a sobering incident. Since his words seemed to confirm Mary's own sense of doom, she was overwhelmed by a desire to go home to Nazareth at once, to take Jeshua out from under so many watchful eyes and live like anyone else in quiet obscurity.

The others remarked upon the prophecy, and wondered at its meaning. Then they brushed it aside as the ravings of a pitiable old man and continued on to the feast, but Mary tucked it away in her heart to be pondered at a later time.

Mary's wish was granted, and once they returned to Nazareth, their life was not different from the other Nazarenes. Her days were filled with household chores. Flax and wool waited to be spun, there were meals to prepare and sewing and mending to do, and of course, Jeshua to tend.

Every morning Mary arose before Jeshua and Joseph stirred so that she might have a quiet hour to herself to pray and ponder on all those things she had hidden away in her heart. As soon as the sun was up she went to the village well with two of her closest neighbors, Mateal and Jacobinus, to draw the water they would use that day and to gossip and exchange the latest bits of news about the progress their sons were making. Mateal and Jacobinus' sons were only a little older than Jeshua, and Mary often caught herself watching them and wondering who these little souls were, and for what purpose they had entered the earth to be born so close to Jeshua. Neither Mateal nor Jacobinus were Essenes, so Mary could not discuss her musings with them, but again could only ponder them in her heart.

So the days passed in idyllic joy. Jeshua's presence dispelled the awkward, embarrassed relationship that had formerly existed between Mary and Joseph, and their mutual love and concern for the child grew to encompass one another. Joseph accepted Jeshua as his own, and no one would ever have guessed he wasn't the boy's natural father. Joseph did not approach Mary physically. It was as though they had reached a silent agreement that the connubial act was unseemly with Jeshua under their roof, and besides that, their whole attention must be concentrated upon the Anointed One. A child born of their union would naturally demand his share of their time and devotion. There would be time enough to bring other souls into the world when Jeshua went to Mt. Carmel.

The Carmelites kept close contact with the little family in Nazareth. A meticulous record of Jeshua's progress and growth was kept in the library at Mt. Carmel, and each new tooth became a cause for rejoicing. Jeshua drew them to Nazareth like a magnet. He was a merry, affectionate baby who laughed with glee and held his chubby arms out to anyone who would pick him up. Judith became his special friend, and the mere sound of Josie's voice sent him clamoring for her soft lap. They tried not to go to Nazareth too often lest they arouse the suspicions of Mary's neighbors, but to stay away for long was a real sacrifice, and Josie especially would grieve when it was time to leave him.

For a long time they refrained from telling Mary and Joseph of the disturbing letters the community on Mt. Carmel was receiving from Judea. Herod was furious that the astrologers had not returned to the palace to tell him if they'd found the child they sought, and he had sent his barbarians more than once to Bethlehem to question the people regarding the night of the star. Sodaphe's letters were full of contempt for the soldiers' crudeness and rough manners, but Judith detected a note of hysteria that grew in every one.

Judith didn't like it. Sodaphe wasn't one to panic or cringe from Herod. She had always been the one who was most open and forthright about her beliefs and cared not who knew or what others might think. The fact that she was genuinely frightened set off a warning bell in Judith's mind. She didn't like the tone of Theresa's letters, either. They too contained a ring of fear. She warned that Herod was becoming obsessed with finding the child who threatened his throne, and no amount of reason could deter him. Even his beloved sister Salome, who thought the whole thing was nonsense, seemed to have no influence.

Judith's efforts to protect Mary and Joseph from undue worry proved useless, for by mid-spring the rumors of Herod's obsessive quest had even reached Nazareth. Priests and scribes were being ordered to appear at the palace, where Herod personally questioned them about the Messiah. His demands were totally unreasonable, and his manner like one demented. All of Jerusalem quaked in terror beneath his fanatic fury.

Mary and Joseph listened to these reports with horror. No matter how loyal their friends were, Herod had exquisite means of torture available which could force the truth out of the most staunch defender.

Mary clutched Jeshua to her breast and looked to Joseph for some consolation. "We are safe in Galilee, aren't we, Joseph?"

Joseph laughed derisively and without humor. "Who is safe anywhere these days? Galilee seethes with hatred for Herod, Rome, the publicans; our young men preach rebellion and boldly accuse their fathers of cowardice in paying taxes to Rome. Sons are leaving the homes of their fathers and are taking to the hills to join with bands of robbers and bandits to attack and harass Roman contingents on the roads. Sepphoris is a hotbed of unrest. The elders and priests counsel patience and submission, and this only angers them more. The firebrands still brood and nurse their bitterness over the census, and the warm days ahead will only serve to goad them into the hills. The whole land rests on a volcano of hatred, ready to erupt at the slightest incident."

Then, seeing Mary's despair, he pulled her close and held her in his strong, protecting arms, a gesture so unusual that Mary almost forgot her fear.

"Do not fear, Mary. The Lord will not forsake His Chosen One. Herod will never find Jeshua."

Mary was comforted, but as spring turned into summer

the rumors increased, and Herod's questioning became more and more ferocious. Rome was reluctantly drawn into his insane quest and had halfheartedly beaten Apsafar in an attempt to gain information.

The days became a nightmare. The Carmelites met and talked and prayed, but no one could find a way to pacify Herod's rage. Then Joseph and Mary each dreamed a dream in which the Lord said, "Get up, take the child and his mother and flee to Egypt. Stay there until I tell you otherwise. Herod is searching for the child to destroy him."

Mary and Joseph awoke from the dream at the same instant. They never questioned its validity, but arose from their pallet and quickly and silently began to gather together their few belongings.

"We'll need animals. Where do I get them at this time of night?" Joseph whispered.

"Wait," Mary answered. She slipped from the house and ran through the dark to Mateal's. She stole to Mateal's pallet and gently shook her awake. Mateal sat up with a start, and Mary clasped her hand over Mateal's mouth lest she cry out and awaken the household.

"Joseph is in trouble. We must flee Nazareth. We need animals, Mateal."

Mateal stared for a moment in astonishment at Mary's pale face, made even paler by the shaft of moonlight that spilled through the open door. She felt her fear and heard the urgency in her voice. She didn't question Mary. Whatever it was that Joseph had done, it was better she didn't know. She only nodded her head in agreement and crept out into the night to help her friend. By the time they were ready, two gray donkeys stood by the door.

Joseph loaded their possessions on one and lifted Mary and Jeshua onto the other. Before the sun peeked over the hills, the carpenter and his family from Nazareth was gone.

That same morning, as Judith was meditating in her usual place above the sea, she saw a vision of an old man who read to her from the scroll of Hosea. "When Israel was a child I loved him, out of Egypt I called my son."

The vision disturbed her. She told Aristotle and Judas what she had seen, but it wasn't until Mary and Joseph arrived at Mt. Carmel that the meaning became clear.

Jeshua must be smuggled out of the country! But how? The way was long and hard and fraught with danger. They couldn't possibly go alone. Besides, for a single family who just happened to have one little boy, precisely the age of the one Herod sought, suddenly to migrate to Egypt would surely be brought to Herod's attention. They decided that others would be sent before and after Joseph, to afford physical protection for the family and to detract suspicion from them. There was a small community of Essènes just outside Heliopolis who would gladly welcome the Palestinians into their fold, so the problem of where they would stay in Egypt was solved.

The first pilgrims left before a week was out, with more following every few days. Mary's sister Salone was among the first group, and Josie won her heart's desire to go with Mary as her handmaid. When the last small group wound its way down the side of Carmel, it seemed to Judith as if the light had gone out in Israel and a dark cloud loomed just over the horizon. Loneliness settled upon her like a yoke of iron. Her loved ones seemed to be taken from her one by one—Phinehas and Enos by death, Justin, whom, she was told, was in Rome and had gone from her life without a farewell, and now Jeshua sent into exile.

Judith went to the library, but restlessness drove her to the infirmary, and the sight of the sick only increased her grief. She went to the House of Lodgement like a child seeking consolation, but the grief of Elkatma, Ann, and Ismeria, who would live at Carmel until Salone returned, was as great as her own, and they could offer no solace.

She was bereft and alone. Judith could find no comfort.

Chapter 16

Work had always been Judith's weapon against loneliness. The City of Salt was nearing completion, and she threw herself into the task of readying it for occupancy. Eloise was appointed supervisor over the school, and monks from Carmel, Damascus, and other communities of the Brotherhood around the world went to the Judean wilderness to take up the work of preserving the Word of the Lord. It was Judith's responsibility as recorder to organize and set up the procedures for the scriptorium and the school, and she spent most of her time in Judea. But each time she returned to Mt. Carmel, it was with a sense of relief.

The hills surrounding the City of Salt made her think of Justin. His rugged, Roman face seemed outlined in every jagged rock, and the bleak barrenness which stretched as far as the eye could see was a painful reminder of the dull ache of longing in her own empty heart. Even the Salt Sea could give her no solace, as any body of water usually did, for it lay thick and heavy and void of life, and its sluggish, oily surface reflected her spirits. She'd climb to the top of the watchtower and stare into the noxious mists that hovered over the sea like a filmy shroud, as though trying to see what awful secrets of evil it hid there, what portents of doom it breathed into the air, until she became as desolate as the sands of salt around the sea, and then she'd flee to the green living forests on Mt. Carmel.

Carmel received word from Heliopolis that Mary and Jeshua had safely arrived, but there was little time to rejoice. By then it seemed as if Belial and all his demons were taking their revenge for Jeshua's flight, and were making a final effort to destroy the Children of Light before he could grow to manhood.

Herod's search for the babe sought by the astrologers intensified, and Judith sent Elizabeth and John to the City of Salt for safety. Herod elicited the aid of Rome in his search for Jeshua, and Roman soldiers became a common sight on Mt. Carmel. Judith's respect and admiration for Aristotle was boundless as she watched him handle the soldiers with urbane finesse, laughing and joking with them and using their own forms of logic to ridicule Herod's obsession. She saw the surly, overbearing soldiers transformed into congenial, agreeable guests under the influence of Aristotle's opulent, luxurious room. But such tactics were not to last.

Theresa's letters became increasingly frantic. As Herod's cancer ravaged his body, the pain ravaged his mind. He became a raving beast, maddened with the fear of dying, and burning with the obsession to find and destroy the Jewish brat whom the priests said would rule over Israel before he died. The palace quaked at the very sound of his voice. Servants were killed over the slightest provocation, and his wives fled from his sight. His own barbarian guard, and the Romans stationed in Antonia, trembled in fear of his insanity, no more immune to his wrath than the lowliest servant.

Priests and scribes were dragged to the palace where Herod screamed and raved and threatened them with death if the child was not found. The priests did their best to convince him that no such child existed, but their arguments only angered Herod the more, and all of Jerusalem trembled in terror.

The soldiers who came to Mt. Carmel were no longer just sneering and derisive. Their fear of Herod drove them to acts of cruelty and physical abuse until even Judith was struck as she tried to convince them that the people on Mt. Carmel knew nothing of a star, or of events in Judea. No longer could they be mollified with fine wine and delicacies from the kitchens, or by Aristotle's wit and hospitality. Mathias succumbed to his ulcer. Judas lay bleeding and broken in the infirmary. Aristotle looked drained and weary, while all of Carmel prayed for deliverance.

It was not only those at Carmel who suffered, but all of their people throughout Judea. Apsafar was questioned repeatedly, until Sodaphe and the girls were frantic. Sodaphe begged Apsafar to flee from Bethlehem, but he refused, afraid that such an act would only convince his enemies that there was such a child. At any cost they must be made to believe that no babe destined to be king had been born in Bethlehem. He steadfastly maintained that all he knew of the astrologers was that they had stayed at his inn and had studied the star, and where they had gone from there, he knew not.

In their hearts the Romans believed him. Most of them had often stayed at Apsafar's inn and liked the burly, caustic Jew, but their fear of Herod was more real than their concern for Apsafar. They tried to force him to admit to anything, even if it was a lie, that would appease Herod's wrath and give them all a little peace. Apsafar was severely beaten and his whole family threatened, and yet he remained silent. A broken rib punctured his lung and he lay on his pallet unable to move, for his racking cough sent searing flames of torture through his breast.

When Herod learned that his only valid source of information had been rendered speechless, he said not a word but retreated to his rooms in brooding silence. The entire court waited in dread, for they knew from experience that Herod's silences were more dangerous than his rages. When he finally emerged from his self-imposed solitude, his eyes glittered with an insane glee and his mouth twisted in a self-satisfied sneer of such evil that even Salome recoiled from him.

He ordered a lavish banquet to be prepared, with musicians, dancing girls, acrobats, and actors, and decreed that the High Priest and all members of the Sanhedrin and all the influential Jews of Jerusalem be ordered to attend the gala. That done, he then called for a scribe and issued an edict that all male children from six months to two years of age, from Bethlehem to Nazareth, be destroyed that same night.

The soldiers received their orders with horror and disbelief. It was madness! Insanity! They had no stomach for slaughtering children, but they knew if they did not obey Herod they would die.

Theresa gathered her friends about her and managed to save a few Jewish children, but there wasn't time to rescue many. Herod had planned his massacre well, and only a pitiful few escaped his madness.

The soldiers did their job quickly and without thinking, for to think would lead to insanity. They went in the night without warning, crashing open doors and without explanation wrenching children from their mother's arms, strangling and beheading them before their horrified, disbelieving eyes. The destruction swept from Bethlehem to Nazareth, leaving a people paralyzed with horror as the sounds of merriment and laughter floated through the night air from Herod's palace.

Editha, Rebkah, Eunice, Mateal, Jacobinus—all watched as their sons were murdered. Apsafar struggled from his bed and tried to stop the slaughter of his only grandson, but his futile effort caused his lung to hemorrhage, and Apsafar drowned in his own blood.

Indeed in Ramah was heard the sound of moaning, of bitter weeping. Indeed did Rachel mourn her children and refuse to be consoled, for her children were no more! The blood of the innocents cried out from the soil. The groan and cry of the people mingled with the stench of death and flew to the ears of the Lord. But the people could not be comforted, for they did not know that God's right arm was waiting in Egypt until he grew in strength and wisdom, and that he would then slay their enemies with the mighty sword of his mouth.

News of the slaughter sped to Mt. Carmel as though borne on the wings of an eagle. The Carmelites rent their clothes and heaped ashes upon their heads. Their keening cry stilled the soughing pines and hushed the forest life, causing the people in Caesaria to shiver at the eerie, almost inaudible sound that floated through the black, still night.

Nothing had ever come so close to destroying the Remnant as the carnage wrought by Herod on the sons of Israel. Everyone known to be sympathetic to the Carmelite school of thought had especially been sought out. All the girls of the twelve whose sons were not yet weaned lost them in the massacre, and their cry of reproof and recrimination assailed the ears of the leaders of the Elect. Why wasn't more consideration given for their sons! Did their sons not have the right to live? Their sons were dead, and their anguish stopped their ears and hardened their hearts: they turned away in bitterness.

Judith bore the brunt of their anger and accusations. It

had been her plan to anger Herod so that he would commit some deed which would alienate his house from Rome, and though that was precisely the outcome, the price paid was too high. Her guilt drove Judith to the edge of madness. She neither ate nor slept. She refused to speak. She sat in her cell and moaned, her body rocking back and forth like an imbecilic child. Elkatma washed her body and combed her hair. She fed her by forcing a thin gruel down her throat, and led her by the hand to the latrine. But Judith remained oblivious, her soul locked away in an unreachable pit in hell.

From the time when she was but a child and newly arrived at Mt. Carmel, the mood of the Elect had instinctively followed Judith's moods, and now the Mount languished in paralyzing despair. Work at the City of Salt came to a virtual standstill. No one dared to venture into the Judean hills lest they draw attention to themselves, and with Mathias dead and Judith and Judas both wholly incapacitated, the monks milled about like sheep who had lost their leader.

Aristotle did his best to rally their flagging spirits, but without Judith it proved a futile task. There was no one he could turn to for help, no one with whom he could share his frustrations and helplessness. He grew thin and haggard and ill-tempered until everyone shunned him and he was left alone with his own guilt for the role he had played in the slaughter.

It seemed that the plans and work of centuries had crumbled to dust. The torch of knowledge was sputtering and would die without the fuel of faith. Aristotle cried unto the Lord, but heard no reply. He hovered on the brink of despondency, and for the first time in his life questioned his belief that he had come into the world to lead this people. He was at the end of his endurance when a messenger arrived with a letter from Egypt, and a spark of hope and understanding replenished the Light on Mt. Carmel.

When word of the slaughter had reached Egypt, Mary and Joseph and all those who had preceded and followed them into that land went into mourning. Mary recognized the mysterious hand of God working through the carnage, and again it was she who healed the hearts of her people.

The letter from Mary was written to Judith and to all at

Mt. Carmel, reminding them of Isaiah's prophecy. The children did not die for naught. Those little souls had incarnated for the express purpose of bringing that prophecy to pass. Judith was only an instrument used by God to bring that prophecy to fulfillment. Judith must have faith. They must all have faith! If Judith had not been the chosen instrument, then another would have been, but she was chosen because she did have that faith, and also the ability to persevere under adversity. She must look within herself and find those qualities which God had given her. She had the strength and endurance to accept and handle this role, and she must use them and not fail the Lord now! She must use her God-given will to overcome her grief and guilt, and go on to accomplish God's plan.

Aristotle read Mary's letter over and over to Judith until finally some hidden part of her mind began to listen and respond. She began to comprehend the enormity of what had occurred, and slowly she returned to the world of sanity. For a long time she stayed to herself, praying, walking, musing, studying again the lessons she had learned of old, reading Mary's letter again and again, practicing all the disciplines of mind and will she knew so well, until she finally came to accept and submit to the will of God.

Judas recovered. Aristotle's good humor returned. Judith's smile warmed the cold, winter air, and the Essenes heaved a sigh of relief and began to live once again. The Remnant had once again survived. They'd come through the darkest part of the night and dawn would break again. But there are many hours between midnight and dawn, and the Essenes girded themselves with faith to endure the time of vigil.

The Jews' initial grief had turned to seething hatred and uncontrolled rage. Two rabbis, Judas and Mattathias, rallied the Zealots of Galilee, and sporadic rebellion and guerrilla warfare broke out through the land. An elite group of Zealots who were called the Sicarii because of the small, curved dagger, the "sica," they carried, waited in ambush among the hills, and slipped through alleys and back lanes in the night and neatly slit the throats of their enemies, striking terror into the hearts of every Jew or Gentile alike who had ever shown the least sympathy to Herod or Rome. The despised Roman Eagle which Herod had erected over the main gate to the temple became the symbol of all the cruelty and injustice inflicted upon the people, and the rabbis led their band in an abortive attempt to tear it down. Forty Zealots were arrested, Judas and Mattathias among them, and were burned alive in a public spectacle as an example to the others. Jerusalem recoiled from the stench of burning human flesh. The forty brave young men became martyrs to a cause, and the ranks of the Zealots grew.

As Herod's health deteriorated, palace intrigue increased. His son Antipater sailed for Rome with Herod's will naming him as successor to the throne, but while he was gone, Salome uncovered a plot against Herod's life in which Antipater was seriously involved. Herod called him back to Jerusalem where he stood trial before the Syrian governor, Varus, and was found guilty. They threw him into the dungeon in Herod's palace in Jericho to wait until Varus returned from Rome where he had gone to have Augustus confirm the verdict. Then Antipater would incur sentence.

Herod's family moved him to the palace at Jericho in hopes that the warmer climate would ease his pain. He languished there through the winter, in a stupor from the medicines administered to relieve his agony, but he rallied when Varus returned. Varus' verdict was upheld. Antipater was sentenced to death and his body unceremoniously dumped in a grave in the Fortress Hyrcania. It was the penalty for being born a son of Herod.

Herod drew a new will naming his teen-aged son Archelaus as successor, and knowing that his own death was imminent, he committed his final atrocity by ordering the death of Theresa on the unbelievable whim that he didn't wish her to outlive him. Forty members of the Sanhedrin were arrested and held in the vast hippodrome in Jerusalem with orders that they too be slaughtered immediately upon his death.

Five days after Antipater's murder, Herod succumbed to the cancer, and at seventy-three he was at last dead. Salome immediately ordered the release of the members of the Sanhedrin, not out of compassion, but to forestall the riots and rebellions that were sure to follow.

Herod was buried as he had lived, with lavish ceremony and glorious outward appearance, enveloped in the hatred and contempt of the Jews whom he had so unsuccessfully tried to please. His wasted body was borne on a golden litter, studded with precious gems and jewels, and the cortege of mourners stretched for miles as they carried his body to the Fortress Herodium in the Judean hills. Thousands of silent, sullen Jews lined the road, every heart rejoicing over the death of a tyrant, and every mind numbed by fear for what lay ahead.

Archelaus took the throne during the days of Passover, when Jerusalem thronged with pilgrims from all over the world. He was the son of Herod's Samaritan wife, Malthake, and the Jews despised him for his impure blood. When he entered the temple and sat upon a golden throne, he foolishly asked the Jews what favors they wanted of him. They demanded a drastic reduction in taxes, that all political prisoners be released from the dank dungeons in Herod's many fortresses, and most of all, that all those who had taken part in the burning of Judas and Mattathias be punished by death. Archelaus refused, and a bloody riot broke out. Archelaus' guard and the soldiers from Antonia marched into the frenzied crowd with drawn swords, and by the time it was over, three thousand bloody corpses littered the House of God.

Archelaus sailed for Rome to present Herod's will to Augustus for ratification. A delegation of priests and elders also went to plead with Caesar not to seat Archelaus on Herod's throne. Eight thousand Roman Jews joined them in petitioning Augustus for mercy, but Caesar upheld Herod's will.

Archelaus was barely aboard ship when rebellion again broke out in Jerusalem. The Roman General Sabinus had been left in charge of the cohort stationed in Antonia. Sabinus was a greedy, sadistic coward, who, despite the fact that Jerusalem was a tinderbox of rebellion, lusted after Herod's legendary wealth. He stole four hundred talents from the temple treasury and began to loot the countryside for any booty he could find. The people retaliated with fury and succeeded in shutting him up in Herod's palace.

Sabinus panicked. He somehow got a message through to Antonia, and without the slightest plan for battle, the streets became a battlefield of mob warfare. The Jews commanded the roofs and the parapets of the temple walls, raining stones and darts and arrows down on Roman heads until the desperate Romans set fire to the temple columns and the edifice became a funeral pyre.

The whole land rebelled. The Zealots marched on Sepphoris and took the Roman arsenal. Herod's palace at Jericho was burned. Roman and Herodian armies were routed from cities and villages throughout Judea and Galilee until Varus and his legions arrived from Syria.

Varus swept through the land without mercy. Cities and villages were burned to the ground. The people of Sepphoris were sold into slavery. Men, women, and children were slaughtered indiscriminately. The Jews lost heart at the sight of four thousand legionnaires, and the rebellion was brought to an end. Two thousand crucified Jews lined the roads leading to Jerusalem, a gruesome reminder of the might of the Eagle. Others were cast into dungeons where they eventually died of the damp cold and starvation. An uneasy peace ruled when Archelaus returned to take up where his father had left off.

The Essenes huddled in the safety of Mt. Carmel and the City of Salt, not daring to leave. The Romans, Herodians, Zealots and Jews hated them and still placed the guilt of the slaughter of the innocents upon their heads. Judith and the others watched the turmoil with horror and dismay and wondered if there would be a nation left for Jeshua to rule. They were consoled by the knowledge that Jeshua was safe in Egypt and would one day overthrow this era of wickedness, and the Elect would see the promised golden age. They saw the wars and upheavals as signs that the universe was entering into its cycle of destruction when all creation would become chaos, but in the end they believed there would be a new heaven and a new earth and the Messiah would take his place as ruler over a world of peace and prosperity and brotherly love. War and oppression would one day be no more. Belial would be bound and cast into Gehenna, and all men would live as brothers.

Chapter 17

The City of Salt flourished. The reservoirs and cisterns were filled to brimming with fresh, sweet water brought tumbling over the aqueducts by the winter rains, and the irrigated hills began to bloom. The whir of the potter's wheel sang its droning song throughout the day, hard put to keep up with the demand for storage jars and bowls and water jugs used by the ever-growing populace. Parchment and ink were used as fast as they could be produced as the scribes and monks carefully copied the Holy Scriptures and books and stored them for the coming age.

The number of initiates into the Brotherhood burgeoned as men of all ages sought the peace and simplicity of life in the wilderness. A city of tents sprang up in the hills, a city which yearly grew in number until it seemed to be a tiny nation in itself, isolated from the rest of the world by the forbidding hills and wilderness. Whole families travelled to the City of Salt, leaving their life in the desperate world to live and die in the peace and freedom offered by the pious community of the Elect. A cemetery was plotted out on a flat plain close to the monastery where the bodies of the faithful could lie in peace.

Mt. Carmel became more or less the religious center only for the Essenes. The administrative duties of the Brotherhood were still carried out at Carmel, and the feasts were still celebrated in the temple there, but the bulk of the work and activity was concentrated at the City of Salt. The Other Mary brought her little flock of orphans to the City of Salt where they could mingle with other children and live a normal family life with the people in the tents.

The Other Mary was not happy in Judea. With her orphans absorbed into the city of tents, she found time hanging heavy on her hands and no express purpose to her life. She spent much of the time with Elizabeth, and would have liked to assume some of the care of temperamental little John, but Adahr and Sofa made it clear that John was their charge, and jealously guarded against any intrusion. Like Judith, she missed the soughing of the great pines on Mt. Carmel, and the smell of the sea borne on the breeze. There was nowhere to escape the relentless sun that beat upon the hills in montonous regularity. When Zebedee asked her to join his household as nurse to his new born daughter Naomi, the Other Mary grasped at the opportunity to escape and to live in a normal family for the first time since she'd left her mother's house in Cana as a child.

There was no such escape from boredom in sight for Judith. Her duties as recorder kept her in the quiet confines of Mt. Carmel. She seldom ventured to the City of Salt, for she was well known as a leader of the Essenes and was regarded with suspicion by the Romans and by Archelaus' band. They rarely appeared on Mt. Carmel any more, and Judith had no desire to encounter them on the roads.

The long, slow days of orderly ritual and work grated on Judith's nerves as she waited for a sign from the Lord that it was safe for Jeshua to return to Palestine. She sometimes daydreamed of Justin, or visualized Jeshua as a growing boy, sitting at her feet as she taught him all the things that he must know. She pored over the schedule of learning she had set up for him, and chafed with impatience at the years ahead before she could begin.

Communications flowed steadily between Egypt and Mt. Carmel. The Egyptian community of the Elect was near the city of Heliopolis. Joseph had opened a carpentry shop as soon as they had arrived, and Mary found life in Egypt little different from in Nazareth.

When Jeshua was weaned, Mary left him in Salone's care, and she and Josie journeyed to the great library in Alexandria to study the ancient records and prophecies regarding the Messiah. They were amazed at the volume of detail they found, and meticulously copied the records and sent them to Carmel. They found that the ancients had foretold the physical descriptions and character traits of all those who would be in close contact with the Messiah, and it thrilled them to read their own descriptions, from Joseph's occupation to the color of Mary's eyes. The records indicated the character and personality which Jeshua would develop, and they gave Mary and Josie a valuable insight into the manner by which they should teach and guide the boy.

They found a prophecy that clearly described Herod's early hopes and aspirations as king of the Jews, and of his failures and frustrations. Mary felt a rush of pity for the man whose flesh and spirit were so at odds with one another, and was saddened by the knowledge of man's slavery to his passions. The scroll told of Herod's final illness, caused by a hatred and jealousy that consumed him all his life, and of the insanity which had culminated in the slaughter of the sons of Isreael. When Judith received the copy of this prophecy, the last burden of guilt was lifted from her shoulders, and she knew she had been the instrument used to bring this prophecy to fulfillment, and if it had not been she, then it would have been another.

Most of what Mary and Josie studied was written in obscure symbology. It was easy to read and understand the events which had already come to pass, but much of it they could only wonder at. They copied everything that seemed to relate to the Messiah, and as soon as Jeshua was old enough to learn, they taught him to memorize all, for one day these events also would come to pass and when they did, their meaning would become clear and Jeshua would know that this too, was foreordained by the Lord.

The Carmelites studied the records from Alexandria with exacting care, but it was the homey, loving letters from Mary that warmed Judith's heart. Mary wrote as any adoring mother would write, letters filled with pride at her son's accomplishments, his first tooth, his first word, his first tottering step.

Jeshua was strong and healthy in both body and mind, and showed an intelligence exceptional in a child his age. He was merry and affectionate. He feared no one and loved everyone. He took special delight in inventing antics which would force sober Josie to laugh, and though he was always obedient, he teased her unmercifully. He was popular with children of all ages. His golden curls would flash beneath the hot Egyptian sun as he joined in all their games and frolics. Salone had given birth to a daughter, and from the day she was born, Jeshua had made her his special friend. Myra's eyes followed him wherever he went, and the mere sound of his voice made her chortle with glee.

But there was another side to Jeshua's personality, a depth of wisdom and feeling which set him apart from other children. He showed an extrodinary tenderness and concern for his mother, and his respect and love for Joseph knew no bounds. He often astonished the elders of the community by the profound questions he asked, and by the understanding he displayed.

Mary and Josie watched Jeshua carefully and saw many things that convinced them that Jeshua was no ordinary child. A time of famine fell upon the land, when the rains did not come and the Nile failed to overflow its banks, leaving its rich deposit of heavy black soil. What grains had grown that year were eaten by locusts that had descended in black, evil clouds from the sky—deafening, horrible little insects which crazed man and beast alike before they disappeared as suddenly as they had come.

Before this, Jeshua had begged for a few grains of wheat to plant in his "garden," a small wooden box Joseph had made for him and which Jeshua had dragged into the corner of the house. Mary had indulged him in his childish whim and they had all laughed at the boy's diligent care of his "garden."

The wheat had grown and was ripe for harvest when the locusts had come. All through that terrible time Jeshua's little garden had fed them. Each morning Josie had stripped the full, fat grains from the fragile stems, and each morning she found them renewed.

How did that happen? Was it the child's absolute faith that his garden would not fail them? Did Jeshua have some unknown power that compelled the wheat to yield day after day for months? They only knew that the wheat had kept them and any who came to them in need alive during that time.

Even more astounding was the time when Nathaniel bar Tholomew, a neighbor child, had been found dead in his bed one morning, and his frantic mother had rushed with him to Mary's house where Josie had laid him on Jeshua's bed. The little body was already cold, and his skin turned white and waxy, but after only a few moments in Jeshua's bed, the boy had returned to life.

What had happened? Nathaniel's mother simply assumed in her joy that she had been mistaken, that the lad had not died at all. But Mary and Josie knew better. They had both thoroughly checked the lad for any sign of life and had found none. It had all happened so quickly that neither of them had had time to pray consciously. It could not have been the presence or faith of Jeshua that time, for Joseph had taken Jeshua to the shop with him. Was it Jeshua's bed? Could some vibration, some residue of energy present in Jeshua linger in his bed clothes, even though his body was not there?

They had seen Jeshua heal wounded birds and small animals he kept as pets, and this was not an unusual gift among the Essenes. Judith herself had manifested this gift when she was little older than Jeshua, but this child had no longer been living!

Nathaniel bar Tholomew had lived, but baby Myra had not. They had all been bitterly grieved by the passing of Salone's first-born, all except Jeshua. He had simply laid his cheek against Myra's and said to Mary with knowing eyes, "She had finished."

Why did one child receive his life back and another not? How did a child of Jeshua's tender age understand that one child's mission was finished and another not? These were all mysteries that they recorded and pondered over, but told no one except those at Mt. Carmel.

Judith lived from letter to letter, and with each one her impatience grew. When would Jeshua come home to Galilee? Then her days of tedium turned into days of joy, for Justin returned to Mt. Carmel.

Chapter 18

It was a hot, sultry night and Judith had slept fitfully, awakening with a dull headache that persisted even after the cold ritual washing. She intoned the prayers and hymns during morning worship without fervor, then trudged to the library and wearily took up her daily tasks.

The morning dragged on with little accomplished. She took her morning meal in the communal dining hall, grateful for the rule of silence. The meal of bread and fruit seemed flat and tasteless, and she only picked at it. Even the little salted olives seemed shrivelled, and the tepid water failed to quench her thirst.

She returned to the library and hung a piece of linen over the open window to cut the heat and glare from the midday sun, but only succeeded in preventing what little air there was moving from coming in. She moved the scrolls and ink to the far end of the table away from the window in the vain hope that it might be cooler there, but her tunic was soon damp with sweat and the heavy coil of hair at the nape of her neck tortured her throbbing head. She doggedly kept at her tasks until a young monk summoned her to the Roman-styled receiving room. Grateful for any interruption, Judith hurried down the passageway. All her weariness and boredom and headache vanished as she looked into Justin's face.

Judith stared at him in shock. A sea of emotion washed over her, rocking her with its intensity, leaving her so dizzy and trembling that she had to cling to the doorway to keep from staggering. Her tongue seemed to swell and cleave to the roof of her mouth. Her mind whirled with incoherent thought. How did he feel about her? Had his feelings changed since last she'd seen him? She stood stock still, afraid to move, afraid to speak, afraid to betray her joy at seeing him, lest he think her a silly, infatuated woman and reject her with his mocking laugh.

She drank him in with her eyes. He seemed older. The ringlets in front of his ears were salted with gray and the planes of his face had sharpened. Tiny lines were deeply etched around his eyes and across his brow, and his lips had lost some of their fullness, giving his mouth a more mature, thoughtful look than the open sensuality it used to have.

Judith saw that Justin was studying her as closely as she studied him, and she flushed to the roots of her hair. She tried to duck her head in embarrassment, but his eyes held hers and would not allow it. His slow, disarming smile began to creep across his face to his black, twinkling eyes, and he held his arms out to her. Before she could think, Judith had flung herself forward and was clutching him to her as though she'd never let go.

Justin laughed, not his sardonic, Roman legionnaire's laugh, but a gentle, loving, merry laugh which dispelled the heat and made the birds sing, and Judith's heart bubbled with such joy she thought she would burst. She drew her head back and looked him full in the face and laughed with him.

Aristotle, who had watched them with unconcealed amusement, cleared his throat and mumbled something about "urgent business to attend to" and discreetly left the room. Justin and Judith were so absorbed with one another they never heard him or noticed him leave. There was nothing for them in the world but this time, and this place, and each other.

Judith disentangled herself from Justin's arms and said crossly, "So you came back!"

"Obviously. I am not a ghost," Justin answered defensively.

Judith slid her hand down his thick, muscular arm. "No, that you are not," she said tenderly.

Her gesture was so intimate and possessive that Justin's blood warmed in his loins and he didn't trust his voice to speak.

"Why did you come back, Justin?" Judith said softly. "You were gone so long I didn't think you would ever come back."

Justin cleared his throat, but still his voice sounded hoarse and unnatural. "Let us walk and talk."

Judith nodded. They left the temple compound, walking stiffly apart under the knowing, smiling gaze of the Carmelites. Judith thought she'd perish of embarrassment as she realized that everyone had been aware of her feelings for Justin. She couldn't get to the cool, shadowed refuge of the forest fast enough, and walked with long, hurried strides. Justin had to quicken his pace to keep up with her, and hooted with laughter when he saw the smiles of those who watched and realized the cause of Judith's discomfiture.

Once in the privacy of the tall silent pines, Justin took her hand and they walked in silence until they came to the bluffs above the sea. The sea was a glassy calm. Only a few brightly colored sails cut the vast expanse of blue, bobbing listlessly upon the water as they waited for a breeze to nudge them on.

Judith sat down on her favorite rock and looked up at Justin. "Why did you come back, Justin?" she asked again.

Justin studied her for a moment, as though hesitant to answer. He was leaning over her, one foot upon the rock, with his elbow resting on his knee. He brushed a stray, damp strand of hair back from Judith's face. He took a deep breath, and his words came in a rush.

"I came back to marry you." He held up a hand as though to prevent her from speaking, and hurried on. "I know you'll have a thousand arguments for me, all of that nonsense about your work and dedication and your determination never to marry, and—"

"I will," Judith interrupted.

"What?"

"I will," Judith repeated softly.

"You will what?" Justin asked stupidly, irritated by her interrupting his well-planned speech.

"I will marry you!"

Justin was flabbergasted. He'd expected to have to spend weeks convincing Judith that her marriage to him needn't interfere with her work and life on Mt. Carmel, and he'd planned every detail of his argument and now she'd simply said, "I will." He didn't know what to say, and could only stare at her in bewilderment.

Judith laughed uproariously at him, but when his face darkened and he looked as though he'd like to throttle her, she muffled her laughter and tried to look contrite. She stood and put her arms around him and buried her face in his neck.

"Justin, my dear," she murmured. "For two years I have given myself every argument you could possibly conceive of. I've prayed and anguished and spent untold sleepless nights wrestling with the thought of what I'd do when, or if, you ever came back. I've wearied my mother to death with my moanings"—she raised her head and looked at him with a distasteful grimace—"and everyone else, too, it seems," she said dryly.

Justin wanted to laugh, but his male pride forced him to keep a pretense of anger. He pushed her from him and held her by her shoulders at arm's length. "Well! By Jupiter, you could give a man a chance to finish his proposal!" he exploded.

Judith frowned. Her eyes flashed and turned glacial. "There will be no more 'by Jupiter' if you marry me!" she shot back.

They stood for a moment locked in a battle of wills. Justin thought that life with this woman would be no easy undertaking. She wouldn't be a serene, docile Roman wife whose only concern was the happiness and comfort of her husband and children. A fleeting memory of his sweet, uncomplicated mother and sisters flitted through his mind, but he also remembered his boredom with their conversations about fashion and gossip and household duties, and his momentary doubts vanished. He relented and sat down on Judith's rock, pulling her down beside him.

"I know that. I'm sorry. That's only habit. There are many things I'll have to change. I'm a Roman, and I think and speak as a Roman, even though I no longer believe as a Roman. You'll have all to be patient with me. Old habits are not so easily broken."

Judith relaxed against his shoulder and her eyes deepened to the blue of the Galilee. "I know that, and I'm sorry too," she said. "I've thought about that also during my sleepless nights. I know how hard it will be for you to give up everything you've ever known and cherished, and all your old attitudes and beliefs. Are you absolutely sure you'd be happy here?"

"Yes!" Justin said emphatically. "I know this is where I belong. It's not only you who draws me here. I am pulled to this life by a force beyond my understanding. I thirst for something that my very soul knows I'll find only with this people. I spoke to Aristotle at some length before he summoned you, and he is satisfied that my desire to become an Essene is sincere and is not influenced by my desire for you. I want to learn and study and come to know the God of the Jews whether you marry me or not."

Judith couldn't speak. She wanted to weep for happiness, and she didn't for a moment doubt Justin's sincerity. She'd always been aware of his restless, searching quest for truth and meaning to life, and she could only silently thank God that He'd drawn Justin to be numbered among the Saints. She clung to him and waited until the lump in her throat disappeared, and then said slowly, without looking at him, "You'll never be first in my life, Justin. My work must always come before you, and Jeshua will always be foremost in my thoughts and actions. His needs and demands will always have priority over yours. Can you live with that and accept it without resentment?"

"Jeshua? Who is Jeshua?" Justin asked in bewilderment. An icy finger of fear crawled down his spine as he wondered if some other man had captured her love in his absence.

Judith straightened and looked fully into Justin's questioning eyes. She chose her words carefully, knowing full well that her life with Justin hung on the thin thread of his acceptance.

"Jeshua is a child," she said softly. "He is the Messiah whom the ancients foretold and for whom the world has waited untold generations. He was conceived by the glory of God, and born of a young, innocent virgin who was taught and nurtured by all of us here on Mt. Carmel. It is my destiny to be his teacher, to bring to his conscious mind all the things that his soul already knows. Husband, mother, friends, my very self must never interfere with that purpose."

Justin looked at her in wonder. "Conceived by the glory of God? Born of a virgin? I know your people sometimes speak in strange symbols and that your words often carry a hidden meaning, but—"

"Not this time," Judith said firmly. "This time my terms are to be taken literally. I mean exactly what I said." She watched Justin struggle to understand, and waited for his reaction.

"You must explain this more fully. No one can seriously believe a virgin can give birth. What do you mean by it?" Justin asked incredulously.

"I believe it. Without the slightest doubt. I know it! So do many others, though there are many of our people who do not. I've told you of the hopes and purposes of the Elect in preparing for and waiting for the coming of the Messiah." Justin nodded. "Well, the time of waiting is over. The Messiah has entered into the earth. Maybe it would be easier if I started at the beginning."

Justin had moved away from her, disturbed by the fantastic tale Judith obviously expected him to believe.

She sighed. She wanted so desperately for Justin to accept what she had to tell him. She prayed to God and all His hosts to help her. Justin leaned forward and listened intently as Judith told him of her own birth and the prophecy given to Phinehas by the angel. She told him of Mary's birth, and of Ann's calm faith under the burden of ridicule. She drew a visual picture of the selection of the twelve girls, of their lives and their education by the Essenes which had climaxed in the beautiful choosing of Mary on the stair.

Justin was enchanted by the wondrous tale Judith wove. She told him of the day the angel had appeared to Mary in the House of Lodgement and of how his message had filled them all with bewilderment and joy. She told him of Elizabeth and Zachariah, and of the birth of John. Her voice quavered and broke as she recalled the horror of Zachariah's murder, and Justin, remembering, touched her hand to comfort her and felt an unaccustomed lump in his own throat.

Judith gave life and substance to all the characters in her story until Justin could feel their pain and experience their joy, and seemed to share in all their victories and failures, and they became as his friends and loved ones under Judith's magic.

Justin listened with awe as Judith told of Mary's miraculous pregnancy, and sympathized with Joseph's distress and reluctance to make her his wife. He marvelled at the carpenter's faith, and wondered what his own reaction would be in like circumstances. When Judith spoke of the astrologers and of her plan to send them to Herod, her face turned ashen and her voice faltered and struggled for release from her throat. She couldn't bring herself to confess the outcome of her action. She couldn't bear the thought of seeing accusation and condemnation in Justin's eyes. Some day when his understanding of all the complexities of the situation was more complete, she would tell him, before they were wed, certainly, but not today. Not today when his very presence warmed her more than did the blazing sun, and the sound of his voice was like angels' song to her ears.

Justin recoiled from the torture in Judith's eyes and wondered what could possibly have happened that would cause her such agony in merely remembering. He wanted to ask, but her suffering forestalled him, and he soon forgot the question as Judith began the tale of Mary and Joseph's trek to Bethlehem.

"Apsafar planned well," Judith continued. "No one in the inn that night had the slightest suspicion that the Nazarenes were known to him. Never, except for that one brief appearance in the inn, did anyone other than a few of our own trusted people see Mary, and afterward no one remembered a young Jewish girl heavy with child. Sodaphe settled them into the cave beyond the inn and Jeshua was born just at the midnight hour."

Judith's voice became tinged with awe, as though even now she found her tale a mystery beyond understanding. "The greatest soul ever to enter the earth arrived unheralded by any except the beasts in the stable and a few lowly shepherds who were tending their flocks in the fields above. Only a handful of men, those who are counted among the Saints, knew that that night was a night of all nights, which future generations would revere for ages to come. The heavens proclaimed its glory, and angels sang out the glad tidings, but men neither saw nor heard, but persisted in walking in the stubbornness of their hearts, and refused to acknowledge the mercy of God.

"We at Mt. Carmel had been keeping a nightly vigil from the roof of the temple tower, and that night was filled with ghostly voices and music which drifted from every direction across the land—music like nothing ever

before heard on earth. It played in perfect harmony, high
notes and low, blending in an unearthly song that made
our flesh crawl with its beauty. It was elusive, first here,
then there, first loud, then so low we had to strain to hear
it. Sometimes we could hear voices singing—high, clear,
pure voices, as though a world-wide choir of children sang
somewhere in the Judean hills. We thought it came from
the stars, and then from the trees, and sometimes it
sounded as though it came from the depths of the earth."

A memory stirred in Justin's mind, and he felt a tingling sensation start at the base of his spine and crawl
toward his scalp. He strained forward, his muscles tense
and his hands clenched.

"We were watching the planets which the astrologers
had charted as they sailed from the east across the sky.
Closer and closer they drew together, until suddenly over
Bethlehem they converged into one vast star."

Justin's body convulsed and he gasped, "It was mammoth! Brilliant! Its rays reached down to the earth and
bathed all of Judea in a wash of silvery light."

Judith stared aghast at Justin. The veins in his brow
showed vivid blue beneath the glistening sweat that bathed
his face. His eyes were wide with wonder.

"I saw the star! That night! I saw!" he cried.

He grabbed at Judith with hands like bands of iron. She
winced in pain from his grasp and tried to twist free.
"Justin—"

"I was in Caesaria. On a high parapet. I saw it! It
moved like a giant beacon, an unearthly, guiding light. It
came from beyond Jerusalem and moved across Judea.
The hills were all lit up. I was afraid, Judith," he moaned.
"I was so afraid. I thought the world had come to an end."

He released her arms and dropped to his knees, burying
his face at her waist. "It frightened me so I cried out,
'What is it?' I heard a voice. I didn't really hear—it came
from inside of my head. It said, 'It has begun.' I begged
for the voice to tell me more but it wouldn't!" Justin's
voice broke with grief. "It wouldn't say. It wouldn't tell.
Only, 'It has begun.' "

Judith sank weakly down upon the rock with Justin still
clinging to her waist. His great shoulders shuddered and
his breath came in rasping sobs. She tentatively touched
his head, feeling the wiry curls spring back against the

palm of her hand. A look of wonder and then of exquisite tenderness passed over her face. The Lord did work in such wondrous ways. She stroked Justin's hair and shoulders until she felt the tension flow away from his body. His grip relaxed and he became still.

A peace flowed through Justin, cleansing, changing, renewing his very core. He slowly raised his head and looked long and deep into Judith's eyes. His face seemed changed, softer and completely at ease. His eyes were liquid with inner knowledge. His slow smile spread across his face, a smile of such tenderness and love that Judith drew her breath in sharply and had to swallow to keep from crying out.

Justin slowly reached out and pulled the wooden pins from Judith's hair, and the coil fell down her back in a long thick rope. His fingers worked lanquidly as he undid the braid until her wheaten hair fell free around her shoulders. He gently smoothed the tangles and spoke in a low voice, almost crooning.

"I also cried out for you that night. It's curious, but even then I somehow knew that you would be the one who could tell me the meaning of the star. Your God is subtle. A sudden flash of revelation or some spectacular vision of the mind would only convince a Roman that he was losing his sanity. But to touch his curiosity, to disrupt the Roman sense of law and order—" Justin shook his head and chuckled. "Your God, I think, has a sense of humor, Judith."

Judith smiled. "Our God, Justin."

"Our God," Justin repeated. "Yes. And 'our' Messiah. Where is Jeshua?"

Chapter 19

J ustin and Judith were married, and after a long, intense examination by the General Council, Justin was accepted as a candidate for membership in the Brotherhood and began his first-year probationary period. Some of the elders had been wary of admitting a Roman into the community, their fear and hatred of the legionnaires overriding the fact that he had married their recorder and was sponsored by Aristotle himself. But Justin had answered every question candidly, hiding nothing of his life and thoughts and feelings, and they finally believed in his sincerity of heart.

He found it surprisingly easy to adjust to his new life. His military training served him well. Most postulants coming in from the world found it difficult to submit to authority and to accept the fact that they were regarded as the lowest in rank, but Justin had been subject to authority all of his life and it was no problem to him.

He was assigned to a supervisor and spent the mornings working in the gardens, cleaning the latrines, and doing all the other menial jobs that were designed to teach humility and submission to authority. Justin didn't mind. The feel of the hoe in his hand and the hot sun on his back reminded him of his childhood when his father had insisted that his sons work in the fields, and he felt as lighthearted and young as a lad again. The distasteful chores made him think of his first years in the army, and he had the curious feeling that his life was beginning over again.

In the afternoon he would go to the library or sit beneath the great, swaying oaks in the courtyard to study the Scriptures and learn the teachings of the Elect. He had a quick, avid mind and his Roman training quickly cut through the trivia of detail and reached the heart of the matter. The monks delighted in him as a pupil, and enjoyed the sessions as much as he.

All of Justin's past studies of science and philosophy paled as he studied the ancient truths. Here was meat for a man's soul! Each day his excitement grew as he learned of the beginnings of the soul, and of its sojourns on the earth; of its struggles and frustrations and its growth and backsliding as it slowly climbed the ladder to spiritual perfection. He felt his old self ebbing away. The self-assured man of the world fell away, and he saw himself as a little child. How much time he'd wasted in the pursuits of the world!

As for Judith, she would one day look back on these years as the happiest of her life. She bloomed under Justin's tender love. The sun shone brighter, the grass seemed greener, and the profusion of flowers around the temple had never had such vivid color. Her work came to life with new meaning as she became caught up in Justin's excitement. She looked at the old, familiar teachings with new eyes as she saw them through Justin's fresh approach and enthusiasm.

They lived in a tent beneath the trees and met in the dining hall at the foot of the compound to take their meals. There was always so much to talk about. Their minds met and sparred and thrust, and words and thoughts were like a heady drink. Their love was tender and undemanding, more a gentle release of the tensions and excitement brought on by their eager discussions than the passionate urgings of the body.

The General Council quickly approved Justin's second year of probation. Before returning to Mt. Carmel, he had relinquished all claim to his share in his father's estate and had sold all of his personal goods and property. When he turned this over to the treasury supervisor at the beginning of his second year, they had been astounded by the amount.

"You never told me you were rich!" Judith had gasped.

"I didn't want you to marry me for my riches," Justin teased.

According to the rule, the Brotherhood could not use the money until Justin was initiated into full membership of the Elect, but Judith already had visions of how that money could be used to further the purposes of the Essenes. Finances had always been a problem. They didn't call themselves the "Poor" for nothing, and Justin was proving to be a boon to the sect in more ways than one.

Judith's first son was born that summer, and Justin named him Servilius after his own father. Justin adored his tiny, black-haired son, and spent every free moment he had in the tent. But Judith was impatient with the long confinement dictated by Law, and was soon bored with nothing to do but feed and play with a baby. The birth had been easy, and within a few days Judith arose from her cot and took up her household chores.

"You give birth like you do everything else," Justin had laughed. "Quick and to the point, and with as little fuss as possible."

They moved into a larger tent, which was divided into two rooms. Elkatma came to live with them and care for Servilius, but she was very old, so Judith sent for a young girl from the school in the City of Salt to help her.

As soon as her forty days of confinement ended, Judith resumed her work in the library and was often irritated when she had to interrupt her work to nurse Servilius. He was a good baby and Judith loved him, but she did think that he was something of a nuisance. She felt a good deal of guilt over her attitude, but try as she might, she couldn't help it.

It saddened Justin to see Judith's lack of enthusiasm for their son, but he remembered her early warnings that she had no strong desire for motherhood, and so he said nothing. He tried to make up for Judith's lack of interest by lavishing love and attention on the child, and Servilius soon learned to take advantage of the situation. He became a petulant, demanding child, prone to use tantrums and tears to get his way. Judith saw what was happening but knew of no way to stop it except by giving up her work, and that she could not do.

Justin swore the oath of allegiance to the Brotherhood and became a full member. His knowledge of the Greek and Roman languages was a valuable asset to the Essenes, and he journeyed often to the City of Salt to help the scribes with their translations of the holy books. Since he was a Roman, Justin could move freely through the land, and the Brotherhood used him as an emissary and messenger to their members in the villages and cities throughout Judea and Galilee. Judith missed him terribly when he was gone, but the work of the Elect, as always, took precedence over her own needs, and she worked harder than ever to keep from dwelling on her loneliness.

More and more of the decision-making seemed to fall to Judith. In the last year, Aristotle had taken to musing and long walks. He often sought the solitude of the mysterious forest, and more and more he deferred to Judith's judgment on administrative decisions. She wondered at the change in Aristotle. He seemed vague and unenthusiastic, like a man who had lost his zest for challenge. Judith and Judas agreed that with Herod dead and his pleasure-loving son Herod Antipas ruling Galilee, it was safe enough to bring Jeshua home from Egypt, but each time they broached the subject to Aristotle, he only smiled enigmatically and answered with a vague, "We'll see."

Aristotle's seeming lack of interest was maddening. Jeshua would soon be old enough to begin his studies, and it was imperative that his education be guided by the Essenes. Judith's frustration made her snappish, and poor Servilius bore the brunt of her impatience. It was with great relief that the Mount welcomed Justin home for the annual review.

The morning that the Council met dawned cool and bright. Judith awoke before the others and smiled when she saw that Servilius had crept into their bed and lay nestled beneath his father's chin. A momentary wave of remorse assailed her as she realized that the boy had never stolen into her bed when Justin was away, but she pushed the thought aside and made her way quietly out of the tent and to the baths.

She met Justin with Servilius in the inner court for the morning worship. The service seemed especially joyous that morning, and even Servilius responded to the atmosphere of good fellowship and high spirits.

Aristotle, as Prefect, was presiding at the podium that Joseph had carved so long ago, and waited until they were all seated according to rank, first the priests and then the elders. Judith took her place among the higher-ranking elders, and smiled at Justin across the room. The assembly stood as one body as Aristotle, arms upraised and palms open to the Lord, raised his voice in the opening prayer.

"Lord of all the Universe, God of our father, Abraham, shed your holy spirit upon this congregation of Israel, the Remnant you have preserved for yourself to cleanse the land of all iniquity and wickedness, and to preserve your teachings and your covenant for all future generations. Shed your Holy Spirit upon us that we might discern your will and be of one accord with you and all your celestial hosts. Your Holy Spirit can pass not away. The fullness of heaven and earth attests it, and the sum of all things stands witness to your glory."

The priests intoned the blessing for the Prefect of the Community, and Aristotle in turn blessed the priests and laymen, and then raised the first order of business for the day.

The morning flew by. There was nothing of great importance on the agenda, and all of the administrative business had been taken care of by the time the Council recessed for the morning meal. They maintained the rule of silence during the break and reconvened an hour later when the sun was at its zenith. God blessed them with a cool breeze blown in from over the sea, and the hall was cool and airy when they returned.

The examination of the first- and second-year initiates went quickly. Justin had come to know many of them well, and he was often called upon to attest to their character and intelligence. He felt a sense of pride when they were all accepted.

The third-year initiation took much longer, for these men were brought into full communion with the congregation with ceremony and ritual. After the postulants had sworn the oath of allegiance, the priests rehearsed all the bounteous acts of God and recited all His tender mercies toward Israel. The Levites counted all the sins of the children of Israel, and pronounced the curse upon all who entered the Covenant with an insincere heart.

"Cursed be every one that has come to enter this covenant with the taint of idolatry in his heart and who has set his iniquity as a stumbling block before him so that thereby he may defect, and who, when he hears the terms of this covenant, blesses himself in his heart, saying, May it go well with me, for I shall go on walking in the stubbornness of my heart! Whether he satisfy his passions or whether he still thirst for their fulfillment, his spirit shall be swept away and receive no pardon. The anger of God and the fury of His judgments shall consume him as by fire unto his eternal extinction, and there shall cleave unto him all the curses threatened in this covenant. God shall set him apart for misfortune, and he shall be cut off from the midst of all the Children of Light in that through the taint of his idolatry and through the stumbling block of his iniquity he has defected from God. God will set his lot among those that are accursed for ever!"

The Council answered, "Amen. Amen!" and the initiates took their place at the far end of the room, their faces radiating their joy at being admitted into the Elect of God.

Aristotle resumed his place at the podium. The congregation waited in happy but weary silence for him to begin the closing ceremony. He stood for a long time without speaking. His eyes had a faraway look as though he were seeing and hearing things no one else saw or heard. A bemused smile played at his lips and then he closed his eyes and seemed to be absorbed in some private communication with God.

The congregation waited patiently. Judith hoped he would bring up the subject of bringing Jeshua home. A bee found its way through the open windows and lazily droned over the silent, unmoving heads.

When Aristotle finally opened his eyes, he looked over the assembly like a tender father observing his children. An almost visible outpouring of affection rose up to meet his gentle gaze. A loving, somewhat sad smile spread to his eyes, impelling the assembly to smile back at him in return. Judith looked across the room to Justin, who was watching Aristotle intently, and then to Judas, whose brow was knit in a look of puzzlement, at the first priests' table. Something was taking place; what, Judith couldn't guess. A warmth, a oneness, seemed to envelop them like a soft, protective cloak. Aristotle spoke, and his voice was so filled with peace that Judith felt a tiny lump appear in her throat.

"My brothers and sisters. My dear Children of the Light. God brought me to you many years ago, an alien, a Jew from Rome, a stranger out of exile, and set me up before you as your leader. Many wondered at that." He smiled. "I did myself. How could a man of my background, wealthy, influential, how could such a man be able to guide the Poor? But you and I bowed to the will of God, I came and you accepted, both trusting in the wisdom of the Lord. As time went by, the wisdom of the Lord's choice became manifest.

"We have just passed through a time of great distress. Our children have been slaughtered, our wives and daughters defiled, our strong young men and beloved elders persecuted and hounded from their homes. The land has run red with blood, and the instruments used for this destruction were my own countrymen."

The pain of remembrance made all eyes drop as Aristotle continued.

"It is written that the Kittim from the land of my birth shall be the instrument used by God to test Israel by fire and sword. When this shall be, we know not the exact date, but it will be soon. This time of woe which we have just passed through is but a warning for the time to come, and I, a Roman, was found most fit to deal with Romans.

"But now we are entering into a time of peace, a time when Belial shall be held in check while our Messiah grows in strength and wisdom. We enter a time of teaching, of preparing our people for the coming age, and a Roman Jew has lost his usefulness as leader of the Elect."

An audible intake of breath was heard as the members gasped in surprise.

"God has called me on to other work. He calls me to the City of Salt, to oversee the work of the scribes, to accelerate the copying of our holy books, for in the coming age we will once again be forced to flee, and the Word cannot be lost as in the days of Ezra.

"But God has raised up another to take my place, another who, like myself, is destined to the times. It was prophesied before her birth that she would one day lead her people, and that day has come upon us. Again God makes manifest His inexplicable wisdom."

A weakness flooded Judith's flesh and she could not breathe. Aristotle's voice rang in her ears.

"I speak of Judith, daughter of Phinehas, teacher of the Messiah, who by the will of God will lead this people to their salvation!"

A stunned silence descended upon the room. Judith's mouth went dry and she was overcome by an uncontrol-

lable trembling. Waves of fear washed over her, and her
mind screamed, "I can't! I can't!"

A low murmur began at the priests' tables and spread
throughout the room until it became as the muffled rumbling of an approaching storm. Pandemonium reigned.
Hands were flung frantically into the air. Calls for permission to speak rang out. A woman? How could a
woman—! Unheard of! Never before— . . . the sins of
Eve—

The old strength flashed out through Aristotle's eyes
and he pounded the podium for silence and order. The
room gradually became quiet and the congregation shrank
at the anger in his eyes. In icy silence, he looked out over
the assembly into sullen faces, and faces suffused with
bewilderment, some of eager excitement. He struggled to
control his rage and finally said in a voice ringing with
authority, "We will enter the silence! We will search our
inner vision and discern the will of the Lord!"

The room was thick with tension and it took some
moments for those present to still their emotions and enter
into a state of deep meditation.

It was hardest of all for Judith. She knew that Justin
was frantically trying to catch her eye, but she couldn't
look at him. She closed her eyes and forced her body to
relax. She blocked out every thought of husband, child,
home, fear, until peace descended and she floated in a sea
of warm, liquid love.

How long she sat that way, she didn't know. When she
opened her eyes the hall was completely silent; only the
soft rise and fall of shallow breathing could be heard. A
bird sang outside the window, and the sweet, fragrant
odor of violets filled the air.

She was peaceful, serene, and filled with conviction.
This was what she had been born to do. This was the
purpose she had been given to accomplish. All doubts and
fears and self-deprecation vanished. She was the Lord's.
His will be done. She saw that Aristotle had left the podium and was sitting with the priests. She quietly rose and
took her rightful place.

One by one the heads came up and saw the tall,
wheaten-haired woman standing behind the podium. She
met their eyes with a steady gaze, strong, assured, authoritative. Justin stared at her, wondering at this woman who

was his wife, and thought he would burst with pride at the glory of her.

Judas stood and raised his arms and palms to the Lord and began to chant the blessing for the Prefect of the Community. Wood scraped against stone, and then the entire assembly was standing, their voices blending as one voice, joyful, gladsome, ringing with affirmation:

"The Lord lift you up unto the summit of the world, like a strong tower on a lofty wall. May you smite nations with the vehemence of your mouth. With your rod may you dry up the fountainheads of the earth, and with the breath of your lips may you slay the wicked.

"The Lord favor you with a spirit of sound counsel and with perpetual strength and with a spirit of knowledge and with the fear of God.

"May righteousness be the girding of your loins and faithfulness that of your thighs.

"May God make your horns of iron and your hoofs of brass, and may you gore the iniquitous like a steer and trample nations like mire in the streets.

"For God has appointed you to be the scourge of rulers. They shall come before you and make obeisance unto you, and all peoples shall serve you. By His Holy Name may He give you power that you be as a lion which ravens and as a wolf which smites the prey, with none to retrieve it. And may your chargers ride abroad over all the broad places of the earth."

Judith was the leader of the Essenes! And the first thing she did was to bring Jeshua home from Egypt.

Chapter 20

Judith's certainty that the time was right for Jeshua's return to Galilee was confirmed by an angel who appeared to Joseph in a dream, and the exiles returned as they had gone, in small groups and at different times, settling in various towns and cities throughout Palestine to avoid suspicion.

Joseph did not return to Nazareth, wisely guessing at the bitterness and resentment which would greet them if they appeared with a son whole and hearty and of the same age as those who had been slaughtered would now have been. His brother Alphaeus urged him to come to Capernaum as a partner in his carpentry shop, and the Essenes agreed. Capernaum seemed an ideal place to raise Jeshua. It was a large town, a center of commerce, and the main port on the Sea of Galilee for merchants and traders coming into Palestine from the lands to the east. Its streets and market place were filled with men from every race and creed, and its inhabitants were a mixture of Jew and Gentile who lived peacefully side by side as they aided one another in lining their pockets with silver and gold. Joseph's family could easily be absorbed into the bustling maelstrom without note.

Alphaeus suggested that Mary and Joseph share his home, for Capernaum was grossly overcrowded; finding a separate abode for them would be nearly impossible. Judith understood Alphaeus' wife Mary's lukewarm response to his generous invitation, and politely refused the offer, hiding her smile at Mary's obvious relief.

Alphaeus was a gregarious, boisterous soul whose door was ever open to friends and kinsmen and business acquaintances until his house was more like a public inn than a private home. He employed many servants, and

Mary of Alphaeus had her hands full running such a household while trying to raise her own growing brood of sons without the additional burden of another family under her roof. Besides, the chaotic atmosphere of such a home was hardly one that encouraged the study and quiet contemplation which was essential to Jeshua's training. Judith turned for help to Marcus' father, Cleopas.

Cleopas was recently widowed and was living in Capernaum, having accepted the unpopular position of overseer to the publicans there. The publicans were notorious for extorting taxes far in excess of the amount required by Rome, with which they then lined their own pockets. The practice was becoming so widespread that the Jewish authorities feared an open rebellion on the part of the poor they so blatantly exploited. Being one of their most revered members, and knowing he was honest to a fault, the Sanhedrin had asked Cleopas to try to rectify the situation. Cleopas had agreed, but found such a task was easier said than done. Extortion was a difficult charge to prove, as it was usually one man's word against another's, so Cleopas was trying to slowly replace the thieves with men of integrity. The position did not win him the love of his fellow Jews, for the very word "publican" stirred their hearts to hatred and closed their ears to any explanations as to what Cleopas was trying to do. It did, however, procure a home for Joseph and Mary.

The house Cleopas obtained was next to his own on the outskirts of the city. It was an adequate unpretentious house, two-storied, with a flat, tarred roof that became Jeshua's favorite place to study as he gazed out over the panorama of the Galilean hills and over the low thatched roofs of Capernaum to the sparkling blue of the Sea of Galilee. A small, walled courtyard acted as a buffer between the street and the house, and provided the privacy and quiet that Mary so desired. A small side gate opened into Cleopas' own courtyard, giving them easy access to one another's homes without having to venture into the street.

An Essene family lived on the other side. The woman of the house, Sophia, and her married daughter, Esdrella, became fast friends with Mary and Josie and introduced them to other Essene families in Capernaum. The remote location of the three houses was ideal for members of the sect to come and go without notice, and soon became the center of Essene prayer circles and meetings.

Unlike the Orthodox Jewish synagogues which separated men, women, and children, the Essenes encouraged the entire family to meet and pray together. Jeshua was always included in these gatherings. That, plus the Essene teaching that God is no respecter of persons, resulted in Jeshua's growing up free from the prejudices regarding sex, age, and class which were so prevalent among other schools of thought.

Jeshua did not attend the synagogue school. He was taught the Torah at home by his parents and Josie, guided by Judith who made regular visits to Capernaum to oversee his instruction. The Essenes augmented Joseph's income so the family could afford servants, which freed Mary and Josie to spend the greater part of each day with him.

Jeshua was a precocious child who absorbed his lessons with ease. He was eager to learn, looking forward to Judith's visits and each new scroll she brought, burning with impatience to discover its contents. He was particularly adept at languages. Aramaic, with its peculiar Galilean slur, was the common tongue used at home, and of course, the classical Hebrew was used for his lessons. But in addition to these Jeshua learned Latin from Justin, and, from his exposure to Romans who frequented Cleopas' house, Greek, Persian, Indian, Egyptian, and many others gleaned by his finely tuned ear from the streets and market place in Capernaum.

As impatient as she was for Jeshua to come to Mt. Carmel, Judith realized the value of the experiences he gained by living at home during those formative years. It was essential that the Messiah, whether priest or king, be exposed to all types and temperaments of souls he would one day rule, and his home in Capernaum offered far more opportunities for gaining insights into his fellow man than the exclusive isolation of Mt. Carmel. Jeshua was a strong-willed child with definite preferences regarding what to study and what to do. He reminded Judith of herself at that age, and, remembering Enos' wisdom in letting her follow where her soul would lead, she counseled the same for Jeshua.

One of his favorite pastimes was to go to the shop with Joseph, where, perched on a stool, he watched a vast cross section of humanity pass before his youthful, knowing eyes. Jew and Gentile, the pious and the unholy, the wise and the foolhardy, the peacemakers and the warmongers, the righteous and the sinner—all mingled in the city square in front of Alphaeus' shop. Jeshua saw the greed of the rich and the desperation of the poor, the arrogance of the powerful, and the helplessness of the weak. He heard the moans of the suffering, the boasts of the cruel, and the judgments passed over all by the just and the unjust.

Jeshua said little about the impressions these scenes left upon his sensitive mind and soul, but, like his mother, preferred to ponder them privately in his heart.

His own large family provided ample opportunity for Jeshua to experience the trials and joys of living in the flesh. Mary and Joseph would not leave Capernaum during the years that Jeshua lived under their roof. Archelaus was as much the tyrant as his father Herod (who some were now calling "the Great"), but without Herod's restraint and uncanny talents for subtle intrigue. He was a dangerous youth, rash and impulsive in his attempts to prove his ability to rule, and his unchecked passions led him to disregard the Law by marrying his brother's wife, an act which brought down the wrath of every Jew upon his head. Mary and Joseph would not even consider exposing Jeshua to the dangerous chaos in Archelaus' territory, so their kinsmen came to them in Capernaum.

For five years Jeshua lived the normal life of any Jewish boy. He learned his father's trade as any son was expected to do. He listened to Salone's and the Other Mary's husbands discuss their fields and flocks, absorbing the frustrations of the poor farmer trying to eke a living through high costs and poor prices, always dependent upon the weather and the taxes levied each year. Uncle Zebedee introduced him to the life of the fishermen, who voiced the same complaints as Timothy and Uncle Zuriah.

Uncle Marcus and Aunt Josie usually stayed with Cleopas when in Capernaum. Cleopas' position brought many Roman officials to his house, and no one paid any attention to the small, golden-haired boy who listened avidly to their tales of graft and intrigue and battles for power by those in high government office. From his cousin Syrus of Bethany he learned of the Sanhedrin, and of the Pharisees and the Sadducees and the scribes who used the Temple of God for their own ends, quarreling among themselves in a continuous jostle for power and prestige.

He was the favorite among his aunts and female cousins. They lavished him with affection and plied him with sweetmeats and delicacies from the kitchen. Only his mother realized how much of their chatter about a woman's plight in a world dominated by men found a sympathetic, understanding ear in Jeshua.

He played with his cousins and listened as they compared their schools and their ways of life in Jerusalem, Galilee, and the City of Salt, paying particular attention to Roael's and James' description of another cousin, the enigmatic John at the City of Salt. Alphaeus' sons—Simon, James, and Matthew—were more like brothers than cousins, but his dearest friend was Lazarus ben Syrus.

Jeshua had an uncanny empathy for everyone around him. He innately understood each individual, and shared the many emotions displayed by any large family. He felt the sorrow of separation when his grandmother Ann and great-aunt Ismeria died peacefully in their old age, and shared the depth of grief suffered by Lazarus when death claimed an untimely victory over his mother Eucharia.

Jeshua was only seven when Eucharia died while giving birth to a daughter whom Syrus named Mary, for Jeshua's own mother, and Jeshua learned firsthand the tragedy and hardships caused by the loss of a wife and mother. Fifteen-year-old Martha was forced to forego her girlish dreams of a home and family of her own and assume the responsibilities of her father's house. Syrus retreated to his library of scrolls, living a life of remote mysticism, while Lazarus wandered in a world of solitary loneliness.

John ben Zachariah's nurse Sofa came to live in Joseph's house during Jeshua's last year at home to acquaint him with the nature and character of the cousin who was destined to be his forerunner. When Elkatma died just prior to Jeshua's tenth year, Sofa agreed to come with Jeshua to Mt. Carmel to act as nurse to Servilius and Judith's second son, Phinehas.

Mary and Joseph took their only child to Mt. Carmel with mixed emotions of pride, expectation, and grief. They watched their son, the long-awaited Messiah, enter through the gate of Judah for the first time—an occasion celebrated by the Carmelites as exultantly as they had celebrated his mother's being chosen on the stair but returned to an empty, joyless house, a prison of silence.

They turned to one another for comfort, and passion was born out of their grief. When, two years later, Jeshua reached the age of manhood and went with his parents to Jerusalem to be questioned by the priests in the temple there, Mary's womb was swelling with child.

Caesar Augustus had finally yielded to the desperate pleas of the Jews and Samaritans and had banished Archelaus to Vienna. Archelaus' ethnarchy was reduced to a Roman province, and a Roman of the equestrian order by name of Coponius was sent as Procurator over Judea and Samaria. No one knew what the future held under Coponius' rule, or how he would use his power of life or death over the Jews, but few doubted if life could be worse than when under Archelaus' erratic hand.

The caravan that wound its way from Galilee to Jerusalem in Jeshua's twelfth year did not worry about such mundane matters as a drastic change in government. They were on their way to celebrate the glorious feast of Passover in the holy City of David, and their minds were filled with thoughts of friends and kinsmen and joyous revelry. Tomorrow was time enough to worry about the consequences of a Roman ruler, today was sufficient unto itself. The only thing that Coponius' rule meant to them right now was that finally it was safe to bring Jeshua into Judea.

All of Jeshua's kinsmen from Galilee were in that caravan, eagerly anticipating the first time the family would all be together in Jerusalem. They rejoiced over Mary's pregnancy, and looked forward to watching their beloved Jeshua prove his maturity when questioned by the priests. They were a happy, joyful throng who wound their way along the eastern shore of the Galilee and down the banks of the Jordan. They sang the joyful Psalms of David, accompanied by lutes and harps and pipes and the clash of cymbals. The sun smiled upon them during the day, and the stars lit their camps at night. Children laughed and chased and played, while the women gossiped and exchanged the news and searched the crowds for their wandering young.

The evenings were spent around the campfires where the men took turns telling stories of the heroes of old and the history of this people whom God had chosen for His own. Their sonorous voices would blend with the night, to curl and drift through the silent, listening host. Their voices rose and fell and moved and swayed until the tale became a song, a chant, pulling the memories of a long-forgotten past from the very depths of their souls.

Babes slept in their mothers' laps, and older children huddled close, enthralled by the heavens so close above and the flickering fire before them. They shivered in fright when God called upon Abraham to slay his only son, and sighed with relief at Isaac's reprieve. They thrilled to the courage of young David as he slew the giant Goliath, and wept when Joseph's brothers sold him into Egypt.

They became caught up in the magic and life of days long ago. They lived again with Moses and Joshua in the wilderness, shared the splendor of Solomon, and triumphed with Elijah in his victory over the priests of Baal.

Jeshua knew those stories by heart and could have repeated them as precisely as any man there, but never before had he heard them told in such a setting or in such a company, and he too listened with childlike awe. The memory of those nights under the open skies became forever etched in his soul, and wherever his destiny might lead, his heart would ever belong to the simple, carefree Galileans of his boyhood.

The caravan entered the mountains between Jericho and Bethany, and the company became quiet with the effort of climbing. The sun shone hot on their backs and the dirt and dust swirled in their faces. The sun was almost at its zenith when Joseph clapped his heavy hand on Jeshua's shoulder and panted, "At the top of the next hill you will see Jerusalem."

Jeshua shot a glance at his weary mother, and she smiled and nodded, knowing her son's question without his having to ask. Jeshua broke free from his father's clasp and began to run up the rocky incline. Joseph started to call him back, but Mary laid a restraining hand upon his arm and said, "Let him go. He follows an inner compulsion to experience his first sight of Jerusalem alone."

At the crest of the hill Jeshua slid to a halt and stifled a cry of wonder and anguish. The city lay before him in the distance, white and shimmering in the noonday sun, with the temple rising up from the sea of white limestone like a crown of glory towering over the city, dazzling and glorious, a splendor of blazing white and flashing gold, soaring over the thick, winding walls like an awesome monarch, commanding, demanding, majestic and regal against the stark Judean sky.

Jerusalem! A city of splendor and poverty, of piety and hypocrisy. A city where Synagogues and pagan theaters stood side by side, where magnificent, lavish palaces arose amidst the hovels at their feet, and pious, holy priests pulled their heavily fringed skirts aside lest they touch the filthy rags of the beggar. It was a city of clamor and silence, of righteousness and evil, of gaiety and anguish. Her history reeked with violence and death, with victory and celebration. The ghosts of her children long dead cried out in their triumphs and failures, and laid bare their transgressions and infidelities.

Jeshua's knees gave way and he fell to the ground, his eyes still riveted upon the city before him. Every human emotion raged through his being, until the sweat of his fear mingled with the tears of his love and sprinkled the dust at his knees.

His parents reached the crest of the hill before the others. Joseph lifted the boy up into his arms and carried him to the shade of a rock where Mary tenderly wiped his flowing eyes and rocked him in her arms, crooning and soothing until he lay quiet and calm.

Joseph was bewildered and distraught. He couldn't understand what had brought Jeshua to such a state. But Mary knew, and through that silent, unspoken communion which existed between mother and son, she brought him the peace of understanding and acceptance. By the time the others reached them, Jeshua was himself again, a twelve-year-old boy eager for the adventures that lay ahead.

The family stayed at Zebedee's estate outside the walls of Jerusalem. Roael, James, and Lazarus took their Galilean cousins on a tour of the city, drinking in the sights and sounds and odors until exhaustion sent them trudging wearily home to sprawl beneath the shady trees in the courtyard and gorge themselves on Salome's sumptuous meals, too drained even to talk of all they'd seen and heard. Jerusalem assaulted Jeshua's senses with her complexities and incongruities until his nerves were drawn taut as a bowstring, his eyes burned with scenes of unfathomable contrasts, and his ears rang with her clamor and din. Only when he entered the temple precincts did Jeshua relax. His reeling senses became calm, and a sense of belonging settled over him. The urban maelstrom of the city rattled him, but the House of God was his own true element, and he felt confident and in control.

His examination by the priests went well, as everyone had known it would. The priests were surprised by Jeshua's knowledge, and questioned him as to what school he attended. They knew he was not a student from a Jerusalem academy, and thought he must be a student in one of the rabbinical schools outside of Palestine. They were astounded to learn he was only a poor carpenter's son from Capernaum taught by his parents and his mother's handmaid, for Jeshua did not tell them of his schooling at Mt. Carmel. They marvelled that the boy was so favored by God as to receive the gift of such wisdom.

Once the examination was over, Jeshua was free to roam the temple at will. The Court of Gentiles, with its booths and stalls, pens and cages of sacrificial animals and birds, seemed little different to Jeshua from the market place outside Uncle Alphaeus' shop. Money-changers hawked their prices, and merchants advertised their goods. Roman soldiers patrolled the wide promenade at the top of the high temple walls, and the temple guard mingled with the people below, ever watchful for the slightest hint of disturbance. They all seemed to Jeshua to be a defilement of this most holy place.

The Court of Women was almost as bad, as the women's high, piercing voices rent the air in an indistinguishable babble of gossip and cries of greeting. Only when he reached the Court of Israel did Jeshua feel he was truly in the House of God.

Only male Jews over the age of twelve were allowed in the Court of Israel. Any Gentile who ventured beyond its sacred gates did so under the threat of death. No business deals were transacted here, no worldly matters were dis-

cussed within these walls; only the Law and those things
pertaining to God found entrance to the Court of Israel.
The court thronged with Jews, from the lowliest, rough-
clad shepherd to the haughtiest, silk-clad priest, all gathered in large and small groups to discuss and expound the
Law.

Two great rabbis had arisen during the reign of Herod
the Great. One, Shammai, was the rector of a leading
Jewish academy and held to the strictest interpretation of
the Law. He was rigid and unbending, giving no quarter
to the life and times of the common people, but held that
the Law must be fulfilled to the last letter if men were to
receive salvation.

The other, Hillel, was only a poor woodcutter in Jerusalem. He had taken a more liberal, humane stand, relying
more on the mercy and love of God to save His people
than on the oppressive, difficult practice of ritual. Hillel
was as humble and compassionate as Shammai was fiery
and harsh, and the sect of the Pharisees had split their
ranks to follow the thought of one or the other.

Any man could aspire to the rabbinate. There were
great rabbinical schools, not only in Jerusalem but elsewhere in the world, where young, intelligent men with a
burning zeal for the Law who were willing to devote
many years to concentrated study in almost abject poverty
could pass the difficult examinations and be admitted into
the rabbinate. These young men became the rabbis and
scribes in the sect of the Pharisees, for only by inheritance
could one be considered a Sadducee. Thus the majority of
the Sanhedrin were Pharisees, but the overriding power of
the High Priest came from the ranks of the Sadducees.

Each rabbi had his own following of disciples, and
lively arguments over whose rabbi was the greatest and
which possessed the most mystical powers assailed the air.
Men would move from group to group, questioning each
teacher on a point of Law and then argue among themselves which teacher had given the wisest answer.

Lazarus had taken Jeshua in tow and introduced him to
all the great rabbis of the day. Syrus was a Sadducee of
great wealth and influence. He was revered for his piety
and great wisdom by both schools of thought, and was an
honored member of the Sanhedrin. He was renowned
as a just man, humble and exceedingly charitable, and his

advice was sought by rich and poor alike. As Syrus' only son, Lazarus would one day inherit both his father's wealth and his position, and so the lad was treated with the utmost courtesy by all the priests, and was made welcome wherever he went in the temple precincts.

Jeshua and Lazarus moved from group to group, listening to the various interpretations of the Scriptures, and Jeshua had been surprised to find that even Essene teachers held forth, their identity only thinly veiled by their words. They sat at the feet of Gamaliel, the foremost disciple and successor to the gentle Hillel, and Jeshua thrilled to the compassionate, loving teachings of the revered sage.

Jeshua became so caught up in the excitement of such heady, intense discussions that he burned with questions until finally, no longer able to contain himself, he'd given voice to the ragings in his heart.

At first the priests and rabbis had been surprised at the boldness of one so young to enter into such discussions with his elders, and tolerated his intrusion only because he was Lazarus' friend. But their condescending indulgence soon turned to open respect at the depth of Jeshua's questions and his profound understanding of the Holy Scriptures.

Jeshua spent every moment he could with the rabbis and priests in the temple. He became so absorbed with all he heard and saw and learned that his mind could think of nothing else. When the week was over and it was time for the caravan to leave Jerusalem and return to Galilee, he didn't even hear Mary tell him that they would leave on the morrow, and instead of joining the others, had returned to the temple. Mary and Joseph assumed the next morning that Jeshua was with Josie, and it wasn't until nightfall that they realized that Jeshua was not in the caravan. They returned to Jerusalem at once, frantic with worry and fear. They searched for him at Zebedee's, then at Bethany, and at Josie's, when finally on the third morning they found him sitting in the midst of the teachers in the temple.

Mary's fears dissolved into parental indignation that her usually so considerate and obedient son had caused them such anxiety.

"Son, why have you done this to us?" she asked. "You see that your father and I have been searching for you in sorrow."

Jeshua seemed surprised at her question. "Why did you search for me? Did you not know I had to be in my Father's house?"

Neither Mary nor Joseph understood what Jeshua meant, but they refrained from further scoldings, realizing again that their son was in some inexplicable way not their son, but belonged to a destiny and time they could not understand.

They rejoined the caravan and returned to Capernaum, and Jeshua went back to Mt. Carmel. A few months later Mary gave birth to a son whom Joseph named James. A year later their daughter Ruth was born, and two years after Ruth, Jude.

Jeshua studied under Judith until there was nothing more she could teach him. When the strange Egyptian she'd met at the Pyramid appeared to her in a dream, Judith sent Jeshua to Egypt. He was fifteen years old, and those men of great wisdom found him to be of remarkable wisdom and intelligence, and in turn sent him on to India where for three more years he learned the stringent disciplines of mind and body and the ancient technique of bringing them into one accord with all the universe. From India they sent him to Persia, where other-worldly, mystical men taught him the ancient arts of mind over matter and the complete subjection of the flesh to the will.

It was while he was in Persia that Jeshua learned that Joseph was dying. He took the first ship home.

PART II
RUTH

Chapter 21

J ude stirred in his sleep and coughed a short, childish hack, disturbing Ruth, who lay cured around his back with one brown arm flung across his shoulders. She rolled over to put her back between the irritating sound and her dreams, and the thin woolen blanket slipped away from her body, letting the predawn chill penetrate her flimsy shift. She groped for the blanket, still in a half-sleep, and then bolted upright as the memory of last night banished the wispy dreams from her mind.

The room was shadowed and cold. The streets were quiet and the only sound was her brothers' shallow, even breath. Ruth strained to hear any movement from the kitchen and courtyard below, and the silence assured her that even Josie wasn't stirring.

She was fully awake now, and the memory of last night made her heart pound with excitement. She brushed the blanket off her ankles and got up, pulling a tunic over her head in one fluid movement and quickly tying a rope belt around her waist. The floor was cold beneath her feet and she glanced at her sandals, but decided against them. She carefully picked her way around the sleeping boys to the open arch which led to the outside stairway. She crept down the stairs, placing each foot with deliberate care lest she disturb a pebble and awaken her mother or Josie.

The grass was wet and cold on her bare feet, its dryness sharp and prickly as she ran swiftly across the yard to Cleopas' house and climbed the outdoor stairway as cautiously as she had descended her own. She paused at the doorway, searching the sleeping bodies until she found Susane. She slipped into the gray dimness like a ghostly wraith and shook Susane until the girl awoke with a start.

Ruth quickly put her hand over Susane's mouth and put her finger to her own lips. She motioned to her to follow and then crept back out of the room and down the stairs.

A grapevine covered the wall between Cleopas' house and Joseph's, forming a leafy bower which Susane and Ruth used as their private, secret, hiding place. Ruth ran across the short space from the house to the vine and dropped to her knees and crawled in. She waited only a few moments before Susane's sleepy face appeared among the branches. Ruth grabbed her by the shoulders and pulled her in also.

Susane seated herself on the smooth, packed ground and rubbed her knuckles across her eyes. "What's the matter?" she asked with a yawn.

"Sh!" Ruth warned. "He came!" she said dramatically, and waited for Susane's excited response.

Susane looked at Ruth dully, her mind still fogged with sleep. "Who came?"

Ruth looked at her in disgust and shook her roughly. "Wake up! He came! Jeshua. Last night!" she said triumphantly.

"Jeshua? From Persia? When did he get here? Did you see him? What is he like?" The words tumbled from Susane's mouth in a rush.

Ruth sighed with relief. At least Susane was awake.

Susane flung her tangled blond curls back from her face and looked at Ruth with huge, questioning blue eyes. "Did he speak to you?" she asked excitedly.

Ruth took a pose of casual indifference. "No. It was late when he came. We were already in bed, but I wasn't asleep yet. I heard him come and then Mother and Josie talking to him. I sneaked down the stairs and watched."

Susane gasped at Ruth's audacity, and then said in an unbelieving tone, "How do you know it was him?"

"Because Mother kissed him and wept. Then Josie hugged him and got him something to eat. I couldn't hear what they said, but I know it was Jeshua."

"What does he look like?"

"I couldn't see his face, but he's very big. He's much taller than Mother or Josie."

"Everybody is taller than your mother!" Susane scoffed. "Even I."

"Well, I still say he's big. Bigger than Father, even,"

Ruth said defiantly. "And you're not taller than Mother!"

"Almost!" said Susane.

For a moment Susane was quiet, deep in thought. Joseph was very big, tall and broad-shouldered, and if he didn't have such kindly eyes and such a gentle way, Susane knew she would be afraid of him. Could Jeshua really be bigger than Joseph?

The sky had lightened and was streaked with pink and lavender ribbons. Susane squirmed, knowing she should get back to her house before the others awoke, but there was so much more she had to ask Ruth. She opened her mouth to speak and then a movement caught her eye. She looked toward Ruth's house and dug her fingers into Ruth's arm. "Look!" she whispered.

Jeshua had come out of the house and was washing his hands and face in water from one of the large, open-mouthed, earthen jars which stood outside the door. He washed his face first, his lips moving silently, and then poured the water over his hands, intoning the ritual cleansing prayers to greet a new day washed free from sin.

He turned and faced the rising sun. It broke free from the confines of the hills and bathed the courtyard in a wash of gold. Jeshua raised his arms and opened his palms to the Lord. The girls watched breathlessly, a look of awe and wonder on their faces.

Jeshua was tall. He wore a rough, dun-colored cloak tied with a hemp-rope belt. The full sleeves fell back from his upraised hands, exposing his thick, sun-browned, muscular arms. He wore his hair long to his shoulders and parted in the center like all Galileans, and his beard was full and neatly shaped. The sun caught the gold in his hair and beard and pulled it into a gauzy halo that framed his face. He said his prayers aloud, his voice deep and rich and melodious like Mary's.

The girls shivered and clasped one another's hands. There was an unearthly quality about Jeshua. The sun diffused the misty, early morning air and seemed to glow around him in a golden aura. Fragments of memory flitted through Ruth's mind of strange stories and events she'd overheard that surrounded the life of this grown man who was her brother.

The girls sat mesmerized until Jeshua finished his

prayers and lowered his arms. Then Susane whispered, "I've got to go," and before Ruth could stop her, she'd crawled out of the secret place and was flying toward home.

Jeshua turned and looked with suprise at Susane's fleeing figure, then his eyes turned to the hard-packed earth before the opening to the bower.

Ruth's heart sank. There was nothing to do but crawl out. How embarrassing to meet her long-awaited elder brother for the first time with her hair uncombed and her feet bare, and on her knees! She pushed the branches aside, cursing the traitorous Susane under her breath, and emerged flushed and dusty to face the man whom so many whispered about in tones of awe and sometimes derision. Her blood pounded in her ears and she was afraid. She reminded herself that she was no coward, and forced herself to stand straight and defiant before Jeshua.

Jeshua tried to hide his amusement at Ruth's discomfiture. There was no mistaking who she was. She had Joseph's dark, thick curls and long, soft lashes framing her large gray eyes. Her skin was a golden hue, tanned nearly olive by the summer sun, and the stubborn, defiant look was entirely like her father's. Only her size betrayed that she was also a child of Mary's—small, diminutive, with a look of femininity that sharply contrasted with her determined air.

Ruth studied Jeshua as closely as he studied her. She saw his face and coloring were exactly like her mother's and James', and she felt a stab of jealousy. She'd always wished that she'd been the one to look like Mary, not James. Mary was the most beautiful woman Ruth knew, and she bemoaned the fact that James had inherited Mary's glorious red-gold hair while she and Jude had had to settle for the ordinary black. Now when she saw that Jeshua, too, had been blessed with Mary's extraordinary coloring, she felt even more bedraggled and unkempt.

She expected a scolding, or at least a look of disapproval from Jeshua, and was surprised to see a merry twinkle in his eye and a small, conspiratorial smile play about his mouth. She relaxed her determined stance a little and wondered what she would say to him. Finally, in as dignified a voice as she could muster, she said, "Peace be with you."

Jeshua's smile spread and he slightly lowered his head toward her. "Peace be with you. You are an early riser, my sister," he answered.

"How do you know me?" Ruth asked.

"I remember you well," Jeshua said gently. "You were only a babe of two when I left, and so cannot remember me, but I was fifteen and so remember you well. We were great friends then, you and I."

Ruth looked at him wonderingly. How could she not remember him? His voice was tender and appealing, like her mother's, and Ruth felt a definite attraction to him. And he said they had been friends. James was so serious and superior, and Jude was such a baby; maybe this brother could be a friend, even though he was so old.

"How old are you?" Ruth blurted, and then clamped her mouth shut, mortified by the rudeness of her question.

"I am twenty-one years," Jeshua answered gravely, not seeming to notice that the question was impolite. "And you are eight. Not so long a span that we cannot be friends."

Jeshua moved to a low stone bench beneath a tree and sat with his hands upon his knees. His hands were long and narrow, his fingers finely tapered with well-shaped nails. He patted the bench beside him. "Come. Sit with me and tell me of our family."

Ruth hesitated. She still was a little awed by him, though no longer afraid. There was something different about him, and she couldn't forget the whispered comments she'd overheard. She walked slowly toward him and sat down gingerly, keeping a goodly space between them.

Jeshua looked toward the grapevine. "I see you've found my secret place. I'm glad. The vine must have been lonely without a child beneath its branches."

Ruth was stunned. "Your secret place?" she asked incredulously.

"I had no friend to share it with, only a puppy, but I spent many hours there in its friendly shade studying the Torah and thinking. Who is your friend?"

Ruth was amazed. She couldn't imagine Jeshua as a boy her own age sitting in her secret place. She stammered, "Her—she is Susane, daughter of Cleopas. She lives in the next house and is my closest friend."

"Ah, yes. I remember when Cleopas married and that his wife gave birth just prior to our mother."

"We study the Law there, too. Josie and Mother are our teachers. Mostly Josie, since Father has been ill."

"They taught me also," said Jeshua.

"James attends the synagogue, but Josie also teaches him. He is almost ten, and then he'll go to the City of Salt. He wishes to become a monk like Roael."

"And Jude?" Jeshua asked.

"Jude is just a baby. He's only six and he doesn't like to study. He only wants to go with Father and be a carpenter. James gets disgusted with him. He says to be a scholar and a teacher is the finest thing, that anyone can be a carpenter."

"If all men were teachers only, who would they teach?" asked Jeshua. "To be a carpenter and to be of service to others in providing the tools and homes and furnishings others need is also a fine thing. Is not our father Joseph a carpenter?"

"Yes," Ruth nodded. "But he was a monk first."

"He was also a carpenter while he was a monk. All labor glorifies the Lord when it is done in the spirit of giving service to His children, no matter how lowly the world thinks it to be. The simple shepherd who cares for the creatures created by God, the Father of All, is as exalted in the eyes of the Lord as the greatest of the rabbis and priests."

Ruth thought about that and then answered, "But man is the Holy One's greatest creation. Did He not set man above the animals of the earth and the fishes in the sea?"

Jeshua looked into her serious little face. "You answer well, sister. Yes. He endowed man with reason and free will and set him over all the earth, but with the intention that man should care for the rest of the Lord's creation, to be a servant of the Lord. Is it not written, 'The Lord's are the earth and its fulness; the world and those who live in it'? Man is as a steward of the Lord. As a landowner sets his son to manage and care for his estates, so are we set over the world."

This was more food for thought than Ruth could digest immediately. She'd have to think about it. She changed the subject.

"Will you stay home now?" she asked.

"For a time," said Jeshua.

"Will you be a rabbi?"

Jeshua didn't answer immediately. His blue-gray eyes clouded with sadness and seemed to see far beyond the hills of Galilee. When he spoke, his words fell heavy and sorrowfully from his lips. "I will be as the Father wills."

Ruth saw the burden of sadness in Jeshua's eyes and wondered what their father willed for her brother. His answer seemed mysterious to her, and she sensed it best not to question him further. She thought about the reason she had been so anxious for Jeshua to come home, and fought a battle with herself as to whether she should ask the question burning in her breast. She remembered the whispered stories of strange happenings and healings which had occurred in Jeshua's presence and decided to ask, her need to know greater than her fear of asking.

"Will you heal our father?" she blurted."

Jeshua started and looked at her with surprise.

"They say you have the gift of healing, even more than Judith," Ruth rushed on before she lost her courage, "and I thought you could heal our father and then he wouldn't die!"

Jeshua didn't answer. Ruth's heart pounded and she was aghast at her own temerity. She fought the tears which threatened to form and clenched her fists in defiance. Why shouldn't she ask! she thought angrily. Joseph was his father as much as hers. If Jeshua could heal others, than surely he had come to heal his own father!

"I come to do the will of our heavenly Father," Jeshua said gently.

Ruth tossed her head and pushed on stubbornly. "Will you heal Joseph?"

"Joseph is old, he has accomplished all the Father had sent him to do. Would you keep him from his rest for your own sake?" Jeshua asked tenderly.

His answer was one Ruth had feared. The tears had their way and stung her eyes. She didn't want to be selfish, but she loved Joseph so. She was the only daughter and as such, was Joseph's pet and favorite. She couldn't imagine life without Joseph's cozy lap and tender arms. She swallowed hard, her voice barely audible.

"I don't want him to die!" she cried desperately.

Jeshua's heart broke at the grief in the child's eyes and

at her valiant struggle to contain her tears. He suddenly lifted her from the bench and cuddled her in his lap. His action so startled Ruth that for a moment she stiffened in his arms, and then all the weeks of pent-up fear and hope broke loose, and she clung to Jeshua and sobbed wildly into his breast. He had been her last hope. She'd pinned everything on his arrival, and had made herself believe that Joseph would live if only Jeshua came home. But now he gave no encouragement, and she was filled with despair.

Jeshua rocked her in his arms and crooned soothingly into her hair. He kissed her wet cheek and brushed her tangled curls back from her face. He was comforting and tender and Ruth nestled closer to him, her violent sobs subsiding .under his gentle, understanding caresses. She quieted, and they sat motionless for a time. It was peaceful and safe in Jeshua's arms, and resignation slowly seeped into Ruth's aching heart.

She wiped her eyes on her bare arm and said in a low voice without looking up, "Where will the soul of our father go?"

Jeshua sighed. How was he to answer a child the question which men have asked through the ages? He put his finger under Ruth's chin and tilted her little, tearstained face up to meet his eyes.

"Our heavenly Father's house has many mansions. Even now, His heavenly hosts prepare a place for our father, Joseph."

Jeshua felt his answer to be so inadequate, and yet, little did he know that one day he would use the same analogy to men mature in years, but childish in understanding.

Ruth looked into Jeshua's eyes, eyes that were so filled with compassion and love that she felt swallowed up in them, warm and safe and more peaceful and protected than she had ever been before. Her mind's eye saw a huge palace, more glorious even than the holy temple. A palace of gold and precious gems with large, airy rooms that smelled of lavender and sweet incense. She saw a myraid of white, resplendent angels hurrying to sweep and air the wonderful room which Joseph's soul would occupy.

She was comforted. She smiled tremulously at Jeshua and wound her soft round arms about his neck. He was indeed her friend. A well of love rose in her breast and she suddenly felt very happy.

A clatter of pots came from the house, and Jeshua untwined Ruth's arms and set her on the ground. "I hear Josie. Come. We must go and greet the others."

Ruth looked down at her dusty tunic with dismay. Her hair was tangled and her face was dirty and tearstained, and her feet were bare. What would she say in explanation to Josie and her mother?

Jeshua seemed to read her thoughts. He laughed merrily. He took her hand and led her to the water jars and tenderly washed her face and feet. He brushed the dust from her tunic and whispered, "Run upstairs and find a comb."

Ruth flew up the outside stairs and returned with a comb and a ribbon. Jeshua struggled through the tangled mass, his clumsy efforts making them both giggle softly. He finally got all the snarls smooth and tied the ribbon around her head as she held her hair free from her neck.

Jeshua held her out from him by her shoulders and made a great pretense of inspecting her, his brows knit and his lips pursed. Then he seemed satisfied and smiled. "That's better. Now you are quite beautiful again."

Ruth flushed, and Jeshua took her hand and they walked into the house together.

Chapter 22

The very sight of Jeshua caused Joseph to rally. His voice became stronger and his eyes lost their cloudy, fevered gaze, and Ruth's hopes soared. She shot Jeshua a look of triumph and ignored the imperceptible shake of his head, convinced if only she could believe hard enough that Joseph would live, he would.

The news of Jeshua's homecoming sped throughout the Essene community, and soon the house was filled with kinsmen and friends who came to welcome him home and with a few who were simply curious to see the grown-up son of Mary.

Ruth had mixed emotions over all the turmoil and excitement. She normally loved company, times when the family would gather for weddings or circumcisions or to celebrate the feast days. Being the only girl among the cousins her age was a definite advantage as far as the amount of attention she received was concerned. Her aunts would smother her face in their ample bosoms and cover her cheeks with wet, loving kisses. They'd examine her needlework with cries of approval, and lavish praise on her attempts at baking the sticky, sweet, honey cakes. Her uncles and older cousins cuddled her in their laps, amazed at what a young maid she'd become, and, tickling her neck with their soft beards, they kissed her cheek and declared they would marry her themselves.

Naomi was a teacher at the Jerusalem temple, and Lia, the Other Mary's daughter, taught at the City of Salt. They let Ruth listen to all the funny and sometimes sad stories about their students and fellow teachers. Josie's daughters, Rhoda and Mary, let her hold their babies in her lap, and taught her the proper way to feed and care for them, and Ruth resolved to have as many of the adorable little creatures as God would permit.

Being the only girl also had its disadvantages, for the boys were allowed to do many things that Ruth was not, such as go fishing on one of Uncle Zebedee's boats, which Ruth longed to do. The boys did let her join in the games they played in the courtyard, and even included Susane, since she was almost one of the family, thanks to John ben Zebedee. James thought it was improper for a girl to run and chase a ball and climb trees, and lively arguments over the matter often broke out among the cousins. John was a few months older than James, and Joses ben Alphaeus even older than John, though not as tall or handsome, Ruth thought. The older boys usually sided together and James was overruled.

John was Ruth's favorite. He was a warm, generous, outgoing boy with a high temper that vanished as quickly as it flared, leaving his oval face bathed in smiles as he laughed the merriest laugh of all at his own occasional outbursts. He was gregarious and displayed none of James' superior attitude toward Ruth and Susane, but treated the girls as friends and equals.

The only thing Ruth disapproved of in John was his obvious infatuation with Martha, Sophia's daughter, who lived next door to Ruth. Martha was eleven, beautiful and feminine; she would never dream of climbing a tree. Ruth and Susane liked her when the boys weren't around and she wasn't putting on feminine airs, but all she had to do was step foot in the courtyard and the boys forgot that Ruth and Susane existed.

This time the family gathering was different from the others. The atmosphere in the house was solemn and subdued. The women spoke in whispers, and the children were hushed and chased out of the house. Ruth felt lonely and left out. No one paid any attention to her, and she felt as though she were in everyone's way. Her lessons with Jude had come to a halt, much to Jude's delight, but Ruth missed those intimate hours with her mother. Mary was always with Joseph or talking in subdued tones with the aunts, and except for an occasional gentle caress, Ruth hardly saw her at all. Jeshua spent most of his time at Joseph's bedside or in deep discussions with his uncles and the cousins who were his own age, and even beloved Josie, who was like a second mother, was too busy supervising the servants in preparing the large quantities of food needed to feed everyone to pay any mind to Ruth.

Her uncles and older cousins made short, embarrassed visits to the sickroom, shuffling their feet and making awkward attempts at levity. What did one say to a dying man? They patted Mary's shoulder and made inane remarks which were intended to console, but only resulted in embarrassment for everyone. Ruth hated it all.

Sometimes when James was bent over his studies, John wheedled permission from Aunt Salome and Mary to take the girls to visit James ben Zebedee. James had married Abigale, one of the eleven girls chosen with Mary, and they lived in Capernaum, where James supervised Zebedee's fishing enterprises. Since John was the apple of his mother's eye, and a favorite with all the women, no one could resist his teasing pleas, and permission was granted. John's vivid imagination turned those outings into high adventure that temporarily banished Ruth's fear and worry over Joseph, but those occasions were rare, and Ruth was mostly left to her own devices.

Josie charged Ruth and Susane with the task of entertaining John Mark and keeping him out from underfoot. John Mark was Aunt Josie's miracle baby. Mary and Rhoda had already grown to young maidenhood when he was born, and even the fact that his left foot was twisted and withered at birth had cast only a fleeting shadow over their joy at having a son.

The girls didn't mind looking after John Mark. He was an adorable child. His bright blond curls gave him the look of a cherub, and his sunny disposition was reflected in his merry, dark blue eyes. He was a teasing, laughing child who didn't seem to notice that he couldn't run and climb like other children.

One day when Ruth and Susane were playing with him, Jeshua had come out into the courtyard and stood watching them. When Ruth saw him, she'd gone to his side and looked up at him imploringly. If he couldn't heal Joseph, maybe he could help John Mark. Jeshua had read what Ruth was silently asking, and shook his head, saying, "My time has not yet come, Ruth. One day, perhaps, but not yet."

Ruth was disappointed, but at least Jeshua had given her hope this time.

As the weeks went by, Ruth began to resent all those who had come. She wished they'd stay home and let Joseph die in peace. She could hardly bear to think of Joseph's dying, and everyone milling about was a constant reminder. She couldn't imagine the house with only Mother and Josie and the boys. She worried over how they would live, who would earn the money they needed for food and oil and clothing? James couldn't—he was only nine, and besides, he talked of nothing else than going to the City of Salt and becoming a monk like Roael. Maybe they would have to leave their home and go to live with Uncle Alphaeus or at Mt. Carmel!

Ruth shuddered at the thought. She didn't want to go to Mt. Carmel and live in a tent, nor did she want to live in Uncle Alphaeus' house, which was a constant turmoil of activity and loud male voices. Her cousins were always arguing about the Law and the plight of the Jews and the political situation, and Aunt Mary had a high, shrill voice which reverberated throughout the house as she scolded and ordered everyone about in a futile attempt to bring order. Ruth despaired at having to live in such clamorous turmoil.

Nor could she bear the thought of living with Aunt Salone, or Uncle Zebedee, or Aunt Josie, for to do so meant leaving Capernaum, and leaving Capernaum meant leaving Susane. Even though Ruth was often exasperated by Susane's timidity and fear of getting into trouble, she couldn't remember a time when Susane had not been her friend, and to lose her father and her best friend all at once was just too much.

Ruth's worry and fears made her cry, and she hated that. She'd hide under the vine in her secret place to cry so no one would see what a baby she was. She didn't sleep well at night, and her appetite waned, but no one seemed to notice. She held out a thin thread of hope that maybe Jeshua would stay and work in Uncle Alphaeus' shop, but somehow she knew that Jeshua's life would not be spent as a carpenter.

So she fretted, longing to throw herself into Mary's arms and sob out her fears, but her stubborn little will refused to add to Mary's burdens, and she kept her suffering to herself.

Then one morning Roael arrived from the City of Salt with Elizabeth and Adahr. It was the first time Ruth had ever seen her mother abandon her calm serene manner as she ran across the courtyard like a young girl and threw herself on Elizabeth's breast. The whole household erupted into a frenzy of excitement and Ruth's tears vanished like the morning dew.

Elizabeth rarely left the City of Salt. When she'd fled to the Judean hills with John as a babe in arms, the world had seemed to her a place of madness where men murdered their friends simply because they held a different thought, and children could be slaughtered on the whim of a despot. It had seemed to her as though the Lord had turned His face away from His whole creation and had given it up to the pleasures of Belial.

Elizabeth feared and despised the world. She'd never been able to accept the fact that Zachariah had been murdered with his hands on the very horns of the altar. That, to Elizabeth, had been the ultimate sacrilege, the final proof that God despaired of the world and that the end was near. She'd been terrorized by the slaughter of the innocents. She'd recoiled in horror when her friends had been deprived of the fruit of their wombs. She'd clung to John with the fierceness of a lioness protecting her cub and vowed never to subject her son to the evil world.

For fifteen years they'd stayed in the safety of the City of Salt, Adahr even more bitter and vengeful than Elizabeth, but John's fiery will had proved too much for the women. John was a child of destiny, a soul born with a purpose and a work to do, and not even the overprotective, suffocating love of his mother and sister could deter him from fulfilling his mission on earth.

John had taken the vow of the Nazirites as his father had prophesied, refusing to cut his hair or to drink strong spirits. His zeal for the Law bordered on the fanatic, and he'd spend weeks alone in the barren hills, living on nothing but locusts and what grasses and roots he could find. He subjected his body to every rigorous torture of the flesh he could devise in the attempt to subject the flesh completely to the will.

Even as a young lad he was alarming and fearsome. His long hair blew wildly in the Judean wind, and he garbed himself in hairy animal skins that scratched and irritated his skin and tested his will to the extreme as he forced his mind to concentrate on his prayers and to ignore the pain and discomfort of his flesh. Those who didn't know him recoiled from him in fear and awe, thinking he was mad, but those in the City of Salt knew the depths of his love for men and how he anguished over the sins of his people which separated them from the Holy One. They knew his terrible aspect was only the manifestation of his zeal for the Lord and his love for men.

Judith had taken Jeshua to the City of Salt one time to visit John so that he would know the character of the man who would prepare the way for the Messiah. The contrast in the two boys was so remarkable that all the Essenes had marvelled at the ways of the Lord.

Jeshua also wore his hair long, but it was brushed to a high sheen and lay in soft neat waves to his shoulders. His clothes were of soft, flowing materials, spotlessly clean, and well-cut. His voice was soft and low and had the unusual quality of carrying over the wind so that sometimes even the monks in the field would smile as they tilled the ground and listened to the boy repeat his lessons.

John's eyes were wild and hypnotic with zeal, while Jeshua's were warm and merry. John drew people to him by the sheer force of his powerful personality, and Jeshua with a gentle love which seemed to flow out from his very body and touch everyone with a warm caress.

Despite their differences, there was a bond of affection and understanding between the boys that far surpassed the normal bond of kindship. They walked across the bleak hills together, John gesturing wildly and his voice resounding against the rocky peaks, while Jeshua walked quietly at his side, his step firm and graceful, his retorts mild and profound. Even though Jeshua was the younger and smaller in stature of the two, it soon became apparent that John ceded to Jeshua's gentle wisdom and regarded the younger boy as his superior in knowledge and understanding.

John had followed Jeshua into Egypt and had also been examined by the holy men there as to his qualifications for the priesthood. John was a Levite, and thus could assume the priestly position which Zachariah had held in the Jerusalem temple, a fact which filled Elizabeth with great anxiety. But John had remained in Egypt, furthering his studies under the great masters and preparing himself both spiritually and physically for the great work God had sent him to do. It was only after John had left Judea that Elizabeth ventured out into the world, but even then, it was only to Mt. Carmel for Passover, and never to make social visits. This was the first time in over twenty years that Elizabeth had joined in a family gathering.

Ruth loved Elizabeth. The whole family milled around her, talking, laughing, pressing delicacies of food upon her and urging her to put her feet up, to rest, to sit, and everything else they could think of for her comfort and pleasure. The Other Mary and Timothy, Aunt Salone and Uncle Zuriah came from Cana, and Judith and Justin brought their sons Phinehas and Servilius from Mt. Carmel, just in honor of Elizabeth. Even Joseph had grasped Elizabeth's hand, his fevered eyes filling with tears, too overcome with joy to speak.

She was the most honored guest Ruth had ever seen in the house, except for Jeshua. Elizabeth was wonderful, and best of all, she claimed Ruth for her own, petting her and fussing over her, and always making sure there was a place for Ruth at her side.

Ruth revelled in Elizabeth's reflected glory. Elizabeth was short and round and had the coziest lap Ruth had ever known, so soft and warm that Ruth didn't care if she was too big to sit in someone's lap; she did it anyway. Elizabeth knew the best stories and the games that were most fun and seemed to know exactly how it felt to be an eight year old, frightened, lonely little girl. She insisted that Ruth show her Capernaum, and invited Susane to go along. She bought them sweets and toys in the market place, and they watched the boats set sail in the setting sun. They watched the women clean and sort the night's catch, giggling and holding their noses against the pungent smell, and sailed little leaf and twig boats in the blue Galilee. Those were sunny, fun-filled days, each one holding the promise of discovery and excitement, and each one held Ruth's fears and worries at bay.

One day when Ruth and Susane returned with Elizabeth from one of their excursions, Mary met them at the gate to tell Elizabeth that Syrus and Lazarus had arrived from Bethany. Ruth shot Susane a look of aversion, then asked as innocently as she could, "Did Martha and Mary come with them?"

Mary smiled understandingly, which embarrassed Ruth —her mother could see through her motives too easily. "No. Not this time," she said gently. "Only Syrus and Lazarus are here."

Both Ruth and Susane sighed with relief. They didn't like Mary. She was older than they, thirteen, and was extraordinarily beautiful, as well as being aware of it. Mary was vain and willful and was forever putting on airs in front of the younger girls. She was pompous, and overbearingly sophisticated and worldly, continually boasting of her wealthy friends and of her own popularity among them. She flaunted her fine clothes and beautiful red hair, and flirted outrageously with the men. She filled Ruth and Susane with disgust, but their mothers had ordered them to treat her with kindness and courtesy and to play no pranks!

Martha and Lazarus had extravagantly spoiled their orphaned baby sister. Syrus doted on her, lavishing everything she wanted upon her, and was unable to resist her petulant demands. They all turned a blind eye to Mary's caprices and vanity, and thought her antics adorable and charming. The other women watched her with a wary eye, and Ruth's mother, especially, worried about her. Mary had tried delicately to warn Martha that the girl would bring them to grief if her wild spirit was not curtailed, but her gentle admonishments had fallen on deaf ears and all the older Mary could do was pray.

Martha was a plain, hard-working young woman who had dedicated herself to raising Mary and making a home for Lazarus and Syrus. Everyone marvelled at the sacrifice Martha made for her family, but secretly Martha was only too happy to have an excuse not to marry. She was terrified of childbirth after having watched her mother die in the throes of birth pangs, and she felt a repugnance for men in general. She thought them to be rough and loud and uncouth in their virility, and she looked upon them in hidden distaste. She didn't think of Lazarus and Syrus as being like other men. They were both meticulously clean and somewhat ascetic. They lived in a world of scrolls and learning, and they spoke quietly and kindly at all times. Coarse laughter and angry words were simply unheard of in Martha's house.

Martha was a stern, proud woman. She tried to make up for her lack of beauty and graciousness by excelling in the arts of homemaking. Her home was tastefully furnished and polished to a high sheen, and her table boasted of the finest cuisine. Her hospitality was renowned and her charitable works in the Jerusalem temple were formidable. She loved with a possessive, jealous love which her pride and reticent nature would not allow to manifest in open affection. She seemed harsh and overstrict to young Mary, when in fact it was Martha's only way of showing her love.

Mary was everything Martha wished that she, herself were—beautiful, vivacious, and popular. Martha was fiercely proud of Mary, but she didn't know how to show it. Instead of praising the girl and guiding her with firm gentleness, Martha could only give her attention by picking at her. She was constantly at Mary to comb her hair, straighten her skirts, sit up like a lady, and so on, until Mary rebelled and lashed out at her sister in a fit of temper. Even then Martha found no real fault in Mary, but only laughed at what she termed "Mary's high spirits."

Syrus and Lazarus didn't help the situation. They lavished Mary with affection and gifts, but gave her no solid guidance. They treated her like a precious, empty-headed doll, and never attempted to enter into a serious discussion with her. So Mary had to find her own way, and she used her beauty and willfulness to get the attention she so desperately longed for, even though it was not the kind she needed. The men thought she was adorable and the women thought she was a little tart, and Ruth and Susane thought she was simply obnoxious.

Only Ruth's mother saw the desperate need in Mary, and she didn't know what to do about it. She only saw Mary of Syrus once or twice a year for a day or two at a time, and while the girl seemed to have more respect and real affection for Mary than for any other adult, there simply wasn't enough time for Mary's influence to be very effective. She'd once suggested that the younger Mary come to stay for a few weeks in Capernaum, but she'd received such vehement protests from Martha that she'd reluctantly dropped the subject.

Ruth and Susane exchanged satisfied looks, and their outings with Elizabeth continued uninterrupted.

The days began to cool and the nights became cold and raw. The harvests were brought to the storage barns and the earth snuggled down for her annual rest.

Joseph grew steadily weaker until Ruth could hardly bear to stand by his bed and look at his thin, emaciated face. She held his limp, withered hand, calling his name in her high childish voice, but couldn't penetrate the fevered haze that separated her from her father. Ruth then carefully laid Joseph's hand back on the coverlet and walked steadily out of the room. But once outside, she fled to the vine and led the river of her grief flow.

Lazarus and Jeshua renewed their boyhood friendship and spent long hours together discussing the Law. In the early evening while Joseph slept and the sun shed its last warmth upon the day, they would all gather around Jeshua in the courtyard and listen as he explained the meanings of the more obscure passages in the Scriptures and taught them of the gentle, loving ways of the Father.

Jeshua's low, soothing voice enthralled them, and his words touched the very depths of their souls. He wove a picture of a loving God, merciful, everlastingly just. Ruth felt tears prick against her lids as her childish image of God as a fiery, vengeful ruler changed into a kindly, loving, forgiving Father, not too unlike her father Joseph.

Joseph died and Josie closed his eyes in their final sleep. Ruth fled from the house and flung herself into the secret place where Jeshua later found her. He lifted her into his arms, and carried her like a baby. They stood beneath the overcast sky, their tears mingling on their closely pressed cheeks as they wept together.

They laid Joseph to rest in a tomb outside Capernaum. The funeral procession seemed to stretch endlessly behind the wailing, hired mourners, as men, women, and children, some of whom even Mary had never seen before, came to pay homage to the beloved carpenter of Capernaum.

Ruth thought she couldn't bear it, that she simply

couldn't live through this day. She kept her eye on Jeshua's back as he walked next to her mother in front of her, and later her eyes followed wherever he went through the milling, mourning guests, and somehow she made it through.

That night she lay stiff and sleepless on her cot in the upper room. She listened to the muffled voices murmuring in the kitchen below and to James and Jude as they whimpered and tossed in their sleep beside her. The hours of darkness dragged on and on until finally there was nothing to hear but the ringing silence of death.

Sometime between the witching hours of midnight and dawn, Ruth held her breath when she thought she heard the pitiful cry of a kitten coming from Joseph's empty room below. She strained her ears until they rang, and when she heard it again, crept silently down the inside stair and pushed the curtain to Joseph's room aside.

The moon was full and lit the room with a soft, silvery glow. Ruth saw her mother huddled in Joseph's bed, her shoulders shaking and her hands grasping the pillow which Joseph had used. Ruth slipped across the room and slid quietly beneath the coverlet and entwined her arms about her mother's neck. Mary clutched the child to her breast, and then wife and daughter finally slept.

Ruth's memory of the first few days after Joseph's burial was a blur of departures and tearful farewells until only the family and Josie and Elizabeth remained. The house echoed with silence, and Joseph's empty bed lay like a gaping, open wound on their hearts. It was hard to get used to speaking in normal tones in the house, and Ruth was horrified when once she caught herself hushing Jude for fear he might disturb their father. Once or twice Josie forgot and prepared an extra plate of food for Joseph, and angrily scraped it back into the pot.

Ruth didn't know what they would have done without Jeshua. His lap was a haven of comfort which she and Jude used in turn, and even the stoic James nestled beneath Jeshua's comforting arm. Mary leaned heavily on Jeshua's strength and he often took her for long walks across the rolling hills, and each time they returned, Mary's burden of grief seemed lighter.

Jeshua seemed to carry a share of all their grief. His strong, broad shoulders seemed large enough to bear it all, as one day they would carry the sorrows of all the world. His presence was like a balm, and Ruth thought that wherever she might be in the world, and whatever pain and trouble she might encounter in life, if only Jeshua were there, everything would be all right again.

One night as Jeshua helped Mary tuck the children into their beds and heard their prayers, Ruth reached up and stroked his silky beard, sleepily asking, "Will you be with us always, Jeshua?"

Jeshua had looked across the child's head and met his mother's eyes. Their eyes held for a long moment and a look of such profound sadness crossed Jeshua's face that Ruth wanted to cry. But then he'd said, so gently, "Yes. I'll be with you always," and Ruth had gone to sleep.

The season for grief passed and life returned to normal. Elizabeth decided to stay with Mary and not go back to the City of Salt. Ruth's fears about how they would manage financially vanished as the Essenes contributed generously to the needs of the family, and they had more material sustenance than they'd ever had before.

James' tenth birthday passed and Jeshua took him to the City of Salt, the first step in fulfilling James' dream of becoming a monk. Ruth and Jude resumed their lessons, but Jude chafed under Mary and Josie's gentle admonishments until Jeshua finally enrolled him in the synagogue school.

They all went to Mt. Carmel for Passover, and Jeshua's presence made it an extraordinarily exciting time. When the Essenes learned that Jeshua would be there, they flocked to Mt. Carmel to get a glimpse of the young man who was said to be the Messiah. Ruth nearly burst with pride when Jeshua was called upon to speak at the worship services. She was amazed at how the people hovered about him and clung to his every word when he taught in the temple courtyards. She questioned Mary as to why everyone paid Jeshua such honor, and was awed by the story of Jeshua's birth.

She looked at Jeshua in wonder. He was only Jeshua, her dear elder brother—how could he be the longed-for Messiah? Ruth wrestled with that problem for a time and then set it aside. She didn't care if he were the Messiah or not. He was her brother, and that was enough.

One evening after they returned home from Mt. Carmel, Jeshua gathered the family together and quietly told them that it was time he resumed his Father's work. Ruth knew him well enough by now to know that when he spoke of his "Father," he meant the Most Holy One, God, and not their father, Joseph. Ruth swallowed hard, determined not to cry, for she'd always known inside herself that Jeshua would someday leave. Mary kissed him and gave him her blessing, and no one tried to stop him.

When Jeshua set out on his long journey back to Egypt, Ruth remembered his promise, "I'll be with you, always," and she knew he would—if not in body, then in a way she couldn't now understand. She knew for a certainty he would keep his promise. Almost ten years passed before Ruth saw him again, but she knew that, in some mysterious way, he was always with them.

Chapter 23

R uth and Susane grew up, and the idyll of childhood passed away. The Essenes insisted that Ruth receive an education befitting the sister of the Messiah, and Mary agreed, though not for the same reasons. Mary was well aware of her daughter's quick, intelligent mind, and felt that such a gift from God should not be wasted. Ruth was anxious to continue her studies. There were so many things to learn about the world, and, like Judith at a similar age, her interests covered a broad range of subjects which Mary and Josie were simply unable to teach her.

Capernaum was no different from any city in Palestine in that females were not allowed to attend the schools. Only girls whose families were wealthy enough to afford private tutors or pay the exorbitant tuition fees to the Jerusalem temple school received any education at all, and then out of parental indulgence and a desire for social prestige rather than the recognition of any necessity for female education. A daughter was expected to marry and bear children, and had no need to read or write.

The boys in the poorer families were little better off than their sisters. They were expected to follow their fathers' trades, and other than learn the Torah by rote, and perhaps to sign their names, their education came through experience, and not by formal schooling. The majority of those who were fortunate enough to go to school despised the mass of "unlearned rabble," and took advantage of their ignorance at every turn. Ruth was determined not to be numbered among their ranks.

The Essenes, in their belief of the many incarnations of the soul into both male and female bodies, recognized the importance of learning all one could in every life in order to hasten that state of perfection whereby the soul need not incarnate again, except by choice to aid its brothers. Therefore there was no question as to if or when Ruth should leave her mother's home to go to school, but only *where*.

Judith wanted her to come to Mt. Carmel, but Ruth's aversion to living in a tent made her say no, and the stringent Rule of the Order held little enticement for a girl raised in the carefree, lenient ways of the Galileans. Besides, she knew Judith too well, and rightly guessed that Judith would expect more from her than of any other. Judith's own sons had rebelled under her rigid demands for perfection, and were now lost to her, wandering somewhere in the pagan world in an attempt to find out who they were when not beneath their mother's shadow.

James argued for the City of Salt, but again Ruth stubbornly refused. She couldn't say so, but James' domination would be as bad as Judith's, and the City of Salt was so far away! She wanted to learn about the world, not retreat from it.

Aunt Josie and Uncle Marcus arrived at the perfect solution. They invited Ruth to live with them to act as tutor and companion to John Mark, and in return they would pay Ruth's fees to the temple school. The prospect of living in the Holy City was so exciting that it softened the wrench of leaving home and Susane, but once that first excitement waned, Ruth found herself longing for the simplicity of Capernaum.

Jerusalem was like another world. Ruth had never realized the extent of Josie and Marcus' wealth and social prestige, and from the first day she was overwhelmed. She felt awkward and unkempt and definitely a Galilean. In Capernaum her family was highly respected for their piety and reputation for honesty and integrity, but those things mattered little in Jerusalem. Here people were judged by social graces, fine clothes, gracious homes, and by the wealth and position a man held. Ruth had none of those things, and her natural shyness and lack of worldly knowledge made her feel out of place. The fact that she was Marcus ben Cleopas' niece won her acceptance in most circles, but she was never allowed to entirely forget that she was just a Galilean.

The temple school proved a great disappointment. The

emphasis was on charitable works and managing a home such as Josie's, and even though Naomi was one of her teachers, Ruth thought her classes were boring and use less. Ruth was certain she did not want to marry a simple laborer and spend her life as an obscure wife and mother, but neither could she see herself in the role of society hostess and fashionable matron in the world of art and culture.

She found it difficult to make friends. Her classmates' chatter about fashion and parties and possible love matches seemed silly and childish. Her cousin Ulai of Archaus, whom Ruth had never met before due to Archaus' objection to the family's traffic with the Essenes, tried to include her in her circle of friends, but Ruth knew their acceptance was only because of her kinship to Ulai and not because of herself.

The Essene tenet that "God is no respecter of persons" had been drilled into Ruth since childhood, and she found the other girls' division into cliques and social groups repulsive and almost sinful. It shamed her to learn that Mary of Syrus was the main topic for their gossips, for she remembered how she and Susane used to speak of her, and she now saw themselves reflected in the uncharitable, mean way the girls talked.

Not that Mary did not invite scandal. Ruth was shocked to the core by Mary's total disregard for proper decorum. She was notorious for her behavior among the young men, and for overindulging in strong drink at parties, which of course only served to incite even more licentious behavior. No one would dream of not inviting her, and everyone urged her on in all her indulgences, just to provide fuel for their talk and excitement to the occasion. It disgusted Ruth. She quietly withdrew from Jerusalem society, preferring to spend her leisure in Uncle Marcus' library, or playing games with John Mark.

John Mark was dear, and the one bright spot in Ruth's new life. He was always cheerful despite his twisted foot, and so eager to please that it was a joy to teach him his numbers. Ruth was secretly glad that the hundreds of steps leading up to the temple area made it impossible for him to attend the temple school, for John Mark was too pure a soul to be spoiled by the hypocrisy and false values he would encounter there.

When Ruth began to spend more time at home with Marcus and Josie and young John Mark she naturally became involved in the events taking place there, and, to her dismay, found the things she heard and saw even more disturbing than those at school. She could excuse her classmates' selfishness and overindulgence on grounds of their youth, but now she found the same lack of virtue in the adults she encountered.

She was upset and bewildered by the ambivalence in Uncle Marcus' position. Marcus served as a sort of ambassador or diplomat in Jewish-Roman relations, and Romans and Greeks were frequent guests at Josie's table. To a girl of Ruth's religious upbringing, those men and their sophisticated wives and daughters seemed like a pagan intrusion into her aunt's pious home. Their revealing gowns and barely veiled sexual innuendos embarrassed Ruth. Their gossip was far more vicious than that of the girls at school, and yet even as they condemned some poor, misguided soul, Ruth knew they secretly applauded the actions.

She could have forgiven their wagging tongues and bizarre behavior because, after all, they were pagans who followed false gods who promoted such self-aggrandizement, but Ruth found the same shallow values and lack of integrity in the Jewish leaders who frequented Josie's house.

Marcus was a Sadducee by birth and inheritance, and was an important member of the Sanhedrin. His home was often used as the meeting place for lesser committees and groups to gather to discuss the problems of the day. Men such as Ardemetus, Artemas, Joseph of Arimathaea, and Nicodemus, who were the leaders of Jewish religious and business societies, became well-known to Ruth, and for a time she was awed and impressed by their wealth and business acumen and by their seemingly deep religious piety. It wasn't long before she was disillusioned.

Ruth couldn't tolerate the compromises and pandering to the Romans which she witnessed among her fellow Jews. It was all for the "good of the temple and the nation," of course, but young as she was, Ruth saw how it also added to their own social standing and mostly to their personal coffers. They spoke of the poor and unlearned in tones tinged with scorn, though their words conveyed pity and understanding. When they openly condemned the lax Galileans, Ruth grit her teeth and burned with silent indignation.

There was one man whom Ruth particularly disliked. His name was Smaleuen of the tribe of Reuben—an arrogant, outspoken Pharisee. He was narrow in thought and loudly condemned anyone who didn't agree with his point of view, and was a continual source of dissension. He centered his hatred upon the Essenes and took every opportunity to denounce and discredit them. Everyone who came to Marcus' home knew of his sympathies with that outcast sect, for Marcus made no secret of his beliefs, but most refrained from openly censoring him. Marcus was highly respected for his tolerance to all men, and for his fairness and wise judgments in all matters. Even those who cared nothing for such virtues remembered that he was the son of Cleopas, and through marriage, the kinsman of Syrus of Bethany, and thus feared him for the power he held by his wealth and connections.

Ruth couldn't reconcile Uncle Marcus' ties to the Romans and Greeks and Jews of high office with his deep involvement with the Essenes. There was a large secluded upper room in Marcus' house where weekly the Essenes met for communal fellowship and prayer. During those sessions Marcus was relaxed, open, and free in manner like the beloved uncle who visited her in Capernaum, and not the compromising, placating diplomat she saw during the rest of the week. As she watched him during those meetings, it seemed as though Marcus was two men, lived two lives, and embraced two separate sets of values. She began to question his sincerity and to see him as a hypocrite also, and her disenchantment with all of Jerusalem increased.

It took a long time and many explanations from both Aunt Josie and Uncle Marcus before Ruth came to fully understand the precarious path Marcus walked between Jew and Gentile, and good and evil.

"The sands of the sea did not appear all at once, Ruth," Marcus once told her. "It grew slowly, grain by grain, and so must the hearts and thoughts of man change. The seed of change must first be sown, by a word here, an action there, and then one must exert patience and wait until God in His season brings forth the increase."

Aunt Josie used Ruth herself as an analogy of what Marcus was trying to do. "You attend your classes and mingle with those of whom you disapprove, yet you treat them with kindness and refrain from open recrimination. You refuse to attend their parties and take part in their excessive galas, and yet they see you grow more lovely and gentle with each passing day. They see how the young men curb their tongues and treat you with quiet respect. Perhaps by your example they will grow to know that modesty and kindness is by far the better way."

Josie had smiled. "Your uncle works in the same way. He quietly counsels honesty and justice, and by his example promotes fellowship and acceptance among the different races and creeds. Sometimes they follow Marcus' way, and then he's won a victory for God. Sometimes they ignore him and go their own way, but Marcus does not despair. He continues on, line upon line, in patience and long-suffering, to do the work the Lord has set before him."

"But what can he do? He is all alone, the only one who tries!" Ruth had wailed.

Josie shook her head. "Not so, Ruth. What of you and me, your mother and brothers? What of all those who meet in the upper room? Even some whom you think to be unjust and hypocritical, such as Joseph of Arimathaea, are in their own way, trying."

"Joseph is not an Essene," Ruth argued.

"No. But he is open-minded and condemns no man. God will open his eyes to the Light when He deems the time opportune. Nicodemus is another whose thoughts go deeper than he lets others see."

"Nicodemus!" Ruth had snorted. "His superior attitude toward women is insufferable!"

Josie had laughed outright. "I agree. But no one knows when God will see fit to change his attitude, or what method He will use. Patience, Ruth. That is the key."

While Ruth did come to understand and even greatly admire Marcus, she still could not accept the hypocrisy and bigotry which surrounded her every day. When Uncle Marcus came home with the news that Mary of Syrus had suddenly disappeared, Ruth's already downcast spirits plummeted.

The search for Mary spread throughout Judea. Lazarus, Marcus, and Zebedee used every means at their disposal to find the girl, but to no avail. The talk which buzzed throughout Jerusalem was so uncharitable and unsympathetic that Ruth could no longer bear to go to school, but stayed at home with John Mark until the shocking news that Herod Antipas had married his brother's wife, Herodias, rocked the city and banished all thoughts of a runaway girl from everyone's mind.

Herodias had divorced Philip shortly after the birth of their daughter Salome, and now in flagrant disregard for the Law which clearly stated, "You shall not have intercourse with your brother's wife," she and Herod had married. It was the most scandalous event that had occurred in Jerusalem for years, and the whole city was in an uproar. The religious leaders bitterly condemned Herod for his illicit marriage—privately, of course, for no one dared to openly criticize the king of Galilee. Jerusalem society reeled under the shock of such disgraceful behavior, but at the same time vied for invitations to meet the notorious Herodias and her beautiful, nubile daughter, Salome. The whole affair disgusted Ruth, and she was relieved to learn that Marcus and Josie would have nothing to do with it.

Ruth hardly had had a chance to recover from Mary's disappearance and presumed death when John ben Zachariah returned to Judea and sent Ruth's sense of order and rightness reeling into a morass of confusion.

Ruth, like all of John's kinsmen and fellow Essenes, expected John to follow his father and take up his duties as priest. John was a Levite by birth, and according to Law, it was his rightful place to perform all the priestly functions in the Jerusalem temple. But John cast the priesthood aside. He resumed his youthful course of living in the Judean hills, dressed in animal skins and foraging the barren peaks for food as he preached repentance and rejection of sin to all who would come to hear him.

No one knew what to think of John. He often taught in direct opposition to Essene belief, and offered baptism to any and all who would repent, without having to undergo the harsh period of probation traditional to the sect. They tried to remember the circumstances surrounding his birth, when they believed him to be the Forerunner, but John's actions were so bizarre that many began to question.

He caused quite a stir throughout Judea. Some called him a prophet sent from God, and others deemed him a madman. Some went so far as to say he was possessed by a demon, and some, the Zealots in particular, wondered if he was the Messiah. Whatever they thought, there soon were hundreds of people flocking into the barren hills to see and hear this new phenomenon.

Marcus counseled patience and relied on his faith that God would in time make manifest the truth of John. When John came down out of the hills and began to baptize in the river Jordan, Marcus took Josie and Ruth and John Mark to see him, more to relieve Ruth's mind than to dispel any doubts of his own.

Ruth was shocked by John's appearance, and could hardly believe that he was the merry, kindly Elizabeth's son. His feet were bare. A ragged camel's hair shirt covered his body to his bony knees. He was thin and emaciated. His hair was long and wild and his eyes were like burning coals. His voice thundered across the hills, shouting, "Repent! Reform your lives! The Kingdom of God is near!"

The hills and gorges and riverside swarmed with people. John stood in water up to his thighs, baptizing the hundreds who surged forward by scooping up the muddy water with his hands and dumping it over their heads. Some Pharisees and Sadducees sloughed through the water toward him, and Ruth recoiled as John turned on them, screaming at them in anger and accusation.

"You brood of vipers! Who told you to flee from the wrath to come? Give some evidence that you mean to reform. Do not pride yourselves on the claim, 'Abraham is our father.' I tell you, God can raise up children to Abraham from these very stones. Even now the axe is laid to the root of the tree. Every tree that is not fruitful will be cut down and thrown into the fire. I baptize you in water for the sake of reform, but the one who will follow me is more powerful than I. I am not even fit to carry his sandals. He it is who will baptize you in the Holy Spirit and fire. His winnowing-fan is in his hand. He will

clear the threshing floor and gather his grain into the
barn, but the chaff he will burn in unquenchable fire."

The words, "the one who will follow me," struck Ruth
like a telling blow. Who was the "one who will follow
me"? Not Jeshua! Oh, please, Ruth thought, not Jeshua!
She knew only too well the immense power wielded by the
Jewish religious leaders. It was folly to anger them and
dangerous to threaten the validity of their teaching. If
John weren't careful, he could find himself brought before
the Sanhedrin to answer charges of blasphemy, and the
punishment for blasphemy was death. The Sanhedrin
could not invoke the sentence of death, but even Ruth
knew they possessed the power and cunning to bend
Rome to their will in some cases.

They stood on the river bank and watched. Ruth saw
many familiar faces entering the water to be baptized. She
saw faces awash in tears of regret and longing emerge
shining with joy. Faces lined with worry and despair
changed to hope and freedom from care. Ruth didn't
know what to think. Either John was the most holy man
she'd ever seen or he was a charlatan of the worst kind,
using his magnetism and electric personality to exploit the
poor and downtrodden to further his own glory. All afternoon they swarmed to John, their voices crying out in
their need, their desperate eyes reflecting the starvation of
their souls which hungered for his words of hope and
comfort.

When the afternoon sun waned and the crowds began
to disperse, John saw Marcus' group standing on the bank
and came toward them. Ruth stepped back, afraid. As he
came nearer, she saw he was smiling, and his eyes were no
longer burning with zeal, but were kind and compassionate and held a gleam of merriment. Some of her fear left
her, but she gasped a little as John Mark hobbled down
the bank to give him a hand to help him up.

John strode toward them and clasped Marcus' shoulder.
"Marcus! I thought it was you! It's been a long time, my
friend," he said heartily.

Marcus returned his embrace with exuberant affection.
"Too long, John. Too long. You were a mere lad then,
and look at you now!"

They laughed. Water dripped from John's hairy garb

and his feet and ankles were caked with mud. His hair and beard were wet and matted, but his voice was friendly and his eyes warm and happy. Some of his disciples were hurriedly building a fire and watching them, wondering who the family could be that were on such friendly terms with the Prophet. He turned to Josie.

"My dear Josie. You grow more beautiful than ever. The Lord God has been with you. I'd embrace you, Cousin, but I fear I'd drown you."

"Ah, John," Josie laughed. "You've not changed since I held you as a babe. One moment screaming with anger and the next an irresistible cherub whom I could refuse nothing. It's good to see you again."

John suddenly stooped and lifted John Mark high into the air. "And this! My namesake, eh? You do me proud, lad. Did you know you're named for me?"

John Mark flushed with embarrassment. His eyes were filled with hero worship, and he was so overwhelmed he couldn't speak, but only nodded his head. John set him gently back on his feet and looked at Ruth, who cringed a little under his intense gaze.

"And this? Surely not Mary or Rhoda?"

Josie put her arm about Ruth's shoulders and said softly, "This is Ruth, daughter of Joseph and Mary."

John looked at her a long moment. His face softened and his eyes glistened. Ruth thought it couldn't possibly be tears she saw, but some trick of sight played by the setting sun.

"His sister, then," John said gently. "How you must have labored to earn such privilege." He took Ruth's hand and raised her fingers to his lips. Ruth trembled at the reverence he showed toward her. "I love your mother well, and your father, Joseph, may his great soul rest in peace."

He studied her again. "Yes, you are like her. A child of Mary. Your life on earth will not be the easier for it, but oh! the glory of it! You are blest, child, twice blest by the Lord God."

Ruth didn't understand what he meant by his words. A terrible burden seemed to settle upon her shoulders and she wanted to weep with sadness. Then John's face changed and again became merry. He released her hand

and said lightly, "What news of Elizabeth? I'm told my mother lives in your house."

"She's—she's well," Ruth stammered. "I received a letter from Mother and her; all are well. Elizabeth longs to see you. She worries over you."

John laughed. "My beloved mother always worries over me. Tell her for me that God cares for the ones He sends. She need not fear."

Marcus frowned. "Sometimes it is the better part of wisdom to fear, John. Your words angered them today. As your popularity grows, so will their fear and hatred of you. Beware, John!"

"Ptah!" John spat. "Those! I have no fear of slithering vipers such as those. Those will never have my head, and those who will, only in God's season, not their own. Not one will dare to touch a hair on my head until the Lord God hands me over, and then my mission will have been fulfilled, and what matter then?"

John Mark had left them to investigate the river bank and was coming back, dragging his withered foot behind. John frowned, watching him, and then called out, "John Mark! Come to me!"

John Mark looked up and hurried toward John in a hopping little run. John lifted him to a rock and said, "Let me see your foot."

He carefully undid the latchets and removed John Mark's sandal. He took the twisted foot in his hands and began to move it back and forth, turning the ankle in circular motions. John Mark winced a few times in pain, but didn't cry out.

Without looking up, John said to Marcus, "What say the physicians?"

"They can do nothing. The foot was obviously twisted in the womb and the bones grew deformed."

John nodded, still moving the foot. Then he covered it with both hands and smiled up at John Mark. "Your foot is cold. We'll warm it."

He held the foot tightly. A strange look of concentration came over his face. His eyes again had that wild, mad glaze, and beads of sweat broke out on his brow.

John Mark cried out and Josie gasped. "Your hands are hot," John Mark sobbed.

John seemed to come to himself and released the foot. "Warm enough, eh?" he smiled. He put John Mark's sandal back on and retied the latchets. "You're a good lad. God be with you." He looked toward the sun, now only a glowing red rim above the hills. "The light is soon gone. This is no land to journey through in the dark." He clasped Marcus' shoulder. "Take the boy and women and return home. We will meet again."

Marcus returned the embrace. "Peace be with you, Prophet."

John nodded, then laid his hand for a fleeting moment on Ruth's head. "Peace be with you." He paused and then said, "And with yours."

Then he wheeled and strode toward the fire and his waiting disciples.

Marcus and the others spent the night in an inn in Jericho and arose at the first gray streaks of dawn to leave for Jerusalem. They walked in silence, still dulled with sleep and lost in thought of yesterday's events. As the sun rose over the hills behind them, they began to meet small groups of people already on their way to the Jordan to hear John and to have their sins washed away in the running waters.

The sun rose higher and warmed their backs as they climbed the ridge of hills between the Jordan River and Jerusalem. Ruth thought about the words John had spoken to her and wondered what they meant, and why he had treated her with such honor. She idly watched John Mark running ahead and wished she had his boyish energy, and then turned her thoughts inward.

Josie and Marcus were walking behind her, talking in low tones and unmindful of John Mark's antics. Suddenly Ruth came out of her reverie and watched John Mark more closely. There was something different about him. He was chasing a butterfly across the face of a low hill. He always ran with an awkward, hopping gait, stepping forward with his good foot while using the useless one only as a balance, then dragging it forward to take the next step. But not now! Ruth stared in disbelief as she watched John Mark pick up the twisted foot and set it down in front of the other. He was taking normal steps!

Ruth waited for Marcus and Josie to catch up with her

and then pulled Marcus' sleeve. "Uncle Marcus, watch John Mark run."

They watched a moment. Josie clutched at Marcus' hand. Marcus was white-faced, and his lips were drawn into a thin, tight line. He called out, "John Mark! Come here, son."

John Mark ran towards them, swinging his deformed foot out from his body and placing it firmly in front of the other. It was an unwieldy gait with a definite, obvious limp, but he was taking steps! He ran up to them, out of breath and smiling happily. His golden curls lay in tight, damp ringlets around his face and the sun formed a halo over his head.

Marcus swallowed. "Your foot—"

"Yes!" John Mark cried. "Isn't it wonderful? John must have loosened it when he twisted it around yesterday. Look! I can move it, and take steps. Watch!"

He marched up and down in front of them, exaggerating the movement of the foot and planting it down firmly with each step, gleefully triumphant with his accomplishment. They could only stare at him.

"A miracle!" breathed Josie.

Marcus reached out and crushed John Mark to his breast; his eyes filled with tears as he looked to heaven and gave thanks to God. "You walk, my son! You walk!"

They didn't know what to do with such joy. They laughed and danced and ran races with John Mark until they fell helplessly to the ground, exhausted by their hilarity and joy. Passersby looked at them askance, wondering if a whole family could be drunk on wine so early in the morning.

They stopped in Bethany to show Martha and Lazarus, and then at Zebedee's where Salome cried and John ben Zebedee chased a limping, squealing John Mark all over the courtyard. That night Marcus called a special meeting of the Essenes and the thanksgiving prayers had never been as heartfelt and glad.

Ruth was bewildered. How had John accomplished this thing? No one had been able to heal John Mark's foot, not even Judith. Judith and some of the others who had the gift of healing could mend torn flesh and heal diseases caused by a conscience guilty of sin, but to straighten twisted bone? Granted the foot was not perfect now, not by far! But what a vast improvement over the way it had been! What kind of power did John possess? And, Ruth thought, if Jeshua was the Messiah and was greater than John, as John proclaimed, then why hadn't he healed John Mark when Ruth had asked? What did it all mean?

Marcus' intention to relieve Ruth's anxiety only served to add to her confusion.

Many of the monks and holy women began to abandon the City of Salt to follow John—Roael, Lia, and Adahr among them. Ruth was aghast to learn that Naomi had given up her position in the temple to follow John. How could women live in the wilderness under the open skies to follow a prophet as a disciple, like the men? Even Uncle Zebedee followed him! She couldn't understand why, or what was happening. Her protected world seemed to be falling apart around her. All the old traditions and beliefs which had been so instilled in her no longer seemed to matter, and she began to pray for escape.

Chapter 24

Ruth's prayers were answered so promptly that in years to come she often wondered if her yearnings for escape were not simply the Lord's way of revealing His plan for her.

A childhood friend of both Aunt Josie and Aunt Salone asked that Ruth become attached to her household as companion and nursemaid to her two small children. Her name was Agatha, and her husband Jacob held a position much like Marcus' in Jewish-Roman relations. Since Judea had become a Roman province, more and more Romans were bringing their families with them to that land, and it was necessary for their wives to learn the customs and traditions of the Jews. Agatha was commissioned as an instructress to the Roman wives, to acquaint them with Jewish religious rituals, culinary differences, and social decorum and protocol, which would aid them in promoting friendly relations between the two nationalities. As companion to Agatha's children, Ruth would have the opportunity of learning these same things about Roman ways, with the added bonus that she share the children's tutor, thus gaining the education she so longed for.

Ruth had long ago discovered that being the only daughter of the most revered family among the Essenes carried responsibilities as well as rewards. Her role as sister of the future ruler of Israel demanded a more extensive knowledge of the world than she could gain in Palestine, and as head of the Essenes, Judith counseled Ruth to accept Agatha's offer. Mary agreed. Agatha was an old, trusted friend, and Mary had no qualms about her caring for Ruth as though she were her own daughter. Ruth again stepped through an opened door to an alien way of life.

As a member of Agatha's household, Ruth traveled throughout the Roman world, living in Athens and Rome, and becoming acquainted with many influential Roman and Greek families. She found the same attitudes of bigotry and hypocrisy there as she had found in Jerusalem, though, coming from pagans, they were not nearly so devastating as when she experienced the same among her own countrymen. Roman debaucheries were far in excess of those of Jews. Divorce and infidelities were commonplace and casually accepted, but again, Ruth found it easier to hate the sin and accept the sinner when such indiscretions were committed by souls ignorant of the One True God.

Ruth's exposure to the Roman way of life and thought gave her a new understanding of the precarious position held by her homeland. Palestine seemed tiny and insignificant when compared to the vast expanse of the Roman empire. Rome's might was self-evident, her legions were numberless and marvellously equipped. Her laws were precise and strictly enforced. Roman devotion to their gods and Caesar was as strong as the Jews' to the One God and the High Priest. How they would ever live in peaceful coexistence was beyond Ruth's imagination.

For a time these facts greatly disturbed her, and she was as unhappy and confused as she had been in Jerusalem. But as her lessons progressed and she grew in wisdom and maturity, she caught a glimmer of God's plan for humanity and placed her faith in His mercy and wisdom rather than in the endeavors of man.

Jeshua's teachings of God as a loving, merciful Father became increasingly real to her as she realized the Lord's patience and loving care in slowly and deliberately awakening His children to the truth of their existence. She pored over the histories of Herodotus and Thucydides, and absorbed the teachings of the great Greek lawmaker, Solon. She marvelled at the steady evolvement of man, from wanton barbarians to the organized, social beings she saw in Athens and Rome. She also sighed as her mind's eye looked into the future and saw how far man had yet to go. Her heart was saddened as she saw how man's spiritual values seemed to evolve so much more slowly than his social and material values. The Essene salutation, "Peace be with you," came to have new meaning as Ruth realized that peace could only come from within, and not from the troubled, restless world.

They were living in Rome, in the household of a Greek woman named Elcor, when Ruth received a letter from Mary calling her home, for Jeshua had returned to Capernaum.

Elcor's husband was an aide to the newly assigned Procurator of Judea, Pontius Pilate. They had lived in Elcor's house for some weeks as Agatha instructed both Elcor and Pilate's wife, Julia, on the customs and personality of the Jews, and since both families had already booked passage to Caesaria, Elcor invited Ruth to travel with them.

Ruth was in her seventeenth year, and was no longer the bewildered, disturbed girl who had fled Jerusalem, but a young woman of beauty and grace who possessed her mother's serenity and her father's accepting faith. When Justin met her in the port of Caesaria, he felt his age descend upon him, for the child of Mary had grown up.

The weeks aboard ship had seemed an eternity. On the last morning Ruth arose before dawn and stationed herself at the ship's rail, staring across the flashing waves until her eyes burned and her legs throbbed, and no amount of admonishment could convince her to leave. Her excitement and trepidation were unbearable. Could anyone ever come home again and find things unchanged? What was Jude like at fifteen? Had James' superiority softened with the years or grown more set and rigid? Would she and Susane be able to bridge their long years of separation? And what of Jeshua? How different was a mature man of thirty from the gentle, loving brother of twenty?

By the time the ship drew into port Ruth was almost ill with anxiety, but the sight of Justin's beaming face and the feel of his hearty, bone-crushing hug made Ruth know she was truly home again.

They said a hasty good-bye to Elcor and started northward to Mt. Carmel where Ruth intended to spend only the night and then push on for home and Jeshua early the next morning. She had a thousand questions to ask and tried to ask them all in one rush, until Justin threw up his hands in exasperation.

"You're as bad as Judith! You don't give a man a chance to answer one question before you throw another at him!"

Ruth laughingly apologized and tried to calm herself. She chattered excitedly and listened as Justin brought her up to date on Mt. Carmel and the City of Salt. He seemed vague about Jeshua, but Ruth didn't mind. She'd rather learn about Jeshua herself.

It was late fall, and the leaves were nearly gone from the great oaks. The sun warmed the naked branches and filtered through the towering pines in hazy, mote-filled streaks. The air smelled dusty and the treetops rang with raucous birdcalls as they gathered for their annual southward flight. Squirrels scolded them soundly for intruding upon their last-minute rush to store their winter supplies, and the forest floor was alive with small animals who scurried to find a winter resting place.

The path became steeper and Ruth and Justin spoke little, conserving their breath for the upward climb. Ruth drank in the sight and smells and sounds around her.

The dense forest came to an abrupt end, and they were suddenly in the clearing around the Essene compound. Ruth stopped short and sucked in her breath. It was all so beautiful! The buildings gleamed immaculately clean, their dazzling whiteness softened by the worn, red-brick walks. They rose in orderly symmetry, drawing the eye upward to the temple which sat like a dusty rose-and-white crown at the pinnacle of the Mount.

"It's so beautiful!" Ruth breathed. "It's so gentle and tranquil and beautiful. I never saw it from here before. It puts Jerusalem's pretentious temple to shame with its simplicity."

Justin had watched Ruth's childlike wonder with tender amusement, and now touched her arm and pointed. "Look."

A figure was coming down the walkway toward them. He was dressed all in white, and the sun obscured Ruth's view of his face. He was tall and walked with long, graceful strides. When he reached the bottommost step, he stopped and raised his arms toward her, the long, wide

sleeves of his cloak falling nearly to his waist, making him
look as though he had angels' wings. The sun diffused his
red-gold hair into a misty golden halo around his head,
and Ruth was suddenly transported back through time
and space to her mother's garden ten years before. She
dropped the bundles she was carrying and, with a strangled cry, ran towards him.

Jeshua! It could only be Jeshua! Tears began to course
down her cheeks as she ran, and her heart beat wildly. As
she drew near, she had the sudden impulse to fling herself
at his feet and embrace his legs, but just as quickly she
abandoned such a foolish thought and flung herself into
his arms. She sobbed with joy upon his breast and held
him as though never to let go. Her haven and her refuge!
All her fears and doubts and confusions and world-weari-
ness vanished as she rested in Jeshua's safe, strong arms.
She was a child again, and nothing could ever do her
harm as long as her elder brother was with her.

Jeshua held her until her sobs began to subside, and
then raised her face and wiped her tears. He smiled at her
and said tenderly, "My little sister. I always seem to be
wiping away your tears. Peace be with you, little one, and
welcome home."

Ruth looked into his face and couldn't speak. His eyes
and his voice! Did anyone ever have eyes and voice like
Jeshua? His eyes looked into her very soul and his voice
melted her heart. What kind of love was this, this overpowering, all-consuming love which only Jeshua could
evoke, a love that transcended everything and soared aloft
on the wings of the sublime?

Ruth stepped back and looked at him. Again she had
the impulse to sink to her knees and pay him homage. He
was looking at her with a strange mixture of merriment
and compassion. An enigmatic smile played at his mouth
and he seemed to be waiting for her to say something. A
trembling sensation assailed Ruth's flesh, and a terrible
knowledge flooded her mind.

"You are the Messiah!" she whispered.

Jeshua's smile spread. He closed his eyes for a moment
and said nothing. Then the moment passed and he tucked
her arm under his own. "Come. The others wait for you."

Ruth smiled at him and said teasingly, "Will you be
with me always, Jeshua?"

He squeezed her arm. "Yes. I'll be with you always," he said gently.

They waited for Justin, who had hung back, not wanting to intrude upon their reunion, and then the three of them walked toward the temple.

Ruth stayed at Mt. Carmel for a few days before returning to Capernaum. She was anxious to go home, but hated to leave Jeshua. She sat at his feet with the others and listened as he taught the mysteries of the kingdom. Sometimes she didn't understand his meaning, and sometimes he seemed to teach in variance with the tenets of the Essenes, but it didn't matter to Ruth. She trusted him completely and knew in her heart that every word he uttered was of God. She realized that Jeshua's understanding and knowledge of the world of spirit was far above the capabilities of normal men to comprehend.

Sometimes she did understand the truths Jeshua tried to explain. She saw how everything in the earth was but a shadow of the realm of spirit. She began to see that all of nature was a lesson by which man could learn the reality of his spiritual existence. She gained a faint insight into the higher meanings of the tabernacle in the desert and the Twelve Tribes of the chosen people, and how even man's house of flesh was a microcosm of the whole universe.

It was Jeshua who finally sent her home. "Our mother waits, Ruth. It is good to learn of things of the spirit, but better to manifest that knowledge in deeds on earth. Take what you have learned and incorporate it into everything that you do, and your understanding will grow accordingly. And when you fail, pray, and the Spirit will set you right again. Put your life in the Father's hands, and He will guide you in the way you are to go. Even when trouble and adversity assail you, trust that the Father's way is perfect, and be at peace."

Capernaum seemed to have shrunk in size and grown shabby and mean in the years Ruth had been away. Part of the reason for this was Herod's grand new capital city of Tiberias, which he'd built not too far away on the shores of the Galilee. Many of the wealthy Gentiles who had lived in Capernaum had moved to Tiberias, and it was there that Herod held court in a gleaming, marble palace. Anyone who wished to be in Herod's good graces and to share in his wealth and power had followed him to Tiberias.

The Jews had at first stayed away. Tiberias was built over an old cemetery which they considered unclean ground, but it wasn't long until they realized that the money had also moved to Tiberias, and the wealthier Jews had laid aside their religious scruples and followed. The poorer, laboring class of Jews bitterly condemned this action, but Herod couldn't stand the embarrassment of being shunned by the very people he was supposed to rule, and so even the poor were coerced into living there.

Not only the town had changed, but so had the people. There seemed to be an air of desperation hanging over Capernaum, as though everyone were waiting in fear for an hour of doom to fall. Ruth had always thought of the fisherfolks' loud, boisterous ways as signs of high spirits and zest for living, but now they seemed tinged with hysteria and near panic.

The Zealot party had grown in numbers and were ever bolder in criticizing the luxury-loving Herod and the oppressing laws of Rome. They advocated open rebellion, and caused both Herod and the Romans to use even harsher methods in controlling the masses, which in turn sent more of the young people to join the Zealots. Ruth wondered how long that wheel of cause and effect would turn until it erupted into violence, and shuddered to think of its disastrous results.

The whole land seemed to be in a state of instability and confusion. Herod and the Roman Procurator were in a constant, subtle struggle for power. Herod considered himself the true ruler of the Jews by right of inheritance, but Rome thought of him as only a puppet king with Rome in control of the strings. Herod would issue a law, and soon Rome would proclaim an edict in direct opposition to it, and the poor Jews were caught in the middle. The people were expected to obey the laws of Rome, and the laws of Herod, and the Law of Moses enforced by the Sanhedrin. They were taxed by Rome, by Herod, and again by the temple, until their freedom vanished and their pockets were empty.

The common people didn't know who to obey or even what to believe in anymore. They were bombarded on all sides with pagan gods and Gentile customs. The Pharisees taught one thing, and the Sadducees another. The Essenes condemned the Jerusalem temple, and the Zealots ridiculed the peace-promoting Essenes. The Samaritans condemned them all and fought for their right to worship at Mt. Gerzim. Then there was John the Baptizer who proclaimed a kingdom of God and of One to come who would lead them to that kingdom.

John ben Zachariah wasn't helping the situation. His preaching against all authority was becoming more bitter and fanatical every day. The Sanhedrin both feared and hated him, and Roman soldiers watched his every move. John's most bitter enemy was said to be Herodias, Herod's illicit wife, for John's favorite theme was their unholy union, and Herodias was determined to get rid of him. John ridiculed her publicly, denouncing her as a harlot and an adulteress, inflaming her to a murderous passion. Herod's steward, Chuza, and his wife Joanna, had joined the sect of the Essenes, and Chuza warned John not to venture into Galilee.

The only place Ruth found to be tranquil and free from strife was home. Mary had not changed at all, except to grow more beautiful. There wasn't a gray hair growing among that mass of spun red-gold, nor a line of worry to mar her perfect face.

Josie was still Josie. A little rounder and with a few strands of gray peeking through at her temples, Josie would never change. She wept and scolded because Ruth was too pale and too thin, and pressed food upon her until Ruth thought she would burst. Ruth saw Josie through her newly adult eyes, and marvelled at the total dedication and loyalty she had given to a family not her own. Josie was the pillar of strength, the anchor of stability about whom the whole family revolved. Her earthy common sense provided the balance to Ruth's often mystical, idealistic family.

Jude had changed. His resemblance to Joseph made Ruth gasp. He was tall and strong and smelled of new wood, and when he picked her up and danced around the room with her, Ruth wanted to cry from sheer joy. Jude was a true Galilean, happy, exuberant, optimistic, and definitely uncomplicated. He worked as an apprentice in Uncle Alphaeus' shop and wanted nothing more from life than to be a good carpenter like his father before him, to

give an honest day's work for an honest day's pay, and to
rest at night with his children upon his knee.

James was another matter. He came home from the
City of Salt for a few days to see Ruth, and at first she
had warmed to him, for his likeness to Jeshua was startling. But it wasn't long before his austerity and dogmatic
lecturing became wearing, and Ruth was glad to see him
go.

Elizabeth had returned to her old home in Ain Karim
to provide a resting place and retreat for John and his
disciples. Adahr followed John wherever he went, looking
after his bodily needs and helping in every way she could
with his ministry. She came to her mother's house only
when John did, and left when he left, but Elizabeth
understood Adahr's possessive devotion to John and didn't
mind.

Ruth's fear that she and Susane would no longer find a
common ground for friendship proved to be ungrounded,
though it seemed their childhood roles had reversed. Susane was now the aggressive, involved one, while Ruth
had grown to serene acceptance.

She was shocked to learn that Susane was involved with
the Zealots. She attended their political meetings and even
took part in some of their skirmishes. Simon ben Alphaeus was the leader of the Capernaum group, and his
brother James his right hand. It was through them that
Susane had become interested in the movement, and Ruth
questioned the wisdom of her commitment to their war-
like philosophy. She tried to point out the dangers and
futility of opposing Rome by overt tactics, but Susane
was so full of their few small victories that she couldn't
see the disasters ahead. She spoke in glowing terms of
their leader, one Judas Iscariot from Judea, until Ruth
began to wonder if Susane might be a little in love with
him. That fear, at least, was laid to rest when Ruth met
Jonas.

Jonas was a physician. His mother and father were of
Greek descent, though Jews, as were many in Galilee.
After years of study in Alexandria, Jonas had returned to
the land of his birth determined to bring relief to the
suffering poor he remembered so vividly from his childhood. Where or how Susane had met him and joined in
his crusade against poverty and disease, Ruth was not

clear, but one look at them together made Ruth know that
while Susane's political thoughts lay with the Zealots, her
heart belonged to Jonas.

Ruth liked Jonas. She admired his honest concern for
the poor, and enjoyed the lively conversations she had
with him on her theory that a healthy, happy mind made
for a healthy, energetic body. It didn't take much persuasion for Susane and Jonas to convince her to work with
them. When Ruth saw the enormity of the task laid before
them, she solicited help from some of their old childhood
friends until they had a sizable group fighting against the
forces of Belial.

The Evil One seemed to be having a heyday. The
masses of poor were in such throes of despair and hopelessness that they left the door wide open to violence,
anger, and hatred which sowed the seeds of rampant disease. Ruth tried every way she knew to uproot those noxious weeds of despair. She found work for the unem-
ployed, homes for the homeless, food for the hungry, and
clothes for the naked. Once she'd made their earthly lives
a little more bearable, she tried to give them back their
faith and hope and love for one another. She tried to give
them something to believe in again and a purpose to their
lives, but it was an uphill job and she often wept at the
futility of it all.

Mary kept her going. When Ruth's gentle reasoning
and argument failed, Mary went with her to some poor,
ramshackle abode, and it was as though she had only to
look at them with her deep, understanding, compassionate
eyes that were so like Jeshua's, and they became transformed with hope and a determination to try. Her quiet
voice and serenity seemed to instill them with the strength
to endure, and Ruth could only marvel at the magic of
her mother's presence.

Ruth's days grew into weeks and months. The debaucheries and sophistications of Athens and Rome faded to an
almost-forgotten memory, and it seemed as though she
had never been away.

Chapter 25

I t was winter. The wind was raw and damp as it whipped across the narrow dirt street. The sky was overcast with leaden clouds and the air was heavy with an icy mist. Ruth pulled her heavy woolen cloak closer about her shoulders and ducked her head into the wind. She'd been up since dawn and was bone-weary and nearly faint from hunger. The number of sick seemed to multiply at an astonishing rate during the cold winter months. She and Susane and Jonas had seen so many sick and troubled during the day that their faces were only a blur in Ruth's mind, and she could only remember their sore-infested, trembling bodies and hacking coughs and fearful eyes.

Ruth pushed her body to use its last reserves of energy. It was nearly dark and she was alone. It was dangerous to be out alone after the sun went down, but she'd lost her sense of time during the gray, sunless day. She knew Jonas would have taken her home, but he was more weary than she, and she'd slipped away without his knowing.

She turned the last corner and almost sobbed with relief as she saw her mother's house with a candle glowing in the window. A strong gust blew her hood back from her head and whipped the cloak around her legs. The mist changed into a cold, driving drizzle that stung her face like tiny pieces of flying glass. She squinted against the rain and ran toward the house. She struggled against the thick oak door and nearly fell headlong into the room when Jude pulled it open.

Jude caught her and helped her regain her balance. He looked out into the dismal darkness before he banged the door shut. "Are you alone?" he asked incredulously. "Why didn't you come to the shop and come home with me? You shouldn't be wandering about the streets in the dark!"

"I'm sorry, Jude. I lost track of time. I knew you'd be gone already," Ruth sighed wearily.

Josie appeared in the doorway and gasped. "You're soaked through, and chilled to the bone! Jonas will soon be treating you! Get those wet things off."

Jude helped her with the cloak and hung it on a peg near the door. "James and John ben Zebedee are here. They're in the other room with Mother. We've been waiting for you. They have news of Jeshua."

A strange twinge of anxiety crawled up Ruth's spine. "What news? Where is Jeshua?"

"I don't know. They just got here a little while ago and wanted to wait until you came home. I think they've come from the Jordan River, where John is baptizing. Hurry and change so we can hear."

Ruth ran upstairs and quickly changed. Her weariness and hunger had vanished. She roughly dried her hair on a coarse linen towel and hastily pulled a comb through it. It was cold in the room, and she grabbed a woolen shawl from a peg, threw it around her shoulders, and ran down the stairs.

James and John were sitting on the long bench behind the plank table. Mary and Jude were opposite them, and Josie was busy ladling hot lamb stew into wooden bowls. The room was warm and cozy. Braziers added their glow to the oil lamps which sat in little niches carved into the white stone walls.

James and John rose when she entered and greeted her enthusiastically. "Peace be with you, Ruth!"

Ruth returned their greeting and hugged John. It was the first time she'd seen him since she came home, and, like Jude, he'd become a young man since she'd seen him last. She kissed Mary's cheek and apologized for causing her worry.

Mary touched her cheek. "I wasn't worried. The Lord is with you in all you do. Come and eat. You look so tired."

"I was tired, but not now," Ruth said as she took her place beside Mary. She looked across the table at James. "Jude says you have news of Jeshua?"

"We'll eat first. James and John have come from Judea and are hungry and weary," Mary interrupted gently.

Ruth swallowed her protest and bowed her head as Jude gave thanks to God for their meal. The men ate heartily, but Ruth could hardly force down the stew. Josie frowned at her and motioned to her to eat. She made herself swallow and chew, for no one disobeyed Josie.

"What is the news from Jerusalem? Are your parents well?" Mary asked.

"Yes. Both are very well. Father sends his love, as do Naomi and Roael," James replied. "I do have news. Roael and Lia are betrothed!"

"Roael!" gasped Jude. "I thought he was a monk and would never marry!"

"He is," said John. "But because of John's teaching and of their love for one another, he and Lia have decided to give their bodies as channels so souls may enter the earth. They believe this age is the most wonderful age of all ages for souls to be in the flesh, and so want to be vessels which will make their entry possible."

"That is wonderful news," Mary said happily. "I'm surprised that I haven't heard this from Salone. She and Zuriah must be delighted!"

"I don't think they know. The decision was made only a few days ago and Lia hasn't been home," said James. "Ruth, I hear you've met our new Procurator. What kind of man did you find him to be? He must be a fool to have brought Caesar's effigies into Jerusalem, and a coward to do so at night. The Sanhedrin is furious with Pilate, and frantic that the incident is only a foretaste of what is to come. Caiaphas worries over how long he'll remain High Priest under Pilate's rule."

Ruth frowned. "I don't think Pontius Pilate will concern himself with religious affairs. Pilate is difficult to describe. He is typical of those Romans who are of the lower social classes and have risen to positions of power and authority. He takes great pride in the fact that he has risen above his plebeian ancestors and is now on nearly equal standing with the old patrician families. He is wealthy and powerful, and is on intimate terms with Caesar Tiberius. Yet I detected an undercurrent of fear and lack of confidence in Pilate which he tries to hide under a facade of great bravado and ruthlessness. He plays the role of a sophisticate, a man of the world, and a benevolent ruler, but I'm sure he wouldn't hesitate to use any means of deceit and cruelty to obtain his ends. He is overly jealous of his reputation and of his friendship with Caesar. If he is ever confronted with the choice between justice and retaining his favor with Caesar, you can be sure he'll choose the latter."

"Hmm," James mused. "We can deal with that as long as he doesn't enjoy the suffering of his subjects. If we can hold the Zealots in check and keep the peace, it might not be too bad."

"I wish you could convince Simon and James ben Alphaeus of that!" Jude snorted. "Alphaeus' house is like an armed camp. Simon and James preach rebellion and war, and despise Matthew for collecting taxes for Rome. Matthew argues for survival, and says that war with Rome would annihilate our people. He thinks the only way to survive is to cater to Rome and live with them in peace."

"What of Thaddeus and Joses?" asked James.

"Joses is like me. He only wishes to be left alone and to be a carpenter. Thaddeus says little. His counsel is to wait for the Messiah and follow his lead."

An uncomfortable silence fell over the room at the mention of the Messiah. That strange prickle of anxiety again crawled on Ruth's flesh. She wondered how Jude could speak so blithely of the Messiah, knowing that Jeshua was expected to be the Messiah. She looked into Jude's face, which was so like her own, and sighed. Jude simply didn't have faith in Jeshua. He loved him, but he didn't see Jeshua's uniqueness.

Mary broke the silence and said gently, "Tell us now about Jeshua."

James shot John a sidelong glance and cleared his throat. "John was baptizing on the eastern shore of the Jordan, above Jericho at the Place of the Crossing Over where Joshua led the Twelve Tribes into the Promised Land. We were all there—myself, Father, Naomi, Roael and Lia, Adahr of course, and even Editha."

"Editha!" Mary exclaimed.

"Yes. And Matthew had also come down with me from Capernaum, and some of the men who work for me."

"I was not there," interrupted John. "I was at home with Mother. I arrived at Bethabara later."

James nodded and went on. "The news that John was in the area had spread far. The crowds were greater than I had ever seen them. There was an air of desperation about them, as though this was their last chance to receive John's blessing. They pushed and shoved their way forward and we had a time keeping them in orderly lines."

"You know how John preaches that his baptism is to prepare the Jews for the coming of the Messiah, that they will know him and recognize him when he comes. This sticks in the craw of our learned leaders. They are blind to the signs that the time has come, and cling to their positions of authority for fear that if it is true, the Messiah will strip them of their unearned prestige and wealth. They also fear the loss of their friendship with the Romans and shrink from the thought of bodily suffering and deprivation." James voice was bitter. "The fools! They'd rather be a friend of Rome than of God!"

Jude shifted uncomfortably on the bench and stared at the table with embarrassment. He secretly wondered if the Pharisees weren't right. Who needed war with Rome?

James continued. "We had been there a few days when the Pharisees sent a committee of priests and Levites to question John, to find out who he was. John told them he was not the Messiah. They pressed him further. 'Who, then? Elijah?' John answered, 'I am not Elijah.'"

"Not?" Mary said, wonderingly.

James nodded. "We were also surprised. We've always considered John to be Elijah, but he said he was not. The only answer he'd give was to quote Isaiah. 'I am a voice in the desert, crying out: Make straight the way of the Lord.'

"This didn't satisfy the priests. 'If you are not the Messiah, nor Elijah, nor the Prophet, why do you baptize?' they asked. John said, 'I baptize with water. There is one among you whom you do not recognize, the one who is to come after me, the strap of whose sandal I am not worthy to unfasten.' That's all he would tell them, and they had to be satisfied with that.

"The crowds listened to this exchange and it made them bold to question John too. 'What ought we to do?' they asked him. John told them, 'Let the man with two coats give to him who has none. The man who has food should do the same.' Matthew asked him, 'Teacher, what are we to do?' He said, 'Exact nothing over and above your fixed amount.' "

"So Matthew has always done," said Jude. "Too bad his brothers didn't hear that answer."

James smiled at Jude. "Even some Roman soldiers who had come to watch got into the spirit of the thing and asked, 'What about us?' John told them, 'Don't bully anyone. Denounce no one falsely. Be content with your pay!' "

They all laughed. "Our cousin fears no one, not even Rome!" John cried in a voice filled with admiration.

"He'd best hear Herodias!" Josie snorted. "If what Joanna says is true, she'll be John's downfall as Jezebel was almost Elijah's!"

"Almost," said John, "but not entirely."

"She failed to win once, but she might not fail this time. John should beware," warned Josie.

"But what of Jeshua?" Ruth asked impatiently.

"It was the next day when Jeshua suddenly appeared among the crowds. I spoke to him, but he seemed preoccupied and disinclined to talk. John saw him from the middle of the river and cried out, 'Look! There is the Lamb of God who takes away the sin of the world. It is he of whom I said: After me is to come a man who ranks ahead of me, because he was before me.' "

The others looked at one another in puzzlement. Ruth sighed. John always spoke in such riddles. She remembered the day Marcus had taken them all to hear John preach. His words had been heavy with unknown meanings even then. She turned her attention back to James.

"Jeshua didn't acknowledge that he was the one John pointed out. In fact, he didn't even seem to hear John. Jeshua acted strangely. Agitated, nervous. You know how calm he always is, but that day he paced the river bank and kept looking toward the sky as though searching for something amid the clouds. When night fell, Jeshua didn't join us around the campfire, but withdrew by himself into the hills."

James looked apologetically at Mary. "I wanted to follow him, Mary, but I feared he'd send me back. He was not himself at all."

"You did right, James," Mary said softly. "Please, go on."

Ruth could feel a tension building in the room. James' face had become drawn and his voice strained. John was watching him intently, as though making sure each word was said as he had first heard it.

"The next day the sky was overcast and the temper of the crowds was restless and apprehensive. There was a feeling of anxiety in the air such as one feels when a storm is brewing. Jeshua again appeared among the crowds and again John cried out, 'Look! There is the lamb of God'

"Jeshua seemed even more distraught than he had been the day before. He'd speak to no one, but brushed us aside as though he were irritated with us. He seemed to be listening, searching, for what I don't know. The sky became ominous with rolling, black clouds, and the crowds began to disperse. I was watching Jeshua and at about four o'clock, he suddenly stopped his pacing and stood still. He was watching the sky overhead, and his face seemed to become suffused with joy, as though he were hearing or seeing something I couldn't see.

"I looked toward John. Everyone had come out of the water except him, and he stood as though waiting for someone. Then Jeshua came down the bank and stepped into the water and walked toward John. I followed a way so I could hear. Jeshua stopped just in front of John and John said, 'I should be baptized by you, yet you come to me!' I had to strain to hear Jeshua, he spoke so softly, but it was very still and I heard him clearly. He said, 'Give in for now. We must do this if we would fulfill all of God's demands.'"

James paused. He reached for a goblet and took a great draught. Beads of sweat stood out on his forehead and his hand shook as he lifted the cup to his mouth. He wiped his mouth on his sleeve and went on.

"John dipped into the water and began pouring it over Jeshua's head. Then it was as though the sky was rent apart in a terrible explosion. Thunder crashed and lightning tore across the sky as though to set the universe aflame. I thought I would die from fright. The rolling clouds were rent apart and a blazing shaft of light descended from the heavens and came to rest on Jeshua and John. A white dove seemed to come from nowhere and hovered over Jeshua. Then I heard, I swear before God I heard a voice like thunder, like nothing I ever heard before, say, 'This is My beloved son. My favor rests on him.' "

They were stunned into silence. No one spoke. They couldn't even look at one another. Ruth's mouth was dry and her blood pounded in her ears. Only Mary seemed calm as she said, "Go on, James."

"Then the clouds were gone. The thunder and lightning had vanished. The sun bathed the whole scene in a greenish-yellow light. Everything was in such sharp focus it hurt my eyes. Jeshua turned away from John. He walked by me through the water but didn't see me. His face was terrible. I could hardly look upon it. It shone as though the sun reflected on it like a mirror. His expression was terrible—tortured, agonized, filled with an unfathomable grief. I ran after him. I wanted to weep, to comfort him. I called his name but he didn't heed me. He walked swiftly, almost running. He pushed through the other of John's disciples who had watched by the shore. They were his friends, his family, and yet it was as though he didn't know them.

"He was heading in the direction of the Judean wilderness, and I motioned to Andrew, a man who works for Father and me and is a disciple of John's, to follow him. They disappeared into the hills."

John quickly took up the story. "In the meantime, I was on my way to Bethabara to join James and Father, and I met Jeshua in the hills below Jericho. I saw him from afar and knew at once it was he—only Jeshua has such hair, that glows so red and gold in the sunlight. I ran forward, overjoyed to meet the rabbi in such an unexpected place. I called to him, expecting him to welcome me with a warm embrace as he always does, but when I reached him, he didn't seem to recognize me.

" 'Master,' I cried. 'It is I, John.' He stared at me as though he'd never seen me before. Then he drew in his breath in a sort of anguished sob, such as a man will do when he hears terrible news. His eyes were awful. He looked at me with such grief, such agony. I was paralyzed with fear. I thought something horrible had happened, that John, or Father, or one of the others had met with death.

"I grabbed his arm and cried, 'What has happened, Jeshua! What is wrong?' He only stared at me and then pushed me aside and began to run into the hills.

"Then I saw Andrew. I ran to him, sick with fear. Andrew clutched my shoulder and said it was all right, to go to James and Father and they would tell me. 'Has someone died?' I asked. Andrew shook his head and said, 'No. No. Go now. I must follow before I lose him. They'll explain,' and then he ran after Jeshua. I ran most of the way to Bethabara and there they told me what had happened."

What had happened! Anguish filled Ruth's heart. She looked at her mother. Mary was very white and still. Her eyes were closed and her hands clasped. Ruth knew she was in prayer, so didn't speak. When Mary raised her head, her eyes were filled with tears. "Blessed be the Most High," she whispered.

Jude exploded. "Mother! How can you say that?" He catapulted from the bench and glared accusingly at them all. "What are you all doing to Jeshua?" he shouted. "Why don't you leave him alone! From the time he was born you've drilled it into his head that he was the Messiah, that he was the Promised One. You even gave him over to Judith, who is a fanatic on the subject."

"Judith!" he continued scornfully. "She's so obsessed with Jeshua that she ignored her own sons for years. Phinehas and Silvanius are both emotional cripples because of her obsession. Disease racks them and they have no direction, all because she's so sure that poor Jeshua is the Messiah!"

"Jude!" Josie cried. "Stop this!"

"I won't!" Jude flung at her. "Somebody has to put a stop to this nonsense before you destroy him."

Jude dropped to his knees beside Mary and grasped her hands. He looked at her imploringly. "Please, Mother. Please stop this," he begged. "Can't you see what's happening? Jeshua is a kind, gentle man. He is no warring Messiah! Jeshua could never kill a gnat, let alone men. He is a teacher, a rabbi, not a general. If you force him into this role you'll destroy his sanity and maybe his soul. Leave him in peace. Let him teach and bring his hope and comfort to the people he loves so much. He is such a gentle, loving man." Jude sobbed, "Don't hurt him, please, Mother. You can save him. I beg of you, don't let them harm my brother."

Mary gently pulled her hands from Jude's and rested them on his head as though in blessing. She looked long and deep into his eyes and then said quietly, "I cannot, my son. I cannot do as you ask. Jeshua came into this world willingly, knowing the path he would lead. I do not know, nor does Judith, nor even John, but Jeshua knows God's plan. All will happen as God ordains. The voice said, 'This is my beloved Son!' A son knows the will of his father. Have faith, Jude."

Jude wrenched free from Mary's caress and with a strangled cry bolted out of the room into the cold rainy night.

Ruth was shaken. She stood, uncertain if she should follow him or stay with Mary. Her heart ached for them both. She shared Jude's fear for Jeshua, and yet shared her mother's faith that all that would be was meant to be. She started toward the door, but Mary's hand on her arm stopped her. "But Jude—" she began.

"Leave him be," Mary counselled. "Jeshua will take care of Jude in his season." She looked across the table at James. "Jeshua didn't return, then?"

James cleared his throat. He and John had watched Jude's outburst in embarrassed silence. "No. I—" He looked at John, hoping he could think of something to add.

John took James' cue and spoke. "When I reached Bethabara, I talked with John about what had happened. He was awed by it all, and exulted. He confessed to me that he hadn't been sure that Jeshua was the One, that he didn't recognize him as the Messiah even though the reason he'd come baptizing with water was that the Messiah might be revealed to Israel.

"John gave this testimony also. 'I saw the Spirit descend like a dove from the sky, and it came to rest on him. But before that, I didn't recognize him. The One who sent me to baptize with water told me, "When you see the Spirit descend and rest on someone, it is He who is to baptize with the Holy Spirit." Now that I have seen for myself, I testify, This is God's Chosen One!' "

Ruth held her head in her hands. John's words were thrilling. An unbearable excitement welled up inside of her. The words were confirming, absolute! There could be no doubt. Jeshua was the Messiah! Where would it all lead? Here was the beginning, but what would be the end? She remembered what John had said to her, "How you must have labored to earn such privilege!" Oh! to be alive in this day and this place. To be a child of Mary and a sister to the Promised One! Ruth couldn't contain herself. She got up and began to pace back and forth across the room. Her emotions ran wild: excitment, joy, exultation, humility, gratitude, an engulfment of love, and a hard, cold fear.

The Messiah would be hated by the world, despised, feared, an outcast from the established order. She bled for gentle Jeshua, and at the same time wanted to laugh at all the fools who would think him so easy to destroy because of his gentleness. He had strength and courage and wisdom beyond their powers of comprehension. To try to stop him would be like chasing the wind.

Ruth whirled about in her ecstasy, and laughed aloud. She dropped to her knees where Jude had knelt in such torment only moments before, and threw her arms around her mother's waist. Her eyes were bright with tears of pure joy. "You're right, Mother," she cried as she hugged her. "You are always right. Jeshua knows, of course he knows. Who is like Jeshua? There is no other, has never been another like him!"

Ruth's excitement caught them all, and they burst forth with incoherent, excited babbling. What now? What next? Who would believe and who would follow and what should they, themselves, do? There were so many plans to be made.

They decided John should carry the good news to Mt. Carmel and the City of Salt. Judith was the leader. She would know what to do and how to do it.

Josie wept. James and John thumped one another on the back and kissed all three women. "Behold the Lamb of God!" John cried. "The reign of God has come!"

Chapter 26

They heard nothing of Jeshua for the next few weeks. James explained Andrew's absence to his wife and family by saying he'd sent Andrew to Judea on a mission for himself. Andrew's brother Simon grumbled over the loss of a hand on his boat, but James mollified him by promising to pay Andrew well for his mission.

Jude refused to discuss Jeshua's baptism by John. He stayed away from the house as much as possible, staying at the shop long after Alphaeus and Joses left, and then stopping at a tavern with his friends and not coming home until late at night. Ruth and Josie worried over him, but Mary counselled patience. "Jude will come to understand. Jeshua loves him also, remember, and will not allow his brother to be lost."

Ruth wondered what James ben Joseph's reaction had been to the events at the Jordan. She'd only seen James once since her return from Rome, and then he'd seemed a little antagonistic toward John's baptizing. James held to the very letter of the Essene teachings, and John's interpretation of those teachings sometimes varied quite drastically with the traditional understanding.

James would soon be twenty years old and would receive his first initiation into the Brotherhood, and Ruth knew he secretly hoped that one day he would replace Judith as leader of the community. James led a harsh, ascetic life at the City of Salt, depriving himself of every comfort, and stringently fasting and mortifying his flesh. John also practiced these disciplines, but Ruth knew that Jeshua considered them unnecessary, and felt that the discipline of the heart and mind was of more importance than that of the flesh. Ruth wondered how James would reconcile his rigid standards to the more relaxed, simple way of Jeshua.

She found little time to indulge in worrying over her brothers. The Other Mary and Timothy had asked Mary to prepare the wedding feast for Lia and Roael. Zebedee was a very important personage in the social and business circles, and the marriage of one of his sons would be one of the main social events of the year. All the wealthy and prestigious leaders of Jewish society would expect an invitation, and in such cases it was the custom to ask the most prominent member of the bride's family to be in charge of all the festivities. Mary was honored that both the Other Mary and Zebedee considered her in this light, but it also meant a mammoth amount of work and planning.

Ruth found herself thrown into the center of all the activities. Mary called upon the Essenes for help, and, the last week before the wedding, Mary's house overflowed with women who were frantically sewing and cooking and taking care of all the final preparations.

A few days before the wedding, they moved all the preparations to Cana. Hundreds of guests would be coming, and the Other Mary's neighbors opened their homes as places of lodging. Cana had never seen such an important event before and probably would not again, and the whole village was agog with excitement. The festivities could last anywhere from three to eight days, and the amounts of food and wine needed for such a multitude was staggering. Everyone helped. All of the eleven girls chosen with Mary were on hand, as well as friends and family members from all over Judea and Galilee.

The guests began arriving the day after the Sabbath, and the little village was turned into a carnival. Musicians played in the streets. Long trestle tables laden with food filled every tiny courtyard. It was spring, and the winter wheat and barley fields rippled in golden waves in the gentle breeze, and the rolling green hills were blanketed in a riot of color. The air was heavy with perfume from blossoming figs and olives and grapevines, and the sun shed its warmth and light from a clear, azure sky.

Lia was kept in seclusion. No one would see the bride until she was borne from her mother's house upon a litter and took her place beneath the marriage canopy.

At midnight Lia's bridesmaids filled their oil lamps and went to the village gate to await the arrival of the bridegroom. They didn't actually expect Roael and his entourage until morning, but it was an ancient custom the bridesmaids performed, to light the bridegroom's way, lest he appear in the dark and the bride miss his coming.

At dawn the guests and villagers began to line the streets and road leading out of Cana toward Capernaum. Heralds were posted along the way and musicians waited with pipes and timbrels to announce the glad arrival of the bridegroom. The streets were strewn with thousands of scented blossoms, and the crowds were decked out in their best and newest finery.

It was drawing close to mid-morning when the first cry of welcome split the air. Roael led the procession, resplendent in finely embroidered white linen, and with a golden crown upon his head. His groomsmen followed behind, James and John among them, and then Zebedee, Salome, and Naomi, and, behind them, Marcus and Josie and John Mark, and all the others of Roael's family and friends. The lines of cheering onlookers fell in behind as they passed, and by the time they reached the village gate, the procession had turned into a long, snakelike, joyful dance.

The procession halted at the marriage canopy and the company became quiet as they waited for the bride. The lilting, haunting strains from the Song of Solomon was heard, floating upon the warm gentle breeze, and then Lia came into view. The litter was beautiful, silk-embroidered and studded with colored stones, led by her singing, dancing bridesmaids. Timothy helped her alight from the litter and a murmur of approval went up from the crowd.

Lia was breathtakingly lovely. Her white, silken gown shone, and the tiny jewels and fine gold threads which were sewn into the rich, floating fabric flashed in the sun. Her veil was of the finest gauze and hid her face, but her long dark curls showed through and caught the sun. She wore a simple crown of tiny rosebuds which seemed to emphasize her youth and innocence.

Timothy led her proudly to the canopy and tenderly laid her hand in Roael's. The old rabbi from the tiny synagogue in Cana raised his hands over their heads as they knelt before him, and pronounced the Blessing of

Yahweh upon them. They exchanged rings, a circlet of
gold with no beginning and no ending, as symbolic of
their love and faithfulness, and then drank of the cup of
wine which Roael then smashed underfoot.

They were wed! Roael and Lia were man and wife as
God ordained from the beginning of man's existence. "A
man shall leave his mother and father and shall cleave
unto himself a wife, and the two shall become one flesh!"

A clash of cymbals rent the air, and the well wishers
roared with cheering. The men grabbed Roael and formed
a huge circle around him and began to dance. The women
watched and clapped their hands, and then bore Lia away
to form their own circle. The woman under Mary's charge
brought out trays laden with food—great clusters of
grapes, bowls of tiny salted olives, plates of figs and dates
and pomegranates and melons; roast fowl and fresh and
salted fish, heaping bowls of tiny green onions, tangy cu-
cumbers soaked in vinegar and oil, beans and leeks and
lentils, honey cakes and other breads both dark and
creamy white, and the crowning glory of whole roasted
lamb, prepared with herbs and spices as had been done
since Moses' day.

Young lads who acted as stewards filed into the courtyard bearing great earthen jars of cool, sweet wine upon
their shoulders, and a cry of joyous welcome went up
from the hot, perspiring dancers. They abandoned the
exhausted musicians and made a rush toward the groan-
ing tables.

As soon as everyone had been served and were reclining
on the gaily dyed rush and straw mats, James sought out
Mary and pulled her aside.

"Jeshua has returned to Capernaum," he said in a low
tone.

Mary's face glowed. "Is he well?" she whispered.

"Yes. He seems very well. Changed somehow, though.
More confident and sure. Andrew returned home the day
you came to Cana. He'd left Jeshua with John at the
Jordan and came home before him. Andrew was elated.
He told Simon that he'd found the Messiah. The next day,
Father and I and John were on the shores of the Galilee
below Capernaum supervising the men in mending the
nets when Jeshua suddenly appeared on the shore. John
saw him first and nudged me. Jeshua was smiling happily,

and before we could speak he motioned to us and said, 'Come! Follow me!'

"How can I tell you what we felt? We've waited so long! We, John and I, dropped our nets and immediately went to him. Andrew and Simon were on their boat washing their nets." James laughed. "Simon was more owlish than usual even, for the night's catch had been poor and Matthew had taken most of his profit in tax. Andrew had been trying to convince Simon that Jeshua was the One, but Simon would have no part of it and shouted at Andrew that he was sick of his pious preaching.

"Jeshua waded into the water with John and myself following, and climbed aboard Simon's boat. Poor Simon nearly burst with indignation, yet he knew Jeshua was Father's nephew and so dared not be impolite. Jeshua grinned at him and said, 'Put out into deep water and lower your nets for a catch.' Simon looked at him as though he were a madman. 'Master,' he fairly growled, 'we have been hard at it all night long and have caught nothing at all.' Simon looked over at me and then shrugged his shoulders and said, 'But if you say so, I will lower the nets.'

"I must admit, Mary, that I too wondered at the wisdom of trying for a catch at midday, but we caught so many that the nets were near the breaking point and we had to signal for help from another boat. The catch filled both boats until they nearly sank. We were all speechless, but Simon most of all. He began to tremble, and looked as though he's seen a ghost. He fell to his knees before Jeshua and cried, 'Leave me, Lord. I am a sinful man.' Jeshua raised him to his feet and said, 'Do not be afraid. From now on you will be catching men.' We put to shore and followed him to Capernaum."

Mary had listened with rapture, her hands clasped tightly at her breast. "He has four disciples then!"

"Six," James corrected. "Philip of Bethsaida and Nathaniel bar Tholomew followed him from the Jordan."

"Nathaniel!" Mary whispered in awe. She felt the rush of tears as she remembered the child she'd laid in Jeshua's bed. "Nathaniel. Of course! I should have guessed. Where is Jeshua now?"

"John and I left him at Simon's house."

Mary stood quietly for a moment, wishing she could

escape the celebration for a while to think and ponder this news alone. She sighed and said reluctantly, "I must get back. There is much to see to." She turned to go, but James caught her arm.

"Aunt, may I make bold to ask—" James' voice held a pleading note. He rarely used the intimate title, "Aunt." Mary smiled affectionately at him. He reminded her of Jude when he asked permission for something he feared she would refuse. "You may ask me anything, James. I'll tell you if I can."

James words tumbled out in a rush. "How does he do it? How did he know that Simon did not get a catch, and how did he know the fish were there at midday? Did he call them up from the bottom of the sea? And Nathaniel! Philip says that Jeshua called him first and then he, Philip, ran to tell Nathaniel. Nathaniel was back in the hills, completely out of sight of Jeshua, yet when Philip brought Nathaniel to him, Jeshua knew that he'd been sitting under a fig tree reading the Holy Scriptures from a scroll. Jeshua even knew the very passages Nathaniel was reading! How does he do that, Aunt?"

Mary smiled and shook her head. "I cannot explain these things. How did Elijah increase the widow's meal and oil? How did he make the iron axe float upon the water? These are mysteries that we do not understand, and yet are natural gifts given to man by God. One's consciousness must be open and ready to receive them. God gave man dominion over all the earth, but through his willfulness, man has forgotten how to use his gifts. The soul knows these things, but the mind of flesh has forgotten.

"There are many gifts of the Spirit, many of which those in the Brotherhood have retained and handed down the teachings of through the centuries. Judith can heal. She has the gift of prophecy. She has the ability to leave her body of flesh and travel in the spirit to realms not of this world. Have you not heard how the Essenes are reputed for their ability to endure excruciating pain without flinching and with a smile of joy upon their faces? This is how. Man has the ability to bring his mind, spirit, and flesh into one accord with God's will. When he reaches this state of perfection, all things are then possible to him, then he will master the universe as God ordained to souls from the beginning."

"And Jeshua? And you, Mary?" James asked.

Mary shook her head. "The Father will lead and the Son will follow, where, I do not know. Follow Jeshua and you will see."

It was long after sundown before the last of the merry-makers fell into an exhausted sleep, and well before dawn when Ruth awoke to Mary's gentle nudging. She groaned as she rolled over and struggled to sit up. Her body ached as though she'd taken a beating and her eyes were filled with all the sand along the Galilee. She sat for a moment with her legs sticking straight out before her, and her head dropped to her chest as she tried to orientate her mind as to where she was and why.

"Come, awake, Ruth," Mary urged. "The first day is the worst. Today will not be so frantic."

Ruth felt better after she'd splashed cold water on her face, and the morning prayers washed away the cobwebs in her mind. She was surprised to find Martha of Syrus busy supervising the ovens. "She didn't sleep well," Naomi whispered. "I'm sure she's thinking of the marriage feast she once planned for Mary. It helps her to be busy."

Ruth felt a stab of pity for Martha. She was close to her mother's age, and yet looked years older. Her hair was streaked with gray, and her skin was dry and pulled tightly over the bones in her face. She looked hard and defiant. Strange, Ruth thought, how some reacted to grief and disappointment with a gentle softening, and others became hard and bitter and found no comfort from any quarter.

By mid-morning the tables groaned again with hot breads and fresh fruits which quickly disappeared as the company broke their fast. The early afternoon was spent with games and dancing, until the heat of the day drove them to find a shady spot beneath the trees, to fan themselves and indulge in quiet gossip.

Ruth was helping the young stewards dispense the wine and caught snatches here and there of the men's talk. John the Baptizer was the topic of the day, and heated speculation as to whether or not he was a true prophet was foremost in their minds. Sometimes she heard Jeshua's name spoken, but her presence cut off their words and they waited in embarrassed silence until Ruth had passed before they resumed the conversation.

She saw Susane and Martha, Sophia's daughter, sitting alone in an olive grove and went to join them. Martha had married Nicodemus while Ruth was in Rome, news which had startled Ruth at the time and filled her with apprehension. Ruth remembered Nicodemus well from the time she'd lived in Aunt Josie's house, and wondered how gentle, demure Martha could be happy married to a man so much older than she, and so pompous and domineering in his attitude toward women.

"Ah, Ruth," Susane said as she approached. "You will know. Do Roael and Lia intend to establish a home of their own?"

Ruth looked across the grove to where Lia sat amid a group of women. She shook her head, wondering how the night had passed with Lia. She looked radiantly happy, praise God. Ruth had seen brides white with shock after their nuptial night, but Lia fairly glowed. "I think not. They intend to follow John, until a babe is born anyway, and then I don't know. I'd guess Lia would stay with Zebedee and Salome, and Roael continue as John's disciple." She turned to Martha. "How is it with you, Martha? It seems so short a time ago that we were girls together and now you are a married woman. Susane and I seem destined for spinsterhood, unless Jonas has his way," she added teasingly.

Susane blushed and they laughed, and then the laughter died on Martha's face. "I am well. Nicodemus is a good man. He treats me kindly and is generous. I have everything I want, and more." All the gladness had vanished from Martha's eyes, and though the words were right, her voice was unconvincing.

"But you are not happy," Ruth said flatly. "I'm sorry, Martha. Remember, we've been friends for all of our lives. Susane and I know you well. Tell us, for it often helps to unburden oneself to a friend."

Martha's chin quivered, and for a moment Ruth thought she was going to cry. Then she straightened her shoulders and lifted her head. "You are right. I am not happy. I'm not so unhappy, just not happy. Nicodemus is a good man, but he's much older than I and treats me like a charming child instead of a wife. Nicodemus is a Pharisee and regards women in the same light as his friends do. I'm to stay always in the background. My opinion on any matter is of no value. He discusses nothing with me of any importance except the running of his household."

"Perhaps that will change when you have a child," Susane said sympathetically.

Martha shook her head. "No. I think not," she said resignedly. "It is the same in his friends' households, and they have been wed for years and have many children. It's not so much the difference in our years, it's the ingrained attitude those men have toward women. I was raised in an Essene household where women have equal status with their brothers and husbands. I am well-educated and knowledgeable, but not in my husband's eyes. My schooling, as far as he is concerned, was only a childish whim, to keep me occupied until I married. He never confides in me. I know nothing of his thoughts and feelings. I am little more than a paid servant and," she added bitterly, "a well-kept woman."

Ruth looked at Susane in consternation. She didn't know what to say to Martha, and finally said, lamely, "Can we help?"

"No. There's nothing. I can endure the silence and his condescending manner, but of late there is arguing and anger, and that I cannot endure!"

"Over what?" asked Ruth.

"John. And—" She shot Ruth a pointed look. "Jeshua!"

A tight knot formed in Ruth's chest. "Jeshua?" she stammered.

"Remember how we used to play, to pretend how it would be when the Messiah took the throne of Israel? Remember how I used to plan how he would look, and the fine, princely robes he would wear and what we would wear? I know those were children's games, but I still dream of those times, and it is now so close." Her voice had risen in excitement and her face was intent and urgent.

"I heard what happened at the Jordan. Oh, not from my husband, you may be sure, but from the other wives. Nicodemus scoffs at it all. I shouldn't speak of it to him, but how can I help it? The kingdom creeps up on him unawares! He will not discuss it, and when I press him, he reacts with shouting and anger. He's forbidden me to mention Jeshua's name!" Martha buried her head in her hands. "How can I endure it!" she cried.

Ruth was troubled over Martha. The cool evening brought on more dancing and games and imbibing of wine, but Ruth found no joy in the hilarity. She longed for Capernaum. The wine made the men bold and more than once she heard Jeshua's name spoken in derisive tones. That night she fell into an exhausted sleep and her dreams were troubled and fearful.

The morning was hot and sultry before the sun broke over the horizon. Mary was still asleep when Ruth awoke, and she slipped quietly out of the room without disturbing her.

She met Editha and Judith on their way to the ovens. Judith mopped her brow with her arm and muttered, "It will scorch us alive today."

"Prophecy so early in the morning, Judith?" Ruth laughed, and Judith gave her a playful shove.

"There's the young miss now," a village woman called as they approached the baking area. The woman was stout and already perspiring heavily. "I'm just saying we needn't bake as much as before. They'll be more for drink than for food in this heat."

"Yes," Ruth agreed. "Cool wine and fresh fruit will be in more demand than hot bread."

"Eh!" the woman snorted. "I've never seen such food and drink. Cana will never see the likes of such a feast again. I'm glad our Mary has only one maid to wed. And you, child! Wait until you stand beneath the canopy. Your feast will put this one to shame!"

"No!" Ruth cried in mock horror. "When I wed, it'll be to a simple carpenter like my father, or a shepherd such as Timothy. None of this for me!"

They all laughed. "Well, it's fitting for your uncle, Zebedee."

Editha called from the back of the courtyard where a shallow cave was dug into the side of the hill to keep chill the great leather skins of wine. "Mary should check the wine. I fear it's running low."

By mid-morning the sun was like a furnace. Rhoda and Mary had taken the children into the hills to play where they could catch a breeze. Mary of Joseph worried over the wine. The supply was running low, and in the heat the wine was already flowing freely among the men. She decided she must send Jude into Capernaum for more. It wouldn't be as rich and aged as that which Zebedee had sent from Jerusalem, but it would be better than none at all.

Before she could summon him, Jude pushed his way through the crowd and whispered excitedly into her ear, "Jeshua comes. He's at the gate!"

Mary's face broke into smiles. She whispered back, "Bring him through the alley to the courtyard."

Mary held Jeshua's warm embrace for a long moment, her eyes closed and her heart too full to speak. Then she released him and held him at arm's length, studying him intently. He was thin, but that was due to his forty days' fast, and not to ill health or anxiety. His eyes were clear, merry even, as he smiled down at her, and his grip upon her shoulders was firm and sure.

Jude and Ruth stood back and watched. Tears prickled the backs of Ruth's eyelids. Only Jeshua could bring such joy to her mother's face. They were so alike. They had the same bright red-gold hair, the same blue-gray eyes, the same gentleness and compassion and fullness of love and life. They seemed to be one soul, one spirit.

She looked at Jude standing as still as granite beside her. His face was a mixture of awe and adoration with a slight shadow of envy, and over all, a terrible longing.

She looked beyond Jeshua to the four men who had come with him. Their eyes were lowered as though they were embarrassed to witness the intimate reunion of their master and his mother. Two she recognized from Capernaum, for they worked the fishing boats for Zebedee, and one was married to Esdrella's daughter. He was of medium height with a square, stocky body, a large head crowned by light curly hair, and a rounded beard which seemed to accentuate his broad, flat nose. His name was Simon ben John. The one beside him was tall and lean; his head long and his face narrow. His beard was dark and full. They were both dressed in rough fishermen's garb and wore rope sandals on their feet. This must be Simon's brother, Andrew, though Ruth could see no family resemblance.

The third man was also dressed as a fisherman. He was short and slight and wore his beard trimmed to a point. His eyes were deep blue, and flashed quickly across the scene, missing nothing. Ruth guessed him to be Philip of Bethsaida.

The last was entirely different from his companions. His black curly hair fell over his ears, and his beard was long and grizzled. His eyes were black and large and stood out against his white skin. He was no poor fisherman. He wore a long white tunic with a purple stripe at the hem, covered by a white cloak with purple gems sewn in the four corners. He looked moneyed and well-learned, more as though he should be teaching in the Jerusalem academy rather than standing in a dusty courtyard in a tiny village such as Cana. If she were right and this was Nathaniel bar Tholomew, then this was his home, but he certainly looked as though he'd outgrown his birthplace.

When Mary released Jeshua, Ruth stepped forward to welcome him, and again had the strange impulse to embrace his feet. Jeshua lifted her from her feet in a crushing hug which took her breath away; he laughed aloud when she gasped.

He introduced his friends, and Ruth had been right in guessing their identities. James and John ben Zebedee joined them, and Ruth noted how changed their attitude was toward Jeshua. They greeted him with the respectful deference a student shows to an honored master, and not as cousins and equals.

Jude hung back until the last, and then shook Jeshua's hand. His manner was stiff and formal, and Ruth's heart went out to him. Poor Jude. He simply didn't know what to think of Jeshua nor where his own place was in the presence of the Messiah. A sadness clouded Jeshua's eyes at Jude's cool welcome, and he looked in puzzlement at his younger brother.

A burst of shouting and laughter floated over the courtyard walls and Jeshua said, "The celebration seems to be a success."

"It will be, if the wine holds," Mary answered. A strange look passed over her face. She remembered Jeshua's "garden" which had fed them all during the famine in Egypt. She remembered the journey back to Galilee when their food was nearly gone and no one would give them more, even though Joseph had begged for the sake of his wife and child. Their meal had never run out. Each day the jar was as full as the day before. She looked intently into Jeshua's eyes. Had not the Voice said, "This is my beloved son"? Had Jeshua not just ten days ago sent Satan away and received ministry from the angels?

She chose her words carefully and spoke them deliberately. "Jeshua, they have no more wine."

Jeshua's mouth twitched as though trying to conceal a smile. He frowned and said in a stern voice, "Woman, how does this concern of yours involve me?" He used the term "woman" in a tone that a pompous Pharisee would use it, and Mary laughed. She knew his time had come! She hugged him and called the stewards. "Do whatever he tells you."

The stewards followed Jeshua to the doorway. Six huge stone jars, which normally held the water for the ceremonial washings, were there. "Fill those jars with water," Jeshua ordered. The stewards did as he bid and filled them to the brim.

"Now," said Jeshua, "draw some out and take it to the waiter in charge."

The young stewards looked at Jeshua and then at one another in fear. Was this man mad? Then one lad, bolder than the others, stepped forward and dipped into one of the jars. He poured the water from the dipper into an earthenware pitcher he'd set down beside him. Ruth and the others crowded around, wondering what Jeshua could possibly mean.

When the water splashed against the bottom of the pitcher, they all gasped. It was no longer clear, but ruby-red with a fragrance like roses and honey and blossoming grapevines.

Jeshua had turned the water into wine!

A strangled sob escaped Jude's throat. The others murmured in astonishment. Ruth groped blindly for her mother's arm. Mary didn't seem surprised at all! Ruth stared at her in wonder. She knew Jeshua could do this thing! What else did her mother know? Ruth felt as though she looked into the face of a stranger.

They followed the steward as he snatched up his miraculous jug of wine and ran to the head waiter. They watched as he tasted it and then heard him call out to Roael, "People usually serve the choice wine first; then, when the guests have been drinking a while, a lesser vintage. What you have done is to keep the choice wine until now!"

Chapter 27

Ruth took a lump of unleavened dough from a large wooden bowl and began to pound it with the heel of her hand into a round, flat cake. The room was hot. Not a breeze found its way through the open door, and the slats of sunlight filtering through the narrow, latticed window were thick with languid dust motes. She was alone. The house was empty and silent, the only sound the rhythmical slap of her palm against the dough. She worked quickly and automatically, her mind free to roam and think at will.

The Sabbath would begin at sundown. Ruth and Josie had been up before dawn, sweeping the house from top to bottom. They'd drawn two days' supply of water from the well, gathered two days' supply of fuel, and bought two days' supply of oil and fruit and meal. Everything they'd need for tomorrow had to be prepared today, for the Law forbade any labor on the Lord's day of rest.

Mary and Josie were in the courtyard with Jeshua and his friends. Judith was there also, and Editha, the Other Mary, Abigale, Sophie, and most of the other of the eleven girls chosen with Mary. They'd all come with Mary from Cana to plan how they could help Jeshua with his mission of teaching God's word to Israel. Jeshua intended to tour all of Galilee, and Ruth sighed, wondering how he would be accepted and what the Jewish leaders' reaction would be to him. If he were a Pharisee or a Sadducee and had been educated in one of their own academies, they might accept his unorthodox teachings, but Jeshua was an Essene, and they would hate him just for that fact alone. Even if they didn't know he was an Essene, surely they'd know he didn't come from one of their own schools, and they'd never accept his teachings as valid.

She remembered Nicodemus' scorn at Cana. It hadn't taken the young stewards long to spread the story of how Jeshua had changed the water into wine. The whole company had erupted like a disturbed beehive. They'd quickly divided into arguing camps, those who believed and those who didn't, with Nicodemus leading those who didn't. Ruth smiled to herself and gave the dough an extra hard blow. Those who didn't believe had certainly stared at Jeshua in awe, and hadn't dared to deride him to his face, even though they denounced the act as trickery behind his back.

Most of the women had believed. Strange how women could see truth where men could not. Maybe it was because their lot was so hard that any change could only be for the better, or since their total existence was relegated to their homes and families instead of business and worldly matters, they had more time to think of truths and things of the soul than men whose minds were so filled with their own selfish desires.

Poor Lia. Her marriage celebration had been cut short as the Pharisees and Sadducees had angrily decamped the next day. Actually, Lia and Roael hadn't seemed to mind, nor even Zebedee. Salome had been disturbed, but dear Aunt Salome, as always, had stood staunchly by her husband's queer family and had bid her temple friends a cool farewell.

John ben Zebedee's voice, high with excited enthusiasm, floated in from the courtyard, followed by a burst of merry laughter. Ruth flipped one of the flat cakes onto an iron griddle and wondered what fantastic scheme John had come up with now. They were all out there planning ways to draw the crowds to listen to Jeshua's teaching, and Ruth wondered if it were all necessary. Andra was making posters and banners for the women to carry and nail to village gates, Editha and Rebkah were planning to sell breads and cakes at the inn in Bethlehem to raise money to finance the mission, and even musicians and singers had been inducted into the cause.

Ruth wondered if her mother would join in the antics of such a carnival-like affair, and decided not. Mary was

far too private a person to join in such clamor. She always
stayed in the background and shunned any kind of public
notice. Strange, how even so, her presence always dominated any gathering.

Jude wouldn't go, of that Ruth was sure. Jude's belief
in Jeshua had been considerably strengthened when he
saw with his own eyes how the water became wine as it
was poured out, but his fears still outweighed his faith.

Ruth wiped the sweat from her eyes and walked to the
door in search of a breeze. Strange how the water had to
be poured out before it became wine. As long as it remained in the stone jars, it was only water. Maybe it
was a sign for all of them. If they did nothing with the
time given to them to spend on earth, then they were like
the water, tasteless and flat, but if they moved, poured
themselves out, gave their love and concern and talents to
help others, then they became like the wine, fragrant and
sparkling with life, an acceptable gift to the Lord. She
shook her head. It was too hot and there was too much to
do before sundown to ponder mysteries of such depth.
Maybe she'd ask Jeshua someday.

It was a long, full day, and a relief when the sun sank
below the hills. They all ate the Sabbath meal together
and then everyone but Mary and Ruth hurried off to the
synagogue. Mary pled weariness and Ruth stayed behind
to wait for Susane. She'd seen little of Susane in the past
weeks. First there had been Lia's wedding, and now with
Jeshua and his friends, and Judith and the other women
all in the house, Ruth had felt compelled to stay at home
and help her mother.

Susane was late and burst into the house with a breathless account for her tardiness, and hurriedly helped Ruth
with her cloak.

"Are you sure you don't want to come with us, Mother?"
Ruth asked.

Mary smiled. "I'll relish some time to myself. You girls
go ahead, I'll be fine."

They bid Mary a hasty farewell and hurried out. They
walked quickly along the deserted, dusty streets, wanting
to run but not being able to because it was the Sabbath.

"Philoas is back," said Susane.

"Philoas?"

"The Roman I wrote you about. The one who's been so

helpful to Jonas and me. You remember," Susane said impatiently.

Ruth nodded abstractedly and Susane rattled on. "He was born in Rome, but lived for some time in Heliopolis. His father was apparently some high official in Caesar Augustus' service, and so Philoas was educated in both Rome and Athens. He seems to be an intimate friend and even a favorite of Tiberius. He acts as a personal representative of Tiberius and has absolute authority. His task is to travel through the empire and recommend the manner in which the peoples under the various schools should be taxed according to their religious influences. He's not a tax collector, but more or less judges groups or individuals as to their ability to pay tax. He's also to judge their patriotism to Rome and if their work is in the best interest of the people in general."

Ruth began to show some interest. "How did you come to meet him?"

"Through Father and Matthew. Philoas had been to Mt. Carmel and had interviewed Judith extensively about the Essenes. He told Father how impressed he was with 'the sect' and was highly interested when Father admitted to being of that thought. He was Father's guest while he was in Capernaum and consequently met me and Jonas."

"Do you trust him?"

"Not at first, of course, but we had some lively discussions about the work Jonas and I do, and Philoas showed a great deal of insight and sympathy for our problems. He made some very useful suggestions and gradually became more and more involved with our project."

Ruth raised her brows skeptically.

"Really, Ruth. Philoas has a sincere concern for the lot of the common people. He displays none of that Roman superiority that most of the others do, and has an insatiable curiosity about the 'One God' of the Jews."

Ruth wasn't convinced, and her face showed it. "Maybe. I'll have to judge for myself," she murmured.

"Isn't Justin a Roman? And what about your friend Elcor?" Susane demanded.

Ruth sighed. "They are only a few, Susane. There are far more Pontius Pilates than Justins among the Romans, believe me. Few Roman minds can understand the Jewish mind."

They came to the market square and hurried toward the synagogue. It was long and rectangular, built of white stone with a faintly Roman look to its architecture, having been built by money donated by a Roman centurion whose sympathy lay with the incomprehensible Jews. Tall, thick stone columns supported the two-storied roof and formed a porch over the great double doors. Ruth was surprised to see a large crowd gathered on the porch, all straining to get closer to the doors. The synagogue was the center of Jewish life and there were always a few curious Gentiles listening from the porch, but she had never seen so many.

She and Susane skirted the porch and entered the synagogue through the women's door on the side. It never failed to irk Ruth that the lowly women were not allowed to use the main entrance, and a rush of irritation swept over her.

They climbed the narrow stone stairs to the balcony which served as the women's section and found that it, too, was unusually crowded. The acrid smell of incense and burning oil and sweating female bodies was overpowering and almost made Ruth gag. They paused at the top step and listened. Strange, loud noises were coming from the floor below—deep, gutteral, throaty sounds like an animal in agony. The atmosphere was charged with an electric excitement and the balcony buzzed with whispering women's voices.

Ruth looked wonderingly at Susane and they began to thread their way through the women toward the balcony rail where they could see to the floor below. The other women noticed who was trying to get through and began voluntarily to step aside to make a path for them. They all seemed to stare with unreadable expressions on their faces and then whisper excitedly to one another as Ruth and Susane passed by.

Ruth was uneasy. These women all knew her well, and had never acted like this before. A sense of disapproval and distrust, tinged with awe and anger, seemed to follow Ruth and Susane across the room. They reached the high iron rail and peered through to the main floor.

Jeshua was standing in the center of the floor. A deep circle of men surrounded him, pressing back against the walls as though to get as far away from him as possible.

A shattering, wolflike howl split the air, making Ruth's skin crawl in horror. A man lunged at Jeshua from the shadows—horrible, filthy, ragged, foaming at the mouth, his hair long and matted with filth and vermin, and his face contorted with madness. Ruth clamped her hand over her mouth to stifle a scream as the madman lunged and retreated, his hands curled into vulture's talons, clawing the air and reaching out toward Jeshua's face.

Jeshua stood perfectly still. He never flinched as each thrust and parry brought the demon-possessed, subhuman creature closer and closer to his face. Ruth could see Jeshua's eyes clearly. They seemed to dominate his face and glowed like fire in their sockets. His eyes never left the creature. He stood calmly, serenely; no fear at all showed in his face, only an intense waiting.

The man growled and crawled and leaped and danced around Jeshua for what seemed to Ruth an eternity, and then finally came to a panting halt a few feet in front of him. A thick, deadly silence descended upon the synagogue. No one moved; the only sound was the creature's rasping, labored breath.

Then he shrieked at Jeshua. "What do you want of us, Jeshua of Nazareth? Have you come to destroy us? I know who you are—the Holy One of God!"

Jeshua's face was terrible, stern and angry. His voice was sharp and commanding as Ruth had never heard it before. "Be quiet! Come out of that man!"

The man fell to the floor, jerking and grovelling and moaning in a convulsive fit of madness. Then a final, shattering shriek emerged from his gaping mouth and he was still. He lay at Jeshua's feet as quiet and peaceful as a sleeping child. Jeshua's expression changed back to his usual one, and he bent down and tenderly helped the man to his feet. He motioned to two men and they came and led the poor fellow meekly out of the synagogue.

The whole place erupted into a roar of amazement. "What does this mean?" Ruth heard from somewhere behind her. "A completely new teaching in a spirit of authority! He gives orders to unclean spirits and they obey!"

Ruth clutched at the iron rails and fought the nausea in her throat. Jeshua hadn't moved. He stood quietly, listening to and watching the reactions around him. Then he **turned and walked to the ark and selected a scroll. He** carried it up the few short steps to the speakers' podium and unrolled it. The synagogue grew quiet. Again there was that deathly silence.

Jeshua began to read, his voice loud and clear and carrying into every corner.

"The spirit of the Lord God is upon me, because the Lord has anointed me. He has set me to bring glad tidings to the lowly, to heal the broken-hearted. To proclaim liberty to the captives and release to the prisoners, to announce a year of favor from the Lord and a day of vindication by our God, to comfort all who mourn; to place on those who mourn in Zion a diadem instead of ashes, to give them oil of gladness in place of mourning, a glorious mantle instead of a listless spirit. They will be called oaks of justice, planted by the Lord to show His glory."

Jeshua rolled up the scroll and handed it to a man nearby. His eyes moved slowly across the room and then up into the balcony where they rested for a moment on Ruth, and then continued their sweep of the silent, waiting Jews.

Then he spoke, again in that clear, authoritative voice. "Today this Scripture passage is fulfilled in your hearing." Then Jeshua sat down.

For a moment there was shocked silence, and then pandemonium broke loose. Angry cries and shouts came from all corners. "Who does he think he is? Blasphemy! Throw him out of the place of worship!"

The coppery taste of fear filled Ruth's mouth. She clutched Susane's arm and whispered hoarsely, "Stay here. Watch what happens. I'm going for Mother."

She spun around and fought her way through the milling, angry women. She fled down the stairs and out the door and began to run. She stumbled and would have fallen, but someone caught her. She pushed herself back from her rescuer's grasp, mumbling an almost incoherent word of thanks, and a wash of relief flooded her as she looked into Jonas' white, tight-lipped face. "Jonas!" his name emerged in a sob.

"Come on," he whispered roughly. "Let's get you out of this mob." He put his arm around her and they pushed their way through.

It wasn't until they'd left the synagogue behind and were in the dark, deserted sidestreets that she noticed the tall Roman who flanked her other side. She couldn't see his face for the darkness, but he was tall, and she could smell the leather girdle that all Roman soldiers wore, and his iron-soled sandals trod heavily on the dusty street. She guessed he was Philoas.

Jonas relaxed his grip on Ruth's shoulder and spoke over her head. "The man in the synagogue is her brother. This is Ruth, of whom we've told you. This is Philoas, Ruth."

Philoas' voice startled her and caused a strange warmth to wash over her. It was deep and gentle, vibrant with compassion and tenderness, not like the usual nasal Roman twang. "Your brother is an extraordinary man. I wish I could have witnessed for myself what occurred inside. Unfortunately your law forbids the entry of a Gentile."

The last was said without rancor, and for the first time in her life, Rush experienced a flush of shame for her peoples' exclusiveness. They heard the muffled clank of iron against stone and she knew a Roman contingent was on its way to the synagogue. She shivered and wondered if Jeshua would be arrested. As though to read her thoughts, Philoas put a comforting hand on her arm and said, "Don't fear. They won't arrest him. They'll only send the crowd home and prevent any further disturbance."

His touch sent little shocks of pleasure up her arm, and Ruth believed him. Her fears disappeared and she relaxed, slowing her pace a bit. They turned the corner and she could see her mother's lighted window. She forced her mind away from Philoas and planned what she would say to Mary.

Mary was sitting quietly with a bit of embroidery in her hands when they entered. She looked up and smiled with pleasure and welcome. "You're early. Jonas! How good of you to bring Ruth home." Then she saw the Roman and the concern in Jonas' and Ruth's expressions, and her smile faded. "Is something wrong? What has happened?"

Ruth kissed her cheek. "It's all right, Mother, for now, anyway. There was an incident at the synagogue, but the Romans have restored order by now."

Mary drew in her breath. A look of resignation mingled

with foreboding crossed her face. "Jeshua was involved. Tell me."

Philoas stayed in the shadows by the door. Ruth had flung her cloak aside and knelt at Mary's knees. An oil lamp burned on a table at Mary's side and cast a golden glow on Ruth's upturned face.

How beautiful they are, Philoas thought wonderingly. The daughter's face is an exact replica of the Mother's—the same small, perfect nose and wide eyes, the same full, compassionate mouth and delicate but strong line of jaw and chin. Only their coloring differed. The lamplight caught the gold in Mary's hair and it danced like flickering little tongues of red and gold flame, while it drew a blue sheen from Ruth's dark curls. Mary's skin was white, translucent pearl, while Ruth's was more like olives ripening in the golden sun.

Philoas expected the mother to become quite hysterical over the disturbance her son had caused, at least to weep and even perhaps to faint, as most well-bred Roman women would have done, but she sat quietly while Ruth recounted what had happened. Only a thin, white line around her mouth betrayed the tumult of emotions which raged through her heart. When Ruth had finished she only said, "I see," and then looked questioningly at the strange Roman who stood in the shadows.

Ruth had forgotten all about Philoas in her concern for Mary. She blushed and said in an apologetic rush. "I'm sorry! Mother, this is Philoas, Jonas' and Susane's friend."

Philoas stepped out of the shadows and bent formally over Mary's hand, noticing how soft and smooth and white, and how delicately formed and tapered it was, the hand of blood and breeding—not a peasant's hand. He felt strangely humbled and awed by this simply dressed carpenter's wife, and a rush of affection reddened his thick neck.

Ruth watched him. He is really most handsome, she thought. He was clean-shaven and bronzed by the sun. His bare arms and legs were thick and muscular and covered by a fine mist of soft black hair. His thick black curls were crisp and cut short in the fashion of the Romans. He straightened and smiled at her and she blushed, hoping he didn't again read her thoughts. His eyes were large and black, sparkling with good humor and kindness, and she noticed that his Roman nose was not quite as Roman as most. His mouth was full and sensuous and somehow enticing, and her flush deepened.

Mary poured out goblets of cool wine and set little dishes of olives and almonds and honey cakes on the table. Philoas looked around the room which was simple, homely, and immaculately clean. The few pieces of furniture were fashioned of wood without the comfort or adornment of plush cushions, though the wood glowed in the lamplight and he could see the mellow grain of lemonwood and cedar. He paused at the stairway and passed his hand over the delicately carved rail. He turned to Mary with an appreciative look.

"My husband was a carpenter. He carved that for me when I was but a bride," she said softly.

"It's exquisite!" exclaimed Philoas. "Your husband was a talented artist." He took the goblet Mary offered, sniffed the heady aroma, and then let a small sip roll over his tongue. He nodded and smiled. "The Jews also make an exquisite wine. I can tell it is from the vineyards of Galilee. The world can boast of none better."

He sat with the others at the table and relaxed. He felt comfortable and completely at ease in this humble little cottage. There was a warmth and peacefulness here that he seldom enjoyed, and he was so enrapt in lazy contentment that for a moment he forgot the disturbing event that had brought him to this house, until Mary's question reminded him.

"What will the Roman authority make of my son's teaching?" she asked in an extraordinarily musical voice.

Philoas regarded the serene woman across the table for a moment and decided she was not one for soothing platitudes, but would expect and want an honest answer. "I doubt they will be concerned this time. Your people are volatile and excitable, particularly in matters of religion, so they will probably treat it as only another incident resulting from religious zeal and then forget it. If, of course, it is only an isolated incident."

"And if it is not just an isolated incident, if Jeshua continues teaching in the manner in which he did tonight and causes further disturbances?" asked Jonas.

Philoas straightened his shoulders and glanced at Ruth. She was leaning forward, waiting for his answer, a look of fear in her eyes. He recoiled from giving credence to the lovely girl's fears, but he sensed that she too expected honesty from him. "That would be another matter. Caesar's order to keep the peace has top priority, and Caesar's orders are not taken lightly. Tiberius is a just man and has an avid interest in the customs and traditions of all the people in his realm, but he will not stand for sedition of any kind. He might consider personally the circumstances that promoted a disturbance, but he is in Rome and his officers will not want their records to carry reports of undue disturbances occurring in their jurisdictions and will use the quickest and most proficient means of preventing it." He looked soberly at Mary. "If your son continues to cause near riots such as tonight, he could very well be arrested and tried for sedition."

Jonas and the women were silent. Ruth's face was drained of color, and Jonas nervously played with an olive pit. Only Mary showed no sign of concern. Her eyes remained serene and her voice calm. "Thank you for your honesty, Philoas. God's will be done. Nothing will deter Jeshua from doing his Father's will, the Lord will see to that." She put her hand over Ruth's. "We needn't fear for Jeshua."

Philoas's brows knit. Was the woman being unrealistic, or was she showing an extraordinary faith in her God? What did she mean, "his Father's will"? What did a long-dead, poor carpenter have to do with this? He was about to ask when the door opened and Susane and Jude entered.

Susane was flushed with excitement, but Jude was white-faced and surly. "Jeshua is at Simon's!" she cried. "It's incredible! There is such a crowd there you cannot get through to the door."

The memory of angry calls and hate-filled eyes flooded Ruth's mind and her mouth went dry. "What are they doing there? Are they trying to harm him?" she asked, aghast.

"No! No, they love him! It's unbelievable. Jeshua is healing them!"

"But they were so angry!" Ruth said incredulously.

"Not everyone," Susane answered. "After you left, some began to cry that Jeshua be heard, but the soldiers came and ordered everyone to their homes. Jeshua,

Simon, and James and John and the others left the synagogue and went to Simon's house. I found Judith and
Abigale and the others, and we followed." Susane paused
and took a deep breath. She looked to Jude as though
expecting him to take up the story, but he only looked
sullenly at the floor and said nothing, so she went on.

"We went in Simon's house. Esdrella was lying on her
pallet." Susane looked at Philoas. "Esdrella is Simon's
mother-in-law. She's been desperately ill with fever," she
explained.

"I've been unable to help her," Jonas interrupted. "I've
used all the known remedies, but I fear Esdrella is dying."

"No more!" Susane cried triumphantly. "Jeshua simply
walked over to her, took her hand, and told her to get up.
She did! The fever left her, just like that! Esdrella simply
got up and started to get everyone something to eat and
drink!"

"Impossible!" Jonas blurted.

"It seems your remedies worked after all, my friend,"
Philoas smiled.

"Wait! Everyone was amazed. We just stared in disbelief. Then some who had followed us to Simon's house
and saw what happened ran to their homes and came
back with their sick—even some who were possessed with
unclean spirits, like that horrible man in the synagogue.
Lame people walked, fevers disappeared, boils vanished,
wounds healed, and the possessed became calm! If I
hadn't seen for myself, I couldn't have believed it. Tell
them, Jude!"

Jude looked at Mary and nodded. "It's true," he said
woodenly. "I saw. Now they will truly hate him. They'll
condemn him for a sorcerer, for being Beelzebub himself,
for how can hypocrites and pompous, selfish, learned men
recognize an angel!" Jude's voice was harsh and bitter.
"They'll kill him. Sooner or later they'll find a way, and
they will kill him!" He looked at Mary in anguish. "And
then your precious dreams of a Messiah will be naught
but cold ash!"

Chapter 28

Jeshua left Capernaum and began his tour of Galilee, teaching the healing in the impoverished, unadorned little synagogues in small towns and villages where Roman and Herodian authority would take little note of an itinerant, sectarian preacher. The women carried through their plan to precede him, drawing the villagers out to hear, tending to his needs by collecting alms to finance his ministry, and procuring food and shelter for him and his followers. As Ruth had guessed, Mary did not go with them, though Josie did. Ruth wanted to go, but felt she couldn't leave her mother alone in the house with no one but Jude for company.

The house was eerily quiet after weeks of constant activity. Both Mary and Ruth found this to be a relief, and with the house devoid of female chatter, and Jeshua no longer in Capernaum to constantly remind Jude of his anxiety over his elder brother, Jude forgot his sullenness and became his old, optimistic, cheerful self. They settled into a pleasant, companionable routine. Mary dismissed her few servants and kept the house herself. Jude left for Alphaeus' shop each morning at dawn, and Ruth resumed her work with Jonas and Susane. Ruth was content and soothed by the busy days and tranquil nights, until her association with Philoas began to grow beyond a friendly involvement, and she found herself in an uneasy battle of wills with her mother.

Susane's assessment of Philoas' character had been right. Philoas had an honest concern for the poor and powerless. He used his authority to intercede on their behalf when their desperate circumstances brought them afoul of the law. He exerted the pressure of his position to force the publicans to collect their taxes fairly, to extend

347

the tax deadline when circumstances made it impossible for them to be paid on time. He helped Ruth find employment for those who had no income, going so far as to create public building works when no other work could be found. Ruth worked closely with Philoas, seeing him nearly every day, and her initial flush of attraction grew into a lasting, woman's love.

There was no doubt that Philoas returned her love in full measure. It shone in the gladness of his face whenever Ruth appeared in his sight, in the gentle pressure of his hand over hers, and in his dark eyes which melted her heart with their tender regard, and caused her knees to turn to water.

Ruth was blissfully happy. She rose each dawn with his name on her lips and slept amid dreams warm with his comforting love. Jonas and Susane watched their deepening relationship with happy approval, and Jude teased her unmercifully and made her blush. But Mary became cool and aloof, unwilling to listen to Ruth's praise of Philoas, until the situation exploded in the first open confrontation Ruth had ever had with her mother.

Dislike and mistrust of any Roman were deeply ingrained in the Jews, and Ruth was shocked that her mother proved no, different. Mary denied that she had such prejudice against the Romans, and declared her only concern was for Ruth's happiness. Who would accept a marriage between a Jew and a Roman? Not the Jews, and certainly not Philoas' aristocratic friends and family! Could Ruth bear a life of criticism? Could she be content with no friend other than her husband? Ruth thought yes, but Mary's eyes were full of doubt. What of their children? Neither Jew nor Roman would accept them. Were they being fair to the little souls they would bring into this world?

Little good it had done Ruth to point to Justin and Judith. They lived in the isolation of Mt. Carmel, and one could not say that Phinehas and Servilius were particularly happy, though Ruth agreed with Jude that their problem stemmed far more from their mother's early neglect than from their Roman-Jewish blood.

Ruth deplored the rift between herself and Mary. Jude declared that he liked Philoas and had no objection to a Roman brother-in-law, but flatly refused to enter into an argument with his mother on Ruth's behalf. "I have my own problems with Mother over Jeshua. I don't intend to create another!" he said adamantly in reply to Ruth's pleas.

Mary did not deny Philoas the hospitality of her home, and treated him with polite deference, but her manner was cool and her disapproval obvious. She admitted that she admired and liked Philoas, but as a friend and not as a future son-in-law!

Ruth was torn. She couldn't deny her love for Philoas, and neither could she marry without her mother's blessing. Her blissful days came to an end. Her sleep was restless with vague, disturbing dreams. She implored the Lord to change her mother's heart, and fervently wished that Jeshua would come home.

When Jeshua did come home, neither Ruth nor Mary found an opportunity to speak to him in private. He stayed at Simon's house along the waterfront and everywhere he went he was followed by the hopeful and the curious. His disciples were always with him, except when he stole away to the hills to pray.

The women had all returned to their homes, and Josie's familiar figure was once more bent over the oven. She brought Ruth and Mary up to date on all that had happened during Jeshua's tour of Galilee, and Ruth could hardly believe the miracles Jeshua performed and Josie's accounts of the hundreds who thronged to hear him.

Ruth did find an opportunity to introduce Philoas to Jeshua one night when Jeshua was visiting Mary at the house. They seemed to get along well, to like one another. Anyway, Philoas professed to be impressed with Jeshua, particularly with Jeshua's knowledge of the world and its affairs. Jeshua's years of travel and schooling in distant lands had surprised Philoas. He'd expected Jeshua to be something of a religious fanatic like John the Baptizer, and was surprised to find Jeshua quite worldly and completely aware of political and economic issues. Jeshua had also impressed Philoas with his religious teaching, using logic and reason to emphasize truths in the manner so dear to a Roman's well-ordered mind. Ruth had smiled to herself at that, remembering Judith telling how she'd used the same methods in converting Justin to the God of the Jews.

On the Sabbath, Ruth and Susane went to the synagogue to hear Jeshua preach again. This time Ruth did not feel uneasy at the women's curious stares. She knew Philoas was just outside the doors and that no harm would come to Jeshua as long as he was there.

The women again made way for Ruth and Susane until they stood before the tall wrought-iron railing. The lower floor was filled to capacity and Ruth recognized some of the Pharisees and scribes who'd come out from Jerusalem to investigate for themselves this strange teacher who was reported to have all of Galilee agog with his so-called miracles. They stood in a tightly knit, sullen group off to one side, their faces all alike with their closed-minded looks of scorn.

Susane nudged Ruth's arm and pointed to Matthew standing next to James ben Zebedee. Ruth nodded and exchanged a knowing look with Susane. What a furor Matthew had caused! A few days before, Jeshua and his disciples had been walking along the shore and had come upon Matthew sitting in his tax collector's booth. Matthew hadn't seen Jeshua since his return to Capernaum, and the cousins had embraced warmly. Then Jeshua had said, "Come, and follow me!" None of them had known how Matthew had secretly longed to be included in Jeshua's intimate circle of friends, nor how he'd thought his position of publican would never allow it. He'd abandoned the booth on the spot, and that night had given a lavish party to celebrate his joy.

Jeshua was, of course, the guest of honor, and pious Jews and pompous Pharisees had been outraged that Jeshua would stoop to eat with tax collectors and sinners. Ruth suppressed a giggle as she remembered Jeshua's scathing retort to their indignant accusation. "People who are in good health do not need a doctor; sick people do. Go and learn the meaning of the words, 'It is mercy I desire and not sacrifice.' I have come to call, not the self-righteous, but the sinners." Philoas had been there and had told Ruth how the Pharisees had nearly choked on that rebuke.

This afternoon those same Pharisees had denounced Jeshua and his followers for picking grain to eat on the Sabbath, and again Jeshua's answer had left them speechless. "Have you never read what David did when he was in need and he and his men were hungry? How he entered God's house in the days of Abiatharthe, the High Priest, and was permitted to eat? He even gave it to his men. The Sabbath was made for man, not man for the Sabbath. That is why the Son of Man is lord even of the Sabbath."

Now they stood together in their righteous little group, and with them was an old man who was a familiar character along the piers of Capernaum. He was a beggar whose hand had been withered and useless since birth, and Ruth wondered why he stood with the Pharisees. Was there some plot under way to force Jeshua to heal on the Sabbath? The poor man was obviously upset and so nervous he could not stand still.

Jeshua had been reading from the Scriptures, but every eye was on the Pharisees. Jeshua finally rerolled the scroll and handed it to an assistant. He looked steadily at the Pharisees for a long moment and then, beckoning to the old man, said, loudly enough for everyone to hear, "Stand up here in front!"

The old beggar shuffled his way to Jeshua, his fear so palpable Ruth could almost smell it. He stood pale and trembling before Jeshua, a pathetic, innocent pawn of the Pharisees.

Jeshua looked at him with pity, and then his eyes flashed with anger as he turned his gaze to the Pharisees. "Is it permitted to do a good deed on the Sabbath, or an evil one? To preserve life, or destroy it?"

The silence in the great hall was heavy. The Pharisees didn't answer. Jeshua turned to the old man. "Stretch out your hand."

Sweat poured into the poor man's eyes and he looked ready to collapse. He never took his eyes from Jeshua's face, and slowly he raised his arm, reaching out toward Jeshua. His hand moved and seemed to grow before their eyes, and then the old man cried out, a cry of such exultation that it tore at Ruth's heart. "It moves! It truly moves! Look! Praise unto the Almighty One who has sent such a one among us!"

A great sigh rose from the hall and the Pharisees were frenzied with anger. They pushed their way roughly through the crowd and left. Ruth felt a smug satisfaction that Jeshua had outwitted them again, but then she saw a group of Herod's flunkies get up and follow the Pharisees out, and her smugness changed to apprehension.

Jeshua waited a few moments and then he too left, with almost the whole congregation in his wake. By the time Ruth and Susane emerged into the street and found Jonas and Philoas, Jeshua was nowhere in sight. They followed the crowd to Simon's house, but the throng was so great they couldn't even get near the door. Philoas looked around in amazement. "These aren't all from Capernaum, Ruth. I recognize men from Tyre, Sidon, the Decapolis, all over. Look there!"

Ruth looked to where Philoas pointed. Four men were carrying a man lying on a mat. When they saw there was no way to get through to the door, they skirted the crowd to the side of Simon's house and carefully eased the man and the mat up the outer stairway to the roof. Ruth and the others stepped back and watched in amazement as the four began to tear a hole in Simon's roof.

"I know that man!" Philoas muttered. "He's paralyzed and cannot walk. This time I intend to see for myself!"

He used his Roman authority and ordered the pressing crowd to make way. Ruth, Susane, and Jonas followed, and they entered the house just as the paralyzed man was being lowered through the roof. Everyone was staring upward and pressing back against the walls to make room for the wasted, frail body descending from the ceiling.

Jeshua looked as surprised as any, and then an amused smile spread over his face as the little man landed with a soft thud at his feet. The man returned Jeshua's smile, pleased with his friends' ingenuity and his own small moment of triumph. There was no fear or trembling in this poor soul, only a jaunty, confident expectation. He was young and brash and looked at Jeshua with a gleam of challenge in his eye. Jeshua looked up into the four youthful faces which lined the ragged hole in Simon's roof and saw they mirrored their friend's merry, challenging expression. His eyes returned to the paralyzed lad waiting patiently at his feet.

"My son," Jeshua said softly, "your sins are forgiven."

Some scribes were sitting close by where Ruth stood. "Why does the man talk that way? He commits blasphemy! Who can forgive sins except God alone?" they whispered.

Ruth didn't think Jeshua could possibly have heard their low whisper, but he turned to them and said sternly, "Why do you harbor these thoughts? Which is easier, to say to the paralytic, 'Your sins are forgiven,' or to say, 'Stand up, pick up your mat and walk again'? That you may know that the Son of Man has authority on earth to forgive sin"—he turned to the man still lying on the mat —"I command you: Stand up! Pick up your mat and go home."

The lad grinned up at Jeshua and tentatively tried moving his useless legs. They moved! He tried again, slowly drawing his knees to his chest, then straightening them out again. He wiggled his bare toes in his sandals, and then with a cry of pure joy, he hopped up and gleefully picked up the mat, flung it jauntily over his shoulder, and strode triumphantly out the door to the cheers of his friends peering through the roof.

It was very late when Philoas took Ruth home, his mind a turmoil of confusion and question. They'd listened to Jeshua's teaching for a long time and had witnessed many cures. The streets were eerily quiet in the predawn, and Philoas kept his voice low.

"How can he do that, Ruth? I know some illnesses and paralyses are caused by hysteria, but I know the man they lowered through the roof. I know of the accident that broke his spine and robbed him of his legs, and that is not hysteria! And the old beggar in the synagogue! Can a babe in the womb be accused of hysteria?"

Ruth slipped her hand into his and squeezed it. "We believe there are no accidents, that everything is a result of past deeds, whether good or bad. Each sin committed, either by thought or deed, must be paid in full. Who can tell what sins the old beggar once committed with his hand? His soul chose a body this time with a hand that could not be used in such a way again. And your friend, the paralytic—perhaps he once committed a violent act against another which robbed that soul of his legs. What better way to learn of the anguish he once caused than by experiencing that anguish for himself?"

"I understand that, Ruth. It is logical and reasonable if one believes in the immortality and continued lives of the soul, but it doesn't explain how Jeshua heals them!"

Ruth sighed. "I don't really know, either," she admitted. "Many Essenes heal through prayer and by the laying on of hands—"

"But Jeshua forgives their sins!" Philoas interrupted.

"I know, but I cannot understand that, either. I understand how God's mercy and forgiveness can wipe away the debt for past deeds, but I don't understand how Jeshua can, unless, as he said tonight, 'The Son of Man has authority on earth to forgive sins,' and Jeshua is the Son of Man."

"What does that term mean, the Son of Man?"

"In our Scriptures, Daniel describes 'One like a son of man coming on the clouds of heaven,' in his vision of the four beasts. Enoch also uses the term as meaning one who was created before the world and who will reign gloriously at the end of time. But before this happens his existence will be revealed to the Elect."

Philoas stopped and looked at Ruth increduously. "Your brother believes he is this incredible personage?"

Ruth shrugged. "How then does he heal?"

Philoas had no answer; indeed, he had no answer to anything regarding this baffling brother of Ruth's. The man was an enigma, unlike any other he'd ever encountered, either in the flesh or in myth. And he, Philoas, intended to marry the man's sister! Well, Philoas thought, he will make an interesting brother-in-law, that is certain.

The next day Jeshua was forced to teach from a boat rowed a short way from shore in order to keep from being crushed by the crowds. The following day he led the throngs into the hills, where there was room for all as he stood at the top of a high mount and preached to the thousands reclining on the grassy slopes around him. His unusual, carrying voice was borne by the gentle Galilean breeze to every ear, and the crowds were held spellbound by the love and gentle understanding in his words and tone.

Philoas came with Ruth and Josie and Mary, and he was moved by Jeshua's simple message of God's love for man.

"How blest are the poor in spirit; the reign of God is theirs. Blest too are the sorrowing; they shall be consoled. Blest are the lowly; they shall inherit the land. Blest are they who hunger and thirst for holiness; they shall have their fill.

"Blest are they who show mercy; mercy shall be theirs. Blest are the single-hearted, for they shall see God. Blest are those persecuted for holiness' sake; the reign of God is theirs.

"Blest are you when they insult you and persecute you and utter every kind of slander against you because of me. Be glad and rejoice, for your reward is great in heaven. They persecuted the prophets before you in the very same way."

Jeshua spoke in the language of the simple man, using the events and sorrows and joys that touched every man's life as the means to explain the Father's will for His beloved children. He taught them how to live happily in this world, by loving one another, even their enemies, by not divorcing their wives with foolish excuses, by not judging one another or counting their worldly possessions as valued treasures. He taught them to pray, simply and from the heart, and assured them that any who sought would find, and for any who knocked, the doorway to God's love would be opened to them. "Treat others the way you would have them treat you: this sums up the Law and the Prophets!"

The sun had begun to dip below the hills when Jeshua came down from the mount and led the throngs back toward Capernaum. Halfway down the mount a leper suddenly emerged from a cave hidden by an overgrowth of weeds and brush. The crowd gasped and recoiled from the horrible, unclean, once-human form. "Sir," he quavered, "if you will to do so, you can heal me."

Jeshua stretched out his hand and touched him. Somewhere in the crowd a woman shrieked. "I do will it," said Jeshua. "Be cured."

The man's skin began to clear. The horrible, weeping, open sores began to fade as though sinking beneath his flesh. A sigh went up from the crowd. Ruth looked at her mother and saw no surprise in her face, only a look of fathomless love.

As they entered Capernaum, the Roman centurion who had donated the money for the synagogue hurried forward to meet them. He saluted Philoas and then said to Jeshua, "Sir, my serving boy is at home in bed paralyzed, suffering painfully."

"I will come and cure him," said Jeshua.

The centurion shook his head. "Sir, I am not worthy to have you come under my roof. Just give an order and my boy will get better. I am a man under authority myself, and I have troops assigned to me. If I give one man the order, 'Dismissed,' off he goes. If I say to another, 'Come here,' he comes. If I tell my slave, 'Do this,' he does it."

Jeshua was amazed and said to his followers, "I assure you, I have never found this much faith in Israel. Mark what I say! Many will come from the east and the west and will find a place at the banquet in the kingdom of God with Abraham, Isaac, and Jacob, while the natural heirs of the kingdom will be driven out into the dark. Wailing will be heard there, and the grinding of teeth." He turned to the centurion. "Go home. It shall be done because you trusted."

Ruth left Philoas and went home with Mary and Josie. She was overcome with weariness and longed for sleep. The emotion-charged atmosphere and excited, milling crowds had drained her of any feeling except a desperate longing for solitude. She fell on her mat and tried to sleep, but images of suffering, desperate faces, mingled with faces of unbelievable joy and those of scorn and hatred, all paraded behind her closed lids. Cries for mercy and surcease from pain, and cries of disbelief and exaltation echoed in her ears until she pulled a blanket over her head in a futile attempt to choke them off.

When she did finally sleep, it was only to fall into a nightmare world where faces became grotesque and contorted with hatred, and voices were a gutteral, animal-like groan, all belonging to creatures of evil who tore at the flesh of a bloodied, innocent lamb who seemed resigned to his fate and accepted his agony with sad, suffering eyes— the blue-gray eyes of Jeshua.

She fought her way out of the nightmare and jerked awake in the cool, gray hour before dawn. She was drenched with the cold, clammy sweat of terror. Her heart thudded with fear and horror, and her hands trembled as she pulled a cloak around her shoulders and stumbled down the outside stair, fleeing the scene of the nightmare like one pursued by Belial.

She flung open the gate to the courtyard and was startled to see a figure sitting on the stone bench beneath the palm tree. She held her breath and waited, letting her eyes become accustomed to the predawn gloom, and then let her breath out in a sob as she recognized Jude's slight young form. Her heart was wrung with pity at the sight of him, and she forgot her own fear.

He was the picture of total dejection, his shoulders drooping and his head sagging almost to his knees. His arms were crossed over his lap and his hands dangled listlessly beside his legs.

Ruth slipped noiselessly up behind him and put her hand on his shoulder. "Jude?" she said tentatively, "why are you out here all alone?"

Jude started and jerked his face toward her. His eyes were red and swollen with suffering. "What are you doing here?" he asked impatiently, and turned his face quickly away, ashamed that she had seen his weakness.

Ruth sat next to him, so close their bodies touched. "I had a nightmare and awoke early."

Jude laughed, a short, harsh, mirthless laugh. "Ah, yes. A nightmare! And don't we all have nightmares. Walking or sleeping, it's all a nightmare. They'll kill him, you know."

Ruth couldn't deny it, not after her dream. She searched for words to comfort him, but found none. She wanted to weep for the finality and conviction in Jude's voice. She covered his hand with her own and said nothing.

"He's chosen the rest of his disciples. Now they are twelve, that mystical, magical number of twelve! Twelve tribes of Israel, twelve girls on a stair, twelve centers in which consciousness became aware in the body of the earth itself—" He looked at Ruth's surprised expression. "I've learned my lessons well, after all."

Ruth smiled at him and said teasingly in an attempt to lighten his mood, "You never seemed to."

"Oh, I did, though. I listened very carefully to all that Josie and Mother taught, and I thought it all exciting and wonderful until I realized that Jeshua was to be their Messiah, and then it wasn't so exciting. In fact, it became quite grotesque!"

"They didn't pick him out, like you'd choose a pup from a litter, Jude. They prepared themselves to receive the one God would send. He sent Jeshua," Ruth admonished.

"Oh, I know. 'The virgin shall bear,' 'I'll call my son

out of Egypt,' 'Rachel cries for her children.' I know all the prophecies, too, and they've all seemed to have come to pass so far, but what of those still to come? They'll kill him, you know," he repeated dully.

"Perhaps they will," answered Ruth, "but if you know the prophecies, don't you think Jeshua does also? He too knows."

There was no answer to that. Jeshua's knowing didn't prevent it, and they both knew it. They said nothing for a time until Ruth finally said, "Are you one of the Twelve?"

"Me?" Jude said in surprise. "Not me! I'll not help those precious prophecies come to pass."

"Who, then?"

"Simon, Thaddeaus, and James ben Alphaeus; Simon and Andrew ben John; Nathaniel and Philip; James and John ben Zebedee, Thomas from Cyrene, Matthew, of course, and Judas Iscariot."

"Judas Iscariot?" Ruth asked incredulously.

"The same. The Zealot leader."

"I thought the Zealots looked to John ben Zachariah to lead them."

Jude nodded. "I think they are becoming disillusioned with John. He keeps pointing to Jeshua as 'The One.' 'He will increase and I must decrease,' John says. They also like Jeshua's miracles. They like the way Jeshua can suddenly disappear from sight, out of harm's way, and besides, Jeshua is growing more popular with the people than even John. Jeshua is softer, gentler, more easy to sway and direct than John. They probably think he'll be far easier to use than John, and I'm sure they intend to use him to the fullest."

"They may be in for a surprise, then. Jeshua is not so easily convinced, or used," Ruth said ruefully.

"They don't know that. I don't like this Judas Iscariot. He strikes me as devious and sneaky. He knows more than he tells, and feels more than he lets on. He's very quiet, but all the same, I get the feeling that his mind is ever busy. He's like a snake, hidden in the grass and coiled to strike without warning. Jeshua should beware."

Ruth looked at Jude and thought, He is not so young. In many ways he's already very old. His insight into Judas Iscariot disturbed her and added to her fears, and she hoped Jude was wrong.

Chapter 29

Jeshua decided to go to Jerusalem to celebrate the feast of Passover, and this time both Mary and Josie went with him. Ruth did not. She was weary and confused.

Jeshua's presence in Capernaum had sent her emotions soaring to the heights, then plummeting to the depths as she witnessed the miraculous works Jeshua performed and afterward saw the hatred and jealous self-righteousness those same deeds evoked from those in authority. She was torn between her fear for Jeshua's life, which she shared with Jude, and her faith that all would go according to God's will, which she shared with Mary. She felt tossed and battered, bounced from the extremes of intense elation to overpowering despair, and, underlying all, the strain of being pulled between her love for Philoas and her obedience to her mother.

Ruth was drained, spent. She was drawing on her last reserves of emotional and mental strength and grasped at the chance to be alone, to sort out her thoughts and feelings and bring them into some kind of accord. Even when Philoas told her that he, too, was going to Jerusalem to observe the feast and send a report of it to Tiberius, Ruth's determination to remain behind did not waver. In fact, she was relieved to see Philoas go, for how could she think clearly and objectively about him when her heart thudded and her blood pounded in her ears as it did whenever he was near?

Jude steadfastly refused to take part in Jeshua's ministry and so remained in Capernaum with Ruth. He and Ruth had formed a silent, mutual understanding since their talk that morning. They ate their evening meal together in easy companionship, their talk only the desultory talk of the day, both content with long, companionable silences.

The days passed serenely. Jude left the house early each morning to go to Alphaeus' shop, leaving her free to roam the hills or putter about the house, to work with Jonas and Susane or do whatever she wished. There was nothing or no one to pressure her into anything she did not want to do. Capernaum was quiet, the market uncrowded. She could dawdle over the fruits and fish, taking her time and talking with the merchants without being pushed and scolded for taking too long. The milling crowds were gone, either to Jerusalem or home to their own cities and lands, since the miracle worker was no longer there to attract them.

Ruth found time to turn inward, to search her own soul and find contact with herself again, and to listen to that small, still voice which is ever there for anyone to hear who will listen. Her days became prayerful; her spirit grew and expanded and found new strength. She felt renewed and content and at peace. She laid her fear for Jeshua aside, convinced that, as the Messiah, no harm would befall him and he would take his rightful place on the throne of Israel according to God's plan. As for her dilemma over Philoas and her mother, that too she'd leave to time and the Lord to solve. Faith and acceptance banished her fears and confusions, and she resolved to leave all in God's loving hands.

Mary's and Josie's account of the events taking place in Jerusalem added to Ruth's conviction that all would be well. Jerusalem had been more crowded than it had ever been before. Herod and his entourage had come from Tiberias, and Pontius Pilate from Caesaria, inciting the political factions to near riot. The Jews despised the blubbery, adulterous Herod, and hated the spiteful, brutal Pilate. It was rumored that Pilate intended to use the temple treasury for funds to build an aqueduct to the Fortress Antonia, and the Jews were furious. Even Herod was upset over this last proposal, and it was said that he and Pilate had exchanged angry words over it and were barely on speaking terms.

The members of the Sanhedrin and other elders and men of influence converged upon the city to debate this latest threat of sacrilege to the House of God, and the common folk and rabble used the feast as an excuse to get a glimpse of John the Baptizer and of the new prophet, Jeshua of Nazareth. The temple courts were packed to capacity with people wanting to hear the teachings of that curious rabbi, hopeful of seeing him perform the wonders they had heard of. Jeshua had not failed to give them something to talk about.

The first morning Jeshua entered the temple, the crass commerce carried on in the temple precincts angered him beyond endurance. He made a kind of whip of cords and drove the sheep and oxen out of the temple. He turned on the money-changers, upsetting their tables and pulling down their tents and canopies, shouting, "Stop turning my Father's house into a market place!"

It was a chaotic scene, bringing the temple rulers into the court, their faces flushed and bodies trembling with anger. "What sign can you show us authorizing you to do these things?" they demanded.

"Destroy this temple and in three days I will raise it up!" Jeshua answered.

They retorted, "This temple took forty-six years to build, and you are going to raise it up in three days?"

The rabble delighted in Jeshua's conduct, and the Zealots became convinced that Jeshua could lead them against Rome. Judas Iscariot especially was smugly pleased by Jeshua's action, and slipped away to confer with his cohorts.

Jeshua taught in the temple every day, and the crowds pressed to hear him. The Pharisees, Scribes, and other members of the Sanhedrin became incensed at Jeshua's increasing popularity. They challenged his teachings and his authority, but Jeshua always had an answer for them, answers which pleased the crowds and further infuriated the rulers.

Not all of those of influence and authority were so angered, however. There were those few who listened, who were willing to set aside their prejudices to hear another man's point of view and carefully consider what he had to say. Nicodemus proved to be one of these.

Mary and Josie had visited Martha, Nicodemus' wife, in her luxurious home in Jerusalem. Martha had welcomed them with profuse joy and immediately led them to a small room in the back of the house where she kept her loom. She and Nicodemus had heard how Jeshua had healed Esdrella of her fateful fever, and Martha had begun to weave Jeshua a robe of fine gray wool, woven in one piece without a seam to mar its beauty, as a token of her gratitude for saving her sister's life.

Nicodemus had outwardly scoffed at such an idea as a "miraculous cure," but the tale had had a profound effect upon him. His appetite waned, his nights were often sleepless. He became impatient with his dogmatic friends in the Sanhedrin, and was prone to pick arguments with them and treat them with thinly veiled contempt.

At home he was moody and short of temper; he made unreasonable demands upon Martha and the servants. It irritated him to see Martha working at the loom, and he snapped and complained until she finally set it aside.

When Nicodemus heard that Jeshua was on his way to Jerusalem, he became even more tense and agitated. He heard Jeshua teach in the temple and saw him chase the merchants and moneychangers from the court. He vent his fury on poor Martha, blaming her for the actions of "her friend," and storming and railing through the house until the servants fled from his sight.

Martha was a wise young woman. She recognized Nicodemus' erratic behavior as symptomatic of an inner turmoil. She held her counsel and treated him with patient understanding. It wasn't easy. She knew their friends were whispering behind her back, blaming her for his unhappiness because of her decidedly lower social standing and her rumored friendship with the despicable Essenes, but she ignored them and did her best to keep her house in order and called on all her early training by the Essenes to keep her marriage intact.

On the night before Mary's and Josie's visit, Nicodemus had left the house at an unusually late hour. He gave no explanation as to where he was going, and it was hours before he returned. Martha had been frantic with worry. Passover week was no time to be abroad alone at night. She imagined all sorts of disasters had befallen him. When she heard him let himself into the house, she was furious with him for the worry he'd caused her, and threw all her well-learned lessons to the wind. She intended to have it out with him, to demand that he show her more consideration, but the look of joy and wonder on his face stopped her short, and she quietly listened to his flood of words until dawn.

He'd gone to see Jeshua, secretly in the night so none of his friends would know. Jeshua's teachings had nagged at him with their ring of truth until he had to talk with Jeshua, to question Jeshua himself and satisfy his gnawing need to know the truth. He and Jeshua had talked for hours. Jeshua reminded him of all the ancient teachings Nicodemus had learned as a youth in the rabbinate and then, like the others of his group, had set aside as mystical, magical legends.

The world spun too fast for men. The political and economic pressures left no time to contemplate the hidden meanings of the Scriptures, and they only saw the mundane, worldly, obvious sense to the Word of God. Under Jeshua's gentle prodding and sometimes deliberately harsh accusations, Nicodemus began to see again. The excitement of discovering truth, of feeling in his very soul that "this is right," a feeling that he had forgotten ever existed, began to wash over him in cleansing waves of joy.

Jeshua also spoke with him about the joy and fulfillment of married love, and Nicodemus had almost wept for the months he'd wasted by regarding Martha as little more than a prized possession. He had talked and talked until he'd fallen into an exhausted sleep, with his head lying heavily on Martha's breast. It was a beginning. This too would not be easy, but it was such a glorious beginning!

Nicodemus was not the only one who began to have a change of heart toward Jeshua. Ardemetus, Artemas, Joseph of Arimathaea, men whom Ruth remembered from the time she'd lived with Josie and Marcus, had come to Marcus' home to question Mary on her son's teaching. They'd treated her with the utmost kindness, and their questions were ones of genuine searching. There was no ridicule or pompous indignation in their tone, or hidden traps in their questions. They were honest men of high integrity, and Jeshua's words stirred them deeply. They were bewildered and confused; their old beliefs and attitudes were shaken. They had left Mary profoundly disturbed, for it wasn't easy to discard the habits and attitudes of a lifetime.

Unfortunately they were only a few, and the vast majority, led by Annas and Caiaphas, saw Jeshua only as a threat to their secure order, and hated and feared him as much as the poor masses revered and loved him. It was heartening, though, to know that Jeshua had at least a few friends in the Sanhedrin. Ruth had flippantly commented to Jude, "Given enough time, Jeshua may sway the whole Sanhedrin."

"Yes," Jude had smiled, and then had added cryptically, "Given enough time."

After Passover, Jeshua and his disciples had joined John ben Zachariah at the Jordan, where James and Simon and the others also baptized the repenters with water, though Jeshua himself did not. John's disciples became upset when Jeshua drew a larger following than John, but John told them, "I am not the Messiah; I am sent before him. It is the groom who has the bride. The groom's best man waits there listening for him and is overjoyed to hear his voice. That is my joy, and it is complete. He must increase, while I must decrease."

Mary and Josie and the rest of Jeshua's family from Galilee had left him there and returned home. Philoas had not returned to Capernaum, and Ruth was surprised when Mary volunteered the information that he had gone to Caesaria with Pilate to try to dissuade him from building the aqueduct with temple funds. She didn't question her mother, but surmised that Mary had spoken to Philoas, and she hugged that small sign of acceptance on Mary's part to her heart. They heard nothing more of Jeshua's movements until the day Esdrella burst into the house and blurted that John ben Zachariah had been arrested and that Roael ben Zebedee was dead!

It was days before they could piece together the garbled and often hysterical accounts which reached Capernaum regarding the Baptizer's arrest. Mary's house became the meeting place where Alphaeus and Mary, Abigale, Esdrella, and the others in Capernaum waited for news. Joses was sent to Cana and brought Timothy and the Other Mary, and Uncle Zuriah and Aunt Salone back with him, and the tension of waiting was nearly unbearable.

Each rumor which sifted into Capernaum seemed more bizarre than the last. One said that John was also dead, and all of his followers; another that the women had been spared and sent to their homes; and yet another that though the women were spared, all had been arrested and thrown into the dank dungeons of Herod's fortress, Machaerus. The only thing they were certain of was that Jeshua had left John at the Jordan and was coming home by way of Samaria, a fact which brought them little comfort, for that was a hostile, dangerous land for any Jew to enter. It wasn't until Cleopas went to Tiberius, and, by using the force of influence merited by his position, that they finally learned the truth.

After his last meeting with Jeshua at the river Jordan, John had thrown all caution to the wind and had moved on into the region of Perea which was under Herod's jurisdiction. His condemnation of Herod's unholy union with Herodias was more vehement and scathing than ever before, giving Herodias the very excuse and opportunity she was waiting for to have her vengeance against her old archenemy.

Herodias had planned her stratagem well. Herod's flunkies had waited until John was well into Perea with no chance to escape across the border before they confronted him with the charge of treason and declared him under arrest. The Zealots among John's followers had taken up arms to prevent Herod's men from taking their master, but Herodias had taken that possibility into account, and the sheer numbers she'd sent to arrest the Baptizer quickly overcame his few disciples. Roael was the only casualty in the short scuffle, which somehow made his death even more tragic than if there had been more. It seemed ironic that peace-loving, gentle Roael, who lived most of his life as an ascetic, pious monk, should be the one to die so violently and senselessly.

The women had not been molested. John's old nurse, Sofa, who had been the first to be baptized by John, had begged the captain of Herod's guard to let her go with John, to tend to his needs and care for him. The captain had relented, considering an old, bent woman harmless enough, and besides, she would free an able-bodied man for higher duty. Adahr had also begged to go with John, but her pleas were refused, her age and cunning against her. She had fled into the hills with the Zealot members of John's following, and no one doubted but what she would find some way to be in contact with her beloved brother.

Naomi had taken Lia home to Zebedee and Salome. Ruth wept for Lia, childless and widowed, and not yet thirty. Some said she was young, that she would forget and love again, but Ruth wondered. If that had been Philoas, would she forget? Would she love again? She thought not.

The family and all their Essene friends mourned the death of Roael, and waited and prayed for word of John and of Jeshua. They decided it was too dangerous to go to Judea to comfort Lia and Elizabeth. John's arrest had stirred the people into an unpredictable mood, and the Zealots were angered beyond all caution.

They were bewildered by John's arrest. He had been warned again and again not to enter Herod's territory, and his action seemed almost deliberate, as though he moved toward the inevitable and accepted his fate as destiny. How did his arrest and Roael's death fit into the order of things to come? It was a disturbing question, and no one knew the answer.

Chapter 30

I t was early morning, and Ruth was in a poor cottage just outside of Capernaum helping Susane attend a woman in the throes of childbirth when one of the woman's children ran into the house shouting, "Romans are coming!"

Ruth left the woman and went to the door. It was a small contingent of only three or four, as far as she could tell through the cloud of yellow dust. They were cantering easily along the road and seemed to be in no particular hurry. She decided there was nothing to be concerned about, and turned to go back into the cottage when something about the front rider arrested her. She shaded her eyes with her hand to get a clearer view, but the sun reflected off their golden helmets and she couldn't make out his face. As they drew near her heart began to pound and she took a few steps toward the road. The ground trembled with heavy hoofbeats and the yellow dust swirled around her, but she didn't care. It was Philoas!

How magnificent he looked upon his great, glossy, black horse! She'd never seen him mounted before, and she was full of pride at the sight of him. She stepped to the edge of the road and Philoas reigned the great horse in sharply, causing the others to dance sideways in order to avoid running into him. His face was a study of surprise and unguarded happiness.

"Ruth!" he cried. "A good day to you!" He twisted in the saddle to face his followers. "I know these people. Go on, and I will join you later." The second in command saluted, and they thundered away as Philoas leaped from the saddle.

They could only stare at one another, too full to speak and too shy to touch. Ruth wanted to rush into his arms and to feel them close tightly around her. She wanted to tell him everything she thought and felt and, most of all, how much she'd missed him. Tears came to her eyes and she finally said in a faltering voice, "Welcome home, Philoas."

Her voice broke his trancelike stare and he reached for her hands. "To find you here!" he said, almost in awe. "I was just musing about how quickly I could dispatch my men, and where I could find you. It seems a miracle of the gods that I should find you standing beside the road! How do you come to be here?"

Ruth laughed at him, thrilled that he should be thinking of her, and delighted at his obvious joy in seeing her. He was so handsome! Even if he was covered with dust and smelled of sweat and leather and horse. "I am with Susane. A woman is giving birth." Ruth sobered. "It is her ninth child and her age is against her. I fear a difficult birth."

"Can I help?" Philoas asked.

"No. I think you might frighten her."

Philoas looked toward the cottage where a huddle of small, underfed children cowered in the doorway. He nodded. "I see. I'll go on, then, and leave them in peace. When will I see you, and where?"

"Tonight. Come and join us for the evening meal," Ruth said softly.

Philoas hesitated, wondering how Mary would receive him, but as though to read his thoughts, Ruth added, "Mother will welcome you. Please come."

There was something pleading and a faint note of urgency in Ruth's voice, so Philoas squeezed her hands and smiled. "Later, then." He swung into the saddle and gave her a jaunty, Roman salute and was gone in a cloud of dust.

Ruth was waiting in the courtyard when Philoas arrived. The evening was unseasonably warm, and Ruth wore a simple dress of pale blue linen, cut squarely across her throat and cinched at her waist with a deeper blue velvet ribbon. Her brown arms were bare, seeming even browner against the pale blue, and her small, narrow feet were encased in soft kid slippers. Her hair hung free, the dark curls tumbling down her back held away from her face by a ribbon which matched the one about her waist.

She wore no adornments or jewels; no bracelets disturbed the beauty of her round, firm arms, nor were there earrings or neckpieces to detract from the youthful loveliness of her face and throat. Her skin glowed with a healthy sheen, and the simplicity of her toilette accentuated her petite femininity.

Philoas was struck by her smallness and youthful vulnerability. His voice caught in his throat as he greeted her and he was overcome with a sudden desire to protect her and keep her from every hurt for all of his life. Her hands in his were soft and yielding, her eyes warm and trusting without a trace of the usual feminine coquetry he'd encountered in other women. Her voice, like her eyes, was warm and honest. Her former timidity was gone and her tone carried a mature assurance that caused a rush of desire to warm his loins.

He was relieved as Jude's approach forced his attention away from Ruth. A servant brought a basin of water so he could bathe his hands and feet, and Jude expansively invited him into the cool shade of the tiny garden. A low table had been laid in the shade of a date palm. Colorfully dyed rush mats ringed the table, and Jude gestured for him to take the place of honor to his right.

Ruth excused herself and went into the house, soon returning with a pitcher of wine. She poured a little into Jude's goblet. He tasted it, then nodded, and she filled it and then poured one for Philoas. Philoas praised the wine. It was delicate and sweet and chilled to perfection. Delicious odors were coming from the house, and he found he was suddenly ravenous. The wine warmed and relaxed him. Jude offered him salted almonds and olives which enhanced the delicate flavor of the wine. He was languid with contentment when Mary's appearance caused him to leap to his feet.

She seemed to float across the lawn towards him. The setting sun diffused the golden lights in her hair and seemed to form a halo about her head. Her grace and carriage made her seem taller than she was, and the simple white dress she wore added to the illusion that a spiritual wraith crossed the garden toward him.

Philoas stumbled as he stepped toward her, and cursing himself inwardly for his awkwardness, stammered as he bowed over her hand. Mary was dismayed by his fluster.

Did it mean so much, then, to this Roman to be accepted and liked by the mother of Ruth? Mary felt a stab of pity for the Roman who so obviously longed for her approval, and suppressed a sigh of resignation. "Peace be with you, Philoas," she said kindly, "and welcome to our house. I trust my children have made you comfortable?"

"Indeed, and the cool peacefulness of your lovely garden is like a tonic after the heat and clamor of Jerusalem and Caesaria," Philoas answered.

"Ruth tells me you return only today. I trust you found the journey fruitful."

"In some ways, yes. Others—" Philoas hesitated. "It was all most interesting. I was moved by the solemnity and grandeur of your feast of Passover. I hope my written account to Caesar Tiberius conveys the deep emotion and reverence that the Jews feel toward their God. Perhaps you would help me by explaining the meaning of some of the symbols and rituals of the feast."

"Of course," Mary replied politely. Was he only trying to flatter her? Surely he'd consulted with more learned minds than hers.

Philoas continued, "Sometimes those who are the closest to such a complex ritual become too engrossed in detail and appearances. Tiberius wished to know the hearts and minds of the people and not only of those in authority. I hope to present the feast to him as seen and felt by the common people as well as by the priests and scribes. My experience in such matters has led me to believe that a poor cobbler sometimes sees more clearly than the High Priest."

Mary smiled and nodded. This Roman was either very cunning or very wise, she wasn't sure which. If it hadn't been for his interest in Ruth, Mary thought she would like him very much.

Josie was coming across the garden with her hands laden with trays, followed by a servant who was likewise burdened. Mary took Philoas' arm and allowed him to take her to table. Jude intoned the blessing over the food and they reclined on the mats. It was a simple, peasants' meal of fish and lentils and dried fruits accompanied by hot steaming breads, but each dish was subtly seasoned with herbs and delicate sauces, and Philoas found it absolutely delicious. Josie joined them at the table, and Philoas

ate heartily, relishing each dish and praising it highly.
Mary's answer to his praises surprised Ruth. "My daughter has many talents. The preparation of food is only
one."

Philoas smiled appreciatingly at Ruth, and Jude ducked
his head to hide his amusement. His mother sounded like
any other mother trying to marry off her daughter!

Conversation flowed easily during the rest of the meal;
only Josie seemed to have little to say. She disliked Ruth's
"entanglement" with a Roman even more than Mary. When
the meal was finished, she coolly excused herself and disappeared into the house. The others dawdled over their
last glass of wine and nibbled languidly on a dish of
sugared almonds and other sweets, enjoying the cool twilight and the peaceful evening song of little night creatures.

Philoas felt relaxed and carefree. Mary had been exceptionally kind and friendly throughout the meal, questioning him politely about his home and family, and display-
ing a genuine interest in his work. He basked in the close
proximity of Ruth, his eyes absorbing her serene beauty,
and his ears delighting in her low, gentle voice. He
laughed at Jude, liking the lad immensely for his brash
opinions, and found a keen intelligence and depth of
thought hidden beneath the surface of his irony. He asked
about James, and wondered to himself how he could win
the favor of that unknown member of the family whom
they all described in such formidable terms. He wished he
had known Ruth's father whom they spoke of with such
reverence and remembered love. His own father had been
aloof and austere, commanding respect and admiration
but not the tender affection and devotion which the simple
carpenter had evoked from his family. He looked at Ruth
and vowed to himself that he would be such a father, that
his own children would one day speak of him in such
loving terms.

Mary's voice broke into his reverie and he brought his
thoughts back to the tiny garden. "Would it be indiscreet
for you to tell us Pilate's reaction to John's arrest?" she
was asking.

For a moment Philoas didn't know who she meant, and
then realized she spoke of the Baptizer. "No, of course
not, though his reaction was little enough. He and Herod

are at odds over Pilate's desire to invade the temple treasury and Pilate's temper flares at the mere mention of Herod's name. He only called him an amorous fool and dismissed the subject."

"Is there any way that Rome could interfere on John's behalf?" Mary persisted.

Philoas shook his head. "I fear not. John was arrested in Herod's judicial territory. If John were a Roman citizen, or even a friend of Rome, Tiberius would have a plausible excuse to interfere, but John is not. His livid public condemnation of Herod's affair with his sister-in-law is treasonous in Herod's eyes, and since the marriage is perfectly legal by Roman law, Caesar has no legitimate grounds on which to reverse Herod's action.

"There is little Pilate could do, even if he wanted to, which he does not, simply because he has no interest in the incident. If he and Herod were on friendly terms, then perhaps Pilate could subtly point out that the anger and disturbance caused by John's arrest outweighs in political importance the slurs made upon his reputation by the ravings of a religious fanatic. He could use his influence, under the guise of simple, friendly advice, to convince Herod of the wisdom in freeing John, thus showing himself to be a benevolent friend of the Jews. But they are not on friendly terms right now, and Herod would take Pilate's interference as an insult and an affront to his authority, and more harm would be done than good."

Philoas saw the discouragement and pain in the eyes of Ruth and Jude, and the quiet resignation in Mary's. He felt sorry for them all, for they were John's family, and Mary's nephew had lost his life defending John. He knew they were all in mourning over Roael's death, though, following Jeshua's example, had set aside the outward appearances of mourning to continue Jeshua's work of spreading the Word of God. He wanted to give them some comfort, some hope, and though he hadn't intended to tell them that he had visited Herod, he decided now to do so.

He put his hand over Ruth's and said gently, "All is not lost. I paid an unofficial, friendly visit to Herod in Machaerus before I returned to Capernaum. I subtly sounded him out on the subject of John, and I think he fears John. Herod is a Jew also, remember, and his conscience tells him John is right. He may let John languish in prison until he decides he has been suitably punished for his treasonous remarks, but being a Jew, he will not dare to kill a possible prophet of his God."

Ruth looked relieved, and Philoas felt a flush of pleasure at the tender gratitude in her eyes. But Mary said, "And what of Herodias? Does she also fear him as a 'possible prophet' of the Lord?" She shook her head. "Who will Herod come to fear most, the wrath of Herodias, or the wrath of God?"

Philoas had no answer. Mary had perceived the very heart of the matter, and there was nothing Philoas could say to contradict that truth. They were silent, each lost in his own thoughts. Philoas wondered at the mystery and perception of a simple, peasant woman. Mary's thoughts turned to Adahr and Elizabeth. Ruth studied Philoas' face and felt a stabbing pain at the terrible grief Lia was going through, and Jude's thoughts turned to Jeshua.

Philoas became a familiar figure at Mary's table. She didn't hide her pleasure in his company, but told Ruth firmly, "My position remains unchanged. I like Philoas. I respect him and trust him and judge him to be a good man. I believe his love for you to be genuine, without guile, but my heart grieves for the unhappiness such a union will bring you. You are a grown woman and must follow your own heart, but I implore you to take care. Think this through carefully, and discern the will of the Lord in this matter."

Ruth wished she could allay her mother's fears and convince her that she was fully aware of the obstacles in a marriage between Jew and Roman, that her love for Philoas and her faith in their future together were strong enough to overcome them. She knew her mother's loving support would not fail; but it grieved her to cause Mary more anxiety. Didn't she have enough worries over Jeshua and Jude, and now even James?

James was home. He had reached his twentieth year, had passed the examinations and entered his first probationary period prior to his admittance as a full member of the Brotherhood. The required ten years of intensive study were behind him, and he had taken the first major step toward fulfilling his dream of becoming a monk of the Elect.

Roael had been James' childhood idol, and his death and the imprisonment of John ben Zachariah had been a terrible blow to him. The City of Salt had reeled under the shock of losing two of their foremost leaders, and news of Jeshua's preaching was also often disturbing. James found himself in a curious position among his fellow monks. They questioned him constantly about his elder brother, and James found it highly embarrassing to have to admit he knew as little as they.

So James had come home, driven by instinct to find solace for his grief in the bosom of his family, and to witness for himself the wondrous events surrounding his elder brother.

His presence in the house was upsetting, to say the least. His resemblance to Jeshua was striking, so much so that a stranger would find great difficulty in telling them apart, but their likeness stopped at physical appearance. James had taken the vow of the Nazirites. He refused strong drink of any kind, refused to cut his hair, which threatened to become as long as Samson's, and disdained all use of any oils—the merciless Judean sun had burned his skin until it was as dry and lined as leather. His knees were a mass of thick, hard callouses from the arduous long hours he spent in prayer. He was thin and sinewy, eating only the amount necessary to keep him alive, and taking no pleasure in that small amount. Indeed, James took no pleasure in anything, save for his prayers which he mumbled at any hour of the day or night, and his family found him a little tedious.

James was a far cry from the social-minded Jeshua, who took pleasure in everything. Jeshua loved company. He enjoyed his food and a good glass of wine. He liked a joke and laughed merrily at the wit and outrageous humor made famous by the Jews. He liked to sing, was adept on the harp, and often drew the little children to him by his deep, rich voice. Jeshua loved children above all. They sensed this immediately, and wherever Jeshua stopped to preach, a flock of youngsters surrounded him, climbing onto his lap and hanging about his knees. Once his disciples had tried to keep them away, but Jeshua had rebuked them, saying, "Let the children come to me. Do not hinder them. The Kingdom of God belongs to such as these."

James, on the other hand, seemed to see children only in the light of potential adults. He was kind to them, of course, if he found himself unavoidably in their presence, but he had no real affection for them and never sought them out. He was concerned for their education and was zealous that they be brought up in the discipline of the Lord, but he found no pleasure in their playful antics and no joy in their innocent prattle.

Ruth and Jude avoided James as much as politely possible. At first they'd been delighted to have him home again, but his constant exhortations to prayer and piety soon became exasperating, and Ruth and Jude found themselves making polite excuses and slipping out of the house. They secretly giggled together over the excessive zeal of "the Saint," and were ashamed of themselves for leaving poor Mary and Josie to contend with him alone—but not ashamed enough to stay.

Ruth had more than one reason for avoiding James. He had bitterly condemned her for "consorting with a Roman!" and his tirades had become so vehement that Mary had been forced to interfere and ordered him to keep his counsel. He bowed to his mother's command, but refused to eat with "a Gentile!" and his absence at the table when Philoas was there was conspicuously uncomfortable. Mary, bless her, had taken Philoas aside and had explained her son's beliefs and attitudes toward him as best as she could, and had insisted that he was as welcome in her house now as before. Philoas had brushed aside Mary's apologies for her son's behavior and had assured her that he understood. Wasn't James' attitude simply a reflection of what most Jews felt toward Gentiles? Of course he understood! He had met with such resistance many times before. It needn't embarrass or upset the family in the least.

So Philoas continued to visit the house as often as before, while James sulked in his self-righteousness in the kitchen. But it was embarrassing and uncomfortable, and Ruth guiltily wished "the Saint" would take his monkhood back to the City of Salt.

Chapter 31

Jeshua returned to Capernaum. John ben Zebedee came directly to his aunt's house to tell her that Jeshua was on his way home, but even more for the opportunity to tell her all that had taken place since Mary had left them at the Jordan.

It was the news of John's arrest and Roael's death which decided Jeshua to avoid Perea and return to Galilee through Samaria. They knew it was a dangerous route, and the journey was tense and watchful. They travelled quickly until the lack of provisions forced them to stop at Jacob's well outside the walls of Sychar, where Jeshua sent Simon and Andrew and the others into the city to buy food, keeping only John at his side.

The well was deserted except for a lone woman who stared in astonishment when the two Jews approached. The sun was high overhead and the haste of the journey had tired Jeshua. He asked the woman for a drink and she stared at him wide-eyed, for no Jew would normally speak to a Samaritan! "You are a Jew! How can you ask me, a Samaritan and a woman, for a drink?"

"If only you recognized God's gift and who it is that is asking you for a drink, you would have asked him instead and he would have given you living water," Jeshua replied.

"Sir," she challenged him, "you do not have a bucket and this well is deep. Where do you expect to get this flowing water? Surely you do not pretend to be greater than our ancestor Jacob, who gave us this well and drank from it with his sons and his flocks?"

Jeshua replied, "Everyone who drinks this water will be thirsty again, but whoever drinks the water I give him will never be thirsty. No, the water I give shall become a fountain within him, leaping up to provide eternal life."

The woman's name was Jodie, and she and her two sisters, Selma and Josie, were daughters of Pagosius, one of the rulers of Samaria. Jeshua, with his ability to see into another's mind, told her everything that had ever happened to her, even that she was now living with a man to whom she was not wed, and that she'd had no less than five husbands in this life.

The woman was amazed. "Sir," she said, "I can see you are a prophet. Our ancestors worshipped on this mountain, but you people claim that Jerusalem is the place where men ought to worship God."

Jeshua told her, "Believe me, woman, an hour is coming when you will worship the Father neither on this mountain nor in Jerusalem. You people worship what you do not understand, while we understand what we worship. After all, salvation is from the Jews. Yet an hour is coming and is already here, when authentic worshippers will worship the Father in spirit and truth. Indeed, it is just such worshippers the Father seeks. God is Spirit, and those who worship him must worship in spirit and truth."

The woman said to him, "I know there is a Messiah coming. When he comes, he will tell us everything."

Jeshua replied, "I who speak to you am he."

When James and the others returned, they wondered at seeing Jeshua speaking with a woman, but they knew better than to question her in Jeshua's hearing. Jodie left them and soon returned with her sisters and an elder of the city named Pleadila and some others who were curious to see the prophet who could read one's mind. They questioned him extensively and were intrigued by his teachings. They begged him to stay with them a while, that they might hear more. Jeshua stayed with them for two days, bringing love where there once had been only hatred, love to those despised of men for weakness of the flesh, understanding that those not of a pure race could be cleansed by the giving of self.

The people of Sychar absorbed Jeshua's teaching as one released from an arduous fast absorbs his first meal. Prayer circles were formed, and one woman, Idailie, was commissioned by Jeshua as a messenger to carry his teachings throughout Samaria. It was a tremendous victory for Jeshua's mission to convert the hostile, unbelieving Samaritans to the good news. John's account was ebullient, his exhilaration dampened only by the shadow of Roael's death.

Once they'd left the borders of Samaria behind, they had gone directly to Cana to comfort and console the Other Mary and Timothy in their grief, but even there the magnitude of Jeshua's power was made manifest. A royal official from Capernaum had come to Jeshua in Cana to plea for his son who was critically ill, begging him to hurry to Capernaum and heal the boy. Jeshua had wearily replied to his entreaties by saying, "Unless you people see signs and wonders, you do not believe." But the official didn't give up until Jeshua said, "Return home. Your son will live." The man trusted Jeshua and did as he was bid. Of course the child lived; his fever vanished the very moment Jeshua spoke, and Capernaum had one more wonder to add to its long, ever-growing list of wonders.

Since John's arrest, Jeshua's teaching held a new theme, "Reform your lives! The kingdom of Heaven is at hand," and the crowds clamored for him day and night. They followed him everywhere, bringing their sick and possessed, beseeching him to extend his healing hands, and Jeshua's compassion for them was so great he could turn no one away. The family became concerned for his health. The people gave him no time for rest or peace, and his meals were hastily gulped or forgotten altogether. Mary, Jude, and James went to Simon's house one day in a futile attempt to lure him home for a good meal and a rest, but the crowds were so intense they couldn't get near him, and Mary had to send word to him through the crowd that she wished to see him. Jeshua ignored her summons, saying, "Who is my mother? Who are my brothers?" Then, extending his hand toward his disciples, said, "There are my mother and my brothers. Whoever does the will of my heavenly Father is brother and sister and mother to me." They'd come home discouraged and hurt, not understanding that his words had been meant as a lesson to the crowd, and not as a rejection of his family.

He no longer taught in the synagogues; the crowds were too great and the moods of the rulers too unpredictable. He led the throngs to the lakeside and taught as he sat in a boat rowed a short way from shore.

One day as evening drew on, Jeshua said to his disciples, "Let us cross over to the farther shore." Leaving the crowd, they took him away in the boat in which he was sitting, while the other boats accompanied him. It happened that a bad squall blew up. The waves were breaking over the boat and it began to ship water badly. Jeshua was in the stern through it all, sound asleep on a cushion. They finally woke him and said to him, "Teacher, does it not matter to you that we are going to drown?" He awoke and rebuked the wind and said to the sea, "Quiet! Be still!" The wind fell off and everything grew calm. Then he said to them, "Why are you so terrified? Why are you lacking in faith?"

As usual, it was John ben Zebedee who brought the report of this last wonder to Mary's house. His young, oval face had beamed with pride in his Master's power, but his voice had rung with mature awe. "Who can this be that the wind and the sea obey him?" John had cried. The Messiah of the prophets, the Anointed of the Lord, the Son of Man as seen by Enoch and Daniel, but who else? The suspicion took root and grew in each of their minds that there was more than this to Jeshua. Brother, son, nephew, cousin; rabbi and master of the mysteries, all of these and yet more. Each one of them who listened to John's questioning cry silently carried the remembered words of another voice who said, "This is my beloved Son!"

John also related how after they had landed on the opposite shore in Gerasa, Jeshua had cast a legion of demons from a poor soul who had been possessed by them for years, and had sent the lot into a herd of swine which had then hurled themselves over the bluff to drown in the sea of Galilee. When the residents of Gerasa heard of this, they feared Jeshua and his followers, and begged them to leave their district, and so they had. They went on to the ten cities of the Decapolis, teaching and healing as they went, and then came back to Capernaum.

Jeshua's boat approaching Capernaum caused a roar of excitement, and the family and Philoas followed the throngs to the shore to greet him. A man whom Ruth recognized as Jairus was at the very edge of the water, impatiently pacing up and down the sandy shore, obviously greatly upset and agitated. Ruth knew why.

Jairus was a Jew and one of the high officials in the synagogue, but he was also the captain of Herod's garrison in Capernaum. He was a man of great authority in the city, in charge of the commercial, social, and political relationships in the whole area. A few years before, Herod had sent him on a mission into Turkey where he had married a daughter of those dark-skinned "Children of Ishmael." Her name was Maipah. The young bride had followed him into his native land full of fear and trepidation for the alien ways of the Galileans. She'd borne her first son at the age of twenty, and then another a year later. Her third child and only daughter was now at twelve an image of herself.

Jairus doted on the child whom Maipah had named Toupar, and was yet almost foolishly infatuated with Maipah. He had heard the teachings of John the Baptizer, and then those of Jeshua of Nazareth, and because of his great love for his wife and daughter, had found it an easy matter to manifest those teachings in his own home. He wished for Maipah to be an equal companion to himself, but Maipah feared and doubted those new ways. She had been raised to believe that women were as nothing, only slaves born to carry out the wishes of men and to bear their offspring. Jairus was patiently trying to convince her of the joys to be had by following the teachings of the Nazarene, but Maipah feared.

Now Toupar had sickened and was near death. Jairus was frantic. He'd called Jonas to attend her, commanding him to stay at the child's side day and night, but all of Jonas' efforts were of no avail. Maipah was again big with child and was no longer young. Her grief and anxiety over Toupar was so intense that Jonas feared for her safety also. Ruth guessed that Jairus had come to elicit Jeshua's help.

As soon as Jeshua stepped from the boat, Jairus fell at his feet and appealed to him. "My little daughter is critically ill. Please come and lay your hands on her so that she may get well and live."

Jeshua's eyes filled with pity at the anguish and suffering in Jairus' voice. He raised Jairus to his feet and they started toward his house.

Philoas had also recognized Jairus, and he motioned to Ruth to follow. They made their way into the crowd with James and Jude close at their heels, trying to pick their way carefully so they could come closer to Jeshua. Ruth was suddenly roughly jostled from behind and turned to see who treated her so rudely.

It was one of Jonas' patients, a woman named Lois whom Ruth knew had suffered from a constant hemorrhage for many years. She looked at Ruth with apologetic eyes and said, "If I just touch his clothing, I shall get well." Ruth gave her a forgiving smile and stood aside, watching as, when she was near enough, Lois reached out her hand and touched Jeshua's cloak. The look of joyous wonder that came over her face told Ruth that her blood no longer flowed.

James had listened to the exchange between Ruth and Lois and had also watched and seen. "Does one need only to touch his clothing to be healed?" he whispered incredulously. Ruth took a step toward Lois, but Jeshua suddenly wheeled about and asked, "Who touched my clothing?"

Lois looked stunned, too frightened to answer. Simon said to Jeshua, "You can see how this crowd hems you in, yet you ask, 'Who touched me?' "

Jeshua ignored him and kept looking over the crowd. Lois was trembling with fear, but finally gathered enough courage to creep forward and fall to her knees at Jeshua's feet. She confessed that it was she, and falteringly explained why she had done so. Jeshua raised her up and said gently, "Daughter, it is your faith that has cured you. Go in peace and be free of this illness."

Before Jeshua had finished speaking, some people from Jairus' house rushed forward with the awful news that Toupar was dead. The blood drained from Jairus' face and it contorted in a spasm of grief. Jeshua disregarded the report. Taking Jairus' arm, he said, "Fear is useless. What is needed is trust." He bade the crowd to stay, and took only James and John ben Zebedee and Simon ben John with him. As they approached the house they could hear the cries and wailing of hired mourners already gathered to bury the child.

They entered the house and Jeshua said, "Why do you make this din with your wailing? The child is not dead, she is asleep." At this they began to ridicule him and even Jonas thought, This time the Master is mistaken.

Maipah was on her knees in the middle of the floor, rocking her swollen body back and forth and keening as only a mother who has lost a child can keen. Jeshua and Jairus lifted her up and Jeshua, after ordering everyone except his disciples from the house, led them all into Toupar's room.

The child lay waxen and still. No pulse beat at her fragile temples, and no gentle rise and fall disturbed her breast. Jeshua bent over her, took her hand, and said, "Little girl, get up."

Toupar's long lashes fluttered and then she opened her eyes and smiled at Jeshua. There was no fear or astonishment in her eyes at seeing a strange man bent over her bed, only a look of one seeing a familiar, trusted friend. She sat up and wondered what all the fuss was about, for the others were crying and laughing in astonished jubilation.

Toupar's release from the bonds of death caused such an uproar that Jeshua took his disciples and fled to the country. They went to Nazareth where Joseph had brought his bride and first-born son to live over thirty years before, but the people rose up in anger against him. Jacobinus reminded the Nazarenes that this was the child of Joseph the Carpenter, the child who had escaped when theirs had been slaughtered by Herod. What right had he to grow to manhood when their sons had been taken from them? With whose authority did a mere son of a carpenter heal and cast out demons? Only Mateal listened and watched with silent joy, realizing her son had been a sacrifice of glory.

Jeshua shook the dust of unbelieving Nazareth from his feet and turned his face toward Jerusalem.

When Mary received word from Jeshua that he intended to return to Jerusalem for the feast of Pentecost, James decided that he would meet him there. He wanted to see Lia, and also to witness for himself how the Judeans received Jeshua's teaching and leadership.

No one, except perhaps Mary, realized how deeply James grieved for Roael. From the time James had been a small boy, Roael had been his idol and his inspiration. Roael was the model of all the youthful James wished to be, though in his zeal to emulate Roael, the mature James had carried Roael's piety and devotion to extremes. Roael's love for the way of the Lord was tempered by compassion and flexibility, whereas James, in his determination to live up to the childish image he'd formed of Roael, had become rigid and narrow in thought. Roael's

death, and now Jeshua's breaking from traditional thought
and ritual, had shattered James' sense of order and con-
stancy, casting him adrift on a sea of confusion. He had
come home to Capernaum hoping to find in his mother the
anchor on which he could secure his floundering faith, and
in his brothers and sister a balm to his grief. But instead he
learned that Mary not only condoned, but applauded
Jeshua's unorthodox ways, and his sister fancied herself in
love with a Roman!

The solace and understanding James sought was not to
be found in Capernaum, so his heart turned to Lia who
knew and loved Roael as much as he did himself. Lia had
been with John's disciples when they had brought Roael's
body to the little cemetery at the City of Salt to lie in
peace beside Aristotle, Enos, Philo, Anna, Judas, Mat-
thias, and all the other Saints who had completed their
work and gone with God. James had yearned to speak
with Lia then, but those had been days of shattering grief
and numbing shock, and not the time for gentle memory
and quiet reminiscing.

To their surprise James asked Ruth and Jude to go with
him to Jerusalem. Jude wanted to go, but Ruth hesitated.
She guessed that James' motive in asking was to separate
her from Philoas, and she stubbornly refused to allow him
to dictate the manner of her life. Philoas solved the problem by suggesting that he escort them to Judea, an offer
which Mary readily accepted, for she'd been uneasy at the
thought of their travelling alone. James wasn't at all
happy about the arrangement. A warning look from Mary
silenced his objections, and there was nothing he could do
but accept the situation.

It wasn't a particularly joyful journey. James was taciturn and moody most of the time. He ignored Philoas,
and when he was forced to speak to him, he did so in a
tone one would use when speaking to a hired servant.
Ruth, Jude, and Philoas tried to ignore his bad manners
and sullen moods, but Ruth found it increasingly difficult
to hold her tongue.

They went straight to Zebedee's, and Philoas left them
there and continued on to the Fortress Antonia. Ruth
watched him go with a heavy heart, knowing this was how
her future with Philoas would be—she being admitted
into Jewish homes, and Philoas left standing without. She

knew that because of their love for her, Zebedee and Salome would welcome Philoas under their roof, but the scandal it would cause among their friends and neighbors simply wasn't worth the gesture. Philoas understood and didn't seem to mind, but it hurt, nevertheless. James' smug smile and curt nod of dismissal didn't help, and Ruth was more determined than ever to follow her heart.

Ruth's attitude softened a little toward James during their stay with Zebedee. He seemed to know exactly the right things to say to comfort them, and his manner toward the grieving family was one of deep compassion and genuine concern, which surprised Ruth and Jude by coming from one they only knew as rigidly austere. Lia particularly responded to James' tender ministrations. She also felt a need to speak of Roael in the light of his beliefs and the work he chose, something beyond the fond memories of his childhood of which his parents spoke. James was the perfect one for easing that pain, and they seemed to bring to one another a calming, soothing comfort.

James and John ben Zebedee came home and told them Jeshua and the twelve disciples were staying at Bethany, and that all were invited to a feast in Jeshua's honor at Lazarus' house—Philoas also; the Master had specifically asked for him. Zebedee declined for his family because of their period of mourning, but he insisted that Ruth, Jude, and James go, and sent a messenger to Philoas in Jerusalem. Philoas met them at Zebedee's and they walked the short way to Bethany.

Bethany was a sleepy village nestled among the hills, about an hour's walk from Jerusalem. Its inhabitants were mostly shepherds and olive growers, common laboring people who worked hard for their material sustenance. Only a few wealthy families like those of Syrus and Archaus had settled in the village for the sake of peace and quiet and relief from chaotic city life.

The evening was soft and mild. A gentle, cooling breeze flowed down through the hills, carrying the melancholy sound of lowing cattle and bleating sheep. Somewhere a dog barked, followed by the high, shrill laugh of a child.

There always seemed to Ruth to be an air of tragedy about Lazarus' house. The mystery of Mary's disappearance had never been solved. The family assumed the girl was dead, but no proof had ever confirmed it, and Ruth never failed to wonder. Syrus had aged quickly after the loss of Mary, and had died after a few short years. Neither Martha nor Lazarus had married, each existing in a private world, which somehow seemed unnatural. It was as though they were suspended in time, waiting—for what, Ruth couldn't guess. But she shivered as she entered the gate, and was glad to see everyone else was already there; her mind was soon occupied with other thoughts than those of Mary.

It was an intimate family gathering. The only guests who were not members of Jeshua's family or of the Twelve were Susane's father and Lazarus' neighbors Thelda and Larue and their young niece, Mariaerh. Three tables had been laid beneath the waving palms and huge gnarled oaks—a large host's table and two smaller guest tables, each laden with sumptuous dishes borne forth by Martha's numerous servants in a never-ending procession.

The meal was festive and gay. The talk flowed easily in an atmosphere of companionship and warm familial love, dampened only by James' contrariness. He refused to eat at the same table with Philoas and Pathaos, Ulai's husband, who was of both Jewish and Roman blood, making a point of removing his dish and finding a place for himself among Alphaeus' sons. He refused to eat of the rich dishes and fine wines, accepting only a few lentils and a crust of bread, which he washed down with tepid water. His disapproval of the merriment was so obvious that Ruth was embarrassed and wished her mother had kept him home as a boy and had taught him some manners.

Jeshua reclined at Lazarus' right hand, and Ruth at his left. John ben Zebedee had quickly taken his place next to Jeshua, with his brother James at his other side. Archaus and Josaida were also honored at the host's table, seated discreetly at Martha's left hand, where she could personally wait on her aging aunt and uncle. Philoas, Jude, Ulai, and Pathaos shared Ruth's side of the table.

Ruth watched Jeshua relax in the company of his close friends and family. He looked content and happy, his face free from the lines of weariness and concern which Ruth had noticed of late. He teased Ruth and Jude, joked with John and James ben Zebedee. He laughed heartily as Ulai regaled them with tales of her children's latest antics, and drew Philoas into the conversation as though he were already a member of the family.

How we all love him! Ruth thought. Every eye was on him, adoring, loving, delighting in every word and gesture. Every face was alive with eager excitement at simply being in his presence. Her eyes met Philoas', and his, too, glowed with happiness, and she knew he felt a part of them.

She looked across John's head, which was resting contentedly against Jeshua's breast, to the other table where James ben Joseph sat in stony silence. Ruth pitied him. He should have been at Jeshua's table, but his own stubborn pride would not let him. Ruth saw that Jeshua also watched James, and Ruth caught a look of puzzled hurt in Jeshua's eyes.

When the meal was over, Simon ben Alphaeus brought out a harp and they all formed a ring around Jeshua and sang all the old psalms and hymns while he played. James ben Joseph joined them for a short time, and then rose and began to bid them all farewell. The sun was sinking low behind the hills and he wanted to reach Zebedee's before full dark. He'd declined an invitation from Ulai to stay at her home for the night, probably because Ruth and Jude and Philoas had accepted, but Jeshua didn't let him go. He laid his hand on James' arm and said, "Stay with me this night, my brother." There was something so infinitely tender and pleading in Jeshua's tone, and so compelling and compassionate in his eyes, that James could not refuse him. He flushed, then swallowed, and numbly took the place which Jeshua made for him next to himself.

Ruth never knew what passed between her two older brothers after everyone else had retired that night, but the next morning when she and Jude and Philoas had left James at Zebedee's, he'd offered his hand to Philoas and had bid him a stiff and embarrassed farewell. It was a momentous step for James to take, the first outward act toward abandoning his old, rigid habits, and Ruth was nearly moved to tears.

They walked the rest of the way into Jerusalem in contemplative silence, each wondering what manner of man was Jeshua that he could change the heart of one like James.

Chapter 32

Pentecost was a far quieter feast than Passover, and didn't draw nearly as many people, but even so the streets would be crowded. They left the road at the foot of the Mount of Olives and crossed the Kidron and Hinnom valleys to enter the city by the Essene Gate, which was close to Marcus' and Josie's house. Philoas left Ruth and Jude at the wide avenue which ran by Josie's house and went on through the city to the Fortress Antonia.

It felt good to be at Josie's again. The servants were as happy to see Ruth as Josie and Marcus, and John Mark. What a tall, handsome lad he had become! At sixteen he was as boyishly playful as ever, fairly hopping with joy, and teasing Ruth mercilessly. His bright gold curls framed his cherubic face exactly as Ruth remembered. He didn't seem changed at all! There was only a year's difference in age between him and Jude, but Jude seemed a grown man beside the sunny, cavorting John Mark. His limp was still noticeable, which reminded Ruth of a promise made long ago, and she thought to herself that the time had come for her to exact payment of that promise.

The first days of the festival passed without incident. Each morning Ruth and Jude met Philoas in the Court of Gentiles. They mingled with the crowds, pausing to listen to the various rabbis exhorting on the Scriptures, watching the pomp and ceremony performed by the priests, or simply finding a rarely vacant bench and watching the parade of costumes pass before them.

Ruth saw many of her old schoolmates and friends from the time she'd lived with Josie. It was fun to renew old friendships and introduce them to her "little brother" Jude. Most of them thought nothing of Ruth's being in the company of a Roman. Times were changing. The younger generation in Jerusalem was growing up in the midst of Romans, and Roman influence and custom touched every aspect of their lives. They thought their parents' hatred and bigotry toward Rome to be old-fashioned and silly, and for them to flaunt their modern ideas before their elders was rather exciting. To have a Roman escort was considered quite chic and fashionable, and some of the girls looked at Ruth with a tinge of jealousy. But not all. Some greeted Philoas coolly and then made a polite excuse before vanishing.

When the three entered the temple area on the third day of the feast, they found an argument raging between Jeshua and some Pharisees and scribes. It seemed that Jeshua had healed a man at the pool of Bethesda on the Sabbath, and the man had told the Pharisees, who were livid over Jeshua's disregard for Mosaic Law. "My Father is at work until now, and I am at work as well," Jeshua was saying in answer to their accusations.

As the argument progressed, it became apparent that the temple rulers were using the fact that Jeshua broke the Sabbath law only as a shield for the true cause of their anger. They were really furious because Jeshua spoke of God as his Father, thus putting himself on an equal standing with God. This was nothing short of blasphemy.

Ruth was uneasy, and moved a step closer to Philoas as though she needed the reassurance of his protective presence. Philoas was concentrating on Jeshua. A deep frown drew his eyes together into narrow slits, and a tiny muscle knotted by tension twitched in his jaw.

Jeshua's voice rang over the temple. "I solemnly assure you, the Son cannot do anything by himself, he can do only what he sees the Father doing. For whatever the Father does, the Son does likewise. For the Father loves the Son and everything the Father does He shows him. Yes, to your great wonderment, He will show him even greater works than these."

"Dangerous!" Jude muttered. "They can't let him get by with such talk in public or they will lose their stranglehold on the masses. Dangerous!"

They stayed in the crowds and listened until Jeshua left the temple for the day. Philoas walked part way to Mar-

cus' house with them. "What do you think?" Jude asked
him.

"I agree with you. It is dangerous talk. It's the same in
the army. If an officer is allowed to speak sedition publicly and nothing is done, you soon have mutiny on your
hands. The rank and file see that the officer goes unpun-
ished, and it emboldens them to follow his lead."

"What would you do in such a case?"

Philoas hesitated, then said harshly, "I would act
swiftly and without mercy. Without discipline, all is lost."

They knew his answer was honest, and because it was
the truth, all the more frightening. He left them at the
Upper City, and they watched his back until he disappeared among the tangled streets.

"He's a fine man, and a good friend. I'll welcome him
as a brother-in-law," Jude said quietly.

Ruth swallowed the lump which had arisen in her
throat, and she squeezed Jude's hand. If we ever marry,
she thought sorrowfully. She sighed. Where would Jeshua
lead them all?

As though in answer to her unspoken question, Jude
said, "He has cast his bread upon the waters. There is no
turning back." Then he smiled at Ruth and said cheer-
fully, "And where he goes, we follow, eh, my lovely sister?"

Ruth looked at him, her younger brother who was yet
so old, and then laughed and hugged him. "Absolutely!"

That night they were invited to a party at Elcor's. Elcor's husband, Barrian, was in charge of the Fortress
Antonia and was the highest Roman authority in Jerusalem except when Pontius Pilate was in residence. He liked
the stiff-necked, inexplicable Jews, and admired their
courage in defending their religious views, even though he
often thought them antiquated and impractical for life in
the modern world. He was a devoutly religious man himself, scrupulous in his daily prayers and devotions to the
gods, and found little difficulty in accepting the idea that
there was perhaps One God above all others, which to his
mind did not lessen the importance or validity of the
lesser gods. He took great pains to study the Jewish Scriptures and found no reason not to believe that someday,
with patience and benevolent rule on the part of his coun-

trymen, Romans and Jews could mesh their religions and live in peace as one.

He worked hard toward that end. He was always available to the Jews, willing to concede to their Law on many points, such as their refusal to enter a Gentile abode, and would, without complaint, meet them in the courtyard of the Fortress instead of insisting on the convenience of having them brought to his quarters. More than once he'd used his tact and diplomacy to soften Pilate's policies toward the Jews.

The Jews knew this and were grateful. They respected him and considered him just and fair. They disagreed with his idea that one day the Jews could accept the Roman gods in an inferior role to the Most Holy One, but did so gently and politely. Not all, however. Caiaphas and his intimates were outraged at such an idea, and condemned such a thought outside of his hearing, while grovelling for his friendship in his presence. Barrian was no fool. He knew them to be two-faced and ingratiating, and did not cultivate their friendship outside of matters of government.

Elcor's guests were a mixture of Jew and Roman. She'd summoned Agatha from Caesaria to help her with the preparations to be sure that every detail of Jewish protocol was strictly observed. Agatha helped her plan the menu and prepare the foods in accordance with Jewish Law, and advised as to seating arrangements and the lavish, colorful decorations which had turned the garden into a festive, carnival-like arena. All the statues of the various Roman gods were removed. The atrium was stripped of any likeness of Tiberius or any other human image, and the Golden Eagle disappeared from above the door. Agatha's swift little body had been everywhere for days, ordering the servants about in her sharp, little sparrow's voice until she was satisfied that nothing remained or was left out which would affront the Jewish sensibilities.

Elcor was happy. Nothing gave her more pleasure than a party, and the most insignificant event was excuse enough for her to indulge in her favorite pastime. She loved gossip, and delighted in scandal. As soon as Barrian told her that Philoas was staying at Antonia, she'd immediately begun plans for a party, and when she'd learned that an affair of the heart was blooming between him and her adored little Jewish friend—well!

Philoas carried absolute authority from Tiberius. It was said at court that the Emperor regarded him as a son—and to think he'd fallen in love with her own darling Ruth! The very thought sent her into such an ecstasy that more than once she'd had to call for her salts to revive her.

Then Barrian, that dear, indulgent man, had brought her the news that the infamous Jeshua of Nazareth was teaching his peculiar tenets in the temple. The whole city had been agog with the extraordinary things he'd done during Passover, and now he was back! She knew, of course, that he was Ruth's elder brother, and she immediately decided that Jeshua would be the other guest of honor. What a marvelous entertainment he would be! Perhaps he could even be persuaded to perform a few of his famed miracles for them. She was sure this would be the most talked-about party of the season.

Elcor was frenzied with excitement. It took hours and a whole battery of maids until she was dressed to her satisfaction, but everything was perfect. Barrian declared she looked like a cool, Grecian goddess, which made her blush, since it came from a man whose compliments were usually few and far apart. Indeed, she felt like one, and the sweet compliments to herself and the approving cries over the garden decor all confirmed that fact.

Ruth had also taken special care in dressing. Josie's seamstress had made her a simple white dress of the softest linen, with a gossamer silk overdress that matched the blue of her eyes. A golden girdle encircled her waist, and tiny gold slipppers adorned her feet. She wore no jewels or bangles, and her long, dark curls were swept away from her face and held with a cord of gold and blue. The effect was one of stark simplicity and virginal innocence which heightened her natural beauty and youthfulness.

Elcor was delighted with Ruth's appearance. Every eye followed them as she presented Ruth to her guests. Elcor, tall, blond, and regal, vivid in magenta, purple, and gold, was a striking contrast to the tiny, demure, dusky beauty of Ruth. They complemented one another and drew a rippling murmur of approval from the guests.

Philoas' hand trembled as he took Ruth's in his own and bowed over it. His voice stuck in his throat and he was forced to cough before he could speak. Elcor left Ruth in his care, for more guests were arriving at the gate. He took Ruth's arm to lead her away to meet some of his Roman friends, but their eyes met briefly; Ruth flushed and her blood pounded in her ears when she saw the stark look of naked desire in his eyes.

Jeshua was already there and embraced Ruth fondly, then looked upon her with frank admiration. "You are very changed from that dusty little girl who crawled out from under our secret place. Your appearance reflects the beauty that lies within," he teased softly.

Ruth recognized many of Elcor's guests as friends of Marcus'. Ardemetus, Artemas, Sylvanus, Alphus, all had been in Marcus' house when she had lived there. She saw Nicodemus and his friend Joseph of Arimathaea talking with James and John ben Zebedee, and she looked around the garden until she found Martha sitting beside a fountain with Rhoda and Mary.

She brought her attention back to Philoas, who was introducing her to a group of Roman soldiers from Antonia. She repeated their names as each bowed over her hand and stared at her in frank appreciation. Phlons, Apolois, Philose, Puburus, and the last, Ponticales, she recognized. He had been on the ship when she returned from Rome. A suspicion took seed in Ruth's mind, for this was the guard in charge of Pontius Pilate's epileptic son. Would Elcor presume upon Jeshua to—? Of course she would! Nothing would delight Elcor more than to be the perpetrator of such a wonder. What a furor it would cause among her friends if Jeshua were to heal Pilate's son!

Philoas had left her to gossip with Martha and Josie's daughters when Jude came up behind her and said in her ear, "Did you know our brother James is here?" Ruth was aghast. James here? At a Roman feast? She couldn't believe it, and followed Jude's eyes to where James sat next to Jeshua. What miracle had Jeshua performed that would bring James to mingle with "froward men"? James looked highly uncomfortable. His eyes shifted from group to group and he looked as though he expected Belial himself to jump out from behind a tree. Ruth covered her mouth to stifle a laugh and shook her head in astonishment.

The feast was lavish and gay. The wine flowed freely, and when the Judean hills hid the sun from view, leaving the garden in total darkness, Elcor's servants emerged from the mansion in a procession, carrying flaming torches and lighting hundreds of lamps and lanterns scattered throughout the garden. It was an impressive sight, and the guests cheered and applauded. Ruth looked for Jeshua to see his reaction, and finally saw him just as he disappeared into the house, flanked by Elcor and Ponticales.

Musicians began to play beneath a gaily striped canopy, and the Jews formed a circle to dance. There was much hilarity as the Romans gamely tried to match the Jews' intricate steps, and Ruth was proud when Philoas seemed to catch on more quickly than the others and was soon stepping and leaping as high and as gracefully as the Jews. Ruth joined in the merrymaking, but kept one eye on the house. A burst of applause drew her eye to the circle, and she was astonished as Jeshua was pulled into the center and the others danced around him. When had he come out of the house, and how had he done it without her seeing him?

Ruth looked for Ponticales. She didn't see him, but did see Elcor watching the dancing as though she'd never been absent. She was clapping her hands in time to the music and her face was flushed and her eyes aflame with excitement—brought on by something more than the dance, Ruth thought grimly. Ruth edged her way to Elcor's side and said in a low tone, "Does Pilate's son visit you also tonight?"

Elcor gasped and looked around, frantic lest anyone had heard. Satisfied no one had, she stammered, "What do you say?" Ruth didn't repeat her question, for she knew Elcor had heard her the first time. "What a silly question, Ruth!" Elcor said quietly as she gained control of herself. "Why do you ask?"

"I recognize Ponticales from the ship."

"I commend your marvelous facility for remembering faces, my dear," Elcor said gaily, deliberately ignoring Ruth's question.

"How fares the boy? I pitied both him and his mother and have included them in my prayers," Ruth persisted.

Elcor saw that evasion was of little use and sobered, giving Ruth a long, meaningful look. "How kind of you. It is rumored the child is recovering. Give thanks to your God, for I believe your prayers are answered."

Ruth knew Elcor well. She knew her words meant that Jeshua had healed the child, but no one must know. She felt weak, but nodded and said gently, "And you, Elcor? Do you give thanks to the God of the Jews?"

Elcor sighed, long and deeply, and then replied without looking at Ruth. "Perhaps I do. Your God has given me much to ponder." Then she looked at Ruth and said gravely, her voice carrying an unspoken warning, "Pontius Pilate would not be pleased to give credit to the Jews for the recovery of his son. It is better that he praise his physicians and his supplications to his own gods."

Ruth understood and nodded. She pressed Elcor's arm and moved away to find Philoas, her face composed and serene, but with emotions raging in her heart.

The musicians were resting, and the guests were lounging upon the lush grass. Someone had brought up a question of the Law to Jeshua, and they were sitting before him listening avidly to his answer. Voices were heard from beyond the garden walls, and a servant ran up and whispered in Barrian's ear. He looked disturbed and somewhat angry as he excused himself to the guests and followed the servant to the gate. Jeshua continued his discourse, but the voices at the gate became louder and more disruptive until he was forced to stop.

Philoas whispered to Ruth, "Stay here. I'm going to see what's happening."

Ruth nodded, but when she saw Jude slip away to follow Philoas, she too slipped into the shadows and caught up with Jude. They stopped in the shelter of a clump of bushes, close enough to hear but not to be seen. There were some Roman soldiers and a few Jews outside the gate who seemed to have a prisoner in their midst, but they could not tell for sure. Barrian sounded angry. "Why have you brought me this nonsense tonight? Can't you see I have guests? Why not wait until morning?"

One of the Romans stepped forward and spoke in a low tone to Barrian, and then the two of them moved away from the others toward the bush where Ruth and Jude were hiding. They spoke in whispers, but were close enough for Ruth and Jude to hear.

"It is the Magdalene, sir, the proprietress of the bordello in Magdala."

"So what!" Barrian said harshly. "What has that to do with me?"

"Please, sir," the Roman pleaded. "We have evidence the woman is a spy."

"A spy!" croaked Barrian. "Then why—"

"It seems she cares not who she spies for as long as the money is ready. She wheedles information out of our poor besotted men and then sells it to the Jews. Then she does the same to them and sells it to us. I've often wondered what charms the lady had that brought her so many riches."

"And I suppose you never found them out for yourself!" Barrian said sarcastically.

The soldier drew himself up in indignation. "I did not, sir!" he retorted stiffly.

"All right. All right." Barrian waved aside his indignation and said wearily, "But why now? And why are the Jews involved in this?"

"They also suspected her, and came to us with the information. They'd hoped to handle the situation themselves. The Pharisees sent a small contingent of the temple guard to bring her in, but found it hopeless without arousing our garrison there, and so were forced to appeal to our captain for help. He brought her to Antonia this evening."

"Does Caiaphas know of this?" Barrian asked.

"Apparently not. You know the rivalry between the Pharisees and the Sadducees. Evidently the girl knows matters which the Pharisees would rather the Sadducees didn't find out. In fact, the girl knows enough to embarrass us all! It was the Pharisees' suggestion that she be stoned under their Law for harlotry, rather than being brought to trial for treason, where she would have a prime opportunity to endanger all concerned by her knowledge. The Pharisees got together a quorum of their own people and condemned her to death for adultery. Of course they cannot carry out the sentence without your approval, and that's why they are here now. They wish to have the matter finished by daybreak, before Caiaphas and his co-horts find out."

Barrian spat a string of epithets hat made Ruth flush to the roots of her hair. "How old is the girl?"

"Twenty-three, sir."

Barrian swore again. "Twenty-three! I detest a world where a young woman can be stoned for trying in the only way she knows to survive in it. What of the men who whispered secrets in her pretty ear while taking their pleasure from her body? They are blameless, of course! Is it not the nature of man to lust? But what of women? Are they without passion simply because they are female?" Barrian's voice was thick with disgust and rang with sarcasm.

"What will you do, sir?"

"I don't know," Barrian said wearily. "I doubt the girl knows any state secrets. What could she know that could harm Tiberius? More likely she knows that which could embarrass only the social standing and reputation of impeccable men of authority. She probably knows of the graft and thievery and dishonest business practices which all our fine, upstanding leaders of the community indulge in, and which everyone knows except the poor fools whom they dupe. However, I suppose if all of that became public, Tiberius would have our heads for the disorder and hue and cry it would cause. The girl will have to be silenced, but damn! death by stoning seems a horrible way of doing it!"

The Jews at the gate had become restless and their murmuring became louder. Barrian turned toward them. "The pack becomes impatient for blood." He walked swiftly back to the gate with the soldier scampering at his heels in an attempt to keep up. Ruth and Jude crept closer, keeping in the shadow of the brick wall.

"Bring the woman forward!" Barrian barked. There were sounds of a scuffle and a man swore, answered in kind by a harsh female voice. The street was dark. The torches on the gate post threw their light upon the woman's body, but didn't reach above her shoulders. Ruth couldn't see her face. She was barefoot and dirty. Her once vividly colored dress of fine silk was filthy and torn. One white, firm young breast was fully exposed and gleamed like alabaster in the flickering torchlight. The girl

had not been taken without a fight. Cuts and scratches
marred her arms and shoulders, and tiny rivulets of blood
shown stark red against her pure white flesh.

Ruth winced and felt a rush of pity for the girl, who
was only a few years older than herself. Philoas was
standing next to Barrian, and Ruth saw her own pity and
distaste for such a spectacle reflected in his face.

"What are you called?" Barrian asked in a more gentle
tone. The woman didn't answer. "You must answer. What
is your name?"

One of the Pharisees stepped forward. "Sir. This woman
is a Jewess and an adulteress. According to our Law,
given by our own lawmaker, Moses, she has been found
guilty of that heinous crime and must be stoned. She was
taken in the very act of fornication and has no defense."
The Pharisee's voice was filled with self-righteous piety
and made Ruth sick because of his hypocrisy.

Barrian grasped his chin in his hand and pondered.
"Your Law, eh! Well, it happens that one of your own
rabbis, a Master of your Law, is my guest this evening. I'll
see what he has to say about your Law!" He motioned
to one of his servants and said. "Ask Jeshua of Nazareth
to attend me."

Ruth gasped and clutched at Jude's arm. "Oh, no!"
Jude groaned.

Jeshua came into the torchlight, followed by the
Twelve and most of the other male guests. James ben
Joseph stood beside him. Barrian nodded politely to
Jeshua and then said to the Pharisees, "This is Jeshua ben
Joseph of Nazareth. You recognize him, I'm sure, as one
of your most learned scholars and teachers. Present your
case before him."

The woman gave a strangled cry. The spokesman for
the Jews seemed to choke, and turned to his fellow con-
spirators for support, but they shrank back before Jeshua.
The Pharisee faced Jeshua and stammered, his voice
quavering with outrage at Barrian's trickery.

"The woman is a harlot, taken in the very act. You know
the Law. She must be stoned!" he rasped.

"Bring her into the light!" Barrian ordered. The soldiers
grasped her arms on either side and shoved her forward.
Her head was down, her tangled hair hid her face. "Look
upon your accusers!" Barrian roared.

One of the soldiers grasped her hair and pulled her head up to face Jeshua.

Ruth cried out as her knees turned to water and her blood to ice. "Merciful God! It's Mary of Syrus!" she moaned. Jude grabbed her to keep her from running out to Mary's side. James and John ben Zebedee lurched forward, but Jeshua's hand stayed them. James ben Joseph seemed to shrink, and put his hand on Jeshua's shoulder to steady himself.

Mary's hair glowed like flame. Her blue eyes blazed with anger and defiance. She jerked herself free from her captors and planted her feet firmly in the dirt, jabbing her fists at her waist in an arrogant stance of pure defiance. She flung her hair back from her face and thrust her chin high, pushing her breasts at Jeshua as though daring him to look upon her nakedness.

Ruth was trembling so she could hardly stand. Tears coursed down her face and she made no attempt to stifle her sobs. Mary's voice ripped through her like a rusty sword, and she clawed Jude's shoulder in her pain.

"What say you, Master?" Mary's voice dripped venom. "They speak the truth. I am as they say!"

Jeshua said nothing. He looked at her a long moment, his eyes filled with such sadness that Mary's finally dropped before them and her shoulders sagged the least bit. Jeshua bent and began tracing with his finger in the dust.

There was complete silence, save for Ruth's sobs. They waited for Jeshua to speak, but still he wrote. Finally a Pharisee cried out. "Come, Rabbi! Give us your decision. The strumpet admits her sin!"

Jeshua straightened. "Let the man among you who has no sin be the first to cast a stone at her!"

Ruth's sobs stopped in her throat. The men looked from one to another in bewilderment. Some of the Romans began to step back uncertainly. Jeshua again bent and wrote in the sand. One of the guests came up behind him and looked over Jeshua's shoulder to see what it was that he wrote. His eyes widened and his face paled. He stared at Jeshua for a moment with his mouth agape and then went back into the garden.

The others were curious. What did he write that caused such an astonished reaction? One by one they approached

Jeshua and read, and one by one they slunk away into the shadows until there was no one left but Barrian, Philoas, James, and the Twelve.

And Mary—standing alone in the street, her face crumpled in anguish. Her shoulders sagged and her head dropped until her body was almost bent double. She'd crossed her arms over her breasts to hide her nakedness and tears made muddy courses down her cheeks. She was pitiful, dejected, beaten. Ruth hid her face in Jude's breast and moaned.

Jeshua stood up and said gently. "Woman, where did they all disappear to? Has no one condemned you?"

Mary swallowed and tried to speak. She sniffed, and her voice was barely audible, like a tiny, fearful child's. "No one, sir," she whispered tremulously.

Jeshua reached out and rubbed away a tear from her cheek with the edge of his thumb. He looked at her with eyes so filled with compassion, and a voice so tender and forgiving that Ruth didn't think she could bear it. "Nor do I condemn you. You may go. But from now on, avoid this sin," he said softly.

Mary wept openly, softly, tears which cleansed and restored her, tears which washed away all the hate and avarice and self-pity and selfishness and vanity which had possessed her soul for so long. Jeshua let her weep a while, and then motioned to James and John ben Zebedee. "Take her home. Her loved ones have waited a long time to welcome back their sister."

Ruth watched James and John tenderly lead Mary away. She turned away from the scene and leaned against a tree, drained and weak. Jude patted her shoulder awkwardly and offered her a handkerchief. Ruth gulped and smiled through her tears and wiped her swollen eyes and mouth. Philoas was beside her, and he took her in his arms. There was nothing to say. She rested against Philoas for a while and then pushed herself out of his arms and looked to where Jeshua had been standing, but no one was there. Only the sputtering, failing torchlight and the faint outline of the wall and gate were to be seen.

Chapter 33

Mary of Syrus the notorious Magdalene! How could one born into a priestly family of wealth and position fall so low! What had happened to her that fateful day when she had disappeared without a trace, Had she been kidnapped and forced into such a life of depravity and evil? No one knew, and probably no one would ever know, but they could talk of nothing else.

Josie's daughters and Martha of Nicodemus bitterly condemned her, and refused to have anything to do with her. Ulai was livid with indignation and disgust. How could Martha and Lazarus accept her into their home after what she had done? Why, she was nothing more than a slut who brought disgrace down upon the heads of her entire family! How would she, Ulai, ever show her face to her friends if Mary's identity became public? Josie drew her lips inward to a thin tight line, but she and Marcus remained silent out of loyalty to Lazarus and Martha, as did Zebedee and Salome.

Ruth listened, but said little. She couldn't forget Jeshua's look and tone of voice when he had addressed Mary. He forgave her completely, without condition, and Ruth suspected that Jeshua expected them all to do the same.

The men didn't talk about it. When the women brought the subject up, they seemed to squirm and avoided one another's eyes. Ruth asked Philoas what it was that Jeshua had written in the sand, but he too had looked embarrassed and had evaded her question. It was Jude who finally pried the answer loose from Alphaeus' sons and James and John ben Zebedee. Jeshua had written only a few words, but it seemed as though each man who had read them saw them differently. Each one had seen his own sin, that particular deed or thought that ate away at his own conscience, written boldly in the sand. How did Jeshua know the innermost, secret thoughts of them all?

Another thought bothered Ruth. How did Jeshua know that the woman brought before him was Lazarus' sister? Ruth was sure that Mary had never met Jeshua before, and yet he'd said to James and John, "Take her home. Her loved ones have waited a long time to welcome back their sister."

Those questions also nagged at James ben Joseph, and many more. He shut himself in his room at Josie's house and refused to see anyone. Everything he'd ever believed seemed to be tumbling down around his head. From the time he had been only a lad of ten, James had eagerly embraced the tenets of the Essenes. He memorized every word of the Rule of the Order, and was determined to become a living manifestation of that Rule.

The Rule covered every aspect of life in the flesh, from spitting during public sessions to betraying the community, and each infraction of the Rule carried the proper form of punishment, from having one's food rationing cut, to total expulsion from the Brotherhood. James chastised himself for the merest deviation from the Rule, kneeling on the hard, rough stones until his knees bled, begging God's forgiveness for imagined sins, and pleading for strength and endurance to accomplish his ends. He knew the other monks thought him a fanatic and whispered about him behind his back. He remembered how angry he'd been when Aristotle had summoned him to his deathbed and had gently warned him not to let the Rule become the master of his soul. He'd thought Aristotle lax, and blamed his weakness on his Roman ancestry and upbringing, and had redoubled his own efforts towards holiness.

The great cycle of ages was coming to a close. The Great Year was upon them when Belial would be given full reign and the world and the universe would writhe in agony. Floods, fire, earthquakes, and war would soon consume all; all would revert to chaos as it had been in the beginning, and when it was over a new heaven and earth would be born. Only the Remnant would escape annihilation. The Sons of Light would march against the

Sons of Darkness, led by the Messiah, the Anointed One, and with all the heavenly hosts at his side, they would emerge victorious to rule the new earth.

James was a part of that Remnant. He would return to help rule the new order, and men would see by his example the way in which to live in peace and honor with his fellow men and God. The stage was set, the hour drew nigh, the Messiah had come, and all was in readiness. But was it?

James never doubted for a moment that Jeshua was the Messiah. He knew his grandmother had given birth long after Joachim had died, and how that child, his own mother, had been chosen on the stair and become with child before his father Joseph claimed her as his wife. One by one the prophecies were being fulfilled. It wasn't a coincidence that Jeshua's birth had taken place in Bethlehem, or that the family had been forced to flee to Egypt. All those events had been preordained and foretold in the Scriptures. Jeshua gave signs and performed wonders that no other since Elijah and Elisha had performed. No, he didn't doubt that Jeshua was the Chosen One, but he did doubt Jeshua's teachings.

Jeshua seemed to disregard both the Rule and the Law. He met and made friends of froward men. He openly consorted with sinners. He failed to observe the ritual washings, and ate and drank forbidden things. He broke the Sabbath time and again, and now had prevented the stoning of an adulteress.

Where was Jeshua leading them? The Zealots hoped to find in him a military leader. The Essenes looked to him to assert himself as King and High Priest. What did Jeshua see when he looked at himself? The Son of Man, a shepherd of the lost sheep of Israel, a spokesman of the Lord to whom the Father invested all authority in His name. What did that all mean? Jeshua showed no signs of gathering an army. He gave no indication of winning the friendship of the powerful Sanhedrin which would hand him the crown of High Priest. Indeed, he seemed to go out of his way to antagonize them, to make them his enemies as he condemned their arrogant, hypocritical ways.

James agreed with Jeshua's condemnation of the temple

priesthood, but thought he should use more tact and diplomacy if he were to use them to gain his ends.

It was written that the Messiah would bring new revelations, a new understanding of the will of God, but Jeshua's teaching seemed to contradict the teachings of old. "An eye for an eye," the Scriptures said. Jeshua said, "If a man smite you on one cheek, turn the other," and "I have not come to destroy the Law, but to fulfill it!" But how? how? James agonized.

James was not the only one who wondered. Adahr and Sofa came to Jeshua, sent by John who languished in Herod's dungeons, to ask of him, "Are you 'He who is to come,' or do we look for another?" Jeshua had answered, "Go back and report to John what you hear and see. The blind recover their sight, cripples walk, lepers are cured, the deaf hear, dead men are raised to life, and the poor have the good news preached to them. Blest is the man who finds no stumbling block in me."

Adahr and Sofa took Jeshua's answer back to Machaerus, and James left Jerusalem and returned to the City of Salt. He had to think, to search his inner vision. He feared Jeshua's words, "Blest is the man who finds no stumbling block in me." He had to listen for that small, still voice which could whisper truth in his ear, and he could only hear it in the eerie silence of the barren, desolate Judean hills.

Jeshua went back to Galilee, but not before Ruth reminded him of his promise concerning John Mark. Jeshua had laughed at her and rumpled her hair as though she were still a child of eight, but John Mark now walked steadily and sure without a trace of his limp.

Ruth, Jude, and Philoas went home to Capernaum and life resumed its normal routine. There had been so much to tell Mary and Josie. When Ruth heard her own voice recounting all that had happened in Jerusalem, it seemed to be a dream. John Mark could walk, James was changing his attitudes, Mary of Syrus had returned home—so many things had happened that such a short time ago seemed impossible.

Susane's reaction to Mary of Syrus echoed Ulai's. "She's acting!" Susane said emphatically. "No one can change so overnight." But Ruth wondered. Didn't James change? Not in such a dramatic way, of course, but still, for James it had been a great change.

"I think you're wrong," she said to Susane. "We stopped at Lazarus' on our way home. Mary is not the vain, pompous girl you and I knew, nor is she the hardened, bold harlot I saw standing before Barrian. She even looks different, soft and kind, with a glow of quiet joy about her. She is not humble or contrite, but rather assured and confident and at peace with herself."

But Susane wasn't convinced and neither was Josie; only Mary agreed with Ruth that a soul could be healed completely of sin and be born anew in one life.

Jude went back to Alpheaus' shop, and Ruth resumed her work with Susane and Jonas. Days melted into weeks. The summer sun burned the Galilean hills and they blessed the cool breeze which blew in from the sea.

Ruth saw Philoas nearly every day, and Mary seemed resigned to their eventual union. Even Josie relented and spoke to him in her sharp, chastising way, but cooked the foods he was particularly fond of, and blushed when he flirted with her in the overly affected way which Roman men were reputed to do, and laughed at his comical impersonations of a court dandy.

Peace and tranquility are fleeting moments during life in the flesh, and Joanna of Chuza shattered theirs with news that John ben Zachariah was dead.

John beheaded! The knowledge shrank their souls with its grisly horror. Herodias had had her way. Herod had given a lavish birthday party for himself, and Herodias' daughter Salome had danced for him, a dance so sensuous that Herod had been consumed with lust for her and promised the girl anything she wanted, even half of his kingdom. Herodias had seen her chance, and ordered Salome to request John's head. There was nothing Herod could do. He had given the promise in front of all his friends, and a king couldn't go back on his word! John's head had been presented to Salome on a platter.

Mary and Josie made the journey to Ain Karim with the Other Mary and Timothy. John's disciples had asked Herod for his body, and the murdered son lay at rest beside his murdered father.

Thaddeaus and Matthew came to Capernaum and told how John's disciples had brought the news to Jeshua.

Jeshua had wept and beat his breast in anguish, then turned back to the crowds and said, "What did you go out to see in the desert, a reed swayed by the wind? What really, did you go out to see, someone dressed luxuriously? Remember those who dress in luxury and eat in splendor are to be found in royal palaces. Then what did you go out to see, a prophet? He is that, I assure you, and something more. This is the man of whom Scripture says, 'I send my messenger ahead of you to prepare your way before you.' I assure you, there is no man born of woman greater than John. Yet the least born into the kingdom of God is greater than he."

Jeshua had then called the Twelve together and sent them out two by two to proclaim the reign of God and to heal the afflicted. "Take nothing for the journey, neither walking staff nor travelling bag; no bread, no money. No one is to have two coats. Stay at whatever house you enter and proceed from there. When people will not receive you, leave that town and shake its dust from your feet as a testimony against them." Then Jeshua had taken his grief and gone alone into the hills.

The weeks passed. Rumors began to filter into Capernaum from all over Galilee about the healings and other wonders performed by the followers of the Nazarene. Thaddeaus and Matthew stayed in the area around Capernaum, and Ruth and Jude listened and watched as they taught as Jeshua taught, and healed the sick and cast unclean spirits from the possessed.

When Jeshua met them all again in Capernaum, he looked tired and thin; his eyes were sunken in their sockets and the skin was tightly drawn over his cheekbones. He took the Twelve and they went off by themselves in a boat, to rest and get away from the great numbers of people who thronged around them wherever they went. But the people saw them go and guessed at their destination. When Jeshua disembarked at Bethsaida, he saw a vast crowd waiting for him and took pity on them because they were like sheep without a shepherd.

He took them away from the seashore up into the hills where they could sit on the grass beneath the trees. He preached to them from early morning until the sun began to sink. They'd had nothing to eat all day, and the Twelve became concerned that some would collapse from hunger on their way home. Jeshua wanted to buy bread for them, but Philip snorted, "There are five thousand men here, not counting women and children. Not even with two hundred days' wages could we buy loaves enough to give each of them a mouthful."

Andrew approached with his son Ardoen. "My son's friend has five barley loaves and a couple of dried fish, but what good is that for so many?"

"Get the people to recline," said Jeshua.

The Twelve got everyone to sit in groups of fifty or so, and then Jeshua took the loaves and fish, gave thanks over them, and gave them to the Twelve to distribute. They broke chunk after chunk off each loaf, but the loaf never disappeared. The same thing happened with the fish. When the crowd had finished eating, Jeshua told them to gather up the crusts so none would go to waste, and they filled twelve baskets.

No one could keep such a secret. Word flew through the crowd that Jeshua had fed them all on only five loaves and a couple of fish. There were Zealots among the crowd, and they began to move from group to group, quoting the Scriptures and recounting Jeshua's wonders, convincing them that, "This is undoubtedly the Prophet who is to come into the world!" Their excited murmuring became louder until the hillsides rumbled like distant thunder. The men began to leave the women and children and congregate together.

Jeshua realized that they would come and carry him off to make him king, so he fled to the mountains alone.

Judas Iscariot was beside himself with frustration. Why had the Master fled? There might never be another opportunity so perfect to assert himself as king as now! Five thousand men, willing and eager to proclaim him king and follow him into battle, and all of Galilee would have followed their example! Within days they could have had an army which would have made Herod's barbarians look like children playing at war, and the Master had let the chance slip through his fingers!

Simon and James ben Alphaeus were also disappointed, but they knew Jeshua far better than Judas Iscariot did. It had seemed as though God had made the moment for Jeshua to snatch Herod's kingdom from under his nose, and what a delight that would have been, he was such a

spineless, murdering swine. But Jeshua knew the will of
God better than any of them, and if he said the time was
not right, then it was not right!

Their argument raged until nightfall. They waited at the
boat for Jeshua, but the wind came up and the sea was
becoming rough. Simon ben John decided they had better
go without him before the storm grew worse, and they
were forced to spend the night there.

They began to row toward Capernaum. The wind grew
stronger and the waves higher until after only three or
four miles they were all exhausted. The waves crashed
against the boat, tossing it about like a child's toy. By
three in the morning they had made little headway and
they fought the wind and waves with the last reserves of
their strength, their fear driving them on as Judas Iscariot
screamed over the roaring winds that it was God's punishment for not proclaiming Jeshua as king. They despaired,
knowing they were about to die, when Philip suddenly
grabbed Simon ben John's shoulder, pointed out across
the foaming sea and howled, "A ghost! We are lost for
sure!"

Their fear turned to panic. They watched the eerie form
approach, and they dropped the useless oars and fell to
their knees in the water at the bottom of the boat. They
prayed, babbling like idiots with fear until the apparition
spoke. "Get hold of yourselves! It is I. Do not be afraid!"

It was Jeshua! He stood on the surface of the roiling
waves—no boat, no raft, nothing but water beneath his
feet. Simon cried out to him, "Lord, if it is really you, tell
me to come to you across the water."

"Come!" Jeshua called.

Simon crawled over the side and began to walk toward
Jeshua. The sea was a frenzy around him, and the wind
roared in his ears and whipped his cloak around his legs.
He was afraid and began to sink. "Lord, save me!" he
screamed.

Jeshua caught him and pulled him back to the surface.
"How little faith you have!" he exclaimed. "Why did you
falter?" He helped Simon over the side, and as soon as
they were both in the boat the storm faded and the sea
was calm. Within seconds they were on the shore at
Gennesaret.

The others stared at Jeshua in awe, completely amazed

by what they had witnessed. Their eyes were wide with wonder and their voices filled with reverence. "Beyond doubt you are the Son of God," they whispered.

There seemed to be no limit to Jeshua's popularity. Hundreds followed him from town to town throughout Galilee. Men closed their shops and businesses, left their flocks under a servant's care, planted their seed and left it to come up alone, and why not? The Kingdom of God was nigh! What did it matter if a business flourished or not? So what if wolves ran off with the lambs? The end of the age had come, and who would need these things after all reverted to chaos!

Women also followed, leaving their homes and children in the care of grandmothers or servants, or bringing their children with them to be blessed by the Teacher. It was a common sight to see a babe at the breast and toddlers clutching their mothers' skirts, and a gaggle of youngsters at Jeshua's knee. They slept in the open beneath the trees on the grassy hills of Galilee, and depended on villagers to provide them with food. Jeshua and the Twelve did the same. "The foxes have lairs, the birds of the sky have nests, but the Son of Man has nowhere to lay his head," Jeshua said.

Andra, Editha, Sophia, all the Essene women who had followed him from the beginning were still with him. They were called "Holy Women," and though they no longer had to precede Jeshua to draw the crowds, they provided and cooked his meals, found places for him and the Twelve to sleep, mended their clothing, and provided the money for his ministry.

The people were frenzied by Jeshua's teaching and the wonders he performed. Every village market square they entered was littered with their lame and blind and deaf and diseased, and Jeshua healed them all. His fame spread to all the outlying districts, and people from as far as Idumea and Perea flocked to Galilee to hear the Master and watch for the chance to touch his cloak that they too might be healed.

Jeshua maintained that he had come to the Sons of Israel, but many times those who were not of Jewish blood prevailed upon his mercy. Once, on a tour of Tyre and Sidon, a Syrophoenician named Anilen approached

him. Anilen's wife begged Jeshua to free their daughter
from the clutches of a demon, and Jeshua had said to her,
"My mission is only to the lost sheep of the house of
Israel. It is not right to take the food of sons and daughters and throw it to the dogs."

Anilen had started to turn away, but the mother
pleaded, "Please, Lord, even the dogs eat the leavings that
fall from their masters' tables."

Jeshua had been amazed at the Canaanite woman's
depth of understanding and at her faith in himself. He
could not refuse her, and the daughter was healed.

But Jeshua's popularity was only an illusion. It was true
that the poor and humble followed him by the hundreds,
even thousands, making it look as though the whole world
was following in the steps of the Master, but the ruling
class, the rich and influential, the businessmen, and priests
who ordered the way of life in Palestine feared and hated
him.

The Pharisees and scribes came out from Jerusalem and
watched his every move, challenging his teaching before
the crowds and keeping a record of all his transgressions
against the Law. He didn't fast, he healed on the Sabbath,
he ate unclean foods, and he disdained the ritual washings.

"It's not what goes into a man's mouth that makes him
impure, it's what comes out of his mouth," Jeshua retorted to their accusations. "You Pharisees! You cleanse
the outside of the cup and dish, but within you are filled
with rapaciousness and evil. Fools! Did not he who made
the outside make the inside too?" And to the scribes and
lawyers, he cried, "Woe to you lawyers also! You lay
impossible burdens on men but will not lift a finger to
lighten them. Woe to you! You build the tombs of the
prophets, but it was your fathers who murdered them.
You show that you stand behind the deeds of your fathers, they committed the murders and erect the tombs.
That is why the wisdom of God has said, 'I will send them
prophets and apostles, and some of these they will persecute and kill,' so that this generation will have to account
for the blood of all the prophets shed since the foundation
of the world. Their guilt stretches from the blood of Abel
to the blood of Zachariah who met his death between the
altar and the sanctuary! Woe to you lawyers! You have

taken away the key of knowledge. You yourselves have not gained access, yet you have stopped those who wished to enter!"

When they railed at him for healing on the Sabbath, he said, "O you hypocrites! Which of you does not let his ox or ass out of the stall on the Sabbath to water it?"

The Pharisees were scandalized by Jeshua's scathing retorts. The crowds roared in approval and the scribes and lawyers were humiliated. The temple authority was losing its ironclad hold on the masses of the poor. For years they had ruled through fear, cowing the people with their contempt and disdain for their ignorance and poverty, convincing them that all of their troubles stemmed from their failure to observe the letter of the Law.

Then came Jeshua of Nazareth. He ridiculed the established order, flagrantly broke the Law himself, and undermined the very foundations of the temple authority. The people applauded Jeshua's retorts and jeered at the red-faced scribes and Pharisees, and there was nothing they could do, for Jeshua spoke the truth and both they and the crowds knew it.

The priests used every approach to try to disenchant the crowds with Jeshua. They came to him in friendship, inviting him into their homes under the pretense of wanting to hear his teachings, and all the while waiting for the chance to trap him. They denounced him publicly, calling him a blasphemer and a false prophet, warning the people that the man was leading them astray, weaving horrible tales of the fate which awaited them in the fires of Gehenna if they continued to follow the Nazarene.

The rabble, thieves and drunkards and murderers, men and women who thrived in a world of violence and depravity, despised Jeshua and wished him dead. His message of brotherly love and peace threatened their existence. They feared to see themselves as they really were, and the gentle Nazarene was like a festering thorn in the flesh. His goodness and mercy and love for all life only served to remind them of their own evil sinfulness, which they could not admit even to themselves or they would be forced to change and give up the life of perverted corruption which they loved so much or admit that their souls were lost.

The Roman authorities watched him with a wary eye, ever alert for signs of insurrection. As long as he kept his teaching to religious matters, they left him alone, but they too sent their spies to infiltrate the crowds and listen for the slightest hint of opposition to Rome. They didn't fear him, or hate him. They prided themselves on their policy of peace and benevolent rule. They allowed the Jews to worship as they wished, and even bowed to their foolish Law in many instances, but they would not tolerate rebellion, and the sheer numbers and the zeal of the crowds made them uneasy; they kept a careful watch.

Herod Antipas feared him. He was a Jew and knew the prophecies as well as any, and the prophecies proclaimed the Anointed One would be the King of the Jews. Herod was as jealous of his throne as his father before him had been, and if the Nazarene was the Chosen One, Herod's throne was in jeopardy. But there was more to Herod's fears than the loss of his kingdom. John the Baptizer's murder ate away at Herod's conscience, and he feared for the salvation of his own soul. He fantasized that Jeshua was John returned to life, or at best, that he was Elijah and would bring doom and destruction down upon his head as Elijah had done to Ahab. He was terrified by day, and horrified by his dreams at night. He wanted nothing more than to see the death of the Nazarene, but his fear of God's wrath overrode all others, and he didn't dare murder another prophet of the Lord.

So Herod also sent his spies, who watched and listened and reported back to their master. Jeshua had many followers who walked with him from town to town and openly proclaimed themselves as apostles of the Anointed One. But for every friend there was an enemy—hidden, cunning, wary, waiting for the time to strike and rid themselves of the threat to their established world.

The Zealots also watched and plotted and planned, and met in secret to calculate when the time would be ripe to overthrow them all and set the Nazarene on the throne of Israel.

As the numbers of his followers increased, Jeshua's teaching became more profound. He began to move away from the method of using parables to describe the Kingdom of Heaven, and to teach them how to live in peace in the present world, and his message became more subtle and fraught with hidden meanings.

"I am the bread of life. No one who comes to me shall ever be hungry, no one who believes in me shall ever thirst. I myself am the living bread come down from heaven. If anyone eats this bread he shall live forever, the bread I will give is my flesh, for the life of the world."

Those were hard words to understand. "How can he give us his flesh to eat?" they asked. Even his disciples questioned such statements. "This sort of talk is hard to endure! How can anyone take it seriously?" they murmured, and many no longer followed him.

The Twelve remained loyal, as Jeshua knew they would. "Did I not choose the Twelve of you myself? Yet one of you is a devil," he said, cryptically.

Chapter 34

Ruth didn't follow Jeshua. She stayed at home with Mary and waited until Jeshua and his friends returned to Capernaum. Their house was a place of retreat and rest for all the Holy Women, who kept them up to date on Jeshua's whereabouts and actions. Judith often came to visit when Jeshua was in Capernaum. She was getting old, almost sixty, but was young in mind and still the leader of the Essenes. Her body tired easily and rebelled at sleeping on the hard ground and tramping over the dusty roads, so she rarely joined the other women in following Jeshua from village to village. She was as tall and ramrod straight as ever, and her eyes still flashed with the blue of the Galilee, but her long, wheaten hair was now silver and caught in a bun at the nape of her neck instead of cascading down her back in a river of gold.

The years of trial and overwhelming responsibilities had brought a serenity and an air of peaceful acceptance to Judith which made her seem more beautiful than ever. Her inner life of the spirit had deepened and expanded. Her gifts of the spirit were a source of wonder to everyone. She saw what no other could see; she heard what no other could hear; she communed with forces outside of the realm of normal men and understood things no other could understand. Only Mary and Jeshua surpassed her in holiness, and when Ruth was in the company of the three of them, she felt as though she were in the company of angels.

Those were tender moments for Ruth, those rare times when Jeshua came alone to the house and only herself, Jude and Philoas, and Mary, Josie, and Judith were there with him. Ruth would sit on the floor at Jeshua's feet with her head against his knee, his fingers sometimes playing idly in her dark curls, and she listened to the sweet, soft voices of the others, basking contentedly in the presence of those she most loved.

Mary, Josie, and Judith—the three women who had nurtured and taught and guided the young Jeshua, surrounded him with love and tenderness, gently prodded his conscious mind to awaken to the knowledge of his soul. They had given everything to Jeshua, every moment of their lives had been dedicated to thoughts of Jeshua. Everything they did and every ounce of energy they possessed had been done for and given to Jeshua. Ruth would sit at Jeshua's knee with Philoas close at her side and marvel at the courage and complete unselfishness shown by these women who looked at Jeshua with such adoration in their eyes.

And how he loved them in return! Ruth often thought of John ben Zachariah's words to her that day at the river Jordan. "How you must have labored to earn such privilege." For privilege it was to be able to sit in the cooling twilight and feel the vibrations of almost holy love that filled the tiny garden. Philoas felt those vibrations also. His eyes sometimes met Ruth's, and a silent communication of such profound understanding passed between them that Ruth was brought close to weeping, her joy so overwhelming she could hardly bear it.

Those times were rare, and the more precious for their rarity. They were moments Ruth would carry in her heart and which would sustain her through trials which her mind could not then even imagine.

Jeshua didn't go to Jerusalem for Passover that spring. He stayed in his beloved Galilee, leading the throngs up into the mountains where he walked among them, healing the sick and crippled, and teaching them beneath the deep blue sky while newborn lambs gambolled and played nearby. The green earth was his synagogue, the sun and moon his lamps; the stars winked their approval and the gentle breeze served as his ritual bath.

They stayed in the hills for days, and again the people had nothing to eat; again Jeshua fed them with only a few loaves, and the crusts left behind filled seven baskets.

Ruth could sense a tension building in Jeshua. His teachings became more urgent; his eyes, as he looked upon the sick and maimed, became sadder. He went away

by himself more often, and when he came back his eyes
held a haunted look, a look of dread and fear and infinite
sorrow. He spent hours alone with the Twelve, teaching
them mysteries on a level the people could never understand, at a depth that often the Twelve didn't understand,
though Jeshua assured them that the day was coming
when they would.

One day at Caesarea Philippi, Jeshua asked the Twelve,
"Who do people say that the Son of Man is?" They replied, "Some say John the Baptizer, others Elijah, still
others Jeremiah, or one of the prophets."

"And you," he said to them. "Who do you say that I
am?"

"You are the Messiah," Simon ben John answered,
"The Son of the living God!"

Jeshua replied, "Blest are you, Simon ben John! No
mere man has revealed this to you, but my heavenly Father. I for my part declare to you, you are 'Rock,' and on
this rock I will build my church, and the jaws of death
shall not prevail against it. I will entrust to you the keys
of the Kingdom of Heaven. Whatever you declare bound
on earth shall be bound in heaven, whatever you declare
loosed on earth shall be loosed in heaven."

From then on Simon was known as Simon Peter, Peter
being the Greek word for "rock," and the others acknowl-
edged that Simon Peter was the leader of them all.

Jeshua started to indicate to his disciples that he must
go to Jerusalem and suffer greatly there at the hands of
the elders, the chief priests, and scribes, but they didn't
understand what he was trying to tell them, or perhaps
wouldn't understand because their hearts could not bear
it.

Jude understood. He'd always understood. But he
couldn't understand why Jeshua went out to meet it, why
he seemed to force things to happen. He raged at his own
impotence to stop it, and lived in icy fear of the day. He
said nothing to no one. He went to the shop each day and
vented his anger upon the innocent wood, ripping and
sawing and hurling the axe until his body was sore and his
mind numb, but it didn't forestall his dreams. He ranged
the hills in his loneliness, and wept for his mother and
sister whose broken hearts he'd somehow have to mend.
He was eighteen and a man, but his burden of knowledge

was too much to bear alone, and finally he went to Philoas.

Philoas loved Jude as though he were his own brother. He listened to the boy's outpouring of fear and anguish, and his heart sank. He knew Jude was right. Jeshua had enemies in every corner of authority. Rome was uneasy over the vast crowds that followed the Nazarene; Herod feared him with almost a fanatical fear, and the Jewish rulers squirmed with hate and jealousy. Philoas might be able to use his influence with Tiberius to save Jeshua from Rome, but he was powerless over Herod and the Jews. The only way to save Jeshua would be to get him out of the country, but both Jude and Philoas knew that was impossible. Jeshua would do what he believed he was sent to do, despite the efforts of angels to prevent it. Nor could Philoas save Mary from the torment she would have to endure, though maybe he could protect Ruth somewhat.

He went to Mary and asked that he and Ruth be married. He explained that he would have to return to Rome in a few months, and he wanted to take Ruth with him as his wife. It was a strange interview. Mary listened to all his explanations with calm interest, but Philoas felt she knew why he was so anxious to take Ruth to Rome. She gave her blessing and smiled and embraced him, but her smile was bittersweet and her embrace a little desperate. Philoas left her with a heavy heart. He could take her to Rome also, but he knew she wouldn't go, not as long as Jeshua trod the dusty roads of Galilee.

Ruth walked on a cloud of euphoria. She felt as though her life were just beginning. To be Philoas' wife, to bear his children and make a home for him, that was her soul's purpose on earth. She wanted only to live quietly and unobtrusively, using her hands and mind and talents to serve her family and the others around her, to build a quiet haven of peace in an unpeaceful world. Her home would follow the pattern of her mother's home, be a place of retreat and rest for the careworn and weary. It didn't matter where her home would be, whether in Rome or Palestine or Greece; wherever Tiberius sent Philoas, she would be at his side and their home would be an island of tranquility. Philoas spoke to Jeshua as head of the family, and with his blessing, they were betrothed.

Jeshua spent the summer in his beloved Galilee, going from village to village, teaching and healing the thousands who gathered around him. Anxious mothers brought their children and pushed them through the crowds so the Master could lay his hands upon them and bless them, believing that no evil would ever befall a child blessed by a prophet of the Lord.

Jeshua loved the little ones. He often used the children as an object lesson to the adults. One time someone asked him, "Who is of the greatest importance in the kingdom of God?" He called a little child over and stood him in their midst and said, "I assure you, unless you change and become like little children, you will not enter the Kingdom of God. Whoever makes himself lowly, becoming like this child, is of greatest importance in that heavenly reign."

It was a long, hot summer. Jeshua's fame was spreading all over the world. People from faraway lands returned home with wonderful tales of what was happening in Galilee—tales of a prophet, a Holy One sent from God who wrought unbelievable miracles and taught a doctrine of love. They came back to Galilee, bringing their wives and children with them, hoping the Holy Man would heal and teach them also.

The tension grew. Jeshua came less and less to Mary's house. He was totally absorbed with his mission and taught the Twelve with a note of desperate urgency. He told them how it would be at the end of days, trying to prepare them for what was to come, but they closed their minds and wouldn't understand. Then Jeshua left them and went alone into the wilderness to pray.

One day he took Simon Peter and James and John ben Zebedee and climbed to the top of Mt. Tabor. The rest of the Twelve and a crowd of followers waited all day for them to come down, and when they did, there seemed to be a change in Simon Peter and James and John. Their eyes were huge with wonder, and their manner was sober and greatly subdued, but they would not tell anyone what had happened upon the mountain.

Galilee was like a vast infirmary. Ruth had never seen so many sick and blind and maimed, and Jeshua healed them, sometimes by touch, sometimes by only a word, and sometimes by a physical sign, such as spitting upon

the lids of a blind man. How did he do it? It seemed to
have to do with faith. If you prayed, and asked for healing, you must absolutely believe it would happen. It
wasn't easy.

A man brought his possessed son to Jeshua and begged
him to help him if he could. "If I can?" Jeshua said.
"Everything is possible to a man who trusts." The man
cried out, "Help my lack of trust!"

Yes, Ruth thought, help all of us our lack of trust. That
man's cry would echo throughout the ages.

Even the Twelve lacked sufficient faith. When Jeshua
came down from Mt. Tabor, his disciples were trying in
vain to cast out a devil from a young boy. Jeshua was a
little angry and disgusted with them. "What an unbelieving and perverse lot you are!" he admonished. "How long
must I remain with you? How long can I endure you?"

Faith! Absolute and unwavering faith! But how did one
acquire such faith? He could work no miracles in Nazareth because of the people's lack of faith. They simply
couldn't believe that the son of Mary and Joseph, whom
they knew so well, could do such things. Other towns
such as Chorazin, Bethsaida, even Capernaum, did believe
he could work such wonders, but even though they believed, they didn't let it change their lives. They continued
on in the same old pattern of bickering and petty meanness, retaining their selfish ways and pandering to their
vain desires. Jeshua condemned them soundly. "If the
miracles worked in you had taken place in Tyre and
Sidon, they would have reformed in sackcloth and ashes
long ago!"

So it took more than faith. It took a change of heart
and ways, a compassion for one's fellow man, and a willingness to help and serve. Jeshua tried so hard to make
them understand. He told them parables which illustrated
how they should live. He told them of a forgiving father
who welcomed home his prodigal son, of a Samaritan
who took pity upon a wounded, beaten Jew. He used
stories to tell them what the Kingdom was like, to teach
them of God's mercy and love for them, of how they
should pray and what they had to do to be saved. Many
listened, and carried their lessons home with them in their
hearts and tried to live what they had learned, but many
came to see the wonders and rid themselves of their aches

and pains and sufferings, and then returned to their old ways.

Jeshua came home for Ruth and Philoas' wedding. He was a rabbi, and so he read the Scriptures and blessed their union. Jude and James served as Philoas' groomsmen, and Susane and Naomi as Ruth's bridesmaids. It was an unusual wedding for those times. There was no great celebration or long procession or canopy, nor any of the other traditional fuss. Only close family and friends were invited, and Jeshua married them in Mary's tiny garden with the blue Galilean sky as their canopy and the blazing sun for their lamps.

The Essenes and other of Jeshua's followers had set up altars in their homes and formed small groups to pray together and study Jeshua's teachings. They were slowly breaking away from the old traditions and customs. Jeshua taught that the body itself was the temple, and the place to meet the Father was within that temple. He taught that attitudes and thoughts and the most private and hidden feelings were what mattered the most.

"When you are praying, do not behave like the hypocrites who love to stand and pray in synagogues or on street corners in order to be noticed. I give you my word, they are already repaid. Whenever you pray, go to your room, close your door, and pray to your Father in private. Then your Father, who sees what no man sees, will repay you. In your prayer do not rattle on like the pagans. They think they will win a hearing by the sheer multiplication of words. If two of you join your voices on earth to pray for anything whatever, it shall be granted you by my Father in heaven. Where two or three are gathered in my name, there am I in their midst."

The wedding feast lasted only three days in keeping with Ruth's wish for simplicity. Mary of Alphaeus was in charge of the preparations and Ruth had a difficult time restraining her aunt from planning a marriage that would outdo Lia and Roael's. Ruth felt a little sorry to deprive Mary of Alphaeus the pleasure of planning a social event of the year for Capernaum, but she knew that most of the people there would come out of curiosity, to see Jeshua and to witness the marriage of a Roman and a Jew.

Ruth's marriage to a Roman was a scandal among the Jews, and most of her relatives agreed with her mother that Ruth was making a mistake and would live to regret it. No one openly condemned her, but the concern and sadness in their eyes betrayed them, and their joyful cries and good wishes were forced. James ben Joseph played his role of groomsman with great dignity and fortitude, which made Ruth smile behind her veil and exchange a knowing look with Philoas.

Only Jeshua, Jude, and Lia seemed sincerely glad for her. "If you have love, you can endure anything, even separation by death," Lia whispered to Ruth, and Ruth believed her. Lia had gained a new beauty since Roael's death. There was a softness about her, a deep spirituality which reached out and touched them all. That passionate zeal with which she'd furthered the work of John the Baptizer was gone, replaced by a gentle acceptance of the ways of the Lord.

The cruel murder of the Baptizer had angered the Jews. Even the priests and scribes wondered at the wisdom of killing a possible prophet of the Lord, and shuddered to think of the punishment which could befall them all through God's wrath. The people who had believed in and followed John now followed Jeshua, remembering John's testimony, "He must increase while I must decrease," and his death had only served to increase Jeshua's flock.

Herod also regretted his rash promise to Salome. The gruesome sight of John's head on a platter had quickly cooled his ardor for his stepdaughter, and he'd soon married her off to his brother Philip in Gaulanitis. Rumors from Tiberias said that his ardor for Herodias had also cooled, since it was at her instigation that Salome had demanded her grisly prize, and the royal chamber was beset with quarrels. Herod was haunted by nightmares and stalked the palace corridors at night, which reminded some of the old retainers of his father's madness when he had murdered his beloved Mariamme. Herod saw John's ghost in every corner and heard his words whispered by the very walls. When his cronies reported the wonders worked by the Nazarene, he rent his clothes and declared that John had come to life again.

John and Roael had not died in vain, but their deaths served as a catalyst to further the cause of the Messiah. Lia took comfort from that and dedicated her life to helping Jeshua fulfill his mission on earth, confident that one day her soul and Roael's would be reunited in the kingdom to come.

Ruth and Philoas planned to make their home with Mary until Philoas was recalled to Rome. James didn't go back to the City of Salt, and so the little house was crowded; privacy was hard to find. But it didn't matter. They were together and nothing would ever part them again. They walked over the hills and watched the sun set over the sea. When Jeshua was in the area, they took Mary and Josie and went to hear him speak. They planned their future and dreamed of the children they would bring into the world; they spoke of their childhoods and laughed together over their childish antics and dreams. They began to know and understand one another, and their love deepened and matured with that understanding.

Jeshua's tension and sense of urgency became more noticeable. Mary became quieter and her eyes darker, and she kept to the house more and more. Herod's barbarians and the priests and scribes became bolder and more adamant in challenging Jeshua. The Zealots plotted and planned to make him king, and the Pharisees plotted to kill him. The Romans grew increasingly uneasy. Pilate slaughtered a mass of Samaritans as they gathered to climb Mt. Gerizem in an attempt to find the ark of Moses, and Herod screamed in fury because some Galileans were among those killed.

None of it touched Ruth. Philoas was a gentle lover and a solicitous and protective husband, and Ruth moved through the days in bliss, oblivious to the threatening clouds of unrest which were secretly making their way over Palestine.

Not so Philoas. He felt the tremors beneath his feet, and the prickly sensations on the back of his neck warned of danger. It was hot, unseasonably so, and the rabble was louder and more disruptive than usual. Tempers were short and fights and near riots were commonplace. Crimes of thievery and rape and vandalism broke out in every squalid quarter, and the Romans quelled them with a fierce brutality spurred by the heat and the tension in the air.

Philoas watched and listened. He felt like a ship's captain who could sense rather than see the approach of a storm. He hid his anxiety from Ruth and kept her wrapped in a protective cocoon of love, but he caught Jude watching him with a knowing eye, and knew he'd soon have to take Ruth away before she was caught in the growing maelstrom of violence.

The hot days stretched into weeks. The only breeze was the scorching wind which blew through the valley at Magadon. The sea lay like a blazing mirror, sending shimmering waves of heat and steam upward toward a white-hot sky. The sand burned through Philoas' ironclad sandals, and the merest movement caused the thick yellow dust to fill his eyes and choke his throat. Disease and misery flourished in the steaming air, and only the Nazarene could give the people relief.

The crowds following Jeshua were suffering, miserable, afraid. They too felt the inexorable movement of death and destruction, and trailed after Jeshua in desperate supplication. Jeshua had set his face toward Jerusalem and every step took him slowly and steadfastly in that direction. Philoas and Ruth followed, Ruth starry-eyed and happy despite the heat, proud of Jeshua's popularity and awed by the works he performed. Philoas, however, knew they followed the eye of the storm and began to plan their escape.

The days were like a kaleidoscope of sound and color and heat and dust. Ruth would leave Philoas' warm embrace before dawn and join the other Holy Women in preparing a quick morning meal before the crowds began to assemble, for once the people came there would be no time to eat until the darkness sent them home again. They arrived with the first rays of the sun—miserable, pain-ridden, suffering; the forgotten, lowly dregs of humanity whom no one cared about, seeking a miracle, listening for the word to fall from Jeshua's lips which would give them hope.

From the first arrival at dawn until the last departing at sunset, Ruth's hands and feet never stopped. The Holy Women organized the crowds into groups according to their afflictions, the sick here, the blind there, the crippled to this side, the deaf to that, and the lepers—the walking dead—huddling in an isolated group on the outer fringes of life. Her shoulders ached from the weight of the old and infirm as they used her young body as a staff. Her head throbbed with the heat and suffering cries, and her

feet burned from the white-hot sand. All day they came—
old, young; men, women, children; rich, poor; high and
lowly; sinners and saints, all clamoring for a touch of
Jeshua's robes, his hand of blessing on their heads, pushing and jostling, crying out, "Heal me, Master, bless me,
cure me, help me, notice me," until it seemed the sun
welded their cries into one massive groan of supplication.

Ruth rode the wave of excitement, awed by the crowds
and the miracles Jeshua wrought, bowed down with pity
at the suffering she saw, thrilled to trembling to be a part
of it all. The world had never known such things as were
happening in Galilee.

Souls had wandered far from their Creator, so far that
they no longer remembered that they were souls and a
part of God their Father, who created them in His own
image. They knew only the body of flesh which they could
see and touch with the senses of the flesh, and they
thought it was all. They lived in fear of that body which
they believed to be their entire self. They feared the pain
and disease it suffered. Their thoughts were consumed
with worry over feeding, clothing, and providing the body
with shelter, and most of all they feared the day when it
would stop functioning and would lie consigned to the
worms and corruption, and they would be no more.

The earth was peopled with souls who no longer knew
who they were or what they were, or how they came to be
on earth, or for what purpose. As souls they had once had
the ability to commune with the Source of their creation.
The heroes of old had walked and talked with God and
had called Him Friend. As time passed and they became
more and more concerned with the things of the flesh, this
gift had fallen into disuse and was forgotten. Communication with the Father had become a mindless ritual, words
spoken and acts performed without knowledge of or
thought given to the meaning which lay behind it.
Through the ritual of the Law, as interpreted by the
priests, God had become a vengeful, harsh Master, ever
watchful for an infraction of His Law so that punishment
could come quickly and without mercy.

They were indeed sheep without a shepherd, mindless,
confused, surrounded by thieves and wolves who snatched
away their hard-earned sustenance and threatened them
with torture and death if they dared to raise their voices in

protest. They were without hope. The only path to salvation was to follow the most minute letter of the Law, which they found impossible to do. They believed they were destined to be born in misery, live in misery, and die in misery, and if there was a part of them which would continue on after the body rotted in the grave, it would only be in the fiery tortures of Gehenna, for they couldn't obey the letter of the Law.

Then came Jeshua, the Nazarene. How could they not believe that he came from God? He gave them signs and performed such wonders as the earth had not seen since the days of Elijah and Elisha. "Love one another," he said. "Do to others what you would have them do to you. That is the whole Law and the Prophets."

He showed by his own example that it wasn't necessary to wash one's hands or to watch every particle of food which went into one's mouth to gain entry into the Kingdom of God. He broke the Sabbath law over and over again, but the power of God never diminished in him. "Come to me, all you who are weary and find life burdensome, and I will refresh you. Take my yoke upon your shoulders and learn from me, for I am gentle and humble of heart. Your souls will find rest, for my yoke is easy and my burden light."

They wept when he spoke those words, for his yoke was light. He lifted the burden of the Law from their shoulders and replaced it with the airy admonition to love. He washed away the guilt which hung like a millstone around their necks and replaced it with the feathery joy of hope. The desperate sheep had found their shepherd and he would show them the way home, home again to the Father who loved them, where suffering and death would be no more.

Ruth watched and listened to Jeshua as though she were two people, one a sister with a sister's love and pride for her elder brother, another an insignificant soul, awed and humbled in the presence of the greatest soul of all, the first and only Begotten of the Father. She wiped the sweat from his face and guided his steps to the next cripple. She brought him cool water to drink and a crust of bread to eat, speaking with him, consulting with him, sometimes joking with him as any sister would do, and yet at the same time she wanted to fall at his feet and worship him and pay him homage.

When the sun went down and the crowds drifted away into the darkness, Jeshua led them all away into the silent hills. The women built fires and cooked the evening meal, exhausted and weary, but exhilarated with a kind of quiet joy. After they ate, they gathered around Jeshua and he taught them beneath the stars in the hot, Galilean night, his rich melodious voice flowing in and out among them like a refreshing bath of cool, clean water, explaining the deeper, hidden meanings to the parables he'd told during the day, and describing to them how it would be in the end of days when God would reign over the earth.

Those were nights which Ruth would hug to her heart and cherish as she did those times when Jeshua had come alone to Mary's house. She'd sit on the parched, prickly grass in the circle of Philoas' protective, loving arm, with her legs drawn up beneath her and her head resting against his shoulder. The stars hung so low she imagined she could pluck them if she stood on the highest hill, and the moon was like a giant lamp brought close to the earth by angels to shed its silvery light on the Remnant nestled in the hills. There was an atmosphere of love and unity of purpose which settled over them like a snug, invisible tent, containing the deep peace which eminated from Jeshua, and repulsing the cares and evils of the world.

Chapter 35

The blistering summer waned. The grape harvest was upon them and the crowds faded away like the long summer days to raid the vineyards and steal from the fruit its ruby-red prize. Jeshua chose seventy-two of his most devout followers and sent them in pairs to every town and place he intended to visit. He instructed them in the same way he had instructed the Twelve when he'd sent them on a similar mission, adding, "The harvest is rich but the workers are few, therefore ask the Harvest Master to send workers to His harvest. He who hears you, hears me. He who rejects you, rejects me. And he who rejects me, rejects Him who sent me."

Slowly, inexorably, Jeshua and the closest to him trod toward Jerusalem. In every town they entered, they were met by members of the Seventy-Two, jubilant with their successes in healing and casting out demons. Only those whom Jeshua had sent to Samaria reported failure, for the Samaritans refused Jeshua welcome since he was on his way to Jerusalem.

James and John ben Zebedee were furious with the Samaritans and wanted to call down fire from heaven to destroy them, but Jeshua reprimanded them and chose another route to Judea, skirting the Samaritan border through the Decapolis, going eastward toward the Jordan in Perea.

James and John smarted under Jeshua's reprimand. They couldn't understand Jeshua's showing mercy to the unreceiving Samaritans until one day, as they were entering a village along the border, they were met by ten lepers, all pleading for Jeshua to have pity on them. When Jeshua saw them, he said, "Go and show yourselves to the priests." On their way they were cured, and one of them came back, praising God in a loud voice. The only one to return and give thanks was a Samaritan.

Jeshua said to James and John, "Were not all ten made whole? Where are the other nine? Was there no one to return and give thanks to God except this foreigner?" He raised the man to his feet and said, "Stand up and go your way, your faith has been your salvation."

They pushed on through the western tip of the Decapolis and crossed the Jordan into Perea. It was a somber crossing, every heart remembering a man clad in skins, his feet bare, and his eyes flashing with zeal for the Lord. It seemed as though his cries for repentance still hung in the air, and some dipped their hands in the water made Holy by John the Baptizer.

The days had become cool, the nights almost cold. The grapes were gathered and the olive trees waited to give up their fruit to the children of God. The crowds again increased. Jeshua and his followers crossed the Jordan at Jericho where a multitude waited on the Judean bank. Throngs lined the road leading into the city, cheering and jostling and running alongside just to get a look at the famed Nazarene.

One man, named Zacchaeus, the chief tax collector and very wealthy, was small in stature, and the pressing crowds made it impossible for him to see. He climbed a sycamore tree to gain a vantage point. When Jeshua passed beneath, he looked up and called Zacchaeus by name, "Zacchaeus, hurry down. I mean to stay at your house today."

The crowds and Jeshua's followers began to murmur, for the man was a tax collector, thus a sinner. But Jeshua said to them, "The Son of Man has come to search out and save what is lost."

They stayed in Jericho a number of days and Jeshua's popularity in that important Judean city was astonishing. They were feted and dined by the wealthy rulers, and celebrated by the throngs wherever they went. It seemed only a foretaste of the way it would be when Jeshua assumed his reign, and even Ruth became caught up in the heady, dreamlike scene, and basked in Jeshua's reflected glory as the sister of the coming king.

All of Jeshua's followers seemed bemused by the acclaim and exaltation given them in Jericho. The Twelve argued among themselves about who was the most important. James and John ben Zebedee went so far as to ask Jeshua if they could occupy seats at his right and left hands when he came into his glory, and even their mother, Salome, added her plea to theirs. No one really heard Jeshua's reply, "You do not know what you are asking. Can you drink of the cup I am to drink?"

Judas Iscariot pushed himself to the forefront of importance among the Twelve. The rich palaces and lavish feasts were his element, and he was at ease in such surroundings, whereas Simon Peter, Andrew, and the other Galileans floundered in their ignorance of social graces. He was urbane and gregarious, his black, flashing eyes darting here and there, his smooth tongue wooing and cajoling the Pharisees and Sadducees into accepting Jeshua as the Anointed One.

Even James ben Joseph fell into the trap of false security laid by flattery and rich surroundings. The contrast between the stark Judean hills and the lush palm groves and richness of Jericho was too much, and he allowed himself to be fooled by the heady accolades given him because of his likeness to Jeshua, and the deference paid him as Jeshua's brother. The feast of Booths was soon to be celebrated in Jerusalem, and, under Judas Iscariot's urging, James complained to Jeshua, "You ought to leave here and go to Judea so that your disciples there may see the works you are performing. No one who wishes to be known publicly keeps his actions hidden. If you are going to do things like these, you may as well display yourself to the world at large."

Jeshua said, "Go up yourselves to the festival. I am not going to this festival because the time is not yet ripe for me."

Only Jude and Philoas retained a sense of reality. They watched and listened, and only they seemed to hear Jeshua's words.

"You cannot tell by careful watching when the reign of God will come. Neither is it a matter of reporting that it is 'here' or 'there.' The reign of God is already in your midst. A time will come when you will long to see one day of the Son of Man but will not see it. They will tell you he is to be found in this place or that. Do not go running about excitedly. The Son of Man in his day will

be like lightning that flashes from one end of the sky to
the other. First, however, he must suffer much and be
rejected by the present age."

The two men heard the warning Jeshua tried to impart,
his admonition for caution. They felt the premonition of
doom in his tone and chafed in frustration at their own
inability to convince the others to hear.

They watched Judas Iscariot pander to the temple authority, and exchanged uneasy looks when they saw him
whispering into a suspect ear, or slipping away to confer
with his cohorts. The eye of the storm drew nearer, and
Philoas was only too happy to take Ruth away from Jericho to Jerusalem for the feast of Tabernacles, while
Jeshua went alone to the hills to pray.

The first few days of the feast were quiet and normal.
Ruth and Philoas, James and Jude stayed with Marcus
and Josie, and after months of following Jeshua and sleeping in the open fields, it was wonderful for Ruth to lie in
her familiar, soft, perfumed bed and recline at ease at
Josie's sumptuous table.

Philoas was equally wonderful. He followed Jewish custom and tradition easily and found no stumbling block in
the concept of One God, Creator over all. In order to
fully embrace the faith of the Jews, Philoas would have to
undergo the rite of circumcision, an order not to be considered lightly by a grown man, and a subject far too
intimate to be broached by a modest young bride. Actually, Ruth didn't really care. One could not follow Jeshua
and still believe that such outward signs of faith were
necessary. What lay in a man's heart and mind were what
mattered, and Ruth could find no flaw in Philoas.

Philoas and Marcus had struck an instant friendship.
Their positions held parallel interests in government policy, economics, and, of course, the religious differences
between Roman and Jew. Philoas' study of Judaism and
all its various sects and schools of thought earned him a
broad knowledge of the Holy Scriptures, and even James
was duly impressed and happily joined in their heady
discussions.

The change in James was phenomenal. The months of
following Jeshua and witnessing the signs he wrought had
banished any doubts he'd had regarding Jeshua's teaching.
He still ate sparingly and refused any wine or oils, but his

rigid manner had softened. He came to understand that not all were called to follow the harsh regimen he'd set for himself, and that every soul must worship God with its own talents and place in life. God was no respecter of persons, and the lowly shepherd mumbling his prayers as he tended the creatures God put in his care was as holy as a high priest in the eyes of his Creator. He embraced Jeshua's warning, "Judge not, lest ye be judged," and instead of critical chastisement, regarded the sinner with pity and prayed for the enlightenment of his soul.

Ruth felt a true affection for James. His change of heart led him to accept Philoas, if not as one of God's Elect, than at least as a member of his family. Also, his commitment and devotion to Jeshua was so total and enthusiastic that Ruth forgot her former fears for Jeshua's life, and if any fears at all lingered in her mind, they were soon banished by Jeshua's surprise appearance at the feast of Booths.

The feast was half over when Jeshua appeared in the temple and began to teach. All during the festival the Jews had looked for him, and Jeshua's name had been on every tongue. The controversy which raged over Jeshua had made Ruth smile. Some said he was a good man, a true prophet, while others condemned him for misleading the people, saying he was an agent of Belial. It didn't matter to Ruth what they said, only that they spoke of him. The name "Jeshua of Nazareth" was as well-known in Judea as in Galilee, and God would bring him to his reign without harm.

The chief priests and Pharisees questioned Jeshua's education and were incensed by his reply. "My doctrine is not my own, it comes from Him who sent me." Rumors were rampant that those in authority wished to kill him, and when Jeshua continued to speak in public without interference, the people began to wonder if the authorities had decided that he was indeed the Messiah. Many in the crowd came to believe in him, but many did not, arguing, "We know where this man is from. When the Messiah comes, no one is supposed to know his origins."

Jeshua knew their thoughts and cried out, "So you know me, and you know my origins? The truth is, I have not come of myself. I was sent by One who has the right to send, and Him you do not know. I know Him because it is from Him I come: He sent me."

At this they tried to seize him, but Jeshua seemed to melt away in the crowds. The chief priests and Pharisees became alarmed by Jeshua's following, and sent the temple guards to arrest him, but most of those in the guard were simple men without ambition or lust for power, and Jeshua's message of love and his insistence that he was truly sent from God forestalled them, and they returned empty-handed.

Nicodemus was there when the guard returned, and he tried to assuage the chief priests' anger. He tried to dissuade them in their plan to arrest Jeshua by using their own Law in his defense, but the temple rulers were beyond reason and logic, and taunted Nicodemus until he was forced to hold his counsel.

Ruth and James delighted in Jeshua's verbal victories. No matter who the authorities sent to question him, to trap him and discredit him in front of the crowds, Jeshua emerged victorious. Each time they tried to lay hands on him he eluded them, only to appear again the next day. He was fearless. He spoke with might and power—challenging, accusing, uncompromising. He used the sword of his mouth to slay his enemies. The Spirit of God was upon him; the Son of God had come into his own and no mortal being could stop him.

"I am the light of the world. No follower of mine shall ever walk in darkness; no, he shall possess the light of life. . . . You know neither me nor my Father. If you knew me, you would know my Father too. . . . You belong to what is below, I belong to what is above. You belong to this world, a world which cannot hold me. . . . I solemnly declare it: before Abraham came to be, I AM!"

The Zealots rejoiced. No longer did Jeshua portray himself as a humble shepherd of a lost flock; now he asserted himself! He spoke with authority and assumed command. He left no doubt in anyone's mind that here was a leader without precedence, and the Zealot forces rallied around him.

The Twelve had reunited at his side when he'd first appeared in the temple precincts. His aunts and uncles and cousins, his old friends who had followed him from the beginning, Essenes who had labored to bring this day about, all gathered to cheer his conquests and celebrate his triumphs. The excitement was electrifying. They could speak of nothing else. They returned each evening to their places of abode in exhilarated exhaustion, impatient for morning when the fray would begin again.

Only Jude and Philoas retained a sense of reality. They existed at the outer fringes of the furor in isolated observance, futilely trying to shake off their growing sense of dread and foreboding. It was like watching a tidal wave approach and being impotent to stop it, and having nowhere to run to avoid it. Not that they didn't believe that Jeshua would in the end accomplish all he'd set out to do, but at what price? What would occur before the reign of God became reality on earth?

Philoas could only see riots and war and a death-dealing struggle ahead. The High Priest and his cohorts would fight for their power to the bitter end. And Rome? Rome wouldn't tolerate war for a moment. And what of Jeshua in the meantime? It seemed as though Philoas and Jude were the only ones who heard his warnings.

"I am going away. You will look for me but you will die in your sins. Where I am going you cannot come. . . . I came into this world to divide it, to make the sightless see and the seeing blind. . . . I am the good shepherd. I know my sheep and my sheep know me in the same way that the Father knows me and I know my Father, for these sheep I will give my life. . . . The Father loves me for this; that I lay down my life to take it up again. . . . When you lift up the Son of Man you will come to realize that I AM!"

The term "lift up" settled around Philoas' heart like a shroud of ice. It was a phrase used in connection with crucifixion. Surely Jeshua could not mean— No! That prospect was too horrible to even consider.

When the feast was over, Jeshua withdrew to Bethany to rest under Martha's and Mary's tender ministrations, and to bask in the quiet counsel of his dearest friend, Lazarus. James returned to the City of Salt, no longer confused and unable to meet his colleagues' baffling questions, but assured and confident and full of zeal for the works his brother performed. Most of the Twelve went home to their families, though John ben Zebedee went daily to Bethany to be with the Master.

Jude took Philoas aside. "I'm going home to Capernaum. Someone must tell Mother all that has taken place, and I'd rather it be me than one who would tell it in overblown terms of glory. Somehow I must convey a warning without causing her undue concern."

"That won't be easy, Jude. Your mother is an astute woman. She sees past your words and reads your very heart," Philoas warned.

Jude laughed. "As you well know, brother." Then he sobered. "What of Ruth?"

"Marcus has invited us to remain a while. I'll go to Caesarea, presumably on business with Pontius Pilate, but in truth to ask for recall to Rome. It will take time for my request to reach Tiberius and for his reply to return to Judea. I only hope it comes in time. In any case, I'm determined to get Ruth out of the country before this volcano erupts," Philoas said solemnly.

"Will she go?"

"Yes, if she thinks my duty calls. I'll begin to prepare her for it as soon as I come back from Caesarea."

Jude nodded and turned to go, and then faced Philoas again. His eyes were suddenly anguished and a muscle worked in his jaw. He looked incredibly young, and yet so old. Philoas felt an unaccustomed lump form in his throat and a well of affection fill his breast.

"We part, then," Jude said in a voice close to tears. "Will we ever meet again?"

Philoas felt his Roman reserve crumble. He took a few quick steps forward and hugged Jude tightly to his chest. "In God's time, Jude. In God's time."

Jude sagged for a moment against Philoas and then pushed himself upright, out of Philoas' arms. He grinned, a lopsided, tremulous show of bravado, and said, "Peace be with you, brother."

"And with you," Philoas answered softly, "and with yours." Then Jude turned and fled.

Chapter 36

The cold winter rains came. The land lay fallow, waiting for the break in the overcast sky to herald the bite of the plow and begin anew the cycle of life.

Jerusalem was quiet. Pilate stayed in the more temperate climate on the shores of the Great Sea, while Herod huddled amidst his many braziers in Tiberias. The wealthy abandoned the raw windy city and retired to winter homes in Jericho, which remained a pocket of tropical refuge surrounded by sleet-filled, wind-driven rain. The poor had nowhere to go. They wrapped their shivering bodies in whatever rags they could find, bent their heads to the icy blasts, and went on with the business of staying alive.

Philoas kept his promise to Jude and went to Caesarea where he petitioned for recall to Rome, but by the time his request reached Tiberius, and Caesar's assent returned to Judea, the seas had become high and whipped by the winds. Philoas delayed his departure until the voyage would be less dangerous.

The hush which lay over Jerusalem lulled Philoas' sense of urgency in removing Ruth from Palestine. Jeshua had returned to Jerusalem for the feast of Dedication, a replay of the feast of Booths when his teaching had angered the ruling class to the point of murder. Since then he had withdrawn to the far side of the Jordan River and the controversy over the Nazarene became desultory without new events to fuel its flame.

Ruth was content. She accepted Philoas' recall as a matter of course and made no objection to going to Rome. She spent her days in cheerful tranquility, visiting with Mary and Rhoda, getting to know their children and dreaming of the day when she would have her own. Martha and Nicodemus celebrated the birth of their first child, a son whom they named Theopolus, and Ruth spent hours with Martha learning the proper care of a newborn babe.

The rains abated. The days became warmer and the promise of spring filled the air. Philoas went again to Caesarea to book passage on the first suitable ship sailing for Rome. The feast of Passover loomed ahead, and he hoped to be far at sea by then. Passover was a volatile, unpredictable time at best, and if Jeshua returned and continued teaching in the same bold way he'd done on the last two occasions, there was bound to be trouble. He knew Barrian was uneasy and planned to reinforce the garrison for that week. Their spies among the Zealots reported a heightened sense of excitement moving through their ranks, though as yet they hadn't been able to learn of any definite plan. Philoas pondered the feast with a sense of oppressive doom and hurried back to Jerusalem, anxious to tell Ruth that their plans were laid, only to find that she had gone to Bethany.

Lazarus was ill, critically ill. Mary and Martha had been tending his fever for days, but Lazarus grew steadily worse. Martha had summoned the best physicians in Jerusalem, but their ministrations were of no avail. Lazarus vomited his food and writhed in agony from pain in his back and arms and legs. Mary remembered Ruth's work with Jonas and Susane, and sent a desperate plea for her to come at once.

Philoas barely paused in Jerusalem, but went directly to Bethany where he found Ruth sponging Lazarus' burning body. The room reeked of fever and vomit and the overpowering stench of death. Ruth was oblivious to Philoas' presence until he put his hands on her shoulders and turned her toward him. Her eyes, as they drank in his face, were dark with grief, but without a trace of tears. She laid her head wearily on his breast and clung to him. Then she pushed herself out of his arms.

"I have sent for Jonas," she said quietly.

Philoas pulled the coverlet away from Lazarus' body and saw the red spots on his abdomen. "Better to send for Jeshua," he said grimly. "Do you know where to reach him?"

Ruth had to swallow before she could speak, and her voice was filled with defeat. "Beyond the Jordan. He should be easy to find because of the crowds."

Philoas squeezed her hand. "I'll speak to Martha." He started to leave, but was held by the despair in Ruth's eyes. He took her in his arms again and whispered through her hair. "All will be well, beloved. Lazarus is greatly loved by Jeshua. He'll not allow him to die."

Ruth nodded and tried to smile, but remembered her father who was also greatly loved by Jeshua. "There are times when Jeshua will not interfere with a soul's due release from the flesh," she said falteringly.

Philoas didn't understand what she meant, but said, in an attempt to comfort her, "Then neither must we, my dear."

A servant was sent to find Jeshua, and Jonas arrived with Susane and Cleopas from Capernaum. Lazarus began to vomit blood. His glazed eyes saw nothing and recognized no one. His once healthy, firm flesh seemed to melt away before their eyes, and all of their combined skill could not stay the march of death.

The news of Lazarus' illness reached his friends in the Sanhedrin and every day some came out from Jerusalem to inquire about his progress. The servant returned from across the Jordan, but alone. Jeshua's words upon hearing of Lazarus gave them all a surge of hope. "This sickness is not to end in death; rather it is for God's glory, that through it the Son of God may be glorified." Surely the fever would pass, they thought, but it did not. Lazarus' exhausted, ravaged body gave up the struggle and his soul went to rest in the bosom of Abraham.

Ruth didn't know if their crippling shock was caused by Lazarus' death or by the failure of Jeshua's assurance. Martha and Mary were beyond comfort. Martha's possessive love refused to let Lazarus go, and Mary's grief was fueled by her guilt over the many years of anguish she'd caused her brother. Ulai set aside her long-standing animosity toward Mary and took over the management of Martha's house while Pathoas carried out the mournful task of arranging Lazarus' funeral.

They buried Lazarus in a hillside tomb just outside of Bethany. The hired mourners were more numerous than Ruth had ever seen, and their grief was genuine. Digni-

taries and men of renown from every race trailed behind
the mourners, joined by simple, laboring folk from both
Jerusalem and the surrounding countryside, a living testimony to the charity and compassion of Lazarus ben
Syrus of Bethany. The house overflowed with friends and
family. Letters of condolence arrived from Pontius Pilate
and King Herod, and the High Priest Caiaphas rent his
clothes and poured ashes on his head in an excessive
display of mourning.

Lazarus had lain in his tomb four days when a messenger brought the news that Jeshua was on the road outside
of Bethany. When Martha heard this, she gave a great
cry, and without stopping to tell Mary, ran from the
house to meet him. Ruth ran after her, afraid to let her go
alone in her distraught state. When they reached Jeshua,
Martha fell to the ground at his feet and wailed, "Lord, if
you had been here, my brother would not have died."

Jeshua closed his eyes for a moment when he heard the
accusation in Martha's voice, then bent and raised her to
her feet. "Martha, Martha," he gently chided. "Your
brother will rise again."

"I know he will rise again," Martha replied dully, "in
the resurrection on the last day."

Jeshua sighed, then said, "I am the resurrection and the
life: whoever believes in me, though he should die, will
come to life; and whoever is alive and believes in me will
never die. Do you believe this?"

Martha met his eyes for a long moment and then
straightened her shoulders and said firmly, "Yes, Lord. I
have come to believe that you are the Messiah, the Son of
God, he who is to come into the world." Then she turned
and ran swiftly back to the house to fetch Mary. Ruth
stayed behind with Jeshua and brought him up to date on
all that had passed.

When Martha reached the house she found Mary in the
center of a large group of friends and kinsmen who were
trying to console the weeping girl. She picked her way
through them to Mary's side and whispered, "The Teacher
is here, asking for you."

Mary looked startled and hid her face in her hands for
a moment before rushing from the house at Martha's
heels. Those who had been trying to console her followed,
thinking she must be going to the tomb to weep there.

When they reached Jeshua, Mary did as Martha had done before her, falling at his feet and crying, "Lord, if you had been here my brother would never have died."

Jeshua looked at her with pity, and then at the others—all grief-stricken, their eyes swollen with days of weeping. He singled out those whom he knew and loved—Zebedee and Salome, Cleopas, Susane and Jonas, Marcus and Josie with John Mark standing white-faced and bewildered at their side, Ulai, who couldn't forgive Mary her past sins and couldn't accept Jeshua's teaching, and Lia, whose eyes told him that she relived Roael's death through Lazarus' passing. His own face contorted in a spasm of grief, and he began to weep. Ruth reached out and gripped his arm, suddenly furious that they should cause him such sorrow.

Jeshua wiped his face and said, "Where have you laid him?"

They led him to Lazarus' tomb, and along the way Ruth heard one of the Jewish dignitaries remark, "He opened the eyes of that blind man. Why could he not have done something to stop this man from dying?" She clamped her mouth shut against the scathing retort that rushed to her lips, lest she upset everyone even more. She kept her place at Jeshua's side, seething that these, his friends, should fault him for Lazarus' death. She set her face in a pose of defiance, daring anyone to criticize him again.

They approached the tomb which was a cave hewn into the limestone hillside with a large stone rolled across its mouth. It was the sixth hour. The sun rode high overhead, its faintly warming light falling unobstructed through the leafless branches and glaring against the stark white stone. The air was still. An eerie silence hung over all.

Jeshua was visibly troubled by the site where his dearest friend lay, and again his eyes welled with tears. He turned to some men and said, "Take away the stone."

Martha gasped. "Lord, it has been four days now. Surely there will be a stench!"

"Did I not assure you that if you believed you would see the glory of God displayed?" Jeshua asked.

The men began to roll away the barrier with a painful screech of stone chafing against stone and the clatter of small pebbles scattering at its base. The Jewish dignitaries clustered together, their expressions a mixture of astonishment, reproof, and abject terror. Everyone stumbled back in fear and repulsion. All but Ruth. She stood bravely at Jeshua's side, determined that at least one should show confidence in him. Jeshua gave her a small smile and then prayed, "Father, I thank you for having heard me. I know that you always hear me but I have said this for the sake of the crowd, that they may believe that you sent me."

The stone rolled away. Miraculously there was no stench. Jeshua called loudly, "Lazarus! Come out!"

A sound almost like a moan went up from the onlookers, which changed to a gasp and then a cry of pure wonder. Lazarus came forth from the grave, still bound head to foot in the grave wrappings. Ruth didn't know whether to laugh or cry or simply expire from the unbelievable thing she was witnessing. She hung on Jeshua's arm and stared at the apparition emerging from the cave until she could look no more. She tore her eyes away and searched the crowd for Philoas. She found him standing beside Marcus, his face ashen, shock and disbelief freezing him into immobility as it did those around him. Not a sound was uttered. The eerie silence was oppressive, compressing their fear into an unbearable tension.

Jeshua motioned to James ben Zebedee and Simon Peter. "Untie him and let him go free."

The two hesitated, as though they didn't understand the Master's command, then lurched forward and pulled the grave cloth from Lazarus' face and began to unwind the narrow linen strips.

Lazarus seemed dazed, bewildered, as though he'd suddenly been rudely awakened from a deep sleep. He looked around, puzzled and perplexed until his eyes fell upon Jeshua and he said in a voice that seemed to come from far away, "Rabbi! How come you to be here?"

It was incredible. His question was so like Lazarus, naive, innocent, absurd in light of the enormity which had taken place. Ruth felt a well of laughter building inside of her, part hysteria and part sheer glee. She clung to Jeshua's arm and tried to swallow her mirth, but her body shook with the force of her joy, and when Jeshua smiled at her with a merry twinkle in his eye, she simply exploded in a triumphant peal of laughter.

For a moment there was a shocked gasp at Ruth's outburst, then John ben Zebedee joined her, then John Mark, hopping up and down and clapping his hands like a court clown, then Susane, Ulai, and Zebedee, who roared like thunder, until finally everyone who was near and dear surged forward and surrounded poor bemused Lazarus in a shout of uninhibited joy.

Hands flew to finish unwrapping him, and Martha and Mary fell upon his neck, weeping and touching and assuring themselves that it was real. Ruth let the throng sweep past her and searched out Philoas, who stood aside, shaking his head in disbelief with an imbecilic grin on his face. Ruth threw herself into his arms, exhausted and weak, but happier than she'd ever been in her life.

Martha proclaimed a feast to outdo all feasts. All the women in Bethany came to her aid with Ulai acting as her right hand while her sister Mary, as usual, sat in awe at the feet of the Master. The entire village and all of Lazarus' friends and kinsmen for miles around came to celebrate his release from death. Both Lazarus and Jeshua were feted with more honor than any given to a king, and Nicodemus used the occasion to present Jeshua with the robe Martha had woven.

Jeshua was clearly moved by Martha's gift, and by the fact that Nicodemus presented it. The robe was beautiful, woven of the finest wool, all of one piece with the selvage woven around the neck as well as upon the edge. It was a soft, luxurious, pearl gray, without a belt for the usual pomegranates sewn onto the fabric; instead, the Thummin and Urim were woven into the selvage about the hem. There were no jewels or threads of gold, nor any other color to mar the simple line and richness of the cloth. Jeshua took the robe from Nicodemus' hands and eased it over his head with loving care. The silken folds fell to his ankles and molded itself to his body. The translucent, shimmering gray accentuated the red and gold in Jeshua's hair and beard, transforming the simple shepherd into a King of Kings.

Ruth stood in the doorway and watched Jeshua don the robe. She had seen it often, had caressed its richness and marvelled over the painstaking workmanship Martha put into its creation, but the robe's true beauty had not been revealed until it clothed the one for whom it was made. Jeshua was magnificent!

The impact of Jeshua's splendor made Ruth stagger, and tears shot to her eyes. She was suddenly lonely, desolate. Who was this man whom she called "brother"? He was not of this earth, nor of this time, nor of this place. In that moment he seemed to move away from her, to grow and expand until he was no longer her brother Jeshua, son of Joseph and Mary of Nazareth, but a universal spirit of brotherhood to all men. Jeshua would march on to his glory, while she would remain as she was, and nothing would be the same again.

Ruth turned and stumbled from the house, no longer able to bear the sight of Jeshua's grandeur. She had lost him. Somehow in those few moments she had lost her intimacy with her beloved elder brother, had released him unto the world, and she was bereft to the depths of her soul. She wept until her tears were spent. She moved through the rest of the days of the feast floating over the surface like a casual observer and feeling no part of it.

She listened to Ulai confirm her belief in Jeshua, and watched that faith manifest itself in her total acceptance of Mary, whom she'd ostracized for so long. She said all the right words in reply to Ulai's new-found convictions, but felt no emotion whatever.

She heard the reports on a meeting of the Sanhedrin, and of how the priests and Pharisees feared Jeshua's raising of Lazarus would bring the whole world to follow him, an event which would cause the Romans to destroy the temple, and possibly the whole nation. She felt nothing when she heard how Caiaphas argued for Jeshua's death, saying it was better for one man to die than for the whole nation to be destroyed. There was even talk that they plotted to kill Lazarus, for his miraculous return from the jaws of death caused many to believe in Jeshua. None of it touched her. He who could raise the dead to life had nothing to fear from men such as those.

But the rumors affected the others. The Twelve feared for Jeshua's life. Precautions were taken to protect Lazarus, and Zebedee counselled Jeshua to retire from the area until things cooled down. Jeshua gave in to the pressure from his friends to flee the wrath of the temple authorities and made plans to withdraw to a small town in the desert of Samaria where he knew he would be welcomed.

The hilarity and celebration were over. All who remained were Jeshua's kinsmen and most trusted friends. Everyone was subdued. The threat of the unbelieving Pharisees and elders was foremost in every mind, and their anxiety was a tangible reality.

Jeshua and the Twelve made ready to leave. He wore the robe which Martha had made for him, moving from one beloved to another with quiet dignity and serene assurance, putting Philoas in mind of a king reviewing his troops before the last great battle, instilling them with confidence and strength to endure the tribulations they soon would face.

Ruth hung back until the last to bid Jeshua good-bye. For the first time in her life she didn't know how to approach him or what to say to him. This Jeshua was a stranger to her. Her humble, tender, loving brother seemed to have vanished, leaving this incomprehensible, inscrutable, godlike presence in his stead. When at last he stood before her, she was unable to meet his eyes, but only mumbled an awkward, halting farewell as an intolerable pain filled the void in her soul.

Jeshua said nothing, then turned and bid the others to leave them. When they had gone he led Ruth to a low divan and sat next to her, his voice gentle and soothing. "You are greatly troubled, my sister. I have known this for days. Can you not open your heart to me? Am I not your elder brother?"

Ruth trembled and worked to control her anguish, but she failed and blurted her confession in a heartbreaking, desolate cry. "But I don't know you anymore! You are lost to me and I know not where to find you!"

Ruth's control suddenly dissolved and she wept with wild abandon. Jeshua drew her into his arms and rocked her against his breast as though she were a child again.

"Did I not once promise that I would be with you always?" he chided. "I keep my promises as the Father who is in me keeps His. You do know me, you have known me from the beginning, as I have known and loved you. Though earth and seas and the veil of heaven separate us, I am with you. You need only call and I shall answer. I shall not leave you desolate, either in this world or in the next. Dry your tears. Let my peace replace your doubts, and believe in me, for I shall never fail you."

Ruth's sobs subsided. She rested awhile against Jeshua's breast, letting his peace fill her heart and soul. She pushed herself gently out of his arms and smiled, her eyes meeting his with candor and faith. "Forgive me my lack of trust."

"Your trust was not lacking, only forgotten. Never fail to call it to mind when your life seems fraught with trials too heavy to bear. Keep your faith in me and in the Father, and bear witness of that faith to all you may encounter that they too may be blest as you are blest, loved as you are loved, even when you despair."

The setting sun cast long shadows over the room. It was time for Jeshua to go. Ruth brushed his cheek with the back of her hand and said, "You go to Ephraim and I to Rome. Will we ever meet again?"

A shadow of sadness crossed Jeshua's face. His eyes looked far into the future and his answer was spoken with quiet finality. "Yes. We shall meet again, sooner than you may think. Greet our mother for me, and tell Jude—" Jeshua paused and sighed. "No. I shall wait and tell him myself. Take care of our younger brother. He will need your strength and faith in the days to come, as will many. Remember this hour with me and draw upon it to comfort our loved ones."

Jeshua rose and pulled Ruth to her feet, giving her a final embrace. "Peace be with you, sister mine."

"And with you" Ruth whispered in reply.

Jeshua and the Twelve left at twilight, when all the land lay beneath a lavender velvet sky. The moon remained hidden and only the stars lit their way as they quit Judea like thieves in the night.

Ruth and Philoas went back to Jerusalem only long enough to pack their belongings and leave for Capernaum. Their ship was due to arrive at the port of Caesarea in a matter of weeks, and Ruth wanted to go home for a time before they sailed. They stayed in Capernaum as long as they could, then took the route to Caesarea over Mt. Carmel, where they bid farewell to Justin and Judith.

The morning they sailed was glorious. The Great Sea rippled impatiently beneath the ship and the sails flapped merrily in the breeze. The sun rode above and warmed Ruth's back as Philoas' smile warmed her heart. The great ship groaned and turned its bow toward Tyre and Sidon, as Jeshua left the village of Ephraim and turned his face toward Jerusalem.

PART III
THE
REMNANT

Chapter 37

The approach of Passover was always a time of tension and strain in the Holy City. Pilgrims from all over the known world began infiltrating the city weeks before the actual feast day, burgeoning Jerusalem's normal population of twenty-five thousand souls fivefold. Every rooftop and spare room, any mean filthy space which could accommodate a sleeping body was occupied, while a sea of tents ringed the outer walls. Greedy inkeepers rubbed their palms in glee, knowing they could demand double and even triple the usual rate for sleeping space and a glass of sour wine.

Prices went up all over the city. Merchants from every land, Jew and Gentile alike, flocked to Jerusalem with exotic wares that they sold at exorbitant prices. Housewives were forced to pay far over the usual amount for a simple wedge of cheese, and the lowly fish became a precious morsel. Even the priests took advantage of the necessity of buying the sacrificial animals, and raised their prices accordingly; nothing gave more pleasure to a Sadducean ear than the musical ring of silver flowing into their coffers. Every incoming Jew was required to spend a tenth of his income after taxes in Jerusalem, a law which to his dismay he found only too easy to fulfill.

Every Jewish household, from the magnificent Hasmonean Palace to the meanest hovel in the valley of the cheesemakers, was a frenzy of activity. Every house had to be scrubbed and polished from top to bottom, special foods had to be bought and prepared according to precise instructions set down by the Law, and the family's clothing was laundered and mended and refurbished. Children, bewildered by all the confusion, plagued their mothers with quarrels and whining demands until the already-distraught women were reduced to boxing ears and snapping unjustly in a futile attempt to keep them out from underfoot. Their husbands added to the pressures by grumbling over the money spent and complaining about the chaos in their normally serene households.

The volatile nature of any major feast was evident throughout the entire city. The streets were a mixture of every race and creed and walk of life. Thieves and pickpockets and prostitutes abounded. Oily, unscrupulous confidence men bilked the unwary with schemes which promised easy wealth, while gamblers and drug sellers pocketed whatever they had left. Political factions used the feast as an occasion to expound their cause and recruit new members.

Droves of cattle and sheep, donkeys laden with little wooden cages of doves and pigeons wound their way over the dusty twisting roads to Jerusalem, and crowded the gates to the city, adding their bawling complaints to the already deafening din. The stench of dung and animal fear mingled with that of garlic and onions and sickening sweet incense, of unwashed bodies and yellow dust which clung to one's clothes and seeped through every nook and cranny until there was no escape from the nauseating, cloying odor of Passover week.

Roman soldiers patrolled the streets in force, cracking heads and shouting orders. Barrian had carried through his plan to bring in extra patrols for the feast, and nearly a thousand soldiers were stationed in the Fortress Antonia. The might of Rome was obvious in every section of the city. Golden helmets flashed in the sun as soldiers, surrounding the walls of the temple courts, marched through the streets and alleys, guarding the gates and city battlements, an affront to every Jewish eye.

The temple itself was mass confusion. Every priest and Levite was required by the Law to participate in feast-day activities—a total of almost eighteen thousand men whose duties ranged from killing the sacrificial animals to sweeping the courts. The High Priest Caiaphas was hard pressed to organize this vast number of underlings, and relied heavily upon the help of his father-in-law, the powerful old Annas, and on his trustworthy Captain of the Temple.

The courts were flooded with pilgrims standing in awe before the splendor of Herod's gold-sheathed, marble temple, making it nearly impossible for Caiaphas to organize his stupendous display of pomp and ceremony. He privately cursed them for their provincial manners and ignorance, and ordered the Captain to force them to make way, while publicly he assumed a pose of smiling, reverent benevolence. He was beleaguered on every side with decisions to be made and requests to be fulfilled, with social amenities to dispense and political concessions and compromises to be made. Above all, he had to deal with the possibility that Jeshua of Nazareth would attend the feast of Passover.

Ever since Lazarus ben Syrus had been seemingly "raised from the dead," the number of men among the elders, priesthood, and elite business and social circles who professed a belief in that Galilean charlatan had grown. Caiaphas expected the ignorant, unwashed rabble to be taken in by such an obvious feat of chicanery, but he was alarmed that so many thinking, intelligent leaders of the Jewish community could be duped. Even the revered Gamaliel counselled caution and a "wait and see" attitude. Caiaphas had used brilliant argument to prove the whole affair a scheming plot. He'd drawn an elaborate scenario of how Lazarus had faked his illness, and of how the tomb could be provisioned with airways and stocked with enough food and drink to keep a man alive for four days. Did not the Galileans bring in one of their own physicians from Capernaum to tend the so-called "dying man"? And why did the Nazarene wait so long before coming to Lazarus' aid? If he was as great a friend as all professed, why didn't he come immediately to Bethany? Instead he had waited until he was sure that Lazarus was in his tomb and then appeared to work his "miracle"!

The sheer force of Caiaphas' anger and the power of his office had silenced any open approval of the miracle worker, but it was easy for Caiaphas to see that his argument fell on deaf ears and many were still not convinced that the man was a fraud. Men believed only what they wanted to believe, regardless of truth. Caiaphas believed that Jeshua was dangerous, that if he were allowed to continue to preach that he was the "Son of God," as he'd done in the past, he'd cause the downfall of the temple hierarchy and of the entire nation! The man was notorious for his disregard of the Law, and without the Law, what was a Jew? Nothing! The Sons of Abraham would melt into the conglomerate Gentile world, and Jews as a race and a nation would become nonexistent! The only way to wipe this heresy from the face of the earth was to extinguish its guiding light. But how?

To quietly assassinate the fool was clearly impossible; he was too well-protected, unless, of course, the assassin would be one of his own. So far, however, everyone close to the Nazarene was fanatically devoted to him. They'd already tried public arrest, but that had caused such a clamor among the rabble who clung to his coattails that the attempts had to be abandoned. They'd provoked a public outcry against him, and incited the crowds to the point of stoning him, but the man had an uncanny way of melting into the throngs and simply disappearing.

The only way Caiaphas could see was to take the man unawares and to try him quickly and quietly before a quorum of trusted, reliable members of the Sanhedrin and be done with it before the masses knew what happened. Secrecy and careful planning would be of the utmost importance, but Caiaphas had full confidence in his ability to pull off such a coup. The only fly in the ointment was a need for inside information as to the Nazarene's movements, but that didn't worry him unduly. Every man had his price, and all Caiaphas had to learn was who and how much. Annas had an excellent collection of spies, and at this very moment they were watching and listening all over Judea. It was only a matter of time before they would name his man.

Once the Nazarene was convicted of blasphemy, for blasphemy would be the easiest charge to prove by his own ridiculous claim to being the "Son of God," it was a simple matter to persuade Pilate to condemn him to death on some trumped-up charge. Pilate owed them a favor. If it hadn't been for Caiaphas and his Sadduccean friends, Pilate would never have got his precious aqueduct through temple funds without a riot on his hands.

The only thing that really worried Caiaphas was the element of time. He simply had to know the name of his betrayer before the feast began, and time was growing short. With each passing day Caiaphas became more uneasy and apprehensive. His usual temple duties seemed unimportant in light of the problem before him, for he truly believed he was saving the Jews from destruction. He grew testy and short-tempered, and his irascible mood flared to a malevolent rage when Roman law forced him to go begging to the Fortress Antonia for his ceremonial robes. Six days before Passover, he learned that Jeshua ben Joseph of Nazareth was in Bethany.

All of Jerusalem had been buzzing with speculation as to whether or not the Nazarene would attend the Passover festivities, and word of his arrival in Bethany spread through the city like wildfire. With dismay Caiaphas and his friends watched the exodus of pilgrims flooding the road toward Bethany. Pharisees, priests, elders, and scribes watched with him, and fear leaped from one to another until it became a living entity, clouding their vision and distorting their reason. It seemed they watched the abandonment of David's Holy City, the beginning of the end of traditional Jewry, and thus the end of the unique Jewish nation.

Caiaphas stood at the top floor of the sanctuary with all of Jerusalem and the surrounding countryside spread out at his feet before him. His eyes swept the length and breadth of the city, seeing the flash of golden helmets on every street and atop every wall. He shuddered and groaned aloud in despair. He loved the city over which he held such tenuous control, and it seemed as though her enemies were pressing in from every side. His spies reported that an inordinate number of known Zealots were converging upon Jerusalem, and who knew how many more who were not known? If they proclaimed the Nazarene king, the rabble was sure to follow, and the result would be riot and guerrilla warfare, and the streets of Jerusalem would run red with blood. One man stood between the life or destruction of the Sons of Abraham, and he, Caiaphas, had never felt more alone or helpless. Caiaphas would never know that at that same moment another shared his depth of loneliness, one surrounded by his friends and cheered by the crowds who pressed without the garden gates, but who walked the path of destiny alone.

Jeshua had been alone from the time he left the gates of Ephraim and began the long, arduous climb toward Jerusalem. For weeks his followers had disputed the wisdom of his coming to Jerusalem. The Galileans feared the city and the men who ruled there, arguing that they would take Jeshua and kill him, while the Judeans scoffed at such an idea and declared they wouldn't dare, and if they did, what of it! Didn't the Master have the power to call upon the very angels of heaven to come to his aid? Who could touch the Son of God?

Jeshua knew. For thirty years he had studied the Scriptures. He knew who he was and why he had come, and the Scriptures pointed the way. At each step in his life, Jeshua had watched an invisible curtain rise, revealing a stage properly set for the next event foretold by the ancients, and now the last curtain had risen. The Sons of Belial had entered into places of authority; Rome was poised as the instrument to be used for their destruction, the forces of fear and oppression had spurred the masses to murderous rage, and all that remained was for the Son to make his fateful entry into Jerusalem and set the wheels of destiny into motion. As Adam he had failed in his mission to bring the souls back to their Father-Creator; as Jeshua he must not fail again, or the race of men was lost. He tried to make his followers understand. He told them all that would come to pass, but they didn't hear, they didn't understand, and Jeshua set out to meet that which had been his undoing in the beginning, alone.

In Bethany, Martha prepared a grand feast which all his friends and family attended, while the crowds from Jerusalem ranged outside, clamoring for just a glimpse of the wonder worker who raised the dead to life. It was a joyful day, the first time many had seen Jeshua for weeks. They sang and laughed and spoke of happy times and loving friends, while Martha served and Mary listened, and Lazarus watched in worshipful silence. Zebedee's boisterous laugh bounced off the walls, and John Mark walked straight and sure.

When the meal was over and the tables cleared, they all lay back upon the couches, replete with food and fellowship and lazily content with wine. Mary of Syrus slipped out of the room and returned with a jar of costly perfume made from genuine aromatic nard, with which she anointed Jeshua's feet, afterward drying them with her hair. The house was filled with the ointment's fragrance, and the company watched with amused approval.

Judas Iscariot was not amused, nor did he approve. He was nervous and impatient. He felt the banquet a waste of time. Tomorrow they would go to Jerusalem and plans should be made, allies alerted, arms procured and distributed in case they found a fight on their hands. But the Master seemed oblivious to any such need. He made no plans. He gave no instructions. He spoke in symbols and veiled language which no one understood, but with a fatalism unfitting for a king. Now he allowed a former prostitute to waste the precious nard by pouring it over his feet and wiping them with her wanton red hair. It was more than Judas could bear.

"Why was not this perfume sold?" he asked testily. "It could have brought three hundred silver pieces and the money have been given to the poor."

"Leave her alone," Jeshua replied. "Let her keep it against the day they prepare me for burial. The poor you always have with you, but me you will not always have."

Judas stung from Jeshua's mild rebuke. Again he spoke of death! Would he never assert himself? If the Master would do nothing to proclaim himself king, then others would do it for him! The seed of a plan took root in Judas' mind, prodded and nurtured by Belial himself, as Jeshua knew it would, and that night when everyone slept, Judas slipped away to the house of Caiaphas, unwittingly answering the High Priest's prayer for the name of Jeshua's betrayer.

As Judas gained entrance through the shadowed service door to Caiaphas' palace, another man approached a small, shabby inn on the road beyond Bethany. It was late and the door was closed and barred for the night, but a faint light still glowed in the window. He rapped on the door with a huge fist and listened for the sound of movement from inside. After a moment a female voice called hoarsely through the thick planks, "Go away! I have no room."

He smiled and called back, "It is I, Sara, Bartaemus! Let me in, for I have news."

The heavy bar screeched in protest at being disturbed so late, then the door swung open and the light spilled out over the threshold. Sara stepped back and Bartaemus ducked his head beneath the low doorway and quickly entered, closing and barring the door behind him. He was a huge man, towering over the tiny Sara, barrel-chested, with bulging muscular arms which ended in great, hammerlike fists. He wore no shirt, only a leather vest laced with thongs that strained across his mammoth black-furred chest and failed to hide the pocklike scars left by bits of molten metal flying from his forge. His black hair was long and ill-cut, his beard full and shaggy. He was a frightening, awesome brute until you saw his eyes. They were black also, but sparkled with merriment and glowed with love. His smile was gentle and compassionate, and his voice rumbled from his massive body like thunder sounding far away.

His eyes inspected the state of the inn, which was cluttered and poor, littered with unwashed, ragged scraps of humanity who snored in every corner and sprawled on every bench. His nose wrinkled at the stench of sawdust and sweat, yesterday's fish, and cheap sour wine. Sara motioned for him to follow, and led him through the tangled mass of bodies to a tiny nook curtained off from the rest of the room. A straw mat, smelling of mold and dusty chaff, lay in one corner, covered by a tattered, faded coverlet. A few pegs protruded from the wall supporting Sara's meager wardrobe, and the only piece of furniture was a rickety bench that served her as a table.

Sara set the sputtering oil lamp down upon the bench and poured a thin vinegary wine from a sticky flask into two chipped earthenware cups. She handed one to Bartaemus and said crossly, "What news is so important that you disturb an old woman in the dead of night?"

Bartaemus took the cup and said chidingly, "Sara! You are not old," but his tongue belied his eyes. Sara looked old. Her graying hair escaped the makeshift knot at the nape of her neck and fell in straggling wisps around her face, a face lined and careworn, with eyes dull with poverty and hopelessness. Her nails were cracked and blackened, and her rough chapped hands were embedded with grime from years of labor. She wore a long black skirt, faded and stained, with the hem hanging down and sometimes catching at her heel as she walked. Her shirt was gray with age and had been many times patched and mended. Her feet were bare, thickly calloused, and splayed from never knowing a shoe. She was thin to the point of being emaciated, and her clothes hung limp and tired upon her shapeless body. Bartaemus knew that Sara was not yet fifty, but her appearance didn't startle him, for most of the women he knew looked the same, old and spent before their time.

"I come from Bethany. The Master is there," said Bartaemus.

Sara's head jerked up to look into Bartaemus' face. For a fleeting moment, the despair left her eyes and they shone with hope. "He goes to Jerusalem, to the feast," she said eagerly. Then the desolation returned and she added dully, "He'll not pass this way."

"Then you must go to him!" Bartaemus urged.

Sara tiredly brushed her eyes with the back of her hand and shook her head.

"Why not?" Bartaemus demanded. "All these years you've waited for the Messiah to pass this way, but never would you invite him. Once again he is so near, why can't you go to him? You must go, Sara! You were there at the beginning, now we will make him king and you must be there at the end!"

Sara turned on him in anger. "How could I invite him to this!" she cried as she waved her arm to encompass the room. "Does one invite the King of Kings to enter a filthy hovel? Go to him, you say! In this?" She tore at her worn dress and a sob escaped her throat.

Pity welled in Bartaemus' breast. "Sara, Sara. Do you think the Master cares for the clothes upon your back, or for the house you live in? You've told me yourself he was born in a stable, a lowly cave! What did he see on the road outside of Jericho, a blind, filthy beggar or a man entrapped in darkness whose soul was flooded with faith? I *see*, Sara. 'Your faith has healed you,' he said, and I could see!"

Bartaemus saw Sara's anger fade and her resolve begin to waver. He pressed on in a more gentle tone. "Tell me how you held him as a babe."

"I've told you before, many times," Sara said wearily.

"Tell me again, for I never tire of the tale."

Sara hesitated, then began. At first her voice faltered and her words came short and disjointed, but soon she became caught up in her own tale and she spoke with strength and wonder. She told of the Essenes, and of her father's involvement with that outcast sect, of the census ordered, and of Mary's journey to Bethlehem where her own father, Apsafar, owned the inn. She described the danger and need for secrecy, and of how they prepared the cave for Mary's protection. She described that night with the rabble and the Romans, and then the star. Memory banished the age from her face and Bartaemus saw the beauty that once was there.

"I held him in my arms. I kissed his silky brow. I cannot describe the love I felt, the joy! I knew I held the Messiah, the Holy One sent by God. Even though he was such a babe, he looked at me and knew me! After they killed my father, I came to this place where I could hear of him and perhaps see him pass by, but he has never passed this way."

"Why did you never marry, Sara?" Bartaemus asked softly.

Sara shrugged her shoulders. "I could have. A young man who worked at the census that year wished to marry me, but I couldn't commit my life to a husband and children after holding that babe in my arms. I had to be free, to hear, to follow." She pushed back the curtain and looked out into the shadowed, dingy inn. "Instead I shackled myself to this!" she said ruefully.

The oil lamp sputtered and went out. The silence was as deep as the darkness. Then Sara's voice rang out, sure and strong and full of conviction. "I will go. I will see him again. I will see the Promise fulfilled!"

Chapter 38

Martha arose before dawn, prodding her sleep-drugged servants awake to prepare for the day ahead. She'd spent a restless night, often waking to the sounds of movement throughout the house, knowing her mind was not the only one which refused to sleep, but chose instead to speculate on the coming day and the events that it would bring. Footsteps on the graveled walk in the courtyard had drawn her from her bed to the window. A lone figure passed from shadow to silver moonlight, his pearl-gray coat a vaporous outline in the murky predawn, quietly gliding through the outer gate and following the path which led up the Mount of Olives. She knew Jeshua had gone alone to pray, and she kept vigil at the window, waiting for his return, wondering what lay in his heart and mind. An infinite sadness had suddenly brought tears stinging to her eyes. She prayed for Jeshua, a prayer of feeling without words, for she didn't know what she should ask for him. She thought about his birth, and the years of study and discipline which had prepared him for this day. She swallowed at the lump in her throat when she remembered the sorrows and slanders and terrible frustrations Jeshua had endured, for no one truly understood his mission, not herself, nor even Lazarus, whom Jeshua had rescued from the grave. No one, except perhaps his mother, and she was in Capernaum, too far away to give him comfort now. An idea bloomed in Martha's practical mind. She impatiently brushed the unfamiliar tears from her cheeks and hurriedly dressed. Action was needed, not maudlin sentimentality.

As soon as the servants were up and about their tasks, Martha slipped unnoticed from the house, and with rapid, purposeful strides, made her way to Ulai's. Ulai's eager face met her at the gate and bid her enter, her own house already alive with sounds of bustling preparation. "Has the Master awakened yet?" she asked.

Martha brushed the question aside. Jeshua's lonely sojourn to the Mount of Olives seemed somehow too intimate to divulge. "Mary should be here," she replied instead. "A mother should see her son crowned king. I thought that Pathaos could send someone to Capernaum, someone who could travel quickly and bring her back in time for Passover."

"Of course!" Ulai cried. "We should have thought of that before." Her brows knit and she said thoughtfully, "Mary will hesitate to come away with strangers. You know how she shuns any public display. It may take some persuasion to convince her to come at all. We'll go ourselves, Pathaos and I. We can leave within the hour."

Martha nodded her approval. "I leave it to you, then."

The sky was streaked with pink and lavender when Martha walked back to her own house. The air was warm, alive with the promise of spring, and charged with expectant excitement. Her neighbors called a cheery greeting which Martha answered with a curt nod of her head. She walked with stern, purposeful strides, her hands encased across her waist in the wide sleeves of her mantle. She held her body erect, her eyes straight ahead, pretending not to notice the smell of honey cakes and coarse, dark bread that emitted from their ovens so early in the morning. She deplored the fact that the villagers took advantage of Jeshua's presence by selling food and drink to the many who came out to see him. On the other hand, they had to be fed, and Martha was glad that she didn't have to do it, but it didn't seem moral to make a profit from the appearance of the Messiah.

She reached her gate where her guests were gathering one by one at the huge water jars to perform the ritual washing and intone the morning prayers. Her house was a babble of voices. The harsh, quarrelling tones of her servants mingled with the high, excited voices of her guests, who called morning greetings to one another and clustered in groups to speculate on the day. She bestowed her meager smile on all who greeted her, but her eyes searched for Mary, who obviously still lay abed. She pushed aside the short flash of irritation she felt, and rationalized her sister's lack of concern for all the chores to be performed by reminding herself that Mary was like their father and Lazarus, other-worldly and intellectual, completely unaware of the practical side of life. Martha sighed and silently chided herself for her momentary lapse of charity, but at the same time wondered how she would manage by herself, and for a moment regretted having sent Ulai off to Capernaum.

By mid-morning tiny Bethany was swollen with pilgrims who clamored outside Martha's gate for a glimpse of the miracle worker. Sara and Bartaemus mingled in the crowd, Sara in such a state of nerves that she could not stand still but wrung her hands and paced back and forth, torn between her overwhelming desire to see the child she had once held in her arms and who had now grown to manhood, and her fear and shame of being recognized by any of the Elect. As the hours dragged on, the crowd became impatient. They called for Jeshua to come out until their cries became a chanted litany, and Martha feared that the gate would fail to withstand the strain of pressing, eager bodies. The sun was nearly at its zenith when a great cheer rose up from the crowd and Jeshua appeared at the gate. The Twelve quickly formed a protective circle around him, forcing the throng to make way. They pressed back to let him pass, then fell in behind, a mammoth, snakelike parade, winding its way toward Jerusalem.

The crowds running alongside and ahead slowed the column to a snail's pace. Just outside of Bethpage, Jeshua sent two disciples ahead, telling them they would find a young donkey, and that they should untie it and bring it back. "If anyone says to you, 'Why are you doing that?' say, 'The Master needs it, but he will send it back at once.'"

They found the colt just where Jeshua had said they would, and soon returned. Clearly the colt had never been broken. It bucked and balked and fought all efforts to restrain it. Simon Peter tried to subdue the beast by twisting its tail, and received a swift kick in the shins for his trouble. The crowd was delighted and roared with laughter as a red-faced Simon growled, "Master, you will never be able to seat this contrary beast."

Jeshua joined with the crowd in their glee and then took the bridle from a disciple's hand and began to stroke the colt's muzzle. "There, friend. No need to be frightened. I have need of you this day. One of your kind bore me in the beginning, and now you are chosen to bear me to the ending."

The colt quieted. His ears pricked forward as he listened to Jeshua's tender voice, and then lowered his head in submission. He stood docilely while two disciples threw their cloaks across his back, and never shied when Jeshua mounted. He turned his head once as though to assure himself that it was indeed the Master who sat on his back, and then obediently trotted down the road.

As they began to descend the Mount of Olives, they encountered more and more Jews who had heard the Master was coming and had come out to meet him. Some had brought palm branches which they strewed on the path before him while others pulled reeds from the fields, and some even used their cloaks as a carpet for the Master to tread upon. They sang triumphantly, their hymn resounding across the hills and echoing through the valleys. "Hosanna to the Son of David! Blessed is he who comes in the name of the Lord! Hosanna in the highest!"

Some of the Pharisees in the crowd said to Jeshua, "Teacher, rebuke your disciples," but Jeshua replied, "If they were to keep silence, I tell you the very stones would cry out."

When they came within sight of the city, Jeshua suddenly reined in the colt and sat motionless, staring at the golden splendor before him. A spasm of grief swept over his face and he began to weep. "Jerusalem, Jerusalem!" he moaned. "If only you had known the path to peace this day; but you have completely lost it from view! Days will come upon you when your enemies encircle you with a rampart, hem you in, and press you hard from every side. They will wipe you out, you and your children within your walls, and leave not a stone on a stone within you, because you failed to recognize the time of your visitation."

The crowd was silenced by the Master's suffering. They were bewildered by his words and disturbed by the depth of his grief, not knowing what caused him such pain.

They were relieved when he collected himself and urged the colt forward again.

Caiaphas and his cohorts watched from the high sanctuary porch as the procession approached the golden gate. One of the priests remarked, "See, there is nothing you can do! The whole world has run after him!" The others looked to Caiaphas, wondering what he would say to this, but Caiaphas, remembering his visitor late the past night, only smiled and said nothing.

It was late afternoon by the time Jeshua entered the temple precincts. He walked slowly through the Court of Gentiles and then paused, listening for a moment in the Court of Israel. Because of the late hour, Jeshua decided to go back to Bethany to rest for the night and return to the temple early the next day. As he made his way again through the Court of Gentiles, Philip and Andrew approached him and said some Greeks would like to speak with him.

Jeshua pondered the request for a moment and then shook his head. "The hour has come for the Son of Man to be glorified. I solemnly assure you, unless the grain of wheat falls to the earth and dies, it remains just a grain of wheat. But if it dies, it produces much fruit. The man who loves his life loses it, while the man who hates his life in this world preserves it to life eternal. If anyone would serve me, let him follow me, him the Father will honor. My soul is troubled now, yet what should I say, Father, save me from this hour? But it was for this that I came to this hour. Father, glorify your name!"

Then a voice came from the sky: "I have glorified it, and will glorify it again."

When the crowd of bystanders heard the voice they said it was thunder. Others maintained an angel was speaking to him. Jeshua said to them, "That voice did not come for my sake, but for yours. Now has judgment come upon this world, now will this world's prince be driven out, and I, once I am lifted up from earth, will draw all men to myself."

The crowd objected. "We have heard it said in the law that the Messiah is to remain forever. How can you claim that the Son of Man must be lifted up? Just who is this 'Son of Man'?"

Jeshua replied, "The light is among you only a little longer. Walk while you still have it or darkness will come over you. The man who walks in the dark does not know where he is going. While you have the light, keep faith in the light; thus you will become sons of light."

The crowd began to murmur among themselves and Jeshua took the opportunity to slip away unheeded and returned to Bethany.

Chapter 39

I t was very early when Jeshua entered the temple the
next morning. The merchants and money-changers
were setting up their booths, and the sheep and cattle
and turtledoves all clamored for their morning meal. Few
worshippers appeared at such an early hour, but nevertheless the courts were crowded with workmen and priests
and Levites, all hurrying to complete their preparations for
the busy day ahead. Jeshua walked among them in silence,
the expression on his face clearly mirroring his disgust for
the carnival-like show being displayed in the House of
God.

Caiaphas watched from the sanctuary porch. "The
troublemaker is early," he said musingly. He turned to
one of his chief aides and said, "Are you sure of all your
witnesses?"

The aide nodded. "They will be here. I paid them well."

Caiaphas smiled. "And our new-found friend?"

"He was more expensive. Thirty pieces of silver, but
well worth the price. He demurred accepting payment for
his services, but only for a moment, then mouthed some
nonsense about using it for the poor."

Caiaphas laughed. "I've heard our friend is quite
wealthy. I'm surprised to hear he is in such straits." He
turned his attention back to the courts below. "Today the
Nazarene will be hard pressed to answer our questions
without committing blasphemy. The council will have no
choice but to condemn him."

"Will Pilate cooperate?" asked the aide.

"He has no choice. He needs us as we need him."
Caiaphas pointed his finger at Jeshua. "Look. Already the
rabble gather around him. Collect our questioners and
witnesses and let the battle begin."

Jeshua was teaching in the Court of Gentiles, using parables which the common folk loved so much. Caiaphas' Sadducean priests and elders waited until Jeshua finished a story of two sons, then asked, "On what authority are you doing these things? Who has given you this power?"

Jeshua answered, "I too will ask a question. If you answer it for me, then I will tell you on what authority I do the things I do. What was the origin of John's baptism? Was it divine or merely human?"

The Sadducees conferred among themselves. "If we say 'divine,' he will ask us, 'Then why did you not put faith in it?' while if we say 'merely human,' we shall have reason to fear the people, who all regard John as a prophet." They answered Jeshua, "We do not know."

Jeshua said in turn, "Then neither will I tell you on what authority I do the things I do."

A Herodian sympathizer entered into the fray, hoping to trap Jeshua on a civil law. "Teacher, we know you are a truthful man and teach God's way sincerely. You court no one's favor and do not act out of human respect. Give us your opinion, then, in this case. Is it lawful to pay tax to the emperor or not?"

Jeshua recognized the trap and said, "Why are you trying to trip me up, you hypocrites? Show me the coin used for the tax." When they handed him a small Roman coin, he asked them, "Whose head is this, and whose inscription?"

"Ceasar's," they replied.

"Then give to Caesar what is Caesar's, but give to God what is God's."

The Sadducees were momentarily nonplussed by Jeshua's refusal to be trapped, then posed a question on the long-standing, volatile debate over resurrection. "Teacher, Moses declared, 'If a man dies without children, his brother must take the wife and produce offspring for his brother.' Once there were seven brothers. The eldest died after marrying, and since he had no children, left his wife to his brother. The same thing happened to the second, the third, and so on, down to the seventh. Last of all the woman died too. At the resurrection, whose wife will she be, since all seven of them married her?"

Jeshua said, "You are badly misled because you fail to understand the Scriptures and the power of God. When people rise from the dead, they neither marry nor are given in marriage, but live like angels in heaven. As to the fact that the dead are raised, have you not read what God said to you, 'I am the God of Abraham, the God of Isaac, the God of Jacob'? He is the God of the living, not of the dead!"

Some Pharisees in the throng were delighted by Jeshua's answer, for, unlike the disbelieving Sadducees, they held to the truth of resurrection. They enjoyed seeing their pompous opponents silenced for once, and one of their members, a lawyer, sought to cap the victory by tripping up the wily Nazarene himself.

"Teacher, which commandment of the Law is the greatest?" he asked confidently.

Jeshua said to him, " 'You shall love the Lord your God with your whole heart, with your whole soul, and with your whole mind.' This is the greatest and first commandment. The second is like it: 'You shall love your neighbor as yourself.' On these two commandments the whole Law is based, and the prophets as well."

Then, using their own tactics against them, Jeshua put a question to the assembled Pharisees. "What is your opinion about the Messiah? Whose son is he?"

"David's," they answered.

"Then how is it that David under the Spirit's influence calls him 'lord,' as he does? 'The Lord said to my lord, Sit at my right hand until I humble your enemies beneath your feet.' If David calls him 'lord,' how can he be his son?"

No one could give him an answer, and they no longer dared to question him.

Jeshua turned to the crowd and his own disciples. The sea of faces before him was dotted with those he knew and loved—Editha, Rebkah, Elizabeth, Rhoda, all from the hill country of Judea, standing with Larue and Thelda of Bethany and their relatives, Jochim and Marh and the child Mariaerh whom Jeshua had met in Lazarus' home. His mother's friends, who were more like sisters to her, all the holy women who had mounted the temple steps with Mary the morning she was chosen to bear the Messiah, stood before him with faces eager to hear the Word. His uncles, Zebedee, Marcus, Alphaeus, and all their families glowed with pride and love at this, their own. Cleopas, Susane, and Jonas, Martha and Nicodemus, even Lazarus standing tall and alive between his sisters, and so many others whom Jeshua had cured and healed and filled with hope, waited for him to speak with faith and expectancy glowing in their eyes.

Jeshua was overwhelmed by the outpouring of love and confidence which emanated from those he called friends, and then angered to fury by the priests and elders who did their best to lead them astray. His countenance darkened; his voice held a warning.

"The scribes and the Pharisees have succeeded Moses as teachers; therefore, do everything and observe everything they tell you. But do not follow their example. Their words are bold but their deeds are few. They bind up heavy loads, hard to carry, to lay on other men's shoulders, while they themselves will not lift a finger to budge them. All their works are performed to be seen. They widen their phylacteries and wear huge tassels. They are fond of places of honor at banquets and the front seats in synagogues, of marks of respect in public and of being called 'Rabbi.' As to you, avoid the title 'Rabbi.' One among you is your teacher, the rest are learners. Do not call anyone on earth your father. Only one is your father, the One in heaven. Avoid being called teachers. Only one is your teacher, the Messiah. The greatest among you will be the one who serves the rest. Whoever exalts himself shall be humbled, but whoever humbles himself shall be exalted."

Then he turned on the leaders, "Woe to you scribes and Pharisees, you frauds! You shut the doors of the kingdom of God in men's faces, neither entering yourselves nor admitting those who are trying to enter. Woe to you scribes and Pharisees, you frauds! You travel over the sea and land to make a single convert, but once he is converted you make a devil of him twice as wicked as yourselves. It is an evil day for you, blind guides! You declare, 'If a man swears by the temple it means nothing, but if he swears by the gold of the temple he is obligated.' Blind fools! Which is more important, the gold or the temple which makes it sacred? Again you declare, 'If a man swears by the altar it means nothing, but if he swears by the gift on the altar he is obligated.' How blind you are!

Which is more important, the offering or the altar which makes the offering sacred?

"The man who swears by the altar is swearing by it and by everything on it. The man who swears by the temple is swearing by it and by Him who dwells there. The man who swears by heaven is swearing by God's throne and by Him who is seated on that throne. Woe to you scribes and Pharisees, you frauds! You pay tithes on mint and herbs and seeds while neglecting the weightier matters of the law, justice and mercy and good faith. It is these you should have practiced, without neglecting the others.

"Blind guides! You strain out the gnat and swallow the camel! Woe to you scribes and Pharisees, you frauds! you cleanse the outside of cup and dish, and leave the inside filled with loot and lust! Blind Pharisee! First cleanse the inside of the cup so that its outside may be clean.

"Woe to you scribes and Pharisees, you frauds! You are like whitewashed tombs, beautiful to look at on the outside but inside full of filth and dead men's bones. Thus you present to view a holy exterior while hypocrisy and evil fill you within. Woe to you scribes and Pharisees, you frauds! You erect tombs for the prophets and decorate the monuments of the saints. You say, 'Had we lived in our forefathers' time we would not have joined them in shedding the prophet's blood.' Thus you show that you are the sons of the prophet's murderers. Now it is your turn: fill up the vessel measured out by your forefathers.

"Viper's nest! Brood of serpents! How can you escape condemnation to Gehenna? For this reason I shall send you prophets and wise men and scribes. Some you will kill and crucify, others you will flog in your synagogues and hunt down from city to city until retribution overtakes you for all the blood of the just ones shed on earth, from the blood of holy Abel to the blood of Zachariah, son of Barachiah, whom you murdered between the temple building and the altar. All this, I assure you, will be the fate of the present generation."

Jeshua's face contorted in a spasm of grief. "O Jerusalem, Jerusalem, murderess of prophets and stoner of those who were sent to you! How often have I yearned to gather your children, as a mother bird gathers her young under her wings, but you refused me."

The hushed court moaned under Jeshua's sorrow. His anger spent, he looked upon them with infinite compassion and said in a voice thick with emotion, "Recall the saying: 'You will find your temple deserted.' I tell you, you will not see me from this time on until you declare, 'Blessed is he who comes in the name of the Lord!'"

He turned from the silent multitude and left the temple.

The Jewish leaders were livid with rage. They spun on their heels and stalked back toward the sanctuary. They had been publicly condemned and humiliated by one they considered the lowest of rabble rousers, and their mortification turned to murderous hate. The rabble was gleeful, Jeshua's friends profoundly disturbed, and Judas Iscariot was jubilant.

Jeshua and the Twelve crossed the Kidron Valley and climbed the Mount of Olives. They were halfway up the face of the mountain when one of the disciples looked back and was struck by Jerusalem's splendor.

The city lay like a cluster of jewels, brilliant and resplendent against a setting of taupe and brown. The sun reflecting upon the gold-sheathed temple dazzled his eye; the lofty towers of pink-veined marble on the Fortress Antonia and Herod's magnificent palace seemed to rise as sentinels around it. Even the tiny, boxlike homes of the poor shone white and clean, the filth and squalor invisible from his vantage point.

The disciple touched Jeshua's arm and pointed back at the temple. "Teacher, look at the huge blocks of stone and the enormous buildings!"

Jeshua looked and saw the marvels his disciple saw, then said sadly, "You see these great buildings? Not one stone will be left upon another, all will be torn down."

When they reached the crest of the mountain and paused to rest a while, Peter, James, John, and Matthew questioned him privately about his remark concerning Jerusalem. "When will this be, Teacher? And what will be the sign that it is going to happen?"

Jeshua said, "Take care not to be misled. Many will come in my name saying, 'I am he' and 'The time is at hand.' Do not follow them. Neither must you be perturbed when you hear of wars and insurrections. These things are bound to happen first, but the end does not follow immediately.

"Nation will rise against nation and kingdom against kingdom. There will be great earthquakes, plagues, and famines in various places, and in the sky fearful omens and great signs. But before any of this, they will man-handle and persecute you, summoning you to synagogues and prisons, bringing you to trial before kings and gov-ernors, all because of my name. You will be brought to give witness on account of it. I bid you resolve not to worry about your defense beforehand, for I will give you words and a wisdom which none of your adversaries can take exception to or contradict. You will be delivered up even by your parents, brothers, relatives, and friends, and some of you will be put to death. All will hate you be-cause of me, yet not a hair of your head will be harmed. By patient endurance you will save your lives.

"When you see Jerusalem encircled by soldiers, know that its devastation is near. Those in Judea at the time must flee to the mountains: those in the heart of the city must escape it; those in the country must not return. These indeed will be days of retribution, when all that is written must be fulfilled.

"The women who are pregnant or nursing at the breast will fare badly in those days! The distress in the land and the wrath against this people will be great. The people will fall before the sword; they will be led captive in the midst of the Gentiles. Jerusalem will be trampled by the Gen-tiles, until the times of the Gentiles are fulfilled.

"There will be signs in the sun, the moon, and the stars. On the earth, nations will be in anguish, distraught at the roaring of the sea and the waves. Men will die of fright in anticipation of what is coming upon the earth. The pow-ers in the heavens will be shaken. After that, men will see the Son of Man coming on a cloud with great power and glory. When these things begin to happen, stand erect and hold your heads high, for your deliverance is near at hand.

"Notice the fig tree, or any other tree. You observe them when they are budding, and know for yourselves that summer is near. Likewise when you see all the things happening of which I speak, know that the reign of God is near. Let me tell you this: the present generation will not pass away until all this takes place. The heavens and the earth will pass away, but my words will not pass.

"Be on guard lest your spirits become bloated with indulgence and drunkenness and worldly cares. The great day will suddenly close in on you like a trap. The day I speak of will come upon all who dwell on the face of the earth. So be on the watch. Pray constantly for the strength to escape whatever is in prospect, and to stand secure before the Son of Man."

It was a sobering prophecy, and the four men passed a disturbed, uneasy night.

Chapter 40

According to the calendar used by the sect of the Essenes, the feast of Passover fell on the day before the date followed by orthodox Jewry, so on the fourth day of the week, Jeshua called Simon Peter and John aside and gave them instructions to go and prepare their Passover supper.

"Where do you want us to get it ready?" John asked.

Jeshua smiled and said, "Just as you enter the city, you will come upon a man carrying a water jar. Follow him into the house he enters, and say to the owner, 'The Teacher asks you: Do you have a guest room where I may eat the Passover with my disciples?' That man will show you an upstairs room, spacious and furnished. It is there you are to prepare."

Simon and John wondered at the mysterious instructions, but did as they were told without questioning Jeshua. They found the man just as Jeshua had said they would, and followed him out of the city onto the road which led to Bethany. When the servant entered the service gate to Zebedee's estate, Simon Peter could only stare in astonishment while John burst out in laughter.

"Why didn't the Master simply say he wished to eat the Passover meal at Zebedee's!" Simon sputtered.

John laughed. "Perhaps he wished to teach us a lesson. Remember the colt at Bethpage? We doubted it would be where Jeshua said it was, and then doubted that he would be able to ride it. He proved himself both times, and now proves again that he knows things which we do not. Come along. We'll find the owner of this fine house and deliver the Master's request."

Zebedee's great, roaring laughter reverberated through the atrium when John humbly delivered Jeshua's message and told how they came to be there. He clapped his youngest son on the shoulder, nearly knocking him down, and chortled, "A fine lesson in faith my nephew has given. The room is ready, as he and I planned days ago. Begone, the both of you, and tell your Master all is as he asked."

The next evening when darkness fell over the city, it seemed as though the entire sect of the Essenes had gathered in Zebedee's spacious upper room to eat this meal with Jeshua. Salome had ordered the tables arranged in the traditional manner of the Brotherhood, with the priest's table on a raised dais at the front of the room, and the many smaller tables running the opposite way below it. The curtains were drawn to hide the light from the many lamps from any curious eye, giving the room a feeling of coziness and intimacy.

Jeshua and the Twelve reclined at the priest's table with Jeshua in the place of High Priest, while his other disciples, friends, and family took places below him according to rank.

The room hushed, and every eye turned upon Jeshua as he stood to intone the traditional blessings to begin the serving of the meal. He stood quietly for a moment and looked into the faces and hearts of those he loved. His red-gold hair glistened in the lamplight, and the pearl-gray robe shimmered when he moved. His expression was one of infinite compassion, and his voice was thick with emotion when he spoke.

"I have greatly desired to eat this Passover with you before I suffer. I tell you, I will not eat again until it is fulfilled in the kingdom of God."

Those gathered before him glanced uneasily at one another, wondering what he meant. Then Jeshua raised his cup and offered the blessing in thanks, adding, "Take this and divide it among you. I tell you, from now on I will not drink of the fruit of the vine until the coming of the reign of God."

He waited until the cup had been passed among the Twelve and was handed down to the nearest table below the dais, then took up a loaf, again gave thanks and broke it, saying, "This is my body to be given for you. Do this as a remembrance of me."

The company began to murmur. They were disturbed by his words and the heavy burden in his tone. They couldn't understand what he meant. Judas Iscariot shifted uneasily on his mat, frightened for a moment by the dire warning in Jeshua's statement, but then he remembered all the marvels he'd seen Jeshua perform and reassured himself that nothing could harm the Master without his own consent. The stage was set and the plans laid. Jeshua would have no choice but to take the throne of Israel. The servants began filing in with laden trays, and the atmosphere turned merry. Judas relaxed and joined in the babble, his momentary doubts forgotten.

In addition to the customary lamb roasted with bitter herbs, and unleavened cakes, the guests were served boiled fish, and rice with leeks, all delicately flavored in a seasoned sauce. Salome basked in the glow of many compliments for the luscious meal, but flushed with mortification when she saw that one of the pitchers used for wine sported a broken handle and lip. She quickly ushered the porter out, and the poor man recoiled from the tonguelashing he received.

When the meal was over, Jeshua again raised his cup for the final blessing, and again ended the blessing with enigmatic words. "This cup is the new covenant in my blood, which will be shed for you." Then he removed the one-piece gray robe, revealing his blue and white linens, and tied a towel about his waist. He poured water into a basin and began to wash John's feet and dry them with the towel. The others watched in amazement. What was Jeshua doing? John, and then James, were too stunned to protest, but when Jeshua moved on to Simon Peter, Simon sputtered incredulously. "Lord! Are you going to wash my feet?"

Jeshua answered, "You may not realize now what I am doing, but later you will understand."

Peter pulled his feet from Jeshua's reach. "You shall never wash my feet!"

Jeshua had been kneeling before Simon, and now rocked back on his heels and looked Simon directly in the face. "If I do not wash you, you will have no share in my heritage."

Simon looked at Jeshua for a long moment, trying to understand, then pushed his feet forward. "Lord, then not only my feet, but my hands and head as well."

Jeshua smiled and loosened the latchets on Simon's

sandals. "The man who has bathed has no need to wash; he is entirely cleansed, just as you are, though not all." He glanced pointedly at Judas Iscariot as he said the last, and Judas flinched under Jeshua's gaze. He couldn't possibly know! Judas thought, but nevertheless, he wished he could escape and get it over with.

Jeshua washed the feet of all the Twelve, even of Judas Iscariot, and then put his robe back on and reclined at the table once more. He said to them, "Do you understand what I just did for you? You address me as 'Teacher' and 'Lord,' and fittingly enough, for that is what I am. But if I wash your feet, I who am Teacher and Lord, then you must wash each other's feet. What I just did was to give you an example, as I have done, so must you do. I solemnly assure you, no slave is greater than his master, no messenger outranks the one who sent him. Once you know all these things, blest will you be if you put them into practice.

"What I say is not said of all, for I know the kind of men I chose, my purpose here is the fulfillment of Scripture: 'He who partook of bread with me has raised his heel against me.' I tell you this now, before it takes place, so that when it takes place you may believe that I AM. I solemnly assure you, he who accepts anyone I sent accepts me, and in accepting me, accepts him who sent me."

Jeshua then suddenly grew deeply troubled. "I tell you solemnly, one of you will betray me."

The disciples were startled, and looked from one to another in puzzlement. John ben Zebedee reclined next to Jeshua in his customary place, and Simon Peter motioned to him to ask the Master who he meant. John was clearly the most beloved of Jeshua, and could always ask when the others did not dare. John leaned back against Jeshua's breast and asked in a whisper, "Lord, who is he?"

Jeshua answered, but in a low voice so only John could hear. "The one to whom I give the bit of food I dip in the dish." He dipped a bit of bread in some cold, congealing sauce and handed it to Judas Iscariot, saying, "Be quick about what you are to do."

Judas flushed, then rose and quickly left the room. John was alarmed and would have followed, but Jeshua's hand restrained him. Others who saw Judas leave thought only that since he was the treasurer, Jeshua had sent him on some errand, but later John would remember and know exactly where he had gone.

The huge, high ceilinged room pulsed with the droning murmur of low, contented voices. The guests lay back, lounging against each other and Salome's soft, plush cushions in lazy, happy comfort. They were all replete with food and wine, basking in companionable fellowship behind the safety of Zebedee's sturdy walls. They were weary, physically exhausted by the hectic pace and exciting events of the past few days, but emotionally fulfilled and confident in the future which lay ahead.

All of those who reclined in Zebedee's upper room had followed Jeshua from the first days of his ministry, nearly three years spent tramping over every dusty road and byway throughout the whole of Palestine. Three years spent sleeping in the open fields with nought but stars for a roof over their heads, often hungry and thirsty, footsore, and weary to the marrow of their bones. They'd known heart-rending sorrow, and bewildering confusion. Their hearts had soared to the peaks of exaltation, then plummeted to the depths of despair, only to soar again until they thought they could endure no more.

But they had endured, and now it seemed as though they had gathered together in a feast of love and unity on the very eve of the fulfillment of all the ancients had foretold. The morrow would bring a culmination of centuries of preparation and planning. The years of suffering and sacrifice were over. No more would the Elect be ostracized and humiliated. No more would their prophets be slain, their Saints hounded, and their children slaughtered in a bath of blood. The Messiah had come and now sat in their midst, and Belial would soon be cast into the flame.

Jeshua knew what lay in their hearts and minds, and his soul grieved for their innocence. His heart went out to them, and he began to address them, trying to prepare them for what was to come. The room grew quiet. The murmuring ceased until the only sounds were the sputtering lamps and Jeshua's tender, loving voice.

"My children, I am not to be with you much longer. You will look for me, but I say to you now, 'Where I am going, you cannot come.' I give you a new commandment:

Love one another. Such as my love has been for you, so must your love be for each other. This is how all will know you for my disciples, your love for one another."

"Lord," Simon Peter said to him, "where do you mean to go?"

Jeshua answered, "I am going where you cannot follow me now; later on you shall come after me."

"Lord," Simon insisted, "why can I not follow you now? I will lay down my life for you!"

Jeshua smiled at Peter, his expression so tender and loving it melted Peter's bones. "You will lay down your life for me, will you?" Jeshua said gently. "I tell you truly, the cock will not crow before you have three times disowned me."

Simon gasped and said vehemently, "Even if I have to die with you, I will not deny you."

The other disciples at the table joined with Simon Peter in assuring Jeshua of their loyalty, and Jeshua could only shake his head sadly, then went on.

"Do not let your hearts be troubled. Have faith in God and faith in me. In my Father's house there are many dwelling places; otherwise, how could I have told you that I was going to prepare a place for you? I am indeed going to prepare a place for you, and then I shall come back to take you with me, that where I am you also may be. You know the way that leads where I go."

They were confused and didn't understand. Thomas asked, "Lord, we do not know where you are going. How can we know the way?"

"I am the way, and the truth, and the life; no one comes to the Father but through me. If you really knew me, you would know my Father also. From this point on you know him; you have seen him."

"Lord," Philip said to him, "show us the Father, and that will be enough for us."

"Philip," Jeshua said wearily, "after I have been with you all this time, you still do not know me? Whoever has seen me has seen the Father. How can you say, 'Show us the Father'? Do you not believe that I am in the Father and the Father is in me? The words I speak are not spoken of myself; it is the Father who lives in me accomplishing his works. Believe me that I am in the Father and the Father is in me, or else, believe because of the works I do. I solemnly assure you, the man who has faith in me will do the works I do, and greater far than these. Why? Because I go to the Father, and whatever you ask in my name I will do, so as to glorify the Father in the Son. Anything you ask me in my name I will do. If you love me and obey the commands I give you, I will ask the Father and he will give you another Paraclete, to be with you always, the Spirit of truth, whom the world cannot accept, since it neither sees him nor recognizes him, but you can recognize him because he remains with you and will be within you.

"I will not leave you orphaned. I will come back to you. A little while now and the world will see me no more, but you see me as one who has life, and you will have life. On that day you will know that I am in my Father, and you in me, and I in you. He who obeys the commandments he has from me is the man who loves me; and he who loves me will be loved by my Father. I too will love him and reveal myself to him."

Thaddeus ben Alphaeus asked, "Lord, why is it that you will reveal yourself to us and not to the world?"

Jeshua answered, "Anyone who loves me will be true to my word, and my Father will love him, we will come to him and make our dwelling place with him. He who does not love me does not keep my words. Yet the word you hear is not mine, it comes from the Father who sent me. This much have I told you while I was still with you: the Paraclete, the Holy Spirit, whom the Father will send in my name, will instruct you in everything, and remind you of all that I told you."

Jeshua looked out over the room and raised his arms as though in blessing. "Peace is my farewell to you. My peace is my gift to you. I do not give it to you as the world gives peace. Do not be distressed or fearful. You have heard me say, 'I go away for a while, and I come back to you.' If you truly loved me you would rejoice to have me go to the Father, for the Father is greater than I. I tell you this now, before it takes place, so that when it takes place you may believe. I shall not go on speaking to you longer, the Prince of this world is at hand. He has no hold on me but the world must know that I love the Father and do as the Father has commanded me."

No one moved or spoke when Jeshua finished. A sadness settled over the room. Each wondered what he meant by this farewell, and thought he must be bidding farewell to the intimate, familial closeness they'd enjoyed as they rested in the hills of Galilee, and looked ahead to when the heavy responsibilities of king and high priests would render those private, personal moments impossible. Then Jeshua smiled and called for a harp, and the mood turned merry and festive again. Jeshua's long tapering fingers rippled across the harpstrings, and his melodic voice filled every corner of the vast room. He sang a psalm of faith and refuge, and those he loved added their voices with confidence and joy.

"He who dwells in the secret place of the Most High shall abide under the shadow of the Almighty. I will say of the Lord, He is my refuge and my fortress; my God, in Him I trust."

When the song was finished, Jeshua laid the harp aside. The hour was late, and everyone was weary and ready to rest. Jeshua stood again before them and looked upon them with eyes of infinitely tender regard, then said, "It is finished." He motioned to his disciples and led them from the room.

As Jeshua and his disciples crossed the Kidron Valley and climbed the Mount of Olives to a garden called Gethsemane where they would pass the night, his mother lay awake in a tiny inn outside of Jericho, staring into the darkness and fighting the weight of fear which crushed her breast and squeezed her lungs until she could barely breathe. And at the port of Sidon, many miles north of Mt. Carmel, a young Jew with a curl of woodshaving tucked above his ear as the mark of his trade of carpenter paced the deserted pier and watched the great Roman ship in the moonlit harbor. He waited for the dawn and a boat to row him to her decks where he'd find his sister and bring her back to Jerusalem.

Chapter 41

The garden of Gethsemane lay only a short way up the face of the mountain, but the climb from the Kidron Valley was difficult, and Jeshua's weary disciples breathed a sigh of relief as they entered the gates and threw themselves down upon the ground. The night was unseasonably warm and humid. Young John ben Zebedee pulled his cloak over his head and tossed it aside, letting the night air cool his steaming body. He was unabashed by his near nakedness when Jeshua, with James and Simon Peter, approached and Jeshua bid him to come with them to pray a while. He let the cloak lay where it had fallen and walked beside Jeshua deeper into the garden, away from the others who already snored loudly in their sleep.

Jeshua stopped beneath a clump of trees and said, "My heart is filled with sorrow to the point of death. Remain here and stay awake."

The three sank down on the long cool grass. James and Simon Peter were soon asleep, while John fought to keep his eyes open. He watched Jeshua fall prone to the ground and heard him begin to pray. "O Father, you have the power to do all things. Take this cup away from me. But let it be as you would have it, not as I." Then his lids grew heavy and his head dropped to his breast and he heard no more until Jeshua was standing over them, shaking Simon Peter awake.

"Asleep, Simon? You could not stay awake for even an hour? Be on guard and pray that you may not be put to the test. The spirit is willing but nature is weak."

He left them again, but still sleep overcame them. Jeshua returned to them a second time, and then a third, when his warning jolted them awake and they would not

479

know sleep again for days to come. "Still sleeping? Still taking your ease? It will have to do. The hour is on us. You will see that the Son of Man is to be handed over to the clutches of evil men. Rouse yourselves and come along. See! My betrayer is near."

They looked back to where Jeshua pointed. A long column of temple guards and Herodian flunkies advanced upon the garden, armed with swords and clubs and bearing torches to light their way. The Captain of the Temple guard flung the gates aside with a resounding crash, jolting the sleeping disciples awake. They scrambled to their feet, but were quickly surrounded and held at bay.

Jeshua strode toward them, and John gasped when he saw that Judas Iscariot stood at the captain's side. Judas saw Jeshua step from the shadows and came to meet him. He embraced Jeshua, saying, "Peace, rabbi," in a tone he hoped would tell Jeshua that all would be well. But Jeshua recoiled from him and said, "Judas. Would you betray the Son of Man with a kiss?"

Judas seemed taken aback, confused. He let his upraised arms fall helplessly to his side and took a step back. Jeshua looked at him sadly, then touched his arm and said quietly, "Friend, do what you are here for."

Judas stammered as though attempting to explain, but before he could speak, the captain of the guard pushed him roughly aside and laid hold of Jeshua. Simon Peter growled with anger that he dared to touch the Master. Drawing a short sword from beneath his cloak, he gave a great roar and leaped forward, slashing out at the nearest man and severing his ear, while James sent his fist crashing into the face of another and John dove headlong into the belly of a third. The garden erupted with cries and the scrape of drawn swords, but Jeshua's commanding voice rang out above the din and put a stop to the battle before it had a chance to begin.

"Enough!" He swung on Simon Peter. "Put back your sword where it belongs. Those who use the sword are sooner or later destroyed by it. Do you not suppose I can call on my Father to provide at a moment's notice more than twelve legions of angels? But then how would the Scriptures be fulfilled, which say it must happen this way?"

He turned to the Captain. "Who is it you want?"

"Jeshua, the Nazarene," the Captain answered.

"I am he," replied Jeshua. The crowd retreated slightly at the authority in Jeshua's voice, and he asked again. "Who is it you want?"

The Captain answered, a little hesitantly, "Jeshua, the Nazarene."

"I have told you, I am he," Jeshua said. "If I am the one you want, let these men go."

Jeshua stepped forward into the crowd of armed men, completely unafraid and at ease. He went to where the man with the severed ear lay moaning and raised him to his feet, all the while addressing the crowd. "Am I a criminal that you come out after me armed with swords and clubs? When I was with you day after day in the temple you never raised a hand against me. But this is your hour, the triumph of darkness." He touched the man's ear, holding it back against his head and running his finger along the line where it was slashed. When he took his hand away, the ear remained where it was. Only the stain of blood bore witness that it had ever been severed.

The guard and Herodians stood rooted in shocked disbelief. Those holding the eight disciples at the gate relaxed their grasp and stared in total amazement. Their prisoners wrenched free and fled into the night.

The Captain had heard of such sorcery practiced by the Nazarene before, and refused to be duped. He ordered Simon, James, and John to be released, then bound Jeshua's hands behind him and led him from the garden.

Simon and James fled with the others, but John hid in the shadows and followed at a safe distance. Once he stumbled and was heard by a rear guard who spun about and grabbed at a flash of white, but only came away with John's linen, which he looked at with disgust and tossed to the side of the road. From then on John took more care, keeping deep in the shadows and picking his way carefully through the dark.

They followed the road which led past Zebedee's estate, and John took a shortcut across the fields and raced to the stables. He leaned against the rough stable wall to catch his breath, sucking the fetid air in through his mouth to ease his tortured lungs. He groped through the dark, searching for something to cover his nakedness and found a rough, dun-colored cloak that belonged to one of the stable hands, and he threw it over his head. He peered through a crack in the stable wall. Zebedee's house was dark. The last of the servants had gone to bed. He turned his eyes toward Jerusalem and saw that the column of torches was already entering the gate. His mind raced. He knew the house would be locked, and by the time he aroused the servants to let him in, the column would have reached the temple and disbanded, and he'd have lost Jeshua. He decided to follow on his own, and go for help once he learned where they held Jeshua. He crept from the stable and ran through the paddock, vaulting fences and hedgerows until he slipped unnoticed into Jerusalem.

The city was deserted. As he'd feared, the main body of the column disbanded at the temple, and only a small contingent pushed Jeshua on through the winding streets. John's heart sank when he saw they were taking Jeshua to Caiaphas' palace, then burned with anger when he saw the gates to the courtyard were already opened and the High Priest's bodyguard stood waiting. He hung back in a darkened doorway, wondering how he could gain entrance, for the courtyard and street in front of the palace were a confusion of soldiers, priests, and elders. A small group passed close by where John hid, and he pressed back against the wall, nearly overturning some large water jars behind him. For a moment he held his breath, terrified that the noise had been heard, then breathed a prayer of thanks to the Most High, and hoisted one of the heavy jars to his shoulder. He stepped boldly out onto the street. Who would question a poorly clad youth bearing water to the High Priest's palace?

The ruse worked. Once inside the gate, John set the water jar aside and pulled the hood of the mantle over his head to hide his face. He looked for Jeshua, but the courtyard was a sea of servants and soldiers. A hoot of laughter came from the far end of the court, and John let himself be carried along with a crowd of onlookers who pressed forward to see what was happening. He felt sick and suddenly cold when he saw the cause for their merriment.

Jeshua stood bound and blindfolded in the midst of a group of soldiers. They taunted him and slapped him, saying, "Play the prophet! Which one struck you?" They kept it up, delighting the crowd, spitting in his face, poking fun and ridiculing him until John could no longer bear to watch. He turned back to the center of the court, desperate to find some means of rescuing Jeshua from his tormentors.

The predawn had turned cold, and some of the soldiers were warming themselves at braziers. John edged his way through them and was startled to see Simon Peter standing across from him, holding his hands over the glowing coals. A flood of relief washed over John. He pulled his hood farther over his face. It would do no good to have Simon recognize him now, not while he stood in the midst of Caiaphas' guard. But John's pounding heart slowed, for now at least he knew he wasn't alone, and, when the time came, there would be an ally in the crowd.

The courtyard was filling with rabble whom Caiaphas' cohorts were questioning, trying to find witnesses to testify against Jeshua. John slipped in among them as they were ushered into the palace, and found himself in a large hall where a quorum of Sanhedrin members had gathered, mostly Sadducees, loyal to Annas. The council sat at a great long table which nearly ran the breadth of the room on a raised dais at the front of the hall. They all stood when Caiaphas entered, resplendent in his priestly robes, and followed by his father-in-law, old Annas. The hall quieted as Caiaphas took his seat in the High Priest's throne at the center of the table with Annas at his right hand, and ordered the prisoner to be brought forth.

The rabble murmured as Jeshua stumbled in. The soldiers pushed him from behind and dragged him along by his bound arms. His face was swollen and bruised. His robe was dirty and his hair fell over his face. When he stood below the dais in front of the council table, a guard jerked the blindfold from his eyes and yanked his head upright by his hair.

Annas began questioning him, first about his disciples, and then about his teaching. Jeshua answered, "I have spoken publicly to any who would listen. I always taught in a synagogue or in the temple area where all the Jews come together. There was nothing secret about anything I said. Why do you question me? Question those who heard me when I spoke. It should be obvious that they will know what I said."

One of the guards next to Jeshua gave him a sharp blow on the face. "Is that the way to answer the High Priest?" he growled.

Jeshua replied, "If I said anything wrong, produce the evidence, but if I spoke the truth, why hit me?"

Annas conferred privately with Caiaphas, and they called their witnesses. Smaleuen led the questioning with obvious relish, his hatred for the Essenes the impetus for his guile. His questions were cunning, cleverly put, and far more damning than the answers he got, but it was a poor show at best, since no one could agree with another. Jeshua remained silent through it all until Caiaphas finally called a halt to the charade and questioned Jeshua himself.

"Have you no answer to what these men testify against you?"

Jeshua said nothing. Caiaphas tried again. "Are you the Messiah, the Son of the Blessed One?"

Jeshua was suddenly angry. His voice rang through the great hall. His head was flung high and his eyes blazed with fire. "I am, and you will see the Son of Man seated at the right hand of the Power and coming with clouds of heaven."

The hall gasped. Caiaphas tore his robes and cried, "What further need do we have of witnesses? You have heard the blasphemy! What is your verdict?"

The council shouted, "Guilty!" Some of the rabble and the guards began to spit on Jeshua. They blindfolded him again and hit him, mocking, humiliating him.

Panic rose in John's breast. Blasphemy! That charge carried a sentence of death! He pushed his way out of the hall and ran across the court. He slowed as he neared the soldiers by the gate, lest he arouse their suspicion. Simon Peter was still there, waiting for word of the proceedings inside, but before John could approach him, a servant girl peered closely into Simon's face and said accusingly, "You too were with Jeshua of Nazareth."

"I do not know what you are talking about," Simon answered gruffly.

"This man is one of them!" the girl insisted to the bystanders. Again Simon denied it, but the bystanders took up the challenge. "You are certainly one of them! You are a Galilean, are you not?"

Simon began to curse and swear, gripped by an uncontrollable fear. "I do not even know the man you are talking about!"

He shoved the men aside and began to stride toward the gate and ran directly into John. John stared into Simon's terrified eyes, aghast at what he'd just heard. Simon was just about to fling John aside when he recognized him. Before he could speak, a trumpet from the Fortress Antonia split the air with the call for "cockcrow," the Roman acknowledgement of the dawn of a new day, and both men remembered their Master's words at the supper only a few hours before. Simon's face twisted in a grimace of pain. He uttered an anguished cry of despair and fled from the court.

John started to run after him, but a shout from the crowd rose up and he turned to see the guards leading Jeshua down the palace steps. They pushed and shoved him about as they would a common thief or ragged beggar. John's gorge rose at the sight, and his breast filled with hatred for the haughty, self-righteous priests and scribes who followed with such pious dignity.

He forgot about Simon and fell in with the shouting, mocking crowd and followed the procession to the Fortress Antonia where the priests asked for Pontius Pilate to greet them in the courtyard. The chief priests and scribes could not enter the Praetorium, for they had to avoid ritual impurity if they were to eat the Passover supper that evening.

Pilate was clearly annoyed by being disturbed at such an early hour. He listened impatiently to their accusations against the Nazarene, and when they had finished with their long list of complaints, Pilate said testily, "I do not find a case against this man."

One of the scribes stepped forward. "He stirs up the whole people by his teaching throughout the whole of Judea, from Galilee, where he began, to this very place."

Pilate looked at Jeshua with renewed interest. He summoned an aide to his side, and after a short conference, asked Jeshua, "Are you a Galilean?"

Jeshua didn't answer, so the scribe answered for him, confirming that he was. Pilate smiled. "The man is from Herod's jurisdiction. Let one of your own decide his fate."

Pilate's remark was a direct insult to the chief priests and scribes, for they despised the Indumean who held rule over their heads. There was nothing they could do but go through with the charade, knowing they'd have to come back, for only Rome could incur the penalty of death.

Herod was delighted to see Jeshua, and questioned him extensively, hoping to provoke him into performing one of his famed miracles, but Jeshua held his counsel and would make no answer to Herod's taunts and the vehement accusations of the chief priests and scribes. Herod finally grew weary of the game and sent him back to Pilate.

It was now about two hours after "cockcrow." The sun shone brilliantly from a cloudless azure sky. The streets swarmed with merchants, pilgrims, and housewives, all in a frenzy of final preparations for the feast to begin that day. When the priests and guard emerged with Jeshua from Herod's palace, they immediately attracted a throng of the curious and the rabble of degenerates who were always on the lookout for any sign of excitement. They soon became a pushing, screaming mob, a tinderbox of smoldering passions, wanting only the tiniest spark to ignite them into a monstrous explosion. They followed Jeshua back to the Fortress Antonia where the Romans were hard put to keep them in control.

Pilate came out of the fortress and took his seat on the judgment bench. The cries of the mob died down. John, who had struggled to keep as close to Jeshua as he dared, inched his way forward to hear what was said. Pilate looked alarmed at the size of the mob, yet was not about to give in to their demands. He singled out a spokesman for the priests and said shortly, "You have brought this man before me as one who subverts the people. I have examined him in your presence and have no charge against him arising from your allegations. Neither has Herod, who therefore has sent him back to us. Obviously this man has done nothing that calls for death. Therefore I mean to release him, once I have taught him a lesson."

The crowd roared their disapproval of being denied their amusement, but Pilate silenced them. "Why do you not take him and pass judgment on him according to your Law?"

"We may not put anyone to death," they answered.

Pilate arose and went back into the Praetorium. In a

little while, a Roman soldier came out and took hold of
Jeshua, saying to the temple guard who was reluctant to
let him go, "Pilate wishes to question him privately."

John became desperate with fear that Jeshua would
disappear into the bowels of the Antonia as John the
Baptizer had disappeared at Machaerus. He fought his
way through the milling mob until he found Barrian and
begged for entrance into the Praetorium.

"Don't be a fool, John!" Barrian snapped. "Pilate is
Jeshua's only chance. If you lose your head and cause a
disturbance, you'll anger the Procurator and only cause
Jeshua harm."

"I promise I won't cause trouble," John pleaded. "Don't
you understand? I have to see! I have to hear!"

John's voice broke in a sob. Barrian had little doubt as
to the outcome of this sham, no matter what the lad did.
His sympathy for the Essenes and his pity for John, the
most beloved of Jeshua's disciples, made him relent.
"Come along then, but at your own risk."

He led John through a side door at the back of the long
receiving hall. The hall was dimly lit, and for a moment
John could see nothing until his eyes adjusted from the
glaring sun in the courtyard to the shadowed interior of
the vast, vaulted Praetorium. The hall was empty except
for a few helmeted soldiers who flanked Jeshua's side as
he stood before the Procurator. Pilate's voice carried easily through the marble-walled hall, and echoed from the
immensely high ceiling.

"Are you the King of the Jews?" he asked Jeshua.

"Are you saying this on your own, or have others been
telling you about me?" Jeshua answered calmly.

"I am no Jew!" Pilate spat. "It is your own people and
the chief priests who have handed you over to me. What
have you done?"

Jeshua looked steadily at the Procurator, disconcerting
him with his fearlessness. "My kingdom does not belong
to this world. If my kingdom were of this world, my
subjects would be fighting to save me from being handed
over to my enemies. As it is, my kingdom is not here."

"So then you are a king!" Pilate said triumphantly.

"It is you who say I am a king. The reason I was born,
the reason why I came into the world, is to testify to the
truth. Anyone committed to the truth hears my voice."

"Truth!" Pilate retorted with sarcasm. "What is truth?" He motioned to an aide with a languid wave of his hand. "Who are the prisoners scheduled to be crucified today?"

"There are three, my lord. One is Barabbas, the insurrectionist, and the other two are merely common thieves."

Pilate pondered for a moment, then asked, "Is there not a custom whereby the magnanimity of Rome releases an imprisoned Jew in honor of one of their festivals?"

The aide nodded, and Pilate smiled. "Well, Galilean. Perhaps we'll confound your enemies by using their own traditions."

Hope surged through John as Pilate rose and went out to address the mob once more. He sprinted to the side door where he could hear. The rumbling mob quieted when Pilate appeared. He looked upon them with unveiled distaste and said, "Recall your custom whereby I release someone to you at Passover time. Do you want me to release to you the King of the Jews?"

John groaned. It was a disastrous term to use before this mob, who resented any kind of authority, and they began to shout hysterically, "We want Barabbas!"

Pilate was taken aback by the sheer force of hatred mirrored in the faces of the mob, but he tried again. "What am I to do with the man you call the King of the Jews?"

"Crucify him! Crucify him!" the mob screamed.

Pilate was truly bewildered. "Why? What crime has he committed?"

The mob didn't hear. They chanted over and over again, "Crucify him! Crucify him!" stamping their feet and clapping their hands in rhythmic frenzy.

Pilate was furious. The mob was about to riot. He whipped his cloak about him and marched back to the Praetorium. "Scourge him!" he shouted to the guard. "Flay his back to ribbons and maybe that will satisfy their lust for blood!"

They dragged Jeshua into the courtyard and stripped him of Martha's luxurious robe. They lashed his hands to a cross-beam with his face forced cruelly into the bark-covered trunk. The Roman whip was a fearsome instrument of torture—many long strips of leather with sharp bits of bone tied at each tip, then bound together at the end to form a thick, hefty grip. A huge bear of a man, barrel-chested, with fists like mauls and the vacant leer of an idiot, swung the evil tool with obvious delight. With the first lash, Jeshua's back arched and his head snapped back, but no cry left his lips. Again and again the great arm rose and fell until John could stand it no more and fell to his knees and retched.

Jeshua's back was a purple mass of pulp when Pilate called a halt. "Bring him to the courtyard!" he ordered, and then went out to once more confront the mob.

"Observe what I do. I am going to bring him out to you to make you realize that I find no case against him."

When Jeshua was brought forth, an almost sensual groan went up from the crowd. The soldiers had woven a makeshift crown of thorns which they forced on Jeshua's head. The sharp barbs dug cruelly into his head and tiny rivulets of blood ran into his eyes and down his cheeks. They'd dressed him like a king in a purple velvet cloak. It was a mockery, and a shameful display of savagery.

"Look at the man!" Pilate roared.

The mob was beyond compassion; their frenzy bordered on insanity. "Crucify him!" they screamed.

Pilate screamed back at them. "Take him and crucify him yourselves! I find no case against him!"

One of the Jewish leaders stepped forward. "We have our Law, and according to that Law he must die because he made himself God's Son."

Pilate stared at him with a look of fear, then ordered Jeshua brought back into the Praetorium.

"Where do you come from?" he asked Jeshua in a tone of awe. Jeshua didn't answer, and Pilate said, "Do you refuse to speak to me? Do you not know that I have the power to release you and the power to crucify you?"

Then Jeshua answered, "You would have no power over me whatever unless it were given you from above. That is why he who handed me over to you is guilty of the greater sin."

Pilate was suddenly afraid of Jeshua. He returned to the courtyard, determined to free him, but the priests warned him, "If you free this man you are no 'friend of Caesar.' Anyone who makes himself a king becomes Caesar's rival."

Pilate's fear of Caesar's displeasure overrode his fear of Jeshua. He ordered Jeshua brought out again and then took his seat on the judgment bench. He called out to the mob, "Look at your king!"

They shouted back, "Away with him! Away with him! Crucify him!"

"What!" Pilate exclaimed. "Shall I crucify your king?"

The chief priests cried, "We have no king but Caesar!"

The mob took up the cry and Pilate realized he was beaten. He called for water and washed his hands in front of the whole crowd, declaring, "I am innocent of the blood of this just man. The responsibility is yours."

The crowd laughed and jeered.

Pilate raised his hand and summoned Barrian to his side. He ordered that Barabbas be released and that Jeshua ben Joseph of Nazareth be crucified.

Chapter 42

When the Roman trumpets sounded cockcrow, the silvery, melodic notes floated over the city and hung suspended in the still predawn until they stirred the consciousness of all who slept below, then faded into oblivion as soon as the sun could vaporize the dew. Marcus lay sprawled on his stomach with one arm flung across Josie's back, which was pressed closely at his side. His mind refused to respond to the call of a new day, but Josie stirred. She shifted her body to lie on her back, and Marcus' arm fell heavily across her breasts. She lay quietly for a while, letting her mind drift in and out of sleep until the sun burst through the open window and crept across the room to tease her eyelids open.

She smiled at the warmth of the sun on her face and at the familiar weight of Marcus' arm. She let her mind dwell on the Passover feast of the night before, and the warm contented love she'd felt then once more permeated her very soul. She wondered where Jeshua had passed the night, and what today would bring, and then turned her thoughts to her own busy day.

Tonight while the Jews ate their Passover meal, her family would gather in her upper room to celebrate Jeshua's victory and eat together in loving fellowship as they had eaten the night before. Mary's arrival sometime today would make the family complete. Only Ruth and James would not be here, for Josie hoped that Jude would come with his mother. Salone, the Other Mary, Cleopas, and Susane already slept beneath her roof, and Elizabeth would come later with Martha and Mary from Bethany. Zebedee and Alphaeus' families would also be here, and of course Rhoda and Mary, and Martha and Nicodemus.

Josie was suddenly panicked by all there was to do. She

gingerly lifted Marcus' arm from her breast and tried to slip out of bed without awakening him. Marcus groaned. He rolled to his side and gathered Josie into his arms.

"Marcus," Josie chided softly. "Let me go. I must get up!"

Marcus opened one eye and grinned. "So soon? It's barely dawn." He pulled Josie's face to his by her braids and kissed her soundly.

Josie squirmed out of his embrace and giggled. "Old fool. I have much to do and no time for such foolishness. Go back to sleep."

Marcus raised himself up on one elbow. "Old!" he said indignantly. "Come here and we shall see who is old!"

Josie laughed and shook her head. "Go to sleep. I hear the servants up before me."

Marcus dropped back to the pillow, muttered some complaint, and was soon asleep again.

Josie quickly dressed and said her morning prayers, then met with the servants and outlined the tasks for the day. Three she assigned to go to the market place to buy enough provisions to last two days. As the Sabbath fell on the day after Passover, her guests would all be staying the night, for no one could return to their homes until the sun went down the following day.

The house was soon alive with activity. Mary and Rhoda arrived with some of their servants in tow to help their mother with preparing the feast. Susane, Salone, and the Other Mary had arisen, and the house resounded with female chatter and laughter.

Marcus and his father, Cleopas, had fled the bevy of females and took their morning meal to the garden where they ate in leisure while enjoying the merriment from a safe distance, but their pleasure was short-lived as one of the servants whom Josie had sent to the market place suddenly burst through the gates and flung himself at Marcus' feet.

"Master!" he gasped. "They have arrested Jeshua ben Joseph!"

For a moment Marcus thought the servant had gone mad, for his eyes bulged and his breast heaved; his face was ashen and twitched with fear. Then the full impact of what the man had said penetrated Marcus' brain and he leaped to his feet, overturning the table and scattering dishes to the ground. He grabbed the servant and hauled him to his feet.

"What! What do you say?" he cried.

The servant cowered beneath his master's grasp. "The Master. They have arrested him! The streets are filled with rabble. They take him to the Fortress Antonia!" he sobbed.

"Who arrested him? Who?" Marcus demanded.

"I don't know, master. I asked, but all I know is that they took the rabbi to Pontius Pilate. The priests—some say the priests held a trial in the night and found him guilty of blasphemy!"

Marcus released his hold on the servant so quickly that the poor man stumbled and fell to one knee.

"Impossible!" Cleopas whispered. "He must be wrong. I heard of no meeting called. We were not informed."

Marcus turned to his father, his face pale and his eyes desperate. "They wouldn't call us. Caiaphas has enough friends to constitute a quorum." He turned back to the servant. "You are sure?"

The man nodded. "I didn't see the rabbi. A great crowd followed, all on the verge of riot, running and screaming like madmen—women, too, and even children. They came from King Herod's palace where they say he questioned the rabbi."

Marcus poured a drought of wine and handed it to the servant. "Drink this, then go at once to Zebedee ben Joachim and tell him to meet me at the High Priest's palace. Do not arouse the women, or speak to anyone but Zebedee or Alphaeus ben John."

The servant nodded. He gulped the wine, then fled through the gate. Marcus summoned a maid and said as calmly as he could, "Tell your mistress that Cleopas and I go to the temple and we will meet them there this afternoon." He turned to Cleopas, his voice filled with despair. "Can we stop it?"

Cleopas clasped his son's shoulder. "Only if it be the will of God."

Caiaphas' palace was not far. They hurried through the wide, paved streets, stopping only long enough to get Nicodemus and Joseph of Arimathaea, who was Nicodemus' guest for Passover week. When they reached the palace, the gates were closed and locked, the courtyard seemingly empty. Marcus pounded upon the gate and shouted until a sleepy-eyed servant made his appearance. Cleopas demanded an audience with the High Priest, but the servant would not let them in. He bade them to wait until he asked if his master would see them, then turned and sauntered away.

They waited for what seemed an eternity, pacing the street and fuming with frustration. Their tempers rose with each passing moment at the insult of being forced to wait outside the gates. When the servant finally did return, it was only to tell them that his master had already left for the temple, and they would have to beg audience with him there. Nicodemus began to curse the servant for his indolence, but Joseph pulled him away, saying "Come, my friend. There is no time to waste arguing with a fool."

They left the wide streets of the Upper City and began the long, twisting descent to the temple. They met Zebedee and Alphaeus who were on their way to meet them and wasted no time in stopping for explanations, but talked as they went. When Marcus finished telling them all he knew, Zebedee swore, then asked, "What of the Twelve? Have they arrested them all?"

Cleopas stopped and looked at both Alphaeus and Zebedee with pity. Six of the Twelve were these men's sons. "We don't know, Zebedee. Our man only said Jeshua. We know nothing of the others," he said quietly.

As they neared the Lower City, the streets became congested, and they slowed their pace. They could hear the cries from the mob at Antonia, and fear drove them on. They were breathless by the time they reached the grand staircase which led to the Court of Gentiles, and they had to pause a moment to give Cleopas a chance to catch his breath.

It was nearly the third hour. The sun rode high over the eastern wall, flashing against the golden walls and magnifying the brilliant colors of the booths and canopies which lined the court. The court itself was chaos. Priests and pilgrims and merchants and money-changers spun in an eddy of movement that blurred before their eyes, and the incessant, excited babble bombarded their ears, obscuring the cries from Antonia. They pushed and shoved their way through the milieu to the Court of Israel which was as crowded as the Court of Gentiles, making it nearly impossible to find someone of authority close to the High Priest in the massive crush of bodies. When they did, he sent them on to see another, and that one on to see someone else, until Zebedee nearly exploded with wrath.

At last they were led from the noise and confusion to a small anteroom off the High Priest's offices, where again they were told to wait, only to learn that Caiaphas had left the temple and was now at the Hasmonean Palace in conference with old Annas. Zebedee's roar of frustration reverberated through the halls, while the others groaned in disappointment and cursed the time already wasted.

There was nothing they could do but face the crush in the courts again. This time fear and panic over the time lost drove them to disregard courtesy, and they ignored the chides and insults thrown at them as they rudely shoved aside any who stood in their way. Cleopas was tiring. Once he stumbled and nearly fell. Marcus wanted him to wait at the temple, but he refused, arguing that his presence would carry more weight than anyone else's, and that his prestige and influence were vital. Marcus and Nicodemus supported him on either side while Zebedee strode before them, forcing the crowd to make way.

Once out of the temple, the high walls muffled the din from within, and riotous screams from the Fortress Antonia again assailed their ears. The sound was subhuman, bestial, mad—it struck terror into their hearts.

"Where is Iscariot and his Zealots?" Zebedee roared. "He's preached rebellion and warfare for months, and now when he is needed, he's nowhere in sight! Let me find him! Let me gather an army!"

Marcus swung on Zebedee and shouted into his face. "Stop it! Control yourself! To fight would be useless. Look!"

Zebedee raised his head to where Marcus pointed. The temple walls were ringed with Romans. In every doorway and at every cross street, golden helmets flashed in the sun. Zebedee groaned and sagged with despair. "It is lost!" he sobbed.

"Not yet," Cleopas panted. "Do not give up hope."

They pushed on through the streets. The Hasmonean Palace loomed ahead. They were exhausted when they arrived, and they were thankful to be admitted immediately and not have to wait outside. The high vaulted room was cool and blessedly quiet. A servant brought them goblets of cool, refreshing wine, which they gulped with unembarrassed relief. It wasn't long before they were led to Caiaphas.

Caiaphas and Annas were standing behind a long table strewn with scrolls and sheets of papyrus, their heads bent together in deep discussion. Protocol demanded that visitors wait for the High Priest's acknowledgment, but Cleopas used the strength of his prestige and cast fine manners aside. "Annas, old friend," he called as he strode across the room. "Forgive the intrusion on such an important day, but I must speak with you on a matter of utmost urgency."

Both priests looked up with feigned expressions of surprise on their faces, and Annas shuffled around the table to meet Cleopas with outstretched arms.

"Shalom, Cleopas. The pleasure of seeing you outweighs any inconvenience," he cried expansively.

Zebedee flinched at Annas' cleverly veiled admonishment. Caiaphas joined his father-in-law and greeted Cleopas with cool but polite disapproval. Their greeting to Joseph, Nicodemus, and Marcus was no less welcoming than their greeting to Cleopas, but Zebedee only received a curt nod of recognition, and Alphaeus was ignored altogether.

Annas launched into what would be a long discourse on the infinite problems to be confronted that day, but Marcus politely cut him short. "We realize the fullness of the day before you, Annas, and so as to not cause you undue delay, let us state our request and be on our way and leave you to deal with the burdensome duties of state."

"We come about Jeshua ben Joseph of Nazareth," Cleopas said quickly, before Annas had a chance to avoid the subject again.

"Jeshua ben Joseph?" Caiaphas mused, then said with pretended remembrance, "Ah, yes. The miscreant convicted this morning."

Annas laughed softly and clapped Cleopas' shoulder. "What can you have to do with that rabble rouser?"

"He is my nephew," Marcus said tersely.

"And mine!" Zebedee growled.

"And mine," Alphaeus added.

Caiaphas looked coolly from one to the other. He rested his eyes on Alphaeus and said with studied disinterest, "Really."

Annas became contrite. His voice lowered with sympathy and concern. "I am sorry," he said to Marcus. "A pity. These are difficult times, I know. There are so many pagan influences assailing the young people of today. One cannot help but wonder that more of our youth are not led astray, and can only thank the Blessed Most High for those who keep their hearts faithful to the God of their fathers."

Zebedee nearly choked with indignation, and only Joseph's warning look prevented him from exploding with wrath.

Nicodemus stepped forward. "I hardly think that is the case with Jeshua ben Joseph. His teaching is filled with love and adoration of the Creator, and of service and love to one's fellow man. Surely you can find no fault with that!"

Caiaphas raised one hooded lid and said softly, "None whatsoever, my dear Nicodemus, if he had confined himself to those teachings only. However, he also taught total disregard for tradition and ritual, which is the foundation of our Law, and incited the ragged unlearned to ignore, even to rebel, against all authority."

"You are mistaken, Caiaphas," Cleopas warned. "Jeshua never taught sedition, quite the contrary, and his disregard for ritual was only when the ritual had lost its meaning and had become an outward, empty gesture."

"Perhaps. Perhaps," Annas said in a placating tone. "Unfortunately, the common people did not understand it in such a light. They saw only the sorcery your nephew performed. They were so awed by his magic that some came to believe he was the Messiah, and were in danger of losing their souls."

"How do you know that he is not the Messiah? How do you know that his 'magic' is not the power of God?" Zebedee cried. "Can you dare to take the responsibility for murdering the Son of God?"

Caiaphas' cool facade dissolved, angered by the charge

of murder. He pounded his fist upon the table. "I can and I do!" he shouted. "As High Priest, I am charged by Heaven above to keep His Laws and bring His chosen ones safely through the temptations in the earth. Do you think that I would cast them aside simply because some ragged carpenter's son proclaimed himself to be the Messiah? Am I to destroy all that was handed down from Adam through all the Patriarchs simply because some fool Galilean declares himself to be the 'Son of God'?"

Caiaphas groaned aloud and tore at his robes. "Son of God! Blasphemy! He makes himself equal with the Most High with such a claim. For that he must die. It is the Law!"

Alphaeus had remained quiet throughout the proceedings, for he was a Galilean and held no influence with these pompous Judeans, but now he was angered beyond endurance and could no longer hold his tongue. "Die! You have no authority to condemn a man to die; surely not by some sham of a trial held in the dead of night and kept secret from any who would see justice done!"

A scribe had slipped into the room as Alphaeus spoke, and he whispered into Annas' ear. Caiaphas turned livid with rage and swung on Alphaeus. "Who are you to criticize the Sanhedrin? The trial held this morning"—he emphasized *this morning*—"was attended by a legal quorum of just, unbiased men who listened to each witness called and weighed the evidence with utmost care. Your nephew had no defense for himself. He refused to speak in his own behalf, and could call upon no one to speak for him. He condemned himself by his very silence!"

"Gentlemen! Gentlemen!" Annas said soothingly. "Such argument is futile." He turned to Marcus with great sympathy. "I am sorry for you, and understand your concern for your kinsman. The matter is out of our hands. The scribe tells me that Pontius Pilate has also found him guilty, and at this moment the Nazarene hangs from a cross on Golgotha."

A shocked silence followed. Caiaphas moved to a chair and sat down, watching the reactions of the men before him. Marcus and Cleopas were staring open-mouthed at Annas, in horror and disbelief. Nicodemus looked stunned. Joseph of Arimathaea covered his face with his hands in a gesture of unbearable grief. Alphaeus looked lost, bewildered. "Golgotha?" he asked in a whisper.

"The Place of the Skull," Zebedee said stupidly. "They have crucified our Lord."

Zebedee sagged beneath the weight of his suffering. He looked old, beaten. His towering height seemed to shrink before Caiaphas' eyes. His broad chest caved inward, drawing his massive shoulders forward until he looked hump-shouldered, bent, grotesque in shape. He began to whimper like a child; the tears flowed freely down his cheeks. His hands trembled, and he weaved unsteadily back and forth on his feet. Even Annas was touched by the total disintegration of a once proud, vital man, and turned his back to gaze out of the window.

Joseph heard the childlike weeping and took his hands from his face. He went to Zebedee and put his arms around him, cradling his massive head upon his shoulder as though he were comforting a child. Nicodemus pulled himself out of his stupor and went to Alphaeus, who was grinning idiotically, from shock. Nicodemus spoke softly into his face, trying to bring him back to reality, but Alphaeus continued to smile and babble incoherently. "Jeshua was always in my shop. He was a good lad. Joseph would bring him in tow and Jeshua would carve little toys out of wood. He was very good at it. He made some remarkable likenesses of lambs and doves. I have kept some of them. I'll show them to you sometime."

"Yes, yes," Nicodemus crooned. "I would like to see them."

Cleopas' heart nearly broke as he saw Marcus stunned to immobility and speechlessness. He swallowed at the torturous lump in his throat and asked Caiaphas, "What of the Twelve? What of Jeshua's followers?"

"I know nothing of any 'twelve.' The Nazarene was the only one to stand trial. No others were arrested."

Cleopas nodded and took Marcus' arm. "Come, my son. It does no good to tarry here. Let us go home." He motioned to Joseph and Nicodemus. Alphaeus let himself be led docilely from the hall, but just before they reached the doorway, Zebedee stopped and turned to Caiaphas. "His mother comes to Jerusalem today. What do I say to my sister?"

They waited for Caiaphas to answer, but he would say nothing and so they left and closed the door gently behind them.

Once outside the palace gates, Joseph asked Cleopas, "Do we go to Golgotha?"

Cleopas shook his head. He said in a voice of infinite weariness, "Let us take them home. Nothing will be accomplished by witnessing the horror. Besides, the women must be told."

They turned their steps toward the Upper City, not knowing that they would find the house empty, and that their women now wept at the Place of the Skull.

Chapter 43

Pathaos brought the horses to the door of the inn before dawn. He helped Ulai, Josie, and Mary to mount, and by the time the sun broke over the hills, they had left the gates of Jericho and were leisurely cantering along the road to Bethany. Ulai and Josie were in high spirits, eager to reach Martha's and learn what had taken place in their absence. Mary tried to join in their gay chatter, but her head ached from lack of sleep, and the fears which had assailed her throughout the night clung to her mind like shadowed wisps of gray clouds. She lapsed into silence, oblivious to the warm, spring day and the laughter of her companions, conscious only of the jarring pace of the horse beneath her and the enormous weight of her depression.

Their arrival in Bethany caused a stir of excitement among the villagers. Mary was bewildered by the attention she drew, and embarrassed by the reverent awe she saw in the faces of the many who spilled from the tiny cottages to watch in respectful silence as she passed. She breathed a sigh of relief when Martha's gate closed behind her. Pathaos lifted her down from the horse and she found herself enveloped in Elizabeth's ample, familiar arms.

Mary's joy at seeing Elizabeth again momentarily banished her fears. She greeted the others with genuine delight and allowed Lazarus to lead her to Martha's lavishly laid table. At first she ate with relish, but as she listened to the excited, animated accounts of all the events which had taken place in the last few days, her appetite fled and she could only pick at the delicacies Martha heaped upon her plate. She was disturbed by the glowing accounts of Jeshua's popularity, and grew increasingly uneasy as they all regaled her with tales of his scathing victories over the

Jewish priests and scribes. Her sense of foreboding grew with every tale, and when the meal was over, she pled weariness and asked if she might rest for an hour or so before they left for Jerusalem. Martha led her to a quiet room at the back of the house, and once alone, she gave way to her fears. She paced the floor and clenched her hands until her knuckles went white, trying to define the terror that mounted within her.

Why could she not share the others' enthusiasm and certainty that Jeshua would soon be crowned King of Israel? Why did she see Jeshua's entry into Jerusalem as the first step toward calamity, instead of the triumph the others proclaimed it to be? Why did every tale confirming his popularity with the masses only increase her apprehension, instead of filling her with motherly pride? Why did she dread this day with such debilitating fear that it numbed her mind and made it impossible for her even to pray?

She was suddenly assailed by a desperate longing for Joseph. She flung herself across the soft, sweet-smelling bed and wept, whispering Joseph's name through wracking sobs until she slept from sheer exhaustion. When she awoke she felt calmer, able to pray. Elizabeth found her on her knees, her face serene, her body relaxed. A shaft of sunlight spilled through the window and formed a golden halo over her head. She was incredibly beautiful, angelic. It took Elizabeth's breath away just to look upon her. She watched her for a long moment, then touched her shoulder and said, "Come, Mary. It is time to go to Jerusalem."

The short walk to Jerusalem was festive, as most of Bethany followed to join in the Passover activities taking place in the temple. Lazarus remained behind. His presence in the temple would be a jarring reminder to the Jewish authorities of Jeshua's reputed powers, and could only serve to inflame their hatred.

Sara was again in the procession, far to the back where she wouldn't be noticed. She had recognized Mary as soon as she saw her, for Mary had not changed at all since the night of the star, and the love Sara had felt for her then bloomed anew in her heart. She looked down at her own shabby dress, and hid her grime-imbedded hands in the folds of her skirt. How she longed to approach Mary, to see her eyes light up with recognition and to hear her say her name, but she couldn't bear the thought of seeing Mary's smile of welcome turn to pity when she saw the low state to which she had fallen.

Sara had been bitterly disappointed when Jeshua had not been crowned king on the day he made such a triumphal entry into Jerusalem, and couldn't understand why Jeshua seemed to exert so little of his power to help those who were sick, or in doubt, or were afraid. She knew many who had been healed by Jeshua before, and was puzzled that he did not use this opportunity to manifest his gifts before thousands of witnesses. Today her hopes soared again. Surely Mary's presence was a sign that the prophecies were to be fulfilled.

Mary and her cousins parted from the procession at Zebedee's estate. Sara was in a quandary as to whether to follow the crowd into Jerusalem or to wait for Mary. She hated to lose sight of her, and feared she'd not be able to find her again in the crowded temple courts, but to linger without Zebedee's gates meant taking a chance on discovery. She could hear the muted rumble which seemed to come from the temple area, and the sound stirred her to excitement. Something out of the ordinary must be taking place, and Sara knew it must have to do with Jeshua. She decided to go on into the city.

Mary also heard the muffled roar which rode the air waves over the city walls like faraway rolls of thunder, but to her the sound was frightening, ominous. The sense of dread had returned at her first sight of the city, gleaming white and gold beneath the brilliant morning sky. It lay ahead in all its splendor, enticingly beautiful, luring her onward with its false promise of glory while her heart pounded with its knowledge of the evil that lurked behind those walls. She remembered the first time she had entered the city, when Jeshua was just beginning to stir in her womb, and Zachariah had met his death with his hands on the horns of the altar. She remembered when she and Joseph had brought their first-born to be ransomed from the Lord and the old man, Simeon, had prophesied to her, "And you yourself shall be pierced with a sword." She shuddered in fear and dread. She was not afraid to die, if Simeon's prophecy was meant to be taken literally, but

she feared the events that would lead to her death, the
dangers and suffering brought to those she loved, and
especially to Jeshua.

She nearly groaned aloud at the thought of Jeshua.
Where was he? If only she could see him, touch him,
know that he was well. She was cold with fear. Her mouth
and throat were dry and her shoulders shot with pain
from tension. She breathed deeply, trying to calm the rise
of panic. She forced herself to respond naturally to Salome's effusive greeting, and swallowed her disappointment when she learned that Zebedee and Alphaeus had
already gone to Jerusalem. She embraced her female relatives in turn—Mary of Alphaeus, Abigale, Lia, Naomi,
and Adahr—hiding her anxiety behind a gentle smile. It
was the tenth hour when they left Zebedee's and entered
the city by the Fountain Gate below the temple compound.

Marcus and Cleopas had been gone nearly two hours
before the servants whom Josie had sent to the market
place returned with their dreadful account of what was
taking place in the city. The women dropped everything
and fled toward the fortress, holding their skirts high as
they ran, oblivious to the stares and catcalls they elicited
from the rabble who watched them bolt by. They took the
shortest route possible, racing down the narrow, twisting
streets, their lungs bursting and the cries from the mob
screaming in their ears. Josie led, shoving and clawing her
way through the crowd like a woman gone mad, as the
others struggled to keep her in sight. She fought through
the deep ring of bodies until she burst through to the
forefront of the crowd, and a long, tearing scream erupted
from her throat like a jagged knife.

The street was lined with Romans on either side, their
long spears held to form a barrier to keep the mob at bay,
and in the center of the street, four mounted soldiers
formed a circle around three staggering, stumbling men,
each bearing two great rough-hewn beams lashed together
to form a cross. One of those men was Jeshua.

Josie was consumed by an uncontrollable rage. She
flung herself against a spear, forcing it to give way, and
tried to run to the center of the street to yank that shameful load from Jeshua's back. A Roman caught her and
hauled her back. Josie fought with a maniacal strength,

spewing words she never thought she knew. Her fingers curled into talons, clawing at any bare flesh she could see. She kicked and spat and screamed until the Roman slapped her senseless, and the last thing she saw before blackness crashed down upon her was Jeshua's loving, piercing, gray-blue eyes, pleading with her to let it be.

Josie regained her senses to find her daughters and the Other Mary and Salone sponging her face and weeping in hysteria. She brushed their efforts aside, hauled herself to her feet, and looked for Jeshua. The sickening procession had passed them by and was making its way slowly up the street. Josie threaded her way through the crowd, ordering them to make way with such a ring of authority in her voice and such command in her plump little body that the rabble could only stare in amazement and do as they were bid. The others followed close behind, and soon they were once again abreast of Jeshua. Josie marched staunchly at the perimeter of the crowd, just behind the Romans' backs, her face set with contempt and fury. She never took her eyes from Jeshua's face, willing him to have strength, to endure. She ignored the blood running in tiny rivulets down his face, and the crimson stain that slowly spread across his pearl-gray cloak. She looked only at his face, transmitting waves of love and support directly to his mind.

Jeshua laughed aloud at his aunt's valiant show of defiance. He became merry, joking with the thieves who bore their burdens beside him, and calling out to faces he recognized in the crowd. He seemed joyful, glad of heart, as though he had won a great victory and marched to collect his prize. But his physical strength was waning. More than once he stumbled and nearly fell, only to be prodded to his feet by the cruel Roman whip. The cries of the rabble became less bestial, their blood-lust finally sated and changing into repulsion. Women began to weep and beat their breasts, lamenting over him. Jeshua turned to them and said, "Daughters of Jerusalem, do not weep for me. Weep for yourselves and for your children. The days are coming when they will say, 'Happy are the sterile, the wombs that never bore and the breasts that never nursed.' Then they will begin saying to the mountains, 'Fall on us,' and to the hills, 'Cover us.' If they do these things in the green wood, what will happen in the dry?"

The procession crept on. The monstrous cross-beams thumped over the cobbled street, playing a funeral dirge to the rhythmical clop of the horses' hoofs. The sun was a white glare; the heat from the pressing crowd was suffocating. The narrow streets cut off any air, and the mournful, keening cries of the women rose and fell like the groan of an animal in agony. Jeshua stumbled and fell again. The whip sang out, whistling through the air and ending in a nerve-shattering crack, but he couldn't get up. One of the soldiers laid hold of a Cyrenean who was coming in from the fields, and they put Jeshua's cross-beam upon his shoulders and ordered him to carry it on to the hill.

They passed through the city gate and the press of the crowd thinned out. It was easier to breathe, and an occasional breeze stirred the air. Jeshua now walked upright, his eyes straight ahead, his arms at his side and his step more sure. His blood left tiny pools in the dusty path, but the following crowd quickly trod them into oblivion. Josie paced her steps to Jeshua's stride. She too held her head high and marched with a fierce pride and devotion.

When they reached the crest of the hill, the cross-beams were thrown to the ground, and the prisoners stripped to their loincloths. Martha of Nicodemus gasped in dismay when Jeshua's robe was cast aside like the filthy rag it had become, and she began to sob uncontrollably. One by one the prisoners were held to the beams, their wrists and ankles lashed to the wood and then pierced with nails driven mercilessly through their flesh. The two thieves screamed in agony, but Jeshua set his teeth and endured the torture in silence.

Three deep holes had been dug in the earth. The soldiers slid the beams with their infamous loads over the rough ground until the foot of each hung over a hole, then raised the cross-beams skyward until the base fell into the hole with a sickening, jarring thud and stood upright. The pain to the prisoners was excruciating. Even Jeshua cried out as the jolt tore his hands and the block of wood between his thighs rammed cruelly into his pelvis.

It was too much. Josie simply gave way. Her knees would no longer support her and her eyes could no longer see. She began to weep, and pitched headlong to the ground with her face in the dirt, and prayed she could die with the taste of earth and brine in her mouth.

Sara was on the opposite side of the street when Josie's rage drove her to fight the Romans. She recognized Josie as Mary's sister immediately, for they looked much alike, and the face of every Essene was indelibly etched in Sara's mind. She recoiled in aversion at the abuse Josie received from pagan hands, and all her horror and sick disappointment at seeing Jeshua reduced to the state of a common criminal vanished. Only one thought consumed her mind. Mary must not fall into the unclean hands of these Sons of Belial, to be subjected to the same degrading abuse which her sister had just endured. Sara let herself be edged back to the outer rim of the crowd where she ducked into a doorway and waited until the main crush surged by, then fled back toward the temple, praying as she ran for the Lord God to guide her steps to Mary.

Sara's prayers were answered. Just as she rounded a corner of the towering temple walls, she saw Mary and her relatives about to mount the grand staircase that led to the Court of Gentiles. She called out to her, forgetting her reluctance to be recognized, obsessed by her mission to save Mary from harm. Mary heard her name called out and turned, puzzled by the poorly dressed, dishevelled woman who hurtled down the street calling her name.

Sara was breathless by the time she reached Mary, and could hardly speak. She grabbed Mary by her forearms and gasped, "Mary! You must go back. You must return to Bethany! It is dangerous for you to be here!"

The women stared at the frenzied Sara in astonishment. Mary peered into Sara's face, trying to discover who she could be. Martha stepped forward, indignant that this stranger should lay hands on the mother of the Lord, and was about to push her roughly aside when Mary recognized her.

"Sara! Sara, can it possibly be you?"

Mary's cry of recognition stopped Martha's action. Mary took Sara's face in her hands and kissed her on both cheeks. "Sara! It is you. So many years have passed. My heart is filled with joy at seeing you again."

Sara pulled her face from Mary's hands and turned to

Martha. "Take her back! Get her out of Jerusalem," she sobbed.

The joy vanished from Mary's face. She took Sara's arm and swung her about. "What is wrong, Sara?" she asked with quiet command. "Tell me why I should leave Jerusalem."

Sara could only shake her head. Tears began to course down her cheeks and she couldn't look into Mary's eyes. Mary shook her by her shoulders. "Tell me!" she demanded.

"Jeshua," Sara whimpered brokenly. "They take him to the Place of the Skull."

Mary didn't comprehend what she meant. She turned to Elizabeth and to Mary of Alphaeus who looked as puzzled as she, but the Judean women knew. Martha's face drained of all color. Mary of Syrus clasped her hands over her mouth to stifle a scream. Salome gasped; her hands fluttered helplessly in the air. "The hill of crucifixion! God have mercy! They mean to crucify him!" she moaned.

The world reeled beneath Mary's feet. The source of all her fears came crashing down upon her. She fought against the nausea and blackness and dug her fingers into Sara's arm. "Where is this place? Where have they taken my son?"

Sara pointed back along the route she'd come. "Beyond the walls, through the Fish Gate north of the fortress."

Mary began to run. She ran as Josie had run, without thought or sight or feeling, hurtling through the streets, letting her soul give wings to her feet. Beyond the temple area the streets were eerily quiet, now nearly deserted. Somehow she instinctively knew the way, following the dolorous path which Jeshua had trod, gathering every suffering moment he'd known into her very self as she ran.

"My son, my son. Absalom, my son." David's haunting cry of despair whispered in her ears, pursuing her in a ghostly, mocking refrain.

She ran until her lungs could take no more and she was forced to stop. She gulped for air through her opened mouth and clutched at the searing pain in her side. She was vaguely aware of the sound of pounding feet behind her, but she couldn't wait and ran again as soon as she had breath enough to take her.

The gate loomed ahead and gave her new strength. She plummeted through the gate towers, running now at a steady, measured pace, her light steps sending little eddies of dust swirling into the air. She could see the hill in the distance, and the three minute crosses outlined against the sky. She called on all her early discipline beneath the gentle guidance of the Essenes, and forbade her mind to dwell on what those crosses held. She had her second wind and never faltered in her pace, but slowly closed the distance between herself and her son.

John had followed Jeshua's every step, from his arrest at Gethsemane through Pilate's verdict, to his final, infamous march through the teeming streets amid the jeers and ridicule of his fellow Jews. Desperation and grief had overwhelmed John to the point where he moved in a trancelike daze, his senses dulled, his emotions numb. He didn't see Josie or Salone and the others; indeed, he saw no one or nothing but his beloved Master bent beneath the cross. He watched in drugged paralysis when they lifted Jeshua up, and felt neither rage nor sorrow when they mocked him by nailing a sign "King of the Jews" above his head.

The Romans formed a ring around the prisoners to keep the crowd from coming too close. John stood just outside the ring, as close to Jeshua as the guard would allow. He looked upon Jeshua as long as he could bear, then turned to gaze back along the way they'd come. He stared at Jerusalem, so bright and gold in the morning sun, and felt the weight of bitter defeat bear him down into total darkness.

He watched without thought the lone figure who ran along the path toward the hill, but as it neared the base of the slope, his mind registered the brilliant flash of spun red-gold, and with an anguished cry, John raced down the hill to meet her.

Mary saw him coming and stopped. She was trembling and faint and gave herself up to John's strong arms with a strangled sob of relief.

"Aunt! Aunt!" John wept.

Mary pressed his face to her own and whispered, "Help me to go the rest of the way, John."

John glanced back and saw his own mother and the other women from Bethany, but he didn't wait. He put his arm around Mary's waist and nearly carried her to the crest of the hill. He spoke to a guard. "My aunt, Jeshua of Nazareth's mother. Let us through."

The guard looked with pity at the grief-stricken woman on young John's arm and stepped aside.

The murmuring crowd hushed. Mary's feet dragged. A pain took seed and grew in her breast as though someone was slowly piercing her heart with a sword. They stopped at the foot of the center beam. Mary slowly raised her head, her eyes travelling past the bleeding feet, past the ugly red welts on his chest, until they came to rest upon his blood-caked face, and she gazed into the eyes of her first-born son.

Chapter 44

The sun beat mercilessly down upon Jeshua's head, congealing the blood on his face and back until it pulled his skin so taut that every movement tore it apart to form a fresh wound. Flies swarmed to the feast of blood, adding their torment to the agony he already endured. The rabble taunted and jeered, goaded by the chief priests, scribes, and elders whom Caiaphas had sent to witness his death. "So you are the one who was going to destroy the temple and rebuild it in three days! Save yourself, why don't you? Come down off that cross if you are God's Son! . . . He saved others but he cannot save himself! So he is the king of Israel! Let's see him come down from that cross and then we will believe in him. He relied on God; let God rescue him now if he wants to. After all, he claimed, 'I am God's son.'" Even one of the thieves who hung at his side reviled him, saying. "Aren't you the Messiah? Then save yourself and us." But the other thief rebuked him. "Have you no fear of God, seeing you are under the same sentence? We deserve it, after all. We are only paying the price for what we've done, but this man has done nothing wrong. Jeshua, remember me when you enter upon your reign." And Jeshua replied, "I assure you, this day you will be with me in paradise."

By midday most of the rabble drifted away, bored by watching the long drawn-out process of death by crucifixion. Their throats were parched and their bellies rumbled. They wandered back to Jerusalem in search of food and drink, and, if they were lucky, some new event to rouse their passions. Those who remained were mostly women, and Caiaphas' friends. The Romans relaxed their guard and let the Holy Women come close to the foot of the cross, where they clustered around Mary in a tightly knit group, shielding her from the eyes of curious strangers. They seldom spoke to one another, for their grief was too profound for speech, but only wept quietly in helplessness and despair. The soldiers were also bored. Some started a game of dice, nearly breaking Martha of Nicodemus' heart when they used Jeshua's pearl-gray robe as the prize to add interest to the game.

Mary couldn't weep. She suffered beyond the release of tears. She leaned against John for support, staring into Jeshua's face, willing the burden of his pain to fall upon her own self. Jeshua met her gaze, his eyes liquid pools of tenderness and love. He saw how John supported her, cared for her, the only one of the Twelve with courage enough to see his trial to the end. He rallied his strength and said to Mary, "Woman, there is your son." Then shifting his gaze to John, "There is your mother," thus charging John to care for Mary for all of her life.

Every moment seemed to drag on for an eternity. The sky became an ever-deepening blue. The sun's brilliance began to fade, slowly, as though the wick of a lamp burned down, not the sudden shadow of a cloud mass passing by. A grayness seemed to settle over the earth. The breeze died down. Voices and sounds seemed to tarry and echo in the heavy, oppressive air. Birds abandoned the freedom of the skies and took refuge wherever they found a place to light. They stopped their song, and hid their faces beneath their wings as though afraid to see what happened in the world. The soldiers' laughter sounded with a hollow ring and the die clattered against the stone with a grating, overloud clink.

Jeshua painfully raised his head and saw the shadow of the moon move slowly over the sun. The time of death was near. He looked down upon the women who wept at his feet and knew their bewilderment and waning faith. He gathered all his remaining strength, and in a final attempt to make them understand, cried out, "My God, my God. Why have you forsaken me?"

His cry startled everyone who watched on the hill. The weeping ceased. The dice lay still. The priests and elders involuntarily drew together as they recognized the hymn Jeshua sang.

"My god, my God, why have you forsaken me, far from my prayer, from the words of my cry? O my God, I cry out by day, and you answer not; by night, and there is no relief for me. Yet you are enthroned in the holy place, O glory of Israel! In you our fathers trusted; they trusted, and you delivered them. To you they cried and they escaped; in you they trusted, and they were not put to shame.

"But I am a worm, not a man; the scorn of men, despised by the people. All who see me scoff at me; they mock me with parted lips, they wag their heads; 'He relied on the Lord; let him deliver him, let him rescue him, if he loves him.' You have been my guide since I was first formed, my security at my mother's breast. To you I was committed at birth, from my mother's womb you are my God.

"Be not far from me, for I am in distress; be near, for I have no one to help me. Many bullocks surround me; the strong bulls of Bashan encircle me. They open their mouths against me like ravening and roaring lions.

"I am like water poured out, all my bones are racked. My heart has become like wax melting away within my bosom. My throat is dried up like baked clay, my tongue cleaves to my jaws; to the dust of death you have brought me down.

"Indeed, many dogs surround me, a pack of evildoers closes in upon me. They have pierced my hands and my feet; I can count all my bones. They look on and gloat over me, they divide my garments among them, and for my vesture they cast lots."

Jeshua's clear, resonant voice surged across the hill, raising the purposes in the minds and hearts of those who were gathered about him with that wonderment and awe that made them know not what was come to pass. David's prophetic Psalm had come to pass before their eyes. The Jewish leaders shrank back with fear. A centurion declared, "Clearly this man was the Son of God!" Then Jeshua said, "I thirst," and a soldier ran to a jar filled with common wine. He snatched up a sponge, dipped it into the jar, then stuck it on some hyssop and raised the sponge to Jeshua's lips.

The sky had become so darkened they could no longer see the city walls. Jeshua took the wine, then raised his head one last time. He watched the small remaining sliver of sun slowly shrink and then become a brilliant ring enclosing total darkness. He cried out into the darkened day, "It is finished," then bowed his head and delivered over his spirit.

A rumbling began in the very bowels of the earth. The ground trembled beneath their feet. The rumble grew until it became a great roar, crashing, breaking in tremendous waves upon their ears. The people screamed and fell to the ground as the earth rocked and bucked and rent apart. The waves of the quake rolled through Jerusalem, tearing in half the heavy veil which hid the Holy of Holies, opening tombs, splitting boulders, stopping the call of the shofar which had just begun to signal the slaughter of the Passover lamb. Jerusalem erupted with panic and terror. Buildings swayed. People trampled one another as they stampeded from the buildings into the heaving streets.

Tremors were felt throughout Judea. On Mt. Carmel, on the cliff overlooking the sea, Justin watched the gathering gloom with growing apprehension. He stood guard over Judith who had knelt in a state of trance for hours. He knew her spirit roamed free of her flesh, he'd seen her thus before. He didn't understand it or know how she entered this state, but he somehow felt it was dangerous to disturb her. He watched the sun being slowly blotted from sight, and was torn between trying to bring Judith's spirit back into herself and fearing the consequence of doing so. He felt the trembling of the earth and heard the leaves rustle in the swaying trees. He reached out to Judith, his fear overriding his caution, when she suddenly moaned and pitched forward in a faint.

The quake jolted Jeshua's uncles from their stupor of shock and grief. They abandoned Marcus' trembling house and fled toward Golgotha, afraid for the women's safety.

The earthquake lasted for only a few moments. The damage was minimal and no lives were lost, but the streets were thronged with people spilled from their homes, and were littered with rubble from levelled booths and market stalls. By the time Marcus and the others reached the Fish Gate, the darkness had become a twilight gloom which gradually lifted until daylight reigned once more. They met the priests and elders hurrying back toward Jerusalem, followed by a parade of nearly hysterical women. Their own women were not among them. They reached the crest of the hill and recoiled in horror and repulsion at the sight of Jeshua's lifeless body hanging broken and limp upon the cross, then went to comfort the women.

Since it was the Preparation Day, the high priests did not want to have the bodies left on the cross during the Sabbath, for that Sabbath was a solemn feast day. They asked Pilate that the legs be broken to hasten their deaths and the bodies be taken away. Accordingly, the soldiers came and broke the legs of the two thieves, but when they came to Jeshua, they saw that he was already dead and they did not break his legs. One of the soldiers thrust his lance into Jeshua's side, to make certain he was dead, and blood and water gushed from the wound.

It was past the tenth hour. Jewish Law demanded burial before sundown. Joseph of Arimathaea returned to Jerusalem and asked Pilate for Jeshua's body. Nicodemus went with him to buy the spices and linens they would need to prepare him for burial. When they returned, they took Jeshua down and laid him in Mary's arms.

There was little time for Mary to mourn, for the hour grew late. She wept over Jeshua for only a moment, then busied her hands by helping Mary of Syrus, the Other Mary, and the ever-faithful Josie prepare the spices. Jeshua's aunts ripped linens into strips, while Andra hastily prepared the napkins which would cover his face. There were many women at the foot of the cross: all of the girls who had mounted the stairs with Mary; Lois, whom Jeshua had healed of the hemorrhage; Beatrice, Herod's danseuse; Susane; Sara; and so many others, all working quickly to bury the Master before the sun went down.

Joseph of Arimathaea owned a new, unused tomb in a garden close by the Place of the Skull and they laid Jeshua there. The high priests demanded that a huge stone be rolled over the mouth of the tomb and that a guard be posted to watch day and night. They took no chances on another miraculous return from the dead, but assured themselves that Jeshua of Nazareth would not rise again.

Mary refused to return to Jerusalem, but chose instead to go home with Ulai. No one could bear to leave her. The sun sank slowly behind the hills of Judea and the grief-stricken band of mourners left Jeshua alone in the tomb on the hill and wound their way home to Bethany.

They skirted the walls of Jerusalem. The streets and the temple were silent. The lamb had been slaughtered, the sacrifice made, and every believing Jew sat at table to recall their passage to freedom. No one saw the Remnant pass by—none but one man who moaned in despair and tore at his flesh, then hanged himself from a tree.

No one in Bethany slept that night. The Elect drew apart, each isolated in a solitary desolate shell, fighting the phantoms of shattered faith. Centuries of planning had come to naught. Centuries of sacrifice, study, and toil; of bloodshed, and ridicule endured; of expulsion and ostracization from their fellow Jews, had resulted in death and despair. The Sons of Darkness had won; the Children of Light were brought to their knees. What had gone wrong? Where had they erred? Was Jeshua not the One after all? Had they sinned through pride and vanity by thinking they could bring the Promise to pass? The Remnant groaned beneath the weight of hopeless desolation.

Chapter 45

The Sabbath dawned gray and gloomy with thick overcast skies denying the earth the light and warmth of the sun. Bethany lay in silence. The streets were empty, the courtyards vacant. The inhabitants huddled behind closed doors, shrouded in grief and despair as damp and chill as the morning air. Zebedee, Josie, and Salone kept vigil at Mary's side, helpless to comfort or soothe. Ulai brought food that remained uneaten upon the plate. John wandered in and out, conscious of Jeshua's charge to care for his mother, but powerless to ease her suffering. Sometimes Mary slept a little, but to watch her in sleep was more painful than to see her awake, for then her conscious control was relaxed and she moaned and wept and cried out in her agony.

The hours crawled by. Questions, spoken and unspoken, tortured their minds with relentless probing. An epidemic of doubt raged through the sect until some even made so bold as to question Mary as to the circumstances concerning Jeshua's conception. Mary reminded them of the angel's words, "The Holy Spirit will come upon you and the power of the Most High will overshadow you; hence, the holy offspring to be born will be called Son of God." Elizabeth told how John had leaped in her womb when Mary had come to Ain Karim, and how she herself had been filled with the Holy Spirit and had cried out, "Blest are you among women and blest is the fruit of your womb. But who am I that the Mother of my Lord should come to me?" Sara recounted the night of the star, of the heavenly choir and voices heard, of the testimony given by the shepherds in the field. "This day in David's city a savior has been born to you, the Messiah and Lord." But still they doubted, for Jeshua lay in the tomb.

The setting sun signalled the close of the Sabbath day, and Jeshua's disciples ventured forth from their hiding places and straggled into Bethany. They were shamefaced and wracked with guilt at the cowardice they'd displayed, but no one had heart or energy enough to condemn them. Their own consciences were punishment enough. Someone brought the news that Judas Iscariot had hanged himself from a tree, but no one cared or issued comment; what was done was done.

Ruth, Philoas, and Jude arrived a few hours after the sun had set. It had been nearly midday before Jude had gained access to Philoas' ship, and their race to Jerusalem had been a nightmare of fear and frustration. They'd ridden all day, stopping only to get fresh horses, but sundown had found them only as far as Sebaste, where they had been forced to stay through the Sabbath. As soon as the sun had gone down they resumed their flight, going at once to Josie's home where her servants told what had happened. Ruth was hysterical by the time they found Mary in Ulai's house. She was prostrate with grief and lay inconsolable with her face in her mother's lap, while Jude stalked the grounds in a rage. He'd warned them, he'd warned them all, but his pleas has fallen on deaf ears and innocent Jeshua had been sacrificed for their dreams.

Philoas was also angry. He was a Roman and knew Roman law and he intended to find out just how Pontius Pilate thought he could condemn an innocent man without having to answer for his actions. He was up before dawn, and, taking Cleopas with him, went to Jerusalem in search of Barrian.

Philoas had already left when Ruth awoke. The sun shone brightly and filtered through the latticed shutters, casting a crisscrossed pattern of shadow on Ulai's whitewashed wall. Ruth moaned and struggled to sit up. Her head throbbed and her throat ached; her eyes were swollen slits that refused to open to the light from the sun. Every movement was one of pain as her body reacted to the torture it had endured for hours on the back of a galloping horse. She pushed herself to her feet and walked painfully across the room and threw open the shutters. The villagers were up and about. Children played in the courtyards and women drew water from the common well. Everything seemed so normal, so commonplace, as though no one knew that goodness had been removed from the world.

Ruth sighed and closed the shutters. She picked up the dress she had worn for two days and shook it out with distaste. They hadn't waited to retrieve their possessions from the ship and all her clothes were now on their way to Rome. She slipped the soiled garment over her head, wrinkling her nose at the smell of horse and sweat. She pulled a comb through her tangled curls and carelessly tied a ribbon around the mass to keep it out of her face. Lifelong habit led her feet to the wide-mouthed jars outside Ulai's door, where she washed her hands and face and intoned the ritual prayers. Ulai urged her to eat, but all she could manage was a piece of fruit, which felt cool and soothing to her aching throat. She suffered her aunts' inept attempts to console, and her uncles' pitying looks, and as soon as politely possible, escaped the house to find Susane.

She met Susane just outside Martha's gate, where they embraced without a word of greeting. Tears glistened in Susane's eyes as she said. "I was just now coming to you. What can I say, Ruth?"

Ruth managed a small smile and squeezed her hand. "Nothing. There is nothing."

"Let's walk where we can be alone a while," Susane suggested.

Ruth glanced at the Mount of Olives and hesitated, a shadow of fear and dread in her eyes. Susane understood and said quietly but firmly, "There is nowhere in the land you'll ever be able to walk without the memory of Jeshua to haunt you. You might as well do it now."

Ruth sighed and nodded, then looked down at her dress. "First though, do you have something I can wear? I am suffocating in my own odor."

Susane laughed. "Of course. I was only being polite by not mentioning it myself."

They went into the house and Ruth again had to endure clumsy words of comfort. Susane tried to smoothe the awkwardness by chattering away about mundane things while trying to avoid mentioning Jeshua's name.

"The house is quiet. Where is everyone?" Ruth asked.

"Father went to Jerusalem with Philoas," Susane answered.

"I know. Ulai told me."

Susane hesitated, then went on. "The Other Mary, Salome, and Mary of Syrus have taken oils and spices to the tomb."

Ruth sharply sucked in her breath and Susane plunged on. "John ben Zebedee has taken Simon ben John to show him where Jeshua lies. Do you know about Judas?"

Ruth nodded and stammered as she forced Jeshua's name to her tongue. "Jesh—Jeshua would forgive him, but not I, not yet. It serves him right!"

When Ruth was dressed, they went out of the house and walked on the mount, avoiding the garden of Gethsemane. Susane told Ruth all that had come to pass, relating only the facts with as little emotional embellishment as possible. Ruth sometimes wept and often clenched her fists in anger and pain, but hearing the account from Susane in an orderly sequence was somehow soothing, and seemed more real than the garbled, emotional outbursts she'd heard the night before. They sat at the crest of the mount for a long time. Jeshua's presence seemed so near at this place he'd loved so much, and the terrible tension Ruth had known since Jude first set foot on the ship seemed to flow away from her body. Her head no longer throbbed, and the searing pain was gone from her breast. She felt only an aching loneliness, a great sadness, and a gaping void in her heart. She was weary to the marrow of her bones.

The sun rode high in the sky. Ruth stood and turned her gaze toward Jerusalem, and then beyond to a place she couldn't see, but knew was the Place of the Skull. "The last time I saw Jeshua, he said, 'Though earth and seas and the veil of heaven separate us, I am with you. You need only call and I shall answer. I shall not leave you desolate.'" She turned to Susane, her eyes awash with tears, but able now to smile through them. "I believe him, Susane, I believe he will answer when I call, but right now my heart is too heavy to hear. Someday—"

Susane swallowed and took Ruth's hand. "I know, and you are right. I think Jeshua knew all along that this is how it would end. He carried that awful beam of wood almost with joy. I know—I watched. I saw him laugh, I heard him call out, happily, to those of us he knew. Only his physical strength gave way, never his mental or spiritual. 'I come to do the Father's will,' he once said. Why the Father willed his death we don't know, perhaps we never will, but Jeshua knew and did it joyously. Remember how Jeshua wept when Lazarus died? Surely he knew he could, and would, raise him back to life. I've thought of that often. Why did he weep? Perhaps as an example to us, to show he shared our pain at separation even while knowing that separation to be a fleeting thing, and that reunion follows close behind. At any rate, the possibility gives me comfort."

"And I," Ruth smiled. "We'd best go back. I wanted to leave Mother alone with Jude for a while. Poor Jude. How can I help him? Ulai sent a servant to the City of Salt early this morning. We expect James some time today, and how I dread that reunion."

They walked slowly back to Bethany where they found everyone in an uproar, for Jeshua's tomb had been opened, and his body had disappeared.

Salone and the Other Mary were the first to return from Golgotha with their breathless account of what they'd seen and heard. John and Simon came soon after, and to all who mourned in Bethany, their tale seemed impossible, a distortion of vision and understanding wrought by the depth of their grief.

The three women had been first to arrive at the tomb. The guards were all fast asleep, as though drugged or senseless from too much wine. They had found the stone rolled back, and when they entered, Jeshua's body was gone. They were at a loss as to what to think. When they came out of the tomb, two men in dazzling garments had appeared beside them. Terrified, the women bowed to the ground. The men had said to them: "Why do you search for the Living One among the dead? He is not here; he has been raised up. Remember what he said to you while he was still in Galilee, that the Son of Man must be delivered into the hands of sinful men, and be crucified, and on the third day rise again."

Salone and the Other Mary had fled back toward Bethany, meeting John and Simon along the way. They told what they had seen, and the two men ran all the way to the Place of the Skull, where they saw for themselves that what the women had said was true.

No one knew what to think. The only logical explanation anyone could come up with was that for some inexplicable reason, the followers of Caiaphas had removed Jeshua's body. But why, why? John couldn't accept that explanation. The linens in which Jeshua had been wrapped lay undisturbed, as though Jeshua's body had been simply slipped through. The shroud had not been unwound and tossed aside, and the napkin which had covered his face was neatly folded in a place by itself. Why would anyone remove his grave clothes, and how could they do so without cutting or unwinding them?

Mary of Syrus had not returned with the others, and when she did come, her account was even more amazing than the others'. After John and Simon had left the tomb, Mary had stood weeping beside it. She'd peered inside and there she saw two angels in dazzling robes. One was seated at the head and the other at the foot of the place where Jeshua's body had lain. "Woman," they asked her, "why are you weeping?" She answered them, "Because the Lord has been taken away, and I do not know where they have put him." She had no sooner said this than she turned around and saw a man whom she thought was the gardener. "Woman," he asked her, "why are you weeping? Who is it you are looking for?"

"Sir, if you are the one who carried him off, tell me where you have laid him and I will take him away," she'd answered. Then the man had said, in a voice so familiarly tender, "Mary."

His voice had been like a stab in her heart. She'd dashed the tears from her eyes so that she could see, and her heart leaped into her throat.

"Teacher!" she'd cried out, rushing to him with arms outstretched, but Jeshua had said, "Do not cling to me, for I have not yet ascended to the Father. Rather, go to my brothers and tell them, 'I am ascending to my Father and your Father, to my God and your God!'" And then he was gone.

They told their stories over and over and over again. Hope soared. Tears were banished. Could it be possible? Philoas and Cleopas came back from Jerusalem, for Barrian had gone to Emmaus and would not be at the Antonia for another two days. However, when they heard the women's account, they couldn't wait for Barrian's return, but left immediately for Emmaus.

When James arrived from the City of Salt he was met with exultation instead of grief, and he too didn't know what to think. They called on their lessons of ancient truths and decided to gather together in one room, to create an atmosphere of prayer and desire where a manifestation of Spirit might enter. They went to Zebedee's house, to the large upper room where they'd eaten the Passover meal with Jeshua.

Darkness had fallen by the time they had all assembled in the upper room. The Holy Women helped Salome prepare food for them all, and they were just about to eat when Philoas and Cleopas returned with the most astonishing tale of all.

They had been joined on the road to Emmaus by a young physician named Luke, and their conversation had been of all the events that had taken place during the past week. A few miles outside of Emmaus they were joined by yet another, whom, later, Philoas and Cleopas would be dumbfounded at their failure to recognize. He had said to them, "What are you discussing as you go your way?" Cleopas had answered, "Are you the only resident of Jerusalem who does not know the things that went on there these past few days?" "What things?" he'd asked.

"All those that had to do with Jeshua of Nazareth, a prophet powerful in word and deed in the eyes of God and all the people; how our chief priests and leaders delivered him up to be condemned to death, and crucified him. We were hoping that he was the one who would set Israel free. Besides all this, today, the third day since these things happened, some women of our group have just brought us astonishing news. They were at the tomb before dawn and failed to find his body, but returned with the tale that they had seen a vision of angels who declared he was alive. Some of our number went to the tomb and found it just as the women said; but him they did not see."

Then the man had said to them: "What little sense you have! How slow you are to believe all that the prophets have announced! Did not the Messiah have to undergo all this so as to enter into his glory?"

Then, beginning with Moses and all the prophets, he had interpreted for them every passage of Scripture which referred to the Messiah. By now they were near Emmaus and the man had acted as if he were going farther. But they pressed him, "Stay with us. It is nearly evening, the day is practically over." So he went in to stay with them.

When he had seated himself with them to eat, he took bread, pronounced the blessing, then broke the bread and began to distribute it to them. With that their eyes were opened, and they had recognized him, whereupon he vanished from their sight. They left the food on the table and returned at once to Zebedee's.

Who could not believe Cleopas, a man revered for honesty and integrity all of his life, and certainly not given to hysterical imaginings? And Philoas, a Roman by birth and a sceptic by nature, declaring his belief in the risen Lord!

The room erupted in chaotic babbling. They clustered about Philoas, Cleopas, and the young physician, inundating them with questions, anxious to hear every detail. Everyone spoke at once, each voice calling out more loudly than the last in an attempt to be heard. Suddenly a woman's high-pitched scream cut through the din. The babbling ceased in mid-sentence. They turned to see who had screamed, and one great gasp filled the room.

Jeshua stood in the center of the floor, his eyes twinkling with merriment. "Peace be with you," he said with a smile.

They recoiled from him in terror. He must be a ghost! The doors were bolted, securely locked, and guarded by servants, for they still feared reprisals. Who had let him in? How had he entered? They stared at him in shocked silence, unable to respond to his greeting.

Jeshua knew their thoughts and said gently, "Why are you disturbed? Why do such ideas cross your mind? Look at my hands and my feet, it is really I. Touch me, and see that a ghost does not have flesh and bones as I do." He held out his hands, and lifted his sandaled feet. The wounds were there, raw and unhealed. They were still incredulous with sheer joy and wonder, so he said to them, "Have you anything here to eat?"

Martha snatched up a piece of cooked fish, which he took and ate in their presence. "Recall those words I spoke to you when I was still with you: everything written about me in the law of Moses and the prophets and Psalms had to be fulfilled." He opened their minds to the understanding of the Scriptures, relating them one by one as he had done on the road to Emmaus. "Thus it is written that the Messiah must suffer and rise from the dead on the third day. In his name, penance for the remission of sins is to be preached to all the nations, beginning at Jerusalem."

They rejoiced in jubilant celebration. Word flew to the City of Salt and to Mt. Carmel, and to each Essene house throughout the land. Messengers raced to every Essene community, to Egypt, Persia, India, wherever a soul of Israel made his abode. Prayers of thanksgiving rose heavenward like the mists of the sea. The Messiah reigned triumphant, King over the forces of Belial! Death in the flesh had been conquered, the First Fruits of all souls had returned to the Father as One with the Father. As Amelius, pure, spotless, perfect, he had once willingly come into the world, but by falling into the snares of temptation had become separate from the Father, tarnished by the sin of self, no longer able to unite with the Father in unblemished oneness. And so he had come into the world of flesh again and again, fulfilling the Law of cause and effect, each life spent purifying mind, body, and soul, until at last, as Jeshua of Nazareth, he once more stood before the Maker, pure and holy, as he had been created in the beginning.

Jeshua stayed in the earth in his body of flesh for fifty days following his triumph over death. He met with his followers often, in Jerusalem, Bethany, and his beloved Galilee, teaching, strengthening, and preparing them for the trials to come. On the fiftieth day he led them, more than five hundred of his followers, friends, and family members, to the Mount of Olives, where he gave them his final instruction.

"Go to Jerusalem and wait there for the fulfillment of my Father's promise. John baptized with water, but within a few days you will be baptized with the Holy Spirit. You will receive power when the Holy Spirit comes down on you; then you are to be my witnesses in Jerusalem, throughout Judea and Samaria, yes, even to the ends of the earth.

"The measure of the years of Satan's power has been fulfilled, but other terrible things are imminent. Yet it was for the sake of sinners that I was handed over to death, that they might return to the truth and sin no more, and inherit the spiritual and immortal glory of justification in heaven.

"Go into the whole world and proclaim the good news to all creation. The man who believes in it and accepts baptism will be saved; the man who refuses to believe in it will be condemned. Signs like these will accompany those who have professed their faith: They will use my name to expel demons, they will speak entirely new languages, they will be able to handle serpents, they will be able to drink deadly poison without harm, and the sick upon whom they lay their hands will recover.

"Full authority has been given to me both in heaven and on earth; go, therefore, and make disciples of all the nations. Baptize them in the name of the Father, and of the Son, and of the Holy Spirit. Teach them to carry out everything I have commanded you. And know that I am with you always, until the end of the world!"

When he had finished speaking, the heavens opened, and a shaft of light, like a brilliant cloud, descended upon Jeshua and then rose again, taking him aloft until he disappeared from their sight. They were still gazing up into the heavens when two men dressed in white stood beside them. "Men of Galilee," they said, "why do you stand here looking up at the skies? This Jeshua who has been taken from you will return, just as you saw him go up into the heavens."

The eleven disciples, along with Mary, Ruth, and his brothers, and all the other of his kinsmen and closest friends returned to Jerusalem and waited in Josie's upper room, where they devoted themselves to constant prayer. Judith was with them, drawing upon her vast storehouse of knowledge gained from years of study and many experiences of spiritual insight, to give them a better understanding of how woman had been redeemed from a place of obscurity to her place in the affairs of the nation, the world, the empire, and the home itself. She taught how the evolution of man's experiences is for the purpose of his becoming more and more acquainted with relationships with his fellow man, as a manifestation of Divine Love, as was shown by the Son of Man, Jeshua. She taught that each and every soul must be the savior of some other soul, to comprehend the purpose of the entrance of the Son to the earth, which was that man might have a closer walk with, yea, the open door to, the very heart of the Living God.

They were gathered together in prayer when the feast of Pentecost fell, and suddenly from up in the sky there came a noise like a strong, driving wind, which was heard all through the house. Tongues as of fire appeared, which parted and came to rest on each of them. All were filled with the Holy Spirit. They began to express themselves in foreign tongues and make bold proclamations as the Spirit prompted them.

Jews from every nation who were in Jerusalem for the feast heard the sound and gathered around Josie's house. The disciples came out to greet them, and the crowd was much confused because each one heard the men speaking his own language. They asked in utter amazement, "Are not all of these men who are speaking Galileans? How is it that each of us hears them in his native tongue? We are Parthians, Medes, and Elamites. We live in Mesopotamia, Judea, and Cappadocia, Pontus, the province of Asia, Phrygia, and Pamphylia, Egypt, and the regions of Libya around Cyrene. There are even visitors from Rome, all Jews or those who have come over to Judaism; Cretans and Arabs, too. Yet each of us hears them speaking in our own tongue about the marvels God has accomplished." They were dumbfounded, and could make nothing at all of what had happened.

Peter, the "Rock" to whom Jeshua had given the keys to the kingdom, stood before them and addressed them.

"You who are Jews, indeed all of you staying in Jerusalem! Listen to what I have to say. You must realize that these men are not drunk, as you seem to think. It is only nine in the morning! No, it is what Joel the prophet spoke of: 'It shall come to pass in the last days, says God, that I will pour out a portion of my spirit on all mankind: Your sons and daughters shall prophesy, your young men shall see visions and your old men shall dream dreams. Yes, even on my servants and handmaids, I will pour out a portion of my spirit in those days, and they shall prophesy. I will work wonders in the heavens above and signs on the earth below; blood, fire, and a cloud of smoke. The sun shall be turned to darkness and the moon to blood before the coming of that great and glorious day of the Lord. Then shall everyone be saved who calls on the name of the Lord.'

"Men of Israel, listen to me! Jeshua the Nazarene was a man whom God sent to you with miracles, wonders, and signs as his credentials. These God worked through him in your midst, as you well know. He was delivered up by the set purpose and plan of God; you even made use of pagans to crucify and kill him. God freed him from death's bitter pangs, however, and raised him up again, for it was impossible that death should keep its hold on him.

"David says of him: 'I have set the Lord ever before me, with him at my right hand I shall not be disturbed. My heart has been glad and my tongue has rejoiced, my body will live on in hope, for you will not abandon my soul to the nether world, nor will you suffer your faithful one to undergo corruption. You have shown me the paths of life; you will fill me with joy in your presence.'

"Brothers, I can speak confidently to you about our father David. He died and was buried, and his grave is in our midst to this day. He was a prophet and knew that God had sworn to him that one of his descendants would sit upon his throne. He said that he was not abandoned to the nether world, nor did his body undergo corruption, thus proclaiming beforehand the resurrection of the Messiah. This is the Jeshua God has raised up, and we are his witnesses. Exalted at God's right hand, he first received the promised Holy Spirit from the Father, then poured this Spirit out on us. This is what you now see and hear.

"David did not go up to heaven, yet David says, 'The Lord said to my Lord, Sit at my right hand until I make your enemies your footstool.' Therefore let the whole house of Israel know beyond any doubt that God has made both Lord and Messiah this Jeshua whom you crucified."

Some three thousand souls were baptized and added to the ranks of the Brotherhood that day, and it was only the beginning. The Elect spread the Good News into every nation, and for generation after generation the numbers of the Remnant grew, until their members were found in every corner of the earth.

And it was at Antioch that they first became known as Christians.

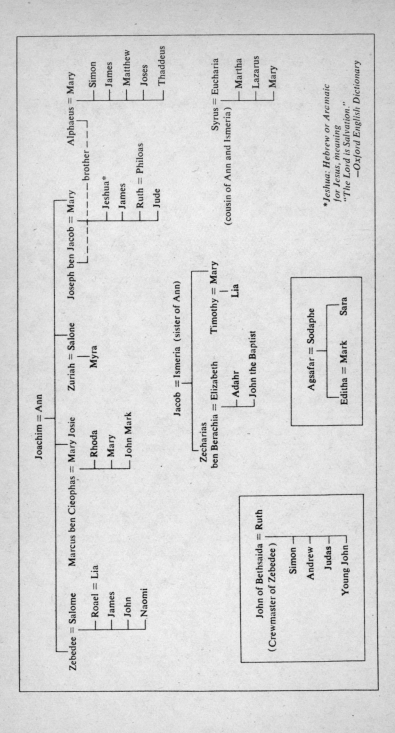

Joachim = Ann

Zebedee = Salome   Marcus ben Cleophas = Mary Josie   Zuriah = Salone   Joseph ben Jacob = Mary   Alphaeus = Mary

Roael = Lia
James
John
Naomi

Rhoda
Mary
John Mark

Myra

— brother —

Jeshua*
James
Ruth = Philoas
Jude

Simon
James
Matthew
Joses
Thaddeus

Jacob = Ismeria (sister of Ann)

Zecharias
ben Berachia = Elizabeth   Timothy = Mary

Adahr
John the Baptist

Lia

Syrus = Eucharia

Martha
Lazarus
Mary

(cousin of Ann and Ismeria)

Agsafar = Sodaphe

Editha = Mark   Sara

John of Bethsaida = Ruth
(Crewmaster of Zebedee)

Simon
Andrew
Judas
Young John

*Jeshua: Hebrew or Aramaic
for Jesus, meaning
"The Lord is Salvation."
—Oxford English Dictionary

Disciples of Jeshua

Simon ben Alphaeus	first cousin of Jeshua
James ben Alphaeus	first cousin of Jeshua
Matthew ben Alphaeus	first cousin of Jeshua
Thaddeus ben Alphaeus	first cousin of Jeshua
James ben Zebedee	first cousin of Jeshua
John ben Zebedee	first cousin of Jeshua
Simon ben John	son of Jeshua's Uncle Zebedee's shipmaster
Andrew ben John	son of Jeshua's Uncle Zebedee's shipmaster
Phillip of Bethsaida	
Nathaniel bar Tholmen	
Thomas from Cyrene	
Judas Iscariot	

Judith's family

Phineas	father
Elkatma	mother
Judith	daughter, Essene prophetess
Justin	husband of Judith, former Roman military tribune
Servillius	child of Judith and Justin
Phineas	child of Judith and Justin

Essene Community at Mount Carmel

Enos	head of order
Aristotle	successor to Enos
Judas	member of the order
Mathias	member of the order
Shalmar	teacher of comparative religions
Philo	recorder and librarian
Zermada	astrologer
Eloise	head of young girls
Margil	teacher of Mary
Anna	teacher of Mary

Maidens

Andra
Abigale
Sophia
Rachel
Editha
Josie
Zipporah
Keleth
Hannah
Rebkah
Mary (sister of Elizabeth)

Scripture Index